WRITERS REPUBLIC

COLD BLOODED

HALEY DIXON

WRITERS REPUBLIC L.L.C.
515 Summit Ave. Unit R1
Union City, NJ 07087, USA

Website: *www.writersrepublic.com*
Hotline: *1-877-656-6838*
Email: *info@writersrepublic.com*

Ordering Information:
Quantity sales. Special discounts are available on quantity purchases by corporations, associations, and others. For details, contact the publisher at the address above.

Library of Congress Control Number: 2021914250
ISBN-13:   978-1-63728-100-0   [Paperback Edition]
                  978-1-63728-101-7   [Digital Edition]

Rev. date: 07/13/2021

For my Uncle Timmy.

May your name live on forever, never forgotten but always missed. I wish you were here to see this; I love you, and I hope you're smiling down at me today.

Prologue

The blackness of the night couldn't even shield me from the fate I had chosen. I had one order to follow....to stay away from *her*. How was that even possible after everything we'd been through: From wanting to put a bullet through her skull to not knowing how to live without the feisty sass only she ever dared to give me. Everyone near me was scared to speak out of line. But from the moment I met her, that sharp tongue managed to amaze and anger me at the same time.

The thing I never believed a killer like me could have was causing me to run for my life. Love. It's an evil thing. It's not always warm and comfortable. It's dangerous. Maybe even more dangerous than I was before she sank her claws into me so deep there was no escape.

I turned the corner into an alley, I hid at the side of an old beaten-up garage. My chest heaved up and down from the blocks I had ran. My lungs burned with the need for oxygen, my feet screamed at me to collapse onto the icy January pavement. I couldn't let my body give out, not until I got to say my final goodbyes to her. I glanced around the garage edge to see the headlights of the car chasing me, cut through the night air. Moments later the Hummer that held my death in the backseat followed. I watched it slowly roll past as the gangsters inside searched the streets for me. I stood in my hiding spot recovering for just a moment, giving them a head start. I quickly ditched my winter coat, threw my hood up from my sweatshirt, and jogged down the alley. Once I hit the street, I walked normally to keep any attention from coming my way.

I was two blocks away from the love of my life, the only person I cared that I would leave behind. You're probably wondering how I got into this trouble. It took different events to put me here, but I wouldn't change it. Go back almost three years ago and tell me that a curly haired, feisty, Colombian girl would become the love of my life and the reason for my death; I would have laughed and put a bullet in your skull for damning me to, such a thing like love. Now, even in my final moments, she was all I could think about.

Finally, the house I'd been searching for came into view. It was all lit up telling me that she and her family were still up. Probably playing some stupid game, that I always hated when she forced me to play. But now I wish I had more time for one more game. The old, rusted gate was swinging in the wind just like I knew it would be. Now I wish I had put up more of a fight to fix it. To know this was going to be my final moment with the only person I've loved more than myself killed me more than any bullet ever could.

Before I was able to snap out of thoughts about the improvement, to the family home I wish I had done, I felt the cool metal of a pistol press against the back of my head. Then came the click of the hammer. The only panic in me was not being able to say goodbye. I didn't give two shits about that gun or the gangster I knew was holding it.

"You just couldn't stay away, could you?" His deep vicious voice was eerily low. It rang in the night almost as a whisper. I knew it had to be him to end it, just like the law stated. I knew the guys in the car weren't going to kill me, they were going to take me to him.

"If you're going to point a gun at me, you better kill me because I won't hesitate to kill you." I growled that low intimidating growl that made people shake with fear.

"That was the old you though, right? Trip?" he asked mockingly. I knew if I made one movement, I'd be dead on the spot. He was just waiting for something, but what?

"You let my daughter soften you and now you're going to die for it," he laughed what I think was supposed to be an intimidating laugh, but he didn't scare me: no one ever did.

"All that you had to do was stay away and all of this could have been yours" he whispered just as the front door to the house opened. I watched her walk into the night. Everything in me wanted to scream at her to get back inside because I didn't want her to see this. Before I could ask him to spare her the impending violence, her chocolate brown eyes cut through the darkness to meet mine. Just like that, a bang rang through the air and the last words I heard were...

"TREY'VON" Screamed an angel's voice that was corrupted by the devil.

Chapter 1

The Great Eleanor

ELEANOR

I watched out of the small porthole-like window of the plane as it landed, bringing me back to the country and the state I grew up in. Los Angeles California is a place of dreams where anything is possible. As happy as I was to be back, I couldn't help but think about the people I had to leave behind. I didn't know when I'd see them again. My grandma, grandpa, cousins, aunts, Uncles, even the friends I made. Over the summer, I had gone back home to Colombia. My friend Zeke sent me there. He paid for everything without even asking. He just offered to send me home to Colombia for the summer. The only catch was that I go and see his family every day, especially his mom who I loved.

Finally, the plane came to a stop, and everyone stood up to. I stayed put in my seat letting the isle clear out a little. I turned on my phone, plugged in my headphones, and turned-on music. Once the plane cleared out a little bit, I stood up and grabbed my backpack from the overhead compartment. Once I was off the plane and had some elbow room, I grabbed my passport and ID then slung on my backpack. I walked through LAX went through customs, security and all that junk. When I finally cleared everything, I went over to baggage claim and grabbed my two suitcases. I walked to the waiting area allowing my eyes to scan the crowd and found my mom and dad sitting in plastic chairs waiting for me.

"Mom, Dad" I called with a smile walking over to the sitting couple.

"How was Colombia? We missed you so so much!" my mom squealed standing up and wrapping me up in a bone crushing hug. I smiled hugging her back nuzzling my nose into her hair taking in its fruity scent.

"I missed you too. Colombia was amazing, it's been far too long since we made the trip home," I told her after pulling away and hugging my dad. His strong toned arms were more comforting than what I remembered. The scent of a fresh construction site still lingered on his shirt.

"Dad, did you just come from work?" I asked, pulling away with a smile.

"Yeah, I got a half day off. I couldn't miss my middle daughter's homecoming," he smiled while ruffling my already messy hair and making me giggle. I grabbed his hand. My parents were a good match, they looked good together. My dad was 6ft, his dark brown hair was always styled but messy from his construction hat. His hazel brown eyes showed nothing but pride every time he looked at his family. He had sandy color skin that looked good with the dark stubble on his face. His smile was always bright and made you wonder what crazy idea he'd come up with next. My dad was very muscular which was the result of his hardworking job.

My mom was beyond beautiful. She was only 5'2 which gave them an appealing height difference. She had beautiful golden skin. Her hair is different than when I left, it's lighter brown with blonde streaks. She has beautiful chocolate brown eyes like mine, and plump lips that were always pulled back into a motherly smile. My mom was a MILF with those curves. No wonder they have 3 kids.

"Let's get you home. I'm sure your sisters are dying to see you," Mom smiled squeezing my shoulder. My dad kindly took my suitcase as we walked out of the airport with one another. We easily found my dad's old beat-up pickup truck, I got in the backseat with my bags.

"Mateo misses you like crazy, Elly," my mom said looking back at me with a smile, but I just hummed.

"She better have stayed out of my closet!" I crossed my arms stubbornly. Mateo was my younger sister, and she was a clothes thief. My parents laughed at me shaking their heads, but I was serious. Just as my dad pulled out of the parking lot he turned on Prince Royce making me smile and sing along in the backseat.

I saw the white run-down two-story house come into view. Surrounding it was a black rusted fence. The gate never closed the right way, so it was left to sway in the wind as it pleased. My dad pulled into his usual parking spot right in front of the house. I wasted no time jumping out of the truck and looking around my East LA neighborhood. There were kids playing kick ball in the streets, more kids riding their bikes, some guys drinking in their yards and shooting dice. I couldn't help but steal a glance at the bar two doors down from my house. It sat on the corner. It's where all the Los Prophets gang members hung out. It was like their home base. Los Prophets was the gang that ran East LA, but that didn't stop people from challenging them, which made East LA unsafe. From the drive-by's, drugs, prostitutes, tagging, to rivals trying to take over, or accidentally seeing somebody getting jumped into the gang when you turn the corner. They ruled this area, it was their kingdom and that's just the way it was. My eyes caught the white Rolls Royce sitting out front of the bar which told Zeke was there.

"Let's go in, yeah?" Mom sent me a small smile as her eyes followed mine. I smiled while nodding and following her through the broken gate. We walked up to the old creaky wooden porch and through the white door that had Los Prophet's symbol spray painted on it. I sighed, shaking my head at the three crosses and walked inside.

"WE'RE HOME WITH YOUR SISTER!" Dad yelled. No one responded to his yelling. He sat down my bags as I walked into our small well decorated living room. We had a grey small sectional against the wall, an older wooden coffee table that held different décor my mom would set out. On either side of the couch was in tables. On the left side of the room was my dad's lazy boy recliner. Then, on the front wall was the TV stand with our large flat screen. Pictures of my siblings, and myself hung on the walls. I grabbed the yellow piece of paper on the table which said that my sisters went out with friends and would be home later.

"Welp, they ditched me for their friends. After two months of being gone I thought I'd be more popular," I joked waving the piece of paper between my fingers. Mom sent me another small smile, sighed and took the paper.

"I guess 'stay here, we're going to get your sister' wasn't clear enough," Mom said. I laughed running my hand through my hair shrugging.

"It's no biggie. I want to see my friends before the first day of school tomorrow anyways," I said, and she nodded tucking a lose curl behind my ear. I grabbed my suitcases and struggled pulling them up the stairs.

"And who needs a man? Not this girl!" I smirked, flipping my long curls over my shoulder and grabbing my suitcases on the way to my bedroom. I threw open the door. I looked around my room letting out a sigh going over to my bed collapsing on it. How good it felt to be home. My mind went to the bar and to Zeke. I wanted to tell him about my trip. You're probably wondering who Zeke is since he's been mentioned a few times. Zeke is the leader of Los Prophets and kinda like a father figure.

When I was around 7, I was outside playing by myself with my dolls. A car pulled up at the bar and there was some yelling. A guy that clearly wasn't from our hood had a crowbar and started smashing the bar windows. Zeke came out of the bar and shot him right in the head. Later the police came and asked me questions: like if I had seen anything and who did it. Even at that young age I knew what happened to rats, so I lied. I looked Zeke right in his eyes and said the shooter wasn't there. The police believed me and left Zeke on the streets for another day. After that, Zeke kinda took me in under his wing. I worked at the bar clearing tables for a generous amount of money. He taught me how to place bets, play dice, to gamble really. Then he taught me how to run numbers but that didn't last long before he stopped letting gamble and run numbers for the gang. He didn't want me involved in the gang life. As I grew older, Zeke's power grew and now he runs everything.

I looked around my room one more time and decided I was going to sneak down to the bar. Clearly, my parents didn't want me down there because it's a bar and gang central, but I never listened. Nothing stopped me from sneaking down there the moments my parent's backs were turned. My dad was pickier about it than my mom. She only acted picky about it around my dad. I went downstairs to find my parents snuggling on the couch.

"Hey, I'm going to Gabby's house," I told them while standing at the bottom of the stairs.

"Do you need a ride?" Mom asked leaning up to grab her keys.

"No it's fine I can walk. It's only a couple of blocks and I miss the neighborhood" I shrugged it off sending her a smile.

"Ok be safe honey," she said. I pushed past the gate and went straight to the bar. I opened the door, which looked like a door to a home, I seen Los Prophet members everywhere. Zeke was at his usual back table with Young Lord, Lil Ugly, Blade, and a guy I didn't recognize.

Zeke wasn't a nasty looking guy. Don't get me wrong, he was covered in tats but he didn't look fresh out of prison like you picture a gang leader. Zeke was 6'1, he had the same russet skin tone as me, his black hair that held the same unruly curls as mine was shaved down into a buzz cut with a perfect lineup. His eyebrows were bushy and, if we're being honest, could use some love. But he managed to pull off the unruly look with class. We shared chocolate brown eyes. His nose and cheekbones were narrow in a good way. Above his pink full lips was a small black mustache to match the stubble growing on his face and neck.

His body wasn't huge with muscles, but they were there. His arms were big, but lean, like with his chest and abs. I always teased him and said he had that "Ken Doll" body. His arms were covered in tattoos but none of them mattered more than the three crosses on his neck labeling him as a Los Prophet. I smiled as I went over to his table. The guy I didn't recognized tapped his shoulder nodding his head towards me.

"Princesa, you're back!" Zeke smiled moving his hood half off.

"Zeke, Colombia was so amazing. Your mom says "hi", and she misses you. I have some stuff she made you at my house. Customs took the brownies she made you. I'm sorry," I told him, genuinely feeling bad for his loss of presents his mom sent him. He chuckled at me shaking his head.

"It's fine. Those fat fucks are probably eating them right now. Ugly get up and let her sit," Zeke snapped harshly to his boy who jumped up right away. I smiled at the man and took the seat.

"So what was your favorite part of your trip?" Zeke asked me kicking his feet up on the table and looking at me with a smirk as he drank from his water glass.

"The beach. I got some illegal fireworks from one of your smuggling connections and we went to the beach one night. We had this huge family day and then that night we set off all the fireworks. It was magical," I told him while smiling and gathering my curls behind my shoulders. I looked over to the boy who I didn't recognize. He stared ahead as if I wasn't even sitting there. I watched closely as he sipped whatever was in his cup.

"You truly are mine, smuggling fireworks!" Zeke teased, making me giggle.

"It was so nice being home and seeing my family and yours but I'm like dying for McDonald's," I told him making him laugh and shake his head.

"You got school tomorrow, right?" He asked me and I nodded my head looking at my nails that could use some love.

"It's the first day of Senior year and I'm so nervous" Honestly high school had been pretty easy for me. Everyone knows I'm affiliated with Los Prophets, so they don't mess with me too much. I looked back up to "unknown guy" to catch him looking at me. The moment he caught my eye, he looked away and lean over and whispered something to Young Lord.

"Shit, I'm being rude. I didn't even think about introducing you guys. Elly this is Trip, he's my new right hand and next up to take my throne. Trip, this is Elly. She's like my daughter so she'll be around a little bit." Why would anyone want to be called Trip? Maybe it's the same thing as Lil Ugly. He hated his street name but was stuck with it. Trip glanced over at me, his eyes looking down at my boobs and then back to my face and he looked back to Young Lord who was rolling a joint.

I couldn't help noticing how attractive he was. It made me wonder where he was from because you'd remember someone that looks like him. His bronze skin seemed to have a heavenly glow. His black silky curls were long on the top and fell just slightly into his eyes. The sides were shaved, and his line up looked fresh like he had just come from the barber shop. His eyebrows were well groomed and were perfectly shaped. His eyes were dark brown-nearly black. His cheekbones fit his face perfectly, but something about his nose seemed a little off. Maybe it had been broken before but, regardless, it was off in just the cutest way, and the small shiny diamond stuck in the side of one of his nostrils caught my attention. His plump pink lips were eye catching and anyone who said they weren't was a liar. I only wished to me. I saw the three crosses on his neck, and he managed to pull them off better than the rest.

I couldn't see much of his body, but I could tell he had muscles. Not like Zeke's, Trip was even more lean. His arms looked strong, as if they could feel like the safest place to be when you were wrapped up in them. His arms were covered in what seemed like random tattoos. There wasn't much skin showing through the black and red inked sleeves. I couldn't help but wonder if his chest and stomach was covered with just as many tattoos as his arm were. The only tattoo on his neck was his Los Prophet tattoo. I could tell he wanted it proudly displayed and that was his way of displaying it. I didn't miss the huge diamond studs in his ears, the sterling rings on his fingers, or the diamond bracelets around his wrist. He was beyond attractive, but I could already tell even though he was gorgeous he was going to have the ugliest personality.

"What happened to Mad Max?" I asked Zeke curiously. That earned me a large exhale of annoyance from Trip and a side glance.

"He was shot by one of the El Diablos" Zeke told me. I nodded slowly. I didn't even know he had been killed, no one told me. When did it happen? How was the family? I needed to send flowers to his family, he had a newborn daughter. I shook away my thoughts as I looked over at Trip. He looked too young to be so high up in the gang.

"Hi Trip," I smiled at him hoping to get his attention. He put the joint to his lips and lit it up and looked over at me. His eyes scanned over me as he inhaled and then blew the smoke at me. I coughed fanning away the smoke that he had rudely blown my way.

"Don't let him get to you. He's a dick," Zeke said getting a smirk from Trip.

"Clearly. Some people just can't handle a promotion and the power that goes with it," I snapped glaring at the obnoxious man that sat in front of me. He couldn't be much older than 19 or 20. He looked at me arching a perfect eyebrow, his lips parted as if he was going to speak but they closed just as fast, and he looked away. Zeke laughed shaking his head.

"You want a drink?" He asked me.

"Just a bottle of water" I told him, and he waved to one of his boys to go. Zeke's mouth opened to speak but was cut off by the bar door slinging open and the sounds of men barking followed. Everyone in the bar jumped up pulling their guns. It only took me seconds to follow the action. I turned to see several huge, white, bald headed men walking in. One of them had tattoos all over his face and the top of his head. It was a scary look if we're being honest. I moved closer to Zeke, and he wasted no time shoving me between himself and Trip. Trip's eyes found mine for just a split second before he focused on the men again.

"I think you guys have the wrong bar." Trip's voice wasn't what I excepted. When you took away the deadly growl that sounded natural, it was smooth, it wasn't too deep or too high just that perfect volume. If velvet made a sound, it would be his voice.

"Nah we have the right one" The white guy with a tattoo on the top of his head snapped at Trip. I assumed that one was the leader.

"Let me restate then. You gringos aren't welcome here." He growled, grabbing the table we had all been sitting at with one hand and throwing it out of his way making drinks and food spewed all over floor.

"Trip, keep your temper!" Zeke warned him. But when I looked up at Trip's nearly black eyes moments ago, they were now completely black. It looked as if a demon was taking over his body.

"You heard you're Papi, boy. Keep your temper!" The scary guy with the face mask of tattoos mocked Trip. Before I could even process what was happening, a deafening bang filled the bar along with my scream. I watched as "Scary Face Mask Tattoo Guy" grabbed his stomach and Trip shot again causing another scream to escape my lips as a bullet went through Face Mask Tattoo's skull. The smell of gun powder burned my nose. It made me almost want to gag but I held it back. I tucked behind

Zeke shaking in fear, hiding my face in his back as yells came from Los Prophets and the white men.

"AYE, AYE WAIT, WAIT!" Zeke yelled. I peeked out to see him stopping what would have been a fight with just his words. The power Zeke held just in his voice alone always amazed me.

"We don't have to fight, what brings you into my bar?" Zeke asked his tone cooler and more dangerous than what I've ever heard it before.

"I need to talk to Zeke Santiago!" The leader said and Zeke nodded looking back at me. I watched him lick his lips and look at Trip who was face to face with one of the white guys.

"Trip, get her out of here!" Zeke ordered. Was he crazy? This guy just murdered someone for mocking him and now he wants me to go with him?

"I am not going with him!" I crossed my arms looking up at Zeke.

"Boss, come on. Look at everyone here that can babysit" Trip groaned and I sent him a glare.

"You aren't babysitting shit. If anything, YOU need a babysitter puto gilipollas (fucking asshole)!" I snapped at him. He sent me a glare, took a step closer to me. But I just looked at him raising my eyebrows.

"BOTH OF YOU STOP. Trip, I'm not asking. NOW!" Zeke yelled. Trip rolled his eyes waving his gun telling me to go forward but I just challenged him with my look.

"Baby girl, just go before you get everyone in here killed" Trip growled at me but I just rolled my eyes as I pushed through the white boys, one grabbed my butt, but Trip pushed his gun against the guys temple.

"Would you like to join your friend?" He growled harshly while nodding for me to go. I walked out of the bar and seconds later Trip came out tucking his gun into his waist band as more white guys walked into the bar. I knew Zeke could handle whatever was thrown at him. I looked at Trip as he sent a deadly glare to the men.

"Well, it was nice...actually it was horrible meeting you," I said turning on my heels and starting toward home, but he grabbed my wrist pulling me back. I looked up at him annoyed already, I didn't want to be around him. He just killed somebody right in front of me. I couldn't help but notice how tall he was, he had to be like 6'3.

"Leave me alone!" I snapped with force at him as I walked away but he pulled me back, again.

"Get in the car!" He ordered me pointing towards a shiny black Audi R8. It looked brand new, I couldn't help but be shocked by the expensive car and I knew the shock was all over my face. I quickly shook away my shock.

"No, I'm going home!" I argued with him. He groaned grabbing my arm so tight it hurt.

"Ouch, Trip that hurts. If you leave a bruise, Zeke will kill you," I threatened him. He tugged me over to his car. He still hadn't spoken one word to me. He pulled open his doors and to my surprise they were suicide doors. He shoved me into the car roughly and slammed the door almost taking my ankle out in the process. What is this guy's issue? He was beyond rude in the bar, he barely spoke to me. What the hell was that whole "baby girl" thing about? Now he's practically kidnapping me. He got in the car and peeled out of the parking spot.

"What the hell is your issue?" I snapped at him. He glanced over me, his eyes raking me up and down and then focusing back on the road. I groaned throwing my hands up in the air in annoyance.

"So you're going to kidnap me and then not talk? Amazing!" I rolled my eyes shaking my head. The car fell silent. I rested my head against the glass trying to get as close to the door as I could. Flashbacks of what happened in the bar kept replaying in my head. That was the second person I'd seen die. The one Zeke shot and now the one Trip shot. I couldn't help but notice how Trip didn't even seem remorseful. It was like snatching that life didn't mean anything to him. I'm sure to be where he's at, at his young age, he's killed plenty of people but to become so numb to it didn't make sense. He reached for the radio turning it on. Right away I recognized the song as All Me by Drake.

"You don't seem to upset about killing someone." I said glancing at him. He just shrugged his shoulders leaning farther back into his seat. I felt the quiet consume us once again. I didn't want to get on his nerves, but he wasn't talking. Did I really want him to talk? The way his eyes looked back in the bar flashed across my mind. It was scary, it was almost like he was possessed but that was clearly just him. He pulled into a gas station and up to a pump getting out. I got out of the car following behind him. I was scared of Trip after seeing how cold he was when it came to killing someone, but I was even more scared of El Diablos, Los Prophets rival gang, or those men that came into the bar. I knew I was protected by Zeke. Trip couldn't hurt me even if he wanted too. I caught up to him just as he walked into the gas station. He looked over his shoulder at me with a look of annoyance.

"Will you wait for me while I grab a water?" I asked him, this gas station was in the center of the gang territory fight. He waved his hand impatiently in the air telling me to go. I quickly ran back to the fridge grabbing a bottle of Fiji water. I made my way back up to the front counter where Trip was staring at his phone. The moment I reached him he snatched the water sharply from my hands.

"Go get your own!" I snapped going to snatch it back, but he set it on the counter along with his debit card.

"Oh...thank you," I whispered. He handed me the water and walked out. I followed standing beside him as he pumped the gas.

"I hate the smell of gas," I commented leaning against his car taking a drink out of my water. He glanced at me and then looked back at the pump. Does he not like me? That's impossible. Today is the first day we've ever seen each other. Well, I guess it's not impossible. I most definitely do not like him. His phone began to ring, he looked down and then waved me away once again. I sent him a glare walking around the car getting in, buckling up. Who does he think he is waving commands at me like that? Why am I listening to them? Well probably because he'd leave me at this sketchy gas station if I didn't.

"Yes boss. I got it." He said while getting in the car and then hanging up.

"That was Zeke. Is everyone ok?" I asked him, but once again I got nothing. He pulled out of the gas station, and I decided to just stay silent for the ride to wherever we were going. I was tired of being ignored. He played different rappers, some I liked and others I didn't. I wasn't going to waste my breath telling Trip my musical opinions. Soon enough he pulled up in front of my white run-down house. I grabbed my phone and slammed his stupid expensive car door shut. I wasn't going to thank him for that ride because I never even wanted to go in the first place. I stormed inside my house slamming the door just as my dad walked by. I couldn't help but giggle as he jumped at the sudden bang.

"What's wrong with you? Did you and Gabby have a fight?" Dad asked pouting his lip but I just cut him with the corner of my eye. It wasn't meant for him, but Trip had me so mad. Who is he to be so nasty when he doesn't even know me?

"I don't want to talk about it." I said going past him and up the stairs. I went into my bedroom locking the door. I sat on my bed as the image of "Face Mask Tattoo Guy" laying dead and Trip's unemotional look floated through my head. That's how the night went before the start of my senior year. Nightmares of a murderous new gangbanger in my neighborhood and "Face Mask Tattoo Guy".

Chapter 2

Tempers Fly

ELEANOR

I groaned covering my face with my thick comforter as the alarm on my phone screamed directly in my ear, reminding me it was the first day of senior year. Ugh...senioritis was already taking over, and I haven't even walked into the school yet. I sighed as I rolled over and turned off my alarm. After a couple moments of sitting up and just staring into the darkness of my bedroom, I reached over and turned on the lamp next to my bed.

The light illuminated a bedroom was unique to me and me only. The brick walls were old and chipped. The bricks were different sizes, and they were kinda laid awkward it gave an old vibe to the room, but I loved how it also gave it character. The floor was a newer polished hardwood, I had a white fake fur rug covering the hardwood. In the center of my bedroom against the wall was my full-size bed dressed in a tie-dyed comforter and black sheets. On either side was two small white in-tables which held a phone charger and a small lamp on each. Across from my bed against the wall was a black TV stand that held my flat screen TV and pictures. To the left of the TV was a black door which hid my packed closet. To the right of my bed was probably one of my favorite things. I had a wall sized bookshelf. It was stacked with great novels and records. On the top shelf I had an old vintage box that held a mountain of cash that I had earned working with Zeke. (There was also one of those pretty little roller latter connected to the bookcase itself.) To the right of the shelf in the corner

13

was a desk that would soon be covered in school projects. The desk also held a makeup mirror. Above the desk was black box wall shelves that held all my makeup and hair things. The centerpiece of the room was the huge window that swung inward. Right outside is the tree that I use to sneak in and out. A window bench sat in front of the window with purple seat covering and white and black fake fur pillows. Lastly, sitting catty cornered in the upper left corner of the room was a tall dresser which held a record player and a couple candles.

I sighed pushing my comforter off my body and got up. I walked over to my closet grabbing a pair of light high-waist ripped skinny jeans, a black off the shoulder long sleeved crop top, and my all-black Nike Air-Max. I went over to my dresser grabbing a pair of underwear, with this top a bra looked funny so I'd just skip it. I made my bed and laid my outfit out perfectly, grabbed a towel, my body soap and went down the hall to the only bathroom in the house. I locked the door and looked in the mirror. My long thick black curls were piled into a bun on the top of my head, but it looked more like a rat's nest than hair. My face clearly needed to washed, I looked like something that had risen from the dead. I quickly brushed my teeth and then got in the shower. I did what I needed to do and shaved what I needed to shave. Once I finished, I got out drying off wrapping the towel around my body and another around my hair. I walked out of the bathroom just as my little sister Mateo approached the door. I went to my bedroom, shut the door and made sure my curtains were shut tight.

It felt like it took more time this morning than usual. Next, I did my usual makeup which consisted of foundation, concealer, contour, blush, highlight (not blinding), eyeshadow which is a nude color most of the time, mascara, false eyelashes, brow filler, lip liner, and lipstick which is almost always a natural pink color and setting spray. I didn't have it caked on, I never did, it always looked natural. I hated that caked feeling on my skin. Once I was finally finished, I changed into my outfit and grabbed my backpack. I walked downstairs to find the kitchen empty, because mom and dad are at work but where is Mateo?

"MATEO!" I yelled but got no answer. I grabbed my black hydro flask from the fridge and saw the time on the stove: 8:00.

"NO, NO, NO!" I yelled grabbing my phone and key running out of the house slamming the door behind me. I wasn't worried about locking it, Isabella was home. At the corner by the bar, I saw the bus and the last person getting on.

"WAIT" I yelled running towards the bus. I guess the driver did hear nor see me because she pulled off.

"NO, WAIT" I yelled running across the street after her, but she just kept going. I groaned resting my hands on my knees catching my breath. Damn, I am really out of shape. Now I have to wake up Izzy and she's going to be the biggest bitch. I stood up to walk across the street when I saw Trip's car pull up to the bar. He got out looking at me with an overconfident smirk, his dark brown nearly black eyes scanned me up and down.

"Looks like you missed you the bus," he commented, I glared at Trip for the obvious comment.

"I would have never noticed. Is Zeke in there?" I asked him nodding towards the bar. I held my backpack straps nervously and walked over to the man that cold bloodily killed a guy with no remorse right in front of me. He looked over his shoulder at the bar and then looked back down at me. His eyes raked over my body once more. I watched him lick his lips before they pulled up into a smirk. Gross, he's checking me out and doesn't even have enough class to cover it up.

"I don't know, he might be" He smirked. I nodded my head stepping around him and his fancy Audi. I started to walk inside the bar and see if Zeke was there. If so, he could give me a ride and I could avoid fighting with my older sister.

TREY'VON

She nodded at me slightly giving me a look of annoyance. I watched her sidestep me and look at my car with the same annoyed look as she started to walk inside the bar. I don't know what it was about this girl, but I kinda liked getting under her skin. Maybe it was because she didn't fight her reaction or maybe it was because she didn't seem scared of me like everyone else. Either way, it was fun watching her get all flustered.

"Or he might not be" I called over my shoulder turning to face the girl who's name I could not remember if my life depended on it. I couldn't stop the laid-back smirk that covered my face as I rested my arms on the top of my car. Something about her chocolate brown eyes caught my attention, I didn't mind her looking at me like I did everyone else.

"Trip, can you just tell me? I don't want to be late for my first day." She sighed giving me a pleading look. My eyes went to her small top that left her stomach, chest, and shoulders exposed for anyone to see. I couldn't help but notice the way her jeans hugged her wide hips tightly. She was sexy, I wouldn't mind hittin it at all, but Zeke would freak out if I fucked his daughter and dipped.

Her long black hair was set into the most perfect bouncy curls. I couldn't help but wonder how she managed to make them look so good. Her russet skin seemed to lack any imperfection, it looked smooth and almost soft. Her perfectly arched eyebrows were full but not too full just kinda perfect. Her eyes didn't seem to bother me as much as I felt like they should. Her cheek bones and nose fit her face better than I had ever seen on a person. Her lips were full, plump, and but painted a rosy, pink color. I knew from yesterday that behind them was a perfect white smile. Her jawline was sharp but nothing too crazy.

Her body caught my eye and imagination more than anything. I knew I could teach her a few new things if it was different with her and Zeke. She had an hourglass shape. It wasn't awkwardly bold like those hoes on reality shows. You couldn't miss the small waist and fat ass even if you weren't trying to notice. Her boobs weren't too big or too small just that perfect size for a nice handful. They were perky which made them even more eye catching and I could already see she wasn't wearing a bra. (She had that upside down heart shape butt that I liked on a girl.) Her thighs were thick but not too thick, they were the perfect size to avoid a thigh gap. She was probably around 5'2 short enough to make all of that even sexier.

"Don't high schools have a dress code?" I asked tearing my eyes away from her body. I looked into her eyes waiting for her to answer me. She crossed her arms which only pushed her boobs up farther making me chuckle.

"Why are you worried about it? You aren't my dad" She sassed me. I smirked licking my lips seeing fire behind her eyes. That Spanish accent she had made it so easy to listen to her talk even if she was giving me attitude.

"Shut up and get in the car" I said opening the door getting in. I looked over seeing her scoff and start to head to the bar, but I laid on the horn. I rolled down the window glaring at her.

"Baby girl, I know you heard me. Get in the damn car" I growled harshly at her. She rolled her eyes storming overthrowing her backpack in the backseat and then got in the passenger seat buckling up.

"What school?" I asked pulling out glancing over at her.

"You're talkative and helpful today. James A. Garfield High School," she told me rolling her eyes. High school, I wonder how young she is? She could have fooled me being at least 20.

"Just your friendly neighborhood lyft driver," I said sarcastically but she just rolled her eyes again staying quiet. I chuckled shaking my head speeding up going towards the school.

"Was Zeke in the bar?" She asked me looking over at me curiously.

"If I thought Zeke was in that bar, do you really think I'd let you in car?" I asked her my tone a little sharper. It was a stupid question, if Zeke was there, I wouldn't have to deal with this but yet here I am. She shook her head looking at her phone tapping away on it. Once I managed to get the dress on got to the high school, I went into the carpool lane.

"Oh, you could have just dropped me at the corner," she said looking around nervously. Oh, so she's embarrassed? This is going to be fun.

"Nah, you're good. The doors are right up there." I smirked nodding towards the drop off point.

ELEANOR

I closed my eyes sinking lower into the leather seat, hopefully nobody sees me getting out of the car. Finally, Trip pulled up to the drop off point and I unbuckled reaching into the back grabbing my backpack. I opened the door just as Trip chuckles.

"What? Not even a kiss thank you?" He smirked looking me up and down.

"You're disgusting" I said getting out slamming the door as he laughed behind me. Right away my eyes caught onto my best friend, Gabby. She was looking between me and the car with wide eyes. I smiled putting on my backpack going to walk over to her.

"BABY GIRL" Trip yelled making me cringe. I turned looking at him with an eyebrow raised. I saw that mocking, cocky smirk plastered on his face.

"LAST NIGHT WAS FUN" He yelled out of the passenger window. My jaw dropped as my cheeks burned a bright red. The people standing around looked at me laughing as they leaned into their friends whispering. He laughed speeding off leaving me there in my state of shock. I hate him, it's official if it wasn't before. I hate Trip. What was the point of yelling that and starting that rumor on the first day? I felt fingers wrap around my wrist and I was pulled back to be met with Gabby's wide eyes.

"Bitch who was that? He stayed at your place last night?" Gabby asked me in shock. I quickly covered her plump lipstick covered lips.

"No, he didn't. He's Zeke's new right-hand guy. I missed the bus, and he gave me a ride to school. He's a dick and I hate him" I told Gabby uncovering her mouth walking towards the school with her following. Gabby was gorgeous, she had long dark brown hair that was left in its wavy state, she had sandy glowing skin, dark brown eyes. Perfect facial features, plump full lips that even caught my attention. Her jawline was sharp and eye catching. She had an average body, but she knew how to flaunt it just right, which made everyone want her.

"He was cute, you're telling me like you guys didn't even kiss?" She asked me as I pushed open the front doors to the school.

"Gabriella, I literally hate him. He's rude, cold, cocky, and just a disgusting person" I told her rolling my eyes. Not to mention he did murder a guy. I know that Zeke kills people and everyone in the Los Prophets did, but no one had ever dared to be so violent in front of me before. There was that one incident when I was younger but that was it, everyone knew Zeke didn't want me exposed to that kinda stuff. I walked into the office as Gabby smirked at me humming.

"That's how every great story starts." She smirked, but I just rolled my eyes.

"Hi, Eleanor Sánchez. I missed orientation" I told the lady sitting in behind the desk. She typed around on the computer and then printed off my schedule and locker combo. I thanked her taking the papers walking out with Gabby.

"How was Colombia though?" Gabby asked me with a bright smile.

"It was so much fun Gabby. It was nice to just be home and see Colombia. Now that I'm old enough to realize where I am and why it's so amazing it was even better" I told her with a bright smile finding my locker with ease. I carefully put in the combination opening it. After going to just one high school for the last 4 years, you know where everything is at.

"Ugh you are so lucky. You get an all-expense paid vacation to Colombia for free while I was working doubles all summer," she said. I pouted my lip at her grabbing her hand squeezing it as she put all of her stuff in my locker.

"I wish you would let me help you. I have the money" I told her seriously. Gabby's mom has cancer and she's not doing well. The medical bills are starting to add up and she has to help her dad with her younger siblings and the bills. It's too much for a 17-year-old girl to deal with. No one else besides me knew about her mom, she kept it from our core group of friends.

"No, I don't take charity and plus you did god knows what to get that money" She shook her head. I laughed shaking my head shutting the locker door.

"I delivered a couple duffel bags and gambled with Zeke. It was nothing, please let me give you some of it" I begged but she just shook her head no refusing to let me help her. I went to argue with her, but she gave me a look that told me she was done talking about it so on that note I changed the subject to our schedules and went on about my day.

TREY'VON

I pulled up to the bar taking my parking spot in front, I put my car in park and got out. I walked inside to see heads were already here. Yesterday Skinheads walked up in here like the owned the place and I'm the one that got chewed out, all because dropped one like the useless piece of shit they are.

"TRIP" One of the runners called my name out laughing already drunk. Disgusting, it's barely passed 8 and that asshole is plastered.

"What can I get you cutie" The lady in her 40's behind the counter asked. I couldn't help but notice how she tied her top up to try to show off her boobs like she worked at hooters. Then the bike shorts she had one wasn't showing off anything flattering.

"Bottle of water. Unopened" I said making a look of disgust as I looked her up and down. I could tell she wanted to snap at me for my look but kept quiet. Everyone knew me and knew how stupid it would be say anything out of line. She slid me the bottle of water and I pulled it open walking over to the table where Antonio, Jose, and Ace were. Antonio and Jose were hit men and Ace was a smuggler. Antonio and Jose were newly moved up as I was, and Ace moved from Mexico to here to transport guns.

"I still can't believe those Skinhead's had the nerve to pull up in my hood" I said shaking my head kicking my feet up on the table.

"The look on their faces when you shot that asshole was priceless" Jose laughed with a thick accent making me laugh.

"Aint nobody about to talk to me like that and live. I don't give a fuck if it's Obama" I said shaking my head grabbing my water taking another drink.

"Yeah, that's something to talk about but what about that fine piece of ass that came in here yesterday?" Antonio asked us. I looked at him raising an eyebrow trying to think about who he could be talking about, but no one stuck out.

"She was hot, but she seemed close to Zeke and I aint tryin to fuck around and get killed" Jose said. I realized they were talking about whats her face. I couldn't help but notice the way my body tensed at the mention of her.

"I don't give a fuck who she close with. The next time she come in here just know I'm smashin" Antonio said confidently making me too well aware of the gun pressed against my stomach in my waist band. I could already smell crisp familiar smell of burning gun powder and I haven't even fired a shot yet.

"How you gonna do it?" Ace asked laughing as my thoughts spiraled about shooting every one of them. I couldn't tell you why the violent images were taking over, what about that girl made this conversation make me so mad. The more vile details that left Antonio's mouth about how he was going to "screw her whether she liked it or not" was just pushing me farther into my madness.

"Actually, none of you muhfucka's gonna touch her and that's a promise" I snapped pulling out my gun sitting it on the table. They looked at me confused raising an eyebrow.

"Since you care about a bitch? Don't you hit and forget about it?" Antonio asked me shrugging. I mean he was right, and I knew that's the only reason their conversation was pissing me off. I wanted to hit it and forget about it, and I didn't want them up in it first.

"I'm hittin it right now and I don't share my shit. She's mine" I growled at them sending harsh glares to all three of them, my hand gripping my gun tighter than before.

"Oh yeah? How you hittin it?" Jose asked me but I just shrugged.

"I mean you know she was suckin this dick while I was drivin" I smirked doing the hand motion. I chuckled as they all yelled out an ohhh.

"Was she good at it at least?" Jose asked me with a smile, and I nodded.

"Bro, she was like a pro. She said I don't do this very often and sucked that shit like a pornstar" I said shaking my head laughing. Suddenly the three men's face paled, and I felt a hand land on my shoulder.

"Is that right?" Zeke's voice came from behind me making me inwardly cringe. I put my gun in my waist band looking up at him to see he was hot.

"Can we talk, Trip" He spat, and I nodded. I stood up grabbing my water following him to the back room. He slammed the door and turned glaring at me.

"You better watch how you steppin Zeke" I snapped harshly taking a step forward.

"Nah kid, you better watch it. That girl like my daughter and you must have a death wish if you think you even touchin her" He snapped at me pulling his gun making me roll my eyes.

"Aint nobody fuckin with her. I don't even like her, she's fucking annoying. Ya'boy Antonio talkin about rapin so I just claimed her. Clearly your wack ass protection wasn't enough" I spat stepping up to him looking down at the gun.

"So, you really about to shoot? Go ahead then what claim gonna protect her? Your word? Yeah, good luck with that. WE CRIMINALS, WE DON'T GIVE A FUCK" I yelled at him. Every bone in my body ached to hit him but he was my higher up. He sent me a glare backing down putting up his gun.

"Just tell Antonio to come in here. We have matters to discuss" Zeke said making me roll my eyes. I stormed out slamming the door telling Antonio to go to the back to talk to Zeke. I snatched up my keys going outside to get some air before everyone really got to see what I was about.

ELEANOR

AFTER SCHOOL

I sat on the bus next to Mateo, I couldn't help but notice how pretty she looked today. She had long black hair that she curled. Her sandy skin that matched our dad's looked like it was shining today. Her eyebrows were styled with a slit through one, she had light brown almost hazel eyes. Her facial features fit her face well, her lips were plump and naturally the prettiest pink color. She had that stereotypical scary movie hot girl body which she pulled off with ease.

"When does Varsity soccer start?" Mateo asked me curiously

"Next week. I'm so ready for it" I admitted, and she nodded. We finally pulled up to our stop, we gathered our things getting off thanking the bus driver. The crowd of teenagers were quick to go their own ways. I saw two guys sitting outside the bar I didn't recognize but they had Los Prophet tattoos.

"Aye mommi, why don't you come on in and let me show you a good time" One of the men called after me. I couldn't help but be taken back because they're all on strict orders not to mess with me.

"Keep your head down" Mateo whispered and I did just that. You never look at a cat calling man.

"You better watch it. That's Trip's girl, aint you hear?" The other asked making me stop dead in my tracks. Mateo grabbed my arm trying to pull me forward, but I ripped away from her.

"What did you just say?" I asked taking a step closer to the Los Prophet members. Why would they call me Trip's girl? We don't even like each other or at least I can't stand him.

"He told us about how you guys fucked in his car" The man smirked at me making my eyes grow wide.

"Sis, let's just go" Mateo begged grabbing my wrist but I pulled away from her.

"Is he in there right now?" I asked and they both nodded. I dropped my backpack storming inside the bar as Mateo took off running home. Just as I swung open the door, I seen him sitting at a table with different guys around him and they were all laughing.

"SO, YOU'RE JUST TELLING EVERYONE WE HAD SEX WHEN YOU KNOW WE DIDN'T" I yelled as I stormed over to his table. He looked up that stupid smirk taking over his face. I wanted nothing more than to slap it off of him at this very moment. His eyes scanned my body making me only roll my eyes.

"Come on baby girl, you aint got to lie about it" He smirked going to reach for a water bottle, but I snatched it off the table tearing off the lid throwing it on him.

"WHAT THE HELL IS WRONG WIT YOU? I WOULDN'T SLEEP WITH YOU IF MY LIFE DEPENDED ON IT" I screamed at him as he gaped down looking at his soaked clothes. He looked up at me, his nearly black eyes were completely black and wild now as his face contorted with rage. I couldn't lie it did scare me, but I wasn't going to back down.

"BITCH YOU BETTER SIT DOWN AND SHUT THE FUCK UP" He yelled jumping up making his chair fall and the table wobble.

"TELL THEM YOU LIED" I yelled at him taking a step closer only making his rage increase and my heart pound harder against my chest.

"AINT NOBODY LIED, YOU'RE JUST A WHORE WHO WON'T ADMIT IT" He screamed back at me. I brought back my hand going slap him but before my hand could connect or he could grab my wrist, my waist was grabbed, and I was being pulled back.

"ELLY, ELLY" I heard my dad yell as I was pulled back.

"JUST CAUSE YOU A BITCH DOESN'T MEAN I WON'T FUCKING DROP YOU" Trip yelled coming closer so we were face to face again.

"GO AHEAD TRIP, SHOW EVERYONE IN HERE HOW MUCH OF A MAN YOU ARE. THE MOMENT YOU DO, ZEKE IS GOING TO PUT A BULLET IN YOUR SKULL!" I yelled at him trying to take a step closer, but my dad pulled me back and put himself between us. He kept trying push me back, but I was fighting against him to get back into Trip's face.

"ELLY ENOUGH!" My dad yelled at me. I looked away from Trip and up to my dad who looked just as angry as the two of us.

"WHO THE FUCK ARE YOU? WHY YOU THINK YOU GET TO STEP IN?" Trip yelled at my dad taking a step towards him sizing him up.

"I'm her father and I don't like the way you are talking to my daughter," my dad stated crossing his arms. Trip laughed shaking his head. Before I could even blink, he pulled his gun pressing it against my dad's head and clicking the hammer.

"I don't give a fuck who you are, I'll talk to that bitch anyway I want too" He snarled at my dad sending a panic through my body.

"TRIP, STOP PLEASE!" I yelled moving in front of my dad pushing at Trip's chest trying to back him away.

"I'M SORRY, I'M SORRY. TELL EVERYONE WE HAD SEX I DON'T CARE ANYMORE. Please, Trip don't do this," I begged him. His completely black eyes looked down at me as his lip snarled up.

"Trip put away the gun," I heard Zeke's cool voice. Trip sent me a cynical smile but put away the gun allowing me to breath for the moment.

"You two get out of here. Trip, me and you in the back" Zeke ordered. I quickly pushed my dad out of the bar and then sent him a glare.

"I had it, I didn't need you to come save me," I snapped at him. My dad sent me that "dad look," making me slink back.

"DIDN'T I TELL YOU TO STAY AWAY FROM THAT DAMN PLACE? I TELL YOU OVER AND OVER AGAIN BUT YOU NEVER LISTEN. YOU'RE GOING TO GET KILLED. ZEKE ISN'T A GOOD GUY LIKE YOU THINK HE IS!" My dad yelled at me shoving me towards the house. I crossed my arms and stormed over to the fence.

"He just saved you," I shot at my dad, but only earned another glare from him.

"STAY AWAY FROM ZEKE AND THAT DAMN BAR!" he yelled at me. I stalked inside the house as my mom walked into the living room letting out a breath.

"Elly, we've told you---" I cut her off snatching up my backpack.

"I have homework," I bit charging up the stairs. I went straight to my room slamming my bedroom door. I threw my backpack at my bed out of anger. I grabbed my hair and slid down the door. There was now a rumor that I had sex with Trip in his car. What was I going to do?

Chapter 3

Lock Down

ELEANOR

My screaming alarm made me groan as I hid my face in my pillows. As I pushed myself out of bed and turned off my alarm. I opened my drawer grabbing underclothes. From the middle drawer I picked a white tight fitting cropped t-shirt. I went over to my closet pairing the top with a pair of light worn high-waist ripped skinny jeans. I made my bed laying out my outfit grabbing a towel and my body soap. I walked down the hall to the bathroom to find the door locked.

"HURRY UP, I NEED IN THERE!" I yelled banging on the door.

"GIVE ME A MINUTE" I heard my older sister Isabella yell, I groaned in annoyance.

"I HAVE SCHOOL!" I yelled back banging on the door. Moments later it swung open to show Izzy wrapped in towels.

"There," she said coming out shooting me daggers with her eyes. I walked into the bathroom shutting and locking the door. I did my usual morning routine and then headed back to my bedroom to finish getting ready for my day. Once I approved of my hair and makeup I got dressed and paired my outfit with my white vans. I gathered my homework and laptop putting it in my backpack. Once I had everything, I walked downstairs to find my mom, dad, and two sisters sitting at the table eating breakfast.

My older sister Isabella was so gorgeous I swear everyone felt their self-confidence drop around her. She had that perfect kissed by the sun glowing skin. Her natural long black curls were dyed blonde. She had perfectly groomed eyebrows, dark brown eyes, narrow facial features, heavy lower lip. Her jawline was sharp and she had a beautiful curvy body. She was 5'5 so about average height.

"Elly sit, let's talk," Dad said motioning to my usual chair my plate was piled high with pancakes, bacon, and fresh fruit onto the plate.

"We want to talk to you about what happened yesterday," Mom said sitting down next to my dad holding his hand.

"It was nothing. I just got into an argument with somebody who's not even important" I hated Trip before, but after yesterday, the fact he pulled a gun on my dad and said what he said, hating him was an understatement.

"How many times have we told you to stay away from that bar?" Dad asked me his tone stern. I looked down at my plate pushing around the fruit with my fork. I shrugged not wanting to answer his question because he had asked it more times than I could count.

"DAMMIT ELLY!" Dad yelled slamming his fists on the table. I looked to the side trying to avoid everyone's eyes.

"I DON'T GET IT ELLY. WHAT IS YOUR OBSESSION WITH THAT BAR AND ZEKE SANTIAGO? WHY CAN'T YOU SEE HE'S A BAD PERSON?" I looked back down at my plate not saying a word.

"ANSWER THE QUESTION!" Tears began to spring to my eyes, but I fought them back. A lesson that Zeke had taught me when I was young was not to cry in front of anyone, don't let them know you have a weak spot because then they'll eat at it.

"Zeke isn't a bad person to me. I mean his job makes him do bad things, but I know Zeke better than anyone. It's like I have two dad's, one that teaches the honest way and how to be a good person and the other that teaches how cruel the world can be and how to cope with it." I told him. But his anger only ignited farther.

"You only have one father and that's ME! You're grounded for being at the bar, being around Zeke and his men, and for everything that happened yesterday." He snapped at me. I just silently nodded.

27

"For how long?" I asked trying not to let attitude slip, but I failed, and it clipped my tone.

"Until I say. Now go before you miss the bus!" He snapped at me. I stood up snatched my backpack and my mom handed me my hydroflask. I thanked her looking at Mateo as she stuffed the last piece of bacon in her mouth. She picked up her backpack and I followed her to the front door. We stepped out onto the porch and it was like God was working against me because there stood Trip, leaning against my rusted fence post. I shook my head, took the lead by pushing open the gate catching Trip's attention. He looked at me with that annoying smirk, but I pretended not to notice.

"I have gym right after lunch, it honestly sucks so bad," I told Mateo trying to strike up a conversation.

"Ew, that probably makes you feel sick for the rest of the day," she said crinkling up her nose. I nodded in agreement as we walked past Trip.

"I swear I almost puked running laps yesterday" which made both of us giggle. Suddenly a surprisingly soft, smooth hand gripped my wrist and spun me around. I stumbled over my own feet. I pushed him away from me as hard as I could.

"Don't you have puppies to put in a blender or anything other to do than Joe me?" I snapped at him turning on my heels. I tried to walk away but he grabbed my wrist again, spinning me around with a chuckle.

"Joe you? Should I understand that?" he asked me. I looked up at him his eyes lit with humor.

"I don't know. Leave me alone," I said jerking away from him. Mateo and I started walking towards the bus stop once again but I heard sneakers against the concrete and moments later Trip was next to me. I couldn't understand what he wanted. I know he had to hate me just as much as I hated him.

TREY'VON

She was so frustrating. That smart mouth, eye roll, and attitude she had made me want to kill her. No one had ever dared to talk to me the way she had or even had the balls walk away from me, but she had and was

28

comfortable doing it. I hated every person I was around, and of course she was no different, but she affected me different than everyone else.

"Baby girl, come on don't walk away from me. I just want to apologize for yesterday. I lost my temper." I couldn't help the slight chuckle my voice carried. No part of me was sorry, she came at me. If anyone should be apologizing it should be her, but Zeke wouldn't hear it. She suddenly stopped walking, she turned to me with her arms crossed and glared her focused on me only heightened my amusement. It took everything inside me not to laugh at this stupid apology and how angry she looked.

"You know when you apologize, you're supposed to mean it," she told me. I gasped dramatically putting my hand over my heart like I was shocked.

"Wait a minute! You mean I can't just say the words?" I asked her sarcastically. Her annoyed look only grew.

"While you bicker with the gang member, I'm going to catch the bus," the other girl she was with said. Fuck, I still don't know her name. Oh well after I apologize, I'll never have to be around her again, but I got to make her believe I actually feel bad.

"Nah, let me drive you guys to school. You seemed to like our last ride," I smirked at "whatever her fucking name is" but she just rolled her eyes.

"I rather spend 5 hours on that bus than be in your car for 5 minutes. You got me grounded by the way," she snapped. I inhaled deeply, attempting to keep my temper in check, as I followed her.

"How the fuck did I get you grounded? How old are you?" I asked her. She looked grown. How was she still getting grounded? And how I was I responsible for her poor decisions?

"Because you started that stupid rumor and then pulled a gun on my dad so thanks. I'm 17 by the way, so you started a rumor you slept with a minor. Have fun in prison, I won't miss you."

"Well lucky for me, I'm only 19. It's only illegal if the gap is bigger than 4 year.s" I smirked looking her up and down. Her outfit was more simple today, but it still didn't cover her flat stomach. Then I realized she brought up that stupid rumor again, she didn't even stop to think about why said it.

"Plus you don't even understand why I did what I did!" I tried to dismiss her, but my tone grew hard. I tried to help her, those guys weren't going to stop just because Zeke said so, but they're scared of me.

"I understand perfectly. I'm done with this conversation and you. Leave me alone, I don't ever want to talk to you again. I don't know why you even want to talk to me." Her tone was sharp. I stopped dead in my tracks in front of the bar. She looked at me raising an eyebrow like she was excepting a comeback. I looked her up and down as her words replayed in my head, I already did what Zeke asked. He said to apologize, he never said she had to believe it or accept it. I could finally just cut my loses with this whole situation and I'd never have to mess with this...girl again.

"You're actually right for once. Zeke just said I had apologize not that I had to make you believe it. Have a nice life, baby girl." She looked at me with wide shocked eyes, her lips parting slightly and with that I walked into the bar.

"Let me get a water," I called out to the lady who needed way more clothing than she was wearing. She slid me a bottle and I walked over to some of the guys.

"What time is Zeke about to get here? I might bounce before he does," I told them honestly. I didn't want the third degree about my apology or to even hear anything about that girl, I just wanted to move on.

"I'm not sure. I know he has some business with a disturber. I guess they ripped off the counterfeit cash," Jose told me. I shook my head putting my feet on the table.

"He better just kill em. Anybody who steals once will do it again and we don't got time to play these games." I said with a careless shrug. A thief and a snitch were the worst kind of people in my book, and you take care of both the same way...with a bullet. It shuts them up and stops them from taking what is yours.

"So, I got word on a party tonight," Antonio said catching my attention.

"Finally! I've been trying to go out for the last few nights. Get a bitch, get a little high," I said we started making plans for the night.

ELEANOR

I slammed my locker shut in frustration. I had been ranting about Trip to my friends. I don't know why he got under my skin so much. That smirk alone was enough to push me over the edge. And that fake ass apology was just so exasperating.

"I've never met a more annoying person. He makes me want to stop going to the bar but that means I wouldn't see Zeke near as much as I do" I fulminate to my friends who just looked at me amused. None of them even knew Trip, of course. Gabby got a look at him when he dropped me off, but other than that they didn't even know who he was.

"What did you say his name was?" My friend Lucas asked me raising an eyebrow. Lucas was so hot, and he was my ex-boyfriend. We dated for a year and 3 months before I broke up with him. I wasn't feeling the same about him anymore. I didn't find myself loving him the way a girlfriend should but more like a friend. I didn't think it was fair to him, so I broke it off. Things got awkward in our group for a little bit but, we're really good friends now.

Lucas was 6ft tall, Puerto Rican. He had dark brown hair gelled up to perfection. I don't think I've ever seen it messy or unstyled. His skin was clear and blemish free, but I knew from experience it was calloused. His were styled and thick brows. His eyes were a brilliant blue I always had loved those eyes. His pink lips that never really seemed appealing to me, but his jawline was crazy sharp. Then he had the craziest muscles. He was the star baseball player at our school.

"Trip. Stupid name, right?" I grumbled kicking a water bottle. All my other friends agreed, but I saw Lucas's face pale.

"You good bro?" Tony asked him slapping his back. Tony was a football player, he was 6'2 and Asian. His black hair was thick and always styled messy, he had the clearest skin I've ever seen. His eyebrows leaned towards the thinner side. His eyes were so brown they were almost black. His thin lips were always plump like they were swollen from kissing. He was muscular as well but not to Lucas's degree.

31

"Uh...um...yeah. I just remembered I forgot my jock strap in the locker room," Lucas said shaking his head. I watched him as he quickly walked away glancing back at me.

"What's up with him?" I asked nodding my head towards my fleeing friend.

"He's been off ever since his brother got out of prison," Tony told us as the first bell rang. We slowly started walking towards our classes.

"What did he get locked up for again? Wasn't it armed robbery?" our other friend Nicole asked curiously. Nicole was very pretty, she had naturally dark hair but kept it bleached blonde. Her paler skin looked good on her, and she kept her eyebrows thin which didn't look too bad. She had dark brown eyes. Her nose didn't fit her face somehow. It was the first thing your eyes went. She had a heavy upper lip, a sharp jawline. Her body was curvy like mine.

"Yeah, he knocked up a corner store," Gabby told Nicole with a shrug. I just hummed.

"I'll talk to him in class," I said as we parted. We all said our goodbyes and I turned down the hall heading towards my first period. Lucas didn't even mention to me that his brother was getting out. I walked into English scanning the room finding Lucas in his usual seat at the back. I walked over and took the desk next to him. He looked at me raising an eyebrow.

"What?" He asked me with a groan making me laugh.

"Are you ok? You walked off kinda sudden," I asked him as I messed with the spine of my notebook. He looked at me like he was thinking about something and then just nodded and looked down at his phone. I knew Lucas better than anyone, he was lying. Something was wrong and he was holding out on me.

"Why didn't you tell me Theo was out?" I asked him curiously as the bell rang signaling passing period was over. Lucas looked at me with wide frantic eyes only furthering my confusion and worry. I felt my face screw up in confusion.

"Who told you about that? How did you find out?" he asked me in a rushed, guarded tone. I watched as his eyes darted around like they do when he's thinking of an explanation on the spot. I leaned over grabbing his hand and sent him a smile.

"Luke, Tony told me. Is something going on with your brother that has you acting this way?" I asked with concern. His brother wasn't the nicest person in the world, he honestly kinda scared me so I'd understand if Lucas was felt unsafe because of him too. I watched Lucas lean back in his seat, he looked at me like he was trying to figure me out.

"You haven't called me Luke since we broke up," he said a with a smile. I blushed covering my cheeks with my hands. I hated when someone brought up our past. I felt like it made things awkward between us...or at least it did for me.

"Miss. Sánchez, Mr. Bow. Since you two seem to be getting along so well you can be partners for this after school project," Mrs. Owens said catching our attention. Wait, what project? After school? Lucas has baseball practice and starting next week I have soccer.

"WHAT PROJECT?" We ended up yelling at the same time which made the class laugh.

AFTER SCHOOL

I sat on the bus trapped between the window and Lucas. He decided he was just going to come home with me so we could start on our project. The assignment was to make a YouTube video where we picked our favorite Gothic poem and made a short movie out of it. Finally, the bus got to my stop, we stood up and I grabbed my backpack. I followed Lucas down the aisle and off the bus. The moment I stepped off, my eyes caught a dark brown pair looking directly at me. Leaning against the bricks on the bar was Trip. He had a blunt between his lips. I didn't fail to notice the way his eyes traveled my body and then flicked over to Lucas. I pulled out my earbuds looking up at Lucas while I ignored the annoying gangster.

"We're about to have the best video in class," Lucas smiled down at me. As I pushed my headphones into the side pocket of my backpack.

"Totally. This neighborhood screams Edgar Allan Poe," I teased him. He chuckled messing with the strings on his backpack as we slowly walked past the watchful eyes of the gangster.

"Who said we were doing Poe? Plus, we already have chemistry which is an advantage" He teased bumping me with his hip. I laughed looking down at my feet smiling. Suddenly I felt Lucas get pulled away from my side. My head snapped up as I saw Trip throw Lucas against the brick wall with his gun out.

"TRIP, WHAT THE HELL IS YOUR PROBLEM?" I yelled at him as he pulled back the hammer on his gun, totally ignoring me.

"You got some nerve being in this neighborhood! What, you thought I wasn't gonna recognize you?" Trip's voice was low and intimidating. It sent shivers even through me. Every warning sign was going off in my head telling me to not push Trip in this moment.

"You got the wrong guy. I don't even know you!" Lucas rushed with his hands up while he sat on the ground. I dropped my backpack to the ground pushing at Trip.

"Trip, he's not whoever you think he is. Please don't do this." I kept my voice calm and soft. I saw how red and glossed over his eyes were. I knew there was no way he could be thinking clearly. Trip looked down at me and scoffed as I tried to push at him harder, but he didn't budge nor say a word.

"TRIP!" I yelled pushing him hard enough to make him stumble. He looked at me with his face reddening from anger.

"HE'S NOT THE PERSON YOU THINK HE IS!" I yelled as I bent down to get eye level with Lucas.

"You ok? I'm sorry, he's a dick," I told Lucas as I helped him up.

"HE'S AN EL DIABLOS!" Trip yelled at me grabbing my arm ripping me closer to him, I pushed him away taking a step back.

"Wait, Trip. That aint the muhfucka that shot at us. He just look like him," Rudy stepped up looking Lucas up and down. I looked at Trip shaking my head grabbing Lucas's arm. I pulled Lucas with me as I walked backwards and then turned pushing him ahead of me. I hurried us into my house shutting and locking the door.

"He's intense," Lucas said making me nod in agreement. I let out a breath I didn't even know I was holding.

"He's more than intense. Are you ok?" I asked him walking over to check his arms and face. There were no marks, I could see.

"I'm fine, he just had the wrong guy," Lucas told me. I looked up at him raising an eyebrow. Why would Trip mistake Lucas for someone else? I knew Trip was high, but Lucas has a distinct look.

"Elle, he was clearly high. Don't think too much into to it. I'm fine" Lucas smiled running his hand over my hair pulling me into a hug. I sighed into his chest hugging him back, happy that he was ok. I pulled away and led us up the stairs. My eyes didn't miss Izzy standing in the living room smirking at me, but I pretended not to notice. We went us upstairs to my bedroom and I tossed my bag on the bed as Lucas shut the door following my lead. I walked over to my bookshelf climbing up the ladder. I selected Emily Dickson, Edgar Allan Poe, Wilfred Owens, and Dorothy Parker books and handed them all down to Lucas.

"I forgot how much of a nerd you are," Lucas teased as he carefully placed the leather-bound books onto the floor.

"Spoken like a true jock. Reading does not make you a nerd, I love the way you can get lost into a good book," I smiled slipping off my shoes and sitting crisscross apple sauce on the floor next to him. He looked at me with a half-smile humming making me laugh. There was a knock on the door stealing our attention. It opened to reveal my mom in her scrubs.

"You're home early," I stated, giving her a confused look.

"Over staffed, so I volunteered to leave early. Izzy told me you were up here. It's so nice to see your face around here again, Lucas" Mom said. Lucas stood up and hugged my mom with a bright smile.

"It's nice to see you Mrs. Sánchez. Sorry for just coming over but the project was kinda sprung on us," he told my mom who clearly loved Lucas. I think my mom cried more over our breakup than I did.

"It's fine. You're welcome anytime, I'm going to start dinner. Leave this door open," Mom told us with a look. It was no secret that me and Lucas was very active in our time together, but that never stopped my parents from being strict.

LUCAS

I smiled at Mrs. Sánchez as she walked away from the open door. I looked back at Elly who looked as good as ever. I couldn't lie, that Colombian sun really brought out an irresistible glow. I missed Elly, I wanted her back. When she broke up with me it hurt my ego a lot. She told me she wasn't in love with me anymore. So I told her I never really loved her. It was the biggest lie I had ever told, I still loved her. I knew once she found out what I was hiding I could kiss all of our chances of getting back together goodbye, maybe even our friendship. That Trip guy almost exposed my secret but thankfully she didn't ask too many questions. Hopefully the time we spend together working on this project will make her remember her love for me and it won't even matter.

"Why are you staring at me?" she asked looking at me with curious eyes as she opened a book.

"I can't look at you?" I flirted. She looked at me confused, laughed, and then looked back at the book.

"So, I was thinking we do *Because I could not stop for death*. I could play Emily and you could be Death" Her eyes lit up brightly with her suggestion. This English stuff was always her favorite, she loved the complex thinking that came with it. I had never seen anyone pass classed with such flying colors.

"Yeah, that could be cool." I smiled, still admiring her facial features. She closed the book looking at me with an amused smile.

"Do I have something on my face?" I shook my head looking down to the books.

"Maybe we should brainstorm our video and then write it out," I suggested. She nodded, while opening her closet and pulling out a poster board and sharpies. She tossed the board and makers down. I watched her lay on her stomach as she drew a circle in the middle writing, ‹*Because I could not stop -ED*›. Her handwriting looked like art in and of itself like it should be show cased in a museum.

"You like?" She flipped her long curls over her shoulder looking up at me, I nodded.

"Yeah, I think I should reread that poem," I said, I never have read it before and I didn't want to sound stupid. She grabbed an open book and handed it to me. I watched her readjust herself and I knew I shouldn't have looked. But her butt jiggled with each movement. I read the poem. Once I finished, I looked up at Elly, she raised an eyebrow at me.

"You didn't understand it did you?" She asked me. I laughed shaking my head no as I closed the thick book.

"LUCAS!" she yelled at me laughing. She hid her face in her arms making me chuckle.

"Come on Elles you know I'm not good at this stuff. Just tell me what it means" I pleaded as I leaned back against her bed. She sighed and explained the poem to me. As I listened to her accented voice break down old American literature, I couldn't help but watch at how consumed she had become. The passion behind her words, the way her eyelids slowly closed making her eyelashes brush against her cheek bones. Then they'd flutter open, and she'd smile as she told me some little fun fact about Emily Dickson. She was so gorgeous. I loved the way she got lost in this shit. It didn't even sound like English to me, but yet she understood it without even trying.

"Are you listening to me?" she asked hitting my foot. I hummed nodding my head even though I couldn't hear anything over her beauty.

"No, you're not. If you don't want to do this poem that's fine," she told me moving to sit on her knees.

"No, I want to. It's just hard to focus when you over there lookin so cute," I flirted. She looked up with wide eyes. I watched her cheeks turn a rosy color.

"Lucas stop. We aren't together anymore," she told me standing up gathering the books we weren't using.

"I'm not doing anything. I'm just being honest," I smiled. She brushed off my comment climbing up on the ladder putting away the books.

"You mean to tell me you don't miss us, like ever?" I asked her curiously. She climbed down off the ladder shaking her head no.

"I don't think about it and I don't like talking about it. We make really good friends and I'm ok with that right now," she told me as she avoided eye contact.

"Do you want to take a break? Go outside and get some air?" she asked me. I must have made her feel uncomfortable. I nodded standing up and followed her down the stairs and out to the front door to the porch.

"I didn't mean to make you feel uncomfortable," I told her as she sat down on the steps.

"You didn't." She whispered. I walked over sat down next to her. I saw her looking toward the bar where the gangsters were playing stick ball with some of the neighborhood kids.

"THAT MUHFUCKA OUT OF HERE!" That Trip guy yelled throwing the stick taking off after the bases.

"Why did Trip think you were an El Diablos?" Elly asked looking over at me. I had to think on my feet, I knew how much those low lives meant to her and I wasn't sure if she'd put herself in their beef or not.

"DINNER IS READY!" Mrs. Sánchez yelled cutting our conversation short. We got up and joined her family at the table. Then got back to work on our project.

Chapter 4

Changes

TREY'VON

Zeke followed me as I swung the bar door open. It has been a busy day already and tonight we have a shipment coming in from the Bahama's which means I'll be at a dope house all night making sure those assholes do their jobs. When I could find a bitch, get my dick sucked, and then go home.

"You have the worst fucking attitude I've ever seen," Zeke's comment was laced with attitude. His patience was wearing thin with me, but I didn't give a fuck. I'm not like these bitch ass pussy dudes in here. I wasn't scared of Zeke. I knew I had to give him a limit of respect because he was my higher up and I'd have his spot one day.

"I don't hear any complaints when we're dealing with fuck ups" I spat back.

"Why don't you get a drink and shut the fuck up?" He asked annoyed banging on the counter. "Hooters want-to-be" poured him bourbon over the rocks, I crinkled my nose up in distaste, shaking my head.

"I don't drink you old fuck. Why don't you have your dusty ass employee put on some clothes?" I growled at Zeke as I went over to the back corner table. I heard him laugh at me, but I was being serious. I got tired of seeing her saggy ass not wearing enough clothes.

"You're a dick" Zeke laughed coming over with a couple other guys. I just sent him a glare.

"She's like fucking 50, no one wants to see that shit. If you gonna make 'em dress like that, why don't you get a bad bitch in here?" I asked shaking my head as I texted some girl, I met at a party last night. I was trying to convince her to come to the bar. I was just gonna nut and go.

"Any other complaints while you're at it?" Zeke asked as he downed the bourbon. I set down my phone looking at him and vaguely nodded my head.

"I don't want to be in that nasty ass dope house all night. Every time I leave one of those houses, I feel like I have to take ten showers to get clean." A shiver ran through my body at the thought of how disgusting all those houses were. I couldn't even sit down without worrying about infesting my whole house with bedbugs.

"Didn't you work in a dope house before?" Javier asked me slamming his beer on the table next to me.

"Yeah, when I was like 15 or 16. Being clean isn't the biggest goal at that age" I said with a shrug, and they all nodded in agreement. My only thoughts back then were bitches, alcohol, weed, and money that was it.

"You're working it and I don't want to hear anything else about it," Zeke said as the door opened. I saw some cholo making a bee line straight for our table. When he finally came into clear view, I realized it was the El Diablo I thought what's-her-face was with yesterday. Within seconds every gang member in the building was standing with their gun pulled except for me and Zeke.

Man, he really looked like that high school kid. He had the same messy black styled hair. His skin was little dark maybe a copper shade. Thin see-through eyebrows that needed work. His eyes were a shade of black, his nose and ears were a little too big for his head. His lips were thin. On his sharp jawline was stumble. He was muscular but not like the guy from yesterday. He wore a black tank top and khaki shorts, on his arm was the El Diablos devil.

"What do we have here? Are you stupid or do you have a death wish?" Zeke asked the guy as I looked him up and down. He looked away from Zeke, his black beady eyes finding me with a harsh glare. I couldn't stop the smirk from spreading across my lips. I could use this kinda fun after my tense day and soon to be tense night.

"I'm only going to tell you one time and one time only. Leave my little brother alone or else you Prophets won't like consequences," he growled at me waving his finger in my face. Right away I felt my temper spike, the thin flood gates came crashing down letting my anger get the best of me. Without a word I stood up throwing the table out of my way not caring about the drinks getting in his face.

"I'll do whatever the fuck I want to whoever the fuck I want. If you hadn't noticed El Diablos, this is MY FUCKING HOOD!" I yelled at him shoving him back powerfully, but he was right back in my face in seconds.

"I'LL MERC YOUR BITCH ASS RIGHT NOW AND YOUR BITCH DOWN THE STREET!" he yelled at me. Without a second thought my fist connected to his jaw sending him stumbling back dazed. I grabbed him by his throat slamming him down on a table that had two middle aged women sitting at it. They had nothing to do with the gangs but wrong place, wrong time. Javier, Lil Loco, Gizmo, and Jose rushed over to the table holding down the asshole I knew as Lil Psycho. I laughed as I picked up a knife from the and table slashed his face with it.

"YOU THINK YOU ABOUT TO COME UP IN MY FUCKING BAR AND DISRESPECT ME? NOW YOU JUST PUT A TARGET ON YOUR BACK AND YOUR LITTLE BROTHERS. NEXT TIME HE IN MY NEIGHBORHOOD HE GETTIN DEALT WITH JUST LIKE HE'S ONE OF YOU NASTY ASS EL DIABLOS!" I yelled at him. He tried to fight against my guys, but I held the knife to his jugular pressing it in with a glare.

"I could bleed you like a fucking animal right now. Lil Psycho is what they call you right?" He nodded his head. I licked my lips with a smile and jerked the knife away stabbing him in the shoulder.

"Touch my brother and I promise you Trip, I'll be the one to kill you!" he laughed at me. I smirked chuckled, licking my teeth as I twisted the knife.

"You know I could use some fun right now what about you guys?" I asked my guys. Everyone in the bar cheered making me laugh. I leaned down real close to Lil Psycho's ear.

"It's your lucky day Lil Psycho, we're not going to kill you today but you're going to wish you were dead." I snickered as I took out his gun and tossed it to the side.

"TAKE HIM OUT BACK!" I yelled pulling off my hoodie and tossing it onto a table. I watched my men pull him out back. I looked over to Zeke who had a devilish gleam in his eyes. We walked out together to see the four already beating his ass. Me and Zeke wasted no time jumping in stomping him out, the laughs escaping my lips were enough to send a shiver through even myself. We continued our punches, kicks, stomps, and spitting until he fell limp. I pushed back everyone to see if he was still breathing, and I was still pissed at the way he disrespected me.

"Actually, I AM gonna kill you!" I said with a sinister grin. I pulled out my gun aiming it at him and pulling back the hammer. Just as I started to squeeze the trigger, I heard a gasp from the front of the alley. My head snapped over and I saw the only pair of warm chocolate brown eyes that I didn't mind on me. They were filled with fear, confusion, and shock. Something about her seeing me like this made every nerve ending in my body go numb. The angry thoughts that pushed me to this point were silenced the moment I heard her. A deep part of me wanted to bark orders for them to hide the beaten up El Diablos. I knew this only came from her being like Zeke's daughter. I knew how much it meant to him to keep her innocent and pure. As his right hand and next in command, that became my goal too. I respected how much he cared about her even if she wasn't actually his blood.

As I kept eye contact with her, I lowered my gun carefully releasing the hammer. She shook her head running off. I squeezed my eyes closed. Now I was going to hear about this from Zeke on top of being stuck in a drug house all night long.

"FUCK!" I yelled kicking Lil Psycho in the stomach so hard I had to hold onto the dumpster.

"Get him the fuck out of here!" I barked the order storming past Zeke to go back inside the bar through the back door. He didn't have that usual angry look he has when I mess up around his "kinda daughter." I could see something building behind his eyes. But I couldn't even bring myself to care what he was thinking at the moment.

ELEANOR

Elly, it's no big deal you've seen countless fights in that bar. You've seen Zeke walk away from half dead guys with their blood on his knuckles, it's nothing. Trip pulled his gun; he was going to kill him but why didn't he? Why was it when he saw me, he stopped? It's not like he hadn't killed someone in front of me before. Maybe he got in trouble from Zeke for that when I wasn't around. Zeke has a strict no violence rule around me. I was very sheltered when it came to the gang stuff with Zeke. I got to do little jobs just so I felt like I was earning the money Zeke gave me, but really that was the only gang stuff I was allowed to do.

"What's wrong? You look like you seen a ghost!" Dad asked clapping my shoulder as he sat next to me on the couch. I looked over at him biting my lip nervously rubbing my arms up and down.

"I think you were right. I need to take a break from the bar for a while," I whispered to him. He looked at me shocked raising an eyebrow.

"What happened?" he asked me curiously. I sighed leaning forward rubbing my temples.

"It's this new guy Trip. He's rude, narcissistic, I don't even think he feels even one emotion other than anger. He is just the most annoying person ever and I can't even go and see Zeke without him being there because he's Zeke's new right hand. He's ruining everything," I told my dad burying my face in my hands. My dad wrapped his strong arms around me.

"He doesn't sound like an exceptionally good person. If Zeke is putting those type of people around him it should tell you something about his true character." Dad jumped at the chance to bad mouth Zeke. I don't know why that surprised me; I didn't understand my dad's beef with Zeke. Hell, he could have even worked for Zeke. After I didn't snitch, Zeke offered my dad a job, but he refused it.

"Yeah, I think I'm going to go lay down before Lucas gets here," I told dad pulling away and he nodded. I stood up grabbing my backpack going upstairs to my room when my phone vibrated in my back pocket. It was Zeke, and I couldn't help but smile.

Zeke- Sorry you seen that

I sat on my bed looking at the text biting my lip thinking about the plain message.

Me- Why? What did he do to you?

Zeke- He was El Diablos. Trust me he deserved worse for how he approached us in the bar, you saved his life. I got to go. Business. I'll call you later Princesa

I sighed tossed my phone onto my bed and laid down closing my eyes, trying to block out the horrible images I have seen over the last couple of days.

TREY'VON

A COUPLE HOURS LATER

I was sitting in a chair in front of the bar with a few of the guys rolling a blunt. We had just finished playing basketball with the kids. It was around the time they go in to do homework, eat dinner or whatever the hell normal functioning families did. Of course, those kids left with maybe a little over a hundred dollars in their pockets. It was always fun to have them race and give the winner money or do a shooting contest with the ball and pay them for every shot.

"You think the El Diablos will try to come for us after you guys beating up Lil Psycho," one of the kids in our gang asked me. I brought the half rolled blunt up to my lips licking the shell and glanced over at him. He was only 15. He was young. I think he said he joined like a year ago. I don't know, but he was pretty chill to hang out with. I remember being 15 and in the gang. I was a lot higher up than him though. I had my drug house, but I had put in more time than he had. I shrugged as I finished rolling it.

"I don't know. Probably. Let em come," I said with a shrug looking at the blunt I just pearled.

"Guhdamn look at this bitch." I held it up as Javier and Gizmo walked over. I put the blunt between my lips lighting it. I inhaled deeply closing my eyes letting the smoke fill my lungs. I swear it was like therapy. I moved the blunt from my lips, I held the smoke letting more of it invade my lungs before I opened my lips slowly letting the smoke roll out.

"Trip, I don't have a gun. What if they roll up on me?" The 15-year-old kid asked me. I looked over at him. He was about 5'11 and paper thin. I swear you could see that kid's bones, but he ate 24/7. He had a sandy skin; his light black hair was shaved into a short buzz on the side but was longer on top like mine. When I took him to get his Prophet tat after he was jumped in, he told me he wanted it on his neck like mine because he wanted to be respected like me. We called him Lil Smiley because he was little and always had some goofy grin on his face. I took another hit from the blunt passing it over to him. I let the smoke roll out of my mouth and then grabbed my bottle of water taking a drink. I went over to my car and unlocked it. I opened the door popping the trunk as I grabbed a brown paper bag. I went to the trunk and grabbed the Glock I had back there. I unwrapped the blanket without touching the gun itself and then dropped it into the bag with a full clip. I wrapped it up, slammed my trunk shut, then tossed the gun to Lil smiley. As he passed along the blunt, I took my seat watched him open it as his eyes grew wide.

"It's hot," I told him taking another drink. He nodded setting it to the side. Gizmo passed me the blunt, I took a hit as a tall sleek black truck drove pass. I watched as it stopped in front of Zeke's "sorta daughter's" house. When the door opened, I saw Lil Psycho's brother get out. Right away I got an idea. Lil Psycho came in here making a scene over that kid, right? Maybe beating the shit out of him wasn't enough. I should send him a reminder that no one tells me what to do. I'll just leave a few bruises on the kid. Just as I opened my mouth to tell the guys what we were gonna do I was cut off.

"LUCAS" I heard the Spanish accent that I could have gone the rest of my life without hearing. I watched the extremely attractive but annoying girl dart out of the gate. She had a big smile as she made her way over to the truck.

"That bitch is so fucking annoying." I leaned back in my chair taking another hit from the blunt and passed it to Lil Smiley.

"I don't think so. I think she's nice," Lil Smiley said with his usual smile. Of course, he'd like her. Who doesn't he like?

"I thought you were hitting it?" Javier asked me as he hit the blunt. I nodded running my hand over my hair.

"I hit it. Past tense but you damn near got to gag her to make her shut the fuck up!" I said rolling my eyes. I mean only part of it was a lie, she never shut up, but I never hit it. Annoying or not I still wouldn't mind hitting it. Her russet skin seemed to glow in any light, those bouncy curls would look even better wrapped around my fist. I wanted to feel those rosy, pink painted lips around me. Then to hear that Spanish accent whispering my name and moaning, the idea of it was enough to make me feel like I was going to bust.

"She's sexy, she's like 17 though. I never had the guts to go against Zeke like you did," Gizmo told me. I made a face at him. His nasty ass was like 36 with a whole wife and kid. Still, he was looking at a 17 year old. Fucking pervert, it's one thing for me and Lil Smiley to look. I'm only 19 and his little ass is 15.

"I don't give a fuck what Zeke has to say but I got to get going to the house," I said grabbing my water and unlocking my car. The loud beep pulled a certain pair of chocolate brown eyes over to me, but I pretended not notice. I opened the door and buckled up. I started the car turning up my music and pulled out swerving around the idiot in the truck that was parked in the middle of the road. Then I wasted my whole night in some nasty ass drug house with a bad attitude.

ELEANOR

I sat down on my bed as Lucas set up the camera, we were using to film our video. We're not ready to film yet, but he wanted to leave his camera over here until we *were* ready, for some reason. I scrolled through Instagram and watched soap cutting videos.

"This rare beauty in her natural habit is showing signs of boredom," Lucas said. He was pointing his camera at me as I looked up. I flipped him off and looked back at my phone trying to hold back my laugh.

"This is an extremely rare site. She's giving off her mating call--." I cut Lucas off by throwing my pillow at him.

"Stop it Luke, put the camera up," I laughed. He smiled at me turning off the camera. He moved over to the bed and laid backdown. I smiled flipping to my stomach. I grabbed his camera and began looking at the pictures on it.

"You called me Luke again," he smiled looking over at me as he put his hands behind his head. I returned this look, shrugged, and looked back at the camera.

"Is that an issue?" I asked him.

"No of course not. I'm just saying." I hummed as I set the camera on the side table. I rested my cheek on my arms and looked over at him, he smiled at me pushing a strand of hair behind my ear. My smile slowly grew even wider.

"You gonna come to my game next Friday?" he asked me curiously. I shrugged pulling at my pillowcase thinking about it. I mean I didn't see the problem with going to his game, he was my friend and friends support friends.

"Do you want me too?" I asked him curiously. He nodded his head looking over my body and then back up to my eyes. When he looked at my body it wasn't in a tasteless way like when Trip did it. Nor did his eyes feel heavy or make my body stir in a way I didn't recognize.

"Yeah, I'd like to look in the stands and see you."

"Then I'll be there. Hopefully, I'm ungrounded and we can do something to celebrate your win." I poked his cheek with my shorter nail. I got off the bed standing up and watched Luke sit up. His beautiful blue eyes looked me up and down one more time before he chuckled shaking his head looking down.

"You seem confident in that?" he asked me as I walked over to my dresser. I picked out a pair of black spandex shorts and a tight-fitting grey volleyball t-shirt.

"You're not? Would it be weird if I changed in front of you? I mean you've seen it all a million times, but I don't know because we aren't like anymore and I don't want to make any---" He cut me off laughing.

"Change. Be comfortable" he told me. I smiled biting my lip thinking about how amazing Luke is. I unzipped my crop top pulling it off tossing it into my clothes hamper and pulled my jeans off right after. I felt Luke's blue eyes staring a hole through me which made me giggle.

"Why are you staring at me?" I asked, placing my finger under his chin angling it up so he had to look at my eyes. He smiled at me as his hands went to the back of my thighs.

"You are still so beautiful," he whispered with that adorable little half smile taking over his face. His bright blue eyes shined with nothing but honesty and maybe even love. Luke couldn't still be in love with me, could he? Regardless of that unsure emotion in his eye, a blush filled my cheeks. I rested my hands on his buff broad shoulders as his hands made their way up to my waist. He never broke eye contact with me. It was times like this I couldn't remember why I ever broke up with Luke.

"I never stopped thinking you were beautiful." There was no denying how attractive Luke was and it was almost like I was seeing him in a different light now. My fingers ached to run through hair, his skin was daring my lips to attach to it. His burning blue eyes staring into mine made the dirtiest thoughts fill my mind. His pink lips seemed to catch my attention more than they ever had before. Then just knowing what was under his shirt pushed my thoughts.

My eyes dropped back down to his lips and then flicked up to his eyes. I saw he was thinking, trying to figure out my next move. I bit my lip thinking about whether I really wanted to cross the line I was thinking about crossing. There was no promise that if I did this, we could have this type of friendship again.

"What are you thinking?" he whispered pulling me more between his legs. I felt his warm breath on my stomach. That insatiable burn for him between my legs grew stronger, the only way I could describe the burn was as a hunger. One that needed fed, or it could drive you insane. I into his eyes and touched his jaw. Without a second thought I connected our lips in a rough and rushed kiss. Nothing out of a book ever happened when we kissed but Luke was an amazing kisser. He pulled me down on the bed making me giggle. I pushed his lettermen jacket off of his shoulders letting it fall back onto my bed. I grabbed his t-shirt moving back farther onto the bed pulling him with me. Our lips disconnected allowing us to laugh. Once I was settled against the pillows, he placed his body between my legs kissing me softly but lustfully. Luke was always soft and careful, never rough like I wanted him to be.

"You sure you want to do this?" he asked me peppering kisses down my jaw. I wrapped my legs around his waist running my hands through his hair, tugging at it.

"Yes, I am sure." But the truth was I wasn't sure. I knew how badly I wanted to feel close to him, but I didn't know if I wanted the consequences. Before I had a chance to think it out clearly, I felt Luke's tongue attach to the pleasure spot on my neck. His lips closed around his tongue making my eyes flutter close as I moved, giving him more room. He repeated that action on another spot on my neck as his hands wandered my body, finding the clasp for my bra. I felt him twist and tug at the strap. He always struggled with my bra, and I always tried to pretend not to notice.

"Luke," I moaned as he nipped at the sensitive spot on my neck.

"Babe, these damn bras," he laughed. I couldn't help but giggle. I grabbed his face kissing him passionately. Luke has always had a ton of girls all over him, but he's only ever wanted me. I reached behind my back without breaking the kiss and unclasped my bra. I slide it down my arms and tossed it to the side. Right away his hands went to my breasts palming them making me moan. I ran my hands down his arms and to the hem of his shirt pushing it up feeling the hard muscles under his skin.

"You are so fucking sexy," I moaned. He grinned leaning up pulling off his shirt. Right away I unbuttoned his jeans reaching into them grabbing his length pumping it. Luke wasn't big or small, he was an average size. I moaned as I felt his length hardening and growing in my grasp.

"Ugh, you don't know how long I've waited for you to touch me again," he groaned throwing his head back in pleasure. He leaned down leaving wet kisses on my stomach making me moan in pleasure. I tugged down his pants and boxers letting his friend spring to life. Without warning Luke's cold fingers slipped into my panties massaging my ball of nerves making my eyes roll back.

"Luke, I would love for us to take our time, but we have to hurry before one of my sisters bust in," I told him. He leaned down kissing me passionately pulling my panties off along with his boxers. He pulled out a condom from the pants pocket and I watched him roll it on. I went to move to get face down ass up, but he pushed me back against the bed.

"No, I want to look at you," he told me lost in thought. I nodded laying back adjusting myself. He tapped himself against me. I felt the silky condom brush against me then I felt his fullness fill me.

"Luke," I moaned his name wrapping my legs around his waist once again making him go even deeper as my fingers tugged at his hair.

"Elly, you're amazing" He groaned in my ear as he slowly pulled out and thrust back into me which sent shocks of pleasure through me. He repeated the move again but this time even slower sending another shock of pleasure through me.

"Faster," I whined running my hands down his back. He grabbed my arms pinning them against the bed. His burning blue eyes finding mine as he slowly thrusted into me. It was so satisfying and such a tease at the same time.

"I'm take my time with you," He muttered running his tongue along my collar bone making another moan escape my lips. He slowly started pulling out and then pushed me into faster and harder than before but not quite as much as I would have liked. Luke ran his fingers through my hair tugging just ever so slightly in a teasing manner as his lips connected to mine. He swallowed the moans rolling from my lips as his tongue invaded my mouth in the most pleasurable way.

"Yes, more baby" I begged, and he repeated the action, thrusting into me a little harder. He let go of my wrists letting me wrap my arms back around him. He licked his thumb and then moved it down to my clit massaging the ball of nerves while he thrust in and out of me. I moved my hips to meet his, but I kept my movements slow and steady just like he did his. Between his movement and his finger, I was being pushed to the edge. My body was tensing up, I got that weird pit in my stomach along with the need to pee. My nails dug deeper into his back as I hid my face in his shoulder.

"Cum baby, go ahead and cum for me" He moaned into my ear picking up the pace. With one rushed hard thrust, my body relaxed, the need to pee and the pit in my stomach released. My whole body shook in pleasure, my nails sank deeper dragging down his back, I huffed into his shoulder. They weren't loud but loud enough to be heard in the next room probably. My toes curled as my eyes rolled back.

"I'm gonna cum---Elly," he groaned hiding his face in my neck as his body tensed. I felt him pulse inside, his body shook and relaxed against mine. After a minute to recover he rolled off of me carefully pulling off the condom tying it off and tossing it onto the floor until we were ready to get up. I rolled over laying my head on his heaving chest with a smile. He kissed the top of my head and we lay there cuddled together, recovering.

Chapter 5

History Lesson

ELEANOR

A WEEK LATER

I looked out of the bus window watching the streets pass by. I hated the bus, I really needed to take my driver's test. I had my permit, but I haven't taken the actual test yet. The bus was loud, annoying, and dirty. It was just horrible. A sandy toned hand landed on my thigh. I looked over at Luke as he talked to one of his friends. I grabbed his hand just holding it but taking it off my thigh. I was right. Things were different after we hooked up. At first nothing was different; we were friends and not talking about it. We just let it happen and moved on. Then that next day at school things were going so good until I started wanting him like that again during chemistry. So, we hooked up in the janitor's closet, then when we went back to my house, after dinner, and before he left. It's became a regular thing again. I mean we're not back together, and I don't feel that way about him and I don't think he feels that way about me either. We're just having fun and this last week kinda been nice.

Another thing this past week I haven't been to the bar, and I haven't really talked to Zeke besides a few text messages. I didn't mean for that to happen, but he's been busy. When he's not busy, he's at the bar. It doesn't make much time for us to hangout. I miss hanging out with him and just laughing, but I knew Trip would be there. Trip...I haven't talked to him and thankfully he left me alone just like I asked. There are times when I see him outside, getting into his car, in the alley wherever he might be to catch my attention. I just pretend not to notice him and keep doing what I'm doing but the truth is...I always notice him. I always feel his dark brown eyes on me, they became almost too heavy to ignore. I casually dropped Luke's hand getting back onto my phone, adjusting in the uncomfortable seat. We were getting close to my neighborhood, thankfully.

"What, I can't hold your hand?" Luke asked me raising an eyebrow just as the bus pulled up to the corner by the bar.

"Of course, you can," I forced a smiled standing up grabbing my bag. He gave me a strange look but got up. I followed him off the bus thanking the driver. Right away I felt the heavy stare that could only belong to one person. I looked up from my phone to see Trip standing by his car with Lil Smiley, Trip's dark eyes following my every move. I wanted to say "hi" to Smiley, but I figured it would be better not to right now.

"Tomorrow soccer starts, you excited?" Luke asked as we walked past Trip and Lil Smiley.

"Yeah I am. I got all new pads, cleats. Actually, my cleats are custom, I'll show them to you," I told him with an excited smile. My cleats were so dope, the left cleat was of the Colombian flag and the right cleat had my name on it in the Colombian flag colors. The cleats also had the Los Prophet symbol on it.

"My mom is picking me up from baseball practice tomorrow, we could give you a lift," He offered. But I just waved it off.

"Nah, it's fine. Izzy is coming to get me" I told him opening my gate walking up on the porch going back far enough to block Trip's view of me. Once his heavy eyes were off of me I let out a breath I didn't even know I was holding; I leaned against the railing.

"That was a big sigh. What's wrong?" Luke asked coming to stand in front of me. I couldn't help but look past the neighboring house to Trip. He was still leaning against his car with a blunt between his lips looking at Lil Smiley like he was an idiot. I couldn't help but notice how attractive he looked with the smoke rolling from his plump full pink lips.

"That guy? Is he still messing with you?" Luke asked sending Trip a glare. If Trip had seen it I knew a bullet would have found Luke.

"No, he's not bothering me. It's nothing," I said pushing off the pole. I opened the screen door and pushed open the heavier door as I walked inside.

"MOM, LUKE IS OVER," I yelled walking into the living room stopping short from throwing my backpack on the couch. My eyes grew wide when I saw who was planted on my couch, eating my cookies. His shoes were off, and his feet was propped up on the table. His black zip up jacket was resting on the chair, and his phone was plugged into the wall using my phone charger.

"How was school, Princesa?" Zeke asked me from his place on my couch. What the hell was he doing in here? Do you know how many arguments there have been in this house over Zeke and the bar? Now he's just hanging out in my house!

"It was fine. What are you doing here?" I asked tossing my backpack on the chair, right on top of his jacket. He glanced over at it and then back at me, his eyes flicked up to Luke as I felt him moving closer to me like he was my protector or something.

"You've been dodging me all week Elly. I don't like that so we're going to dinner." He told me with a half grin. I haven't been dodging Zeke, I've been dodging Trip and for good reason.

"I have not been dodging you, I just haven't been to the bar. I can't go to dinner anyways. I have a school project, that's why Luke's here. Where's my mom?" I asked moving away from Luke. I could almost feel him breathing on my neck and it wasn't sexy or comfortable.

ZEKE

Elly stopped coming to the bar. The first couple of days I thought Antonio (her "dad") just caused another one of his scenes about it so she was laying low. After 3 days I knew she wasn't just laying low until he calmed down something was wrong. Then I was outside with Trip one day when she was walking home with her friend Gabby, and she purposely took the alleys to avoid walking past the bar so that's when I knew for sure something was up. Today my schedule was clear except for one little shipment pickup, but Trip could handle it by himself. So, I'm taking her to dinner to find out what was going on.

"Do your project later because me and you are going out to dinner," I told her with a shrug. She went to say something just as Savannah (Elly's mom) walked into the living room and jumped when she saw the two teenagers standing in the living room.

"I didn't even hear you kids come in. Luke, I didn't know you'd be over again," Savannah smiled as Elly crossed her arms eyeing her mom.

"I don't get you. I'm grounded for being around Zeke but yet you're going to let me go out to dinner with him?" Elly asked her with a soft tone. I could see she was confused by Savannah's actions. It was a complicated situation and Elly didn't know a big part of our history to understand it.

"You're not grounded for being around Zeke. You're grounded for getting a gun pulled on your father" Savannah told her. Elly made a face as if she was going to talk back to her mom, but I leaned forward glaring at her.

"Hey, you don't talk back to your moms. She's gonna be the only one to have your back one day," Elly just rolled her eyes going to say something but that boy Luke easily grabbed her elbow.

"Elles go. You were just going on today about how much you missed him, I'll be here when you get back. Izzy should be coming home soon anyways," Luke shrugged. She looked at him for a moment and then sighed nodding.

"Can we get Sushi?" She asked turning to look at me. I nodded standing up grabbing my jacket pulling it on putting my hood up in that half down/half up way.

"You need to get any homework done?" I asked holding her backpack.

"Actually yeah, I haven't understood a word in my math class all week" Elly told me with a blush. I smiled slinging her backpack on over my shoulders. Elly always brought her math homework to me. I was good at it. She'd cry because she didn't understand it but we'd sit at the back table in the bar and get through it together.

"You two have fun!" Savannah called with a smile. Elly hugged her mom kissing her cheek as I walked out of the house. Elly quickly caught up with me as I walked onto the porch. I led us down to my white Phantom ghost Rolls Royce. I unlocked it putting her backpack in the back seat.

"ZEKE!" I heard my name. I looked over to see Trip with a blunt between his lips and his hands up in the air as he looked at me. I swear that kid is always stoned. I don't know how he functions sometimes because he gets stupid high.

"HANDLE IT YOURSELF TRIP. TAKE ANOTHER GUY IF YOU NEED," I yelled out to him opening the door letting Elly in. I heard his loud annoying groan as he stormed into the bar. I got in the car pulling out heading towards our favorite Sushi place in Beverly Hills.

"So Zeke, soccer starts tomorrow. Well, I mean it's just tryouts for varsity so we're picking people to join this year but I'm so excited to finally get back on the field," Elly told me clapping her hands together. I put Elly in soccer once we started getting a close relationship, I knew she'd love it. She's good at it too, I didn't even have to buy her way onto varsity.

"I'll be at all your games like I have been every year. Do you need Volleyball money again this year?" I asked her. That volleyball team was expensive, but I loved that she wanted to be involved in her school and play sports, so I handed over the cash for it.

"Yeah, but I have money for it. I still have money from that time you let me go with you to drop off those duffel bags," she told me with a shrug. But I just scoffed shaking my head no.

"No, go to a concert or something fun with that money. I got volleyball don't worry about it but you do got to tell me what's going on with you and Lucas Bow." I smirked glancing over at the girl next to me. She rolled her eyes as we both burst into laughter. I didn't like boys around Elly by any means, but Lucas I didn't mind so much. He had a lot of good things going for him and he was moving in the right direction, so I liked him.

"Oh my god, Zeke stop. We're friends and have a project together. I love Luke as a friend, but I couldn't ever be with him again like that," she told me shaking her head looking over at me. I sighed glancing at her as I stopped at a red light.

"That sucks because that's the only guy you bring around, I'm ever gonna like. *The rest get bullets!*" I smirked at her. She made finger guns at me pretending to shoot, making us laugh. I shook my head at her as the light turned green. She was more like me than she knew. She had my good qualities and I thank God for that every single day I breath.

ELEANOR

I smiled at the lady as I slid into my chair. Zeke pushed it in for me. I thanked him watching him walk around the table taking his seat in front of me. We were at my favorite Sushi place in Beverly Hills.

"Can I get you guys drinks?" The hostess asked us with a friendly smile.

"A hot tea please," I smiled at her as she wrote down my order.

"Sprite but can I get it in a to go cup?" Zeke asked. He always did that, he always got his drink in a to go cup. He wouldn't touch the actual glasses and I wasn't sure why. He never used the metal silverware either he asked for plastic and then took it with him. If the restaurant didn't have any plastic, he had sets out in his car.

"Why do you always get your drinks in a to go cup?" I asked him curiously once the hostess walked away.

"Because you don't get this powerful without the FBI trailing you. I'm not letting them get my DNA," he told me with a shrug. That made sense, Zeke was very powerful and very wanted.

"Now about this Lucas thing. I noticed you called him Luke and I know you only did that when you guys dated so spill," Zeke said seriously. I laughed rolling my eyes messing with the diamond tennis bracelet on my wrist that my dad got me for my 16th birthday. I mean I couldn't exactly look at Zeke and tell him me and Luke were just having sex. There was no feeling there anymore for either of us, so I decided to play it off all together.

"I didn't even notice I did. We're just friends it's nothing," I shrugged looking up at Zeke with a smile. He hummed nodding his head not believing me.

"Well, I think you guys are good for each other. He's the star athlete of your school which means full ride college, an amazing career. He treats you well, I didn't even have to threaten to kill him. Then you have everything going for you, college, a career. Together you guys can get out of East LA and have a good life," Zeke told me. Get out of East LA and leave him behind? Psh, he clearly doesn't know me too well then. I don't want to leave East LA. I mean, yeah, the driveby's are getting more and more common and it can be dangerous sometimes, but it's my home. Before I could answer the waitress came over with our drinks and handed us menus. We thanked her and I poured hot water into my tea glass adding sugar and a tea bag.

"Zeke; I don't want to leave East LA. I want to stay around because you're here and who could leave the bar behind?" I asked him smiling. He looked at me squinting his eyes taking a drink of his Sprite. His eyes searched my face like he was trying to find something. I gave him a strange look looking at the menu knowing I was going to get California rolls and Godfather rolls.

"Then why you been hidin' away from the bar?" he asked leaning forward. I sighed, closing my menu and looked around the restaurant that was filled with rich stuck-up teenage girls. How was I supposed to tell him I was trying to avoid Trip? What would Zeke think about the whole situation between us? I hated Trip. Maybe it was even more than hate, but I still didn't want to see anything bad happen to him.

"I asked you a question," Zeke pointed out just as our waitress walked over.

"Ready to order?" she asked. I nodded handing her back my menu along with Zeke's.

"Can I get California rolls and Godfather rolls?" I asked her. She nodded writing it and down looked at Zeke.

"Just the spicy tuna," he told her. She nodded as she walked away once again leaving us with Zeke's lingering question.

"Honestly, I've been avoiding Trip," I told him running my hands up and down my arms. Zeke's eyebrows scrunched together as confusion contorted his face.

"Trip? Why? I know you guys had that argument but other than that I thought you guys were cool," I couldn't stop the scoff from leaving my lips. Me and Trip cool? Never in this lifetime will we be cool. He's so arrogant, rude, and just *cold blooded*. I couldn't ever see us getting along let alone be in the same room without trying to kill each other.

"Me and Trip will never be cool," I told him looking into his eyes. His face coated with concern, and I could see his brain working a million miles an hour. I laughed leaning up and grabbing his tattooed hand squeezing it sending him a smile.

"What happened? I like Trip a lot but if he's causing problems for you, he's gone" Zeke growled, making me laugh and shake my head.

"No, no it's not like that. Zeke, he gets under my skin without trying and then the way he pushes me over the edge just makes me feel crazy. I've never been into conflict because I've never cared what people said or did to me. I always turn the other cheek, but he pushes my buttons and I want to explode on him. I want to cuss him out and I really wanted to slap him that day we argued. I just don't like him," I told Zeke with a shrug. I watched as he leaned back into his seat, his eyes were scanning my face as his mind worked something out. I'm sure I didn't want to know whatever was going on in his head, so I just didn't bother to ask.

"Then he's literally the rudest person I've ever met in my life. The very first day I met him, and you sent me away with him. After he murdered someone right in front of me. He even didn't speak a word to me. Like I tried to talk to him, but he'd just look at me or ignore me. He wouldn't say one word. The only time he even really acknowledged me was when he snatched a bottle of water out of my hand. Then, the next day I missed the bus and I saw him outside the bar. I asked him if you were inside the bar, and he had clearly seen me miss the bus. He wouldn't tell me if you were inside or not. He just kept nagging me over my clothing choice. Then when he finally took me to school, he pulled all the way up to the school and yelled 'last night was fun' and drove off," I told Zeke. I crossed my arms at the memory getting annoyed with Trip all over again. He wasn't even here to focus that heavy stare on me while making a smart comment or ignore me and he was still annoying me.

"Trip's just an asshole Elly. You got to ignore him, now that he knows he bothers you he's going to keep doing it until you stop having a reaction," Zeke told me with a shrug, making me groan and put my head down on the white tablecloth.

"How am I supposed to ignore him when he told everyone on the block, I had sex with him in his car?" I asked Zeke. He pinched the brim of his nose squeezing his eyes closed. I crossed my arms waiting for him to give me a good answer.

"Ok I will tell you he had a good reason for that. I was pissed when I heard it too, he can tell you about that if he wants," Zeke defended him. Our waitress returned with our food. I smiled thanking her telling her my food looked good as I took a sip from my tea.

"There is no good reason for that Zeke. I hate him, then he pulled a gun on my dad, do you not hear how long this list is?" I asked him. He laughed nodding his head taking another drink of his Sprite.

"Let me tell you a little bit about him, it might help you understand why he's such a dick," Zeke said too loudly getting us snobby looks which we just laughed off. I would be lying if I told you, I wasn't curious about him. I wanted to know about how he ended up in the gangs, how long he had been a Los Prophet, how he moved up so fast, where he was from. I had so many questions, but I refused to ask him to just be ignored. I took out my chopsticks breaking them apart doing the same to Zeke's for him while I waited for him to tell me about Trip.

"Well, you gonna tell me before I'm 90?" I asked him picking up a California roll with my chopstick.

"Trip joined Los Prophets at 9 years old. When I say "join" I mean the whole thing Like he jumped in and then killed someone. He didn't waste time at all. He did whatever he was told when he was told. There was no excuse or complaint...at first. Now all he does is fucking complain." Zeke rolled his eyes, I giggled at his annoyance with Trip. I pictured the two of them in the bar, Trip complaining and Zeke just trying not to lose it.

"Why did he join?" I asked curiously as Zeke took a bite out of his roll.

"I don't know the whole story. I know he grew up in South Central. His mom wasn't around very much at all. His stepdad was abusive, used to beat on him or his sibling or somebody, I don't remember. Anyways, his piece of shit parents weren't around a lot so he was left to take care of his brother and sister. They were older, but he was more street smart, so he took the challenge of taking care of them. He started getting picked for stealing at 6 years old. He would steal food so they could eat, clothes, blankets because they didn't have heat. That kinda stuff. One day he got tired of his stepdad beating on whoever he beat on. So, he joined Los Prophets," Zeke told me like it wasn't anything. But that was real life trauma that isn't getting any treatment. I still didn't think it was an excuse to be as rude as he is to everyone, to make up rumors that I slept with him, to hold guns up to my dad. Trip has done a lot of unforgivable things to me in the short time I've known him so it's going to take more than a sad secondhand story to make me forget all of that.

"So, he killed his stepdad to join?" I asked curiously and Zeke nodded his head.

"Yeah, Trip rolled up on him while he was out with his friends. Got him alone, shot him, and never looked back. Trip's done a lot since then too. He's extremely high up in the gang and only 19. He's had a rough life. If I lived a third of his life, I would be the biggest and coldest dick ever too," Zeke told me with a shrug. I bit my lip thinking about Zeke's words and trying to find it in myself to be understanding, but I couldn't. Maybe that made me a bad person, but he managed to do all those horrible things in just the first two days I had known him.

"Nobody wants to be like that, Elly but they are sometimes. I'm sure Trip doesn't want to walk around with the weight of the world on his shoulders. He doesn't have anyone, no family or anything anymore. He's taken more lives than what's he affected positively. I'm sure that probably bothers him. He's been forced to do some unspeakable things so he could get up top. I learned quickly that Trip wants power more than anything," Zeke told me. But it made sense that's what Trip wanted. He grew up in an abusive household where he felt like he didn't have any power, so now he'd kill for it. It was his security blanket to be able to manipulate every situation his own way.

ZEKE

I could see the wheels turning in her head as she thought about what I told her. I knew parts and pieces of Trip's story. We were very close friends, but he never told me much about it. When I asked, he told me it was ancient history he buried years ago.

"Wait what happened to his siblings?" Elly asked me but I just shrugged my shoulders.

"He never told me," I told her. She sipped her tea as her eyes darted around the room. Finally, she shook her head, not looking up at me.

"I hate that he went through that but it's no excuse to treat people the way he does," she told me. I sighed nodding my head in agreement. I didn't expect her to want to be around him after that, but I thought it might smooth the waters between them.

"Did he tell you why they call him Trip?" I asked her curiously. She shook her head no looking at me with her eyebrows furrowed together. She probably never thought of the story behind his name.

"I didn't even know there was a reason," she told and I nodded.

"Trip got his name because anything and everything makes him angry. Then, when Trip gets angry, it's not like when me and you get angry it's a deadly rage right away. The way you came into that bar and yelled at him, anyone else would have a bullet between their eyes before they could have finished a sentence. Nothing can a save person from Trip, not even me. That's why he's so feared," I told her. Her eyes grew with the new information. Before she could say anything, my phone vibrated, and I pulled it out to see it was Trip calling.

"Speaking of the devil. Excuse me," I said getting up and walking to the back of the restaurant.

"What's up?" I asked him, licking my lips.

"How the fuck are you going to leave me with Lil Smiley to pick up this fucking shipment. HE'S 15 FUCKING YEARS OLD ZEKE AND WE'RE TALKING 315 KILOS OF COCAINE!" Trip yelled at me through the phone. That deadly rage I was just talking about was evident in his voice.

"Stop yelling at me because I will end everything for you and, yes, I am threatening you, Trip. If Lil Smiley is the only one that can help you, hand him a gun and shut the fuck up. I'm trying to make things better with my daughter. She's avoiding everyone because you're a dick," I snapped harshly at him while rubbing my temple annoyed with his temper.

"I don't give a fuck. My life is so much easier without her around to whine so it's not bothering me one little bit. What's bothering me is all these drugs coming in and the DEA on your ass," he snapped at me. I just sighed shaking my head. A small part of me didn't believe him when it came to him not wanting Elly around. I noticed the way his eyes followed her when he saw her.

"Figure it out. You got this," I said and hung up the phone. I went back to the table sitting down grabbing one of my tuna rolls taking a bite.

"So I got customized cleats for soccer and they're so dope. I even got a little part on them for you. I have the Los Prophet symbol on the side under my ankle," she told me with a bright smile. Elly didn't really shun the gang life, but she never showed an interest in joining, thankfully. She ran jobs every now and then and I paid her, but I wanted to teach her how to earn money, so I just wasn't handing it to her.

"What else is on them? Can you wear them for games and practice with the symbol on them?" I asked her and she nodded her head.

"Yeah, I should. My right one is the Colombian flag and then my left one is my name and then I have the symbol on that one. Look I got a picture actually," she told me getting on her phone and then handing it to me. I looked at the picture of the cleats and they were nice. I nodded my head impressed handing it back to her.

"Those are cool and they're a good brand, they should last all season," I told her as she put away her phone. With the subject changed from boys and my gang members onto a lighter topic, we spent the remainder of our dinner laughing and joking around making up for the time we lost over that happened over the last week.

Chapter 6

Buttons

ELEANOR

I squeezed my eyes closed tighter trying to drown out the sound of my alarm. In my sleep deprived mind if I just refused to move it would stop ringing. After getting more and more annoyed with each second that passed, I rolled over grabbed my phone turned off the alarm and dropped it back down onto the side table. I sat up looking around my dark room tiredly. Friday couldn't get here fast enough. I pushed my covers off and turned on the light. I went to my closet looking for something to wear and grabbed a tight-fitting skin tone bodysuit with wide tank top straps. I paired it with a pair of worn high-waist skinny jeans, then grabbed a bra from the dresser. I made my bed, laid out my outfit, grabbed a towel and my body wash going down to the bathroom just as Izzy walked out.

"Don't forget to pick me up from soccer," I reminded her as she walked past.

"I won't Eleanor," she called over her shoulder, a smirk holding in her voice.

"IT'S ELLY!" I yelled after her. She laughed disappearing into her room. I flipped her off going into the bathroom doing what I had to do and left the bathroom to Mateo. Once I was back to my room, I sat down at my desk locking my curls in for the day, and then did my usual makeup to perfection. Once I approved my look and changed into my outfit. I added a pair of big golden hoops and a diamond tennis bracelet. To complete my look, I grabbed a pair of calf high lace up heeled boots that matched my bodysuit. Once I felt put together, I gathered my homework, laptop and duffel bag. I grabbed my things and headed downstairs as my mom grabbed her keys off the table.

"I'm working late, I have to pull a double," Mom told me before kissing my temple. She was a nurse at the hospital, so doubles weren't anything new around my house.

"Ok have a good day," I smiled as she walked into the kitchen. I got my hydro flask from the fridge.

"We need to go," Mateo said tossing me an apple. I followed her out locking the door behind me. We walked in silence down to the bus stop. Mateo must be just as tired as me. Luke ended up staying late, I don't think he left until my mom said she was going to bed. Mateo and I weren't at the bus stop for 5 minutes before it pulled up. I got on and went to the back, sitting in my usual seat, putting in my headphones, looking out of the window. The ride to school was as annoying as a bus can get. I will never understand the reason people scream at 7:30 in the morning. Once we finally arrived at school, I pushed my way off the loud bus and into the school. I went straight to my locker to see Gabby digging around inside it while Luke, Tony, and Nicole stood behind her. I took out a headphone as I walked over and playfully rammed my body into Tony's.

"What is wrong with you? It's 7 in the morning!" Tony said faking exasperation. I laughed shaking my head tossing my duffel into my locker.

"I feel like I haven't saw you guys in forever!" I complained as I handed my water to Luke right away so I could get my books out.

"I know! We were just talking about how Luke keeps hiding you away from us. Friday, friend's dinner at my house. I got the place to myself, figure out what you're cooking or bringing so we can make a list," Gabby announced. We haven't had a friend's dinner since we did Friendsgiving last year. Friend's dinner was just want it sounded like. We all went over to each other's houses and cooked a dinner together. Like from scratch. Then we ate and played games and just hung out. We've done this ever since we've known each other.

"You should make that chicken Cajun pasta" Nicole told me. I watched as my friends closed their eyes (humming and touching) their stomachs at the mention of it which made me laugh.

"Ok bet. Gabs I'm making pasta," I told her with a smile as I shut my locker. We all got lost into conversation about what we were going to bring. We were cut short by the devil in the flesh...Novah Yates. Following behind her were her two minions, Dior Brady and Yara Fox. Novah and I never got along. We've been in school together since the first day of Preschool and we literally hate each other. The only problem with that is Novah is captain of the Soccer team, so I was going to be stuck with her every day after school for the season. She called herself 'the queen of the school' (which is cringe upon itself) but, honestly, she was only popular also she spreads her legs for anything that moves.

"Eleanor. Today is the first soccer practice. If you miss it, you're off the team," she told me crossing her thin arms. She had shoulder length platinum blonde hair, bright blue eyes, porcelain skin, pink lips, and a sharp jawline. I always thought her head looked a little big. It reminded me of a bobble head. She had that average skinny body type, but she thought was the baddest. She was curve-less and showed off her long back like it was ass.

"I know, I'll be there," I said, an annoyed tone slipping through, even though I tried to hide it. She looked me up and down humming.

"I thought you'd be busy with your little gang," she said in a snobby tone. I looked at her and licked my teeth. Everything in me wanted to lash out at her, but that wasn't me. I stayed quiet just looking at her.

"Cute boots," she smirked, looking at my shoes. I mumbled a thank you looking down at my heels. Suddenly, they were covered in a pink liquid which made me gasp. Anger automatically bubbled in my veins. Every muscle in me wanted to hit her. I wanted to scream at her and tell her how big of a bitch she was, but that wasn't me. Why should I let myself sink low and look stupid over a girl with low self-esteem?

"Oops!" she snickered as she dropped the cup at my feet and walked away with her friends.

"YOU DON'T HAVE TO BE SUCH A BITCH!" Nicole yelled. I just grabbed her arm shaking my head no.

"Don't. She's not worth it. I'm gonna go clean up," I said with a sigh, looking down at my feet again.

"You need to take up for yourself. I know you don't like confrontation, but she's gotten away with enough!" Tony snapped not at me but just at the situation. I shook my head no. I squeezed his shoulder as I walked past them to the bathroom to get cleaned up.

TREY'VON

A COUPLE HOURS LATER

I stormed through the front doors of my Beverly Hills home letting them slam roughly behind me. I was pissed, I spent all night getting that stupid ass shipment with Lil Smiley's dumb ass because Zeke just had to run off to go play daddy. I stormed up my slightly twisted staircase to the master bedroom where I slammed the door hard enough to hear something fall and break. I didn't care. I threw myself down on my bed letting a groan escape my lips. As my body relaxed, I felt how much my back hurt from last night's activities. After we got the shipment, we had to take it to the warehouse, get it weighed out and repackaged to go to the dope houses. That took fucking hours, I couldn't just leave 315 kilos of coke in a warehouse, so I had to stay, and that meant Smiley had to stay. So, all night he drank coffee to keep himself awake and didn't shut up or get out of the fucking way once.

Then when it was time to reload and take the dope to the houses, Smiley's stupid ass kept screaming police, raid, attack or whatever fucking else. He'd freak everyone out and then just laugh and say 'got ya'. It took all of the strength in my body not to kill him last night and the only reason I held back is because I needed his little ass. Zeke was getting a fucking ear full today about pulling that shit. But, for now, I needed a shower and some sleep. Then, I'd go and tell Zeke how much of a fuck up he is. I laid on my huge California king bed for a little longer with my eyes closed. I felt gross after being in those damn dope houses all night. I knew I wouldn't be able to sleep with how my skin was crawling. I finally got up and got a pair of boxers from the drawer in my closet and then walked out going into my en suite bathroom.

I tossed my boxers on the counter and pulled off my shirt as I walked over turned on the shower to let the water warm up. I stripped out of my clothes and just threw them on the bathroom floor. I slid open the glass doors stepping into the warm water. I closed my eyes and let the hot water run over my body relaxing my muscles. I ran my hand over my curls that were hanging low into my eyes and pushed them back.

I needed to relax; I was on edge. I hadn't got pussy in like three days; I knew if I busted, I'd be more relaxed and I'd sleep better. I pushed the pump on the conditioner, I closed my eyes as I gripped my length in my hand. Between my tight grip and the hot the water, I had no problem getting hard as I pumped my hand back and forth. I tried to picture different girls, titties, ass, pussy anything but the only thing coming to mind was her. I squeezed my eyes tighter as I pictured her russet skin under my fingertips, her curls messy, her plump lips wrapped around me.

"Fuck baby girl," I groaned opening me eyes. I almost jumped when I could actually see her kneeling on the shower floor. I knew it was pure fantasy, a subconscious dream while I was awake, but there she was. Zeke's sorta daughter kneeling on my shower floor completely naked looking up at me.

"You want me don't you Trip?" Even light Spanish accent was perfect in my head. I bit my lip looking down nodding my head swallowing hard. I swear I felt the ghostly touches on my thigh as she laughed.

"Nice to know what you dream about, pendejo," she laughed as her lips brushed against my tip making me inhale sharply.

"This is my fantasy, how the fuck you get to insult me?" This only made her laugh.

"I guess you like it," she smirked taking me between her lips into her warm wet mouth.

"Fuck!" I moaned as I watched the fragment of my imagination push her head back and forth fast as her small hands worked the lower half. I heard a whimper of a moan escape her lips and then she pushed her head all the way back taking me into her throat while she moaned loudly. I couldn't stop the slurs of curses and groans leaving my lips. I felt my lower abs and back tighten up. She moved faster making my body grow more tense until I couldn't take it anymore.

"Baby girl," I groaned feeling my body release. Pleasure filled my body as my eyes rolled back. My knees shook but supported me as I felt the warm cum fill my hand. After my blissful orgasm passed, I opened my eyes to see the water rushing the cum out of my hand. I washed my hands still breathing hard. Even in a fantasy she's annoying. I finished my shower, dried off, and threw on my boxers. I wasted no time getting in bed trying to ignore the burning in my ears to hear that light Spanish accent in person.

ELEANOR

LAST BELL

I was so thankful to hear that unnecessarily loud and long bell ring, signaling that the school day was over. I've had a horrible day; Novah giving my shoes a smoothie make over was just the tip of the iceberg. I got written up twice: once because I raised my hand, got called on and asked to go to the bathroom. Mr. Andrews started screaming at me for interrupting his class and told me to get out. The second write up came from lunch: Dior decided it would be funny to send Collin Mathews over to me and ask what my mouth does. I got up and tried to just walk away to avoid the situation all together and the principle wrote me up for being out of my seat.

Then, in Criminal Justice class we're learning about street gangs. I always stay quiet during that class because everyone knows I'm associated with Los Prophets even the teachers. One of the boys in that class decided to pick me out for it and, when I just rolled my eyes and ignored his stupid remarks, everyone started making them. Even the teacher-he would just laugh along with them. I'm not ashamed of being around Zeke or what he does, he's good at it. But they were commenting on something they knew nothing about. I just put in my headphones turned up my music and tuned them out for the remainder of the period. That's not even everything that happened today.

I got to my locker to see Gabby already had it opened, I roughly slung my books and papers in which made Gabby jump.

"Your day didn't get better?" Gabby asked me with soft eyes. I shook my head no ripping my duffel and backpack out of my locker. Without another word, I walked away going towards the athletic building, so I could change in the locker rooms. After making my way across campus and into the athletic building, I went straight back to the locker room to see everyone already there.

"Ouch, 5 minutes late. I'm going to have to dock game time," Novah smirked as she crossed her arms and looked me up and down. I sent her a glare and was going to snap at her but, just as my lips parted, I stopped. I didn't want problems with anyone. Novah could take away all my game time and make me like 3rd string and I wanted play. I took a deep breath nodding my head.

"Do what you have to do," I said going over to a locker and stuffed my backpack inside it. I took my duffel into a changing stall. I only changed in the stall because I couldn't wear underwear with my bodysuit and had to put some on. Once I completely changed into the tight-fitting grey, black and lime green spandex t-shirt, black spandex shorts, my pads, and cleats I walked out and locked my my duffel in the locker. I pulled my curls up into a ponytail while walking outside with the rest of the team. I sat and stretched on the field next to Veronica.

"It's bullshit she took your playtime. I think she does that because she's threatened by you. You're prettier than her," Veronica told me. I just shrugged. I wasn't the type to bad mouth someone about their looks. Personality and morals...if they were horrible then I'd say so but not about looks.

"It is what it is. I can't change anything about it," I said as the girls who wanted to try out for varsity came onto the field to sit down and stretch.

"I don't even know why she's captain. You're the best on the team," Maria commented. I looked over at her with a small smile nodding. Part of me believed Novah's dad bought her spot and then another part believed

I didn't get it because of my ties to Zeke. Either way I didn't care, I still played, and I didn't want to lead the team.

"I don't care. I don't want to lead the team, I liked just being a player. I'm captain of the volleyball team anyways," I said with a shrug. I heard a loud scoff, I looked up to see Novah stomping over in front of me.

"Not for long. I'm trying out for that position this year," she said proudly crossing her arms. I looked up at her raising an eyebrow.

"Yeah, well there isn't even tryouts for that position," I told her, but she just shrugged.

"Don't worry. My daddy will make sure there is!" She told me flipping her hair over her shoulder and flouncing off. Every part of me wanted to tell her one of my father figures could end her life with just a look, but I kept my mouth shut and just shook my head. I was more than ready to get this practice over with.

I ran down the field kicking the ball, my head was on a swivel for my next move. As I saw opposing teammates closing in on me, I passed the ball to Maria. I took off running even faster down the field watching her. She made eye contact with me and just like that we connected, and she knew what I wanted her to do. The moment I got positioned for a goal Maria fired the ball my way. I ran over bringing back my foot about to power kick it into the goal when I felt cleats connect to my ankle knocking me off balance. A gasp escaped my lips as I began to fall with Novah under me. She brought her knee up as I when down. Her knee connected to my cheek bone making my head snap back as I hit the turf with a hard painful thump. I rolled over onto my back with a groan and then back onto my stomach hiding my face in my arms.

"Oops, you should watch your blind spots better," Novah snickered as I heard her get up. I laid on the turf groaning in pain. Soon enough the rest of the team was surrounding me asking if I was ok. When my senses finally came back, Maria and Veronica helped me up.

"Are you ok?" Amy asked me and I nodded my head. I wasn't ok, I was pissed. She did that on purpose, she tried to take me out for the whole season on an injury. I was seeing red flash. I wanted to run over and beat her ass for what she just did, but then I'd be the one in trouble.

"Sánchez, 20 laps for that foul. We can't have that in a game," Novah sneered. I opened my mouth to say something but then I just snapped it shut. I stormed past Novah's shoulder, checking her so hard it hurt my own shoulder.

"WHERE ARE YOU GOING? THE TRACK IS THE OTHER WAY!" she yelled at me as I went into the locker room. I ripped open my locker grabbed my bags and stormed right back out of the locker room not even bothering to change back.

"IF YOU LEAVE, YOU'RE OFF THE TEAM!" Novah yelled. But I didn't even care if I was off this stupid team or not. I stormed off the field and down the walk to the parking lot to see my older sister's Honda sitting in the parking lot. She was on her phone snapchatting. I ripped open the back door threw all my things in and got in the passenger seat.

"Whoa what happened to you?" Izzy asked me. But I just shook my head no. I knew if I talked, I'd end up snapping on her and I didn't want to be that person. She nodded and let our drive be silent. I was so mad I couldn't even think straight, my whole body was shaking, I was ready to just go home and lock myself in my bedroom and call it a day.

TREY'VON

I stood outside the bar eating a bag of Hot Cheeto's. I had the munchies like a muhfucka. We just had this huge smoke circle and had like 3 blunts going around. I was fucked up; I couldn't even focus on what these dumb asses were telling me. My mind was on these chips and my shower from earlier. I wanted to hear her voice; that little Spanish accent yelling at me like I was supposed to be scared of her. I wanted to bug her, I wanted to get on her nerves and get that reaction from her. I wanted her to scream my name, I wasn't gonna get her to scream it the way I wanted her to, so I'd settle for a scream out of irritation. I wanted to see those chocolate brown eyes filled with annoyance and anger as they glaring at me. I wanted to watch her curls bounce as she spun around to tell me how irritating I was. It was a weird feeling and not one I'd ever admit to having if I wasn't blowed.

"Trip you listening to us?" Julio asked me, which made my head snap up from the chip I was staring at.

"Huh?" I asked, looking at the group of men in front of me.

"You're stuck," Lil Smiley laughed at me. I went to defend myself, but I saw a shitty tan honda civic coming down the street. I knew it belonged at her house, I watched it pull in front of the house she hid in. After a few moments, I saw the oldest get out of the car. She was bad but not like her sister. Moments later here she came out of the passenger seat. She had on a tight spandex t-shirt, short sexy spandex shorts, knee pads, cleats. Her bouncy curls were piled into a bun on the top of her head and she already looked angry, but it wasn't going to stop me from messing with her.

"YO MA!" I yelled over at them. I saw the chocolate brown eyes I wanted to see find me along with her sisters. I watched her roll them and turn away. I smirked pulling up my pants and jogged over to them, trying to think of a way to get on her nerves. Then I got the perfect idea.

"What's up wit you ma?" I gave the older sister a smug look. Baby girl whipped around glaring at me.

"Leave me alone I'm not in the mood for you or anyone!" she barked. I forcefully hid my satisfied grinned as I looked over at her with a calm cool look.

"I wasn't talking to you Baby Girl. I'm tryin to see what's wit you," I flirted with the older one looking her up and down. She looked at me shocked and then over at Zeke's sorta daughter. How the fuck do I not know her name?

"Me?" The older one asked and I nodded amused.

"Yeah, I've you seen comin in and out" I shrugged at her as Baby Girl scoffed.

"I don't mess with bangers. That's all her," she motioned toward Baby Girl. Trust me I plan on her messin with a banger but first I want to piss her off.

"Trip leave us alone," Baby Girl voice was sharp as she pulled out bags from the backseat. I looked that sexy little outfit up and down again. It was hugging those curves so perfect. Fuck all she got to do is let me in that house one time and it's over.

"You can go, I'm not talkin to you," I bit back sharply at her. I watched as the glare spread across her face and she zeroed in on me.

"You're fucking disgusting, really get away from us," she shot harshly. I stepped around the older one finally getting the attention I wanted from the girl I wanted the attention from.

"I don't think you want me to get away," I said with a shrug, taking a step closer to her.

"Why would I want you around? You told the whole neighborhood we fucked and now you're trying to get with my sister," she pointed out. I raised an eyebrow taking another step closer to her. She looked at me squinting her gorgeous eyes.

"You're high," she stated while noting her sister had left her alone out here with me.

"Baby Girl you don't got to be jealous. You're still my favorite and yes I'm fucking fried," I told her with a grin as I touched her chin. She firmly smacked away my hand pushing me back. I glared at her feeling the anger rise through my foggy state.

"I DON'T WANT TO BE YOUR FAVORITE OR EVEN IN YOUR MINDSET. WHAT DON'T YOU GET? I FUCKING HATE YOU TRIP!" she screamed at me shoving me back one more time, but I grabbed her wrists with a glare. She tried to fight against me, but I easily pushed her against that shitty tan car pinning her against it.

"Go ahead, tell me what you hate about me. If you hate me that fucking much," I snarled at her. I don't care if she likes me or not because honestly, I think she's annoying she just has a nice body. That, and that reason only, is why I've taken such an interest in her. I just want to hit it and move on.

"I HATE HOW RUDE YOU ARE, HOW TEMPERAMENTAL YOU ARE, EGOISTICAL, NARCISSISTIC. HOW YOU TRY TO

ACT SO COLD LIKE YOU DON'T CARE ABOUT ANYTHING OR ANYONE. OR HOW YOU THINK EVERYBODY OWES YOU SOMETHING!" She yell at me. I don't think she even realized it, but while she was yelling, I let go of her wrists and she closed in the little space between us. She was just centimeters from me, I felt her body brushing against mine. Her brown eyes stared intently into mine. That russet skin seemed to glow even more because she was sweating, her full painted lips were catching my attention. She clearly noticed because she pulled the lower one between her teeth. It was little things like that I was noticing about her, and it drove me crazy with lustful thoughts.

"You're right. I am all of those things, but I think you like it," I whispered confident I was right. I looked down at her shirt that hugged her chest perfectly and to her shorts that showed off her wide hips and perfect legs. My fingers ached to reach down and touch her legs, her hips, to trace her flat stomach but that was even a line I wouldn't cross with anyone. I licked my lips looking back up to her chocolate brown eyes. Her breath catching in her throat, I could see the pulse point in her neck speed up. I smirked running my fingers along her neck feeling her pulse.

"I'm probably the star of your wet dreams at night if we're being honest. You look sexy in those knee pads, let's put them to use," I flirted going to close in the space but she shoved me back harder than she ever had before. I stumbled barely catching my balance. I looked up to her with a glare as nothing, pure rage pumped through my veins.

"YOU'RE DISGUSTING. YOU REALLY EXPECT AFTER YOU LIE TO EVERYONE ABOUT US HAVING SEX THAT I'M REALLY GOING TO SLEEP WITH YOU. YOU'RE STUPIDER THAN I EVEN THOUGHT YOU WERE. WHY DON'T YOU GO BURN OFF MORE OF YOUR BRAIN CELLS AND SMOKE AGAIN? I ALREADY TOLD YOU I NEVER WANTED TO TALK TO YOU AGAIN BUT YET HERE YOU ARE. AFTER EVERYTHING YOU FUCKING DID, YOU PULLED A GUN ON MY DAD, YOU CALLED ME WHORE AND TRIED TO GIVE ME A REPUTATION. FUCK YOU TRIP, I'VE NEVER DISLIKED SOMEONE AS MUCH AS I DISLIKE YOUR DUMB ASS!" she shrieked at me snatching her bags off the ground. That's when I saw the bruise on her cheekbone. It was almost like someone hit her. That jock she hangs out with isn't dumb enough to put his hands on her, is he? She went to storm passed me, but I grabbed her arm spinning her around.

"You're face. What happened?" I asked her looking at her seriously. I went to grab her chin to get a better look, but she jerked away.

"Don't worry about it, Trip. Go find some random hoe to bother just leave me and my sister alone," She grumbled storming through the gate in front of her house. I watched her curvy figure disappear inside the door. I couldn't stop or hide the smile that spread across my face. She was so feisty, and I really liked that. I licked my lips heading back towards the bar to see Zeke leaning against a pole watching me with curious eyes. I knew I was pissed at Zeke for something, and I knew I had a bunch of shit to say to him, but even after getting screamed at I was too high to remember.

"What was that about?" Zeke asked me as I walked back over. I looked up at him a smirk taking a seat in a chair, snatching up my bottle of water.

"Just having some fun," I shrugged taking a drink of my water. I expected him to lecture me about bothering his sorta daughter, but he just nodded his head. I could see the wheels in his head turning, but I didn't question it.

Chapter 7

Stuck Like Glue

ELEANOR

I picked up the pack of raw chicken breast and put it inside a giant bowl filled with ice. I popped the lid onto the bowl and put it into the cardboard box. I looked over everything in the box making sure I had what I needed to make Cajun chicken pasta over at Gabby's house. Today was our Friends dinner, which also meant it was Friday, thankfully. Soccer hadn't gotten get any better, and to make matters worse I had a big ass bruise on my cheekbone from Novah's knee. Once I was positive, I had everything I tucked my house key into my back pocket, letting the Nike lanyard hangout.

"I'm heading over to Gabby's," I told dad as he walked into the kitchen. He nodded kissing the top of my head.

"Have fun. Elly, I'm proud of you for staying away from the bar," Dad smiled at me. I smiled back and nodded as I walked out of the kitchen.

"LOVE YOU!" I yelled over my shoulder. I walked out of the front door still stressing that I didn't have everything, but I did. As I walked down the steps of my porch, I heard loud music from a car. I looked over to see Trip's shiny black Audi pull up. I quickly looked away from the car hoping not to draw his attention as I balanced my box in one arm and opened the gate.

"YO ELLY!" I heard my name yelled. I looked down the street to see Zeke looking at me and back to Trip who was walking around his car looking at his phone. Zeke waved over. I couldn't spend forever talking, but I had to go that way nonetheless.

"Hey Zeke," I said once I got over to him. He looked at me raising his eyebrow as he looked inside the box.

"Donating to charity?" Zeke asked me which made the guys around him laugh. Me and Zeke both shot them displeased looks. He's not that funny but they always laughed like he was Kevin Hart.

"No, friend's dinner at Gabby's house. It's been a while so I'm making Cajun chicken pasta," I smiled proudly at my box of things. He nodded looking into the box seeing I had everything needed.

"Trip come here!" Zeke barked. The most obnoxious groan left Trip's lips but he came over to Zeke anyway.

"The feud with El Diablos is growing more intense thanks to our friend here," Zeke said clapping Trip's shoulder. Of course, he'd find a way to ruin the fragile peace agreement Zeke had worked so hard to make. I don't know why Zeke even kept him around. He was a liability, and he was annoying.

"Surprise!" I mocked. Trip flipped me off. Mature as always and expected.

"They know you're a weak spot for me. You're like my daughter so I need to make sure you're safe at all times. Trip is going to hang out with you all of the time now," Zeke said. Our eyes grew wide. I didn't want to be stuck around Trip all of the time. I didn't need a babysitter. The El Diablos had never come for me before so, I didn't understand why they would come for me now.

"NO!" We both yelled, and then turned to glare at each other.

"I don't know why you're yelling "no". You're the one that is infuriating," Trip accused. My mouth gapped open. I'm infuriating? Has he never met himself? If anything, he's the infuriating one with his angry at the world facade.

"I'm shocked you even know what that word means," I snapped back at him. Zeke stepped between us and shot us a look that sent a shiver down my spine. But, we stayed quiet.

"I'm not asking if either of you want this" Zeke growled at us but I just shook my head no.

"I don't need a babysitter," I retaliated at Zeke. He sighed grabbing my shoulders, his dark brown eyes looking into mine.

"Don't think of it like a babysitter, think of it like a bodyguard. Just until the feud settles, a couple weeks tops," Zeke told me. But I shook my head "no". I'd rather come face to face with 50 angry El Diablos then spend one minute with Trip. He just wasn't the drama I wanted or needed in my life on top of everything I already had going on.

"Pick someone else. That's below my paid grade. Try Lil Smiley, he'll do about anything," Trip snapped as his eyes traveled over my body. Every time he did that, I felt so exposed no matter how much clothing I had on. I moved my box to hide my upper body from his eyes. Zeke turned to glare at Trip. But I saw the rage building in Trip's eyes. I knew it too well from our previous encounters. Zeke snatched my box and shoved it into Trip's chest making him take it.

"YOU'RE GOING TO DO THIS. I DON'T GIVE A FUCK IF IT'S BELOW YOUR PAID GRADE OR NOT. I TOLD YOU TO DO IT NOT SMILEY!" Zeke yelled. Trip scoffed, giving me back the box and turned to walk towards his car.

"You don't do what I tell you to do, or you'll be at the dope houses until someone kills me," Zeke barked which stopped Trip dead in his tracks. He turned with a hard look but stormed over to me and snatched the box.

"No, I don't need his protection, nor do I want it," I told Zeke, but he shrugged as he looked between us.

"Well, you got it now, I have things to do. *Don't hurt each other!*" Zeke said turning away and getting into his car with two other guys. I groaned in annoyance looking up at Trip who looked anywhere but at me. I couldn't lie, he looked so amazing today. His bronzed skin holding a different kinda glow to it. His nearly black eyes weren't red or hung low, telling me he was completely sober for once. He had on black skinny jeans, a white pull over hoodie, a black beanie that said "Trippin" across it, which hid his mess of curls. He had his hood over his beanie as well. He matched the outfit with a pair of white Nike Air Forces. I noticed he had on his usual silver rings, diamond studs in his ears. But today he had on an iced-out chain.

TREY'VON

I felt her chocolate brown eyes burning a hole into me. Part of me wanted to lash out at her for staring at me, while the other part wanted to stare right back into them. After a couple seconds of suffering their burning, I looked over at her.

"Well, he's gone so have a nice life," she said sarcastically snatching the box of food from me and walking away. I groaned while I pinched the brim of my nose. I knew she was going to do this. I knew she was going to make my life way harder than it had to be.

"Yo, Baby Girl come on, wait up," I complained as I followed her, but she spun around glaring at me.

"My name is Elly not Baby Girl, and you're not coming to my friend's house with me," she flared with such confidence. Elly. Finally, I know her name...Elly. I low key really liked it. I couldn't help but let a smirk slip. I was actually kinda excited that I knew her name now, but I didn't understand why I was so excited.

"Uh...that's not how this shit works. You heard Zeke, I got to stay with yo annoying ass or I'm in the dope houses. Guessing you never been to a dope house, they're nasty so, 'hi bestie'," I said walking over, taking the box from her. I walked over to my car opened the door to the backseat and put the box in.

"Can't we just lie and say you went?" she asked me as she came over. I shook my head looking over at her and damn. She had on a soft pink strapless crop top. It was one of those crop tops that only covered the boob area. She also had on worn tight fitting high-waist skinny jeans. Her long curly hair was put up into a messy bun, but she left some curls out to frame her face. She was already easy to look at but having her hair pulled from her face made it even easier. She had on black strappy sandals that looked impossible to get in and out of. Her makeup was done like it always was, but even through her efforts to hide the bruise on her cheekbone I could still see it. For Lil psycho's brother's sake, he better hope and pray I never find out he's the one that left that bruise because if he is, I have a bullet with his name on it.

"And let you walk through this neighborhood on your own? Dressed like that?" I asked looking her up and down. She blushed as my eyes scanned her body. So, she did like my attention?

"Just get in the car. We don't have to make this harder on either one of us," I sighed opening the passenger side door. She looked at me like she was thinking about making it hard, but she didn't. She just slid onto the leather seat letting me shut the door. I walked around the car getting in the driver's seat looking over watching her buckle up. I noticed how loose it was around her waist, it wasn't securing her in at all. I felt the strange urge to reach over and tug it tight. I bit my lip really thinking before I moved. Trey'von, don't do it. Who gives a fuck if her seat belt is loose? What if we get into a wreck? Will she fly from the car or get hurt? Stop, Trey'von you don't care what happens to her, JUST MOVE ON!

"Why are you staring at me?" her tone dripping with venom. I licked my lips shaking my head looking away to the steering wheel. She's always staring at me but suddenly when I do it, it's a bad thing.

"Because yo annoying ass hasn't told me where we goin and you don't know how to put on a seat belt. Fix it!" I spat, reaching over pulling her seat belt tighter. She gave me an odd look but gave me the address we.

"Why you got all that shit?" I asked her after several minutes of complete silence. I glanced over at her as she stared at her phone.

"We're having a friend's dinner," she told me as I stopped at a stop sign. I looked over at her with a blank expression. She looked over at me, a small smile breaking through on those painted pink lips.

"It's where all my friends get together and we all cook together, eat together, play a game after or just watch a movie. It's just a way for us to hangout" she told me with a shrug. I nodded my head taking off back down the road. I leaned up turning on the music, quietly rapping along with it. Soon enough, I pulled up in front of the house she was going too, I turned off the car, unbuckled, and looked at my phone. Elly got out, opening the back door grabbing the box slamming the door shut. I sighed adjusting in my seat, getting comfortable. Who knew how long I would be sitting here waiting? Suddenly, the passenger side door opened. I looked over to see Elly staring at me with an expecting look.

"You coming?" I was taken back by her invite inside. She didn't even want to get in the car with me and now she wants me to go inside to this little dinner thing?

ELEANOR

I watched Trip's eyebrows lace together, his plump eye, catching lips slightly parted in confusion. I knew he was a little slow but what was so complicated about 'you coming' like come on.

"I think it would be better if I stayed out here. I can make sure your safe better, see anything coming," he told me. I nodded, slowly looking him up and down. He was lying and giving me a bullshit reason. I put the box on the floorboards and got in the car with him. I felt his heavy stare on me, but I just ignored it making my hands into binoculars pretending to look for something.

"What the fuck are you doing?" he asked, laughing. I looked over at him with my hands still cupped as binoculars.

"Looking for this threat. If you're not going in then neither am I," I said going back to my childish mocking. He laughed at me once again shaking his head. I couldn't help but smile a real smile this time.

"Baby Girl, they're not gonna want me inside that house. I'm the big scary monster remember?" he asked me with a smile. It wasn't big. You couldn't see his teeth, but it made it past the smirk stage into a smile. His face was a little brighter.

"Well, I don't think you're scary at all and I'm not the type of person to let you sit in this car or leave you out when you came with me. If they have a problem with you being here then we'll both leave," I told him with a shrug. I didn't care what differences we had. I didn't care about my ill feelings towards him. He brought me here, he was stuck hanging out with me and I wouldn't ever make someone feel like they weren't worth my time. I would never leave someone out or force them to sit in a car. I wanted to include everyone and make sure they were having a good time.

"You sure?" he asked me raising an eyebrow. I smiled, reaching over to grab his hand to squeeze it. But the moment our skin touched, I felt something I hadn't ever felt before. It was like electricity shot through my arm. Butterflies erupted in my stomach and floated into my chest. I quickly pulled my hand away in shock. I looked up to his face to see him staring at his hand in shock. Did he feel that too? What was that?

"Yeah, I'm sure but you're carrying the box," I said, playing it off like I didn't feel anything. I got out of the car and he followed seconds later. He came around with the box and I led us up to Gabby's door. I just opened it and walked inside.

"YOU'RE FAVORITE'S HERE!" I yelled with a smile as we walked towards the kitchen where I could hear laughter coming from that direction. I saw I was the last to arrive.

"You look amazing," Luke said, coming around the table towards me.

"Yeah well it's not easy being a bad bitch," I mocked, pretending to flip my hair that was up in a bun. Trip scoffed from behind me and sat the box on the table making me laugh.

"Got that right" Luke smiled leaning down going to kiss me. I looked away pretending not to notice. I casually went to stand next to Trip hoping no one noticed. I didn't want all of our friends to know we were hooking up. It wasn't like that for me.

"Guys this is Trip, he's going to be hanging out with us today. Trip that is Luke, Tony, Nicole, and my bestie Gabby," I told him pointing to each. He nodded, sitting down at the table pulling out his phone. I sighed, grabbed the box and went over to the counter.

"I need the stove, is anyone using it?" I asked, seeing somethings was already cooking.

"So, this is the Trip we've all heard about. He's cute girl," Nicole bit her lip looking over at me. I glanced at Trip seeing him smirking at me, but I just shook my head.

"So, you talkin about me Baby Girl? All good things though, right?" he asked me with a cocky smirk making me dramatically roll my eyes.

"No, I tell them how much of a cabron you are," I told him as I washed my hands then grabbed the pack of chicken.

"Why would you bring this guy to my house? I thought you hated him," Gabby whispered, as I washed off the chicken. She grabbed a cutting board and knife and put them on the counter.

"It's a long story that I don't want to get into, but I had to and I wasn't leaving him out. Trip would you like to help?" I asked looking over my shoulder at him. He scoffed glancing up at me.

"I don't cook for hoes," he answered me with an attitude. I bit my tongue, not wanting to explode on him in front of my friends.

"I just don't like having a gang banger in my house. It makes me nervous. What if he robs us? We can't afford that," Gabby whispered to me, stressed. I smiled as I reached over, grabbed her hand, and squeezed it.

"He won't, I promise. Just chill Gabby," I told her. I felt an arm wrap around my waist. I looked up to see Luke drinking a juice, watching me pull peppers from the box.

"I love that pasta," Luke told me. I smiled, twirling out of his arm.

"Who doesn't like my pasta? I'm an amazing cook," I bragged, putting the peppers on the cutting board and cutting them up. Luke moved to touch me again. I set down my knife and walked away like I was going to look at my phone.

"You ok?" Luke asked quietly, coming over to me going to put his hand in my back pocket. But I moved, aggravated with his touchiness.

"Stop fucking touching her. She's keeps moving away from you and you followin her like a pussy whipped dog. Lay another fucking finger on her and I'll shoot it off," Trip growled that low dangerous growl. Luke raised both hands up and moved away. I sent Trip a thank you smile. He nodded, and I went back to cooking.

TREY'VON

I watched her move back towards I think her name was Gabby or Gabe or somethin. I couldn't figure this Luke guy out. He was Lil Psycho's brother. I knew Elly didn't know he was tied to El Diablos. She's too loyal to Zeke to be around anyone associated them. I wonder what would happen if I just blurted it out right now. Would Elly flip shit or just dismiss it? It would tell me a lot about where she stands with Los Prophets, but I decided to keep the information to myself in case I needed it. He was touching her a lot. It made me wonder if something was going on between them. She seemed uncomfortable by it, so I'd step in. I couldn't help but wonder what made him feel like he could touch her so much.

"Would you like something to drink?" a blonde headed girl asked me. I couldn't remember her name and didn't even try to.

"Sure. You got water?" I asked and she nodded, skipping over to the fridge. Moments later she handed me a bottle of Just Water. I nodded my head twisting it open taking a drink as I pulled out my phone and scrolled through my social media. I ignored the friend's gossiping, not really caring about what was going on in their shitty high school.

"We should play music," the Asian guy said pulling out his phone. I swear if he plays that k-pop shit I'll air this bitch out. I rather listen to "Turn them lights down low" than that bullshit.

"I WANT TO PLAY IT!" Elly yelled, jumping up waving her arms in the air. I smirked, watching a bright smile pull over her face as she scrambled for her phone.

"No! You and Tony aren't playing it. Tony is going to play hair rock and you over there sellin drugs and pimpin hoes," the blonde girl laughed shaking her head. Elly shrugged turning back to the counter.

"I'll play it," that Gabby girl said, but Luke scoffed.

"No, because then only you and Elly will understand it. You only listen to Spanish music," Luke argued. I raised an eyebrow at he assumed I didn't know Spanish, but I just let it go not really caring. They all burst into bickers over who was playing music.

"WAIT STOP!" Elly yelled shooting her friends daggers.

"Trip will play music since we can't decide. Trip do you mind?" she asked me. I shrugged not caring. She smiled coming over taking my phone from me easily. After a couple minutes I heard a dig from a bluetooth speaker. She handed it back and I played 'Worst Behavior' by Drake.

"YOOO, YOU GUYS LISTEN TO THE SAME MUSIC" the Asian guy yelled. Elly smirked going back to cooking. I chuckled shaking my head at how she played every single person in this room to get her way.

"Call it gang trait" She snickered. I shook my head getting up walking over to her and leaning on the counter, watching her as she finished cutting the bell peppers. I couldn't lie, she was fucking that up, but I wasn't here to teach her how to cut peppers. She reached into the box pulling out a bag of raw shrimp on ice. I made a face looking away from the seafood. She must have noticed because I heard musical like giggles escape her lips.

"What? You don't like shrimp?" she asked me. I shook my head no, cringing as she opened the bag. The smell even bothered me.

"I won't eat stuff with seafood," I told her, shaking my head no. She looked over at me curiously.

"Are you allergic?" she asked me curiously. Her smile was taking up her face, but my eyes caught onto that bruise. I couldn't help but wonder how it got there, was it that Luke kid? Was it someone else, like her dad? Did she run into something maybe? Did it hurt?

"No, I just don't like seafood. It's gross," she nodded adding seasoning into a bowl with the shrimp.

"Then I'll leave it out. They can add it if they want it," she said with a shrug. I scoffed looking away from her. Why was she being so nice? She was just pissed I had to come with her. She was going to lie to Zeke, so I didn't have to come, and now she's trying to cater to my liking of things? This was a different side of Elly then what I'm used to, and I didn't know how to react to it.

"You don't got to do all that. I got a feeling I'm not even welcome here," I said glancing over to Gemma and Lil Psycho's brother who were standing next to each other sending me stink looks. Elly sat down her wooden spoon with a smack, her chocolate brown eyes burned into mine. It wasn't with the usual anger or annoyance. I couldn't tell you what was in them this time.

"Well, I want you here. We're stuck together until things settle so, therefore, I want you wherever I am and if it's to big of a problem I won't go somewhere that you can't. I'm never going to be the type of person to leave someone out because I don't like them or the people around me don't. I'm not that type of female. You will eat and hangout," she told me the last part coming out as a demand. I was taken back by the idea of her wanting me here but I guess she's trying to just make something good out of a bad situation.

ELEANOR

I poured the sauce over the pasta making sure to leave the shrimp out just for Trip. I still didn't like him, but I wasn't going to make him uncomfortable. He came with me as my guest, so it's my job to make sure he's comfy. My mom raised me to be a good person and a host. The pasta made a wet noise as I mixed it together, making all my friends laugh.

"That's what good pussy sound like," Nicole laughed from where she sat by Trip. I think she was tryin to slide on him, but he wasn't having it. Everyone in the room chuckled as I smirked.

"That's what mine sound like," I joked making the room explode. I laughed, my face turning red as everyone laughed at me.

"I'M JUST JOKING...well not really" I said making them laugh harder as my blush grew. I turned my back away from them as I set the bowl of pasta on the counter and the shrimp next to it.

"She just exposed herself," Tony giggled like a 10-year-old boy. We all turned looking at him, I raised an eyebrow not sure what I really exposed. It wasn't a bad thing. It was actually good. It made sex better.

"What the fuck are you talking about? That's a good thing, when you hit it and it start squishing you know you doin it right and it feels better," Trip said looking him up and down. Tony blushed looking away scratching the back of his neck. Tony's never dated before, so I don't think he's ever done anything. I'm sure the only naked girl he's seen is me, and that's because he walked into the bathroom on me.

"Why did you leave the shrimp out? That's my favorite part," Nicole complained, picking up the bowl of shrimp.

"Trip doesn't like shrimp. You can just add it in," I said with a careless shrug. My friends looked at me funny. I just ignored it.

"Ok so here's the real question. After we eat are we playing a game or Netflixing?" I asked them all seriously.

"I say we Netflix and chill," Luke said suggestively coming to stand next to me. He sent me a flirtful wink, but I pretended not to notice even though Gabby and Tony totally did.

"What do you want to do?" Nicole asked Trip, but he shrugged.

"Get some fucking peace and quiet from you," he spat at her, I didn't expect anything less. Gabby's mom's liquor cabinet caught my attention, I walked over to it and grabbed a bottle of whiskey.

"Or else we could all get drunk" I smirked holding up the bottle getting some snickers.

"I'm so down," Gabby smiled at me. Suddenly the bottle was snatched from my hands, and I looked up to see Trip glaring at me.

"You're not drinking," he snapped at me.

"Well, you're not my boss and I'll do what I want" I challenged him snatching back the bottle with a glare. He took a step closer, making me take one back hitting the liquor cabinet.

"No, you're not. If something goes down, I need you to be able to react," he growled at me. I went to tell him off, but the bottle was taken from my hands. Me and Trip looked over to see Luke with his own challenging look.

"You've clearly never met drunk Elly. She's fun" Luke mocked. I laughed stepping away from Trip.

"She's only fun when she's your girlfriend," I teased Luke with a smirk. His eyes scanned me up and down as he took a step closer.

"Yeah? And what's the difference now? I'm already pulling it down every night," he said smoothly. I felt time stop as my eyes grew wide and my lips parted in shock. Gasps filled the rooms followed by questions getting thrown at us by our friends. I didn't want everyone to know me, and Luke was hooking up. I knew it would become this thing about us getting back together, and I didn't want that. I just wanted his sex. It wasn't that great, but it was familiar, and I couldn't be labeled a hoe. Then he asked "what's the difference" he didn't think I felt anything for him, did he? Was I leading him on with it? I blinked rapidly pulling myself out of a state of shock, sending him a glare.

"Where's the fucking popcorn," I heard Trip, but I was too angry to even comprehend what he said and how much I didn't want him commenting on my life.

"I think Trip's right. Maybe we shouldn't drink." My tone was cold as I sent Luke a glare shaking my head. I snatched the bottle roughly from him shoving it towards Trip. I tried to walk away but Luke grabbed my arm.

"Elly," he said I ripped away. He yelled my name once more as I stormed over to the back door slamming it behind me.

Chapter 8

Connecting

TREY'VON

The back door slammed hard enough to shake the cabinets. Everyone was silent and just staring at Lil Psycho's brother, who was staring at his shoes. It didn't shock me they were sleeping together. I kinda thought something was up by how touchy he was. The only thing I want to fucking know is how lied and said we were sleeping together and got cussed the fuck out, but he does it and she just walks away? What type of backwards bullshit is that? I was trying to protect her, and he was just being an asshole.

"Now how come when I told people I slept with her she cussed me out?" I asked putting the bottle back in the cabinet. I looked up to see everyone in the room looking at me, shocked and confused for some reason. I raised eyebrow unsure of why they were staring at me like I grew a second head.

"Elly? Cussed you out?" Gabby asked me like she didn't believe me. That girl was always cussing me out over something. I don't know why that was such a big shock. She's feisty about everything which is sexy as hell, I can't lie to you.

"Yeah? So?" I asked, my tone coming out more clipped than I intended, but oh well.

"Elly doesn't like confrontation. She lets people walk all over her, there's no way she's cussing you out," that annoying blonde bitch said, as I sat down at the table. I shook my head. These people really didn't know her then.

90

"You could've had me fooled. She be talkin to me like I'm 5'1, don't got a gun, nor a reputation. I don't know what you talkin about," I said shaking my head, and taking a drink out of my water. That blonde girl came and sat next to me at the table. They all just looked at each other with their mouths gaped open in surprise. I didn't know Elly that well, so maybe that wasn't a part of her that many had people seen?

"Whatever. I'm goin out here, I don't even like you bitches," I said, standing up and grabbing my bottle of water. I pulled open the back door stepping out onto the wooden porch that creaked under my weight. Right away, I seen Elly sitting on the stairs with her face hidden in her arms.

"Go away, go finish telling everyone how we had sex," she said her tone laced with anger. But she wasn't lashing out like she normally did. I couldn't help but worry. I knew the feisty, lashing out, annoying Elly, not this one that hid away when someone did something she didn't like.

"Well the last time I did that you almost beat my ass," I partly joked. Her head shot up and she looked back at me, letting out a sigh of relief which shocked me even more.

"I'm so happy it's you. I never thought I'd say that," she laughed. I walked over and sat next to her on the steps. Man, she already tellin me how happy she is to see me and I've barely even said anything. I could get used to this Elly, this calm not trippin out version.

"Yeah, it's just me. So, you and frat boy?" I asked, mockingly. She laughed shaking her head hiding her face in her hands. I laughed licking my lips looking at that top that barely covered anything.

"It's complicated. We dated for a while, like a year but I lost feeling. I wasn't in love with him like he was with me, and I knew I'd hurt him, so I broke up with him. We stayed friends, so it was never weird. Then we got paired up for this stupid English project. He came over and I was changing and the next thing I know I'm in bed with him. Then I wanted it again the next day and he was there. It became a normal thing and, honestly, it was just because he was the one there that day," she told me. I nodded my head taking in what she said. I didn't think her as the hooking up type but that's good to know she was in a way, it could work out well for me.

"Lucky dude, right place right time but I got a question," I said, leaning against the stair railing looking at her. She looked over at me with those chocolate brown eyes waiting for me to ask.

"How the fuck do I get cussed out for saying we had sex and his bitch ass doesn't? I know I'm scarier than homeboy," I said laughing. She burst into laughter, leaning back on her hands shaking her head looking up at the sky. She sighed, licking those beautiful plump lips I was dying to taste.

"Because you drive me crazy. You push buttons I didn't know I had. You make it easy for me to scream and defend myself when I can't do that with anyone else," she told me. I looked over that curvy body. My imagination going wild with all the things I could teach her. I know that kid isn't putting it down the right way.

"So it's easy for you to scream at a guy who's killed people since he's been 9 years old?," I asked her, chuckling. She laughed as she nodded her yes. It was interesting to see how defending herself to Luke was hard but the crazy guy with a gun wasn't. We ended up in a comfortable silence. She just stared up at the clouds as I stared at her face, trying to figure her out. I've never met someone who never feared me, let alone was fine flipping out on me but not anyone else in their life.

ELEANOR

I watched the clouds move above me as I tried to ignore Trip's heavy stare. I felt my skin tingling from his eyes which was a new but exciting feeling. I tried to ignore it, and just enjoy our silence together.

"I don't love him," I told Trip, ripping my eyes away from the sky. I expected to see a judgmental look. That same *'you're a hoe'* look that anyone would have given me. Hook ups give guys street cred, but me...it makes me a whore because I have a vagina.

"You don't have too. It's just sex," he told me with a shrug looking out towards the yard. I bit my lip nervously, nodding, looking up to the sky once again.

"I've never really been the hook up type of person. There was one random guy, and then this time with Luke. He made that comment about me kinda being his girlfriend and I don't want that. I think he still has feeling for me that I didn't know about before and now I feel like if I was to break it off, I'm gonna be forced to pick between my friends or being with him romantically," I told Trip. I was sure he didn't want to hear all of this, but the great thing about venting to someone I hated was...I didn't care what he thought about me. When he didn't say anything, I looked over to him to see that he looked like he was in deep thought. He reached into his hoodie pocket and pulled out perfectly rolled blunt out of a baggie. Great, he's going to get high. I watched him put the brown stick between his lips. I looked away trying not to get annoyed with him.

"Here," he said tapping my shoulder. He was holding the blunt towards me. I laughed, looking at him like he was crazy.

"I've never smoked anything in my life," I told him. He rolled his eyes taking another hit.

"It'll help. You're overthinking and it will chill that the fuck out. Come on, just try it. You don't like it, that's fine" he told me. I bit my lower lip looking at the tightly rolled drug. After a few seconds of going back and forth in my head I took it from him.

"Put it to your lips and inhale. Small because it's your first time and that's straight gas, then swallow or inhale again," he told me. I nodded, putting the drug between my lips. I inhaled, closing my eyes, feeling the smoke fill my lungs. I pulled away the blunt, inhaling deeply again, blowing out the smoke. A small cough left my lips, but that was just from the odd taste and how dry it made my tongue.

"It really does make your mouth dry huh?" I asked looking at it. I put it back to my lips repeating the process, just taking a bigger hit and then passed it back to Trip.

"Here, drink. It will help with the cotton mouth if you drink water while you smoke." He handed me his bottle of water. I opened it taking a drink. When he went to hand me back the blunt, I offered him the water, but he shook his head no. I took another hit closing my eyes as this odd calm came over my body. I didn't feel like my mind was going a million miles per hour about the whole Luke situation anymore. It actually didn't seem that big of a deal anymore. I took another hit, passing it to Trip.

"So, what's your real name? I know your mom didn't name you Trip," I asked. He looked at me raising an eyebrow, pushing the water towards me again. I took a drink still looking at him.

"Why?" He asked me blowing out smoke.

"I'm just curious. I'm not going to go look for your kid or girlfriend or anything," I told him with a shrug. A lot of the time a nickname was to protect their family. Trip chuckled, shaking his head, and passed me the blunt again.

"I don't have a kid and I don't date. It's Trey'von," he told me, and I nodded taking another hit.

"I like that. Trey'von. It sounds better than Trip," I told him taking another hit, passing it to him.

"I didn't know your name until today. That's why I called you Baby Girl," he told me. I looked over at him as I took a drink of his water. He smirked taking another hit.

"You always gonna be my Baby Girl though. Aint thing changing," he flirted, making my eyes grow wide. I fought a smile looking at Trey'von. He was so cute and right now he sounded like the best idea I've ever had.

"Oh yeah and why is that?" I asked him with a smirk. He chuckled looking over at me handing me the blunt.

"Finish that shit off," he told me. I nodded and finished it off. He watched me with each puff I took. Once it was burning my fingers, he took it and flipped it off into the grass, then looked at me again making me laugh.

"Why are you staring at me, weirdo?" I asked, hearing my voice slur just slightly. He laughed, moving closer to me.

"Because you a bad bitch and I like what I see every time I see it," he flirted. I blushed looking away from him. I felt surprisingly smooth, soft fingers glide along my jawline turning my head. Right away I was met with Trey'von's nearly black eyes staring directly into mine. His face was inches from mine. I felt my breath hitch in my throat, my heart sped up beating against my chest so hard I wondered if he could hear it.

"Don't be shy with me," he whispered, his pink tongue peaking out wetting his eye-catching lips as his eyes dropped down to my body. I didn't even catch myself leaning in as I stared at his lips. I looked back up to his nearly black eyes that were rimmed with red.

"You're gorgeous," he whispered, leaning in. His lips brushed against mine sending electric shocks through my body. It was a feeling I never felt before, but I was starting to realize that wasn't uncommon with him.

TREY'VON

I could smell her fruity perfume mixed with the smell of marijuana. It was a heavenly smell, not even one I knew I longed for before this moment. My lips brushed against her full, plump, painted ones. A visible shiver followed by tingles ran down my spine. She giggled, making me smile as her hand ran up my chest to my neck. Just as I went to close the space between our lips the back door swung open.

"Elly---oh," I heard Lil Psycho's brother speak, just as Elly faked a cough pulling away from me.

"Am I interrupting something?" he spat, crossing his arms with a glare. I leaned back against the pole fixing my hood as Elly giggled.

"Your head looks funny," she giggled, making me burst into laughter. Elly gasped making my head snap up. I looked over at that Luke kid to see what she gasped about. Suddenly two hands landed on my upper thigh, I looked over at Elly as she smiled a bright smile at me.

"I'm starving and there is pasta inside. Let's go eat," she said standing, making me laugh and shake my head. I grabbed my water, taking a drink and handing it to her.

"Hey, can we talk real quick?" Luke asked her, as I stepped into the house.

"After I get food," she pushed his arm off and followed me in. I moved, letting her go over to the food. I walked over and sat on top of the table with my feet in a chair, as I pulled out my phone to get on Snapchat.

"Are you high?" I heard Gabby...Gemma...whoever ask Elly as she piled two plates high with food. I looked up as whats his face walked in and all her friends got closer. I saw her trying to play it cool, but she failed, bursting in laughter.

"It actually feels sooooo good," she told them laughing, making me chuckle and shake my head.

"Next time you payin for that shit then. Whether you got to suck dick for it or got paper," I teased her. Her eyes were wide, and she burst out into laughter.

"Then make your own plate," she said, sitting down the plate, laughing.

"No, Baby Girl come on. I'm hungry," I complained. But she just shook head no.

"You said I had to suck your dick if I wanted more," she laughed when I knew she should be yelling at me. Her friends looked at her confused, and I was right there with them.

"I mean or you could just suck it for the hell of it. I don't care either way, I just want food," I complained. She rolled her eyes finished filling our plates, bringing me mine with a fork. She sat in the chair my feet where in, but shared it, without a complaint. I liked high Elly, she wasn't annoying.

"Well, this is new. Elly is a full-blown stoner guys," the annoying blonde threw her hands in the air. I spun my fork in Elly's pasta, taking a bite. I hummed at the flavor. I was pleasantly surprised to find out she could cook. I heard the front door slam shut, and moments later a Hispanic man walked into the kitchen. His clothes were covered in filth, he had a lunch box in his hand, and work boots on. He looked around smiling at everyone and then his eyes landed the Los Prophet's tattoo on my neck. I nodded my head at him and looked down at my plate as Elly pushed my legs off the chair, sending me a stink look. I flipped her off going back to eating.

"Elly, who's your friend?" the man asked eyeing me.

"This is my friend Trip. Trip this is Mr. Lopez, Gabby's dad," Elly told me, and I nodded my head.

"What's up?" He nodded a hello at me.

"Gabby, a word?" he asked. I watched the father/daughter combo walk out of the room together. Elly started talking to her friends about the food.

I couldn't lie, everything but for the food Elly made was gross. There was something wrong with each thing, either it was over spiced or didn't have enough. It was watery, dry, burnt, under cooked, or frozen before it was cooked. Elly's was the only one cooked with fresh food and had the right amount of everything. Gabby walked back in with her dad glancing at me.

"Baby Girl, you the only one here who can cook," I said, pushing around the other food.

"I made the chicken. You don't like it?" the annoying blonde said coming over to me with a smile. She rested her hands on my leg, but I roughly shoved them off sending her a glare.

"No, it tastes like shit. It's dry and you didn't season it," I said setting down the plate. She looked at me, shocked, her eyes narrowing.

"That's rude," Elly said, but I shrugged, not caring. This bitch was annoying. She hasn't left me alone since we got here. Elly got up and went over to Gabby. I put my feet back up and got on my phone. That blonde girl sat down in the chair I had my feet in making me groan loudly and move.

ELEANOR

I sat on the counter staring at Gabby. She was talking to me about something, but I have no idea about what. It was such an odd feeling. Everything seemed funny. I felt way more relaxed. I could almost go to sleep if my mouth wasn't so dry.

"Are you even listening to me?" Gabby asked. I shook my head clear of all thoughts about how I was feeling.

"I'm trying," I admitted with a blush, making her sigh. She looked me up and down, then shook her head at me.

"I can't believe you got high," she said, shaking her head as Lucas walked over to us.

"Same. I thought you had better judgement," Lucas scolded coming over but I just waved them off. Lucas just told everyone we were having sex. I was upset, and Trey'von said it helped him, so why the hell not try it? I can honestly understand why he smokes it so much. He's so angry and this calms you down so much.

97

"How about we all play never have I ever?" I suggested, getting off the counter. Everyone agreed, but Trey'von who let out a loud annoying groan. but in this state, not even he could bother me.

"Let's go into the living room," Tony suggested, tossing me a bottle of apple juice. He handed Trey'von another water and we walked into the living room. We sat on the floor in a circle, to the right of me was Tony, and to the left was Gabby. Trey'von was directly in front of me with Nicole on his left and Lucas on his right. They both seemed uncomfortable, but they'll get over it.

"I'll start. Never have I ever peed in the shower," Nicole said, clapping her hands. I made a face, watching Trey'von, Lucas, and Tony all drink.

"You guys are gross," me and Gabby said. They just shrugged.

"So, you get out of the shower to pee?" Trey'von asked, clearly not believing me.

"I've never had to pee while I'm in the shower," I argued, but he just scoffed waving me off.

"I'm calling bullshit," he said. Tony and Lucas agreed. They all burst out calling us liars which led to a huge bickering match. Before anyone could make it serious (translation: before me and Trey'von killed each other) we broke out into laughter even Trey'von.

"Ok I got another one," Nicole said as we sobered up from our laughter. We all looked at her, waiting for her to ask.

"Never have I ever had butt ass naked sex in a pool," she said. I brought my juice to my lips taking a drink to see Trey'von mocking me but no one else.

"YOU'VE HAD SEX IN A POOL? AND YOU NEVER HAVE?" Gabby yelled, pointing at Lucas as he glared at me.

"With who?" he spat at me, but I just shrugged laughing.

"I don't kiss and tell like you, or lie like you" I said, pointing at Trey'von and Lucas. Trey'von just shrugged, not even caring.

"Ok my turn. Never have I ever had mind blowing sex," Tony said. I gave him a look squinting my eyes as everyone took a drink, except for me and Tony.

"You're a virgin," I accused him. He just laughed

"And you just said Luke sucks in bed," he snickered at me making my eyes grow wide. Luke sent me a glare, but I just smiled.

"I mean it's average it's not mind blowing. Never have I ever had a wet dream about anyone in this room," I said, and everyone took a drink. Even Trey'von making my eyes grow wide but he just shrugged.

"You're hot," he told me, making my eyes grow wide and a blush fill my cheeks.

"Never have I ever been tied up during sex," Gabby said, cutting mine and Trey'von's conversation short. He's had a sex dream about me? Interesting. No one took a drink except Trey'von, making my eyes grow wide.

"TREY'VON!" I screamed, making everyone but him jump. He just looked at me with wide questioning eyes.

"You've been tied up? Nobody ask another question yet!" I said, stopping anyone from changing the subject. He nodded his head fixing his hood. He was probably confused about my excitement. 50 shades of grey and all that rough sex is like my fantasy, but come on, you've seen what I was working with.

"Oh my god! Is it fun?" I asked him, leaning forward to listen to what he had to say. He raised an eyebrow at me nodding his head again.

"Yeah. Tied up, blind folded and got a bitch with ice between her teeth running it down my body. That's that sex that could lowkey make a man crazy if the pussy hit right," he laughed hitting Lucas's arm, but trust he wouldn't know anything about that. I couldn't lie that sounded like so much fun. I hated Trey'von a lot but maybe one night couldn't hurt? No, nope. Zeke would kill the both of us. And then, Trey'von will take our night as he can disrespect me whenever he wants too.

"You've always been into that 50 shade shit," Gabby laughed, and I nodded my head leaning back.

"You really gonna act like that don't look fun. I'd put it down every night, period and all for some shit like that," I said shaking my head making the whole group except for Lucas laugh.

"Ight I got one," Trey'von said glancing at Lucas, smirking at him and then looking at me. His nearly black eyes piercing mine.

"Never have I ever hidden my gang affiliation," he said confusing me. We all took a drink except for Lucas, making me look at him, confused.

"Never have I ever pictured somebody I knew while masturbating," Gabby said boldly. I looked around to see Tony and Trey'von drinking.

"TONY!" Nicole screamed, making us laugh but he just shrugged.

"I saw Elly naked one time! I couldn't help it," he defended himself.

TREY'VON

I looked at the Asian guy in shock and then over to Elly as she shrieked shaking her head no and moving even further away. I couldn't help but chuckle at her reaction, but then it reminded me of the time I pictured her in the shower with me. She seemed really interested in my sex life earlier. I know I can bag her, just wait. It's gonna take time, but thanks to Zeke that's all I have.

"TONY THAT'S WEIRD. Nicole move. Trade me," Elly demanded crawling over. She moved sitting next to me making me laugh. If only she knew she'd be joining me in the shower later tonight.

"I can't help it. Every other guy in here said you're hot but I do it and oh no," he mocked Elly making her eyes grow wide.

"They said I was hot, not that they were jerking off to me," she defended, and I decided to fuck with her a little bit.

"Well...I mean I might---" She cut me off

"TREY'VON WHAT THE FUCK. That's sooooo gross" She complained trying to crawl away from me. I laughed grabbing her waist pulling her onto my lap wrapping my arms tightly around her holding her into place as I chuckled.

"NO LET ME GO!" she yelled playfully laughing, as I chuckle.

"I'm kidding," I laughed, and she hummed, still fighting against me, but I held her even tighter.

"STOP BEING SO LOUD!" Gemma's dad yelled, making them all stop and giggle quieter. Elly tried to get off me, but I just held her tightly, she glanced back at me with a weird look.

"Let me go, ya'nasty," she giggled at me but I just laughed shaking my head.

"I was kidding. If anything, you probably gonna be the one with fantasies now that you know I'm down to tie you up any day," I purred in her ear. Right away I felt her breath hitch. I saw her pulse speed up telling me her heart was pounding against her chest. She squeezed her eyes closed like that would stop any reaction she had. Her palms touched my leg as she adjusted herself and I felt the sweat.

"Uh...I um...need to pee," she gulped. I let go letting her up with a smirk and she quickly walked away.

"I thought you guys hated each other?" Gemma asked me the moment Elly was out of sight and earshot.

"Oh, we do, but she's sexy and high. It makes it easy to flirt and her not to take my head off," I shrugged carelessly. My phone started vibrating in my pocket. I pulled it out to see Zeke. I stood up walking into the kitchen answering it.

"Yo," I said carelessly leaning against the table.

"Where are you and Elly at right now?" He asked me, his voice rushed and angry.

"At one of her little friend's house why what's up?" I asked him curiously. I was the hothead between us, so it was different for him to be mad.

"The DEA just caught one of our shipments coming from Mexico. I think we got a rat. I need you at my house, now," he told me and right away I felt my temper spike. I thought about Javier. I never really trusted him that much.

"I'm on my way and I have an idea who it might be," I said and hung up.

"FUCK!" I yelled texting a couple guys to get Javier for me and take him to Zeke's. I stormed into the living room ripping up all of Elly's shit.

"BABY GIRL COME ON" I yelled, anger slipping through my tone. Elly quickly walked out looking at me with wide eyes.

"We got to go now," I snapped.

"Why, what's going on?" She asked me with an attitude lacing her voice only making my anger rise.

"The DEA just got a shipment from Mexico. I have a bullet to put through someone and you need to be at home, now let's go," I growled, grabbing her wrist and pulled her out of the house not even letting her say goodbye.

"TREY'VON. STOP, YOU'RE HURTING ME!" she yelled as I got to the car and opened her door. She got in rolling her eyes. I slammed the door walking around getting in the car and ripped out.

"I don't want to go with you," she spat harshly at me.

"You aren't," I snapped. She crossed her arms looking away from me out of the window.

"And stop flirting with me. I don't like anything about you, I don't want you to kiss me or say little things to get a reaction from me," she spat, but I didn't even give a shit about that right now. I was more worried about my cocaine and heroin.

"Last I checked you leaned into me first," I argued with her. She turned with a deadly glare. I don't know why she thought she scared me.

"I WAS HIGH. I COULDN'T FUCKING CONTROL IT! YOU GET HIGH ALL OF THE TIME YOU CAN CONTROL IT," she screamed at me. I knew the moment we left there was going to be nothing but war between us.

"YOU NEED TO SHUT THE FUCK UP AND SMOKE AGAIN. FUCK! YOU'RE ACTUALLY TOLERABLE HIGH," I yelled at her as I flew through stop lights and stop signs.

"THAT'S GOOD TO KNOW YOU ONLY LIKE ME WHEN I'M HIGH AND PUTTING UP WITH YOUR SHIT. I'M NOT THAT

GIRL THAT'S GOING TO LET YOU WALK ALL OVER HER," she screamed at me as I pulled up to her house.

"Get the fuck out of my car before I shoot you," I threatened. She squealed getting out slamming my door so hard if I wasn't mad, I'd be worried the window was going to shatter. Once I seen her annoying ass get inside the house, I pulled out speeding towards Zeke's to take care of the situation at hand.

Chapter 9

Feisty

ELEANOR

I stepped out of the shower drying off. It was Saturday and I didn't have any plans. Right now, I was thinking about hanging out with my sisters but I didn't know if I wanted too. I always felt like I missed them but 5 minutes into sister day, I remember why I don't like hanging out with them. I wrapped the towel around my body and another around my hair. I walked down to my bedroom, shut the door, and sat down at the desk. I pulled my hair out of the towel putting it in two french braids down my back. I did a "no makeup" makeup look, which I did on lazy days. Once finished, I went over to my dresser looking for something to wear. I changed into grey baggy Nike sweatpants, a white, tight, sorta see through, long sleeved shirt that had a few buttons at the neckline which I kept unbuttoned. I made my bed quickly. I grabbed my phone going downstairs to see my dad on the couch watching "Cupcake Wars".

"What's up Pops?" I said, sitting next to him on the couch. He smiled looking over at me and got more comfortable.

"Enjoying my day off. You look comfy," he said, eyeing my outfit. I shrugged messing with my braid and looked up at the TV.

"Gordon Ramsey's shows are better," I said making him laugh and shake his head.

"BLOODY HELL IS THIS? IT FUCKING MOOED AT ME!" Dad yelled, mocking Chef Ramsey's accent which made me burst into laughter and push at his shoulder slightly. My mom walked into the living room to see what all the yelling was about.

"I don't care how rude it is, it's funny." My dad agreed with me. I didn't get to spend much time with him, so it was nice to just hangout.

"I thought something was wrong," Mom hissed at us storming off. We smiled shrugging. I leaned into my dad bringing my knees to my chest and focused on the TV.

"I'm proud of you for staying away from the bar," he told me as he hugged me more into his side. I have stayed away from the bar, but I've been around Zeke and Trey'von. I've gotten high. I've been in Trey'von's car I almost kissed him. I've gotten into screaming matches with him. How much I was separating myself was questionable, but my dad didn't need to know that.

"I out-grew it," I lied. I was keeping the peace. He didn't know I was going there, so that meant TV cuddles with my dad and that was just fine with me. We let a silence fall over us and just watched TV. After two episodes of "Cupcake Wars", Izzy walked in with Mateo following after her.

"Oh "Cupcake Wars". I love this show" Mateo said plopping down next to me. Izzy moved to lean against the couch.

"That's impressive," Mateo said and we hummed agreeing.

"I couldn't do it," I mumbled. My dad and Izzy agreed with me.

"I could," Mateo said, making us all roll our eyes. She over-cook's noodles, let alone make these kinda cupcakes.

"Oh shoot, Elly, there's a guy on the front porch waiting for you. I told him I'd get you," Izzy told me. I looked at her raising an eyebrow, who the hell could be out there waiting for me?

"Who is it?" I asked, licking my lips.

"He told me to tell you it's the man of your dreams," Izzy told me. I looked at my dad who looked at me with questioning eyes. I got up and fixed my sweats.

"Want me to look first, kid?" Dad asked, but I just waved him off.

"I have street cred," I mocked which made them laugh. I walked out of the house and onto the creaky porch. I didn't see anyone, so I walked over to the L part of the porch to find Trey'von sitting on the swing. I crossed my arms, he smirked as his nearly black, heavy eyes traveled my body. Oddly enough, goosebumps followed the tingles his eyes left on my skin. I ran my hand over my arms like I was cold but, really, I was trying to wipe away the evidence of him having an effect on at me at all. I didn't understand my body's reaction to him. Yesterday I thought it was just because we had a moment. We were getting to know little things about each other, but they were carrying over into today and I didn't like that.

"Hey Baby Girl," he said in a husky voice.

"Man of my dreams? Really?" I asked him. Annoyance laced my voice as he leaned back into the swing. Izzy had seen Trey'von before with the whole flirting with her thing but yet still repeated what he said?

"Yeah, don't act like you didn't come home last night with your mind spinning with thoughts about me and the things we could do together," he snickered. He's so gross. He clearly took me asking questions as 'I want to sleep with you' when I wouldn't sleep with him if he was the last person on Earth. Yesterday, those thoughts come from the pot and only the pot. It wasn't me. If I had had a clear head, I wouldn't have had those repulsive thoughts about him.

"Not even if we were the only two people on Earth," I told him rolling my eyes making him chuckle and nod.

"Keep telling yourself that, but what are we doing today?" he asked me while messing with his mop of curls.

"WE aren't doing anything together," I said pointing between us. He looked at me tilting his head to the side in the most irritating way.

TREY'VON

She was so annoyed with me even though I had just got here. I couldn't lie, I was living for this reaction from her. I knew she wasn't as fed up with me as she acted. I knew she wanted me just as much as I wanted her but, she tried to cover it with irritation. She was only fooling herself with this act, but I'd let her lie to herself for a while.

"Zeke said I'm supposed to be with you so whatever you're doing turns into what we're doing, so don't make it something lame again," I rolled my eyes at yesterday's events. The 'never have I ever' game got interesting but became boring just as fast.

"Why do you want to hang out with me? I don't see Zeke around. Is it just so you can flirt with my sister right in front of me again?" There it was. With her attitude laced accusation, she revealed how jealous that action truly made her. The funniest part was, I did that for her attention and her attention only. I didn't give a fuck about her sister.

"So you're jealous?" I asked. She huffed, then started to walk away, but then turned right back around and stormed up to me. She stood directly in front of me with her hands resting on her thin, tiny waist. Those chocolate brown eyes ignited in rage as they burned into me. My smirk only grew as I looked over the sexy "lazy" outfit she had on. This outfit was one of the best I had seen on her. Baggy sweats, a shirt that covered her stomach but gave off a perfect amount of cleavage. She didn't have on any makeup up and her hair was pulled back out of her face. She looked good, I couldn't even front. It made me want to rip those clothes off even more.

"Trey'von are you even listening to me?" she snapped as she grabbed my jaw in her hand lightly, forcing me to look up to her face. Her touch was soft, her skin was warm and smooth. It made me want to feel her pressed against my body even more. I blinked away my lustful thoughts.

"You didn't even say anything and don't ever fucking touch me!" I spat harshly at her knocking away her hand. I did want to feel her touch, but I was stubborn and would never admit that.

"I did too! You just don't listen. I said, I will never be jealous over anything you do, Trey'von," she spat at me. I couldn't help but enjoy the way my name slipped from her tongue mixed with her Spanish accent.

"What happened to Trip?" I asked her curiously. She groaned closing her eyes as she pinching her nose making me laugh.

"Go home Trey'von!" she snapped as she walked away. I got up, grabbed her wrist, and spun her around. We stood inches from one another. Her chest almost brushing against my stomach. She only came to the bottom of my chest, it was a desirable height. Her chocolate brown eyes were staring up at me, but I didn't see any emotion in them. I leaned down within inches of her ear, really.

"I asked you a question Baby Girl," I growled lowly. I felt her shiver as her hands went against my stomach as she tried to push me away, but I grabbed her waist and pushed her against the railing, pressing our bodies against one another.

"Trey'von, stop," she whispered weakly. I smirked cupping her russet cheek feeling how soft her skin truly was.

"Do you really want me to?" I asked her leaning in. I licked my lips, looking at her soft unpainted pink ones. They were parted slightly as I felt her eyes burning into my skull.

"Elle's you ok?" I heard a deeper voice and the screen door slam open. I groaned, hanging my head low as she pushed me away hard enough to make me shuffle back a couple steps.

"Yes, *Trip* was just leaving," Elly said looking at the man I assumed was her dad. She looked back at me with pleading eyes making me roll mine. I couldn't help but notice the way she called me Trip instead of Trey'von. It was a different kind of disappointment, not one I've ever felt before or wanted to feel again.

"Whatever, Baby Girl. I tried but don't call me when those bitch ass punks get a hold of you," I snarled at her and stormed off the porch and threw the gate open that never truly shut. I stomped right back down to the bar and inside to see Zeke playing cards. I walked over slapping all of the cards off of the table glaring at him.

"Find someone else to babysit the little brat" I growled at him. He looked at me raising an eyebrow, putting down his cards.

"She's a handful huh?" He asked me and took a drink from whatever the fuck he was drinking. It took everything in me not to slap the cup from his hands as well.

"She won't let me do my job and I'm not going to bicker with her like she's my bitch," I snapped at Zeke. He nodded his head, set down his cup, and then looked at the cards on the floor and then back to me.

"Ok that's fine," he told me. I looked at him, shocked. He was really giving me my way easy this time. I nodded turning to walk out of the bar when his cool, calm voice spoke up.

"You can work the dope houses then," he told me. I turned and glared at him storming over as my lip snarled.

"Do you want me to shoot you?" I asked him.

"Either you watch over Elly or dope houses. Follow her around without her seeing you if you have to." He told me with a shrug, motioning for Julio to pick up the cards I threw down. Of course, like the bitch he is, he picked every single of them up as I glared at Zeke and he gave me a calm, collected look.

ELEANOR

I pushed open my bedroom door with Mateo and Izzy following behind me. I decided to try sister day since none of us had anything to do and I didn't feel like going anywhere or seeing any of my friends since Lucas told everyone about us. Plus, just listening to music, watching movies, and gossiping with my sisters sounded like the move.

"This shirt is so annoying. I'm about to just wear my bralette or is that weird?" I asked them, tugging on the shirt as Izzy walked over, sat on my bed and looked around my room. I never let them in my room because it's my space and I don't go into theirs. Mateo walked over to my bookshelf and touched all my books as I went to my desk to grab my Bluetooth speaker. Just as Izzy's lips parted to answer me, a huge bang came from my window which made us all jump and stare with wide scared eyes.

"Fuck." I heard the smooth-as-velvet voice that could only belong to one person. Suddenly my curtain was ripped down to expose Trey'von crawling through my window. I crossed my arms as he pulled himself through the window into my room and tripped over my curtain. He looked up at me at with a cocky smirk as I glared at him, no longer scared.

"Shit, I wouldn't mind if you lost the shirt," he smirked looking away from me and around my room.

"What are you doing in here Trey'von? How did you know this is my room?" I hissed at him as he pulled open my top dresser drawer. Before it registered what drawer it was, he had pulled out a black lace thong with a smirk. My eyes grew wide as I stared at him, horrified for holding my underwear up in the air.

"Sexy," he smirked as he smelled them which disgusted me and my sisters.

"Ok pervert, get out!" I snapped climbing across my bed, and snatched my panties away from him, put them back in the drawer, and shut it. His eyes traveled over my body making goosebumps and tingles fill my skin all over again. Was this going to be a new thing for us? I hoped not.

"It's either you or a dope house. Baby Girl, you are so much more fun to look at. So what are we doing?" He asked, kicking off his shoes and moved around me, laid on the bed with his hands behind his head.

"Is this your boyfriend?" Mateo asked me, eyeing Trey'von. I couldn't help the belly laugh that left my lips as Trey'von looked at me amused.

"Nah, I don't date. But one night with me and you'd be wishing I did," he smirked sending me a wink.

"Never in my life. Trey'von get the fuck out of my room now!" I snapped at him as I grabbed his arm tried to pull him from my bed. But he just laughed at me. I grabbed a pillow and hit him in the stomach.

"Whatever, stay. I don't care" I grumbled as I walked around the bed and looked at my sisters.

"Great, girl's day is crashed," Izzy rolled her eyes.

"No, it's not. What do you want me to play?" I asked going over to the desk to turn on my bluetooth speaker and grabbed my phone.

"Justin Bieber!" Izzy said taking her spot back on my bed while trying to ignore Trey'von, who was behind her. I rolled my eyes turning on a song making him whine annoyingly loud.

"Ok Izzy, spill about mystery guy," Mateo wiggled her eyebrows at her from where she stood in front of the bookshelf.

"I knew you were talking to someone, hoe," I said as I tapped Trey'von's legs. He bent his knees, letting me sitting on the bed in front of him. I crossed my legs smiling at my sister, who blushed.

"Why don't you tell us about yo new mans?" Izzy smirked wiggling her eyebrow as Trey'von put his legs over my mine, and I messed with his pants leg.

"Well for starters, he's not my man. I don't even like him, he's annoying" I waved off her question only to make Trey'von shake his head.

"How dare you say that? I thought we had something." he said as he pulled his gun from his shirt and put on my table.

"Anyways, your dude?" I asked Izzy, but she just shrugged.

"It's not serious yet. We go to school together. I'll tell you about him when it gets serious," Izzy said as she closed her eyes and ran her hands through her curls.

"What about you and Lucas? He's been around more," Mateo asked me with an excited smile. She loved Lucas, if she had it her way, I'd have his babies and he'd be around all of the time.

"We were hooking up but that's over. He's got loose lips," I said with a shrug looking down at Trey'von's track pants leg and playing with the zipper.

"Can you just have his babies already? Like, dang, those would be cute kids," Mateo playfully whined, making me laugh.

"Never would I ever," I said. Trey'von laughed from where he lay on the bed. I smiled with a blush hoping, he didn't bring up our game.

"Can I have this?" Mateo asked, pulling out my copy of "Wuthering Heights".

"No. Grandpa gave me that. It's a first edition. Now put it back before you ruin it!" I complained. Trey'von rose his dirty foot to my face. I grabbed it throwing it off of me while sending him a glare.

IZZY

I watched my sister glare at the gangster that crawled through her window. He looked at her with a smile that took up his face and then burst into laughter while he covered his face with a pillow. As much as she claimed to hate him, I could see some kind of connection between them. Maybe they didn't feel it yet because they were too busy getting on each other's nerves. He tossed the pillow, sat up whispered her in ear.

"No, we got way too flirty last time and then had that big blow up fight," she shook her head no. He groaned and laid back down. Me and Mateo shared a knowing look as she stepped down from the shelf. I went to say something, but the gangster cut me off.

"Then can we at least put something on worth listening too. FUCK!" He yelled, annoyed. Elly rolled her eyes pushing him off her and got up. She walked over to the desk, grabbed her phone, and turned on "Pour it Up" by Rihanna.

"Ohhh so twerking music," Mateo snickered making me and Elly look at her with confusion.

"You can't even twerk, no ass" I said. She flipped me off making me laugh.

"And you can?" Elly asked me. Her look was pure amusement, which only made me laugh harder. I glanced over at the gangster. He was looking at his phone.

"I can only do the hip swirl thing," I said with a shrug. I couldn't twerk. I didn't know how to make my butt bounce.

"Wait, can you twerk?" Mateo asked Elly. I looked up at her, curious, as she looked at her phone and nodded her head "yes".

"No way. Like full on throw it back?" I asked shocked. Me and Elly never party together. We aren't really as close as we should be. None of us are, we see each other only in passing. We have our own lives, and we like it that way.

"Yup," she nodded nonchalant. I felt the gangster behind me move. I looked to see his eyes wondering over my sister's body. They're totally hooking up, the way he's looking at her, I know he's hittin.

"No way, show us," Mateo said. I didn't really think she was going to, but she put down her phone and pulled up her sweats a little more. She started by moving her hips in a circle in the sexiest way I've ever seen from her. She laughed and then started throwing it back. Me and Mateo screamed, and jumped up as we watched her.

"GOT DAMN!" the gangster yelled from where he sat on the bed. His eyes were wide, his mouth gaped open.

"ELLY!" Mateo screamed as Elly giggled, dropping it low and still twerking. Suddenly money went flying in the air over her, and I see the gangster pulling money from his wallet.

"Ok I'm done," she laughed while sitting on the floor and covering her face in her hands, probably a little embarrassed.

"Yoooo how'd you learn that?" I asked her as she picked up the cash on the floor.

"Some girl showed me when I was a freshman," she said with a shrug while she threw the money back at the guy.

"I can twerk on beat too. Is this yours?" Elly asked indicating to the bottle of water, and he nodded. I watched her take a drink without any concern about his germs. They're so messing around.

"My friends just texted me. I'm out," Mateo said waving her hand as she walked out of the bedroom.

"Stop, you're going to spill it," I heard Elly. I looked over to see What's-his-Face trying to hit the bottom of the water bottle while Elly held it.

"Yeah, I'm gonna dip out too. You two have fun with whatever you do," I said, getting up. They both mumbled a goodbye and went back to bickering over the water. I walked out shutting the door while texting my little boo thang.

ELEANOR

Trey'von went to snatch the water bottle from my hand, but I smirked jerking it away and holding it over my head. Was it childish to fight with him over *his water*? Yes, it was very childish. But it sounded fun, so that's what I was gonna do.

113

"Give me the damn bottle," he barked. But I just took a step back, taking a drink from it with a smirk.

"Take it from me" I teased him. That fire was igniting in his eyes, telling me I was about to get a reaction from him. That's exactly what I wanted. Before I could move, he was centimeters away from me grabbing my waist picking me up in the air.

"Trey'von!" I squealed as I dropped the water bottle while trying to grab a hold of him. Before I could get a grip, or fight against him, he threw me roughly onto the bed. I felt that hunger pit form in my stomach. I felt the fire of the needy tingles between my legs. Before I could cross my legs to try to ease some of the wanting Trey'von climbed on top of me grabbing my wrists and pinned them to the bed. His nearly black eyes burned into mine. I felt my breath hitch in my throat, my pulse sped up as my heart pounded against my rib cage. I felt the intense pulse between my legs and this position was not helping with that.

"What was that last thing you said?" He asked me, his voice a low husky growl. Every part of my body screamed at me to get his pants off and right now. Every part of me wanted to tell him to just take me and do whatever the hell he wanted to. I swallowed hard looking over his beautiful facial features down to his body that wore too many clothes. How badly my fingers ached to rip them off and feel every inch of his body.

"I-I-" Couldn't make a sentence. I was too distracted by him and my fleshy need. I bit my lip looking up his tattooed arms and back to his face, my eyes catching on the three crosses on his neck.

"Come on Baby Girl, use your words," His voice was a low, rough, and so sexy. He slowly leaned down closer until his nose brushed mine which only drove me crazier.

"I want to..." I was struggling so hard to get out any words. He looked at me with wide eyes. I couldn't help but see the burn of need for me behind them. He smirked as his nearly black eyes looked over my body and back to my eyes. He leaned down kissing my jaw and then planting the nastiest kiss on my neck. I closed my eyes moaning at the wet warm feel that came with his lips. I felt his smirk grow even wider as he left another wet, hot kiss on my neck.

"But we can't," I gasped with no conviction in my voice, and unable to stop from rolling my head to the side to give him more room.

"Come on Baby Girl, I see how much you want me," he whispered in my ear, nipping at my earlobe. He let go of my hands. Right away I brought one of my hands to his head, lacing my fingers through his hair. While the other gripped his tattooed forearm in pleasure. His tongue licked a bold stripe up my neck. My eyes rolled back as my hips bucked up just so slightly. He smiled grabbing my thigh placing it around his waist. Right away I felt his length press against my area that I'm sure was as wet as a fucking lake.

"Don't you feel what you're doing to me Baby Girl?" he whispered in my ear. His wet lips lined my collarbone as he nipped at the sensitive skin.

"I can feel that pussy begging for me," he groaned against my skin. My body was begging for him, but I couldn't cross this line with Trey'von knowing it was just a matter of time before we exploded on each other again. I allowed one more moan to escape my lips at the sound of the dirty words leaving his lips. I pushed at his shoulders lightly, not really wanting him to stop or get off of me. He sighed, hovering over me and looking down. I watched his eyes search my face. I couldn't help but shiver as the goosebumps took over.

"You're so fucking gorgeous," he groaned running his long fingers down my cheekbone and then rolled off of me onto the bed. I got up swallowing hard, fanning myself. I walked over to the window looking at anything but at the man I wanted at that moment.

"Stop, come here." Trey'von's usual strong voice was whiny and needy. I closed my eyes one more time taking a breath. I moved walking over to him, he smirked grabbing my hips pulling me down on the bed next to him. I looked at his arm tracing different tattoos with my eyes. One on his forearm was of a women's eye, but inside of it was an outline of death. It was like she was looking at death. Above that was snake that looked like it would attack and, between those tattoos, in bold clear lettering it said *'GODLESS'*. There were other tattoos surrounding those but those three were heartbreaking enough. They were telling a story of a lack of hope, and it was a story I didn't care to hear til the end. On his upper arm in handwriting, it said *'The soul that sees beauty may sometimes walk alone'*. I was curious about what that meant, but I was scared to ask him as well.

I felt his fingers brush my cheekbone stealing my attention from his tattoos. His eyebrows were scrunched together as if he was deep into thought. I didn't understand this change between me and Trey'von. This morning we were snapping and hating each other and now it's taking everything in me not to rip his clothes off. Then, he was staring at me like I was the finest jewel he's seen, the change is too fast and too much.

"What happened? I've been staring at this bruise for days," he whispered, touching my cheekbone again. I had forgotten about the bruise Novah so kindly left me.

"Soccer. I got kneed in the face," I whispered to him reaching up touching his warm hand. His dark eyes found mine. They looked at me suspicious, almost like he didn't believe me.

"That kid didn't do it?" he asked me. I knew he was talking about Lucas. He thought Lucas was hitting me?

"I'll fucking kill him," he whispered his tone soft and almost adoring. I shook my head no, reaching up and brushing his curls from his eyes.

"No, it was a girl named Novah. We've hated each other ever since I can remember and she 'accidentally' kneed me in the face," I told him using air quotes. I watched his lip snarl up as he stared at the bruising.

"What's going through your head?" I asked him curiously, not being able to pinpoint his emotion or thoughts like I normally can.

"Nothing. I just don't like that you're bruised up," he told me quietly. I looked at him confused, but I didn't push it. He opened his mouth to say something, but was cut off by his phone ringing. He pulled it out with a groan answering it.

"What the fuck do you want?" He was so hostile when he spoke. A few moments of silence passed as he sat up staring ahead.

"I'll be there in 20 minutes," he sighed and hung up. I watched as he stood up and grabbed his shoes.

"I got to get one of my boys. They got picked up, put your number in my phone and text yourself. If you leave, text me and tell me where you are going." He demanded as he tossed me the phone.

"I'm an adult I don't need a babysitter!" I snapped back putting in my number texting myself. He hummed snatching his phone rudely and disappeared out of my window. His mood swings were worse than mine on my period.

Chapter 10

Painful Push

ELEANOR

I woke up to my alarm spazzing out. I sighed, forcing my eyes open, and turned off the alarm. I sat up running my hand over my face and looked around my dark room already tired for the day. I pushed off my blanket, got up and turned on the light. I wasn't feeling an all-out outfit today. Instead, I grabbed a white hoodie that says, *"I don't finish anythi"* and a pair of dark high-waist short shorts. I picked out underwear and a bralette from my dresser, then made my bed and laid out my outfit. Finally, I got a towel and body wash and headed down to the bathroom. I got in the shower and did what I had to do, making sure my legs were hairless, since I was wearing shorts.

Once I finished, I dried off, wrapping a towel around my body and another around my hair. I walked back to my bedroom and sat at my desk. I blow dried and styled my curls figuring it was the easiest thing to do this morning. I finished with my usual makeup. Once I approved of my look for the day, I got up and changed into my outfit. I collected all my homework and school needs and shoved them messily into my backpack. I paired my white Toms with my outfit and threw them on. Lastly, I grabbed my soccer bag. I walked downstairs to see Mateo washing out a bowl.

"You gonna eat?" She asked me, as I opened the fridge grabbing my hydro flask.

"No. I'm too tired," I admitted yawning.

"You're going to be grumpy by second period if you don't eat," Mateo scolded.

"I'm hoping to be asleep in second period. Plus, we have to head to the bus, let's just go," I said with a shrug. She grabbed her things and we walked out of the house. I watched Mateo lock the door. I looked down at my phone as I walked towards the porch steps, before my feet could find them, arms wrapped around my waist. Without a second thought I screamed, dropping my phone and throwing elbows trying to get away from whoever grabbed me.

"GET OFF OF ME!" I screamed, turning in their arms so that I was face to chest, which was the opposite of what I intended.

"Yo, Baby Girl chill," I heard the smooth, velvet voice of Trey'von. I looked up as he smiled down at me. I huffed out, pushing him away roughly while sending him a harsh glare.

"You are so stupid. You better hope my phone isn't broken," I spat at him. I was too tired to deal with Trey'von this early in the morning. Luckily, for him, my phone wasn't broke.

"What would you have done if it was broke? Nothing," he said with a smirk. His heavy dark eyes looking over my outfit lingering at my legs. I felt the goosebumps rise from his eyes which only furthered my annoyance towards him.

"Can you like stop stalking me? Thanks," I snapped storming down the steps and walked through the gate that doesn't close. Mateo followed close behind, probably not wanting to be alone with Trey'von, not that I blame her.

"I am not stalking you. Baby Girl wait up," I heard Trey'von call. Moments later he ended up right beside me which only infuriated me more. It was just too early for Trey'von, his mood swings, and the weird feelings I got around him. I was tired and didn't have the energy to over think every single emotion he brought out in me. Or his weird actions. One minute we were friends and the next we're not. I just didn't get it.

"Let me drive you to school. Both of you," he said stepping in front of me. So, I stepped around him.

"No thanks. We can ride the bus," I dismissed his offer glancing to see Mateo walking behind me.

"Maybe we should, the bus smells bad," Mateo said, catching up beside me. I just shrugged.

"Aye stop, what's wrong with you?" Trey'von cut off my path again. I closed my eyes took a breath trying not to lash out at him. I just wanted him to leave me alone. I opened my eyes to see he was growing more impatient. His eyebrows were laced together, his hands were balled into fists next to him, his lip was snarled as he glared at me.

"It's too early to deal with your mood swings. Just leave me alone. I need to get to school," I told him, pushing past him as my shoulder bump his. He grabbed my wrist, pulling me to turn and face him.

"MY MOOD SWINGS? YESTERDAY YOU WERE ALL COOL WITH ME. YOU WANTED ME YESTERDAY, BUT THIS MORNING IS A WHOLE NEW STORY, YOU ACT LIKE YOU DON'T EVEN WANT TO LOOK AT ME. IF ANYONE IS HAVING MOOD SWINGS IT'S YOU!" he screamed at me. Mateo jumped as she looked between us with wide scared eyes, but it didn't even register. I felt my body begin to shake, my vision blurred, I felt my adrenaline spike. I will never understand how he sets off this type of burning anger in me, but he does.

"YOU'RE ACTUALLY KIDDING ME, RIGHT? YEAH, YESTERDAY WE WERE GETTING ALONG GREAT AND TALKING LIKE NORMAL FUCKING PEOPLE. THEN THE MOMENT I DIDN'T GIVE IN AND LET YOU IN MY PANTS, YOU GOT A "PHONE CALL" AND HAD TO GO. YOUR WHOLE ATTITUDE CHANGED YOU WEREN'T BEING NICE ANYMORE. YOU WERE BEING A DEMANDING DICK AGAIN. IF ANYONE'S ATTITUDE CHANGED! IT WAS YOURS!" I yelled, dropping my duffel bag, and shoving him. He grabbed my arm so tightly I felt the ache all the way to my bone. Before I could even try to rip away from him, he jerked me roughly closer to him. His pupils were blown out and his eyes were completely black. He was shaking with anger. It kinda scared me, but I knew he wouldn't hurt me. Something deep inside me told me he wouldn't hurt me no matter what I did.

TREY'VON

I was seeing red flash my mind was slipping in and out of reality. I wanted to hurt her, and I knew I would have if she was anyone else. I tell myself it's just because who she is to Zeke but, truthfully, even if Zeke himself talked to me like that or touched me, I'd kill him.

"TRIP, YOU'RE HURTING ME!" her accented voice screamed at me, but it didn't register that I was hurting her, or maybe I didn't care.

"WHAT THE FUCK DID YOU EXPECT? FOR ME TO LAY UP WITH YOU LIKE A PUSSY WHIPPED BITCH? I'M NOT SOME FUCKING HIGH SCHOOL KID! THE ONLY REASON I GIVE A SINGLE FUCK WHAT HAPPENS TO YOU IS BECAUSE YOU'RE MY WAY OF STAYING OUT OF THOSE FUCKING DOPE HOUSES. IF SOMETHING HAPPENS TO YOU THEN I'M STUCK WATCHING CRACKHEADS TWEAK OUT. THAT'S THE ONLY REASON I'M HERE RIGHT NOW!" I screamed while shoving her back against my car.

"GET OFF OF MY SISTER!" I heard the little one yell. I looked over, waved her off, and then glared back at Elly. I hated this bitch so much, but something inside me stopped me from lashing out in every way I wanted too.

"Do whatever you need to do to make sure you feel in control, Trip," she spat with so much venom in her voice I could almost taste it. She was daring me to hit her. She stood up taller, standing toe to toe with me. I didn't understand why she wasn't scared of me. Why wasn't she begging me to stop?

"WHY AREN'T YOU FUCKING SCARED OF ME? I COULD KILL YOU RIGHT YOU NOW!" She looked at me shaking her head. I watched her eyes dart up as they glossed over with tears of anger.

"I hate you so much. EVERY TIME I FEEL LIKE I'M GETTING TO KNOW YOU OR WE'RE BREAKING GROUND YOU TURN AROUND AND ACT LIKE THIS!" I looked at her, tilting my head, getting to know me? Did she really think I wanted to get to know her and ride off into the sunset with her? I couldn't help but laugh at the idea. I took a step back and laughed so hard tears were falling from my eyes.

"You're even stupider than I fucking thought," I laughed. She looked at me, shocked, with wide eyes. I wiped my eyes, unable to stop laughing.

"You thought I really liked you? I bet you feel like a dumb bitch right now. I don't date and, even if I did, I wouldn't even think about dating you. You might be a night of fun, that's all you'll ever be. One useless night," My voice dripped with venom as my laughing sobered up with each word that fell from my lips. She looked at me, emotionless, I couldn't read her. Behind her eyes was nothing, there was no emotion. No tears, nothing. Just completely blank. I wanted to see pain behind them. I wanted her to cry and tell me how much she hated me. I wanted her to hate me, when she thought of me. I wanted her to think of how much of a dick I was. I didn't want her close to me in any sense, emotional, or mental. Not in a way that mattered, I wanted her close enough that I could hit one time and that would be it.

"Enjoy your nights at a dope house Cabrón," Her tone was flat, just like her expression. With that, I watched her grab her bag and walk off with her sister just as the bus pulled up. I stood there watching her walk away from me, with each step she took I felt the pit of anger burning inside me start to fade. Her long curls disappeared inside the bus as it pulled away with her inside it.

I didn't know how I felt about what I had said to her. I don't date, and I wouldn't ever date her because it's just not something I do. I don't want someone close to me like that ever again, but Elly wasn't just a useless night. She could be a cool girl, but she just pushed me and pressed every button. She pissed me off on purpose, so I'd have these reactions. She wanted me to blow up and say this stuff to her. She always wanted me to be the bad guy in every situation. She knew if I got angry enough, I'd say things to hurt her.

"Smooth. I thought you cared about her," I heard Ruby say from behind me. I rolled my eyes storming over to my car, getting in and speeding away from the bar. I needed to hurt someone, anyone. I didn't care about the reason. I just wanted to feel the burn of gun powder. I wanted to feel the sting of my knuckles busting. So that's exactly what I was going to feel. We had a snitch problem, so I might as well be productive in my fit of rage and beat everyone's ass until I found out who it was.

ELEANOR

I slammed my locker shut as Trip's words hung in my mind. *"You might be a night of fun but that's all you'll ever be. One useless night"*. Is that really what he thought of me? I was just one useless night to him? I don't even know why I cared so much. I wanted to cry, but his words cut so deep and hurt so bad, I couldn't even find the strength.

"Hey pretty lady" Lucas said with a smile as he leaned on the lockers. I sent him a weak one and took a drink of my water hoping to ease the burn Trip's words inflicted.

"What's wrong?" he asked me, standing up straight with a concerned look.

"Nothing. Me and Trip had a fight this morning that's all," I said with a shrug and putting up my hood. I needed to feel isolated, and that's what a hood does. Having it up makes me feel like I'm in my own space and alone, which is just what I need.

"I don't like or trust that guy," Luke told me shaking his head. I don't know if I trusted him anymore either. All I was, was a useless night to him, so why should I trust him? What do you do with useless things? You throw them away or forget about them, and I refuse to let him use me and toss me to the side. I couldn't be more happy I stopped what was about to happen between us last night.

"That makes two of us," I said taking a drink of my water again. It wasn't helping with the pain, but I could pretend, right?

"Do you want to come over today after practice? We can do the audio recording for our poem. Theo has a whole recording system because he thinks he's a rapper now," Lucas told me. I couldn't help but giggle at the image of Theo as a rapper. I'm picturing rainbow hair, teeth, face tats, the whole nine when it comes to mumble rappers. I shook my head as I took another drink of my water and looked up at Lucas.

"I know we need to get serious about the project, but I just can't today. I'm so exhausted and inside my head," I told him while looking down to my Toms and playing with the top of my hydro flask. I felt Lucas's eyes on me, they weren't heavy, nor did they make goosebumps rise on my skin. They were just normal, which I was thankful for at the moment.

"How bad was it?" he asked me. I sighed, closing my eyes trying to stop tears from. Lucas, being my ex, I'm sure he didn't want to hear about some other guy.

"I bet you feel like a dumb bitch right now. I don't date and even if I did, I wouldn't even think about dating you" Trip's angry words burned the inside of my brain. I don't know why those stung so much. I didn't care if he dated or not, and I would never ever even think about dating him. He's a narcissistic asshole that only cares about himself. He did these things to me he made things hurt that I didn't know would hurt or, he makes me feel things I don't understand but want to feel.

"Whoa, you're crying. It must have been bad," Lucas said. I hadn't even felt the tears sliding down my cheeks. As the wetness traveled down my neck, I sniffled, wiping away my tears only for them to be replaced.

"It hasn't even been our worst fight either. I don't even know why I care what he thinks, I can't stand him," I said looking away wiping away my tears. I started walking and motioned for Lucas to follow. I just needed to move around before I started to feel like I couldn't breathe.

"You don't want to hear about another guy, just forget about it," I said, waving it off when I saw Gabby at her locker. I started slowly making my way through the crowd over to my best friend.

"I mean you clearly care for him if what he says and does affects you. I don't care to listen even, if it's about someone else. I'm always going to be here for you whether we're together or not," he said with a shrug. I grabbed his hand squeezing it and sending him a smile. I was thankful for his offer, but I knew I couldn't listen to him talk about another female.

"Thank you" I whispered and let go of his hand. I walked straight over to Gabby, dropped all of my books, hugged her while hiding my face in her neck letting the sobs, I'd been fighting to fall onto my best friend's shoulder.

"Honey what's wrong?" She asked me, hugging me back tightly and running her hand over my hood.

"It's Trip," I cried into her. She gasped, pulling away and looking at me with wide dramatic eyes. She wiped away my tears and tucked a piece of hair behind my ear.

"Honey, I'm so sorry. When's the service or do you know?" she asked. Service? I couldn't help but look at her, confused.

"What are you talking about?" My voice was weak and wobbly. I wiped away my tears with my sleeve, not even caring about the black stain that would be left behind.

"Oh my god, I thought he was dead!" She let out a breath. I shook my head no hugging her again crying into her shoulder.

"We had a fight this morning. He told me I was one useless night and nothing more," I cried. She hushed me, squeezing me tightly in a comforting way.

"You guys hooked up?" she asked, her tone holding no judgement or shock. Part of me only believed that was because I was upset. I shook my head no against her shoulder. No one will ever understand how thankful I was that I stopped everything yesterday. If I had had sex with him and this happened, I don't even know how'd I cope with it.

"No, we almost did but I stopped it," I cried as the bell rang. I knew we needed to head to class so I pulled away, sniffling, and tried to pull myself together.

I sighed looking into the mirror that was in the girl's locker room. I looked a mess. My makeup was smeared to hell and there were heavy bags under my eyes. You could see in my eyes that I was feeling miserable for myself. I gathered my long curly hair tossing it up into a messy bun leaving some strands out to frame my face. I grabbed my bag and walked out to see Luke waiting by the door.

"What are you doing?" I asked. I looked over his outfit to see he was in sweats and a tank top. He smiled, running his hands through his hair that was messy from practice.

"I wanted to see if you needed a ride home?" he smiled at me. I was just gonna walk but getting a ride sounded even better.

"Actually, yeah, I could use a ride." He took my bag like the gentlemen he is, which made me smile even wider.

"So how was practice?" he asked me curiously. I just shrugged.

"Shit, because of Novah, like always," I laughed, as he pushed open the front door. I smiled thanking him and stepping past him outside to see Trey'von. He was leaning against his shiny black Audi looking at his phone twisting one of his curls.

"Let's have your mom meet us in the back," I said, shoving him back inside the school as my phone went off.

Trey'von 😼😿 - Yo, baby girl I'm out here

"Why is he here? Should we call the police?" Luke asked which made me smirk at how naive he was to this stuff.

"He's here to pick me up. Let's just go," I said, grabbing his hand and pulling him through the school. He called his mom and told her to meet us out back. Just as we walked out of the back doors she pulled up, and I got into the backseat of the giant truck. My phone vibrated again with another text from Trey'von.

Trey'von 😼😿 - Wya. I got a soccer mom checking me out and that's gotta be a no from me

"Am I just taking you home?" Luke's mom asked me. I had completely forgotten to greet her in my moment of "fleeing the gangster" I've been crying over all day.

"Oh. Mrs. Bow sorry for not saying anything. Can you actually take me to this address instead of my house?" I asked showing her Zeke's address. She agreed. I let her talk to me throughout the ride. But I only gave nods and yeahs. I wasn't really listening, but instead I was watching Trey'von blow up my phone. Each text message becoming more impatient and hostile. When we finally pulled up in front of Zeke's East LA home, I couldn't have been more thankful to see it. It was a small white house with blue trim. I never understood why he stayed here, with all of the money he had.

"Thanks," I said jumping out of the truck and shutting the door before either of them could say anything else. I ran up to the door banging on it with the side of my fist, making the bars on the door rattle.

"ALRIGHT, I'M COMING FUCK!" I heard Zeke yell. His door ripped open to show him in only a pair of basketball shorts.

"Elly what's wrong?" he asked me, unlocking the screen door and opening it so I could come in.

"I came to talk to you, and I feel like we never get to hangout, and I could really use a movie night," I admitted as I stepped into his familiar home. I dropped my bags by the door then kicked off my shoes. I shut the door as he walked farther into the living room and grabbed a while glancing back at me with a questionable look.

"Fine, but no TV until homework is done. How was practice?" he asked, looking over my face suspiciously. I knew he was probably wondering where Trey'von was and why he wasn't with me. My phone vibrated and I saw Trey'von had texted me once again.

Trey'von😏😾- Ok bitch, I'm gonna find you and when I do... FUCK. You aren't going to like me

I shook my head at the text message. He never scared me, not even a threat like that scared me. Just as I closed out the messages, Zeke snatched my phone away making me look at him with wide eyes.

"No screen time until homework is done," he scolded, and shoved my phone in his pocket. I rolled my eyes as I picked up my backpack.

"I'm 17," I reminded him. But he just shrugged.

"And my underage daughter," he smirked, making me laugh. I wasn't really his but he took me in as his. I was the closest thing Zeke had to kids and he took that on with so much weight it was insane. I respected him even more for it, even if my real dad didn't. My dad didn't like that Zeke was a part of my life. It caused up roars in my house, though not recently, but I knew it would hit its boiling point.

Haley Dixon

ZEKE

AN HOUR LATER

I looked over at Elly. She lay on her stomach staring at her books with her eyebrows laced together. We were currently in my bedroom. There was less distractions in here than in the living room and dining room. I looked back at my phone from where I laid back on my bed.

"Zeke, I need help," she said, sitting up and handing me her notebook. I looked at the history question.

"Elly, what kind of government does Russia have?" I asked, my tone slipping to be a little harsh. She was smart and was asking dumb questions. She just didn't want to do it.

"Communist," she told me with a shrug, and I nodded.

"What was the United States scared of, that spread like the plague at one point in time?" I asked her raising an eyebrow. She looked at me biting her lip like she was nervous to answer the question.

"Communism," she told me, and I nodded my head.

"The United States was worried communism would spread over here and Russia is one of our greatest threats and they're communist. What started the cold war?" I asked her handing her back the paper.

"Communism," she answered, and I nodded.

"You know my dad doesn't even help me with my homework he tells me to google it," Elly said, looking over her shoulder at me with a smile. I squeezed her ankle making her giggle and get back to work. I knew my presence in her life caused issues around her household. Antonio (her "dad") hated that I was around her, that I taught her my way of life. He hated how I sent her away on vacations. I made sure her bank account didn't drop below 10,000 dollars. I supported her in a way he and Savannah never could. Don't get me wrong, they were amazing parents and did everything right. I just did somethings better. There was also bad blood between me and Antonio but that was ancient history that Elly didn't know. I found myself wanting to tell her about it more and more, but it just wasn't my place yet.

"Zeke, I don't want Trey'von around me anymore," Elly told me sitting crisscross in front of me. I looked at her raising an eyebrow. Who the fuck is Trey'von? I mean I'll kill the kid if he's fucking with her. Where's Trip while someone is messing with her? That's his job to protect her.

"Tell Trip. He'll take care of whoever Trey'von is and if he don't, I will" I told her with a shrug. She looked at me with a smile, and then burst into laughter.

"Zeke, Trey'von is Trip. That's his real name," She laughed. Oh, I didn't know they had gotten to first name basis, or that he'd ever actually tell anyone his first name. That was why I put them together because I saw something there. They could help each other in the best ways.

"What are you guys fighting over now?" I asked with a sigh, closing my eyes. They could help each other, but they fight like an old married couple.

"He's so hot and cold with me. Like sometimes he's so nice, and I'm like oh my god, we can actually be friends. The next minute he's screaming. He's just the worst person I've met. He said something to me this morning that's made me cry all day, and I don't think I deserve to be treated like that." she shrugged. I like that she sees how she should, and shouldn't, be treated but I did need her protected.

"Listen Elly, I put you guys together for a reason. There is something between you guys that I don't understand, and you guys can learn from one another----" She cut me off with a scoff, pushing her books away and crossing her arms.

"I will never learn anything from him because I don't want too," she spat. That right there is what I'm talking about. Before she would have just accepted it and moved on, but she's trying to stand up for herself, which is something she learned from Trip.

"You have already. I put you guys together because he has a hell of a soft spot for you Elly. I watch how he won't hurt someone in front of you. He did one time, but even after that, he wasn't the same for a couple days. I've watched him stop short of killing someone because you were around. He won't hit anyone. He is more patient with people, so he doesn't explode in front of you. He's learning to be not so hotheaded because of you, and that's something a good leader needs" She just shrugged, giving a look filled with attitude. I couldn't help but laugh at the sassy teenager in front of me.

"And you are learning. He lets you get away with more than I've ever seen anyone get away with. You get to yell and fight back. You can almost hit him and not one gun gets pulled on you. It's that soft spot, something about you hits it. You're learning to stand up for yourself more. Before people walked all over you. People at school, mom, dad, sisters, ex's, friends, hell I even did at times, but you're starting to become more vocal. You're learning how to stand up for yourself" I told her seriously. I liked the improvements I was seeing in both of them.

"Zeke, he told me he didn't give a fuck what happened to me as long as he got to stay out of the dope houses. He looked me dead in the eyes and said I would be nothing but a useless one night to him. All this came right after I started to think maybe we could be friends. We were hanging out and talking without fighting. Then look at this text he sent me. I ditched him at the school," she told me. He thinks my daughter is going to be a "useless night," he's not touching her that way. Yeah, there is something there with them, but they will never be together like that. I'd put a bullet in Trip before that ever happened. Elly needed to be with a doctor or a lawyer, not a gang banger. I read the threatening text messages and right away felt anger boil over.

Maybe my plan for them to learn from each other wasn't as brilliant as I thought. I couldn't keep them together at this rate. I didn't mind them yelling and screaming at each other, but these messages and his idea he was going to get her in bed didn't fly.

"Finish your homework. I'm pulling him," I told her. I got up, grabbed my phone and called Trip to tell him to get to the dope houses right now.

Chapter 11

My savior

TRIGGER WARNING: ACTS/MENTIONS OF SEXUAL ASSAULT

ELEANOR

I turned off the water, pulling back the shower curtain and grabbed a towel as another bang came from the bathroom door along with Mateo's yells for me to hurry up. I dried off, wrapping a towel around my body along with another around my hair. I made sure to grab my body wash so she couldn't use it and then swung open the door, giving her a dirty look.

"You need a shower; I could smell you all the way in there," I shot at her. I went straight to my desk, pulling my hair out of its towel. This morning I really took time make sure my curls looked good. I also took some extra time on my makeup making myself look a little glammed up. After my emotional day yesterday, I wanted to look good and feel good. Once I approved of my hair and makeup, I went over to my bed and looked at my outfit. It was a skin tone tight fitting dress that stopped a couple inches below my butt. It was spaghetti strapped and showed off my chest. I slipped on my thong and then my dress. I didn't want to wear a bra because I wanted to feel sexy. I put on my silver strappy heels. I grabbed my bags, making sure I had everything for school and soccer, then went downstairs to see my mom and dad sitting at the table.

"Why aren't you at work?" I asked them, raising an eyebrow and grabbing my water bottle.

"I have a night shift," my mom told me, and I nodded. She was setting a plate of food in front of my dad.

"I called in a couple hours late. I woke up late and I wasn't going to rush," Dad told me. I nodded my head, leaning against the fridge, taking a drink of my water.

"I'm going to Lucas's after school for the project," I told them, and they nodded. Soon enough Mateo joined us, grabbing her water bottle. We kissed our parents on the cheek and walked out of the door. Part of me was anxious about whether Trey'von would be out there. The other part was craving to feel his eyes on me. When Zeke called him last night, he was in my bedroom waiting for me to come home. Zeke told him it wasn't working, and he was at the dope houses for now. I knew he was pissed. Part of me wondered if he truly would make my life harder than it had to be over that. Then another part of me wanted him to be waiting to scream at me. I walked over to the L part of the porch to see that the swing was empty. I looked down the street and didn't see his car. He wasn't here.

I didn't know if I was thankful or hurt. I did ask Zeke to keep Trey'von away from me, but I guess a small part inside hoped he wouldn't actually listen to Zeke that I was really worth more than a useless night to him, but I guess I wasn't.

"Why do you look so sad?" Mateo asked, snapping me from my thoughts. I shrugged, messing with my backpack.

"No reason," I shrugged. She just hummed. She wasn't dumb, but she didn't push it. I couldn't help but walk slowly past the bar. I wanted him to storm out and scream at me for getting him stuck in those houses, but of course he never did because he wasn't here. I got to the bus stop and looked at my phone as I waited. Soon enough the bus pulled up and we all piled on. I went straight to the back taking my usual seat. The ride to school was unusually quiet, but I was thankful for it.

When we finally got to school and filed off the bus, I walked straight in to see Gabby getting in my locker. She used mine and then her own. I guess whatever type of mood she was in.

"Bitch," I sang, going over to my locker and tossing my duffel bag in.

"You lookin like a whole bad bitch. You drop gang friend?" she asked, eyeing me up and down. I smirked, flipping my hair over my shoulder, making her laugh.

"Yup, Zeke told him to stay away," I said smiling. I wasn't sure how much of it was real and how much was fake. I was always conflicted when it came to Trey'von, but I was going to enjoy my drama free day without him.

"Good, I didn't like him the moment he got you high," Gabby complained as Tony walked over to us wearing a goofy smile.

"So, I just heard Amanda Walters likes me," he told us, making us squeal. I grabbed Tony's hands jumping up and down in happiness for him.

"You so got to slide in her DM's tonight" I squealed as he gave me duh look.

"Duh, she's hot too," he told us, making us laugh.

"Now come on don't talk about me while I'm right here" Lucas smirked coming over to stand behind me. I smiled, looking up and leaning into him. He wrapped his arms around my waist, leaning down to kiss my cheek. I blushed at the sweet gesture.

"You wish we were talking about you," I joked, him just chuckled.

"You still coming over for the project, right?" Lucas asked me messing with my curls.

"Yup! Is your mom or dad picking us up?" I asked him curiously as the bell rang, signaling it was time to go to class.

"My mom. She was worried about you yesterday." I turned in his arms playing with his shirt. I felt bad for making people around me worry.

"Aw. I'll have to tell her I'm ok. I'll see you guys after class," I smiled, pulling away from Lucas. I walked away glancing back at him with a smirk as he watched me. Lucas was my first love. Even though I wasn't in love with him anymore, there would always be something special between us.

I walked out of the locker room, zipping up my duffel bag, I was trying to get out before Novah was able to say something that would ruin my whole day. She hadn't been too bad today and I wasn't going to let her mess with me. I walked towards the boy's locker room to find Luke waiting with his friends at the trophy case.

"Luke," I said going over. He smiled opening his arms for me to go into, which I did. His hair was messy from his baseball helmet. His smile told me how tired he was from practice. His arms didn't hang around me lazily though. He had them wrapped around me tightly giving me a sense of comfort.

"How was practice?" he asked me with smile kissing my cheek.

"It was good, how was yours?" I asked him standing on my tippy toes brushing his hair back.

"I have scouts coming to my next game, so I have to be perfect. You ready to go?" he asked, taking my duffel bag. I nodded with a smile pulling away from him. He said goodbye to his teammates, and we walked away together.

"You've been loveable today," Luke commented, glancing down at me. I shrugged, looking up at him smiling.

"I can't be in a good mood?" I asked him playfully. He chuckled, nodding his head as we walked over to his mom's truck.

"I need to get my own car. I have my license" Lucas complained, opening the back door for me. I climbed in and moved over, so he could get in with me. Me and Luke didn't talk about anything important until we got to his house. We thanked his mom and climbed out. Luke took my bags from me, calling out a "see you later" to his mom as she drove off.

"We can just go straight up to my room," he told me. I nodded, noticing as we got closer to the house the louder the music sounded. He opened the door, letting me walk in first.

"LUKE, THAT YOU?" I heard Theo yell. I hadn't seen Theo since he went to jail. Luke had acted funny when he first got out, but we got over that.

"YEAH," Luke yelled, motioning for me to go upstairs as he headed towards the living room. But I followed behind him, wanting to see Theo. When we walked in I saw Theo sitting on the couch with 4 other huge guys. Music was playing loud, the room smelled so strongly of pot, I swore I was already high. There were liquor bottles laying everywhere and the room just looked nasty. I glanced up from the disgusting room to

Theo and the men with the familiar Devil tattoo that marked them as El Diablos. My eyes grew wide, and I stumbled back, hitting a table, which made empty glass bottles fall.

"Oh, look at this Theo. Zeke Santiago's little daughter," one of the men smirked as he walked over towards me. I felt panic wash over me. I was affiliated with Los Prophets and in a house filled with their rivals while they had a giant conflict going on. Theo looked at me, tilting his head.

"Elly, I see you've gotten sexy since I've been locked up. Where's your bitch ass boyfriend?" Theo asked. I knew he was talking about Trey'von. The truth was I had no idea where he was, but I did know he wasn't coming for me.

"He's on his way. He knows I'm here," I lied, looking at all of them swallowing hard. They all burst into laughter as they closed in on me.

"I say we have some fun, what about you?" another guy asked mockingly.

"I think we should show Zeke he's not untouchable," Theo smirked as one grabbed me. I screamed trying to jerk away from him, but he was too strong for me to escape. He threw me to Theo who caught me. He laughed as he grabbed my dress ripping the side, exposing my hip.

"GET OFF OF ME!" I screamed throwing an elbow upwards catching Theo in the nose. He stumbled back grabbing his bleeding nose. I went to take off out of the door, but another guy grabbed me and threw me against the wall.

"YOU STUPID WHORE!" Theo screamed sending me a glare that sent a shiver down my spine. Why wasn't Luke trying to help me? I looked over at Luke to see him staring with wide horrified eyes. He knew El Diablos were here and his brother was one but didn't bother to tell me. He let me walk in blind and now who knows what was going to happen to me. Theo laughed, wiping the blood from his nose on the back of his hand coming over to me.

"I think you need to make that up to me," he grabbed my dress. I tried to push him away, but his two friends grabbed my wrists, pinning them to the wall.

"GET OFF OF ME. TRIP KNOWS I'M HERE. HE'S COMING RIGHT NOW AND HE'S GOING TO KILL EVERY SINGLE ONE OF YOU SUCIO PERRA CULO EL DIADLOS (DIRTY BITCH ASS EL DIADLOS)" I screamed the threat, trying to fight my way free but their grip on my wrists was so tight it hurt, and I knew it would bruise. They laughed as Theo pulled my dress up to my waist, and another ripped it right under my breast.

"Good, let him see our sloppy seconds" Theo growled. I knew Trip wasn't really coming. I needed to buy myself time and get him to come. Theo grabbed the band of my thong. My panic rose even higher.

"I HAVE TO PEE!" I screamed. I don't know why they'd care but it was the first thing that came to mind. They stopped looking at each other and one of them nodded.

"I don't want her pissing on me while I fuck her. HURRY THE FUCK UP!" he yelled grabbing my hair, throwing me to the ground. I scrambled to my feet, but not before grabbing my phone. I ran down the hall to the bathroom. I locked the door grabbing my hair pacing around the bathroom. I ran to the window and tried to pry it open, but it was bolted shut. I needed to get the fuck out of here. I looked at my phone going to the only person's number who I knew could truly help me, if he even would.

TREY'VON

Her thin legs wrapped around my waist as I pushed myself deeper to her. Her loud moans filled her small room as she tugged at the sheet making it come off the bed. I felt the tension in my lower back and abs. I groaned, hanging my head low, thrusting hard into Megan? Molly? Fuck if I remember.

"THAT'S IT, SHIT YES!" she screamed as her walls tightened around me. I groaned throwing my head back as her body shook and she let moans fall from her lips. The tension in my lower back and abs built until I felt like I was being pushed over an edge. With one last sloppy thrust I felt the pleasure of an orgasm. I mumbled curse words as my body shook. I felt myself empty into the condom I was wearing. Once my high was over, I groaned, rolling over onto the small bed. I carefully pulled off the condom tying it shut tossing it beside my pants. I closed my eyes, putting my hands behind my head, trying to catch my breath. I smoke too damn much, fuck.

"That was fun," Megan...Molly...Madison...whatever-her-name-was breathlessly told me. I opened my eyes looking over at the girl. I met her at the gas station while I was filling up my car. She started talking to me and one thing led to the next, and I followed her home.

"Yeah, it wasn't the worst time of my life," I said with a shrug. Now I had to find an excuse to leave without her going all insane on me. Most women didn't like the whole fuck and go method, but that was my routine. As if on queue, my phone started ringing in my pants pocket. I sat up, grabbing my jeans to see the caller I.D said, 'Baby girl😇😗'. I rolled my eyes, answering the call pressing the phone to my ear.

"You have some fucking nerve calling me after the bullshit you fucking pull" I spat harshly into the phone. A sob ripped through from her end making my anger boiling towards her extinguish right away. Elly never cried in front of me or wanted me know she was crying, she wanted to look strong.

"Trip, I need your help. I'm scared and I don't know how much time I have," she sobbed into the phone. I jumped up grabbing my boxers.

"Baby girl calm down. Where are you and what's happening?" I asked her rushing to pull on my pants and buckle the belt.

"What's going on?" Molly...Megan...whatever asked me, worried.

"I went to Luke's house to work on the project and his brother, Theo, is an El Diablos. I didn't know, he wasn't when he went into prison. They're going to rape me Trey'von, I'm so scared. I barely got away. I'm locked in the bathroom but they're banging on the door telling me to hurry up." She cried into the phone as I pulled on my t-shirt and hoodie and stormed out of the girl's bedroom. The anger I was feeling at the moment I haven't felt since I was a kid before I joined the gang. This was the anger I felt as a kid when I saw my piece of shit step-dad beating my mom's crackhead ass. It was the anger that drove me to kill. I can only picture Elly locked in a dirty bathroom scared, crying, praying for me to break in there and save her. I stormed out of the shitty apartment complex my racing mind focused only on Elly.

"Listen to me Baby Girl. You say whatever you got to, you tell I'm on my way and I'll kill every single one of them motherfuckers. Send me your location I will be there in 2 minutes," I told her seriously. No one was getting out of there alive if they touched her and that was a promise.

"IT'S 10 MINUTES FROM THE BAR. DON'T HANG UP!" she screamed as I got in my car, pressed the start button and pulled out, not bothering to put on my seatbelt.

"I said I will be there in 2 minutes. Send me your location. Baby Girl do whatever you have too. Get blood on your hands if you need to, you won't go down for anything," I told her and hung up my phone. I got her location and sent it to a few guys and Zeke, telling them to meet me there right now. I ran every stop light and stop sign. I damn near had my gas pedal floored as I followed the directions to the house that I knew Elly was at. It honestly probably didn't even take me two minutes to get there with how I drove, but I just kept hearing her sobs playing over and over again in my head. When I got to the okay looking house, I saw everyone pull up at the same time.

"Zeke, stay out here. I'll send her your way, someone's dying," I said as I climbed out of my car. I pulled my gun, cocking it back as I ran towards the house.

"GET OFF OF ME!" I heard Elly scream just as I got to the door. I kicked open the door and ran into the living room. They had Elly pinned to floor. She was thrashing around and fighting, trying to get away from them but she wasn't strong enough. Her dress pushed up to hover just below her breasts. On top of her was Lil Psycho. The rage I felt was more consuming than any I had ever felt. I wanted to destroy everyone in this room at this moment, but I knew Elly was in here and I wouldn't let her see me like that again. Once she was outside, they were going to wish they never fucked with her.

"GET THE FUCK OFF OF HER!" I yelled grabbing Lil Psycho's hair, throwing him back, and kicking him in the face so hard that if I wasn't so mad my foot would hurt.

"TRIP!" Elly screamed. I turned to see her running towards me. She hugged my torso tucking her body behind mine. I wrapped my arm around her to remind myself she was right there.

"YOU'RE ALL DEAD. WHO THE FUCK ARE YOU TOUCHING MY FUCKING GIRL?" I yelled, not catching my words nor caring. I kicked Lil Psycho over and over again in the face and throat. I didn't stop until he was coughing up blood. I bent down pushing my gun into his mouth, laughing a deadly laugh.

"Just know once I get her out of this house, you're dead. I promise you it won't be a fast death either," I laughed, pulling my gun from his throat hitting him in the face with it. I felt hands grab my sweatshirt. I turned to hit whoever had the nerve to touch me, but I saw that it was Elly trying to snuggle into me. She looked around in horror as the other men were being beat to death.

"YOU KILL SOMEONE IN FRONT OF HER I'LL KILL YOU PERSONALLY!" I yelled at my guys, and they stopped for a moment. I looked back down at Elly. Her makeup was smeared, her hair was ratted up, but she still managed to look gorgeous. What looked like it would have been a dress that would have made my imagination go wild, was ripped on her hip, under her breasts, on her stomach, one of the straps was completely missing. I shoved my gun in my waist band grabbing her face lightly, making her look up at me.

"Are you ok? Where did they touch you?" I growled looking over her skin for any bruises. The only ones I found were on her wrist. She hid her face in my chest, sobbing and shaking her head "no". I hated seeing her like this and they were going to pay for it. Everyone in this house was going to.

ELEANOR

I hugged Trey'von so tightly it made my arms ache, but I felt like the moment I let go of him he'd disappear, and I'd be pinned to the floor again. I needed him more than I ever thought I would have. He was the only thing making me feel secure in this moment.

"Baby Girl, where did they touch you?" he asked me again, running his fingers through my nappy curls.

"You got here just in time. They busted into the bathroom and took my phone," I sobbed into him trying to get even closer, but I couldn't. I wish he'd wrap his arms around me and make me feel even more secure, but this was Trey'von we were talking about.

"Look at me," he said, moving back as he grabbed my face, making me look at him. His eyes were black. His whole body was shaking from anger. His upper lip twitched up. He pushed a curl from my face, I couldn't tell if he was trying to calm me down with the action or himself. He moved back, pulling off his sweatshirt and put it over my head. I thankfully complied and put on the baggy thing hiding my body.

"I need you to run outside as fast as you can. Don't come back in here no matter what you hear, got it?" He asked me hatefully, I knew this time he didn't mean it so harsh towards me. I shook my head "no", grabbing his t-shirt as my breathing picked up from the panicked state I was feeling.

"No, NO I DON'T WANT TO LEAVE YOU!" I screamed clinging to him. He closed his eyes wrapping a warm strong arm around my waist.

"You have too. Zeke is outside waiting for you, run Baby Girl," he told me, trying to push me away, but I just clung to him.

"No, what if there is more outside" I cried into him. He groaned ripping away from me, kicking Theo so hard he went flying against the wall. I couldn't help but jump. I was in disbelief at Trey'von's strength.

"I'll be right back for you," Trey'von growled at Theo. Trey'von came over grabbing my arm. He wasn't rough about it, but he was firm. I followed close beside him as he led me through the house, his anger was radiating off of him. I knew the people in that house didn't stand a chance because he was going to live up to his reputation.

"Take off your heels. Run straight to Zeke and do not come back in here," he demanded once we got to the porch. I nodded holding on to him taking off my heels. He looked at me and nodded his head, motioning for me to go. I didn't want to leave Trey'von, but I wanted away from the house, so I did just what he said. I ran jumping down the steps straight towards Zeke. He opened his arms for me to come into. The moment I reached Zeke he wrapped me up in his strong fatherly arms.

"Are you ok? Are you hurt? Did they touch you? Do you need to go to the hospital?" Zeke asked question after question as I hid my face in his chest.

"I'm fine. They didn't get a chance. Trey'von got here just in time. He's still inside, you have to get him before something bad happens," I said pulling away staring up at Zeke. My eyes were wide and scared for the man that came to my rescue without even so much as a question.

"Trip, can handle this. Come on, we'll go to the bar, and he can meet us there," Zeke said opening the door to his G-Wagon, trying to push me in. My heart was already pounding against my chest, but it managed to pound even harder against my ribs. Panicked tears fell down my cheeks as I shook my head "no" rapidly.

"NO, I'M NOT LEAVING HIM!" I screamed, ripping away from Zeke. I wouldn't leave Trey'von not until I saw him safely outside.

"ELLY, I'M NOT DOING THIS! GET IN THE DAMN CAR!" Zeke yelled going to grab me, but I dodged him. I heard yells coming from inside the house, my panic became blinding. I could only picture an El Diablos member getting the best of Trey'von and ending him before we could even fix what we broke during our last fight. The idea of that drove me to a point of raw fear I had never felt before. I didn't understand it either. I went to run back towards the house, but Zeke caught me wrapping his arms around mine, pulling me back.

"ELLY STOP THIS!" Zeke yelled at me probably confused by my behavior that all came down to Trey'von still being in that house.

"HE'S IN THERE, WE CAN'T LEAVE HIM INSIDE!" I screamed at Zeke, trying to push him off me, and trying to wiggle out of his grasp, but I couldn't. Zeke's lips parted to speak but he was cut off by a gunshot ringing from the house. My heart dropped at the sound. I knew it was Trey'von they'd find laying dead inside that house.

"NOOOO!" I screamed trying to run inside, but Zeke pulled me back. It was in that moment that I thought I'd never see him again when I realized how much I truly cared for the rude, cold blooded gangster.

"IT WASN'T HIM!" Zeke yelled, the confusion clear on his face at my reaction. I allowed myself to collapse in sobs. Another shot came from the house making my body jerk along with it, and my sobs grew louder.

TREY'VON

I tossed that Luke kid back. We decided to leave him alive, but barely. He brought Elly here knowing what waited for her. I already didn't like him, and he left me with no choice but to show him what I was truly about. I looked over just as Lil Loco cut off Lil Psycho's second hand. He had bruised Elly's wrists, so he'd die without hands. He screamed out in pain as Lil Loco mocked him. Without another word, I pulled back my trigger putting a bullet right between Lil Psycho's eyes.

The only one left alive was Luke, and that was just so he could warn El Diablos what would happen if any of them messed with Elly again. Nobody was going to touch Elly and get away with it. I walked out of the house with Julio, Ruby, Lil Loco, Gizmo, and Lil Ugly. I lifted my shirt as I walked down the steps wiping the blood off my face. Just as I dropped my shirt, I felt a petite curvy body slam into mine, arms wrapped tightly around me as the body shook with tears. My arms went out to my sides, and I looked down to see Elly hugging me, crying.

"I thought you were dead. I thought they killed you," she sobbed into me. I looked up at Zeke, confused at this newfound concern she had for me. She got me sent to a dope house last night but was now terrified I was dead. Zeke looked at me just as confused, shrugging. I lazily wrapped one arm around her waist unsure of what to do in this situation.

"No, I'm here," I said, trying not to sound uncomfortable. I easily pulled away from her looking at her with an eyebrow raised.

"Are you ok?" she asked me, wiping away her tears. I nodded my head, running my hand through my hair.

"Yeah, but we need to go before the police get here," I told her, and she nodded her head.

"Can I ride with you?" she asked me her voice soft and almost childlike. I nodded, looking at Zeke, pointing to Elly telling him I was taking her.

"Let's go," I said, pushing her towards my car. We both got into my Audi quickly, and I pulled out taking a different turn than all the other guys. We had to spread out for a moment.

"Thank you for coming, I didn't deserve it after I got you sent to the dope houses," she told me. I scoffed, waving her off.

"That was fucked up but not to the point where I'd let anything like that happen to you," I told her with a shrug. I didn't understand why she did what she did, but right now I just wanted to make sure she ok.

"You gonna let me go back to babysitting now?" I asked her with a playful smirk. She looked over at me laughing, shaking her head.

"I don't know. I'm so conflicted about you all of the time, can we talk about this another time?" she asked me. I licked my lips, looking over at the girl who managed to look stunning even when she looked like shit.

"How about tomorrow?" I asked her curiously. I needed a shower tonight. I was covered in blood and then I had had sex with that random bitch. I'm sure Elly wanted a shower and sleep, and, honestly, once I was home, I wasn't leaving for the night.

"I have school," she said but I just shrugged.

"Ditch. Live a little" I smirked at her. She looked at me shocked and then, if I wasn't mistaken, she looked as if she was seriously thinking about ditching with me. I reached over tucking hair behind her ear. Our ride was silent after that, only music lowly playing in the background. When I got to her house, I parked in front of it turning to look at her. She looked over at me smiling nodding her head.

"Fine, I'll ditch with you. I'm going to accidentally miss the bus, be out here," she told me. I couldn't lie, I was shocked she agreed to it, but a huge part of me was happy she did. Maybe I could figure out her mood swings. She accused me of having mood swings, but one minute she hates me and the next she doesn't. It's hard to keep up with.

"I'll be here. If you need to talk, you got my number" I told her. She smiled squeezing my hand and then got out of my car. I watched her walk inside and then pulled out driving to my Beverly Hills home.

Chapter 12

Stepping Stones

ELEANOR

I laid awake in my bed staring mindlessly at my TV watching "Aqua Teen Hunger Force". I remember sneaking to watch it as a kid. My parents would walk in on me watching it and I'd get in trouble, but it was so funny. I giggled at the dirty jokes flowing from my TV while I snuggled further into my comforter. I didn't really sleep last night. I only got a couple hours, if that. My dreams were filled with Theo, Luke, and the El Diablos members. So, I've been switching between Amazon Prime, Hulu, Disney plus, Netflix, and Instagram all night long. My alarm went off signaling it was time for me to get up and get ready for 'school' aka my day with Trey'von. I reached under the covers grabbed my phone and turned off the alarm.

I didn't know how I felt about hanging out with Trey'von now that I had calmed down. Yesterday, he came to my rescue without any question. He stopped the worst thing that could have ever happened to me. I was beyond thankful for that, and I had no idea how to repay him. I was conflicted because, once again, I felt something I didn't understand. Before any of that happened, we weren't speaking. He had told me I was a "useless night" and nothing more, and I had him sent to the drug houses. We were probably at the worst place we had ever been. We don't like each other. When that gunshot rang through the air, all I could picture was Trey'von laying inside that house dead, and it sent a panic through me. It was just raw emotion that I had never felt before, and I didn't want him, out of all people, to make me feel that way. A big part of me wanted to just go to school and cancel on him. Every time he shows me a side of him that isn't cruel and cold, he does something to make us fight so he can attack me with his words. I couldn't handle that today. I was still dealing with so much. Then again, I did want to meet with him and just see where his head was at.

I groaned, rolling over, and hiding my face in my pillows. I swear overthinking is my specialty. Fuck it, I already made the plans and I'm not flaking out. I mean he'd probably just show up at my school and rip me out of class to cuss me out for standing him up. I pushed myself out of bed and turned off my TV. I switched on my light and wandered over to my closet to look for something to wear. My first instinct was to wear something that covered my body, but that would just be letting El Diablos have control over me. I refused to let them win. Plus, I'd be with Trey'von, and no one would dare touch me around him. I grabbed a pair of tight-fitting black leather high-waist skinny jeans, a Tommy Hilfiger bandeau, and a pair of underwear. My phone vibrated in my sweat pocket. When I pulled it out, it was Trey'von.

Trey'von😼😵‍💫- Yo baby girl, I just woke up. Don't eat, we finna to go out to breakfast. We got shit to talk about 😋

Ok perfect, he wanted to talk too. Maybe he was feeling things that confused him just like I was. I knew I needed to be honest with myself and him, but I was too stubborn to admit what those feeling meant.

Me-K. I'm getting in the shower now🚿

I made my bed, laying out my outfit for the day. I grabbed my towel and body soap and headed toward the bathroom. I got in the shower and did what I needed to do, shaved what I needed to shave, and got out. I dried off, wrapping a towel around my body and hair. I slipped out of the bathroom to my bedroom. I took a seat at my desk to style my curls, locking them in place. I did usual makeup. It came out better than it usually does, so I was really feeling myself. Once I finished admiring my hair and makeup, I got up and changed into my outfit for the day. I paired it with ankle heeled boots and large silver hooped earrings. My hair looked good, my makeup was the shit, and my outfit showed off every curve I had. I smirked, flipped my hair over my shoulder, grabbing my backpack. I walked downstairs to find that Mateo was already gone, thankfully. I grabbed my hydro flask from the fridge then looked at my phone. I went to Trey'von's text messages so I could tell him I was ready, but I saw the three dots playing in the chat, so I just waited for him to text first.

Trey'von 😼 😺 - I'm out here

Such a gentlemen. I rolled my eyes at the text message, as I took a drink out of my hydro flask and grabbed my keys off the table. I walked through the house and out of the front door, locking it. I turned to see Trey'von's shiny black Audi sitting in front of my house. He was leaning against it while on his phone. He looked absolutely amazing. There was something about his simple but yet trendy style that was so appealing. He had on a red hoodie, black Adidas track pants, and a pair of Yeezys. His longer curls on top were styled to perfection. He had ditched the sterling rings, but still had in his huge diamond stud earrings. I hopped down the porch steps catching his attention. I felt his heavy, dark brown eyes burn into my flesh as they raked my body up and down. Without hesitation, I felt the tingles and goosebumps that his eyes always bring out in me. He smirked, licking his lips as he looked up to my face.

TREY'VON

I heard heels click on the concert sidewalk. I looked up, knowing it was Elly. But when I saw her, I wasn't excepting her to look so good. Not after yesterday, or to hang out with me. I figured she'd be in sweats and ready to fight me on everything. She had on the tightest black leather skinny jeans. The way they hugged her tiny waist and wide hips made her figure stand out. Just from that view there, you knew she had ass and these jeans were gonna show it off. Her top was one of those ones that barely covered her tits and it leaned to the tighter side. Her long black curly hair fell past her shoulders, drawing my attention to her dewy russet skin. She had on makeup, it looked good. But I had this gut feeling that if she took it off, I'd be even more amazed with what was under it.

I don't know what it was about seeing her dress like this. Those tops that showed off her tits, stomach, and shoulders, the pants that were tight and gave away her figure. It drove me insane. It has since that first day I saw her dress like this...the day she missed the bus. At first, I thought it was just because of Zeke, but it was far beyond Zeke. I don't know what it was, but when she was out in public dressed like that, I wanted to wrap her up in my clothes and shoot anyone who looked at her longer than three seconds. I also loved the way it showed off her body. I loved staring and getting the dirty pictures in my head. I just didn't want anyone else thinking about her like that.

"Damn if I knew you were dressing that fine, I would have at least put on a pair of decent jeans," I smirked as I allowed my eyes to wonder over her curvy body. I watched the heat flood to her cheeks as she fought a smile at my compliment. She pushed through the broken gate that, honestly, needed fixed. She needed better security in this shit hole house.

"You know I could fix that gate. A couple new hinges and bolts and it wouldn't stand open," I offered. She looked back at the gate and then at me with an amused look.

"It's fine. It's been broke since I was like 5. I'm actually the one that broke it," she told me with a shrug as she stopped directly in front of me. My fingers ached to reach out and grab her wide hips and trace them. My lips burned at the sight of her nude painted ones, but I tried to fight away my urges, knowing they'd only lead to us fighting.

"How'd you manage that?" I asked her curiously.

"I had a Barbie car. Me and my older sister were arguing, so I tried to run her over. But when I hit her, she hit the gate and it broke," she told me. I looked at her, shocked. I chuckled shaking my head making her giggle.

"And they call me Trip. Why you got yo school shit? I aint takin you there," I said opening the back door and tossing her backpack in.

"So, it looks like I went to school, duh? Did you ever ditch?" she asked me as I opened the passenger side door for her. She blushed, mumbled a thank you as she stepped past me to get in the car. I took the opportunity to look at her ass and...fuck. I think I just nutted in my pants. I swear it looked like it was just scooped into those jeans. It took everything in me not to reach out and give it a smack. I wonder how she'd react if I did? I mean the other day when I was kissing all up on her neck, she could barely get a word out, she wanted me so bad.

"I didn't make it past the 9th grade. I didn't ditch, I dropped out Baby Girl," I said shutting her door. I walked around the car getting in the driver's seat, started it up and pulled out.

"Why'd you drop out?" she asked, being nosy already. I glanced over at her with a smirk and then looked back at the road.

"I was in Los Prophets and moving up fast. I wanted to move up faster, but school was taking up too much time. So, I said fuck it. I mean I got more money and success by dropping it," I told her with a shrug. She nodded her head looking out of the window as I drove. I was just gonna take us to Denny's for breakfast. After a long silence, I decided to speak first.

"How'd you sleep?" I asked her curiously. She went through a lot yesterday. I didn't sleep at all. I had dreams of Lil Psycho on top of her and me not getting there in time. I think that's why I'm so relieved to be with her right now. No one would touch her around me and that's a fact.

"Horrible. I had dreams all night. I barely slept," she sighed. I nodded my head, opened my glove box, and pulled out a blunt.

"Want to smoke it away?" I asked wiggling my eyebrows. She laughed, taking the blunt from me and looked at it.

"I haven't even had breakfast," she told me with an amused look.

"Even better. Food is amazing when you're high. Here light that shit up," I said, pulling a lighter out of my pocket. She looked at the blunt and lighter like she was considering it. She looked up at me and then put the perfectly rolled Mary Jane between her plump lips and lit it up.

"I knew I kinda fucked with you for a reason." She giggled. We passed the blunt between us while I drove to Denny's.

ELEANOR

I laughed, hiding my face behind my menu so that Trey'von couldn't look at me. We were both high, but I felt like I was a little more high than him. Maybe it was because he was used to it, or he had a higher tolerance.

"Stop fucking hiding from me. I want to see your face," he laughed and ripped the menu away from me, which made me laugh harder.

"Aw hell naw," I sang playfully, trying to get the menu back from him, which only made him laugh harder at me.

"That's ugly as fuck," he laughed, giving me back the menu. Our laughter was cut short by an annoyed waitress.

"Are you guys ready to order?" she asked. I tried to stop laughing, but every time I looked at Trey'von we'd burst into laughter again.

"Can we just get the chocolate chip pancake breakfast meal with bacon" Trey'von stated. The girl wrote it down and then walked off leaving us to our fit of laughter. Once we both calmed down and caught our breath, I couldn't help but think about how he told me I was "just one useless night." I wanted him to explain it. By explain it, I mean tell me he didn't mean it, that he was just trying to piss me off.

"Can I ask you like a real-life question?" I asked him. He leaned back, running his fingers through his hair.

"Well, this is real life," he commented sarcastically. I took a drink of my tea.

"You told me I was just one useless night; did you mean that? Then if you did, why did you come when I called? I mean I'm not expecting you to say that you'd date me or whatever, because I know you don't date and I don't want too, but I mean I have to mean something for you to come, right?" I rambled when I didn't mean to, but I nervous about his answer and I was high. The two weren't the best combination but I needed to know, and I had the courage to ask right now. He looked at me like he was trying to figure out what I was thinking and why I asked. He was quiet for a long time, just thinking about how he was going to answer it. Or trying to figure out a way to be mean to me.

"I don't know," he said and looked away from me. His nearly black eyes were cast to the other side of the restaurant. I watched his sharp jawline lock and unlock. I knew he was lying. He knew exactly why he said it, and I wasn't going to let it go.

"You don't have to embarrassed to tell me the truth. Was it me rejecting you? Did it hurt your ego----." He cut me off with a bone chilling glare. I bit my lip, looking at him nervously while waiting for him to lash out at me.

"Reject me? You were practically fucking begging for me," he snapped. I didn't want to argue with him. Before I could say anything else, our waitress returned with our meals. I thanked her kindly for them and she disappeared.

"I don't want to fight with you, I just want to talk," I told him quietly while pushing my food around. It still bothered me that he thought I was "one useless night". I wanted to tell him how much it bothered me, but I could almost put money on the fact that he didn't give a fuck.

"You know I cried for a solid day over that. You told me I was a "useless night" and didn't care what happened to me as long as you didn't end up in a dope house. It hurt because at the end of the day, I care what happens to you." I told him as I took a bite out of my pancakes. He sighed, squeezed his eyes closed, and ran his hand through his hair.

"Of course, I care what happens to you Baby Girl. Hell, I just slaughtered a house full of El Diablos for you. I just get mad and spit shit out sometimes," he told me with a shrug. But I felt like there was more. I took a bite of my bacon and looked at my plate while letting his words sink in. I couldn't help but wonder if he had killed Luke.

"Is Luke dead?" I nervously inquired.

"He should be but no. I left him alive...barely." Trip told me. I nodded my head. I bit my lip while looking up at him, thinking. He raised an eyebrow at me and took a bite of his food. I couldn't help but giggle at him which made him smile.

"You never answered my question Trey'von. Do you really think I'm one "useless night"? Did you mean it?" I asked him again and took a drink of my tea. He reached over and stole a piece of my bacon.

"Eat your own" I joked just to be met with bright amused eyes. His laugh was so pretty. It was soft and relaxing. It was a sound I was sure many people have never heard.

"No, yours is better," he teased. I laughed, grabbed another piece of bacon and I took a bite.

"If I thought you were "one useless night", do you think I would still be hanging around you Baby Girl? I mean fuck Zeke. He can't control as much as he likes to think he can. I'm still around because I want to be around you. You're different from anyone I've met, you aren't scared of me" he told me. I looked into his eyes as they bore into mine. All I saw was fuzzy red and honesty. I smiled proudly and took another drink of my tea. It did make me feel better to know he really didn't think that. We were still far from any kind of real friendship but, who knows, maybe today could change that just a little bit.

TREY'VON

I couldn't help but just stare as a bright smile lit up Elly's face. She had the prettiest smile. I had never cared or noticed things like that about people, but I always notice it on Elly. I noticed the way her eyes lit up when she got excited or laughed, how her smile lit up the room...for me at least. I also noticed the way she bit her lip when she was deep into thought or nervous. It was little things like that, which captivated me. It made me want to learn more about her, but that would mean getting close when she'd just leave after a while.

"Why are you staring at me?" she asked through a mouthful.

"Why'd you get me sent to the dope houses? That was fucked up." I was still pissed that I had to spend another night in one of those dirty ass houses because of her. She looked at me and then back down to her food.

"I didn't mean too. I was over at Zeke's house and was telling him what was going on with us---." I cut her off as my eyes grew wide. If she told him everything, I had bigger problems than a dope house. He'd kill me if he found out I tried to push things farther with Elly. She's a boss's daughter.

"You told him about how us almost fucking?" I asked her, rushed. She looked at me with wide eyes, and quickly shaking her head "no". I took a deep breath, sinking back into the booth and relaxed.

"Thank fucking god. Baby Girl. He'd kill me. You're like his kid and he's a boss," I told her in case she didn't put it together. She reached over, grabbed my hands and looked me right in the eyes.

"Listen, I know you don't trust anyone, but I promise you, even if we did cross that line, I wouldn't have told him. I was upset with you, but not enough to get you killed. I wouldn't do that. I promise," she told me, her eyes serious. It made me want to believe her, but I knew the moment I put my trust in anyone they'd show me something different. I nodded, lacing together our fingers looking at her nails.

"Girl, those looking hella rough. We goin to get them hoes done," I said. She gasped and ripped her hands away from me, laughing. I smiled, shook my head and took another bite of my pancakes.

"They aren't that bad. What are we doing after we leave here?" she asked me curiously. I just shrugged. I noticed she was just playing with her food at this point. She had eaten all of her bacon and only half of her pancake.

"I don't know. We can go shopping. I want a new pair of shoes." I told her with a shrug. She nodded her head, pushing away her plate.

"Is something wrong with your food?" I asked. I'd send it back if there was something wrong with it.

"No, I'm just full but you finish eating," she told me. I looked at her, confused.

"We smoked before we came, don't you got the munchies?" I asked her, confused, as I took yet another bite of my pancakes.

"I don't even feel high anymore," she told me with a shrug. We smoked straight gas. How is she already sobering back up?

"We finna to smoke again when we leave then," I said. She laughed at me and pulled out her phone. We let small talk take over while I ate.

I inhaled the smoke, closing my eyes, enjoying the taste and feel of it. I felt a small hand tap my leg. I opened my eyes to see Elly holding up her snapchat camera on her phone. I was annoyed but leaned over and blew out the smoke as she took the picture.

"We're hot," she commented. I watched her save it and caption it: *'We're friends...sometimes'*. I raised an eyebrow as she took the blunt from me and put it between her lips.

"We're friends?" I asked. She gave me a sass-filled look.

"Sometimes. Right now, we are. We have an off and on friendship. You're not allowed to tell me we aren't friends either," she waved me off. I chuckled, shaking my head as at the light turned green.

"I don't really have friends, just the people that are scared of me," I told her as I glanced over to see the guy in the car next to us gawking at her. I flipped him off, and then easily brushed Elly's hair off her shoulder.

"Well, I'm not scared of you and I'm your friend...sometimes," she told me and past me back the blunt. I don't think I've ever had someone consider to be a friend...even sometimes. I didn't know how I felt about her considering me to be friend, but like everything else, I let her have the title. I pulled into a nail place parking lot, and easily found a parking spot. I heard Elly make some kind of weird bird noise, I looked over at her puzzled.

"I know you said we were spending the day in Hollywood, but I can't afford to get my nails done here, even with the money I got from Zeke," she said. I smiled as I took another hit of my blunt and passed it to her.

"Well lucky for you it's on me," I smirked over at my 'friend'. She shook her head "no" as she took a hit from the blunt.

"I can't let you pay. This place is expensive." I shrugged, grabbed her hydro flask and took a drink of the water.

"Well, I'm damn near a gang leader and a drug lord. I'm good on money, let's go," I said while putting out the blunt in my ash tray as we got out of the car. She followed me seconds later as I took a drink of the hydro flask again.

"Trey'von, I don't want you spending money on me," she whispered as I pushed open the front door to the salon.

"Too late, *friend*," I snickered at her. She rolled her eyes as I went to the counter.

"Two?" The lady asked me. I shook my head no.

"Just her," I said, motioning towards Elly. The lady started talking to her. I walked over to the fish tank and looked at the shark while I waited for them to finish talking.

"So why don't you get super long nails like other girls? You look like you have a job at a lawyer's office" I mentioned, noticing how short she was getting her nails. There was some length, but they weren't like Cardi B long. They were a natural length. I liked it, don't get me wrong, I was just curious.

"I think the super long nails look trashy. Then I just don't know how to act when I have them. I think I'm Joy from *Friday*," she explained. I burst into laughter, shaking my head as I tried to picture her flipping her hair and talking like Joy. I grew up around bitches like that in South Central. Loud, ghetto, and annoying. She was so different, but I could totally see her pretending.

"Why do you always drink water? Even at the bar when everyone else has alcohol you have water," she asked. I debated her question. I wasn't sure if I should answer or not. I looked at the little Chinese girl working on Elly's fingers. Elly got a black holographic nail set and I think they'll be dope when they're done. I didn't really want to let anyone into my past, but I didn't want to fight with her either. After taking a couple minutes to think about it, I decided there was no harm in spilling a bit of my past.

"I used to have a drinking problem. I got sober on my own though," I told her. She looked over at me shocked. I watched her bite her lip as she looked me up and down.

"But you're only 19!" She blurted out. I nodded my head, leaning back in my seat.

"I started drinking at 13. I wasn't a very nice drunk either. At 13 you wouldn't think I could do much damage, but I did. Fights, stabbing, shootouts. At 14 I was pimpin hoes and they'd get the blunt end of my drinking," I told Elly with a shrug. I didn't know if she'd judge me for this or not, but she wanted to know. I saw she was shocked, but she gave me a look of concern.

"Where were your mom and dad?" she asked. That was something I knew I wasn't getting into with her. I wasn't telling anyone about that shit, ever. It's ancient history and I just wanted to forget it.

"I don't want to talk about that." She nodded her head in understanding. I was surprised she didn't push the topic and start a fight, but I was glad she didn't.

"What made you stop drinking?" she continued. I ran my hand over my face, looking at the nosy girl sitting next to me.

"I hit a girl with a closed fist for the first and last time ever. I always said I'd never hit a woman. I was so fucking drunk. I couldn't get hard. She was rubbing me up and trying. I got mad and blamed her. I told her she was disgusted by me, and I beat her up like she was man. That morning I woke up and found her still naked and huddled in the corner, scared. I hated that I did that. So, I bought her way out of state, sent her back to school, and got sober. I won't touch shit now. It's been 3 years," I told her with a shrug. She smiled, her eyes lit up with something, but I wasn't sure what it was.

"I'm proud of you. It's hard to get clean and see what you did was wrong. You could have drunk the memory away, but you didn't." I nodded my head, looking away as I felt the heat flood to my cheeks. I didn't know how to take that. I've never had anyone be proud of me and I didn't ever need it. It did feel good to hear those words, but it would be the first and last time I heard them, so I wasn't going to hang onto them.

"So is that why you don't date? Because of her?" Elly asked. I scoffed, spinning around in the chair and shaking my head no.

"I wasn't dating that bitch. I was just trying to fuck. I've never dated. I've never had a girlfriend," I told her. I watched Elly's eyes search me up and down, her tongue poked out wetting her painted lips. She looked back at her nails. What was she thinking? I wish in this moment I could hear her thoughts.

"That's hard to believe. You're attractive," she told me. So, she did find me attractive. That's just another thing working in my favor. I mean she clearly wanted to hook up with me the other day made that clear. She could barely tell me to stop and, trust me, I didn't want to either. But I wouldn't force anything on her.

"Clearly you've had boyfriends," I snickered. She laughed and nodded her head.

"Yeah, only two, though. There was boy that lived across the street from me when I was 14. His name was Xavi. I lost my v-card to him. Then, you know Luke." I didn't expect that from Miss Perfect. 14 years old and hooking up, that was interesting.

"All done," the Chinese lady said. Elly showed me her nails and smiled happily. I looked at them, nodding. Elly thanked her and I paid for the set of nails which cost more than I thought they would. We spent the rest of our day in the shopping centers just talking and actually having a pretty nice time with each other.

Chapter 13

Family Night

ELEANOR

I looked at my phone to see it was already 6 o'clock, and I was still in Hollywood with Trey'von. We were in Louis Vuitton, and I was refusing to touch anything. I didn't have the money to even really walk into this store, but Trey'von was practically just throwing his bank card around. It did make me wonder how much money he had, but that wasn't my business. A yawn escaped my lips which caught his attention as he tried on pair of shoes.

"You tired?" he asked with concern filled eyes. I nodded my head, running my fingers through my curls.

"But I'm fine. Keep shopping," I told him, waving it off carelessly. I was kinda ready to go home, but today has been so nice with him. I didn't want it to end. I knew the moment it did, he'd go back to being an obnoxious dick. He stood up and walked in a circle, trying out the shoes and then looked at me.

"What do you think?" He asked as I took his seat on the bench. I looked at his shoes and nodded my head.

"Yeah, I like them," I said with a shrug. He looked at me raising an eyebrow. Maybe it was the high wearing off, but I was ready for a fat nap.

"We're going home," He announced as he reached down and pulled off a shoe.

"No, I want to hangout still" I complained with puppy dog eyes. He chuckled as he leaned down to eye level with me. He smirked as he pushed my hair out of my face an ran his fingers through my curls.

"Do you not want to leave me?" he teased. I laughed pushing him away from me and shaking my head no.

"If we're being honest, no I don't. You're actually being nice to me and we're not fighting. The moment we leave, and I see you again, you're going to be mean, and we'll be at each other's throats," I told him honestly. I didn't care how needy I sounded for wanting to be around him. I liked Trey'von a lot when he was like this. He chuckled at me, raising an eyebrow.

"Who said I was leaving just because I took you home? You got Netflix," he said with a shrug. He wanted to hang out with me just as much as I wanted to hang out with him. I couldn't help but smile at the idea. His eyes looked me up and down as he waved for me to follow him. We went to the register, and I waited for him to buy the clothes and the shoes he had. Once he paid and they were bagged, we walked out of the store and back to his Audi. Once I was finally in the car, settled and buckled up, I saw a white surveillance van sitting on the corner labeled "FBI". I squinted leaning forward to make sure I was seeing it right.

"What are you looking at?" Trey'von asked me trying to follow my gaze but failing.

"Right there. Is that a surveillance van?" I asked, pointing. Trey'von followed my finger and saw the van. I looked over to see him cool, calm, and confident. He didn't look bothered by it one little bit.

"If you're not wanted in this game, then you aren't doing it right," he told me with a shrug. We watched as the sliding door opened and Javier got out. My jaw dropped and before I could look over at Trey'von, he punched the steering wheel making it pop.

"I knew it. I KNEW THAT MUHFUCKA WAS UP TO NO FUCKING GOOD!" he yelled while gripping the steering wheel so tight his knuckles were turning white. His nearly black eyes were now completely black. His upper lip was snarled up. He was angry, and I felt myself getting angry as well. Javier was a rat. He was working with the Feds. That would mean Zeke could get locked up.

"Zeke," I heard Trey'von bark. I looked over at Trey'von to see he was already on the phone.

"I just saw Javier get out of a Fed's surveillance van. Me and Baby Girl are in Hollywood. He's the reason our shipment got picked up," Trey'von seethed into the phone. I couldn't help but smile at how he still didn't use my real name. I sorta liked the "Baby Girl" thing but honestly, I didn't know if I'd ever tell him that I enjoyed the nickname.

"No, I don't think he saw us. We were in the car already when we saw him," Trey'von told Zeke. I watched him wait for Zeke to say anything that about we were supposed to do.

"So, what, we're just going to let a rat in? What the fuck is wrong with you old man?" Trey'von snapped. I sighed, seeing his mood sour. I sat back in the seat, knowing my day with him was over.

"I already planned to chill with her for a little bit longer. You better hope your plan works. Tomorrow he's dead, regardless." Trey'von growled as he hung up his phone and put it into the cup holder. I looked out of the window, pressing myself against the door, hoping to keep his attention off of me. He was angry and I didn't want him to attack me. I felt his heavy tingly stare on me. The goosebumps forming on my skin didn't fail to make themselves known.

"Zeke is going to play Javier into telling the police false information," he told me. His tone was calm, but hints of anger slipped through. I looked over and he was still holding the steering wheel tightly, but his face didn't hold any anger.

"Zeke is smart. I trust him," I told Trey'von. He looked down at my hands laying in my lap and then back up to my face.

"I think he's going to get us all locked up," he told me. I reached over grabbed his hand and laced our fingers together. I leaned over and pushed one of his curls out of his eye with my other hand and smiled at him.

"That's not going to happen. Now let's go enjoy the rest of our night without work turning you into a raging lunatic," I whispered. I was trying to calm him down so we could still enjoy our time together. He sighed as he nodded his head and leaned back into his seat. I tried to take my hand from his, but he just held on tighter. I couldn't help but smile and lean back into my seat while I admired all of the tattoos on his arm.

TREY'VON

I parked behind an old beat-up truck that I think belonged to Elly's Dad's, but I wasn't sure. I turned off the car and looked over at Elly as she bit her lip while looking at the cars and then the house. She glanced over at me, and I saw the wheels turning in her head. I raised an eyebrow, waiting for her to tell me what she was thinking.

"My whole family is home," she whispered, but I just shrugged.

"So, we're just hanging out and even if we were coming here to do anything else it doesn't matter because you're an adult," I reminded her as I looked at her nails again and then up her face.

"You held a gun up to my dad if you don't remember," she laughed but I just shrugged, sending her a smirk.

"He got in our business. I was arguing with my top girl not his ass," I teased. She laughed at me. She leaned over and wiped the corner of my eye.

"Fine. Be nice," she told me. I laughed at her because I'm never nice. I finally let go of her hand and we both got out of the car. I walked around the car following her through the broken gate. I stared at her ass that looked scooped and molded to the jeans. I wanted to reach out and give it a nice smack or just grab it. I swear it moved with each step she took.

"Stop staring at my butt," she giggled as she opened the screen door.

"I can't help it. Have you seen it in these pants? Fuck!" I complained. She looked over her shoulder at me with a shy but amused look.

"Go or Imma slap it," I joked. She looked at me, shocked, and turned to face me.

"You wouldn't dare," she challenged. I snickered and moved closer, pretending to wrap my arms around her waist. She squealed as she opened the front door. I followed her inside as she dumped her backpack on the stairs.

"ELLY IS THAT YOU?" I heard a deep voice call from another room.

"YEAH, IT'S ME," she yelled back. She looked at me and then started towards the room. I groaned but followed her to find her whole family in the living room. I'm talking mom, dad, and sisters. I swear, it was like everyone's eyes found me all at once and they froze, just staring at me. I sent them all dirty looks for gawking, and then looked back down to Elly's butt.

"Guys this is Tre--," I cut Elly off by grabbing her waist and pulling her back into me which made her jump slightly.

"Don't use my real name Baby Girl. I don't care if you call me Trey'von, but I don't want anyone else knowing my government," I told her quietly. She looked back at me with her eyebrows scrunched together, confused, but she slowly nodded in agreement.

"Trip. He's just hanging out for a bit," Elly told them. I looked around the family to find the dad glaring at me. I smirked, leaned back and looked at Elly's ass. It was just nice. How could you not stare at it? Elly moved away from me, sat on the floor and patted the spot next to her.

"Only you would want to sit on the floor," I complained as my gun pressed into my stomach. I pulled it out of my waist band and rubbed the area. I set it on the table, and leaned back against the couch, looking at Elly.

"I thought you were tired?" I asked.

"I am but I feel awkward taking you upstairs with them here," she admitted with a blush. I rolled my eyes and closed them.

"The last I saw you guys together you were screaming in each other's faces," the dad commented while looking between us with a suspiciously. Elly shrugged and held up her phone on the selfie camera. I stuck out my tongue as she did a cute little pout and snapped a picture.

"That's actually so cute," Elly cheered. I watched her go to her Instagram as the dad scoffed because neither of us had explained our relationship to him. It's none of his fucking business what goes on between us.

"What should I caption it?" she asked, looking up with big chocolate brown eyes. I looked down at her with a sly smile, holding back a chuckle.

161

"I don't got any PG-13 captions. Last thing I need is Zeke tryin to shoot me over your fine ass," I smirked, poking her side. She jerked hella hard, almost flopping, which made me laugh.

"Stop! I'm ticklish! You're so annoying," she said as she captioned the picture *'I don't got any PG-13 captions -Trip'*.

"It's family game night. How about we play monopoly," the mom said as she turned the TV off. All three girls cheered a "yes". I grumbled at the suggestion, looking away from the family.

"I'm about to bounce," I said as I got up, grabbed my gun, and jamming it into my waist band.

"No stay. Play with us," Elly whined as she got up and tugged at those fucking pants. I licked my lips looking them over.

"Nah, I don't do family game nights," I said, shaking my head. She pouted her lip at me, her chocolate brown eyes practically begging me to stay, but I firmly shook my head 'no'.

ELEANOR

"GIMME MY MUHFUCKIN MONEY!" Trey'von yelled playfully, making everyone laugh, even my dad. He gave Trey'von the 200 dollars and Dad threw it down onto his huge pile of money. How he had so much, I don't know. I honestly think he's slowly stealing all of Izzy's money and she just hadn't noticed yet.

"Give me the dice, cheater," I laughed and took the dice, shaking them, and tossing them onto the board.

"How am I cheating? You just mad you broke," he shot at me as I moved my piece.

"You stealin Izzy's money," I defended but he only shook his head "no" while holding back a laugh.

"Aye, give me back my money!" Izzy demanded as she counted her cash. He looked at her with a sarcastic smile.

"You should have paid better attention. I'm finna to rob the bank once I get my block all set up," he told us. We all sent him a look and then burst into laughter as he adjusted his houses on the board. He was taking over one edge of the board so he had a whole block. He kept telling me it was the gang's territory.

"You're different than what I thought you would have been, Trip," Mom said, rolling the dice. He playfully dusted off his shoulder.

"I'm the life of every party," he proclaimed overconfidently. I looked him up and down trying, to decide if I should disagree with him or not.

"Don't gimme that look. You know you aint goin to the bar for any of them dumb ass," he teased. He was actually in a good mood and getting along with everyone. I figured he'd have a bad attitude and ruin the game, but everyone was actually enjoying him.

"Aht Aht momma Sánchez, pay it up. 300 bucks right here." Trey'von stuck out his hand. She laughed as she dropped the money into his hand. He smiled and looked over at me.

"Here, just cause you're pretty," he flirted as he handed me $200. I blushed as I took the Monopoly money from him.

"I got to piss and charge my phone. Imma plug it up in yo room," he told me as he got up. I nodded, intending to ask him if he knew where it was, but he was already out of the room.

"You don't like him again, why?" Mateo asked me with a confused look. I smiled and ran my fingers through my hair.

"He's not this nice all of time, don't let it fool you. When he's like this I really do like him, but then he becomes an arrogant dick and I hate that side of him. I am about to steal some of his money" I said leaning over and grabbing his huge stack of cash as I threw myself some and put the rest back.

"I still don't trust him or like him. I'd rather you not be with him after he pulled a gun on me," Dad griped, but I just brushed off his comment.

"You did get in their business, Antonio" Mom defended Trip. I couldn't lie, I was taken back by that, but didn't say anything.

"I think you guys would be cute. The other day when I saw you guys together, I thought so too," Izzy told me. I looked at her like she was crazy. Before I could say anything, Trey'von cut in.

"Baby Girl, I'm about to smoke." I turned to see he had a blunt between his lips, lighting it up.

"Actually, this is a smoke free house" My dad said as Trey'von came over and tried to hand it to me.

"Sorry, I don't smoke" I said kindly, hoping he wouldn't call me out. He looked at me confused and then back to my dad.

"You want me to go outside and smoke?" he asked as he took another hit and tried to offer it to me again, but I shook my head.

"I rather you not smoke around my children at all" Dad said sharply. I saw Trey'von's body language change. He looked directly at my dad and blew the smoke in his face.

"Trip," I whispered. He looked at me and motioned for me to follow him. I sighed, getting up while sending my family a smile as I followed him outside. Once the door shut, I took the blunt from him, hitting it.

"Thought you didn't smoke?" he mocked. I blew the smoke in his face, but he playfully sucked it up.

"My parents would have freaked if I took it," I told him as I took another hit and passed it back. He shrugged pulling his hood, up over those amazing curls.

"I think it's sexy you like to smoke," he told me as the smoke rolled from between his lips. I blushed moving closer to him and looking out to the night-time street.

"You've been giving me a lot of compliments today," I noted, looking up at him. I liked his compliments. I just wasn't sure where they were coming from. He shrugged, hitting the blunt again and passing it to me.

"Just saying what's on my mind. You know this whole game night isn't too bad, it's still shit, but" He shrugged. I smiled and blew the smoke at him. He smiled and leaned against the house.

"I thought you'd ruin it, honestly, but you haven't. Hey, I have a game Friday. Do you want to come?" I asked him curiously. He looked down at me as I passed him the blunt.

"Yeah, I'll be there. You nervous to go back to school tomorrow and see him?" He questioned me. I hadn't given it much thought. None of my friends had texted me. I didn't know what Luke had told them.

"I haven't thought about it," I shrugged. He nodded, letting a silence fall over us. We stayed like that just passing the drug back and forth between us getting as high as we could before we walked back inside to finish the game.

"What's your last name? I know your first name is Trey'von, but that's it." My curiosity always got the best of me. Then, once we started smoking, I always felt the need to ask and not just let my curiosity brew.

"Walker. Trey'von Walker. Let's go inside." he said, flicking out the little bit that was left and putting it back into his pocket.

TREY'VON

We walked into the living room and took our seat on the floor as the family looked between us with shocked or suspicious looks. It wasn't hard to tell we were high. Our eyes were red, glossed over, and low. I looked at my stack of money and could see some was gone. I looked at everyone's stack and saw that Elly's was bigger.

"Baby Girl, you stole my cash. Run me my shit," I said, waving my hand. She laughed and slapped my hand as she shook her head 'no'.

"Take it from me," she teased, holding it up. I looked down on that sexy little outfit I couldn't get enough of. I licked my lips and looked back up at her.

"Don't tempt me" I smirked, moving closer to her. She laughed, pushing me away and looking back at the game.

"It's your turn Elly," Izzy said. I watched as she grabbed the dice and rolled. She ended up landing on one of Mateo's properties.

"I'm so over playing Monopoly. I'm hungry, are you hungry?" Elly asked me as she got up and disappeared into the kitchen.

"BRING ME CHIPS BABY GIRL" I yelled after her, not wanting to get up. I reached over and stole all of her money since she thought she could take some of mine.

"What's the real reason you're with her right now?" The dad asked me with attitude lacing his voice while his eyes sent me a glare. I smirked looking at him.

"Does it bother you I'm with her?" I asked mockingly, seeing the anger growing behind his eyes. I didn't give a fuck about this guy. If he wanted ruin game night he could, but I was going to enjoy it.

"I think there is something else behind why you're here. I don't trust you," he spat at me. I laughed as I nodded while becoming really aware of my gun. Elly came back before I could say anything else to him. She tried to hand me the chips, but I just pulled her down onto my lap and hid my face in her neck, enjoying the fruity, marijuana smell that lingered on her.

"What are you doing?" she asked laughing.

"Nothing, I just wanted to be close to you," I smiled at her. She beamed as she fed me a chip. I lightly nipped at her fingertips which only earned me a sweet giggle. I looked up sending the dad a 'what you gonna do about it' look. I saw the anger growing in his eyes as Elly got more comfortable on my lap and leaned back into me.

"I don't want to play anymore. I want to watch a movie," she told me. I pushed back her curls behind her ear.

"Do you want go upstairs? I know you told me you were tired earlier," I asked her. She gave me an odd look, probably wondering why I was being so nice. I glanced over at the dad to see his face turning red which made my smirk only grow.

"Only if you will watch "The Little Mermaid" with me," she negotiated. I groaned, letting my grip on her loosen as I rested my forehead on her shoulder. I didn't want to watch that bullshit, but I wanted to prove to her dad it didn't matter what he said or thought because I'm where she wants to be. I liked getting under people's skin, especially if they gave me a reaction. Just as Elly was about to say something, her phone started ringing. She got off my lap to answer it.

"Hello?" she asked, looking at me as she bit her lip. I mouthed a 'who is it' to her, but she didn't answer me.

"Yeah, he's right here, his phone is charging," she told whoever it was and then looked at me with nervous eyes.

"It's Zeke and he sounds angry," she told me as she handed me the phone. I pressed it against my ear and heard his heavy breathing.

"Yo you're interrupting game night," I said into the phone. He's another one who gave me a reaction.

"YOU'RE SUPPOSED TO BE AT THE DOCKS HELPING ME WITH THIS FUCKING SHIPMENT NOT PLAYING FUCKING BOARD GAMES WITH MY DAUGHTER AND HER BLUE-COLLAR FUCKING FAMILY!" he screamed through the phone. Right away, I felt my tempter spike. I was on my feet in seconds, accidentally knocking the game off the of the table.

"ARE YOU FORGETTING WHO THE FUCK I AM ZEKE? I'LL COME TO THE DOCKS TO JUST TO FUCKING SHOOT YOU FOR THINKING YOU CAN TALK TO ME THAT WAY. I THOUGHT YOUR LITTLE RAT ASS BITCH THAT YOU WANT TO KEEP AROUND GOT THE SHIPMENT TOOK BEFORE IT EVEN ENTERED THE UNITED STATES," I yelled right back at him as I paced around the room getting angrier. Who the fuck did Zeke think he was talking to me like I was a fucking kid?

"TRIP, WATCH HOW YOU TALK TO ME. I DON'T CARE WHO YOU ARE, I AM YOUR HIGHER UP---." I cut him off.

"I DON'T GIVE A FUCK. GET THE SHIPMENT YOURSELF OR HAVE SMILEY HELP YOU, FUCK YOU ZEKE," I yelled, hanging up the phone. I went to throw it but I stopped and just dropped it on the floor.

"You ok?" Elly asked me. I sent her a glare that really wasn't meant for her.

"I don't want to talk about it. I got to get to the docks," I rolled my eyes. She stood up looking me up and down. I could see she was trying to think quickly, but I was too angry to even care what was going through her head right now.

"Are you going to do something stupid?" she asked with nothing but concern and worry in her eyes.

"Don't fucking worry about me. I'm getting my shit and leaving," I spat and stormed out of the living room. I went up to Elly's room, grabbed my phone and keys, stormed right back downstairs and out the front door to meet Zeke.

Chapter 14

Crossing Lines

ELEANOR

I sat on the floor in my bedroom as I stared at the clothing on my bed trying to find the courage to go to school. I knew Lucas would be there, but I didn't know what he told all our friends or if they were even still my friends. What if he spread a rumor about how we were hooking up, or how Trey'von killed his brother? It was all over social media that it was a gang related killing. Taking a deep breath, I got up and went up going over to my bed. I put on my underclothes and then my outfit, which was a simple tight fitting grey crop top that had wide tank top straps and was high necked. It was matched with a pair of worn high-waist skinny jeans that were ripped in the knees. I threw on a pair of Adidas. I put diamond earrings in my ears, gave my curly hair and makeup a once over, approved, and grabbing my backpack. I walked downstairs to see dad on the couch. He's officially on vacation. Every year he gets a week off and today starts that week.

"Do you have practice after school?" Dad asked me. I nodded my head yes walking over to him.

"Yeah why?" I asked him curiously

"We're going out to dinner tonight when you get home. Oh, and Elly stay away from the gangsters. Next time you bring one home I'm not going to just let it slide," he told me with a serious look. I smiled at him nodding my head, not saying anything. If my dad ever did really try to tell Trey'von he couldn't be around me anymore, and there was a fight over it, my money

169

would be on Trey'von. It would always be on him. He was dangerous and he didn't care about anything but his own wants and needs. If he and my dad came to blows, I knew how it would end.

"Shoo, you're going to miss the bus," Mom said coming into the living room in her PJ's. She must be off today too. She handed me my hydro flask. I thanked her, kissed their cheeks, and walked out to catch the bus.

AT SCHOOL

I took a deep breath as I looked up at the huge high school building. I didn't know what was waiting for me inside the halls, but I was going to face it head on. I proudly walked through the doors. I don't know what I was expecting to happen, but no one stopped to look at me. No one was whispering or snickering. They were all just carrying on as if my life didn't almost get ripped apart. Part of me was so happy that no one seemed to know but the other was confused. I knew how fast news spread around this school. That means Lucas didn't tell anybody. I pushed through the crowd going to my locker. I skillfully opened it to find Gabby hadn't put her things in it. I tossed in my duffel bag and started to pull my books out of my backpack.

"Elly," I heard a deep voice sigh almost in relief. I froze at that voice, knowing it could only belong to one person and that I couldn't be caught talking to him. I didn't want to talk to him. He knew the danger I would have been in and didn't care. He didn't even try to help me after he put me in that situation. It was almost like he brought me there just for that to happen. I ignored him like I didn't even hear him call my name as I grabbed my books. I set them in my locker as I hung up my backpack.

"Elly, please talk to me," his voice cracked. I glanced over at him and was taken back by what I saw. His face was beat up bad. His right eye was so purple it was turning green. It was swollen shut and just looked gross. His lower lip was swollen with stitches. He had stitches on his forehead. It looked as if his nose was broken, but it was fixed almost perfectly. A patch of his hair was missing, and black and blue bruises covered his face.

"Theo, they killed him right in front of me. I didn't know they were going to do that to you---." I cut him off, holding up my hand and shaking my head no.

"Lucas we can't talk anymore or be seen together," I said, grabbing my books and shutting my locker. I started to walk away, but he grabbed my arm pulling me back.

"Elly, I don't want our friendship to end over this." He rushed his words out as all the books fell from my arm with a loud thud which caught everyone's attention. I closed my eyes, inhaling deeply as I felt my temper spike. He didn't know what he did. I was affiliated with Los Prophets and even though Theo is dead, Lucas will always be affiliated with El Diablos. It was official. Anything that could have ever happened between us was over and I had to make that known, even if it hurt him. It was for his safety and mine. I spun fast pushing him against the lockers with a loud bang. If people weren't staring before, they were now.

"Our friendship? That's long over Lucas. You clearly don't understand what you have done. You're affiliated with El Diablos now, even though Theo caught a bullet, it doesn't mean anything. You're still connected to them. I'm affiliated with Los Prophets. Everything between us ended the moment I saw Theo's tattoo," I snapped at him, shoving him against the lockers once again. I backed up and shook my head as I looked up. Me and Lucas have had a couple bad fights before, but this was different.

"Stay away from me. You got off easy for what you did. Next time Trip will kill you like the filth El Diablos you are," I spat harshly at him. He was staring at me with wide shocked eyes. I didn't even bother picking up my books. I pushed through the gathering crowd and down another hall away from a man I once loved, but now couldn't even look at without disgust.

"ELLY!" I heard Gabby yell. I turned, looking to see her run up to me just as the bell rang warning us we needed to go head to class. She had my books in her hands. She came over and handed them to me.

"What was that about?" she asked me with a confused look on her face.

"Lucas didn't tell you yesterday?" I took back my books with a small thank you.

"I wasn't here. I had to meet the finance people with my dad. We can't afford my mom's chemo and radiation anymore, so we have to take her off of it," she told me, looking down with a sad look. I looked at her with wide eyes. I didn't say anything I just wrapped her up in a tight hug. I know she didn't want my help with money, but now she didn't have a choice. I was getting her the money she needed no matter what I had to do.

"I'm so sorry honey," I whispered. She didn't say anything. She just hugged me tighter than she ever had before.

"Let me give you the money," I said, pulling away while I pushed back her hair. She shook her head no, wiping her tears.

"I don't take charity, Elly. I don't want to talk about it. Tell me about what's going on with you and Lucas," she said, wiggling her eyebrows at me trying to lighten her own mood. It wasn't charity. I loved her mom too and I was going to help her with this money no matter what.

"And that's the topic I don't want to talk about," I told her looking away. I didn't want to relive Theo's hands on my body...ever.

"You said he was affiliated?" Gabby pushed. I nodded my head, as we started walking down the hall together.

"Theo was an El Diablos. I can't be around Lucas. I'm like Zeke's daughter. The Los Prophets are my people," I told her looking down to my feet. I had to make a choice, people that are like my family. People that came when I needed them or Lucas, the ex that led me into that situation and didn't do shit to help me. It was clear to me which was worth giving up.

"Theo's dead?" Gabby asked, confused. I nodded my head, looking away, I knew I should be sad, but I wasn't. I felt safer knowing Trey'von killed him, and he couldn't come back for me.

"Trip killed him," I admitted, avoiding Gabby's eyes. A gasp left her lips as I had expected. I knew she was going to force me to get into this topic. I felt her slender fingers wrap around my arm as she pulled me into the restroom.

"Gabby, I don't want to talk about this," I groaned as she kicked open each stall door to make sure we were alone, just as the second bell rang.

"No, you're I hate you; I love you, gang boyfriend killed Luke's big brother. Spill on why you are acting like that's ok. I saw him all over your Instagram last night too," she said, sitting her books on the sink and crossing her sandy colored arms. Her eyes were narrow. I saw the disapproval pouring off of her. I sighed looking up at the ceiling tiles, then squeezed my eyes closed.

"Luke is our friend and has been since pee pee pants days. You can't just give that up for something like that...that...gangster. I mean you aren't even----." I cut her off, throwing my books into the sink.

"THEO TRIED TO RAPE ME!" I yelled at her throwing my hands out to the side. Her eyes grew wide as her jaw fell open. Tears filled my eyes at the memory of Theo and his friend's hands on my body, pinning me to the floor, about to have their way with me.

"There it is. The rivalry between the two gangs is bad right now. Theo and his buddies were going to rape me to get back at Zeke. I barely got away. I locked myself in the bathroom and called Trip. He was there so fast, before they could ya'know. They had kicked down the bathroom door and had me pinned onto the living room floor. Theo was about to take off my panties when Trip came busting in. That "gangster" saved me, he killed Theo and his friends for touching me," I told Gabby as sobs raked my body. She quickly came over wrapping her arms around me. I grabbed fistfuls of her sweatshirt sobbing into her shoulder.

"Elly, I didn't know. I am so sorry," she whispered, petting my hair.

"Lucas didn't even try to help me. He just stood there and watched. Theo pushed me against the wall and his friends held me in place. They ripped up my dress and were touching me. I feel so disgusted," I sobbed. My knees began to shake at the memory. I felt them give out, me and Gabby both slowly sank to the floor as I sobbed into her.

"Did he know they were there? Maybe he thought Theo would be out for the night. I'm sure he didn't mean for that to happen. Luke loves you," Gabby said with her voice cracking. Part of me really did believe she was trying to convince herself of that.

"He knew, he didn't care. He didn't even tell me Theo was an El Diablos. When Theo yelled when we walked into the house he could have told me and I could have gotten away" I cried. Part of me wondered if that was Lucas's plan all along. They used him to get me there to set an example. I pulled out of Gabby's shoulder dabbing away my tears hoping to not mess up my makeup anymore. I got up, looked in the mirror, grabbed a paper towel and cleaned the black smudges off my cheek.

"Fuck Luke and Theo," Gabby said getting up. I nodded my head, throwing away the paper towel and looking over at Gabby taking a drink from my hyrdo flask.

"I'm going to class," I told her and she nodded giving me one last hug. We grabbed our things and went our own ways as we headed to our first class of the day.

PRACTICE

I sat on the turf watching all the girls run around the field, practicing drills. I had to sit out since I missed yesterday and refused to give my coach a good explanation as to why. I mean, what was I supposed to tell her? That I was almost gang raped, so my gang friends killed the guys that tried to rape me. Then that the gang member that saved me was the one I only liked part of the time because he gives me mixed messages. Yeah, I bet that would go over well and wouldn't draw police attention.

"HUDDLE UP GIRLS!" Coach yelled. I got up, walking over and stood next to her as all the girls came running over. Thankfully, Novah wasn't here today. She had an appointment, I guess. I was just happy I got a break from her.

"Good practice, this game Friday is going to go our way. Hit the showers and head out," Coach said and we broke. I grabbed my duffel bag and backpack. I walked off the field and down the paved walkway. When I got to the parking lot, I found Trey'von parked in front of the school, leaning against his car looking at his bracelet. I walked over trying to read his body language to find out his mood. As I approached those nearly black eyes snapped up to mine. I watched that cocky, confident smirk take over his lips as those eyes wondered over my body. I felt the goosebumps rise on my skin as he licked his lips.

"You look sexy today," he commented on my appearance as he reached out taking my duffel from me.

"There you go with those compliments again but thank you. You look handsome," I complimented him back, looking at his outfit. He had on a black bombers jacket, a black t-shirt, dark jeans with rips, and then a pair of Jordan's. He wore his rings, a chain around his neck, a diamond bracelet, and then, lastly, his diamond earrings.

"Oh shit, you finally complimented me. Your day must have been good," he joked, tossing my bag in the backseat and opening the passenger door for me. I laughed, rolling my eyes as I slipped into my seat, shrugging.

"It was average," I said. He closed the door and walked around the car to get in.

"So, Lucas tried to talk to me today," I told him looking at my nails, which I was kinda obsessed with. Trey'von pulled out, speeding past my teammates.

"Does he not get it? I'll kill him! Did you talk to him?" Trey'von asked, his tone guarded. I looked away from my nails over to Trey'von who was looking between the road and me.

"I told him we couldn't talk or hangout anymore because he's affiliated with the El Diablos, and I'm affiliated with Los Prophets. I told him he was lucky you didn't kill him and if he didn't leave me alone, you would," I told Trey'von as I pulled down the mirror to look at my eye makeup, which did not look as good as when I left this morning. I glanced at Trey'von to see he was wearing a proud smile. I smirked, pushing the mirror back up. Small talk overtook us. We talked about how I didn't get to practice, Javier still being alive because of Zeke, and just other little things that happened in our day. When Trey'von neared my street, I reached back to mess with my backpack.

"Yo, is that your pops?" Trey'von asked me. I looked up to see my dad storming to the bar with an angry look. He had something in his hands, but I wasn't sure what it was. I squinted my eyes like I could see better that way.

"He looks pissed," Trey'von commented. I gasped, realizing the object in his hand was the box from my room with money in it.

"No, that box has 50,000 dollars in it," I told Trey'von with wide eyes as he slowly...too slowly pulled up to the bar.

"Why the fuck do you have that much money in your room?" he asked me as he parked around the corner on the side of the bar.

"College, what else?" I snapped at him without actually meaning to. The moment the car was at complete stop, I jumped out with Trey'von following me. We took off running around the corner to see my dad was already gone. He must have gone inside the bar already, I looked over at Trey'von as he looked at me.

"Inside," he told me. I nodded my head as we ran to the door. The moment Trey'von threw open the door to the bar, I heard my dad yelling.

"SHE'S 17 ZEKE, SHE DOESN'T NEED THIS. I DON'T APPRECIATE MY UNDERAGE DAUGHTER HAVING A BIGGER BANK ACCOUNT THAN ME!" I heard my dad yell as I tried to push pass Trey'von to get inside the bar faster. He was so slow sometimes; it drove me crazy. When I broke past Trey'von, I found Zeke at his usual back table. My box of money dumped out onto the table and the box thrown to the side, broken. Zeke sat back with a cool calm and collected look as my dad hovered. His breathing was harsh, his shoulders bouncing up and down, his fists balled to his side.

"I offered you a job all those years---." My dad cut Zeke off before he could bring up what happened years ago.

"I DIDN'T WANT YOUR MONEY THEN AND I DON'T WANT IT NOW. I DON'T WANT MY DAUGHTER INVOLVED WITH THIS BULLSHIT. STAY AWAY FROM HER AND KEEP YOUR BUD---." I didn't even realize Trey'von had left my side until I saw him walking up behind my dad with his gun out. It was like time slowed and I was frozen in place. Trip kicked my dad behind the knees making him fall. I watched as Trip held the gun up to my dad's head.

"I'LL FUCKING KILL YOU RIGHT HERE. YOU DON'T WALK IN THIS BITCH TALKIN TO MY BOSS LIKE THAT. THAT FUCKING MONEY DOESN'T BELONG TO YOU AND YOU DON'T CONTROL HER, SHE'S GROWN!" Trip yelled, and it was like his voice broke the frozen state I was in. Without another thought,

I ran over trying to push him away from my dad, but it was like his feet were bolted to the ground.

"NO, TRIP. DON'T DO THIS!" I yelled, still trying to push him away.

"No Trip, go ahead shoot me if you have the balls to do it," my dad dared him, making my eyes grow wide along with Zeke's.

"Antonio, don't say that. He'll do it. Trip, put up the gun," Zeke demanded, trying to deescalate the situation. I looked up at Trip to see his jaw was locked, his eyes were black, his left hand was shaking so violently that I was scared he might go into a seizure. Oddly enough his right hand, which held his gun, was completely still. The only difference was the veins popping out in his hand.

"Don't do this Trip. Not to me, or you, or us. Please we were doing so so so good," I begged him, holding onto his right arm hoping to bring him back from whatever state he was in.

"DO IT!" my dad yelled which only sent panic through me.

"Baby Girl, go wait outside for me," Trip demanded. I pushed him, but he still didn't move.

"NO, YOU AREN'T DOING THIS!" I yelled at him, trying to squeeze between his body and my dad's. He easily shoved me to the side as he glared at me.

"GET THE FUCK OUTSIDE, I'M NOT GOING TO ARGUE OVER IT! GO NOW!" he yelled as if he was my boss, or my dad and he wasn't either.

"NO, FUCK YOU! IF YOU'RE GOING TO HURT MY DAD, YOU'RE GOING TO DO IT RIGHT IN FRONT ME! IS THIS WHAT YOU WANT? FOR US TO HATE EACH OTHER FOREVER?" I screamed. He shoved my dad forward, storming over to me so that we were inches away from each other. His completely black eyes sent fear through me I had never felt before, but I stood my ground against him.

"BITCH YOU KNOW I CAN'T DO SHIT WITH YOU AROUND. LIKE I PHYSICALLY CAN'T, NOW GET THE FUCK OUT OF MY DAMN BAR BEFORE I HAVE YOU DRUG OUT," he screamed at me, his face turning red. I had never seen him this angry, but it was my dad's life on the line and I refused to let him do this.

"THAT'S ENOUGH!" Zeke yelled, stepping pass my dad.

"PISS OFF ZEKE. WHY DON'T YOU GO BLOW YOUR FUCKING SNITCH IN THE BACK ROOM AND LET ME TALK TO MY FUCKING HOE IN PEACE!" Trip yelled at Zeke. His hoe? I wasn't his or a hoe. I shoved him back harder than I thought I ever could. He stumbled back into a table, making it screech backwards.

"I'M NOT *'YOURS'* OR A HOE! RIGHT NOW, I DON'T EVEN FUCKING LIKE YOU. YOU DO THIS EVERY TIME TRIP! WE START GETTING ALONG AND I START SEEING SOME GOOD IN YOU AND YOU DO SOMETHING LIKE THIS TO MAKE ME HATE YOU. YOU DON'T GIVE A FLYING FUCK ABOUT HOW HE TALKED TO ZEKE. YOU'RE JUST TRYING TO PUSH ME AWAY. DO IT A DIFFERENT WAY WITHOUT MY DAD INVOLVED! ERES UN COBARDE (YOU'RE A COWARD)" I yelled at him. He grabbed a chair throwing it across the bar making it shatter against the wall.

"I'm not going to tell you again, get outside Baby Girl," he growled, coming toe to toe with me again, but I just glared at him.

"If this is the choice you're making, you have to live with the fact you did it in front of me," I snapped at him. I knew he wouldn't hurt my dad in front of me. He wouldn't hurt anyone in front of me. If I went outside, it was a death sentence.

"YOU DON'T THINK I WILL? WATCH ME!" he yelled at me as he turned and walked over to my dad, pressing the nuzzle of his gun to the back of my dad's head. For a moment I was second guessing myself. Maybe he would, maybe he was so angry he didn't care if I was here.

"Go ahead," I said, crossing my arms. Everything in me screamed to shut up and just do what he said but the better part of me knew he wouldn't.

"FUCK. GET HER THE FUCK OUT OF HERE!" Trip yelled. Lil Ugly and Lil Loco started to come towards us. I looked at Zeke who was focused on Trip and trying to calm him down.

"Don't touch me!" I snapped at them. But Lil Loco picked me up and threw me over his shoulder.

"GET OFF OF ME!" I screamed, punching him in the back. I knew it was useless to try to fight against them, but I had to. Lil Ugly opened the door, Loco sat me down, pushing me out of the door in front of the eyes of our neighbors.

"DAD!" I screamed, turning to run inside. But they had slammed the door and locked it.

"NO, TRIP STOP!" I screamed, banging my fists on the door and trying the knob. I moved back, kicking it, but it wasn't budging.

"TRIP, ZEKE!" I screamed, grabbing handfuls of my hair as I backed up and stared at the door with wide eyes.

TREY'VON

I could hear Elly screaming my name from the other side of the door. I smirked as I walked over and grabbed her dad by the hair, pressing my gun into his neck.

"Nothing saving you now," I growled at him. I threw his head to the side making it hit the table.

"Trip, you need to calm down. If you do this, neither of us will see her again. You can lie to yourself, but I know you care about her," Zeke said, trying to talk me down. He was right, I did care about Elly. I cared more about her than I thought was ever fucking possible and it scared me. Regardless of my feelings for her, I would do whatever I wanted whenever I wanted.

"You care about her though too, right? That's why you're keeping a whole fed snitch around, fuck you Zeke!" I snapped at him as I looked back at Antonio. I leaned down, coming eye level to him pressing my gun under his chin.

"You seemed to have a lot to say before. What? Nothing now?" I asked him. His eyes were frantic with fear. I laughed, shaking my head standing up and grabbing the stack of money, looking at it.

"She's 17," he told me, but I shrugged.

"Sexy, young, impressionable. She seems to like the whole power trip thing I got going on," I said as my name through from the door again, followed by banging. I turned throwing a stack of money at him in anger.

"THIS WASN'T YOURS TO TAKE. EVERYONE RUNS OVER HER BECAUSE YOU MOTHAFUCKA'S KNOW SHE WON'T SAY OR DO SHIT ABOUT IT. THAT'S DONE; ALL THIS SHIT BELONGS TO HER!" I yelled at him. I brought my gun up, pulling the trigger letting two bangs fill the small bar along with the smell of fresh gun powder.

ELEANOR

I kicked the door, backing up searching the street in a panic trying to find a way back inside the bar. I grabbed my hair unable to even think straight, I was so panicked. There was no one out here that could help me. Trip was uncontrollable. He'd do whatever he wanted to do. Before I could even get an organized thought a gunshot rang from the bar. I felt my heart drop to my stomach, my mind went blank. Before I could react, another shot rang from the bar. Finally a scream left my lips. I ran over to the door trying to open it again and to my luck the door swung open. I pushed Guzman out of my way, to get a clear view of the scene unfolding. My dad was kneeling on the floor in front of Trip. Trip's gun was pointed to the side where Javier laid in a pool of his own blood.

"DAD!" I yelled in relief. I ran over to him, kneeling next to him looking for any injury. The side of his head was bleeding and there was blood on the table like he had hit his head.

"Get the fuck out of my bar," Trip spat at my dad. I helped him up, glaring at Trip as he looked at me with guarded eyes, like he was ready for anything. I shook my head, hugging my dad tightly as tears filled my eyes.

"I hate you," I told him as a tear slipped from my eyes. He shrugged, looking away from me. I stood up helping my dad up. We walked out of the together in silence. I helped him down the street and back to the house, even if he really didn't need it. Once we got inside, I helped him sit on the couch as mom walked into the living room.

"WHAT HAPPENED?" Mom screamed running over to my dad and looking at his wounds.

"Eleanor's boyfriend," Dad spat harshly, glaring at me. I covered my face, quietly crying into my hands. I didn't mean for any of that to happen. I don't even know why he was in my room to begin with to ever find the money.

"He's not my boyfriend. Are you ok?" I asked him, crying, uncovering my face.

"NO, I'M NOT FINE ELEANOR. HE ALMOST KILLED ME AND HE KILLED SOMEONE RIGHT IN FRONT OF ME!" Dad yelled as mom looked back at me with questioning eyes.

"If it makes you feel any better, he was working for the police----." Dad waved his hand in the air stopping me from saying anything else.

"I can't even look at you right now Eleanor. Go" He snapped at me. I looked at him shocked and hurt. I looked at my mom, who looked away from me and back to my dad's wounds. I looked up as a sob ripped through my body. I nodded, taking a couple steps back, watching my mom clean the blood from my dad's head. I turned, ran up the stairs to my room and slammed the door. I walked around my room, screaming out in pain. The pain I felt settling in my chest was a different kind, it was my fault my dad was hurt. Trip hurt him and forced us to take a step back that I didn't want to. Every time I felt like we took a step forward he ripped us back 12 steps. I walked over pressing my back against the wall by the window, sliding down hiding my face in my arms crying harder than I think I had ever cried.

Chapter 15

Makeup?

ELEANOR

I stared across the room at my bedroom door. I cried all the tears I could cry. I screamed all the sobs I could. I knew I caused this, I brought Trey'von around even though I knew how dangerous he could be. I should have stayed away when I said I was going to. I'm so co-dependent on Zeke it makes it hard, but yet he has a bomb around him. A bomb that was ready to blow whenever and didn't care who it took out with it. I wiped away any remaining, and tears picked myself up off of the floor. I went over to my dresser and grabbed a black bralette, a thong, and black spandex shorts. I walked out of my room to the bathroom. I tossed my clothes on the sink counter and turned on the water, letting it get warm. My mom, dad, and sisters went to dinner. I wasn't allowed to go, but I didn't want to go anyways, so that worked out. I stripped out of my clothing, got in the shower and let the scalding hot water rush over my body.

I dried off my body, wrapping my hair up in a towel. I hated letting it air dry naturally, my curls became unmanageable when I did that. I changed into the clothes I brought in the bathroom with me and then walked back to my room. I walked over to my desk sat down and grabbed my things to style my curls. I wasn't going anywhere, but I wanted my hair down and manageable. As I cleaned up my mess, my window swung open. I turned in my chair, looking over, as a duffel bag flopped in.

"Dammit. I should have just walked through the front fucking door," I heard that smooth, velvety voice complain. I couldn't help but notice how much my body relaxed just hearing his voice, even, though I was so angry with him. Seconds later he stepped into my room, fighting with the curtain. I stood up crossing my arms and raising an eyebrow as I watched him shut and lock my bedroom window. He turned with a smirk, looking over at me. His nearly black eyes wondering over my breasts, stomach, hips, and legs. I couldn't help but notice how they lingered at my hips. His pink tongue darted out wetting his plump full lips in the most attractive way. I felt the burn of tingles slide through my skin as goosebumps followed their lead.

"What are you doing here?" I asked him. My voice came out tired and laced with attitude. His eyes ripped away from my body up to my face.

"I brought you back your money. All of it's there, your box was broke though," he said motioning to the duffel bag. I nodded, looking him up and down. I didn't care about that money right now. I didn't want to see him.

"Well, you can leave," I snapped at him as I walked over and grabbed the duffel bag. I hid it on the top shelf of my closet.

"I'm sorry for calling you out of your name. I know I do it too much," he told me. I spun around glaring at him, slamming my closet door.

"YOU REALLY THINK THAT'S THE REASON I'M MAD AT YOU? BECAUSE YOU CALLED ME A COUPLE OF FUCKING NAMES?" I yelled. I took a deep breath, running my hand through my hair trying to calm myself down just a little bit.

"Yo, stop yelling before your parents come up here. I don't want all that drama while I'm dealing with the drama between us. I know you're not just mad about the names, it's over your dad too," he told me with a careless shrug. I shook my head, feeling tears welling up in my eyes, but I refused to let them fall in front of him. He didn't get it. I wasn't just mad about a couple of names, or him losing his temper with my dad. I was mad about the reason he did it. I wasn't sure at first, but I was now. Every time we made progress, he destroyed it by doing something like this, he didn't care how my dad talked to Zeke. He just knew we were getting somewhere, and it scared him.

"MY PARENTS AREN'T EVEN HERE TRIP. THEY WENT TO DINNER, RIGHT AFTER THEY UNINVITED ME BECAUSE MY 'BOYFRIEND' TRIED TO KILL MY DAD!" I screamed at him, using air quotes around boyfriend. He looked at me biting his plump full lip. I couldn't help but lick mine. His always looked so soft and glossy. I always found myself wondering what they tasted like, no matter what he has done.

"So, what, fuck em, I'll take you out to dinner if you're hungry. He shouldn't have come at Zeke like that," he said with a careless shrug. I shook my head walking over to him and pushing him backwards. He stumbled back, landing on my bed.

"IT'S NOT EVEN ABOUT ZEKE, MY DAD, OR HOW YOU ARE SINGLE HANDILY RUINING EVERYTHING I HAVE WITH MY FAMILY. IT'S ABOUT HOW YOU GET SCARED THE MOMENT YOU FEEL LIKE I'M GETTING TOO CLOSE TO THE REAL YOU. TO THE REAL TREY'VON. YOU DO THIS EVERY FUCKING TIME!" I screamed using my hands as I yelled. I was mad about everything he did, but I was hurt by the way he pushed me away every chance he gets. Somehow, the hurt was overpowering the anger right now.

"I'm not scared of shit. You haven't even gotten close to the real me, tell me Baby Girl what's my middle name?" he asked me from where he sat on the bed. He had a beyond arrogant look, it was almost mocking. I wanted to just choke him and scream at him to stop acting like this.

"HOW THE HELL AM I SUPPOSED TO KNOW WHEN YOU WON'T TELL ME ANYTHING TREY'VON?" I yelled, grabbing my curls, pacing around my room. I couldn't even tell you what I was feeling right then because I was feeling too many different emotions.

TREY'VON

I watched Elly pace around the room holding her hair. I was fighting with my temper, but I was losing poorly. I didn't come here to fight with her. I wanted us to be good. I knew everything she was saying was true. I did feel her getting close to me over these last couple days. I was feeling something for this angry girl in front of me that I've never felt before. It did scare me. I didn't know how to react to what I was feeling. I thought about her all the time. It wasn't just sex I thought about anymore. I thought about her laugh, the way her eyes lit up so brightly when she was having a good time. The way she looks down at her homework, biting her lip in concentration, as her curls fall into her eyes. I couldn't even eat with my friends, or alone, without thinking about the cute little shoulder dance she does every time we get food together. Then there was the way she wasn't scared to put me in my place, and, lastly, how she reminded me I wasn't untouchable. When I saw Lil Psycho and his buddies pinning her to the ground, it reminded me of how human I was. I hadn't realized she had opened such a large soft spot in me. But she had, and it drove me to want to protect her so much more. That's why when I saw her dad with *her money*, it pushed me over an edge.

"I don't have to tell you shit," I spat at her. She whipped around, sending me a look I hadn't ever witnessed from her before. One so angry I couldn't describe it. My blood ran cold, and for the first time in my independent life, I wished I was invisible. I swallowed hard as she stomped over standing directly in front of me. She leaned down so her chocolate brown eyes were staring into mine. For the first time I felt a fluttering in my stomach. I hadn't realized how truly easy they were to stare at before. It was like they were sucking me in, pulling me deeper and deeper into a maze I didn't want to find my way out of. I saw the anger, the pain, the betrayal, all of her emotions for the first time. It was like she was a book and her eyes were the opening to the pages.

"That's the problem. I try so fucking hard to be your friend, to stand in your corner and give you somebody who is going to support you. Then you turn around and do something you know is going to push me away from you. Something that's gonna make me stop trying to be your friend. Do you know how tiring that is? After a good day, I always worry about what you're going to say or do to me that's going to hurt worse than the last time. I can't fucking do this with you anymore," she told me as anger and hurt were seeping through her tone as she used her hands to talk to me like that would help me understand. I looked away from her, licking my lips and fighting off my instinctive reaction to her talking to me this way.

I looked back at her, letting my eyes roam her as I fought to keep myself calm. Exploding on her and showing her, I was in charge would only make this situation worse. Her russet skin always held that dewy look. She was glowing as she always does. Her curls bounced with each angry movement she made. Those beautiful pink, plump, unpainted lips were parted in the most tempting way. I wanted to feel them molded against mine. I wanted to teach them tricks that only I could. Her petite shoulders shook slightly from the anger she was feeling towards me. She wore a sexy lace bra that had straps lining her boobs. It squeezed them together and pushed them up. The fact that she was leaning over didn't help how eye catching they were. Her flat stomach had a different attractive appeal to it that I had never noticed before. Those little spandex shorts hugged her wide hips and showed off her attractive legs. My skin burned to feel her touch, to feel her soft, smooth hands that were shaking from every emotion she was feeling right now.

"Of course, you wouldn't hav---." I cut her off looking into those deep chocolate brown eyes.

"Maybe I don't *just* want to your friend," I snapped back at her. I watched her eyes slowly close, her breathing picked up as she stood up straight.

"YOU'VE MADE THAT MESSAGE CLEAR AS FUCKING DAY. IF YOU DON'T WANT ME TO DO BE YOUR FRIEND THEN WHY THE HELL DO YOU KEEP COMING AROUND?" She yelled, not catching the 'just' in my sentence.

"MAYBE I WANT MORE. I DON'T JUST WANT TO BE YOUR FRIEND, BABY GIRL!" I yelled, jumping to my feet before she could even take a breath to recover from her yelling. I watched her freeze in place, her eyes wide with shock and confusion. I think I mocked her exact reaction. I couldn't believe the words leaving my mouth. I had thought about it before and I know I have feelings for her but I didn't know how to be a boyfriend, a husband, or anything. It's not like I had the best person in the world to show me that stuff growing up. I watched her carefully like she was a cornered Pitbull. She swallowed hard her eyes searching my face for anything.

ELEANOR

I felt blindsided by his confession, it wasn't something I had expected. He's told me over and over again he doesn't date, so for him to say he wants something more with me is confusing and shocking. I mean I have feelings for Trey'von too, I never bothered to admit or really let them flourish, because I thought it would be a waste of my energy and just get me hurt in the end. There was so much I liked about him. I liked how confident he was. He drove me crazy at times, but sometimes those were the best times. I loved the way his eyes felt on my body or how he made me feel things no one else had. I could sit and listen to his laugh for hours, or stare at his perfect white smile. It looked like a painting. I knew not many people got to see it, but he privileged me with it. Then that confident, cocky smirk I wanted to smack off him the majority of the time. I found myself missing it after a couple days without him around me. It was everything that drove me to my brink of insanity with him that made me want him.

"I...uh...um," I stumbled over my words. I closed my eyes trying to get a grip to form a real sentence. My shock and confusion was overpowering the anger, hurt, and betrayal. I was on an emotional roller coaster...literally.

"You don't date," I told him, looking up to those nearly black eyes. They were so guarded, I seen the fear in them. It was almost like his slip of words was his biggest fear. He took a step closer to me grabbing my waist.

"Maybe that's changed," he told me with a shrug. My mind was reeling with the idea of him having feelings for me and wanting that level with me. It was pure excitement and confusion I was feeling right now.

"You've changed me," he whispered as his nose brushed against mine. I hadn't even realized he was leaning in. I pushed away my thoughts. I wasn't going to over think this. I was going to live in the moment. Without a second thought, I stood on my tippy toes crashing my lips into his, wrapping my arms around his neck. Just like everything else we did, our kiss was filled with things I had never felt before. Our lips fit together like missing pieces to a puzzle. My head buzzed, giving me a natural high feeling that felt better than any high weed had ever given me. I saw fireworks behind my eyes as butterflies invaded my stomach, fluttering up to my chest. Electricity shot through my veins, sending an oddly relaxing feeling through me. I felt sparks bouncing off of the walls around us, symphonies playing in the background. His lips tasted like mint and marijuana. It was such a heavenly mixture, one that I knew from the first taste could make you addicted for more.

It was slow and tender at first, neither of us sure what to expected. He wrapped his arms more firmly around my waist bringing me even closer to his body. I smiled in the kiss, making him chuckle. He went to pull away, but I only brought him closer to me, deepening the kiss, and making it rougher. I felt his lips turn up into a smirk as his hands fell to my curvy hips tracing them and then going to the dip in my waist. His tongue traced my bottom lip asking for permission. Just as I slightly parted my lips, he shoved his tongue in my mouth, dominating the kiss. I couldn't help but moan as I felt his warm tongue gliding over mine and tracing it. It only fueled his confidence. He dug his long fingers into the back of my thighs, picking me up. I wrapped my legs around his waist instinctively as my hands ran down his back that was covered with too many clothes. As I was about to pull away and complain about his clothing, he roughly pressed my back against the wall. He pressed his body into mine more, letting his hands travel up my legs, over my butt to the waist band of my shorts. With no warning, he ripped them off. I gasped pulling away from our heated kiss as he pulled the shredded shorts off, tossing them to the side.

I laughed, bringing my hands to his neck, leaning down kissing him in that rough passionate frenzy again. That hungry pit in my stomach for him wasn't forgiving and the ache of the needy/wanting tingles between my legs only pushed my need for him. He stumbled back to the bed sitting down. My legs ended up on either side of his lap as I straddled him. I pushed his jacket off of his shoulders tossing it to the side. His hands went to my butt rubbing and squeezing it. I rolled my hips on him, earning a satisfying moan from him. He pulled away from the kiss, trailing sloppy kisses down my jawline to my ear.

"You're so fucking sexy," he growled lowly as his teeth sank into my earlobe, making me moan. I slipped my hands under his shirt feeling along his lean abs and pecks.

"Take it off," I complained as his wet lips connected to the sweet spot on my neck. I moaned, tangling my hands into his shirt as I rolled my head to the side giving him more room. He smirked, biting down roughly.

"Trey'von," I whispered/moaned. He ran a bold strip of his tongue up my neck. He grabbed me, flipping us so my back was pressed against the mattress and he hovered over me. He kissed my lips again, sitting up pulling off his shirt, tossing it to the side. I was taken back by what was hidden under his clothing all this time. His whole front body was covered in tattoos. One caught my attention right away. On the left side of his ribs, it looked like his skin was being ripped away. Inside of it was a little boy's face, with a black eye, and busted lip. He looked purely miserable. Under it, in cursive handwriting, said *'The phoenix will arise from the ashes'*. I made a mental note to ask about the meaning behind the tattoo later.

"You don't know how many times I've imagined this," he groaned, running his smooth soft hands over my body, making me momentarily forget about the tattoo. Goosebumps covered my skin making him smirk as he leaned down leaving a hot, wet sloppy kiss on my stomach.

"I'm taking my time with you. I've been dreaming about this pussy for weeks now," he whispered seductively, kissing the ball of nerves between my legs through my panties. I moaned as my back arched and my eyes fluttered closed. I felt the heat pool between my legs as the soft wetness became apparent. His lips traveled back up my body leaving hot wet sloppy kisses. He let his lips linger between my breasts. He smirked looking up at me, and connected our lips in a passionate kiss. His fingers traveled behind me to take off my bra. I expected him to fumble around, but the moment his fingers touched the clasp it came undone. He was too good at undoing it. I knew that meant he's been with a lot of other girls. A big part of me wanted to push him off me but another craved him too much. I pulled off my bralette tossing it to the side, right away his smooth hands moved, palming my breasts.

TREY'VON

I massaged her boobs as I left sloppy wet kisses on her neck, earning sweet soft whimpers of moans. One right after another, it was like music. I moved sitting up looking over her body licking my lips. She was so fucking gorgeous and all mine in this moment. I ran my hands up her thighs rubbing between her legs. I watched her eyes flutter closed as she squirmed under my touch, moaning. She was so wet that her thong was soaked. I might as well have already had my fingers inside.

"You're so fucking wet, Baby Girl. You're about to feel so good," I groaned, closing my eyes. I slipped a finger around her panties into the soft wetness. I opened my eyes, leaning over her just a little more so I could get a better view of her face. I slowly, teasingly pushed a finger inside of her. I watched as her face contorted in pleasure as moans slipped from those perfect little lips. She wasn't only soaking wet but she was tight and the two together...fuck. This was about to be the best sex.

"Trey'von," she groaned making me smile. I felt her pulse around my finger, her body begging for me as her sweet juices literally drooled around my finger. I cursed under my breath in amazement.

"You've been wanting me for a while now too huh? This pussy is begging for me," I whispered, leaning down kissing around her boobs pushing in another finger. I pushed my fingers into her rougher than before. Her nails sinking into my forearm while her other hand gripped the sheets.

"I want you Trey'von. Please," she begged reaching for my jeans, unbuttoning them. I pulled out my fingers, bringing them to her lips. Without any question she took my fingers between her lips. Her tongue traced them making us both moan at the feeling.

"You like the way you taste don't you?" I asked her, pushing my fingers down her throat, getting a moan instead of a gag, and that was enough to make me feel like I was going to bust. I groaned, pulling my fingers from her mouth, pulling off her panties and tossing them to the side. I pulled off my jeans, leaving myself in my boxers. I moved between her legs leaving hot kisses on her thighs. Finally, I ran my tongue across her opening, moaning at the sweet taste that lingered between her legs. I flicked my tongue over the ball of nerves, just teasing her.

"Stop being a tease," she moaned as her fingers tangled into my hair and tugging at it. It wasn't something I knew I liked before but, fuck, that felt good. Her nails scrapping my scalp as she pulled me closer to her core. I smiled sucking on her clit, making those sexy moans grow louder. I plunged my tongue inside of her. She was so wet, I damn near thought I was about to drown in it. I pulled away blowing on her sensitive area, making her jump.

"Trey'von," she complained as I laughed. I left a sloppy wet kiss on her clit and pushed my tongue back inside of her. I easily pushed in a finger as I licked and sucked on her clit. Her legs began to shake telling me she was close, so I slipped in another finger pushing them in and out of her faster and hard.

"Fuck, Trey'von I'm---oh my god. Yes" She was breathless as her eyes screwed shut tightly.

"Cum for me baby," I whispered and went back to sucking on her clit. Not even seconds later did her whole body tense up as she shook violently, slurs of curses and moans escaped those perfect lips. I felt her tighten around my fingers pulling them almost deeper into her. I made her get to that point a couple more times before I satisfied with the work my tongue and fingers had done. I sat up sucking her juices from my fingers groaning at her taste. I felt like I couldn't get enough of it.

"Baby, that was amazing" She whispered with her eyes closed. I chuckled leaning over her and kissing her passionately. I grabbed her hand slipping it into my boxers wrapping her tiny fingers around my dick. She started giving me slow firm pumps, making me groan in pleasure.

"Do you feel what you do to me? How badly I want you?" I groaned as I felt myself jump in her hands. She laughed, and I made it do it again. I opened my eyes as she started pulling my boxers down. I helped her, letting myself spring to life. Her eyes grew wide as she stared at it. I grinned as I got up to grab my jeans to get the condom out of my wallet.

"You're so big," she gasped, I looked down at it and shrug.

"But you gonna take it," I snickered that confident cocky smirk. She looked up at me with lust filled eyes nodding her head eagerly.

"Yes, Papi," she teased as I rolled on the condom. I leaned down kissing her with a smile.

"You can keep calling me that" I teased her with my tip.

"Fuck me Papi," she whispered in my ear, nipping at my earlobe. I groaned slowly, sliding into her and I've never felt anything so good before. She was wet and tight; the warm combination could easily become an addiction.

"Oh fuck, Baby Girl. This pussy is fucking addictive," I groaned as I slid it all the way inside of her. I hid my face in her neck as my arms shook daring to give out from the pleasure. I had to give myself a minute to adjust because fuck, I've never felt something like this.

ELEANOR

Trey'von was big, like he had to be over 8 inches. He was fatter than what I expected him to be too. I thought it would hurt, but it was nothing but pure pleasure. He thrust into me so hard my whole body bounced.

"Oh fuck" I grunted hiding my face in his shoulder as he mocked his same action which earned another moan from me. He moved, sitting up and thrusting into me faster and harder than before and it was pure ecstasy. I looked up to his face to find his nearly black eyes staring down at me. It was like they were deeper somehow. Pulling me into a new world known only as Trey'von, a world I didn't want to leave. He thrust roughly into me again, but broke eye contact. He pushed so deep inside of me I swore he hit my lungs. I couldn't stop the gasp that left my lips or how my eyes rolled back.

"You like that don't you Baby Girl?" he groaned. I opened my eyes, looking back at him as he thrust into me again, sending me waves of pleasure. All at once Trey'von started thrusting into me fast and hard. It was like he was hitting a magic spot because this felt better than any sex I've ever had.

"TREY'VON, BABY YES!" My moans were screams as my nails dug into his back. He moaned and cursed, letting the dirty words that I adored fall from his beautiful lips. He grabbed my ankles bringing my legs up pinning them by my head going even faster and harder than I knew was possible. It felt so good I couldn't even utter a sound. I looked up at him to see him staring at me in the most adoring way. He slowed down letting my legs go, his hand going to throat squeezing just right as he kept up his rough steady thrusts.

"No one is ever going to fuck you this good Baby Girl, only I can make you feel this way," he growled that dangerous violent growl as he choked me a bit hard, even more pleasure course through my body. He leaned down kissing me roughly shoving his tongue into my mouth making me moan. Without a warning his thrusts picked up to the harsh rough fast pace that I've always wanted.

"Tell me how much you like this dick," he groaned moving his hands to my boobs massaging them.

"Yes, Trey'von. You feel so good inside me," I moaned as my body tensed, I felt the pit in my stomach that makes me feel the need to pee. My legs began to shake and I knew I was close.

"I'm going to cum. FUCK, TREY'VON!" I called out as I felt like I was getting closer to the edge.

"Cum for me Baby Girl, keep your eyes open and look at me," he demanded, thrusting into me even harder. All at once, I felt the tension in my body release being replaced with pleasure. My body shook as my nails dug into Trey'von's back, a strangled moan leaving his lips. My eyes tried to roll back but I fought to keep them focused on Trey'von. Slurs of curses left my lips, my hearing was starting to ring from how hard I was orgasming. My vision blurred slightly.

"TREY'VON, TRIP, BABY FUCK YOU FEEL SO GOOD!" I screamed out in pleasure. Seconds later I felt him pulse inside me. His face screwed up in pleasure, his lean muscles strained under his tattooed skin. His breathing was heavy as his jaw clinched. It was weird seeing him in such a vulnerable state but it was so attractive and I already couldn't wait to see him like this again.

Trey'von clasped down on the bed next to me both of us breathing hard from the pure bliss we both just felt. I've never had sex that good before, it was the kind that could make you stuck on a person. Once our breathing was controlled again, I felt a little recovered. I looked over at Trey'von who laid with his eyes closed and his arms behind his head. He was glowing, and I couldn't help but giggle. He opened his eyes and looked over at me with a questioning look.

"What?" he asked me raising an eyebrow.

"Nothing. That was probably the best sex I've ever had," I told him with a smile. He blushed slightly which made me giggle, but he shrugged it off.

"I told you one night with me, and it would be over," he bragged. I grinned moving to lay on his chest and cuddle with him. I felt him tense up under me, I looked up at him with questioning eyes as he looked at me with almost frantic ones.

"What's wrong?" I asked worried.

"I don't cuddle," he told me uncomfortably. I quickly moved off him with a blush.

"I'm sorry I didn't mean to make you uncomfortable" I said quickly, but he just waved it off looking away. An awkward silence overtook us. I grabbed my blanket, covering my body with it. He sat up ripping away the blanket making my eyes grow wide as I tried to cover myself with my arms.

"Stop, don't do that. I didn't mean to ruin the moment. I just don't like being laid on. It freaks me out," he told me with the reddest cheeks I've ever seen him have. My eyes dropped down to the tattoo of the little boy. I started to ask about it, but I heard the front door slam.

"ELEANOR WE'RE HOME!" My eyes grew wide at my dad's voice.

"You got to go. I'll see you tomorrow, but he can't see you in here," I said jumping up and grabbing Trey'von's clothes, throwing them at him.

"ELEANOR!" My dad yelled, making me cringe.

"IT'S ELLY AND HOLD UP. I JUST GOT OUT OF THE SHOWER!" I yelled back at him, as I grabbed a pair of sweats and pulled them on.

"Eleanor?" Trey'von teased with a snicker, I sent him a warning look.

"Elly. Come on go" I corrected pushing him towards the window.

"Well, gimme a fucking kiss first, damn. Fuck me and then kick me out, how the tables have turned," he laughed. I rolled my eyes grabbing his jaw kissing him quickly.

"Go, please. He will kill me," I begged but Trey'von scoffed, shaking his head.

"Nah, aint nothin happenin to you while I'm here, but fuck I'm going," he said as I pushed him towards the window again. I ripped open the window as my bedroom door started to open. I ran over pushing my body against it to keep it shut.

"I'M NAKED!" I yelled which wasn't a completely lie. My tits were out. Once Trey'von was safely out of the window, I put back on my bra and shut the window. I took a deep breath, preparing to face my angry father.

Chapter 16

Ghost

ELEANOR

I woke up to my alarm screaming. I didn't find myself dreading getting up but, instead, I felt energized and full of life. I sat up with a stretch as I grabbed my phone, turning it off. I pushed my covers off, and as I went over to my closet searching for something to wear. I wanted to look as good as I felt, and I wanted a certain someone's eyes on me. I bit my lip trying to hide my smile as last night replayed in my head. Trey'von, admitting he had feelings for me and that he wanted more with me. Then our sex, oh my god that was a different kind of pleasure. He was rough and dominating, just everything I wanted. I knew it would only get better too, which did excite me. I already found myself wanting him again with just the thought of it. I was still curious about the tattoo on his ribs. My family came home and kinda cut us a little short before I could ask, but I planned to ask today.

I pulled out a pink/nude dress that was spaghetti strapped. It would be tight fitting so it could show off my body, and its mid-thigh length would show off my boobs in a pretty way. I grabbed a thong and bra, laid out my dress and underclothes. I paired it with a pair of skin tone strappy heels. I grabbed a towel and body soap and ambled down to the bathroom. I locked the door, set the towel on the counter and looked in the mirror.

It was the craziest thing, but I swear I looked just a little different. My hair seemed to be shiner, my skin was glowing, my eyes were full of life, my lips still looked a little swollen from our kissing, my cheeks had a light blush from my thoughts of last night. My skin was littered in dark purple love bites. They covered my neck, just a couple inches below my ear, and down by my shoulder. My collarbone and chest looked as if it was poke-a-dotted. My stomach had marks of its own from Trey'von. I knew my inner thighs had mark after mark as well. He really didn't take it easy on my skin. I had a lot to cover to up this morning, but I couldn't even bring myself to care. I ran my hands over the marks closing my eyes picturing his plump full lips attached to my skin again. I smiled taking a deep breath as I turned around and turned on the shower. I stripped out of my clothes and got in.

Once I did what I needed to do, I got drying off and wrapping a towel around my body and another around my hair. I walked out of the bathroom as Izzy walked past me on her phone giggling like a love-struck child. I made a kissy face at her as I went to my bedroom and sat at my desk. I styled my natural curls to perfection and then did my usual makeup which was a little more glammed up. I looked good today and I was feeling my hair and makeup. I smiled flipping my curls as I got up and changed into my outfit. The dress hugged every curve I had, I just really felt sexy and pretty today. I grabbed my phone sitting on my bed and bit my lip as I went to Trey'von's number.

Me- Good morning😘 after I'm done with practice do you want to link?

I reread the text message 10 times before I finally sent it. I don't know why I was so nervous. We talk all the time...well we scream at each other, but either way, it's communicating. I took a deep breath, closed out my text messages and grabbed my homework (which I didn't do), books, laptop, and backpack. I walked downstairs as I shoved my history homework in my bag

"Eleanor?" My dad's calm, but angry, voice spoke the moment I stepped into the kitchen. I looked up from my backpack with wide eyes. He sat at the table, staring down at the place mat. My mom stood next to him with an unreadable look. Izzy looked at me with a smirk as she made her stupid avocado toast and Mateo was holding back a laugh from by the fridge.

"Yes?" I asked looking back at my father who refused to look up at me.

"I've thought long and hard about your punishment. I've decided that since you want to play with dirty money and gangsters after I've told you not to, since you want to act grown, I will be treating you as such now," he told me. I finally noticed the paper in his hands. I looked at him confused, my eyes cast up to my mom who looked away, almost ashamed.

"These are your bills. It includes rent, utilities, groceries," he told me, making my jaw drop. Before I could say anything, he literally threw the paper at me. I watched it float down in front of my feet.

"I don't have a job because of sports," I reminded him reaching down to pick up the paper. I looked up at my dad who was still refusing to look at me. Mom touched his shoulder, sending me a warm motherly smile.

"We'll talk more when you get home. Have a good day honey," Mom said, holding my hydro flask. I nodded shoving the paper in my backpack. She came over giving me the water bottle and kissing my cheek.

"You girls better get going," Mom said shooing me and Mateo out of the kitchen. I decided I wasn't going to stress over this right now. I'd talk to my parents after I got home, and we'd work it out. Right now, there just wasn't a reason to panic.

"Do you think they're really going to make you pay bills?" Mateo asked me nervously. I couldn't help but smile as we walked to the door. I knew Trey'von was probably outside waiting for me, like he is most mornings.

"Nah, he's trying to scare me," I said, swinging open the door and rushing out to the porch. I didn't see his car parked in front of the house, so I looked down to the bar to find his glossy black Audi missing. Strange. He normally is here in the morning. Maybe he was just sleeping in. I'm sure he'll text me later. It's no big deal.

"Who are you looking for?" Mateo asked me as I stepped off the steps.

"No one," I said, looking away from the bar to my little sister smiling. She gave me an odd look, but I just brushed it off, not keeping much conversation as we walked to the bus stop. I was more in my head about last night. I was still spinning from it in the most amazing way.

GABRIELLA

I stood at Elly's locker piling in my things. I use hers because it's closer to all my classes. Every year we end up sharing a locker, so of course Senior year was no different. Then in college, we'd be roommates of course. It was me and Elly in it together for life.

"Bestie," I heard Elly sing. I smiled looking over to see she looked like a total bad bitch. She wore a tight dress that showed off her body. She was glowing, her smile was bright, and that makeup was insane.

"Hi," I said, looking at her shocked. She looked at me with a smile, putting her bags in the locker.

"You look good," I said eyeing her up and down.

"I feel amazing, today is going to be the best day. I already know it, I'm so excited for soccer today too. I'm goalie," she said cheerfully. She hated playing goalie. She complained and threatened to quit the team every time they made her play goalie. I nodded my head, looking at her suspiciously.

"What did you do last night?" I asked her curiously. She looked over at me with a dreamy smile and then looked away. She bit her lip, closing her eyes and looked back at me with bright eyes.

"I had the most mind-blowing sex last night. Gabby, I have never orgasm so hard or so much in my whole life," she told me in a hushed whisper. My eyes grew wide at her words. I couldn't help but smile as I screamed an "ohhh", looking her up and down. She laughed, blushing hard and shaking her head. I was shocked only because I knew her, and Luke weren't talking just yesterday. She was mad over a gang issue that Theo drug Luke into.

"Well, I guess sneaking around with a rival gang member can make it even more exciting," I teased. She looked at me confused, shutting her locker.

"Rival? What are you talking about?" she asked me. I licked my teeth, looking my best friend up and down. I know she was not playing stupid right now.

"Luke" I said in a "duh". She burst into laughter, shaking her head no. She looked away from me trying to fight a smile but failed. Her smile was so big it took up her whole face. It made her eyes light up; and her already glowing skin glow brighter.

"No, I slept with Trip," she told me. My excitement for her vanished right away. She hated him and rightfully. He was an asshole and dangerous, but yet here she is glowing because he manipulated her.

"You what? Why? How? I don't---Why?" I couldn't even think of a proper way to ask her if she was stupid. He only wanted sex from her, he didn't give two fucks about her. Elly is gorgeous, every guy looks at her and flirts, but they just want sex. She's so smart and sees that with almost every guy, but suddenly not this gangster.

"It's a long story that I don't want you worrying about, so I'll make it short. He snuck into my window; we were arguing about a situation that had just happened. I told him I try so hard to be his friend and he was like what if I don't want to be just friends. It threw me off, but the next thing I know he has me pinned against my bedroom wall and we're making out. He literally ripped my shorts off. Let me just tell you, he wasn't gentle either." She beamed telling me the story. I couldn't help but roll my eyes at how desperate she was to be dominated, but that's just a whole other issue. The issue at hand is her acting this way over a guy who doesn't care about her.

"You aren't serious? He doesn't care about you Elly. He wanted sex." I told her as the bell rang. She looked at me offended, taking a step back as if it would stop the sting from my words.

"And since when do you care about him? I thought you hated him?" I asked raising an eyebrow. I couldn't see Elly just using him for sex. She isn't the type. She's the type to get stuck on a guy over something like that.

"Yes, I do care about him. I don't have to explain anything to you Gabby. I do care about Trip and I know he cares about me too. He might have a hard shell when he's around you and everyone else, but that's not the Trip I get. You don't know him or what he's like when he's just with me," she defended herself, sending me a look that could kill. It's already started, she's probably already got her wedding dress picked out for a guy that is just trying to get it in.

"BECAUSE ALL HE WANTS IS SEX!" I yelled at her as the bell rang. She rolled her eyes, sending me a glare.

"Whatever. You're just mad I'm not drooling over Lucas anymore. That's all you care about is if our little group stays together. Hate to break it to you, but Lucas is only alive because of Trip, when really, he shouldn't be. Me and Lucas will never be friends again let alone together because I don't keep trashy El Diablos around," she snapped harshly at me. She tried to walk past me, but shoulder checked me. That was the most confrontational I've ever seen Elly. I knew it was Trip's influence on her. I couldn't help but be shocked by the bitter words that didn't sound like they should belong to Elly.

TREY'VON

A COUPLE HOURS LATER

I groaned, pulling my comforter over my head trying to block out the sunlight blasting through my balcony doors. I forgot to cover them last night when I got home. In my defense, my head was spinning. I mean who's wouldn't be after last night's events. I admitted feelings for Elly and that's way out of character for me. I can't tell you what made me blurt it out. I did have feelings for her, but never once did I even think about telling her. Then after weeks of knowing her and fantasizing about her, I finally got her into bed. Oh god, it didn't feel like normal sex, it was so much better. She was so much better. She was just so tight and wet. Then the way she just took it, all the way down to her moans was perfect.

"FUCK!" I yelled, throwing my blanket off and squinting as my eyes adjusted to the brightly lit room. I rolled over and grabbed my phone to see Zeke already was blowing my shit up. Lil Smiley was already sending me stupid pictures and Elly had texted me. I ran my hand over my face sitting up and opening her text message.

Baby girl 😇😺- Good morning😸 after I'm done with practice do you want to link?

I licked my lips running my hand over my messy mop of curls as my eyes frantically searched over the screen. What have I done? I can't go back around her now; she's going to except something more now. I told her that's what I wanted, but I don't anymore. I mean I do, but I don't. I don't know how to be more than that or how to even act towards a girl I slept with. I shouldn't have even gone to her house last night. I should have just let her think I'm an asshole. At least I'd be able to look at her and do my job. MY JOB? I can't look over her now. It's not just babysitting her now. It was either her or the dope houses. I looked back at the text message, reading it again just as I received another one from her.

Baby girl 😇😴- I missed you this morning, it was weird not to have you waiting outside of my house. I'll talk to you when you wake up 😴

I swallowed hard, shaking my head "no" and deleting all of the text messages. The dope houses it is. I'll just use yesterday's blow up at the bar as an excuse to Zeke about why I can't babysit her anymore. I can't do the sappy text messages, cuddling, loving, geeked stuff. I didn't know how to do that stuff, hell I barely know how to feel anything besides anger. I shook my head in regret about my actions last night. I got up out of bed and went into the bathroom. I got in the shower and let the hot water calm down my panic over the mouthy girl.

I spent a little more time in the shower than usual. I let the hot water turn icy cold. Once I finally did turn off the water, I dried off wrapping the towel loosely around my hips. I walked over to my sinks and wiped off a section on the mirror. I styled my curls into their usual fluff and shaved the little stumble I had growing in. Once I approved, I walked out and went over to my closet. I walked inside looking for something to wear. My closet was huge, but I needed the space. Maybe even a little more if we were being honest. I grabbed a grey supreme t-shirt, faded ripped skinny jeans, boxers, and black Jordan retro 4's. I changed throwing on an iced-out chain and my usual silver rings. I walked out grabbing my phone and went downstairs. I grabbed a bottle of water from the kitchen and walked out of the door heading to the bar. I planned on coming right back and just hanging out until I had to go to the dope houses.

I pulled up and parked right in front of the bar. I knew Elly was at school and I was going to be long gone before she ever got home. I got out of my car and walked inside the bar to see Zeke sitting alone at the back table eating McDonalds.

"Zeke," I said walking over. We shook up and he offered me the McDonald's bag which I assume had food in it.

"Nah, I'm good. I'll eat at the crib. I just came to talk to you," I said sitting down. He raised an eyebrow as he took a drink of his coffee.

"What's up Trip?" he asked curiously. I sighed, shaking my head and running my hand over my curls.

"I can't do this babysitting thing anymore. Can I just work in the dope houses? Either way, it's below my pay grade but I'll take it," I asked. I hated, asking but, after yesterday, I knew he was still a little pissed and I really needed this. He looked at me confused raising an eyebrow.

"Fight pretty bad huh?" he asked me. I shrugged my shoulders, looking away and then back over at him.

"Not really. I just can't do this constant back and forth, and bro her dad is the worst," I complained. He sighed, nodding his head "yes".

"I agree. Antonio oversteps because he's insecure. If I take you off then I'm not putting you back on," he told me. I nodded my head, not caring because my goal was to never see her again. We fucked, I admitted something I should never have admitted, and that would be the end of it. There would be no more "Elly vs. me" fights or us sitting outside getting high. There would be no more forcing her into my car and her telling me what happened at school or how angry I made her. There would also be no more admiring how she did a happy little shoulder dance when our food came out, hearing her sing little words and phrases, listening to that laugh that I couldn't get enough of. No more watching her stare at her homework as she bit her lip, or her screaming at me, putting me back into my place. She wouldn't be there to humble me anymore. She was going to be completely gone. The idea sent physical pain through my chest, nothing inside me wanted to let her go, but I knew I couldn't be or give her what she wanted. I didn't want to.

"Don't, I just can't do it anymore. I'll find anyone else but myself. It's not worth it for me, you, or her," I told him, shaking my head. He reached over the table slapping my shoulder. It took everything in me not to lash out at him for touching me. I fucking hated being touched and he knew it.

"I was wondering which one of you would come to me first after yesterday. Yeah, I'll take you off and don't worry about the dope houses. We have a shipment coming in so of course the next two nights we have to be there but other than that, business back to usual. I'm tired of doing your job. Keeping all of those guys in line and trying to settle conflicts before they turn into wars. It's exhausting. I don't miss my underboss days," he told me. I was so happy to hear I was just gonna do my job from now on. I was still gonna stay away from the bar but that meant no more lower grade shit. The first fucks I'm dealing with is the El Diablos. Zeke didn't punish them enough for what they did to Elly. He thought killing the guys was enough, but it was far from enough. Now that I was back in power, they'd know it.

"Fuck, I'm glad to get back to being me," I said, making him laugh. He took a drink from his coffee as a couple other guys walked in.

"I am too, but you learned and that's what I wanted. You learned patience and how to respect authority a little more," he told me. I scoffed, snatching up my water bottle standing up.

"Keep telling yourself that old man. Imma bounce, I'll see you later tonight to get the shipment in," I said shaking up with him, and he nodded. I started to walk out and then it hit me, Elly has been excepting me to pick her up from practice so her sisters wouldn't be there to get her.

"Yo, Zeke. Elly lowkey might be excepting me to get her from practice still. I have in the past after these kinda fights," I told him, but he just waved me off.

"I'll tell Savannah to get her," he told me, but I raised an eyebrow, having no idea who Savannah was and why she'd pick up Elly. I know it wasn't my place to care anymore, but I did.

"Her mom, Trip," he mused. I nodded, walking out not saying another word. Elly was covered after practice and that meant I could hopefully move on with no more of that kinda drama. I could go back to not giving a shit, being with a different girl every night, and not worrying about anyone but myself. Back to my perfect life. I smirked, getting into my car and pulling out and driving back to Beverly Hills to hang out at the crib for the day until it was time to go.

ELEANOR

AFTER PRACTICE

I smiled looking myself over one more time in the mirror to make sure I looked good. Trey'von hadn't texted me back all day, but I figured he was busy with whatever his actual job is in the gang. I knew he'd be out here waiting for me like he always is. I grabbed my bags walking out of the locker room and out to the parking lot. I looked around not to find Trey'von's shiny black Audi, but Izzy's Honda instead. I shook my head looking over the parking lot for his car again, but it wasn't there. Was he avoiding me? Was he regretting last night? Did he not like something about my body? Did he not like the sex that I thought was amazing? Did Zeke find out somehow and hurt him? I walked over to the tan car trying to hide my anxious thoughts. I ripped open the passenger door to be met with dark nearly black eyes and for a split second I really did think this look alike was Trey'von, but it wasn't him. Just someone who looked sorta like him.

This look alike had bronze skin, but it was missing the glow. He had longer black curls on the top of his head that didn't dip into his eyes like Trey'von's did, and they were tighter. The sides were shaved into a lower buzz cut. His eyebrows were a little messy and looked like they needed touched up. His cheekbones fit his face but oddly enough his nose was kinda off too. It was almost like it was too long for his face. It was pierced just like Trey'von's. His lips weren't near as pink, plump or eye catching. He looked like he was probably just a little taller, but his build was even close to Trey'von's, maybe just a little less muscular.

"Oh, I'm sorry," I mumbled closing the door as I opened the back door climbing in.

"How'd you know to come get me?" I asked Izzy, completely confused.

"Zeke told mom you needed a ride, so here we are" she said looking back at me. I nodded my head buckling up. I didn't do something right last night. Maybe I should have taken charge more. Did I say something wrong? Was he mad I rushed him out or was it the whole cuddling thing? I didn't mean to make him uncomfortable.

"ELLY!" Izzy yelled, making me jump as she pulled me out of my thoughts. I sent her a glare through her mirror as Walmart version Trey'von laughed along with her.

"What? You are so damn annoying," I complained, rolling my eyes in annoyance.

"I said, this is my boyfriend, Anthony." I looked up, nodding my head looking him over.

"Get out while you can. She's annoying," I told him. He laughed as he shook his head.

"I think I can handle her," he smiled proudly, leaning over and kissing her cheek which made Izzy blush. I was shocked at how deep and smooth his voice was. I rolled my eyes looking out of the window. Maybe Trey'von was at the bar. I doubted it, but I was too stupid to give up hope.

"How'd you guys meet?" I asked them.

"School. We had a class together," he told me as he looked at my sister so lovingly. I stared at him trying to figure out how he could look so much like Trey'von. Once we got onto the block, I looked to the bar for Trey'von's car, but it wasn't there and neither was Zeke's. I grabbed my phone as Izzy pulled over.

"Thanks," I said getting out and grabbing my things. I walked up on the porch, set my things down, and brought up Trey'von's text messages. I was hurt and angry at him for doing this. He was once again pushing me away because I got too close or maybe I really was just a useless night to him.

Me- How fucking typical of you. I don't even know why I'm so shocked you're doing this. Do you really even actually have feelings for me or was that your way of getting me in bed? Of course, you lied about it. Somebody like you doesn't even know what feelings are. I

guess I really am just one useless night to you! I didn't lie, I really do have feelings for you but you don't care because you don't give a fuck about anyone but yourself. I'm done playing this game with you Trip. You made this decision to ruin any sorta friendship, relationship, anything that could have come out of us. I hope you're happy with that. I fucking hate you!

I grabbed my bags, walked inside and set them by the door, as I tried to push away the anger that was forming at Trey'von.

"ELLY COME IN HERE!" My dad's sour tone came from the living room. I rolled my eyes knowing it was about the bills he set for me, which were way too expensive for my tiny room.

Rent-$325.00

Lights/Electric-$75.00

Gas-$45.00

Water/sewage-$87.00

Cable/Wi-Fi-$120.00

Groceries-$200.00

I walked into the living room to see my dad glaring at me and my mom looking away with a guilty look.

"Did you look over the bills?" he asked, and I nodded my head sucking my teeth.

"I did. 325 for my tiny bedroom is way too much. I could get a real apartment for that amount. I'm being charged for cable when I don't have a cable box. I have a Firestick so all I use is Wi-Fi, and I'm one person, I don't need 200 dollars' worth of groceries. This is so stupid you're even making me do this. I don't have a job because of sports," I used my hands to talk. The whole plan had been that I wouldn't get a job until after graduation.

"Get out of my house then. I'll make the cable 50 since you don't have a cable box," he shrugged. My eyes grew wide at how little he seemed care. He wasn't seriously telling me, his underage daughter, to get out.

"Antonio!" Mom snapped at him, sending him a glare.

"No, she wants to act grown and not listen. I'll treat her like she is. Your rent is due in a week," he spat at me as he got up. I looked at him a smirk that I could have only learned from one person.

"Yeah? What if I don't pay? What are you going to do about it?" I mocked him tilting my head to the side. He turned sending me the scariest glare I've ever seen.

"ELEANOR I CAN'T HAVE THE DRAMA YOU BRING AROUND HERE. YOU WANT TO RUN AROUND WITH THESE BANGERS AND DO THEIR DIRTY WORK. THIS IS THE SECOND TIME YOU'VE GOTTEN MY LIFE THREATENED. I HAVE TWO DAUGHTERS AND A WIFE TO WORRY ABOUT. IF YOU WANT TO BE NOTHING, THAT'S FINE. THESE ARE YOUR BILLS IF YOU WANT TO KEEP LIVING HERE. IF YOU AREN'T GOING TO PAY THEM THEN PACK YOUR SHIT AND GET OUT OF MY HOUSE!" He yelled storming over closer to me. I looked at him with wide shocked eyes. He wouldn't really kick me out of the house, would he? I thought he was just trying to scare me, but he seemed almost serious. I looked back at my mom to see her crying, looking away from the scene. I looked back up at my dad, laughing.

"You're only doing this to prove to yourself you have some power. Trip stripped you of the power you thought you had and now you need something to make you feel like a man. I'll get you the damn money don't worry about me!" I bit back as I stormed past him and upstairs to the room I was going to have to pay for. It felt nice to stand up for myself like that and just to say what was on my mind. The pride of my small win only lasted minutes before I remembered how Trey'von was completely avoiding me after our most intimate moment. I ended up staying in my room for the rest of the night, lost in my thoughts, overthinking every move I made last night.

Chapter 17

Heartache

ELEANOR

My phone buzzed on the nightstand as I just laid in bed staring up at the ceiling. I looked over at the phone which told me it was time to get up and get ready. I reached over, grabbed it, turned off the alarm, and dropped the phone to my chest. I looked back up to the ceiling that I'd been staring at for hours now, ever since I stopped crying over my dad hating me, my mom not even trying to help me, and Trey'von going MIA. After I finished breaking down over all of that, I plunged into thoughts about whether my dad would ever forgive me. How would Zeke react when I told him about my bills, I would have to. Zeke always keeps my bank account at 10,000 dollars. When it starts disappearing faster than usual, he's going to ask questions. Another thing that plagued my thoughts was that night with Trey'von and any reason I could come up with about why he would disappear without even trying to start a fight with me. He always did, if we got too close. Or if he just wanted me to leave him alone, he'd start a screaming match. He'd say something mean and I'd storm away. We'd leave each other alone for a couple days and then, like magnets, end up together fixing it. Maybe this was his way of saying something mean...he wasn't saying anything at all, only proving how I was one useless night that didn't matter.

I grabbed my phone and went to my camera roll, looking at the two pictures I had of me and Trey'von. I couldn't help but smile at the one where I had a cute little pout, and he had his tongue sticking out in the most attractive way. We took that one in my living room and it was one of my favorite pictures. The next picture was of us in his car, both sets of our eyes were red and glossed over and hung low. I had a huge smile on my face as I looked over at him while he blew smoke out of those plump pink lips that I already missed.

"How does one night have me this caught up on you?" I whispered, looking at the picture. I was fine with him coming and going up until he spoke the magic words "I want to be more with you." I closed the pictures, shaking my head and forcing myself out of bed. I turned on my light and went over to my dresser where I grabbed dark grey baggy sweatpants, and a white t-shirt. I decided to skip my shower today, I didn't smell and didn't have the energy. I changed into my new outfit and walked over to my desk. I looked in the mirror at my appearance. My eyes were red and swollen from the hours spent crying, my skin was pale, and my hair was ratted up. I had heavy purple bags under my eyes. I grabbed a makeup up wipe, using it to clean my face, and then I pulled my long curls into a messy ponytail. I got up randomly picking out my Adidas superstars tossing them, I matched my black Adidas sweatshirt pulling it on over my t-shirt. I shoved my phone in the pocket along with my headphones as I picked up my backpack. I didn't bother with my soccer stuff because I didn't plan to even going to practice. I walked downstairs to find my whole family in the kitchen. I pulled up my hood grabbing my hyrdo flask from the fridge.

"Honey, you look horrible! Are you feeling ok?" Mom asked, rushing over to touch my head, but I just swatted her hands away and nodded my head.

"I haven't see you look this bad since you and Lucas broke up. Did your imaginary boyfriend breakup with you?" Izzy teased. I snapped around and sent her a glare that made the house fall silent.

"Fuck you Izzy. You got hella jokes but when are we going to talk about how your new boyfriend looks just like Trip? What, you didn't think I noticed? Guess what dad, I'm not the only one who likes him," I shot at my sister and dad as I walked out of the house leaving Mateo behind. I put in my headphones and turned up the music loud enough that I couldn't hear anything else. I walked to the bus stop, sat down and closed my eyes waiting for the bus.

I stared into my locker debating if I was actually going to take any books to my classes. I knew I wouldn't do much, but did I want to look productive? Before I could make up my mind, a hand landed on my shoulder. I looked up to see Tony looking at me with a smile. I pulled out my headphone, raising an eyebrow.

"You look like you are going through a mid-life crisis so I came with a chocolate peanut donut and a caramel iced coffee from the school's café," he grinned holding up the cup and white bag as he wiggled his eyebrows. I laughed, pulling out my other headphone and smiled at him as Gabby walked over to me. She didn't look much better than me. I wanted to ask her what was wrong, but I couldn't handle my own problems, let alone hers.

"What would I do without you Tony?" I smiled, taking the sweets from him.

"You look like shit. Gang friend?" Gabby asked me raising an eyebrow as she shoved everything into my locker. I sighed looking at the coffee and bag.

"Not only him. I have a lot going on that I don't want to talk about," I admitted as I avoided eye contact with both of my friends. I was hoping they'd leave it with "I don't want to talk about it."

"Homecoming is in like a month, are you guys going?" Tony asked changing the subject. I looked up sending him a thank you smile. He smiled back, pulling me into his side hugging me. I giggled, hugging him back.

"I'm going. I love dances," Gabby cheered. I felt their eyes on me. I planned on going before everything happened, but I just wasn't in the dance spirit.

"I'm not going this year," I shook my head "no" as I pulled away from Tony and looked down at my feet.

LIL SMILEY

I walked through the hall waving at the kids who were staring at me like I was Brad Pitt. I think it was the tattoos, or maybe they could just tell I was a Los Prophet. I don't know, but it was weird being back in high school. I dropped out as soon as I joined Los Prophets, but Trip made me come back to keep an eye on Elly. I finally found the girl he showed me a picture of and who he said was Elly's best friend. She was standing with a super tall Asian guy and someone in baggy sweats with their hood up. I bet she'll know where Elly is.

"I'm just not feelin a dance this year. I don't have anyone to go with and I'd rather sit at home," I heard Elly's accented voice as I got closer to the group. I realized that she was the one hidden in the baggy sweats. Just as I walked over, I saw her about to take a drink from a cup. I quickly snatched it before her lips touched it.

"Hey that was--," She stopped as she turned to see it was me. I looked at her as I took a drink of the coffee just to make sure it wasn't poisoned. Trip made it very clear. He told me *If one of those silky curls on the top of her head is misplaced I will you nail to the wall and use you as a dartboard."* Trip was my best friend, but he scared me and I took his threats seriously. He wasn't going to get a chance to torture me because I was going to make sure everything was perfect.

Her tired, red, swollen eyes were so wide that the purple bags under them almost disappeared. Her skin was pale, which made her usual pink lips a purple color. They were parted open in surprise. Her usual bouncy curls were pulled back and hidden under her hood. I couldn't help but notice she hid the body she normally flaunts, and she didn't have on a trace of makeup. If I found her in this state, it doesn't fall back on me right? Trip can't use me as a drinking game for this this?

"Lil Smiley? What the hell are you doing here? I thought you dropped out, give me back my coffee!" she barked the last part as an order, snatching it back. I smiled at my friend and looked at her friends who looked confused.

"I'm your new buddy. Since Trip took back his rightful place, he thought you were going to be unguarded too much, so he put me on it. He told me if one of your curls were out of place, he'd use me as a dartboard. So why do you look like that?" I asked her nervously. She rolled her eyes as she shook her head. I saw the agitation on her face. I saw how bad she wanted to lash out, but all at once it disappeared. She looked at me with wide, desperate eyes.

"Wait, he took back his rightful place? He's not hurt or dead?" she asked, taking a step closer. Her words were rushed and filled with worry. I looked at her and shook my head no.

"No, he went to Zeke and actually asked to be in the dope houses after that last fight you guys had. Zeke said he was ready to take back his place as underboss, so he's been trying to find out who Lil Psycho's boss is. Why do you care? I thought you guys hated each other," I asked curiously. They were back and forth. One minute they were friends and the next they were ready to stab each other in the throat. I think they just needed to stop playing games and get together. That's clearly what they both want. She looked at me hurt, nodding as tears filled her eyes. I looked at her shocked and taking a step forward.

"Elly don't cry---," she cut me off, holding up her hands and shaking her head no.

"Tell Trip, I don't need protection. He's hurting me more than anyone else could," she said, stepping around me as she started to walk away. I reached out, grabbing her arm to pull her back, but she jerked away from me with a glare.

"Smiley, I love you and you are my friend but there is so much more going on than you know. I just can't right now. Please, nobody follow me," she begged as she walked away leaving me with her friends who I did not know.

"Y'all know what's wrong with her?" I asked looking between the girl and the Asian boy.

"The last I saw her like that, she broke up with Luke," the Asian boy told me. Luke? Ah shit, that was Lil Psycho's little brother. Fuck, if he did something I'm gonna have to kill him. Trip made it very clear I had to keep him away from her. I groaned, leaning against the lockers and closing my eyes.

"You're right, and she was out of it for weeks after that. Like she even quit coming to school at one point," the girl said in deep thought. I sighed, looking at the pair in front of me.

"I have strict orders about that Luke guy. If he's messing with Elly, I have to handle it. Where is he?" I asked the two who just shrugged as they looked at each other. Before I could say anything else, they mumbled excuses as to why they had to go. Well if they weren't going to help me then I had to find Elly and hope she would help me. If not, then I was going to have to report to Trip directly. He told me not to report to Lil Ugly for any of this stuff just straight to him. If I reported someone was messing with her and I didn't know how to find them, it would end badly for me.

SAVANNAH

I glanced over at Antonio as he sat at the table scrolling on his iPad, reading the paper. I hated what he was doing with Elly. She was only a teenager. Paying bills, school, sports, surviving in this neighborhood, it was too much for her to worry about all at once. I understand why he is upset. I am too. I hate that the love of my life has been threatened so many times, but we all know how these things work. If a gang member like Trip or Zeke find a girl they genuinely care about, taking a life over them isn't anything. It was just something about them, maybe it was because they were in control all the time. If someone came between them and their girl, the consequences were always dangerous and deadly. I placed the last dish into the dish washer, and turned it on.

"Honey, come look at this," Antonio said. I wiped off my hands, and walked to him and looked over his shoulder at a video of a puppy playing with a kitten.

"Aw how adorable. Antonio, I want to talk to you about this Elly thing," I said moving around the table so he'd look at me. He set down his iPad, shaking his head "no".

"It's not up for discussion. She's gotten my life threatened twice. I have two biological daughters to worry about. If she wants that life she can have it, but she can't have that and live in my house for free," he told me. His tone was stern as he walked out of the kitchen. Biological? Her DNA never bothered him before and he wasn't going to hold that against her. It was my mistake and he is the only father she knows.

"She is 17, Antonio, and you are the only father she knows. You are not going to throw that up in my face and you are not going to tell her," I stated matter-of-factly going into the living room where he sat on the couch.

"So, you're ok with her getting my life threatened?" He turned on me. I sighed looking away and crossing my arms.

"Of course, I'm not Antonio. It doesn't change the fact she's 17 and we're her parents," I argued with him. I just wanted the best for my kids and making her struggle and have to drop sports that could give her a full ride into college wasn't ideal.

"She'll realize how hard grown-up life is Savannah. She'll drop all of those gangsters and we won't have these problems anymore," he said with a shrug. I couldn't help but feel irritated at him. He was always so against her being mixed up with those people. I wish as a mother she wasn't, but I understood it. The power they have, the way people bow to them, their influence, the certain sex appeal. Then, Los Prophets are in her DNA. I thought it would have been an environmental trait. I knew I was wrong when she was only 7 and lying to police to cover up for Zeke. I knew then it was in her DNA.

"SHE'S NOT GOING TO DROP THEM ANTONIO. LOS PROPHETS ARE IN HER DNA, SHE'S RIGHTFULLY BORN INTO THEM WHETHER SHE KNOWS IT OR NOT. YOU WOULDN'T BE GETTING THREATENED EVERY TIME WE TURNED AROUND IF YOU JUST STAYED OUT OF THEIR BUSINESS!" I yelled, only getting angrier with him. He should know this by know. He knew what happened when you got in too deep with one of these guys. It's not the first time something like this has happened, but this time it was his daughter.

"YOU'RE SAYING IT'S MY FAULT THAT I ALMOST DIED?" he yelled at me as he jumped up to his feet. He sent me a glare. I could tell he was trying to mock a frightful one, but nothing about Antonio was scary.

"That's exactly what I'm saying. You know how these guys work, they're all the same. They find one girl and one girl only that is theirs. That's the one they kill over, they baby, they protect. It's the only love they feel. You know if you get between them in any way, he'll do whatever needs to be done," I reminded him. He stormed around the table glaring at me. He hated when I brought up this part of our past and normally I didn't, but I saw history repeating itself.

"YOU STILL WANT HIM, DON'T YOU?" Antonio yelled at me. I rolled my eyes as I tugged on my hair trying to calm myself down before I said something I didn't mean.

"YOU'RE MISSING THE POINT ANTONIO. YOU'VE SEEN THE WAY TRIP LOOKS AT ELLY, OR HOW HE TOUCHES HER HAIR, HOW HE WORRIES IF SHE'S TIRED OR NOT. YOU EVEN SAID IT YOURSELF! HE SAID HE WAS TIRED OF EVERYONE RUNNING ALL OVER HER. IF SHE WASN'T HIS GIRL, THE ONLY ONE THAT WILL EVER TRULY MATTER TO HIM, HE WOULDN'T CARE. WHAT I WAS TO HIM IS NOTHING COMPARED TO WHAT I SEE ELLY BEING TO TRIP!" I yelled at him picking up my glass candle holder and throwing it at him. I didn't want anything of my past back and it didn't surprise me he'd accuse me of that.

"SO, WHAT? YOU'RE SAYING I JUST LET HER RUN AROUND WITH THESE GANGS AND GET US ALL KILLED?" he yelled at me his face turning red with anger.

"No, what I am saying is stay out of her and Trip's business. You wouldn't almost die then. If they're fighting, don't get involved. If you find money, leave it alone. Zeke takes very good care of her as he should. You have to let her fight Trip so she can find her breaking point, just like I had to. I love you and I don't want back a single thing from that time in my life, but Elly deserves to feel that way once in her life. The raw burning passion, the excitement, the thrill of this person that does everything they shouldn't but gets away with it. The fiery love, the touch that is so wrong but yet so right, it's addictive. She deserves that, every girl does. I won't let you kick her out over that or let you mistreat her." My tone was clipped with anger and desperation. Antonio scoffed shaking his head as he turned to walk away from me. I watched as he changed his mind and spun around, storming over to me shaking his head "no".

"It's in her DNA to be around those gang members. You knew it the moment she lied to the cops at only 7," I snapped at him. He looked at me licking his lips bitterly laughing.

"If that's what she wants, then she needs to get out or pay up. I won't put up with this a second time," he laughed. I shook my head, snatching my keys off the of the table and storming to the door.

"WHERE ARE YOU GOING?" Antonio yelled at me. I heard his heavy footsteps following behind me. I quickly ran out of the front door onto the porch turning to look at him.

"TO TALK TO ELLY'S REAL DAD. I WON'T LET YOU MISTREAT HER EVEN IF THAT MEANS SENDING HER WITH HIM," I yelled at him. I saw his face pale, but I just turned and walked down the steps to get into my Cadillac that Elly's real father so kindly gifted me. Without a second thought of my husband, I pulled out, driving to meet the only person who could truly help Elly.

ELEANOR

LAST CLASS OF THE DAY

I tuned out my teacher as she rambled on and on about her lesson. My focus was on my phone. I stared at the picture of me and Trip. It was the one where I was smiling, and he was blowing the smoke from his mouth. In his red, glossed over, low hanging eyes you could see a hint of true happiness and my smile didn't hide how happy I was to be with him. I know we were never together or even close to it. We had only hooked up, but I felt like I was going through a real-life breakup. One that hurt worse than mine and Lucas's ever did. The last bell rang, pulling my attention away from my phone. I closed out my camera roll and grabbed my books and hydro flask. I walked out of the room, adjusting my hood that was beginning to fall.

"Elly," I heard a deep voice. I turned see Lucas leaning against the wall next to my classroom door. His face was still busted up badly. He pushed off the wall to jog over to me, his eyes traveling over me. I watched the worry and concern flood them, but it was too late for him to worry about me.

"I'm sorry about everything. I didn't know Theo and his friends were going to do that to you. I thought---" I cut him off shaking my head and

217

looking anywhere but at his face. Even with the disgusting bruises, he still managed to look amazing.

"It doesn't matter anymore," I told him with a shrug. He sighed reaching out to grab my hips, but I slapped away his hands.

"It does matter. I didn't know gang rivals were that serious, I didn't know he'd come for you like that. I'm sorry I didn't do anything. I froze I was so scared. Believe it or not I'm actually thankful you keep Trip around. I don't even know how to repay him," he told me. Tears filled my eyes with just the mention of his name. I closed my eyes as the tears I was trying so hard to fight slipped from my eyes. I wiped away a tear quickly, but another replaced it as a trader sob escaped from my lips.

"Why are you crying? Is Trip ok? Did something happen Elles?" Lucas worried and taking a step closer. I nodded my head trying to get myself under control so I could speak.

"Trip's fine, asshole. He's not going to like you talking to his girl though, and as you already know he's not someone to piss off. Go run back to your bitch ass El Diablos." Lil Smiley growled, walking over to me and Lucas. I sniffled, wiping my tears away and taking a step back from the two boys who were about to have words. I realized Smiley called me Trip's girl. It was too much. I was feeling thrown away, abandoned, useless to him and I didn't want to be labeled as that. I didn't even catch what Lucas said before I cut their bickering short.

"I'M NOT TRIP'S GIRL, SMILEY. IF HE CARED EVEN AN OUNCE FOR ME HE'D BE HERE INSTEAD OF YOU. HE DOESN'T GIVE A FUCK ABOUT ME SO DON'T PLAY IT LIKE HE DOES. BOTH OF YOU JUST LEAVE ME THE FUCK ALONE!" I yelled at them, catching everyone's attention. I stormed away to my locker where Gabby already had it open. I grabbed my backpack, shoving everything in messily, and storming away before she could say anything to me. I walked out of the school to see Zeke waiting for me in the spot Trip usually parks in. I walked overlooking up at him as he looked me over with a concerned look.

"You look like shit," he said eyeing me. I shrugged, looking away. I couldn't tell him about Trip. Zeke would kill him if he found out we had sex. It was just a rule. You leave the boss's daughter alone. I wasn't his real daughter, but I was the closest thing to it.

"Elly, talk to me," Zeke pushed in a soft fatherly voice. I shook my head, moving into a comforting hug. I buried my face into his chest, letting sobs rip out. My knees wobbled and in moments gave out from under me, but Zeke was quick to catch me.

"Princesa, I'm right here," he whispered hugging me tighter which I honestly needed at the moment. I needed a dad, one that wasn't going to freak out on me or demand I pay up right now. I just needed a fatherly hug and for a dad in my life to tell me I'd be ok without Trip.

ZEKE

I poured honey into the cup of tea, stirring it slowly. Elly stopped crying not long after we got to my house, but now she sat in my bedroom on my bed crisscrossed, just staring ahead in complete silence. I didn't know what this was over but I had an idea of what it could be. I carefully picked up her hot tea, taking it upstairs to my bedroom where I found Elly just as I had left her.

"I got you tea with honey. It might help you feel better," I told her as I handed it to her. She looked over at me, sending me a small smile while nodding her head.

"Thank you, Zeke," she whispered, blowing on the tea and taking a sip. I sat down on the bed next to her looking at her trying to figure out what she was truly feeling.

"What's going on kiddo?" I asked her. She sighed burying her face into her hands, shaking her head.

"So much Zeke. I don't even know where to start. My dad is flipping out on me. He created a whole list of bills for me to pay. Then when I told him I had soccer and volleyball in a month, he told me to "pay up or get my shit and get out." I know I can cover the bills with the money you gave me, so I'm not worried about it. My mom hasn't even said anything to him, she's just letting him do this. I just feel like he hates me over what happened with Trip," she told me. I looked at her with wide eyes shaking my head. It pissed me off even more hearing it from Elly herself. I wouldn't let anyone treat her like this. I stood up pacing around my room thinking about how I was going to handle this. I was going to have a meeting with Antonio about this for sure, and I knew my friend, Trip would love to be a part of that meeting. He did care a lot about Elly, and he hated how her dad was always trying to run over her.

"Then on top of all of that, there was this guy. We were getting so close, he told me about these feelings he had for me. We had a moment and then it got cut short by my dad coming home so I had to make him sneak out of my window. He ghosted me. Zeke I really did care about him and now he's just gone," she sobbed, covering her face with her hands. I looked over at her shocked. On top of all of that stress with her home life some asshole ghosted my daughter. Is he blind? Stupid? My daughter is beyond gorgeous, what type of teenage boy would just ghost her?

"Who is he? I'll have him killed," I growled, going back over to her. She shook her head "no," sobbing, I sat down on the bed hugging her. Her nose nuzzled into my neck as her tears made a wet spot.

"No, I don't want him hurt because I still care about him. We weren't even close to being a thing and I feel like I'm going through my worst breakup ever," she sniffled. I hugged her tightly, running my hand up and down her back.

"It's going to be ok Princesa. We're going to get through this," I whispered kissing the top of her head that was covered with her hood.

"This home situation. It's fucked up. You shouldn't have to pay bills, you're 17 and in school. How much is he making you pay?" I asked her. She pulled away to get up and grab her backpack. I watched as she shuffled through the mess. I knew she had homework, but I wasn't going to push the idea of her homework tonight. She pulled out a notebook paper and handed it to me. I read over her bills and the total amount, and it was crazy expensive for one person in her tiny ass bedroom.

"$325.00 for that bedroom? Fuck that. No, you can stay here. I have an extra bedroom right down that hall that can be yours. You've been wanting your own room here," I said, crumpling up the paper. $200.00 for food. She's one girl that's probably only 120 pounds, if that. How much can she possibly eat? He just saw the money I had given her and wants some of it himself but won't work for it. Piece of shit. I swear wait till tomorrow.

"I don't want to bother you with it," she whispered, I couldn't help the sound of disapproval that left my throat.

"Princesa, I want you here. You can move in with me. You don't have to deal with this bullshit. You can bounce back and forth if you want" I told her. She looked at me with her eyebrows laced together. I watched them dart back and forth as she thought about her choices.

"Can I stay here tonight and think about it? I don't think I can handle another night of being the piece of shit daughter," she asked. I smiled, nodding my head. She smiled back, kissing my cheek and grabbing her cup of tea.

"I'll give you a break from homework tonight, but tomorrow we're getting busy, and you're going to soccer," I told her, shaking my finger at her. She laughed, nodding her head.

"Can you have one of your guys go get me clothes and my soccer stuff?" she asked. I nodded, grabbed my phone and texted Rudy to go get her things and bring them here.

"Yeah, let's go into the living and watch a movie. I'll order Chinese," I said. She smiled, getting up and following me into the living room. I turned the TV onto Disney Plus and selected "Mulan," remembering that "The Little Mermaid" and "Mulan" were her top favorite movies as a child.

Chapter 18

Drained

ELEANOR

I woke up to my alarm going off for school. I groaned, reaching over and grabbing my phone to turn off the alarm. I slept for maybe an hour and half last night. It was more than the night before, but I was still exhausted. I was up most of the night crying and just trying to figure out at what point my life went to shit. My thoughts bounced from how my family hates me, to Trey'von, to why I was so stuck on him after one night. I've had hookups before. I know I have feelings for him, but this is so crazy. Then it went to moving in with Zeke and then back to Trey'von. I sighed sitting up looking around the guest room that I wasn't sure I'd let become mine or not. I pushed the cover off, got up, and went over to my bag. I grabbed a pair of leggings, a white baggy hoodie that had a picture of Lilo from "Lilo and Stitch" on it. It was the one where she was laying on the ground and it said, 'leave me alone to die,' which was a total mood. I grabbed underclothes. I looked at the outfit debating if I really wanted to get in the shower. I needed one because I didn't take one yesterday, but I really didn't have the energy to do it. I lifted an arm to smell my pit.

"Deodorant and I can get through one more day," I told myself, shrugging. I looked at myself in my new outfit in the mirror that was connected to a dresser. My hair was crazy, so I just gathered the curls putting them in a very messy ponytail. I looked at myself again to see how much of a hot mess I really looked. My eyes had deep purple bags under them, they were blood shot, swollen from all the tears, and my skin was

222

pale. My lips were the palest pink they had ever been. They were chapped and looked gross, but I didn't even care. My ponytail probably couldn't even pass as one. There were lumps and strands sticking out all over the place. I looked down at my outfit as I pulled on my hoodie, trying to hide my body even more. I wasn't ready to really see my body knowing his memory lingered on my skin. I bit my lip holding back tears as I put on perfume and deodorant. I threw on my Adidas from yesterday. I shoved my phone in my pocket, picking up my backpack and duffel and descended down the stairs to loud Spanish music. I walked into the kitchen to see Zeke dancing at the stove. He wore pajama bottoms and a wife beater. He smiled as he looked over his shoulder at me.

"Princesa, just in time for breakfast. Make a plate and sit," he said, motioning toward the table. I wasn't hungry, but I didn't want to hurt Zeke's feelings.

"I need to go if I'm gonna catch the bus," I told him quietly, looking away from the food as my stomach turn.

"I'll be taking you school. No bus. Sit, eat," he sent me a fatherly look. I sighed, tossed down my bags and grabbed a plate piled with a waffle, sausage links, fruit, and scrambled eggs. It looked and smelled so good. But my stomach felt the need to throw up from just looking at it. I sat at the table pouring syrup over my waffle as Zeke sat down a glass of orange juice in front of me, along with a key.

"I don't know if I will be there to pick you up after practice, but I will have one of my guys there. Don't lose this," he told me. I nodded as I grabbed my keys from my backpack and attached the key. I took a bite of my eggs and looked up at him.

"What are you doing today?" I asked. He glanced at me with a 'don't ask' smile. Honestly, I couldn't handle anything else to overthink, so I just shrugged and moved on.

"Are you feeling ok?" he asked as he rested the back of his hand on my forehead.

"My heart is hurt Zeke. I don't have energy for much right now," I shrugged as I watched as he made his plate and sat down across from me.

"Over things at home? That boy? What is it?" he asked. Honestly, it was over Trey'von aka "that boy," but I couldn't tell him that. I wanted to so bad, I just wanted to scream and cry to anyone who would listen without judging me, but Zeke wasn't that person.

"Everything, I guess. I feel way worse now than when me and Lucas broke up," I told him, taking a bite out of my waffle. He looked at me shocked. I know he remembered the depression I slid into after Lucas. It was worse than the crash of the 1930's. I didn't even leave my bed for like two weeks. Trust me, I didn't want to leave the bed now, but I was forcing myself. I knew a day would come that I wouldn't be able to, but right now I could. We let a silence fall between us and just ate. I took like 5 bites of my waffle, I ate half of my eggs, one and half pieces of sausage, and like two pieces of fruit. I was officially full after that so I just pushed away my plate.

"Done already?" Zeke asked me raising an eyebrow. I nodded my head as I looked away embarrassed that I couldn't eat anymore. It was so good and a hot breakfast in the morning was new, I just didn't have the stomach for it.

"That's ok. You'll get your appetite back," he told me. I nodded, got up and scrapped my plate, washed it and put it away. I watched Zeke do the same as I thought of the question about to escape my lips.

"Zeke, can I stay another night?" I asked hopeful. He looked at me, making a face and laughing.

"Yeah, but you got to go brush your teeth. Damn girl," He waved his nose. I blushed, touching my lips. I can't believe I forgot. I never forget to brush my teeth. I nodded and walked back upstairs to brush my teeth.

ZEKE

I pulled up into the carpool lane at the high school and slowly drove up to the front behind all the soccer moms. I looked over at Elly as she just stared out of the window. She looked horrible. The last time I saw her like this was when she and that Lucas kid broke up, but I think this might be just a little worse. I felt like it was more to do with a boy than Antonio, but she wasn't going to tell me who the guy was. Maybe Trip will know who the boy is. He was with her for a while so I'm sure he saw something.

I pulled up to the drop off point. I watched Elly put up her hood and look over at me.

"Thanks Zeke. I'll see you at home," she told me. Her tired eyes looked around the front of the school where teenagers stood with their friends.

"Have a good day Princesa," I said. She leaned over, kissed my cheek and got out. She grabbed her bags from the back, and I watched her walk up to the door. I pulled out of the school drop off lane onto the street. I tapped my touch screen control panel and called Trip through the car phone.

ring

ring

ring

"Yeah?" he answered. I heard water running in the background. Well at least he was out of bed.

"You still meeting me at the bar?" I asked turning onto a side road so I could go to the gas station next.

"Yeah, I'm in the shower and then I'll be there. What is this even about Zeke? That was one vague ass text message you sent last night. I damn near thought we was takin out the president," he joked. I rolled my eyes at his lame attempt at humor. Elly was right about one thing, Trip was annoying. He was good at what he did though and had a soft spot for her, which I was going to use to my advantage.

"We'll talk about it at the bar. I know it's something you're gonna want to be in on," I told him stopping at a red light. Already there was a tweaker on the street acting like a damn fool. I rolled my eyes in annoyance. I don't understand why people come outside to tweak out instead of staying home.

"Ight bet. I'll see you there," he said, and I hummed. We hung up and I stopped at the gas station before heading to the bar.

I sat at the back table with the bar still closed. I needed a private meeting with some of my guys. I didn't need the public hearing this. All of my guys were here except for Trip. What a surprise that is. The longer I sat waiting for him, the more impatient I grew. He took forever. He lives all the way in Beverly Hills. He didn't stay in the neighborhood like everyone else. We stay close so we know what is going on in our hood, but he refused to live here. Just as I went to complain about him running late the bar door opened to reveal Trip looking at his cellphone.

"About fucking time!" I snapped at him. He looked up at me with that cocky smirk and shrugged.

"Sorry, traffic" he shrugged. I rolled my eyes at the cocky teenage boy in front of me. He was arrogant because he knew no one would say shit to him.

"Will you just sit the hell down," I barked. He put up his phone and sitting down.

"Why the fuck am I here Zeke? I have an El Diablos to kill," Trip spat out harshly, sending me a glare. Always with the revenge. He was trying to find Lil Psycho's boss. He wasn't satisfied with just killing Lil Psycho and the others, he wanted the higher up too.

"It's about Elly," I told him. I saw him freeze. His eyes grew wide as his lips parted slightly. I smirked seeing his reaction, he wiped the shocked/worried expression off of his face leaning forward with a serious one.

"Is she ok? I put Lil Smiley with her. I swear if he let anything---" I cut him off waving my hand in the air.

"She's fine physically. Mentally, I think that can be debated, but that's none of your concern. Antonio decided since she was going to be around me, you, Smiley, whoever else, that she was directly defying him and since she was 'acting grown' she would be treated like that. He gave her this and said if she didn't pay up she'd have to pack her stuff and get out," I told him tossing him the crumpled up paper I stole from her backpack. Trip's lip snarled up as I saw the anger taking over his body. He uncrumpled the paper looking at it and then laughed with his whole body.

"Fuck that. I've seen that bedroom and she isn't paying this or anything. It's his fucking job to take care of her," Trip snapped as he pulled out his lighter and burned the piece of paper. I nodded agreeing with him.

"So what are we gonna do about it?" I asked, leaning back crossing my arms.

"I say we put a bullet in his head," Trip grinned. The others looked at me with wide eyes practically begging me not to take the girls 'father.' I raised an eyebrow at him, Elly would never forgive him for doing something like that so why would he want to.

"Elly won't forgive you," I reminded him, but he just shrugged.

"She already isn't ever going to forgive me. You don't know everything that's happened between me and her. Killing that piece of shit will make her life easier. She hates me for it, fine. We can add it to the growing list of things," he explained with a careless shrug. I saw the way he looked away locking and unlocking his jaw. I watched as he popped his knuckles. It gave away that fact that he wasn't ok with her hating him, but he was going to play like it was fine. Was he the reason she was a walking zombie right now?

ELEANOR

LUNCH

I walked into the lunchroom with Gabby and Nicole. They were going on and on about Homecoming. They were so excited, and I should be too, this was my senior year. My last Homecoming but I couldn't even find the energy to act excited about it. I had no one to go with. I couldn't go with Lucas for obvious reasons. Even if Trey'von wasn't avoiding me, it wouldn't have been his thing. It's not like my parents would be happy to see me all dressed up. I doubt they'd want the cute little pictures. I knew they wouldn't come with me and help me find a dress. It just wasn't in the cards for me. We went through the lunch line. I only grabbed a bottle of apple juice.

"You're not getting food?" Nicole asked me raising an eyebrow. I shook my head "no," holding up my juice.

"Hun, I'm going to have to ask you to take down your hood," the lunch lady said before letting me go find a seat. I rolled my eyes, pushing down my hat exposing my mess of hair. She sent me a small smile letting me go.

I followed Gabby and Nicole to a back table away from our normal table. Lucas had taken it over.

"Yo, this food is trash" Lil Smiley said coming over and dropping his tray on the table. I sat down pulling out my phone and getting on Instagram.

"Can I fix your hair Elly? I'll put it back in a ponytail but make it cute" Nicole asked me in the nicest, friendliest tone she could manage. I looked up at her sending her a small smile.

"No, it's ok. I'm not feeling myself anyways" I told them with a shrug. They all sent me a sad pitiful look. I rolled my eyes and took a drink of the juice as I looked back at my phone, but it got snatched away.

"Ok spill. We know you're all sad over this Trip guy. What the hell happened?" Gabby asked. I glared at her, glancing at Lil Smiley who just shrugged with his mouth full.

"I already know something happened between you guys. He called me cussing me out last night when he found out you were staying at Zeke's house and I didn't tell him," Smiley told me. Who is Trey'von to keep tabs on me after everything he's done? If he was going to throw me away like I was trash, I'd rather not have a spy on me.

"I don't want to talk about it and Smiley don't tell him anything. It's none of his business what I'm doing anymore," I snapped at him with a glare. He put his hands up in surrender, nodding his head fast.

"Well, I'm here for you. What if after school we have a girl's day?" Gabby suggested, Nicole was quick to agree with her. I couldn't help but let the corners of my mouth turn up ever so slightly. I loved my friends and appreciated them trying to help.

"We can do each other's hair and makeup. We can go shopping or get our nails done." Nicole spit off everything we could do. Just as I was about to raincheck them, I felt a tap on my shoulder, I looked over to see Tony smiling down at me. He took a seat between me and Smiley.

"How you feelin today?" Tony asked, but I just shrugged.

"I'm here," I shrugged. He chuckled, nodding his head. I watched him nervously scratch the back of his neck as he looked at me.

"I know you said you weren't going to Homecoming so if you say no that's totally fine. I was...um...just wondering if you'd go with me?" I looked at him, surprised. I liked Tony as a friend and that was it. He was a sweet guy and deserved the world, but I didn't see him in that light. Even if I could see something with him, which I can't, right now wasn't the best time for me.

"Just as friends," he added, quickly running his palms over his pants. I nervously licked my chapped lips. I didn't want to ruin our friendship.

"Why aren't you asking Amanda Walters to go to Homecoming with you?" I asked. They were talking for a minute, but I hadn't seen them together recently.

"She's kinda shallow so I stopped talking to her. I just thought it would be fun for us to go. I mean I don't have a date and you don't have one. Friends can go together, right?" He asked me. I really didn't want to go to Homecoming. I looked up at him to see he had wide hopeful eyes, his lower lip wobbled with nerves. I couldn't bring myself to say no. I sighed closing my eyes nodding my head.

"Yeah, I'll go with you, just as friends Tony," I said pointing at him. His smile grew so bright and joyful.

"Of course, you have the whole heartbroken over a gangster thing going on right now but that's ok. We'll have fun. I'll text you later with details?" He asked me. I forced a smile as I nodded my head. He got up walking away as Nicole and Gabby squealed.

"You and Tony? Ohhh," Nicole squealed. I shook my head making a face.

"I love Tony as a friend only and I'm not in the head space for a boyfriend," I admitted with a shrug. They smirked at each other and started going on and on about why Tony could be good for me.

"I'm telling Trip," Lil Smiley cut into their long pros and cons list. He sent me a glare, which only made my blood boil.

"Suck his dick while you're at it Smiley. Lube up, it's big" I snapped at him as I got up and snatched my juice. I walked out of the lunchroom trying to find a moment just for myself.

TREY'VON

I sat on the kitchen table inside the safe house in Calabasas waiting for a couple of the guys to get here with Antonio. It was my idea to kidnap him. Zeke won't let me kill him, but I was going to scare him. I might not be around Elly or talking to her, but she was still my girl and I wouldn't let anyone hurt her. Him trying to take advantage because he found a couple thousand in her closet was hurting her and I'd put a bullet in him before I sat back and let that happen. I know I hurt her too. I do it way too much, but I don't know how to be any different.

"Why the fuck are we sitting in this safe house instead of talking to him?" Zeke asked me for like the millionth time. I closed my eyes inhaling deeply, trying not to lash out at him. I already told him I had it covered, and he keeps asking me these dumb ass questions. Just as I went to answer his question the front door busted open, and my men walked in carrying a body bag that was thrashing around with muffled screams. The two holding the body bag threw it on the floor with a hard thud.

"Trip, I told you we weren't going to kill him," Zeke rubbed his temples. I looked over at him rolling my eyes.

"I'm not going to kill him Zeke, damn. I'm just gonna scare him. Here, tie him up to this chair, keep his bitch ass gagged" I growled at my guys as I kicked a chair making it fall back. I stayed in my spot on the table. I watched them cut open the bag. Antonio looked around, his eyes landed on me which made his screams grow. I watched as he tried to fight against my guys while he was still bound. It didn't take them long to get him in the chair and tied up.

"What are you gonna do when he calls the police and says you kidnapped him?" Zeke snapped at me. I smirked at Antonio looking him over. He was wearing a tracksuit. Fucking blue collar idiot.

"He won't because he knows what happens to snitches and I don't have anything to lose anymore" I said eyeing him up and down. I mean Elly hated me, there was no question in my mind about that. I fucked and dipped. I knew she was thinking she did something wrong, but I couldn't even face my own emotions enough to let the woman I care about the most know it's not her fault. I'm damaged.

"So, Antonio, I heard you tryin to make my girl pay you to be a fucking dad. What type of shit is that?" I asked. His eyes were wide in panic. He pulled at his restraints trying to get away, but there was no way he could. He muffled through the gag in his mouth. I'll never understand how he made someone like Elly.

"How is she anyways? I haven't seen her in a couple days. The last I saw her was the same night I almost killed you. She wanted me to come chill with her," I mocked him. Of course, I couldn't mock him the way I wanted to because of Zeke, and I couldn't bring myself to talk about her like that. She wasn't a normal bitch.

"Pull out the fucking gag," I snapped at my men. They ripped it out, leaving him breathing hard.

"Antonio man, I just want to talk to you about this. I love Elly and I care about her. I heard something that bothered me. You're doing this because of what happened in the past. You're taking it out on her," Zeke snickered. I didn't know know what happened in the past and I didn't care because all I cared about was her.

"Fuck you Zeke. Fuck both of you," he spat. Within seconds I was off the table and onto my feet in front of him. I brought back my fist and punched Antonio so hard blood splattered from his mouth as his head snapped to the side.

"MAYBE I SHOULD JUST FUCKING KILL YOU. I DON'T HAVE ANYTHING TO LOSE BY ENDING YOU. I'M NOT GOING TO BE DISRESPECTED BY SOME PUNK ASS HOMEBOY LIKE YOU!" I yelled punching him again and making the chair bounce. He coughed as blood drooled from his lower lip. My phone vibrated in my pocket. I pulled it out to seeing Smiley calling me. I answered it as I walked away.

"What's up Smiley?" I asked him as I sauntered into the kitchen.

"Yo, Elly has a date to Homecoming," he told me. I stopped dead in my tracks. My eyebrows lacing together thinking of anyone it could be. I knew it wouldn't be the Lucas kid, so who?

"Who the fuck is it?" I snapped at him. How is she already over me? My mind is consistently on her and how guilty I feel for what I'm doing, but she's just out here right back to dating? Did she even mean it when she said she had feelings for me? How the fuck is she going to play me? I thought for a split second that someone could actually care about me. I was so fucking stupid to believe she genuinely wanted me. No one in my whole life has ever wanted me, so why would she be different?

"It's that Asian kid, Tom, Timmy. Tony, that's it, Tony," he told me. What about a fucking downgrade, the virgin of her friends? I know she can't be serious. She has to be trying to piss me off at this point.

"K thanks," I spat and hung up. I threw my phone across the room. I grabbed the draw strings on my hood, tightening it. I turned and punched a hole in the wall out of anger. She really thinks I'm going to sit back and let her date bimbo the fucking clown. She fucked with the wrong one. I stormed into the dining room going straight over to Antonio punching him in the face so hard his chair fell back breaking.

"TRIP!" Zeke yelled as I grabbed Antonio and slammed him against the wall. He grabbed my wrists trying to pry me off, but I wasn't moving.

"Listen asshole, I'm going to let you live but you're going to do what I say, got it?" I spat at him viciously, in no mood to bicker with him.

"I don't work for either of you. GET THE FUCK OFF OF ME," He screamed. I laughed, shaking my head and slamming him into the wall as hard as I could which cracked the dry wall.

"TRIP, BACK OFF!" Zeke yelled, but I just sent him a glare.

"FUCK OFF ZEKE. WE'RE TALKING LIKE MEN!" I yelled and then looked back at Antonio with a devilish smirk.

"You're right. My little Baby Girl is out of control and you're going to fix that. You aren't going to let her go to that Homecoming dance," I told him. He looked at me, shocked, but if she wanted to date whats-his-face then she'd miss the dance. I tossed him back and took a step away.

"A dance?" Zeke asked confused.

"Yeah, I don't want her there, so you are going to come up with any reason to not let her go," I snapped my order at him. He looked at me with challenging eyes, but I was in no mood for his challenges. This is Elly we're talking about and even though I'm being a fuck up she's still mine.

"And what if I do let her go? The whole point of this kidnap situation is that I control her too much, right?" he asked me with a sly smirk. He thought he had something over me, but he didn't because I'd kill everyone, he ever loved except for her.

"If she does go I'll kill you or one of those pretty little daughters. That way too nice of a wife seems like an easy target. Then I'm sure you have a mom, a dad, somebody else I can find and hurt. She stays home, you live. No one dies," I told him with a shrug. He looked at me and then over at Zeke who was looking at me with questioning look.

"Fine, she won't go to the dance," he told me. I nodded my head, pleased that I had gotten my way.

"I don't want to hear anything else about the past or her paying you to live in your house got it?" Zeke asked Antonio. He looked like he was about to smart off so I took a step forward. He melted back, nodding his head.

"Good. She doesn't need to know about this meeting. Get him out of here, I'm tired of looking at him," I waved him away. My men took him out, leaving just me and Zeke in the safe house.

ELEANOR

I sat on the turf with my knees in my chest and my chin resting on my knees. I didn't want to even go to practice, but I knew Zeke would freak if I didn't. I refused to change out or practice. I'd have to miss the next game, but I don't even care. I was just ready to go back to Zeke's house and go to sleep. I couldn't help but roll my eyes at Novah, Yara, and Dior walking over to me.

"Aw, you look so sad. Did you finally realize you'll never be as pretty or as popular as me? Or did your little gang friends get tired of using you as a toy?" Novah asked me with a snicker once she was in front of me. Her little sluts laughed like it was the funniest thing they've ever heard. I just rolled my eyes and pulled my hood up.

"Go find someone else to torture Novah. I'm not in the mood," I said looking away from the three girls.

"Why would we find someone else when we have a dirty slut like you sitting right in front of us?" Dior asked me. I looked up at her with a smirk, shaking my head.

"I saw you were wearing Gucci today. That's really funny because everyone knows you sucked Roman's dick for it. Prostitute!" I shot at Dior. I watched the rage ignite in her eyes. She looked over at Novah who looked just as shocked.

"Say some shit like that again and we'll make your life hell," Yara threatened me like I was scared of her.

"You can't even pass basic math without fucking your teacher. What can you possibly do to me?" I asked her. She gasped, squealing, and looking at Novah who was holding back a laugh.

"Novah!" Yara complained. Novah looked at them and then at me with a smirk.

"Who cares what the reject says, girls. I'll make sure everyone finds out about the football team," She sneered, walking away from me with her minions. I had no idea what she was talking about, but I didn't even care. I heard Coach calling for a huddle to dismiss us. I grabbed my bags, walking off the field and down the walkway to the parking lot. I saw Julio waiting for me. I walked over and got in his car without a word. Thankfully, he kept our ride silent. When I finally got to Zeke's house, I went straight up to the room I stayed in last night. I got straight into bed ready to sleep away the pain.

Chapter 19

Spiraling

ELEANOR

A WEEK AND A HALF LATER

"PRINCESA, WAKE UP! YOUR MOM IS HERE TO GET YOU FOR LUNCH!" Zeke yelled banging on my bedroom door. I groaned, hiding my head in my pillows. I already told her I didn't want to go out to lunch. I didn't want to leave my bed. I just wanted to lay here. Over this last week and a half, I'd hit my lowest point. I hadn't left my bedroom at Zeke's house in 5 days. I've just been laying in bed crying and sleeping. Zeke's been shoving just enough food down my throat to maintain my weight, but even that's a battle. I stopped going to school. I'm sure I'd been kicked off of the soccer team by now, but I didn't care. I let my phone die so my friends would stop calling me and texting me. When Zeke finally plugged it in, I just turned it off. I haven't moved to shower or anything. I knew I had to smell bad just by how greasy my hair was, but I didn't care. I felt empty, like someone had punched a hole through my chest. It was painful but numb at the same time. I closed my eyes trying to go back to sleep, but there was a knock at my bedroom door.

"Elly, I'm here for our mommy-daughter day," Mom called out, but I just pulled my comforter higher, hoping she wouldn't see me under the mounds of blankets and pillows. I felt the bed dip in, and a hand rub my back.

"Girl, you need a shower," Mom laughed, but I just shrugged.

"It's the smell of my soul dying," I grumbled getting comfortable. Mom laughed, snuggling closer to me.

"Ah, I missed our snuggles," she told me. I stayed quiet hoping she'd just take a nap with me and that could be the end of our mother-daughter day. Moments later, my comforter and pillow got ripped off of my face, making me groan.

"Mom, just leave me alone. I already told you, I don't want to go," I complained, but she just laughed and tried to push me out of bed.

"Nope, you need to get out of this room. It's starting to stink," She commanded, but I just laid there. Moments later I felt her attack me with tickles. I jerked, lunged off the bed and fell face first onto the floor, making her burst into laughter.

"ELLY. Are you ok?" she laughed at me as I groaned. I pushed myself off the floor glaring at her. I did not want to be out of bed right now but, yet here I was.

"Fine, I'm up. Let's go," I rolled my eyes while grabbing my Vans to put them on when my mom stopped me.

"Aren't you going to take a shower?" She asked, but I just shook my head "no." I should, but I just didn't have the motivation to take a shower.

"At least change your clothes?" Mom pleaded. I sighed, nodding my head and motioning towards the door. She smiled and walked out of the room shutting the door behind her. I grabbed a pair of baggy grey Adidas sweatpants, and a baggy Michael Jackson t-shirt that used to be Lucas's. I grabbed new underclothes and changed. I threw my hair up into a messy bun on the top of my head. I threw on my white Vans, grabbing my dirty clothes from the floor. I picked my phone, turning it on shoving it into my pocket as I walked downstairs.

"Savannah, there is something else going on. It's not just Antonio, I'm not sure what it is but she's bad off right now" I heard Zeke tell my mom. I shook my head as I went into the laundry room and tossed my clothes in the washer. I added some of Zeke's dirty clothes and then starting the load of laundry. I walked out to find them both talking quietly in the kitchen about what could possibly be wrong with me.

"Can we just go so I can come back?" I asked mom, fighting against my natural instinct to grab a blanket and just lay down on the couch. Mom smiled at me, and Zeke walked over to me, clapping my shoulder.

"Have fun and actually eat food Princesa," Zeke smiled. I nodded my head as I grabbed my keys, looking at mom. She said "bye" to Zeke, and I followed her out of the house to her car. I got in the passenger seat buckling up as she got in the driver's seat. She pulled out as I looked at my phone to see my friends had blown it up. I scrolled through the text messages reading them, but not replying.

"I think I want comfort food, what about you?" Mom asked, looking over with a smile, but I just shrugged. I didn't care where we went. I wasn't even hungry. I was just trying to get through this stupid lunch so I could go back to sleep.

"How's Gabby doing? It's been a while since we've seen her," Mom asked, just trying to start a conversation. I pulled at the peeling skin on my chapped lips. She was trying hard, and I felt bad that I couldn't find the energy to even talk to her.

"She's ok. I mean she's going through it with her mom, but I haven't talked to her in a few days either," I told her with a shrug. I couldn't help but notice how shocked she was. I don't think she thought I'd actually talk to her. I've been pretty much mute and just laying in bed these last few days. I've been at Zeke's because I couldn't handle my dad's judgmental eyes right now. With the hole lingering in my chest, it would just be too much.

"You should call her, go out and do something," Mom encouraged. But why would she want to hang out with me? It would take one thing to remind me of him and I'd be in tears.

TREY'VON

I laid in bed with my eyes closed trying to figure out where my head was. This last week I've not been myself. I've been meaner, more violent, lashing out faster over the smallest things. At first, I didn't think anyone noticed it, they just cut it up to me being a dick, but then Zeke made a comment about my behavior. I couldn't help it. I couldn't think straight. I felt like I wasn't functioning properly anymore. I've thought about drinking, snorting coke, just doing anything to get my head right, but I couldn't bring myself to do it. I always seen her chocolate brown eyes when I think about it. I heard her accented voice telling me she was proud of me for getting clean. It stopped any thought of drinking or doing a hard drug. Of course, I've smoked weed and I've started doing acid.

For the first time in my life, I missed someone. I missed Elly so much. I missed her screaming at me, I missed listening to her laugh, or her telling me something I didn't give a fuck about. I missed watching her cute little dances when we were getting food, I missed sharing my blunts with her. I missed her non-stop questions. I missed stressing out over her clothing choices or complaining when she wanted to do something I didn't. I wanted to see her and talk to her again, but I couldn't. I admitted I had feelings for her, and I knew she'd expect more to come of it, and I didn't know how to be more. I knew how to be an abusive drunk piece of shit because that's what I grew up around and I didn't want that for her. Elly was so amazing, she deserved someone way better than me. Then we had sex. I didn't know how to be around a girl I had sex with. Ever since my first time, I hit and dipped. I never saw them again. They didn't matter but Elly does. I didn't want to fuck up and I didn't want to be the reason she's fucked up.

Of course, none of that matters now, she already moved on. She's messing with that Asian kid, what's his name? Tony? Tommy? I think it's Travis. Or at least that's what I'm calling him, Travis. I should have known that she didn't feel the same way I do. No one has ever cared about me, not my mom, my siblings, hell CPS didn't even give a fuck about me. I was ok with that, I always thought I could get through life without anyone, but then she just came in and destroyed it all. She made me feel something I haven't before and really made me think she felt whatever the fuck it was too. I was wrong because if she did, she wouldn't already be dating.

I reached over to my bedside table grabbing the framed picture I had of us. I smiled running my finger over her face. It was the picture of us in my car, she had the brightest happiest smile. She genuinely looked so happy to be with me, like it made her whole day. I leaned over blowing smoke from my lips looking at the camera but really, I was looking at her. She was so gorgeous. Her face was lit up in this picture. I loved it, it was my favorite because of how happy she looked.

"What are you doing to me Baby Girl?" I whispered putting down the picture. I opened the bedside table pulling out a strip of acid. I put it on my tongue laying back on my bed closing my eyes, waiting for the effects to take over. It lets me see her, feel her. It gave me her even if it wasn't real. Within 30 minutes after putting the strip on my tongue I felt a weight straddling my waist. I opened my eyes smiling licking my lips, that musical giggle leaving her lips.

"Did you miss me?" her accented voice asked me. I smiled taking in her appearance. It was Elly, just like I knew it would be. She looked as amazing as ever. She had on those leather pants that drove me crazy, a white crop top that only covered her boobs, her curls were down and bouncy. She had on large silver hoops.

"I always do miss you," I told her with a smirk. She laughed leaning down kissing me easily, this was when I remembered it was just a hallucination. When I actually kissed her there was an explosion, a rush of feeling, but when I kissed this hallucination, I felt nothing other than lips on mine.

"I missed you too, Papi," She grinned running a nail down my chest. I licked my lips watching as her finger dipped down to the band of my boxers.

"Why don't you just go see me?" she asked. I looked up at her, raising an eyebrow.

"I'm seeing you, right now," I said as if it was obvious. I grabbed her hips rolling her over, so she was laying on the bed and I was between her legs, hovering over her. She burst into laughter, touching my face. I smiled, leaning down and kissing her. She laughed pushing me back.

"I'm not real and you know that. You're making out with your own pillow. Look," she snickered. Then suddenly she wasn't under me, but my pillow was. I jumped up tossing the pillow away looking around for her, confused.

"See. I'm not the real Elly, I'm just want you want to see," I heard her voice from behind me. I turned to see her sitting on my dresser mocking me.

"Stop doing that. You know this is as close to the real you as I'm gonna get," I bickered with her. She laughed, jumping off of my dresser and looking in the mirror. She leaned over the dresser just slightly showing me her ass.

"This is as close as you'll let yourself get to me. You always are pushing me away, this is just you doing that," she bitched, making me groan. How does my own hallucination call me out on my bullshit?

ELEANOR

I stirred my spoon around in my tomato soup. I also had a grilled cheese sandwich, and soup but I wasn't really hungry. I had taken two small bites out of the sandwich and hadn't really touched the soup. My mom was going on and on about her co-workers and patients. I tried to listen at first, but I just couldn't, so now I was just nodding and pretending to listen. My mind was everywhere but nowhere at all. I just felt like I was lost with whatever thought popped up.

"Elly? Elly? Elly?" I heard my mom calling my name. I looked up at her with wide, questioning eyes. I was so zoned out I didn't even hear what she had asked me. I watched my mom sigh as worry took over her eyes. I knew she was concerned about me. I knew Zeke was too, but I just had to go through it.

"What is going on with you Elly? I'm worried about you." I looked off to the side where a family sat. I grabbed my hood, putting it up tightening the strings, and shaking my head "no."

"Nothing," I whispered lowly, avoiding eye contact. I knew if I looked at her I'd lose it. I'd have a whole breakdown in this restaurant. I couldn't even really tell her what was going on. She'd tell Zeke and then Zeke would kill Trey'von. I'd never forgive myself if I got him hurt. I still cared about him way more than I should.

"Honey, I know it's something. You can tell me whatever it is. Is it you and your dad fighting? Did something happen between you and Luke? Or that guy you brought home, what's his name Trip? Just talk to me please," she begged. Hearing his name was like someone stabbing me and slowly turning the knife. I closed my eyes trying to fight back my tears. I didn't want to do this here or tell her about it. It was embarrassing the way he got what he wanted and ditched me.

"You might be a night of fun, that's all you'll ever be. One useless night." I heard his voice in my head reminding me that's all I was to him. A useless night. I felt so stupid for believing him that day. He told me he said it out of anger. He meant it and he showed me he meant it which hurt more than anything. I should've known he'd get what he wanted and disappear, but I believed that he had feelings for me and he wanted more. Hot tears fell down my cheeks as my thoughts spiraled about how stupid I was.

"Baby Girl---" I flinched at the nickname, shaking my head "no." She never called me that, why she'd do it now? I don't know but I wish she hadn't. I brought my hands up to my face and my knees to my chest letting a sob rip through me. I missed him, I missed him so much it hurt physically. I missed that annoying cocky smirk that I wanted to slap off of him most of the time. I missed his smile, his laugh, the way he made comments to me just to get a reaction. I missed watching how with one look he could have everyone around us cowering in fear. I missed the way his hands felt, the way his curls looked. What I missed the most were the feelings that came with his eyes, the butterflies and goosebumps.

"I miss him so much mom but it's my own fault. I knew I shouldn't have let it get this far," I sobbed into my hands. My body shook violently with each sob. I'm sure people were looking at me but I didn't even care. They weren't the eyes I needed, or I wanted. I felt my mom slide into the booth next to me. Her arms wrapped around me, pulling me into her side as I sobbed.

"What is your fault? Who do you miss?" Mom asked me. I hugged her, crying into her side. She ran her hand over my disgusting hair shushing me trying to comfort me.

"You can't tell Zeke if I tell you. Zeke will kill him," I cried into my mom as she hushed me.

"It's our secret no matter what," she whispered, holding out her pinkie. I interlocked my pinkie with hers unable to stop my crying. I knew I shouldn't tell her, but just maybe if I told one person, I'd feel better.

"It's Trip," I cried, pulling away from her. I wiped my tears taking a few deep breathes. I looked down at my food, playing with it while gasping and trying to calm myself down. My mom stayed quiet waiting for me to speak.

"Well before I really get into this most recent thing, I feel like I need to start from a little farther back. One day me and Trip was fighting, and I had made a comment about every time I start to get to know him, the real him he pushes me away. He literally laughed at me and told me I was nothing but a night of fun. I'd always just be *"one useless night."* I was upset, but we had talked about it, and he told me he was just angry when he said it. I forgave him for it and really just believed he was upset," I told my mom, looking up towards the ceiling and trying to keep it together. She pushed back a strand of my hair, tucking it behind my ear. It was too familiar of a touch and wasn't helping me.

"You're more than one useless night and if he thinks that, he's stupid," Mom told me. I laughed shaking my head "no."

"I'm the stupid one. That day after everything happened with Dad, when you guys went out to dinner without me. He came over. He snuck into my room to bring me back the money. I was so mad at him. I was yelling and for the first time he wasn't yelling back. He was too calm which only made me angrier, but he told me he wanted more with me. He didn't just want to be my friend, he wanted something real. Like an idiot I believed him because I wanted that with him too. I just never thought he could want me like that." I couldn't stop the tears. I felt so stupid and used but I was so heartbroken. I just wanted to go back to how things were before. We'd fight and two days later he was back to annoy me. This time it was different, he wasn't fighting to be around me because he had gotten what he wanted.

"We had sex and oh my God it was so amazing. After we did the deed, I tried to cuddle with him, but he freaked out because he didn't like it, but that was ok. You guys got home, and I rushed him out. I haven't heard from him or seen him since that day. He went to Zeke and asked to be put in the dope houses. He hates them, he says they're gross. He'd rather be in the place he hates the most than around me. I don't know what I did wrong. I didn't mean to make him uncomfortable, and I said sorry. He's just proving how I am just "one useless night" and I can't get over it"

I sobbed, the ache in my chest growing so painful I almost couldn't take it. My mom hugged me tightly, but my body was numb to anything other than that ache.

"For starters was the sex consensual?" Mom asked me and I nodded my head.

"We both wanted it and used words to consent," I told her as I sobbed into her shoulder.

"Elly, you didn't do anything wrong. You were being a teenage girl. The guy you like suddenly likes you back. It's exciting, its him that has the problem. If he can't see what type of amazing girl, you are then he doesn't deserve you. You are more than one night and one day you will find someone who shows you a lifetime, " Mom promised, her voice cracking. I didn't even want to think about anyone else right now. I didn't want to even think about Trey'von but was here I am crying in a diner over him.

"I should have known he wasn't just angry that night. I should have seen through it when he told me he had feelings for me. He can't feel anything. I thought I was special, but he just dipped out. He doesn't even have to suffer at the dope houses, he got back his spot as underboss," I told Mom. I didn't want him to suffer physically but sitting in those houses would be a nice pay back.

"Tell Zeke, get his title taken away," Mom told me. I jerked away shaking my head "no" fast. Her eyes were wide and frantic at my reaction.

"We can't tell Zeke. I'm like his daughter and it's the number one rule. Leave the bosses daughter alone. He'll kill Trey'von, Mom. Please, I can't actually lose him." My breathing picked up and I began to panic at the idea of her telling Zeke about me and Trey'von.

"Calm down, I won't tell, Elly, but he doesn't deserve this much of you," Mom told me, grabbing my hands. I closed my eyes, tears falling even harder.

"He doesn't deserve it, but he has it. I miss him Mom. I miss the things I thought I hated," I wept. She nodded her head, grabbing my hand and kissing my knuckles.

"That's how it normally works. If he cares about you like he said, he'll come back. If not, then you'll get through this stronger and smarter and find someone who will cherish every single moment with you," she seemed so sure, but I didn't know how I was ever going to get through this. Maybe I was just another one of his victims and I didn't know if could survive the notorious Trip.

"He made me feel things I've never felt. He made goosebumps rise on my skin just by looking at me. The butterflies were so intense, and I really found myself happy around him...sometimes...when he wasn't being a raging lunatic, but I even miss those moments. Right now, I feel like I'd take any version of him I can get. There is this hole in my chest, and it hurts, but I know he's the key to getting rid of it." I couldn't believe how everything was just spilling from my lips when I didn't mean to tell all of this. My mom hugged me just promising me I'd get through this even though I didn't feel like it.

"Can you take me home?" I asked her crying and she nodded. She paid our bill and we walked out to her car. She took me back to Zeke's, promising to keep it as our secret. I couldn't be more thankful for that. I said my goodbyes going inside getting right back into my bed and crying myself to sleep.

TREY'VON

I smiled at Elly as she sat on my island bar watching me cook. It wasn't anything special just spaghetti. I looked back at Elly with a smirk as she smiled at me.

"What are you staring at crazy man?" She flirted. I chuckled, walking over standing between her legs, holding her hips.

"Crazy man? That's new and I'm not crazy," I teased, leaning down and kissing her. She giggled against my lips, wrapping her comforting arms around my body.

"You are crazy. We can run through some of your greatest hit from birth," she offered. I looked at her confused. She didn't know shit about my past, how was she going to bring up that stuff.

244

"You know, I'm waiting for you to come make this right for me," she whispered. I took a step back glaring at her. She wasn't real. She didn't know shit about the real situation. She was just a hallucination that needed to stick to the damn script.

"You don't know shit" I snapped back as I stirred my sauce on the stove.

"I do though, Trey'von. I know everything because I'm a part of your subconscious. You're only taking acid so you can see me. You just won't go find the real me," it taunted me. I whipped around glaring at her as she laughed at me.

"Am I making the big bad gangster mad?" she asked pouting her lip.

"SHUT THE FUCK UP BITCH. IF YOU REALLY KNEW EVERYTHING THEN YOU'D KNOW WHY I CAN'T SEE THE REAL HER. FUCK OFF, BEFORE I FUCKING GUT YOU," I yelled at the hallucination and grabbing my knife, trying to scare her. She disappeared letting me take a breath of relief. I turned off my sauce, moving it off of the burner. I mixed it in with my noodles and made myself a bowl. I walked out of my large kitchen and into the dining room almost dropping the bowl in surprise. Laying on my table in just a thin thong was Elly. She had lines of white powder, shuffling them around with my debit card.

"This is what you've been thinking about right? Cocaine. What do you think I'd say if you actually did it?" she mocked me. I tossed the bowl on the table messing up her lines only to get annoying complaints in the process.

"Baby, why are you being so mean to me?" She pouted, sitting up on the table.

"You're being annoying and trying to piss me off," I snapped, but she just raised an eyebrow.

"You're in charge of all of this. It's your subconscious. You just like fighting with me. Do you like my boobs too?" she asked, running her hands over her exposed breasts. I licked my lips looking away. Of course, I liked them, because I loved everything about her.

245

"Put on some fucking clothes, slut," I spat at the hallucination. I sat at the table mixing up my spaghetti some more. Arms wrapped around my shoulders as lips connected to my jawline.

"What do you think I'm doing right now? Do you think I'm fucking Tony right now?" she pushed me closer to the edge. I couldn't even picture Elly like that with anyone else. I'd kill them for touching her.

"She wouldn't do that," I snapped at the hallucination, but it just laughed at me.

"But you're scared she would," It taunted. This isn't how this normally goes, normally she's herself. She's fun, clingy, and wanting me. Today she was taunting and trying to piss me off. She wanted a reaction from me, but I wasn't sure why.

"These curls are so sexy," she whispered, sitting on my lap. She was now back in her clothes. I smiled leaning down kissing her shoulder.

"Stop trying to fight with me, I just want to enjoy you," I whispered, leaving another kiss on her shoulder.

"Enjoy the real me," she pressed. I shook my head "no," pulling her even closer. She giggled resting her forehead against my head.

"I love how your arms feel," she whispered. I smiled touching her chin lightly, earning a sweet giggle. The rest of my night went swung that. My trip being sweet, loving, and enjoyable to this mocking, know it all monster. It was like the moment I figured out one version of it, it turned into the other. It was one of the worst trips I ever had and one that couldn't end soon enough.

Chapter 20

Rumors

ELEANOR

"Princesa, wake up. You're going to school," Zeke called while ripping the blanket off my body. I groaned, rolling over and hiding my face in my pillows. I was not going to school or leaving this bed. I got up yesterday and that was good enough for a week or so.

"No, I don't want to," I whined, holding a pillow to my face. But regardless of my attempt to hold onto it, Zeke ripped it away from me.

"Nope, you're going to school. You've missed enough and I'm meeting with the soccer coach today to get you back on the team," Zeke told me. I groaned loudly and fixed my gaze on him. He was dressed and ready to go. I didn't know why he thought today of all days was the right time for me to go back.

"I don't want to play soccer or go to school. I just want to stay right here," I complained but he shook his head "no."

"Nope. Get up, shower, brush your teeth, change your clothes. Become a human again," He ordered as he walked out of the room taking my pillow and blanket with him. I rolled off my bed. I walked over to my closet where my mom had hung up my clothes after she brought me back. I grabbed a pair of leggings, a white bandeau, and a white and black Nike windbreaker with underclothes. I just dropped them on the floor, not caring. I shut the closet looking at them and really thinking about a shower. I knew I smelled bad, but I just didn't want to take one.

"TAKE A SHOWER!" Zeke yelled, like he could hear my thoughts.

"NO, I DON'T WANT TO TAKE ONE!" I yelled back at him, looking down at the clothing again. Was he really going to make me go to school? I sighed, walking back over to my bed just as Zeke entered my bedroom.

"Aht Aht, don't get back into that bed. Come on, you're taking a shower," he told me, grabbing my arm. I grunted as he pulled me over to the clothes on the floor and grabbing them.

"I don't want to. I just want to lay in my own filth and die," I pleaded as he drug me down the hall. He laughed, looking back at me shaking his head. Once we got to the bathroom he let go of my arm. Part of me wanted to make a run for it back to the bedroom, but the fight wasn't worth it.

"Elly, I have no idea what you're so sad about. You won't talk to me about it and that's ok because you will sooner or later, but sometimes you have to pretend you're ok when you're not," he scolded. Pretend I'm ok? I'm far from ok so why would I pretend like I am? What would I gain from that? I raised an eyebrow looking at him, he chuckled shaking his head.

"Sometimes Elly, if we pretend long enough, we'll start to believe it. It's ok to scream and cry, not leave bed for a little while, but life has to go on. You have to trick yourself into thinking you'll be ok so you can feel ok again. You have to make yourself think, 'whatever is going on is almost over,'" he lectured. His eyes were filled it a different worry. It wasn't anything I had seen from him before and it kinda scared me. I nodded my head as I reached out and took my clothes from him, biting my lip.

"I'll take a shower," I whispered. He nodded and opened the bathroom door. After locking it, I went over to the towel closet, tossed my clothes in there and then went to the mirror. I looked worse than what I knew was possible. My face was dirty, my eyes had purple rings around them because they'd been swollen for so long. The bags under my eyes revealed that I'd been days without sleep. My eyes were red, and my lips were so chapped you could see the skin peeling off. My russet skin was ghostly pale, my hair was so ratted up it looked as if it would be easier to cut than comb. I looked like something off of "The Walking Dead," but I couldn't bring myself to care. I took a deep breath, stripped out of the clothes I was wearing and looked down at my body. Zeke had forced enough food down my throat to keep my weight on, so I wasn't deadly thin. I must have looked for a second too long because I could just see bronze, smooth hands gliding over my curves. Tears filled my eyes as I grabbed my hair, sinking to the floor as sobs racked my body.

"What is wrong with me?" I cried into my arms. My mind was reeling with everything that could be wrong. Maybe he thought I was fat and was disgusted by me. Or maybe he didn't like that my nipples weren't pink or my skin tone. Maybe he didn't like my big lips. Did I not get wet enough, so he thought I was just trash in bed? Maybe I didn't do enough but I was so caught up in the moment I didn't even think about taking control or doing something back. I was so caught up in him and his hands to think of any type of freaky shit. I opened my eyes and looked at my legs. Maybe my thighs are too big, and he didn't like that. I ran my hands over my face, taking a deep breath as I picked myself up off the floor, getting into the shower. I knew I needed to shave, but I didn't care.

I didn't take long in the shower. Once I got out, I dried off by wrapping the towel around my body, I grabbed a comb from Zeke's drawer and combed all the knots from my curls and let me tell you it was so nappy my head hurt after I was done. I put in two French braids and changed into my outfit. I looked in the mirror at myself once more. The shower hadn't made me look better. All it had done was wash away the dirt. I still looked like a zombie. I sighed, walking down to my room where I stuffed my feet into Adidas. I grabbed my backpack and went downstairs. I walked into the kitchen where Zeke sat two plates on the table.

"That's my favorite breakfast," I whispered, looking at it. It was potatoes, peppers, onions, and eggs. It was so good, but I just didn't have the stomach.

"I know, that's why I made it. You have to eat half of your plate," He commanded as he motioned me to sit down. I looked down at the huge pile of eggs. I sighed, putting salt and pepper on them and it grabbed a fork.

"I'm not hungry," I told him as he sat across from me. He raised an eyebrow at me pointing to the plate.

"And it's your turn to dishes tonight. You've been slacking off and I've been letting it slide, but dishes." He jabbed his fork in the direction of the sink. I nodded my head taking a bite of my eggs. A long silence filled us as we ate. It gave my mind a chance to wander to Trip. I couldn't help but wonder how he was doing or how he was liking his spot back? Was he still his cocky annoying self or was he a mess like me? After a moment or two I looked up to see Zeke eating not paying attention to me. I bit my lip as I played with my food, trying to find the courage to ask about him.

"How's Trip doing? I haven't seen him in a while," I asked. He looked up at me probably confused as to why I was asking about Trip, after everything with my dad, and then the fact he had asked to be away from me. I still cared about him, and I missed him so much. I would even take back the silent Trey'von I met my first day back in the States.

"I'm not real sure. I want to say he's ok, but I don't know," he shrugged. I felt a surge of panic fill my body. Why wouldn't he be ok? How wouldn't Zeke know? He works with him.

"What do you mean? How wouldn't you know?" I rushed, the urgency slipping through my tone. Zeke looked at me with a questioning glance, but I just ignored it.

"I don't know. He's been at his house. He doesn't hang out as much anymore and when he does, he's high. It's not weed, it's different. His pupils are giant and he just stares. I don't know what's going on with him." I nodded my head, looking down at my food. My stomach turned at the idea of him being just as bad off as me and not knowing how to cope without drugs.

"Thanks Zeke," I mumbled, getting out of the car as I slung my backpack on. I put up my hood as I walked inside the school. Right away, I felt eyes on me and noticed everyone whispering as they looked at me. Why were they all looking at me? I know I've been gone, but I don't even know who half of those people are. I rolled my eyes, ignoring it and not letting it get to me. I went to push through a crowd of people, but a girl jumped away.

"Don't touch me. Who knows what I'll catch?" She spat at me. I looked at her, shocked. What the hell was she talking about?

"What are you talking about?" I asked, my tone was hateful and annoyed. I just wasn't feeling people. She looked at her friends and they just walked away. I sighed, going to my locker, opening it, putting my backpack in, and grabbing my headphones.

"Oh my god you're back," I heard a squeal. Before I could look arms wrapped around my body squeezing me to death. Nicole was hugging me so tightly I felt like I couldn't breathe. Behind her was Gabby, Tony, and Lucas.

"Yeah, Zeke made me come," I said once she pulled away and I could breathe again. I looked at Tony and Lucas. Lucas looked away from me into a crowd of people, but Tony stepped up giving me a hug. Just as he was about to say something, he got cut off.

"Watch out Miller, you might catch something," I heard Novah snicker. I looked over at her to see Dior and Yara standing behind her. What the fuck are they going to catch from me? Depression? It wouldn't surprise me if those dumb bitches thought you could catch depression.

"Fuck off Novah, I'm not in the mood for you sluts," I my voice coming out as a low growl. They laughed as Novah took a step closer to me with arrogance.

"No? But maybe you're in the mood for the whole football team again. How did you heal up after that?" she asked me with a devilish smile.

"What the hell are you talking about?" I asked her with crossed arms. I saw my friends cringe and take a step back.

"Novah, just back off," Lucas ordered.

"I don't need your help," I snarled at him, but he just shook his head while sucking his teeth and looking up. Novah snickered as she leaned in real close to my ear.

"You fucked the whole football team at once. That's why you weren't here. They really messed you up," She smirked as she moved away. She's unbelievable.

"No one is going to believe that Novah. Are you really still mad over what I said at soccer?" I asked, but the girls just laughed at me looking at one another.

"They all believe me. The football team made a video telling everyone how easy you are," she smiled triumphantly. I felt the earth under my feet shaking and crumbling away. I couldn't believe she'd tell everyone that. Is that why everyone was staring? They can't possibly believe that, can they? The whole football team? At once?

"You're the school whore," Yara snickered, and they walked away. It was like I was frozen in a state of complete shock. I could see my friends talking to me. I could see their lips moving and see them touching me, but I didn't hear or feel anything other than my world ending.

TREY'VON

I watched her long nails trace the tattoos on my stomach as I inhaled the blunt that rested between my lips. Her curls fell into her gorgeous face as she looked at me smiling so brightly. I loved how happy she looked to be around me. I reached up tucking her hair behind her ear.

"You're so gorgeous Baby Girl," I whispered looking over her body. She wore a sexy lace bra and matching lace thong. She laid on her stomach next to me in the bed. I knew it was about to end. My trip was going down and once it knocked me out, it would take Elly with it and I wasn't ready for her to go. I wanted to take another strip to keep her here with me, but I needed sleep. If I didn't sleep, I wouldn't be sharp and anyone could take me out.

"You are too Papi," she whispered to me as she ran her nail over my lips. I nipped at it easily, making her giggle.

"This is nice. Just me and you in bed with a blunt. I could stay here all day," I told her honestly. She laughed, leaning down and kissing my lips easily, while she ran her fingers through my curls. I wrapped my arm around her waist and played with the band of her thong.

"I could too. I love being in your arms," I loved hearing that. It made me feel like the fucking man. The fact that someone as perfect as Elly wanted to be around me was still so unbelievable.

"You're going to go away soon though," I whispered with a pout. She smiled, pushing back my curls and nodding her head.

"I don't have too though. You could always take another one of those magic strips. You'd get me for another 12 hours," She tempted as she kissed my shoulder. I closed my eyes playing with her hair that no longer felt soft, but wiry. It was how I knew she was leaving faster than I expected. I started to feel reality again and that's not what I wanted to feel.

"I can't Baby Girl. I really wish I could, but I have to sleep or else someone can get an advantage on me. You don't want that do you?" I asked her. She flipped her curls over her shoulder moving to straddle my waist. She leaned down kissing me passionately, making me smile.

"Of course, I don't want that Papi. I just don't want to leave you, I always miss you too much and I know how much you miss me," she frowned. It made it so tempting to take another strip. I've never wanted to be around someone so bad or had them want to be around me.

"I never want you to leave but I have to keep myself safe," I tried to remind myself more than her. She rolled her eyes in the most Elly like way, I watched her fingers run through her hair as her eyes cast down on me.

"You really don't give a fuck about me do you Trey'von? If you cared one little ounce about me you wouldn't let me disappear," Her tone vicious. I sat up and watched her walk across the room and into my closet.

"This bitch is always trippin," I groaned, getting up and going to the doorway of the closet to see Elly standing in front of the mirror running her hands her body.

"You're really going to let all of this disappear?" she asked me, swaying her hips. I closed my eyes inhaling deeply. I didn't want to, but I had to meet with Zeke today. The last two times I'd been high and unable to focus because of her.

"I have to go with Zeke. We have things to do, and you distract me Baby Gir,l" I pleaded her, wishing this could be easier. She always made it hard when the high started wearing off.

"I won't distract you. I promise. I'll sit there like a good little girl and, if I don't, then you can punish me" she flirted, walking over to me. I bit my lip at the proposal. It was hot, I will admit that. She dropped to her knees in front of me, rubbing on my length which made my eyes close as I sucked in air.

"Baby Girl" I struggled to get her name out.

"Papi please? I'll make it worth it," she begged letting her lips connect to my boxer band. I looked down to see those innocent chocolate brown eyes looking up at me. I ran my fingers through her hair, groaning.

"Fine," I breathed out. She smiled, moving to her feet and kissing me easily.

"Go take another so I don't disappear, and I'll give you what you want," she pushed. I nodded going into the bedroom with her following me. I watched her dive on my bed looking at me. I grabbed another strip and placed it on my tongue.

"Yay! Now I get a full 24 hours with you," she cheered, throwing her hands up in the air. I sat on the bed, patting my lap. She wasted no time climbing onto my lap, grabbing my jawline.

"And I have plenty of ideas on how we can fill the next 12 hours," she told me seductively. Ok so this just might have been the best decision I made. Fuck sleep, who needed it when I have Elly right here with me?

ELEANOR

LUNCH

"Guy's stop being bitches and show me the video," I pressured my friends as we walked into the lunch line. Everyone has been looking at me, whispering, laughing. I've had a few "whores" and "sluts" thrown my way. I haven't seen anyone from the football team yet, which I was thankful for because I wanted to see the video. Nobody would show it to me. They just kept brushing me off.

"Elly, I don't think you can handle it yet. You just got back to school," Tony told me with concern. But I didn't care what he thought. I couldn't handle Trey'von ditching me after we had sex, the football team lying I can handle.

"Yes, I can. Come on I deserve to know what everyone else knows about me," I complained, following them out of the lunch line and to our old table.

"You aren't even eating. When is the last time you ate?" Nicole asked me as they all sat down. I scoffed, crossing my arms and sitting down. I'm not eating because I'm not hungry, not because of Novah and the football team.

"This morning. Zeke has been shoving food down my throat," I defended myself. This has been the most words I've spoken. I didn't feel much better at all, I was honestly just a little anxious about this video that everyone was talking about. Gabby sighed, looking at everyone else. I saw she was about to break down and show me the video.

"Gabs, I'd show it to you," I pouted my lip at her. She bit hers as well and looked up at Tony, who shook his head "no." She grabbed her phone, and I watched her swipe around. Moments later, she handed it to me with a pitiful look. I looked down to see the whole football team sitting in the locker room. I pressed play on the video sucking in a breath, holding it.

"YO, YO, YO!" Mathew the quarterback, yelled as everyone settled and calmed down behind him.

"We wanted to settle the rumors once and for all about Elly Sánchez," Mathew said as the guys behind him started to laugh and whisper jokes.

"WE FUCKED THAT HOE!" Darnell yelled. He was a running back. My jaw dropped as everyone started cheering and Mathew laughed.

"Hell yeah, we did. Whole ass train," Tommy announced from where he stood on the bench. My jaw dropped in disbelief. I couldn't even get one logical thought through the chaos going on in head.

"We even have proof. Here's the video," Mathew said and then the video switched from them to me. I was wearing sexy lingerie. I was in a dark garage sitting on a weight bench with my legs spread. I remember this, I was dating Lucas and he had taken the video. I was blacked out drunk because we went to a party and then went back to his place.

"Do you like it?" I asked seductively getting up. I laughed running my hands up my body grabbing my breasts. They muted out Lucas's voice, so you'd never know he was there.

"I bet you want to do soooo many dirty things to me," I laughed throwing my head back and letting my curls bounce. I slowly and seductively turned so you could see my butt and it was only a thin little thong. How did they even get this video? Would Lucas have given it to them? Why would he give them this video? I thought he deleted it!

"Baby, put the phone up. I want that you" I laughed my words slurring the worst they had yet. I walked over to the phone bending and down pushing my boobs together laughing.

"You like recording, don't you? Maybe I should let you record yourself fucking me," I teased backing up and moving my hips in a sexy little dance. I dipped my fingers into the band of my panties pretending to pull them down in a teasing way, laughing.

"Turn off the camera so I can feel this" I commanded, as I dropped between Lucas's legs rubbing him through his pants.

"Turn it off," I instructed as I unbuckled his pants, and then the video of myself ended. All I could do was stare in shock. That video was private, and Lucas had promised that he deleted it. Why would he give to Mathew or Novah?

"There's your proof. Elly Sánchez is a whore" Mathew proclaimed as the video ended. I was in complete utter shock. My mind was blank. I felt frozen. I no longer heard the noise of the lunchroom or my friends. It was just nothing.

"ELLY!" Tony yelled, shaking my shoulder breaking me from my state. I gasped for my breath. I hadn't even realized I stopped breathing. Lucas had given Mathew that video knowing what they were going to do with it. First Theo, and now this video. I felt a different type of anger rising. It made my whole body so hot I felt like I was sweating. My body shook, my mouth was so dry it felt like I could choke, but I kept my jaw locked. I wanted to hurt him. I wanted to scream and cause a scene.

"Elly, you look angry, try to breath normal. Maybe it will help you calm down," Gabby voice shook with fear. I hadn't even realized how hard my breathing was until she had said that. I looked across the lunchroom to see Lucas sitting with the baseball team and Novah right next to him.

"I'm going to get him fucking killed," I said between clenched teeth as I stared at him. Lil Smiley walked up to the table smiling as usual. I got up and stormed over to Lucas's table without even saying anything else to my friends.

"HOW THE FUCK COULD YOU GIVE THEM THAT VIDEO AND LET THEM USE IT TO STAY I FUCKED THE FOOTBALL TEAM? YOU WERE SUPPOSED TO DELETE IT LUCAS!" I screamed as I neared his table. The whole lunchroom fell silent and their eyes were drawn me. I didn't care.

"FUCK YOU! YOU KNOW I WAS FUCKING DRUNK WHEN YOU TOOK THAT VIDEO. YOU'RE A BITCH ASS LIAR AND I PROMISE ON EVERYTHING I LOVE YOU WILL REGRET THIS!" I screamed. I grabbed his milk and poured it over his head, making his whole table gasp.

"Elles---" I cut him off by picking up his lunch tray and slinging the food on him and his lettermen jacket and then threw the Styrofoam tray at him. He stood up looking down at his clothes in shock and then to me.

"WHAT THE FUCK IS YOUR PROBLEM?" Lucas yelled at me. Before it even registered in my head what I was doing my fist connected to his jaw. I hit him so hard I felt the ache in my knuckles. Before he could even snap his head back to face me, arms wrapped around me and pulled me back.

"Elly calm down, what's going on?" I heard Smiley whisper in my ear, but I jerked out of his arms glaring at Lucas who stared at me stunned.

"You think what we did to Theo and his buddies was bad. It's nothing compared to what the Los Prophets are going to do to you. That was just Trip, I'm like a daughter to Zeke. I promise you Los Prophets will be at your door. FUCK YOU LUCAS!" I yelled as Smiley tried to pull me away from Lucas. I spit at Lucas just as Smiley was able to make me move. I shoved Smiley off, storming out of the lunchroom away from everyone's eyes. The minute I hit the hall I felt wet tears falling down my cheeks.

"ELLY, WAIT UP WHAT'S GOING ON?" Lil Smiley yelled, running out after me. I stopped wiping my tears and let him catch up to me.

"I need to leave Smiley. Novah and Lucas gave a video of me drunk to the football team. It was from when me and Lucas was dating, and I wanted to have sex with him. He recorded it. The football team told everyone they had a turn with me. I thought Lucas deleted that video forever ago. I need to leave now and talk to Zeke," I told him. He nodded his head grabbing my hood and put it up, hiding me from wondering eyes.

"I'll call Trip," he said, pulling out his phone. I couldn't handle seeing him right now, not with everything else, so I grabbed Smiley's wrist.

"Call Lil Ugly, I can't handle Trip right now," I pleaded, he nodded his head. He walked me to my locker so I could get my things as he talked to Lil Ugly. I had Gabby send me the video so I could show it to Zeke.

"He's on his way, lets go" Lil Smiley commanded. We walked out of the school together and not even 5 minutes later, Lil Ugly pulled up. We got in the car and he pulled out before any of the teachers had a chance to stop us. I was quiet the entire ride. I just sat in the backseat letting tears silently stream down my face while Smiley filled Lil Ugly in. Once we got to Zeke's, I grabbed my backpack and practically ran inside.

"ZEKE!" I screamed, dropping my bag. Zeke came out of the kitchen with wide frantic eyes. I ran straight over to him, hugging him, and hiding my face in his chest, sobbing. He hugged me and played with my braid trying to calm me down.

"Lucas gave Novah a video of me drunk trying to suck his dick," I hiccupped, still crying into him. Zeke pulled away looking at me with wide eyes. He leaned down wiping my tears.

"Now the football team has it and they're telling everyone I had sex with all of them and that the video is proof. I'm the school slut and I didn't do it. That video was from when me and Lucas was dating. He told me he deleted it," I cried. Zeke hugged me I could feel him mouthing something to Smiley and Ugly.

"Princesa, it's going to be ok. I'm going to take care of Lucas, who's Novah?" he asked. I pulled away, going to the couch, kicking off my shoes and I brought my knees into my chest hiding my face in them, crying.

"She's this popular girl. We've never gotten along and one day at soccer I called her on her shit, and she said she was going to make my life miserable and then this happened. The whole school has seen the video," I cried as Zeke sat next to me, rubbing my back.

"What are you doing about it?" Zeke barked at Smiley.

"I don't know. I'm not good at this, I haven't even told Trip yet," he told Zeke, which only panicked me more.

"NO DON'T TELL HIM! What if he believes it?" I cried. Zeke leaned over kissing my head.

"Let me see the video Princesa," he urged. I pulled out my phone bringing up the video and playing it for him. He dismissed Smiley and Ugly. We sat on the couch and talked about Novah, Lucas, the football team, and the video. He promised me he'd take care of it and I shouldn't worry anymore. Zeke spent the next couple hours with me and then told me he was going to go handle business and left me home alone with my thoughts.

Chapter 21

Breaking Point

TREY'VON

I woke up to my doorbell ringing. I huffed, rolling over and burying my face in my pillows trying to ignore it. If it's important they'll come back later. Just as I was about to fall back asleep, my doorbell started going off rapidly. I groaned loudly, throwing my blanket off. I tugged on a pair of sweats and grabbed my gun. Whoever is at my door I'm fucking shooting them. I haven't slept into two days and when I finally let my high come down to sleep, I get woken up. I stormed downstairs to hear someone banging on the door as they rang the doorbell. I stomped across the foyer, ripped open the front door and pointed my gun at whoever it was. I saw Smiley looking at me with wide eyes, his hands were up.

"FUCK! Why the hell are you beating the shit out of my door?" I spat, lowering my gun and putting it in the band of my sweats as I sent him a glare when he walked into my house.

"Because I've been up all night feeling guilty. I feel like I'm betraying you and you're my best friend. I wouldn't do that so I have to go against Zeke, but I know I shouldn't do that either," he rambled so fast my sleep-deprived brain almost couldn't keep up. Best friend? I am not that kid's "friend" he just hangs around and gets on my damn nerves. Betraying me? And Zeke? What the hell is going on?

"Smiley, slow down. What's going on? Come into the kitchen with me." I waved him to follow me. I don't remember the last time I had eaten or drank anything, and my mouth was dry. He followed me into the kitchen where I grabbed a bottle of water, downing half of it. I looked over at him as I sat the bottle down.

"Ok, what are you rambling about? Why are you betraying me and Zeke?" I asked as he sat down at the island. I watched him groan as he hid his face in his arms and then looked up at me with stressed eyes.

"It's Elly and I don't know what to do. I can't do this whole babysitting thing. You were good at it and I'm not. I couldn't even get her out of bed when she refused to leave it for 5 days," He explained. I cringed at his words. He had told me about Elly refusing to get out of bed and just laying there crying. When I asked Zeke how she was, he brushed me off without telling me anything. I wanted to go check on her, but I knew it was over me, and I didn't want to make it worse.

"Is she still in bed? Offer to take her to get sushi, she loves sushi," I suggested with a shrug. The amusement in his eyes was undeniable.

"I can't believe you out of all people remember that, but no she's out of bed. She went to school yesterday, but this girl Novah started this rumor that she had sex with the whole football team--," I cut him off right there. Elly would never do something like that, and I wouldn't entertain that idea of her.

"She wouldn't do that. You don't know Elly the way I do. She's not just gonna give herself to anyone," I snapped. Even if I wasn't around her, she was still my girl and I was going to handle that Novah bitch. I just didn't want him going around spreading that rumor when Elly would never.

"I know, but she didn't but listen to me! That Novah girl and the football team started spreading that rumor around. There is a video going around so everyone thinks she's the school slut. I guess the video they used came from that Lucas kid. She told me she was drunk, and they were dating when the video was taken but he told her he deleted it and didn't. She exploded on him in front of the whole lunchroom and literally threatened his life. I don't know what to do," he told me as my eyes grew wide. Elly exploded in front of the lunchroom on someone? Fuck yeah! That's my muhfuckin girl, lettin know she aint for it. Then she threatened him? Man, she did learn something from being around me and I'd make sure the threats were carried out. I wanted to be mad over the video, but I didn't know how bad it was and it didn't shock me he did some fuck shit like that.

"Let me see the video. I don't know how angry to get and what was her threats? I'll make sure they are carried out." I waved for him to show me the video. He sighed, getting on his phone tapping around.

"She said if you think what we did to Theo is bad, what will happen to you will be worse. That Los Prophets was going to show up at his door," Smiley informed me. I smirked as ideas formed in my head, from burning down his house to terrorizing his family. If Elly was mad enough to threaten someone it was a big deal to her, so I'd take care of it for her. Smiley handed me the phone and I pressed play. I watched the video in pure shock. It was so foreign to hear the dirty words coming from Elly's mouth. They were sexy and I loved hearing them slip through her accented voice. I couldn't help but be jealous. She didn't talk like that to me when we were in bed. I knew it happened so fast and we both did the best we could but damn, I want that. Then she looked sexy, so fucking sexy. I realized mid-way through the video that her whole school had seen this because of that fuck, Lucas. I felt that rage boiling over. No one other than me should see Elly like this, and he was going to pay for it.

My vision was blurring in and out. My hearing was almost gone. I was shaking and I knew if I didn't put down Smiley's phone I'd throw it, so I dropped in onto the counter. I gripped the edge of the counter while my head spun with thoughts. If I didn't dip out like I did none of this would be happening, right? I could have put a stop to it before it got out of hand. How was she coping with all of this? Should I go check on her or would it make it worse?

"I'm gonna kill him. That's my fucking girl, we might be going through it but she's mine and I'm gonna fuck him up," I told Smiley, looking up at him. I couldn't help but laugh at the idea of all of the things I was going to do to that kid.

ELEANOR

I watched as we pulled up to the school. I slunk farther into my seat looking over at Zeke who gripped the wheel so tightly his knuckles were turning white. He was pissed, not at me, but at Lucas, Novah, and the football team. I knew they'd get what was coming to them, especially Lucas. I didn't know what Zeke was going to do, but I didn't know if I really wanted to. Zeke turned to say something to me just as we got stuck in the carpool lane. He was cut off by his car phone ringing, he sighed, pressing the button on his steering wheel, answering it.

"Zeke Santiago," He answered. There was heavy breathing and then a crash of stuff, making me jump in my seat.

"WHAT THE HELL IS YOUR PROBLEM ZEKE? WHY DIDN'T YOU TELL ME PEOPLE WERE FUCKING WITH HER? WHY WAS SMILEY TOLD TO LEAVE ME OUT OF IT? THAT'S BULLSHIT! YOU KNOW THAT NO ONE CARES ABOUT HER MORE THAN ME!" Trey'von's angry, yet velvet voice, screamed through the car. Smiley told him about the rumor. Did he believe it? I felt like the breath was knocked out of my body. Trey'von didn't care about me he just wanted to feel like he could control me. I felt frozen in my seat. I stared at the screen that had his name rolling across it. Why would he say he cared about me when he clearly didn't give a shit about me? I felt the tears well up in my eyes and before I could stop them, they were rolling down my cheeks. I opened my door and ripped out my backpack.

"ELLY, WAIT---!" I cut Zeke off by slamming the door shut. I turned, running up the path and into the school. I was getting looks, but I didn't care about them. It had been almost two weeks since I heard his voice. I've craved the sound of those soft, velvet words falling from his lips but the moment I do, he's spitting out some bullshit lie about him caring about me. If he cared, he'd be here. I couldn't handle this right now. I saw Gabby at the locker pushing her things in. I walked over quickly to her, pulling my hood up. She looked over with a concerned gaze as the sobs shook through my body.

"Honey what's wrong?" Gabby asked, taking me into her arms right away. I hid my face in her neck hugging her tightly. I felt another hand land on my back rubbing it.

"What's wrong Elly?" Tony asked me. My legs shook but I kept myself up-right for the moment.

"Trip--," It was all I could get out. I felt Gabby sigh, but she didn't say anything, she just hugged me. I felt a weight on my back squeezing me against Gabby and I knew it was Tony.

"What did he do now? I thought you guys weren't talking?" Tony asked, but my sobs just grew worse. We weren't talking and his lie was just bouncing around in my head.

"You know that no one cares about her more than me." He didn't care though, that was the thing that hurt the most.

Gabby pulled away grabbing my face forcing me to look into her eyes.

"Come on, let's go to the bathroom," she said, and I nodded, wiping my face. I sent Tony a smile as Gabby grabbed my arm and pulled me through the hall. Hiccups fell from my lips as tears continued to stream down my face. She pulled me into the bathroom, checking all the stalls making sure we were alone. I walked over to the mirror, above the sink Gabby's books were in, looking at myself. I looked just like I had, pale, swollen red eyes, nappy hair, the dirt finding its way back from my lack of showering. I hated looking at my body. I couldn't help but wonder what was wrong with me. I had reclaimed my baggy sweats and sweatshirts. Zeke's method to pretend just wasn't the move today, maybe tomorrow.

"What did this dumb ass do now?" Gabby asked. I closed my eyes, as tears slipped from my eyes. I was so tired of crying over him, but yet here I was crying again, and I knew it would be an all day and night thing now that I had started.

"He called Zeke while I was in the car--," I stopped as another sob ripped through my lungs. Gabby came over, hugging me and waiting for me to be able to explain to her what was happening.

"He told Zeke no one cares about me as much as he does, but Gabby..." I stopped shaking my head as the sobs ripped out hard. My body fell numb and the next thing I knew, we were tumbling to the floor. I heard her sniffle into my shoulder. I knew she hated seeing me like this, but I couldn't help it.

"I care about you way more than he does. I'm the one picking up the pieces," Gabby sniffled into my shoulder. I squeezed her tighter, crying harder.

"He doesn't care, that's the problem. If he did, he'd be here with me" I cried. I knew he wouldn't be at school with me but with me, in general. He wouldn't have dipped out right after he got what he wanted.

"Fuck him, Elly. He doesn't give a shit about you. You don't need him, I got you," Gabby promised, pulling away and wiping my tears. I shook my head "no," hiding my face in my hands.

"I miss him though. I want to be around him. I miss the little things like just sitting in his car smoking. I can't even look at my body without feeling disgusted by myself. I don't know what I did wrong," I sobbed. Gabby pulled me into another hug, trying her best to comfort me.

"Don't say that Elly! You're fucking sexy, everyone thinks so. You have the most attractive body, your personality is the best, you have the most gorgeous face. You are so perfect. I love you Elly, don't say things like that. Just forget about him please," Gabby practically begged, but how was I supposed to just forget about someone who gives me such a rush like he does. No one would understand that part of our relationship. It was the most addictive part of it.

"Oh, what's this? I knew you two were girlfriends?" I heard the high-pitched voice that I could go the rest of my life without hearing. Novah. Following her voice were hyena-like laughs which made me cringe. I pulled out of Gabby's shoulder, dabbing away my tears trying to pull myself together, so I didn't look weak in front of Novah. Of course, the dramatic gasps from trying to stop sobbing wasn't helping my case.

"Don't you have something better to do? Buy a soul? Convince someone of murder or to eat a forbidden fruit?" Gabby bickered back. I stood up going over to the mirror, wiping away my remaining tears and getting my breathing under control. I cleared my throat trying to hide any tears that might have been in my voice.

"Let's go Gabby. She has the same insults as an eight-year-old, anyways," I mumbled grabbing Gabby's books and looking down at my shoes. Gabby rolled her eyes but nodded. Just as I went to step past Novah, she shoved me back, making me drop the books. I looked up at her with a glare. I wasn't in any mood for Novah, and I didn't think I'll be able to just turn a cheek this time.

"Novah, I'm not in the mood. Get out of my way" I snapped. She looked at me like she was amused. I listened to her cackling laugh as her hyena minions copied her.

"No one is scared of you. Just fuck off" I spat as I tried to walk around her again, but she shoved me back. As I stumbled, off balance, I stepped on a notebook which slid from under me as my ankle twisted. I went flying back, smacking my back on the hard tile. I groaned, squeezing my eyes closed as nothing but pain passed through me.

"FUCK YOU NOVAH. ELLY MIGHT NOT FIGHT YOU BUT I WILL!" I heard Gabby yell as I groaned, rolling over onto my stomach and bringing my knee to my chest as I grabbed my throbbing ankle.

"GET OFF ME!" Gabby screamed, but I was in too much pain to even look to see what was going on.

"You're a dirty whore, Sánchez. I mean look at you, you're supposed to be surrounded by these big bad gangsters that scare everyone, but you won't even fight back. You're just their toy. Thankfully, Luke figured out how big of a slut you really are," Novah growled as her pointed toe heel dug into my ribs as she kicked me, making me fall over onto my side.

"Come on girls, I'm done in here," Novah laughed, and I heard her heels click out of the bathroom.

"Elly are you ok?" Gabby asked me, coming over to my side looking at me.

"My fucking ankle," I groaned. I knew it was messed up and if I actually cared about soccer right now, I'd be pissed.

"Come on, let's go to the nurse," she said, helping me up. I tried to put weight on my ankle, but it collapsed under me. Gabby quickly grabbed me. I held onto the sink while she gathered her things and then helped me to the nurse. This would be the last time Novah Yates, and her minions ran over me and that was a fucking promise.

PRACTICE

I sat on the bench watching all girl's practice. The nurse said my ankle had a slight sprain which would work itself out within a week, but I shouldn't do anything to strain it like soccer. So, I had to miss this week's game. I didn't have a bruise on my ribs or back, thankfully. You couldn't even tell that Novah did anything to me. Things were going to be different. She's right, I do surround myself with the most feared people in the city. I needed to act like it, and I would.

"Sucks that you tripped in the bathroom," Novah snickered running past me. I glared at her, shaking my head. I wanted to fight her so bad, but I didn't have the first idea how to fight.

"BRING IT IN!" Coach yelled. I stood up, limping over to her. All the girls ran over making a circle around our coach.

"Good practice, hit the showers and change," Coach said and we broke apart. I walked over, snatching up my duffel and backpack as I stormed off the field. I limped down the walkway to the parking lot. I found Zeke's car sitting where Trey'von used to wait for me. I pushed away the memory as I stormed over and got into his car. He looked over at me, his smile falling when he saw my face.

"What's wrong?" he asked stiffly. Well, I don't have a poker face.

"I want you to teach me how to fight, Zeke," I told him seriously. I crossed my arms as his face contorted in surprise and question.

"Why? Since when do you want to know that?" He asked, shocked. I looked away a little ashamed to admit it, but Novah did get the best of me today. It would be the last time.

"It's Novah. I'm so tired of her and her minions messing with me. She's been doing it since grade school and I'm done," I told Zeke. He looked shocked but still concerned.

"This morning I was in the bathroom with Gabby when Novah came in starting her usual crap. I started to leave, and she pushed me. Then we argued and she pushed me again. I tripped over Gabby's books and when I fell, I twisted my ankle. It's just a sprain, but when I was down, she kicked me. I need to learn how to fight." I watched the surprise fall from his face and turn into hard anger. He nodded his head, running his hand over his face.

"Ok, Princesa. I have a quick thing to take care of and then we're going to gym." I couldn't stop the smile from spreading across my face. I was excited to learn how to fight and to have Zeke teach me. Novah wouldn't ever mess with me again, and that was a promise I intended to keep.

TREY'VON

""Ahhh, someone please help me. He's crazy." SHUT UP BITCH, NO ONE IS COMING TO FUCKING HELP YOU!" I yelled at the lady tied to a chair in front of me. She was gagged, but it didn't stop her from trying to scream. Zeke sent me a look of disapproval, but I just shrugged. I don't know why I'm getting looks when he hit the stupid bitch. We were currently sitting in in the dining room of Lucas's house with his mom tied up. Zeke smacked her a few times to get her under control. Her eye was already swelling and turning black. Her lip was busted but I figured it would scare the kid when he walked in. I swirled my finger around the trigger to my gun as it laid on the table next to me.

"You're a dick sometimes," Zeke reminded me, but I just shrugged.

"You hit her," I countered carelessly. The lady, I assumed to be Lucas's mom, looked between Zeke and I frantically. I smirked, leaning forward and pressing my gun against her temple which made her scream. I laughed, watching her struggle under the restraints.

"Boom!" I mocked, laughing as I pulled away. I saw Zeke giving me a look as he shook his head, but I thought it was funny watching the stupid bitch struggle.

"You know why we're here right now?" I asked her, leaning forward with a wicked smirk. She muffled something I couldn't understand, so I ripped her gag out.

"Theo," she answered, but I just shook my head no.

"Nope, Lucas," I told her. She looked at me with wide eyes still pulling on her restraints. I saw her about to scream, but I pushed my gun into her ribs.

"That would be a mistake mama," I warned. She took a deep breath, looking at me nodding her head so I lowered my gun.

"Luke is an amazing kid. What you think he did, he didn't do," she told me, but I just nodded my head.

"Oh, but he did. So, my Baby Girl used to date him, and she likes to drink when she parties," I explained. Honestly, I didn't even care if Zeke picked up on the fact that I had real feelings for Elly. Let him kill me. It'll be easier than living without her for the rest of my life.

"I guess alcohol makes her horny. I wouldn't have guessed that about her, but your son knew that and recorded it," I told her. Her eyes grew wide with a horrified look. I nodded my head as Zeke huffed out.

"Can you just shut the fuck up?" Zeke spat at me. I glanced at him and then back to Lucas's mom.

"Zeke, I'm pissed at you the way it is. Leave me the hell alone," I growled. I used my gun to push hair out of the mom's face, smirking at her.

"He wouldn't have recorded himself doing that," she rejected the idea which only made me laugh.

"He wasn't fucking her. You wouldn't be alive right now if I seen that, it was just her really wanting it. Then he gave that video to the football team so they could say they all had turned her out. You want to see the video?" I asked, pulling my phone out. I brought up the video, pressed play, as I held it up. She tried to look away, but I grabbed her hair wrapping it around my fist and forcing her to watch it. She started sobbing as she watched it. Once the video ended, I let go of her hair and sat back down.

"You about done?" Zeke asked, eyeing me. I sent him a glare telling him to shut the fuck up. I was letting off steam. I couldn't even look at another female to let out steam that way, so being a little more violent was gonna do the trick.

"I can't believe he'd do that to Elly. He loves her," she cried. But I shook my head "no." I felt my blood boil at the idea of another man even caring for her. She was mine. No one would ever have her the way I have her. I mean hell, we weren't even speaking and I'm about to burn this whole house down for her. I put the gag back in her mouth.

"You need to find a bitch or something, damn. You been a dick lately," Zeke spat at me. I just shrugged once again. I didn't want any other female.

I knew they wouldn't be like Elly. They wouldn't make me feel that bliss. They wouldn't be near as good. They wouldn't matter like she does.

"MOM, I'M HOME!" I heard Lucas yell. I held up my gun pointing it at the mom making her stay silent.

"MOM!" I heard him yell again. I looked at Zeke, who shared my murderous grin.

"IN HERE SON!" Zeke called out. I heard him fall silent, moments later he walked into the dining room to find his mom, me, and Zeke. I watched as fear took over his face, his skin paling as his eyes grew wide. The mom screamed staring at her son. I grabbed her hair, yanking her back.

"Bitch, I told you not to scream!" I snapped as I sent her a glare. Right away, she shut the fuck up.

"Get off my mom!" Lucas demanded. I looked at him amused. I got up wrapped an arm around his mom and pressed my gun to her throat.

"What, you don't like this, Lucas? " I asked him with a sneer. He sent me a glare, taking a step closer. I pulled back the hammer, smirking at him as I pressed the gun harder against her flesh.

"Lucas Bow. I used to really like you kid. You were going places, you seemed so right for Elly and now I can't seem to find a reason to stop Trip from killing you all," Zeke told him, but I just scoffed. He's not good enough for Elly, he never was.

"Just know he can't stop me, and he won't. Mama Bear, so sad your pussy ass son drug you into this," I taunted. I already had a plan about how I was going to do this. Neither of them were dying...today. I was going to take out everything around Lucas that he loved. I was going to start with this shitty house and then I was going to take away the baseball career, then his pops, his mom, and then him. It was going to be slow, but he'd know I was coming. I pushed away from the mom leaning against the table, looking at him.

"You're here over the video, aren't you?" he asked, looking between the two of us. Zeke threw his head back in a mocking belly laugh, making me smirk.

"Oh, so you're smarter than I thought," Zeke mocked. I looked at the mom again who was crying...again. Her eyes were swollen, one from a black eye but mainly from crying. Her hair was ratted up in the nastiest way. Her face red from fear. She looked disgusting, like a slob. I rolled my eyes, pulling a blunt from my pants pocket.

"I didn't think you and Elly were talking right now?" Lucas asked me, as I put the perfectly rolled drug between my lips, lighting it.

"You don't get to ask questions. HAVE A FUCKING SEAT, LUCAS!" Zeke yelled, slamming a chair down next to the mom. I smirked as Lucas looked at me and Zeke, then right back at me. I motioned to the chair. He slowly sat down. I got up walking over, hitting him in the face with my gun which made the mom scream.

"Look at what you're doing to her. She would never have let this happen before," Lucas spat at me. I laughed at him, hitting him again. Elly needed to be stronger. She needed to harden up because then shit like this wouldn't happen. She lets people walk all over her and it gets out of hand like this.

"I like this version of her. You really thought she wouldn't tell us didn't you?" I asked blowing smoke at him. Suddenly a fist connected to his jaw so hard it sent the chair flying back, breaking.

"DAMN" I yelled, laughing as Zeke just started beating his ass. I laughed as I turned mom's chair, spinning it so she had to see it. She screamed, trying to look away but I grabbed her face, forcing her to watch.

"BEAT HIS ASS ZEKE!" I cheered laughing as his mom thrashed around screaming. Zeke backed off, looking at me nodding. I let go of the mom and pulled out my cell phone about to call Julio, Guzman, Loco, and Joker. Just as I looked up to ask Zeke something I saw Lucas punch him in the jaw. My eyes grew wide as Zeke stumbled back, dropping his gun. Lucas hit Zeke with a two piece in the ribs before he could recover.

"Aw hell naw," I said pushing the mom out of my way. Zeke hit Lucas with a clean two piece and an upper cut before I could even cross the room. The moment I was in arm's length, I hit Lucas with a right hook grabbing his head slamming it into the table. Blood splattered from his forehead, and he melted to the ground. Right away I started stomping on his head, as Zeke kicked him. After a couple minutes of our brutal attack, Zeke grabbed me pulling me back.

"You good?" I asked him, and he nodded his head as he wiped his bloody lip.

"You remember what I told you about Snitch's momma?" I asked her, texting the four that it was time. Before she could answer Julio, Guzman, Loco, and Joker came in pouring gasoline all over the house. She nodded quickly with wide scared eyes as Lucas groaned trying to get up, but Zeke kicked him again. Once they finished pouring the gas, I cut the mom free ripping the gag out of her mouth.

"LIGHT THIS BITCH UP!" I yelled as Zeke, and I walked out of the back door to our cars that were parked in the alley.

Chapter 22

Explosive

ELEANOR

A WEEK LATER

I pulled back the shower curtain letting the freezing cold air wash over my body. I shivered as I grabbed a towel and dried off by wrapping it around my body and I wrapped another around my hair. For the first time in weeks, I actually shaved and took a proper shower. I decided to take Zeke's advice. Pretending I'm ok until I believe I am. It was clear Trey'von was fine, and I was the only one crying in bed over us every night. It was hard to realize it, but he posted on Snapchat for the first time since I added him before any of this happened. I spent all night crying and just rewatching his story and listening to his laugh. He looked so amazing in every snap. Not sad or anything. The first video was a loop video of him in his car. He stuck out his tongue in that attractive Trey'von way as he held up the Prophet symbol with his right hand.

Next was a video of him and Smiley at Walmart. The video began with Trey'von smiling a small smile. Then he laughed that beautiful laugh, the one I missed so much. The video was pretty much of him and Smiley bickering back and forth about Smiley jumping into the ball cage. Of course, being the kid he is, Smiley did it and the video ended with Trey'von running off. The last snap was a loop video of him again, this time he was in front of a mirror at a house party showing off those amazing tattoos covered abs. He had it captioned with a broken heart emoji. So I decided I was done letting myself be sad. I was going to fake it until I made it.

I grabbed my blow drier from my bag filled with hair and makeup products. I styled my curls. I put them in their bouncy healthy state. Once I finished my hair and approved, I grabbed my lip scrub and scrubbed away all the dead, flaky, hardened skin. I did my usual makeup, but I did spend a little more time covering the black circles around my eyes from crying so much. I gave myself a glowing look, so I didn't look pale anymore. Once I looked like me again, I glanced over at my outfit, biting my lip. I pulled on a thong, tight red high-waist leather pants, and a matching red leather bandeau. I paired it with a pair of huge red hoops, and black strappy heels.

Once I was dressed, I stepped back looking in the mirror. I knew I looked like the old me, but I didn't feel the same about what I saw staring back at me. I couldn't stop myself from pinching the skin on my stomach. I was fat, no wonder he disappeared. I'm disgusting. My boobs are actually kinda small. I did like their size but maybe that was another problem. My hips were too big, and my thighs were fat and gross. I turned, looking at my butt, it was big, and I always loved it but maybe it was too big or not big enough. My face wasn't any better. My nose was huge, my forehead was too small, and my eyes were buggy. I couldn't blame him for dipping because I would have too. I looked away from the mirror before I could cry. I cleaned up my mess and went to my bedroom. I tossed my things on the bed, grabbed my backpack, and went downstairs to find Zeke setting breakfast on the table. He looked up at me his eyes growing wide and his smile growing even bigger.

"You look like you Princesa," he said, overjoyed. I smiled nodding my head and looking at the food. My stomach flopped around at the idea, I was feeling too fat to eat.

"I took your advice. Pretend to be ok and I will be ok, but I'm not ready to eat yet. I kinda feel gross about myself today," I admitted looking away from the food back over to Zeke. He just stared at me with a lit-up face and goofy smile making, me laugh.

"That's fine. One step at a time, Princesa ugh. It's so good to see you in real clothes and showered, AND MAKEUP" he yelled, making me laugh and shake my head.

"One picture Princesa just to mark the beginning of new," He asked, but I shook my head no.

"I'll eat breakfast instead," I negotiated.

"Aht aht picture," he said pulling out his camera. I groaned, looking at him smiling a non-convincing smile, but he still took the picture.

"Can we just go to school?" I asked. He nodded snatching up his keys. I bit my lip looking at the keys and back up to Zeke.

"Can I drive? I have my permit and I logged all my hours with Mad Max before I left for Colombia and he bit a bullet," I asked Zeke, giving him the puppy dog look I knew he'd give in to. He smiled, tossing me the keys which made me cheer.

"Give me the phone," He ordered, and I handed it to him. We walked out getting into the G-Wagon. I adjusted my mirrors, buckled up and made sure Zeke was too and then pulled out. The ride to school was quiet, aside from Zeke's backseat driving.

This last week hasn't been any easier either. Trey'von and Zeke terrorized Lucas's mom and burned down their house. Zeke has the fire department on the books, so they didn't even respond to the fire. Most of the football team had gotten scared and told everyone they were lying, but, either way, I was still the school whore. I quit soccer. Zeke was upset at first, but he understood why. My ankle was hurt, I was missing games, so I just quit. I have been going to the gym and Zeke has been teaching me how to box. Novah's laid off too. After the whole thing with Lucas's house, I think she got spooked, thankfully.

Once we got to school in the carpool lane, I looked over at Zeke who clapped, making me laugh and shake my head.

"I won't be able to pick you up after school. I'm leaving town for the night but someone will be here," he said as I slowly pulled forward. I actually wanted to go home today, just for a little. I missed my sisters, mom, and dad. I wanted to see them.

"Actually, I want to go home for a little bit. I'll just take the bus home. I miss my sisters. If I decide to stay, I'll just text you and let you know," I told him. He looked at me raising an eyebrow, but just nodded his head.

275

"Ok, I'll let your mother know," he said as I pulled up to the drop off point. I smiled, putting the car in park and leaning over to kiss his cheek.

"Thanks Zeke. Love you," I said getting out of the car as he followed my actions. He yelled a "have a good day" while I walked into the school to became the most talked about whore for the next 7 hours.

LAST CLASS

I sat in the back of class looking down at my phone rewatching Trey'von's story before it disappeared. It was taking everything in me not to cry, but I just needed to watch it. I needed to hear his voice.

"Miss. Sánchez?" I heard my teacher call just as tears had started to form. I quickly closed out Snapchat and looked up with wide eyes. Everyone was looking at me, so I blinked away my tears clearing my throat.

"Yes Mr. S?" I asked, as he hung up the phone on his desk.

"Your older sister will be picking you and Mateo up," he told me. Izzy never picked us up, unless we had to stay after school for something. Why would she now, instead of making us take the bus? My face must have shown the confusion because Mr. S looked concerned as well.

"Is that ok?" he asked, and I nodded my head "yes," sinking back into my seat for the rest of the class, I sat back in boredom, waiting for the bell to ring. After what felt like forever, the bell finally rang signaling the day was over. I let out a breath of relief, grabbing my books as I walked out of class.

"We're still dress shopping tomorrow, right?" Gabby asked as soon as I came to my locker. I nodded my head as I grabbed my backpack and shoved my homework into it.

"Yeah. Me, you, Nicole, and Tony. I'll meet you at your house and we'll go from there. I'm going home tonight," I told her, and she smiled at me nodding her head happily.

"Izzy's waiting on me. I'll text you later," I waved. She nodded as I walked away. I walked through the school out to the parking lot. I saw Izzy's tan Honda sitting there waiting. I went over and got in the passenger seat. Mateo hadn't made it out yet.

"I missed you," Izzy squealed, hugging me.

"I did too. I was going through it, girl," I laughed off my pain. My door ripped open, and arms wrapped around me. I smiled, hugging Mateo back and rubbing her hair.

"I'm so happy you look like you again. I was so worried," she whispered. I buried my face in her shoulder, fighting off my tears.

"Get in the car. Let's go home," I whispered. She pulled away and got in the car. Izzy pulled out and they just began overloading me with how things have been at the house for the last couple of weeks. I tried to listen, but my brain was still off in its own world, so I just pretended by nodding and adding a few 'yeahs." It didn't take us long to get home and for Izzy to pull up front of the house. I got out, grabbing my backpack and putting it on my shoulder as I looked over at the bar out of habit, but I saw the car. The shiny black Audi that plunged into my dreams like a plague. I felt frozen for a second, knowing he was right inside the bar. My shock was replaced by anger faster than it ever had been before. He can hang out at a fucking bar but can't even send me a text message.

Before I had even really caught up to myself, I was dropping my backpack to the ground and storming down to the bar, ignoring the yells that came from my sisters to come back. I got looks from some of the surrounding gangsters as I pushed open the door hard, making it hit the wall with a bang. What I saw was enough to crumple me to the floor if it wasn't for the anger pumping through my veins which was keeping me strong. There sat Trey'von with a girl on his lap, his arm was securely around her waist as he held a bottle of water looking at Lil Smiley. She was gorgeous. Long brown straight hair that had blonde highlights and sandy skin. She was thin, unlike me. Her thighs didn't touch, her stomach sank in, in what I thought was unattractive, but maybe it wasn't. She leaned into him smiling and it was enough push me over the edge. That bitch shouldn't be on his lap. He was supposed to be mine.

"YOU'RE A FUCKING LIAR!" I yelled, storming over to him. His head snapped up. I watched those deep dark brown nearly black eyes grow wide as he looked at the girl on his lap and then back to me. The girl looked at me shocked as well. I felt my body shaking from anger as my hands balled into fists.

"GET THE FUCK OFF HIM, SLUT!" I screamed at the girl. Trey'von looked at me with that cocky, overconfident smirk and tightened his arm around her bring his other arm to follow. It was a deadly action. One I didn't know could hurt this bad.

"What if I don't want her to get up? What you gonna do about it, *Baby Girl?*" Trey'von snickered the Baby Girl part as the whole bar fell silent, staring at us. I sent him a glare and then burst into laughter. Without hesitation or warning, I reached down and grabbed his gun from his pants. I cocked back the hammer, holding it up to the girl's head which made her scream.

"GET THE FUCK OFF HIM!" I yelled at her again, but Trey'von just laughed leaning back in his chair. Would I really shoot this girl? No, of course not. I'm not a murderer, I just needed her off him. I couldn't stand to look at it.

TREY'VON

I couldn't believe she was standing right here in front of me even without an acid tab. God himself has no idea how amazing it is to hear that accented yell, to see the angry fire behind those chocolate brown eyes. Her curls bounced with each enraged movement she made. It was like watching a goddess. Those plump lips I was dying to taste as they parted in anger. Then that fucking outfit it pissed me off that everyone was looking at her dressed like but fuck, she looked good. She wore tight fitting red leather pants. They didn't compliment her as well as the black ones, but these were nice. Then she wore a red leather boob holder top which was tight and squeezing her tits together. That flat stomach was on view, those wide sexy hips were out for everyone to see. I knew that ass had to look crazy.

Then don't even get me started on her holding that gun to this random hoe in my lap. I didn't give a fuck about the girl. I was just trying to move on since she had. I wasn't really going to sleep with the girl. Every time I thought about it, I thought about Elly and I just can't bring myself to do it. Just seeing the jealousy in Elly's eyes, watching her shake from anger with the gun in her hand. I felt my jeans tightening and I know this bitch did too.

"Go ahead Baby Girl, shoot her. This whole jealousy look is kinda hot," I mocked Elly. I knew that girl better than I knew myself and she wasn't a murderer. She looked at me, shocked as the bitch on my lap whimpered in fear.

"Please don't. Let me up, Trip," the girl said moving, trying to get up, but I held her there. I smirked, jerking back the girl's hair making her cry out in pain.

"Right here Baby Girl. It's the sweet spot," I smirked, tapping her temple. Elly looked at me blinking rapidly trying to brush off her shock.

"You don't think I will?" she asked, pressing the gun against the girl's head. I laughed shaking my head "no." It was cute, but she wasn't about to fucking shoot anyone. I watched Elly's eyes look around the bar, taking attendance, and just as I excepted, she lifted the gun shooting two rounds into the empty back room.

"I'LL DO IT. I DON'T EVEN KNOW HOW YOU CAN LOOK AT ANOTHER BITCH!" She yelled at me. Me? She's the one who has a whole new fucking boyfriend. My temper spiked at her in a way I had never felt before. I grabbed the random whore's hips, throwing her off of me and letting her hit the table as I stood up.

"YOU WANT TO TALK ABOUT ME? WHAT THE FUCK ABOUT YOU? YOU'RE OUT HERE ACTING LIKE A DAMN WHORE. NOW RUN ME BACK MY SHIT!" I yelled, snatching back my gun. I watched her take a step back not from fear, but shock. She looked at the girl and then back at me. Her wide eyes growing into a glare.

"I'M ACTING LIKE WHORE? TREY'VON DO YOU NOT UNDERSTAND EVERY----!" I cut her off taking a step forward. She was not going to use my government name in front of all these fucking criminals.

"GET THE FUCK OUTSIDE! YOU IN HERE USING FUCKING GOVERNMENT NAMES. GET OUT, GO!" I yelled at her, but she stood her ground, putting her hands on her hips sending me that damn pushy look which only made my anger grow.

"NO FUCK YOU, FUCK YOUR GOVERNMENT NAME, FUCK ALL THESE GUYS! WHAT, YOU SCARED TO HAVE THEM

HEAR ABOUT HOW YOU FUCKED THE BOSS'S DAUGHTER AND DIPPED OUT LIKE I WASN'T SHIT! DO YOU KNOW THE SHIT YOU'VE PUT ME THROUGH?" Elly screamed at me. I looked around the bar frantically, fuck. One of these assholes were going to tell Zeke. I fucking knew it in my soul.

"I knew you two were doing it," Lil Smiley commented, making both of us glare at him

"STAY OUT OF IT!" We both yelled at him and then glared at each other.

"YOU SEEM TO BE DOING JUST FINE. WHERE'S YOUR FUCKING BOYFRIEND, BABY GIRL?" I yelled at her. I watched her anger turn to confusion, and then right back to anger just as fast.

"YOU'RE FUCKING DELUSIONAL. I DON'T HAVE A BOYFRIEND. I HAVE BARELY LEFT THE BED AT ZEKE'S HOUSE. ALL I HAVE DONE IS CRY OVER YOUR DUMB ASS WHILE YOU'RE OUT HERE FUCKING CRACK WHORES. I CAN'T BELIEVE I BELIEVED YOU WHEN YOU SAID YOU HAD FEELINGS FOR ME. YOU DON'T KNOW HOW TO FEEL ANYTHING FOR ANYONE. I HATE YOU TREY'VON!" she screamed, tears falling from her chocolate brown eyes. I knew they came from anger and that was it. She knew exactly what I was talking about. She knew I was talking about Travis.

"I FUCKING HATE YOU!" she screamed, sobs breaking through. Her fist came flying towards me, but I grabbed her wrist, shoving her back into a table.

"Don't make that mistake Baby Girl. You might scare that bitch but not me," I growled lowly at her. She tried to shove me back, but I didn't budge. I couldn't help but get lost just staring at her face. Her russet skin still looked so smooth and soft. Her plump lips were still the most kissable things I've ever seen. That sharp jawline was enough to drive me crazy. Then those chocolate brown eyes were still as soul-taking as that night. I fucking missed her. She's here right in front of me and instead of trying to explain to her that I really cared, and that I just got scared, I'm fighting with her. What the fuck is wrong with me? She finally pushed me back, grabbing a cup of whiskey and threw it at me, but I moved just in time.

"You lied to me in the worst way. I fell for that "I cared about you and want more with you" shit, I really thought---." she stopped, tears falling from her eyes. But I just shrugged, shaking my head looking away.

"I lied? For someone who supposedly had feelings for me you moved on hella fast. STOP PLAYING LIKE I DON'T KNOW ABOUT THE ASIAN KID YOU'RE GOING TO THAT DUMB ASS DANCE WITH!" I yelled at her. She looked at me shocked and then burst into laughter shaking her head.

ELEANOR

I couldn't help but laugh at him. He's so stupid. I never even thought about moving on and that dance wasn't me doing that. I didn't even want to go to the damn thing, I just couldn't bring myself to say no.

"IT'S A FUCKING DANCE TRIP. I DIDN'T MOVE ON. I'VE BEEN CRYING OVER YOU FOR WEEKS BUT YOU DON'T CARE! YOU NEVER GAVE A FUCK ABOUT ME. I REALLY WAS JUST "ONE USELESS NIGHT" TO YOU, WASN'T I? WAS ANYTHING YOU SAID TO ME TRUE?" I just wanted to hear him say I didn't mean shit to him. That he got what he intended to get and dipped out, then just maybe then I could move on. I wouldn't be faking how happy I was because I could be happy without him. He looked at me scoffing, shaking his head and backing up while waving me off.

"If you really believe that bullshit then just get out," he said shaking his head and starting to walk away. I caught up behind him, grabbing his elbow and making him turn to look at me.

"NO TRIP, JUST ADMIT IT THAT'S ALL I WAS. "ONE USELESS NIGHT!"" I yelled at him. His nearly black eyes were completely black now. He was shaking from anger and his lip snarled. His hand went to his gun and then moved away just to repeat the action. I knew I was pressing his buttons, but I didn't even care.

"IS THAT WHAT YOU WANT TO HEAR? YOU WANT ME TO TELL YOU THAT YOU WERE JUST ONE FUCKING NIGHT TO

ME? THAT YOU DIDN'T MEAN SHIT? THAT YOU WERE JUST
SOME EASY PUSSY? THERE WAS NEVER TO GOING TO BE AN
"US." IS THAT WHAT YOU WANTED TO FUCKING HEAR?" he
yelled at me, taking a step forward. I couldn't stop the tears from falling
this time. I closed my eyes as my hand went to my stomach that was
twisting and flopping around. I felt like I was going to be sick. My whole
body was hot.

"DON'T CRY NOW, THAT'S WHAT YOU WANTED TO HEAR
RIGHT?" he yelled. I opened my eyes and looked up to the ceiling, trying
to find anything to say, but, I mean, what could I say? I looked at him
shaking my head. I needed to just look at him one last time before turning
to walk out of the bar.

"Wait, Baby Girl I---." I cut him off the moment his hand touched my
wrist. I ripped out of his grip as a sob escaped my lips.

"Just leave me alone Trip. I get it, there is nothing here," I told him.
He looked at me, shocked and panicked. But I just turned walking out
of the bar to see my whole family standing in front of our broken gate. I
hugged myself, sobbing as I walked over to them.

"Are you ok?" Dad asked carefully, but he didn't care if I was ok or not.
I just walked right past them into the house. I went straight upstairs to my
bedroom and threw myself on the bed sobbing as our argument replayed
over and over again in my head. Of course, my sisters came up and just
listened to me rant and cry over the man who didn't ever care about me.

Chapter 23

Drugs, Drinks, Regrets

TREY'VON

I pulled up to the house in South Central LA that was already poppin off. One of the guys was throwing a party and I told him I'd slide through. I really didn't want to be here. My mind was far from a party. I kept replaying mine and Elly's fight over and over again. Every wrong thing I said just so she would give up on me. I didn't mean any of that shit and I wasn't actually going to do anything with that girl. I just wanted to hurt her enough to keep her far away from me, because I was scared. Now I ruined everything between us and there was no going back. She really hated me this time. There was no way I could flirt my way back in. She didn't trust me. I said her worst fear when it came to us, and I left her after a vulnerable moment. A banging sound came from my window, breaking me from my thoughts. I looked over to see Smiley trying to look through my tinted windows with a big ass smile. I rolled my eyes opening the door, getting out, and shaking up with him.

"Yo that party is crazy. Strippers everywhere bro," he told me, making me laugh and shake my head.

"They didn't have water or juice or anything, so I went to the store and got some. I know you don't drink," Smiley was truly thoughtful. I don't know why he was so loyal to me but sometimes he's the friend I needed.

"Good looks bro," I said locking my car. We walked towards the house in silence, but I could feel his eyes burning into me. It was taking everything in me not to flip out on him for staring at me. I looked over at him, raising an eyebrow.

"I'm sorry about your fight with Elly today," he said lowly. I just shrugged, not saying anything. I didn't want to talk about our blow up especially with Smiley.

"TRIP!" I heard my name get yelled from different areas of the house as I walked in. I nodded my head in greeting. I shoved my hands into my hoodie pocket, messing with my baggie of acid tabs. I brought them just in case I needed her to appear again sooner than I thought I would.

"Follow me dude," Lil Smiley said, hitting my arm. I followed him through the house to a room. When he opened the door, I saw some of the highest members of our gang sitting there. Men that Zeke went to and discussed big decisions with. I didn't know what their titles were, but they were big. On the table was coke and there were strippers everywhere, already naked.

"We already told you higher gang members only, get the fuck out!" someone snapped at Smiley. I pushed open the door more, sending them glares for talking to the kid that way. They saw me and nodded their heads, letting Smiley in and making him smile even wider.

"Yeah, I got Trip with me. We like best friends," Smiley bragged. I scoffed, grabbing a bottle of water.

"Shut the fuck up," I rolled my eyes. We were friends but I didn't have a best friend. I walked over, shaking up with the men. A hand landed on my shoulder. I looked up to see tits in my face. I could still see the scar from she had had implants put in.

"Hey handsome want a dance?" the stripper asked. I knocked her hand off my shoulder, sending her a harsh, dangerous glare. She backed up almost falling off the table, making me smirk.

"Don't fucking touch, bitch," I snapped at her, sitting on the couch next to Big Rico. Smiley squeezed in next to me and the couch arm with some kinda alcohol in his cup.

"How you been Trip?" Carlos asked me. I nodded my head running my hand over my curls.

"Just fine Carlos. I see still you're a fat fuck," I rolled my eyes, taking a drink of my water.

"I still see you're a dick," he commented, making me laugh and Smiley followed my lead. I shook my head, looking up at the stripper that was dancing.

"Take a line," Daniel urged motioning to the coke, but I shook my head "no."

"I will," Smiley jumped up excitedly. I grabbed him pulling him down with a glare.

"No the fuck you won't. We don't do our own product, that's how yo ass gets killed," I spat at him. He nodded, leaning back into the couch.

"Lighten up Trip, no one is coming for you here. Let the kid live," Big Rico laughed, but I just shook my head "no," taking a drink of my water. They let conversation take over. Smiley being Smiley was trying to get in with the big guys, but that just meant I got to be in my own world. Before I could stop the thoughts, I was thinking about the bar. The pain in her eyes when I told her she meant nothing to me. I didn't mean it, she was just pushing me and pushing me to say it, so I did. The look on her face, the tears, how she walked out without fighting. I didn't want us to end that way. I didn't want us to end with me just ghosting her either. Honestly, I just didn't want us to end, but she had a whole new boyfriend.

My mind wandered to a dangerous place. I could see Travis's hands on her. His big ass kissing her and touching her. I could hear her moaning his name instead of mine. I could see those small hands running over him as her back arched. It pissed me off because no one should see her like that but me, and no one should be making her feel like that but me. Elly was mine and this guy really thought he was just going to fuck her at that dance. The gun pressed against my stomach made it tempting to tear through her friend group until someone told me where that asshole lived. I wanted to kill him before he got the chance to even see her like that.

"Yo, you good?" Big Rico asked, hitting the side of my leg. I looked up at him glaring big bastard touching me.

"Don't fucking touch me yo," I shot looking up at the stripper who was dancing. My mind wandered to that day in Elly's room when she was showing her sisters she could twerk. Man, imagine if she was wearing those black leather pants when she did that. I would have had to have her right then and there. I knew she wasn't going to leave my mind, but I knew the one thing that could drive her out. The one thing I haven't touched in years.

"Where's the fucking alcohol?" I asked standing up. Smiley looked at me wide eyed, but I sent him a glare which told him to not say shit to me.

"Right over there at the bar. Help yourself. Where's Zeke at?" Carlos asked, pointing towards the bar. I walked over looking at all the options. I grabbed my poison of choice. It's always been my go-to drink. Whiskey. I grabbed the bottle, seeing it was aged to perfection.

"He's out of town on some business. Meeting with a supplier," I told Carlos with a shrug as I grabbed a cup, pouring the brown liquor over ice. I spun the ice around in my glass, walking over to the couch to Smiley.

"Cheers to the relapse," I said holding up the drink. Smiley looked at me disappointed, shaking his head. I threw back my head downing the whole glass. The familiar burn felt so good going down my throat. The strong bitter taste was like the best thing in the world. I wanted more, one drink and I was hooked all over again. I grabbed the bottle refilling the glass as I sat down.

"You look like you're drinking with something on your mind," Daniel observed. I looked at him, smirking and taking a drink.

"Or someone," Big Rico pushed. These weren't the guys to let into your personal life. They were dangerous and would fuck up your life over one little mistake. I'd be damned if they came for Elly, so I just shrugged.

A COUPLE HOURS LATER

I drunkenly laughed as Carlos kept messing with the stripper. She'd slap his hands away and he'd smack her ass even harder. I went to take another drink from the bottle. I had given up on the glass a minute ago, but now the bottle was empty.

"WHAT THE FUCK!" I yelled throwing the bottle and letting it crash against the wall. I got up, stumbling over to the bar, knocking a bottle of Fireball off with a crash.

"Shits, nasty anyways," I slurred, grabbing another bottle of whiskey. I ripped it open, taking another drink and laughing at Carlos and the stripper.

"If that bitch doesn't put out, Carlos put her ass out no clothes and all. She's just a fucking whore like the rest of them," I slurred. I watched Carlos stand up smacking her in the face, throwing her out of the room like I said.

"Yo, Trip man. I think you've had enough," Lil Smiley said, coming over to me. I laughed throwing my arm around him pulling him into my side.

"Yo Smiley you really a good friend, you know that? You just always down for me," I said, taking another drink. He hummed, reaching for the bottle, but I snatched it away laughing at him.

"I don't think so you're only 15. Still a little baby," I teased, pinching his cheek laughing, making the others laugh.

"Trip, you're wasted," he told me as I let go of him and moved back the table. I laughed, nodding my head.

"I'm fucking gone, and I haven't felt this good since I quit drinking. FUCK IT, LETS BRING DAY DRINKING BACK!" I yelled, plopping on the couch as the people in the room cheered me on, except for Smiley who just looked disappointed.

"You think that feels good, take a couple lines," Big Rico said scrapping four lines out of the smaller pile of coke. I looked at it, taking a drink of my whiskey, and then nodded. I was handed a rolled up 100-dollar bill. I leaned down, snorting the first line. I couldn't help but make a face and touch my nose feeling the burn of the powder. In like 30 seconds I already started to feel an energizing high. I smirked, leaning down snorting the next three lines.

"WHOA!" I screamed rubbing my nose. Smiley looked at me with disappointed eyes, shaking his head. But I just ignored it. My high took me higher than I've ever been. I couldn't help but jump up and walk around as I took a drink of the whiskey.

"Shits high quality huh?" Big Rico asked, laughing, and I nodded.

"Yo, I've never been this fucking high. Smiley you got to do a couple lines," I said walking over to him and pulling him over to the pile.

"Nah, Trip. I'm good on the real. I think maybe we should go," he suggested, but I just laughed at him. Suddenly hands landed on my shoulders and I looked up to see a stripper smiling down at me.

"You finally ready for me handsome?" she asked. I licked my lips looking over her body and back up to her face. I moved sitting on the chair waving her over to me. She smiled coming over straddling my lap. Right away I grabbed her boobs palming them making her giggle as she got comfortable on me. She started twerking on me. I moved my hands, smacking her ass making her laugh. She moved grinding on me, but she didn't use her leg like most strippers. I smirked pushing up my hips, making her eyes close in pleasure as she balled up her fists in my shirt.

"I think you want more than just a dance," I snickered. She ran her long ghetto looking nail down my cheek. I took a drink of the whiskey, pouring some into her mouth and letting it run down her body.

"You're attractive, can you blame me?" she asked, running her hands down my chest.

"Nah, you just want his money, slut" Lil Smiley barked at her, making me roll my eyes as I ran my hands up her body. She teasingly melted between my legs running her hands up my thighs bringing her lips to where my dick was hidden in my jeans.

"Nice to see after everything that happened with us today you can still enjoy yourself," I heard that soft accented voice laced with attitude. My head snapped up looking back at the door, but she wasn't over there.

"Over here, fuck up," she snapped again as she sat across from me with her legs crossed looking at her nails.

"Oh shit," I said pushing the stripper off, making her hit her head on the table.

"Fuck, you ok?" I asked looking back to see Elly was gone. I stood up looking around for her.

"You seen that shit too, right?" I asked Smiley, but he looked at me confused.

"Dude, you're so fucked up, I don't even know what you're talking about," Smiley shook his head in disappointment.

"He's right. You're fucked up and still can't escape me, how does that feel?" I heard her voice. I looked over to see her standing behind the couch with her hands on Carlos's shoulders. I shook my head, rubbing my eyes and she was gone.

"I need to piss," I lied stumbling out of the room. I stumbled through the house to the bathroom. I walked in, shutting and locking the door. I went over to the sink splashing water on my face. "Elly is not here. Elly is not here. Elly is not here."

"Yes, I am," her voice came from next to me. I jumped, seeing her sitting on the counter.

"I didn't even take acid you stupid bitch. Leave me alone," I spat. It wasn't the real Elly, so I didn't give a fuck.

"You're the one that went and snorted coke and started drinking," she spat back at me, making me roll my eyes. I sighed reaching out to touch her, but my hands went right through her. She looked at me laughing, waving goodbye and then faded away.

"BABY GIRL!" I yelled, looking around but she was gone. I grabbed the counter looking in the mirror. I was sweating so bad my hair was sticking to my forehead and you could see it through my sweatshirt. My pupils were blown out like I was on acid, but I wasn't this time. My mind was wild with thoughts about Elly. I needed her. I didn't care if she was screaming at me and telling me how much she hated me. I needed her. I couldn't function without her. I reached into my pocket feeling my keys. I looked up at myself nodding. I was seeing my girl. Tonight.

ELEANOR

I had only been asleep maybe an hour before I was woken up by loud banging on my window. I jumped awake, staring at my window with wide scared eyes. My mind went from a murder rapist to a possessed clown, to a demon. I slowly pushed the covers off my body. I grabbed my old soft ball bat. I slowly walked over to the window, bringing back my bat as I snatched open the curtain. I almost screamed when I saw Trey'von in the tree looking back at me. I dropped the bat, resting my hands on my knees catching my breath as he began knocking on the window again. I looked at him with a glare ripping open the window.

"You almost gave a me heart attack asshole," I whispered/yelled at him. He chuckled, wobbling on the branch which made me gasp and grab him. His sweatshirt was soaked.

"Watch out Baby Girl, let me in," his usual smooth velvet voice was rough and slurred. I felt my heart drop in my chest as I got the strongest whiff of alcohol. He was drunk. He stopped drinking and now he's relapsed. I watched him wobble through my window, almost falling. Once he caught his balance, he looked up at me with a drunken sloppy smile.

"You're drunk," my voice cracked. He laughed, waving it off.

"Just a little bit. What were you doing at that party?" he asked me coming closer, but I took a step back and crossed my arms. I squinted my eyes. I could see his pupils were blown out. I gasped, reaching over to turn on a side lamp and then grabbed his face. He was sweating like he just ran 10 miles. His sweatshirt was soaked. His hair was dripping wet and in his eyes. Even his pants were wet. His pupils were blown out so much there was barely any dark brown left.

"Are you high?" I asked, my tone coming out harsh. I looked him over as he laughed, grabbing my hips pulling me closer.

"Baby, I only did a couple lines. I'm fine. I swear. I just missed you," he smiled at me. I scoffed at his lie and ripped out of his grip. He stumbled, almost falling, but I was quick to grab him and keep him up. Just as my lips parted so I could ask him if he did cocaine, his lips connected to mine. I was frozen in shock as his hands found their way to cup my cheeks. Without even kissing him back I felt the sparks, the electricity flowing through my veins. Without thinking, I closed my eyes, moving my lips in sync with his, resting my hands on his sweaty hips. The kiss was just as mind blowing as our first. Our lips fit together like they were molded perfectly for one another. My head buzzed, giving me a natural high that felt better than any high weed had ever given me. I saw fireworks behind my eyes as butterflies invaded my stomach, fluttering up to my chest. Electricity shot through my veins, sending an oddly relaxed feeling through me. I felt sparks bouncing off the walls around us, symphonies playing in the background. This was more perfect and explosive than our first kiss. The addictive Marijuana and mint taste was replaced by a minty whiskey taste. I felt him pull me closer as he nibbled at my bottom lip asking for permission. It was that action that reminded me how angry I still was at him and how disappointed I was in him for drinking and getting high. I pulled away, slapping him hard. His head snapped over as the sound rang through my bedroom.

"Damn, I like it rough but not like that," he smirked, starting to kiss me again like he didn't feel any pain. But I ripped away.

"What did you snort Trey'von?" I asked. He groaned, closing his eyes and sighing dramatically.

"Cocaine, now kiss me," he complained, moving closer to me, but I dunked moving under his arm to stand behind him. He laughed, spinning around wagging a finger at me.

"I'm still pissed at you Trey'von," I said, crossing my arms. He groaned, hanging his head low.

"I didn't mean any of that shit I said. I was just being a dumb ass. Come on, baby, forgive me?" He pouted in the cutest way. I moved back from him, shaking my head "no."

"You left me for weeks Trey'von. Right after you swore you had feelings for me. You lied to get me in bed. It crumbled me. I didn't leave my bed for over a week and all I have done is cry over you since. You don't have feelings for me, you don't miss me, you're drunk and high and I'm not a toy," I told him, my voice cracking. I knew I couldn't send him back out there like that. He was going to have to stay with me tonight. Just to make this all hurt so much more. It's like it was God's sick humor.

"Baby Girl, don't say that. I do have feelings for you, shit I can't even function without you properly, look at me. I'm drunk, high, and I just climbed through a fucking window. I need you more than I've ever needed anyone. I just got scared," he slurred. I knew he was drunk because he wouldn't talk to me that way when he was sober. He started to touch me, but I moved away from with a look.

"Stop trying to touch me. What is there to be scared of? It's me," I asked, my voice breaking at the idea of him being scared to feel around me, of all people. He groaned, stumbled and almost fell, but he caught his balance.

"I'm scared of feeling something. I don't know how to be a husband," he slurred, stumbling backwards. I grabbed his arm which stopped him from falling once again.

"Husband? No one was even talking about marriage Trey'von. You skipped steps," I told him, rolling my eyes. He laughed, reaching around me and grabbing my butt. I sent him a glare, moving away from him and smacking away his hands.

"What's the thing you are before that? Boyfriend. I've never been that before. I don't know how to be anything other than this and abusive when it comes to being a boyfriend and I don't want that for you. Baby, how you make your room spin like this? It's kinda cool," he said, looking around. I sighed, shaking my head. He was going to pass out soon. He's never had a girlfriend before? How? He's sexy. He can't even hit anyone else in front of me, so what makes him think he's going to hit me? Him not being confident about something was new. Also, so was expressing his fears. I wanted to comfort him and sooth his fears, but he wouldn't remember in the morning.

"You could have just come to me and talked to me about it," I told him, walking over to the window, closing and locking it. I shut the curtain as he laughed, coming over hugging me from behind, leaving a kiss on my neck. I closed my eyes, letting myself enjoy his arms for just a moment.

"Oh, you want me to stay the night, huh?" he asked, his warm breath hitting my neck. Between my legs started to tingle and burn for him, but I wouldn't let this happen.

"I can't let you leave like this. Did you drive?" I asked him and he nodded his head. I turned to find him with a goofy smile which made me giggle. He leaned down to kiss me, but I moved, sending him a look.

"You have more of these shorts? Man, those last ones didn't stand a chance," he laughed, trying to grab my spandex shorts. I grabbed his hand sending, him a pointed look which only made him laugh. Of course, the guy I'm stuck on would snort coke, get drunk, and climb through my window.

"Sit on the bed," I sighed. He smirked at me, moving over to the bed sitting down looking up at me with a smirk. I rolled my eyes looking at him. That smirk was so annoying but missed it.

"Can you undress yourself?" I asked. He laughed as he looked down, his smile fell.

"Oh. Baby I did coke. I don't think I can get hard. Everything is too numb right now, but I'll make it up to you in the morning," he pouted. I scoffed kneeling between his legs and pulling his shoes and socks off. I started undoing his pants and put his gun on the nightstand.

"That's not what I meant. You're staying the night here. Your clothes are soaked, and they need washed. Plus, sleeping in jeans and a hoodie doesn't sound comfy," I told him, pulling off his jeans which left him in his boxers. He pulled his phone out of his hoodie, shoving it under the pillow.

"That's my side," he declared as I stood, grabbing his hoodie and pulling it off.

"The whole bed is yours," I grumbled, pulling off his wife beater which left him in just his tight-fitting boxers.

"You aren't sleeping with me? I want to cuddle," he told me. I rolled my eyes at how he mocked me. I knew that was one of the issues.

"Just go to sleep Trey'von," I sighed watching him move up the bed. I grabbed the blanket and covered his attractive tattooed body.

"Goodnight Baby Girl," he said and then passed out. I turned off the light and grabbed his clothes. I went downstairs and put them in the washer. I grabbed a bottle of water and Advil. I went upstairs and sat the water and Advil on the table next to him, ready for when he wakes up in the morning. I put the trashcan next to him on the floor in case he had to puke. Then I went down the hall, grabbed extra pillows and blankets from the closet and went back into my room to set up a bed for myself on the floor. Once the room was set up, I went downstairs and watched TV until Trey'von's clothes were freshly washed and dried. I folded them neatly and set them inside my closet on the top shelf. I closed the door and got into the make shift bed on the floor. I laid there listening to Trey'von's heavy breathing until sleep finally took me over.

Chapter 24

Ashes

ELEANOR

"ELLY, BREAKFAST IS READY!" I heard my dad yell from the bottom of the stairs. I rolled over and hid my face in my pillows. I didn't feel my soft bed under me but rather, the hard floor. For just a moment, I laid in confusion but a groan coming from my bed sent the memory of last night running through my brain. Trey'von is here in my bed.

"ELLY!" My dad yelled. His voice was getting closer. I sat up and looked back at Trey'von who was moving around in my bed, waking up. I heard him mumble something as he touched his head with his eyes still closed. My dad was going to kill me when he saw Trey'von. There was no way to hiding him. I couldn't have just sent him back out there in the state he was in. He was way too drunk and high to be behind the wheel.

"Elly, I said break---." My dad stopped the moment he opened the door. His eyes landed on Trey'von who tossed the blanket off his upper body. I watched my dad's eyes find mine as they coated over with anger. I watched his hand slip from the doorknob as his jaw clenched and his cheeks flushed red.

"What the hell---" Trey'von cut my dad off.

"Fuck," he groaned, moving fast as he leaned over the bed throwing up into the trashcan.

"Trip!" I gasped, getting up and practically ran over to my bed. I sat next to him resting a hand on his back and the other on his arm while he threw up the alcohol from last night. His skin was hot, like burning hot. He was clammy but not really sweaty, oddly enough. His body shook not from anger but from a hangover. He cringed as I touched him while he threw up. I saw a tear run down his cheek from vomiting. I didn't want him to be embarrassed even though he should be.

"Hey, I'm right here. It's ok," I whispered, leaning down and kissing his exposed shoulder.

"YOU HAVE TO BE KIDDING ELEANOR!" my dad yelled, making me cringe. I shushed him, waving down his tone.

"Stop yelling he probably has a headache," I snapped, looking back at Trip as his nose started to bleed. I got up and grabbed makeup cotton pads. I went back over to him rubbing his back.

"LIKE I SHOULD CARE ABOUT THAT THUG. I'M CALLING THE COPS!" Dad yelled at me. I looked at him with wide eyes. I felt frozen just for split second, my heart rate picked up, pounding against my chest. My dad started to grab his phone. I started to get up, but Trip's hand landed on my knee as he sat up, groaning.

"Yeah, and what you gonna tell em? 'My daughter snuck in the guy I don't like and he stayed the night.' That's not a crime you dumb fuck," Trey'von coughed out at my dad. I looked to see his eyes were red and squinted like the light was hurting them. His lips were dry and starting to chap as the blood ran from his nose.

"It's breaking and entering. You didn't come through the front door plus I'm sure they have more to pin on you," Dad spat at Trey'von as I dabbed away the blood with the cotton pad. I grabbed Trey'von's hand and made him hold the pad.

"Dad, please please don't. I couldn't send him away last night. He was in no state to drive, please" I begged, grabbing my messy hair. Dad scoffed tapping away on his phone which increased my panic. Trey'von doubled over, throwing up again.

"STOP, I PAY YOU TO LIVE HERE. I CAN HAVE ANYONE OVER I WANT NOW," I yelled, standing up. I felt bad because I knew Trey'von's head had to hurt but I couldn't have my dad calling the police on him. I couldn't get him out of here before the police got here. Look at him. My dad's head snapped up as I grabbed my hair in a state of stress. His glare was hard and heavy on me. I was mad at Trey'von, but I couldn't let him go to jail.

"YOU HAVEN'T PAID ME SHIT ELEANOR. YOU RAN OFF TO LIVE WITH ZEKE INSTEAD!" he yelled. I looked at him shaking my head. I stormed over to my closet and grabbed my duffel bag.

"No, Baby Girl. Fuck him," Trey'von said, trying to get up but his legs gave out and he landed on the bed as he puked into the trashcan again. I unzipped the duffel bag throwing it in front of my dad sending him a glare.

"50K you're paid off. NOW, LEAVE HIM ALONE AND GET OUT!" I yelled, moving to block Trey'von with my body. I didn't want my dad's judgmental eyes on him any longer. My dad laughed at me, shaking his head and grabbing the duffel bag.

"You just paid 50,000 dollars for someone who doesn't give a fuck about you Eleanor. I thought you were smarter than that," Dad said, shaking his head. I knew Trey'von didn't give a fuck about me, but I gave one about him.

"Get out," I ordered, grabbing my door. My dad shook his head walking out and I shut the door looking at Trey'von as he threw up again. I walked over and sat crisscross on the bed next to him, rubbing his back.

"You're burning up," I whispered as he groaned. He laid back on the bed, covering his eyes with his arms.

"Baby Girl, go down there and get that money back and grab a bottle of water," he groaned. I leaned over his lean attractive body, grabbing the bottle of water with a smile. I opened it and handed it to him. He sat up, taking a drink and rinsing his mouth, spitting into the trashcan. He started downing the water which made my eyes grow wide. I grabbed his wrist, making him stop. I leaned over and grabbed the Advil.

"For your headache. I'm sorry for the yelling," I whispered. He looked at me, smiling as he took the pills.

"It's ok. I like watching you stand up for yourself. Fuck, Baby Girl, I feel like shit. I don't even remember coming here," he groaned, laying back. I brushed back his curls, biting my lower lip. He doesn't remember our kiss or the things he told me.

"How long have you been doing coke?" I asked him, unable to hide my disapproval. He looked over at me. I watched him close his nearly black eyes and then open them again.

"That was my first time in years," he told me, and I nodded my head. I watched his body violently shake and his sweating get worse. This wasn't the time to even try to talk to him about his actions.

"Go back to sleep. You'll feel better when you wake up," I told him lowly, getting off the bed. He moved farther up and I threw the blanket over his body, letting him go back to sleep while I faced my angry family.

TREY'VON

AROUND NOON

I woke to the sound of low mumbling and curses. My head still hurt. My stomach was still wheezy and daring me to puke. I was covered in sweat and felt gross. I could smell the alcohol coming from my pores. I opened my eyes slowly, sitting up and grabbing my stomach as I tried to keep everything down. I looked to find Elly standing in front of her closet grabbing clothes out looking at them and then throwing them on the floor. She only had a white fluffy towel hanging loosely around her body, but she held the top ensuring it stayed up. Her gorgeous curls were tied up in another towel. I couldn't help but wonder how girls did that.

She looked beautiful standing there with a scowl on her face. She wore no makeup, her skin was dewy, just as I remembered it to be. Her plump kissable lips were the prettiest pink. I didn't fail to see that everything wasn't perfect, but I knew deep down, that I had caused that. She had deep dark circles under her eyes. There were a few acne marks, like she had stopped taking care of his skin. She wasn't pale like everyone said though. I saw the life in her. Regardless of all of that, she still managed to look like a goddess.

"Good morning beautiful," I said. She jumped at my voice looking over at me with wide eyes. I couldn't help but laugh, shaking my head. I have no idea how I got here. The last thing I barely remember is seeing her in the bathroom at the party. I don't remember anything really before or after that. There were key things like snorting the coke and pushing the stripper off me, because I saw her, but I was missing things.

"You scared me. How are you feeling?" She asked, dropping my favorite pants onto the floor. I licked my lips looking at them. She must have noticed because she picked them back up, tossing them onto a mountain of blankets.

"Like shit," I told her, and she nodded her head. I watched her suck her teeth looking me up and down. I bit my lip looking at that little white towel that didn't hide those curves by any means. I smirked, watching her shiver as goosebumps crawled over her skin.

"Come here Baby Girl. Come snuggle with me," I said, waving her over to me. I wanted to feel her in my arms. I wanted to lay in bed and hold her for real. She wasn't going to disappear and be a mop. It was just Elly.

"You don't snuggle or cuddle and I'm more mad at you now than what I was before," she told me, shutting her closet door and going over to her dresser. I watched her pull out a crop top and a thong. She slipped the thong on under the towel and then then turned her back to me as she put on the crop top. It was olive green and reminded of the boob holder crop tops she wears except this had long sleeves on it.

"Well, I changed my mind. I want to cuddle, please?" I pouted, reaching over touching her arm. She jerked away from, me sending me a dirty look.

"You change your mind a lot," she commented, making me smirk. I loved that little sassy tongue. I licked my lips, taking a drink of my water.

"Just 5 minutes. Who knows? I might hate cuddling and it won't last that long," I said with a shrug. She tossed the towel away completely leaving her in just that thong and crop top that showed plenty of under boob. She rolled her eyes, moving over to the bed and climbing in with me. I laughed, unwrapping her curls from the towel and tossing it away.

"They aren't styled yet," she blushed, but I just shrugged and pushed them out of her face.

"You don't need all of that shit. You're most gorgeous person I've ever seen," I whispered. Her eyes filled with tears, and she looked away. Why is she crying? What did I say wrong? I literally gave her a compliment.

"Wait, don't cry," I whispered as a tear slipped down her cheek. I quickly wiped it away just for it to be replaced with more.

"Then why did you leave? What's wrong with me? Am I fat or is my nose weird? I know I have buggy eyes but maybe with makeup---." I cut her off covering her mouth, shaking my head "no." I couldn't believe the words falling from her lips. She wasn't any of that. She was so perfect. It was me that was a fuck up.

"Baby no. God no, you aren't any of that. You're not fat, your nose is fine. I mean I'm not really looking at your nose. Your eyes are something I could stare into forever, not buggy at all. You are so perfect," I told her, wiping her tears. She shook her head "no," looking away from me.

"If that was true you wouldn't have left me like you did," she told me, a sob breaking through.

"Baby Girl, I didn't leave because of you. I left because of me. I don't know how to do this. I got scared," I told her, honestly. She looked away sucking on her teeth. I groaned, laying back on the bed. I knew her trust was gone but her self-image too?

"You should have told me that. You could have come to me and said 'Elly, I've never had a girlfriend before, I'm scared because of my past.' I wouldn't have held it against you. I would have fought through it with you" She cried, covering her face with her hands. How did she know that I never had a girlfriend before? What did she know about my past?

"How do you know that?" I asked her, raising an eyebrow. Did I tell her something I shouldn't have while I was drunk?

ELEANOR

I hid my face inside my hands, crying over all this stupid shit again. We weren't really cuddling either. I was just sitting next to him while he laid back on the bed looking up at me. I peeked at him through my fingers as he waited for me to answer him.

"You told me last night. You said you didn't know how to be a husband and I tried to tell you that you were skipping steps. Then you told me you had never had a girlfriend and you didn't know how to be a boyfriend, besides what you were doing. Getting drunk and being abusive, but you won't hurt someone else in front me so what makes you think you'd hurt me?" I couldn't stop the question. He sat up running his hand over his face. I saw the anger starting to take over. I didn't want to scream and fight with him. I just wanted to talk and work through every issue in my head. I began to speak again, but his anger had grown fast. His jaw was clenched, his already shaking body was shaking even harder. His nearly black eyes were completely black. He ripped the comforter off his body, throwing it at me as he got up.

"WHY DOES IT MATTER IF I KNOW HOW TO BE A BOYFRIEND OR NOT? YOU ALREADY HAVE A BOYFRIEND! IT REALLY DIDN'T TAKE YOU ANYTIME AT ALL TO MOVE THE FUCK ON DID IT?" he yelled at me. I watched as he clenched and unclenched his fist as he paced around my room.

"YOU'RE ALWAYS SO QUICK TO PUT THE FUCKING BLAME ON ME BUT WHAT ABOUT YOU? YEAH, I SAID I HAD FEELINGS FOR YOU AND I MEANT WHAT THE FUCK I SAID BUT YOU DIDN'T! I DON'T KNOW WHY IT'S SO FUCKING SHOCKING. NO ONE IN MY LIFE HAS CARED ABOUT ME BEFORE, SO WHY THE FUCK WOULD YOU? I'M PISSED, I BELIEVED YOUR LYING ASS, JUST FOR YOU TO GO OUT AND START FUCKING THAT CLOWN REJECT!" I felt frozen in place. I had never seen him so upset before. With each word I could see his rage growing worse. I swallowed hard looking at the ground trying to avoid his black eyes. His lip curled up, as he ground his white teeth. His muscles were tight, and you could see them straining under his tattooed skin. He punched the brick wall in my room with so much force I heard a pop come from his wrist as blood splattered.

"TREY'VON!" I screamed, getting up as he stormed over to me with his hand dripping blood. I tried to hide how scared I was for him at this moment, but I couldn't control my breathing. It was coming out rough and uneven. I felt my heart pounding against my chest.

"WHAT, BABY GIRL YOU SUDDENLY FUCKING CARE ABOUT ME? I DON'T WANT YOU TO CARE ABOUT ME OR LOVE ME ANYMORE. I'VE STRUGGLED EVERYDAY WITHOUT YOU BUT YOU'RE OUT HERE JUST MESSING WITH THE NEXT GUY THAT BATS HIS EYE AT YOU!" he yelled at me. I haven't even moved on. He's driving me crazy with that. Then him struggling without me? Yeah, right, because out of the two of us, he was the one struggling.

"YOU WERE STRUGGLING? I DIDN'T LEAVE MY BED. ALL I HAVE DONE IS CRY OVER YOU. I DON'T HAVE A BOYFRIEND! I AM NOT DATING TONY---!" he cut me off shaking his head

"Bullshit!" he barked at me. I shook my head as tears filled my eyes. I wasn't arguing with him over something he's made up in his head.

"I'm not arguing with you. Take a shower, you smell like a bar," I snapped at him as I grabbed my black leather pants. I pulled them, struggling to get them over my hips. I wanted to look sexy. I wanted to show Trey'von what he was missing, but I didn't know if he'd care.

"I don't have any fucking clothes. I'm sure I didn't show up here naked," he spat harshly at me as I zipped up my pants. I don't know why, out of all comments he's made this is the one that made my temper spike so high, but it did. I stormed over and ripped open my closet.

"I WASHED THEM DUMB ASS. YOU CAME HERE DRIPPING IN FUCKING SWEAT. YOU'RE WELCOME!" I screamed at him, throwing the jeans, wife beater, and hoodie at him.

"NO ONE ASKED YOU TO DO THAT!" he yelled back, picking up the clothes as I threw a towel at him. I grabbed body soap, slinging it at his head but he ducked.

"THAT WHAT IT MEANS TO CARE ABOUT SOMEONE. YOU DO SHIT FOR THEM WITHOUT BEING ASKED. LEAVE ME THE FUCK ALONE," I yelled at him as he grabbed the things, I threw at him.

"Bitch," he snapped, walking out of the bedroom. I rolled my eyes sitting at the desk, my hair was almost dry. I grabbed my spray bottle, wetting it down again. I styled the curls. I spent a little more time on them, so they looked flawless. I did my usual makeup, covering the circles that were still under my eyes along with the acne marks. I left out lipstick, just putting on ChapStick. I was trying to get them soft and healthy again. Once I finished with my hair and makeup and approved of my look, I tied on a pair of green, white, and black Jordan Retro 4's. I sighed, grabbing my hair mask, curl crème, and my blow drier. Trey'von would need it for his hair too. I opened my bedroom door, just as mom started to knock.

"Oh hey, I came to check on you. We heard you guys downstairs," Mom said and I nodded my head.

"Yeah, I'm fine. He's just being a dick," I shrugged, as I walked down to the bathroom, knocking on the door.

"FUCK OFF!" he yelled. I kicked the door out of anger.

"STOP BEING SUCH A DICK. I'M BRING YOU STUFF TO DO YOU HAIR!" I yelled, hitting the door again. I heard mom giggle and I sent her a glare for laughing at me. She looked away, amused, making me roll my eyes. I opened the bathroom door and he ripped back the curtain.

"I'm naked," he snapped as I walked into the bathroom, shutting the door.

"So? This is a hair mask. It really makes your hair feel good," I said, handing him the bottle and setting the rest of the things on the counter.

"Here's a toothbrush. Don't use mine," I snapped, setting it out.

"Too late," he said, making me roll my eyes. I walked out of the bathroom, shutting the door to find mom smirking at me. I rolled my eyes, motioning for her to follow me downstairs.

TREY'VON

I turned off the blow drier and looked at my curls. This shit was better than the stuff I normally use. I ran my hand over my hair to feel how soft it was. I looked at the label to make a mental note to order some when I got home. I grabbed her shit, so I didn't get bitched at and walked back down to her room to find it empty. I dropped everything on her desk. I looked around and moved to the pillow where my dead phone was and my baggie of acid. I quickly shoved the acid in my pocket and plugged my phone in. The door opened and I turned to see Elly walking in with the trashcan and a clean bag. The whole room was actually cleaned up. She looked so fucking hot. She had on those tight black leather jeans that have been plaguing my dreams. That olive green crop top hugged her bust perfectly. I couldn't stop staring at how her under boob dipped out in the sexiest way. I bit my lip, as my mind went crazy with all of the things I still wanted to do to that body, that I hadn't had the chance to do.

"Well, now that you're sober, you can leave?" she asked, her chocolate brown eyes looking up at me. I looked her up and down, raising an eyebrow. She turned, put back the trashcan and bent over giving me a perfect view of her ass.

"Where you goin?" I asked as I sat on the bed.

"Out," Her tone clipped. Her vague details starting to press my buttons. I scoffed, looking at those pants that just made her ass looked scooped into it.

"Where is 'out?'" I asked. She turned, looking at me and crossing her arms which brought my attention to that under boob. I loved when she dressed like that, but I also hated it because I didn't want anyone to see her like that but me.

"With my friends. We're going dress shopping for the dance," she said. I chuckled, looking at her amused. I knew she wasn't going to that dance. Antonio and I had an agreement. He lives and she doesn't go to the dance.

"You aren't going to that," I stated, waving it off. She scoffed, looking at me.

"You're not my dad. I'll go if I want to go," she pushed me. I reached over grabbing my gun and pushing it into my waist band.

"Let's just go get food. I'll take you to that Sushi place in Beverly Hills." I dismissed her comment. She just looked at me, I knew food cured everything with girls.

"Rain check," she grabbed silver hoops and putting them in. She picked up a small Calvin Klein backpack, slinging it on. I watched her walk out of her bedroom leaving me in here. Oh hell no. I walked out of the bedroom, slamming the door behind me.

"Baby Girl, stop. Look you the one running now," I said, reaching out looping my finger in her belt loop. I went to spin her around, but she turned to face me. Because I was already a little dizzy from crashing from the coke and the hangover, it sent me stumbling back.

"I'M RUNNIN--," she stopped yelling at me. Once I recovered, I saw her looking down with wide eyes and her mouth gaped open. I could see she was staring at my baggie full of colorful acid tabs placed perfectly between us. We looked up at each other and I saw her about to run for them. I took off for them too, but she snatched the bag just as I got to them.

"GIVE THEM BACK!" I yelled, grabbing her. She tried to push me away, causing us to struggle. She ended up turning in my arms so her back was to me. She leaned down putting her weight on my arms.

"LOOK AT WHAT IT'S DOING TO YOU. NO!" she yelled, shoving it into her top. I grabbed her shirt, pulling it so the baggie would fall.

"TREY'VON!" she screamed. I grunted in anger, picking her up fully from the ground.

"ELLY?" I heard her mom yell, but I didn't even care.

"GIVE ME THEM!" I yelled. She flung back an elbow, catching me right in the chin. I dropped her, stumbling back and grabbing my chin. The second her feet hit the floor she took off toward the steps. I cursed under my breath, taking off after her. Just before she hit the top step, I caught up to her. I pushed her against the wall, but even in my angry state, I was careful with her. She tried to hit me, but I pinned her hands to the wall and pressed my body against hers so she couldn't kick me.

"Give it back," I ordered, but she just shook her head "no."

"No, is that what you've been doing? Acid? Zeke told me you've been doing drugs. You already said that was your first-time doing coke in years, so acid?" she snapped at me trying to fight against me. I don't know why she cared what drug I was doing, that was my business.

ELEANOR

I tried to get out of his grip, my top was pulled down low enough that I could feel the wind on my nipple, and I felt the baggie slipping out from between my boobs.

"DON'T WORRY ABOUT WHAT THE FUCK I DO. WORRY ABOUT YOUR BOYFRIEND!" He screamed. He made the mistake of letting go of one of my hands to get into my top for the baggie, but Zeke had been teaching me how to box. I brought down my arm, wrapping him up, spinning us, and slamming him against the wall. I pushed off him, running towards the stairs.

"BABY GIRL!" he yelled as I went running down the steps. I looked back to see him close behind me. The moment I hit the bottom step I saw my whole family standing in the living room looking towards the stairs with wide eyes. I looked to see that Trey'von was almost within in arm's length.

"IZZY!" I screamed, pulling the drugs from my boobs and throwing them to her, just as Trey'von grabbed my shoulders, pushing me back. He sent me a glare as he headed towards Izzy.

"Izzy, don't give them to him. He won't hurt you," I said as I ran up and grabbed Trey'von, spinning him around.

"STOP, YOU WON'T UNDERSTAND WHY I NEED IT!" he yelled, but I shook my head "no."

"NO, I UNDERSTAND PERFECTLY! YOU'RE ADDICTED AND I'M NOT GOING TO SIT BACK AND LET YOU THROW AWAY EVERYTHING YOU WORKED SO HARD FOR. YOU THINK ZEKE IS GOING TO LET AN ADDICT TAKE HIS PLACE?" I screamed. I was fighting him so hard because I loved him. I saw mom pushing Izzy towards the kitchen with the drugs while I had him distracted.

"Fuck Zeke, fuck that stupid ass gang, fuck my position. That drug gives me something more than any of that bullshit," he snapped. I shook my head running my fingers through my hair, trying to collect my thoughts.

"Is it enough to lose me? I won't fight you forever," I told him, but he just looked at me shaking his head. He went to snap at Izzy, but she was already gone.

"Shit," he snapped, as he went towards the kitchen. I ran past him to find Izzy and my family looking at it.

"GIVE IT TO ME!" I yelled and she quickly threw it to me. I looked behind me to see Trey'von hot on my heels. I ran to the sink hitting my stomach on the counter, knocking the wind out of myself.

"NO, STOP!" Trey'von yelled, as I turned on the water. Just as he reached me, I shoved the drug down the garbage disposal and turned it on.

"NOOOO!" Trey'von yelled, looking down into the sink to see the colorful paper getting wet and destroyed. He turned, looking at me with black eyes, his body shaking, his breathing violent. He punched a hole in the dry wall making my sisters and mom scream.

"DO YOU KNOW WHAT THE FUCK YOU JUST DID?" He screamed at me, more harshly than he ever had before.

"I SAVED YOU FROM YOURSELF!" I yelled back at him. He closed his eyes, pacing around and grabbing his hair. I swallowed hard watching him carefully. I heard my mom whisper to my dad to stay out of it and that would be for the best because Trey'von would kill him this time.

"NO, YOU TOOK AWAY MY ONLY WAY OF SEEING YOU!" he yelled. I looked at him confused, seeing me? I was right here. Was I his hallucinations?

"I'm right here Trip. You don't need a drug to see me, you know you can come to me whenever you need to," I told him keeping my tone soft and easy. He shook his head "no," punching another hole in the wall. Ok, he's paying for all of this damage.

"STOP, YOU'RE HURTING YOURSELF!" I grabbed his hands. He moved, hiding his face in my neck wrapping his arms around my waist. I froze until I heard his low sniffle in my shoulder. I wrapped him up in my arms, playing with his curls.

"It gave me you when I didn't have you. You were happy to be with me," he told me, his voice showing no sign of tears. I just hugged him tighter. I wasn't happy with him right now and I wouldn't lie.

"You didn't have me by your own choice," I whispered. Suddenly, he had me pushed against the counter. He brushed my hair out of my eyes, cupping my cheek. His sudden gentle touch was confusing. He had just been punching holes in the wall and now he was going to be sweet.

"I don't want that to be my choice anymore," he whispered, leaning in to kiss me as I looked away. He pressed his lips against my cheek in the cutest way, but I wouldn't let him get to me. I pushed him off, shaking my head.

"Then you need to show me you don't want that. I have plans today, go home," I told him, stepping around him. He scoffed, grabbing my hand and pulling me back to him.

"I'm going with you since a certain person couldn't keep his end of the deal," he said, glaring at my dad. I rolled my eyes shaking my head "no."

"No you aren't. You're paying for all of this by the way," I said motioning to my broken house. I turned to my parents, sending them a smile as I fixed my top.

"I'm going dress shopping with Nicole, Gabby, and Tony," I told them, and they nodded, looking at me with wide eyes. I heard Trey'von laugh. I looked over at him to see him shaking his head.

"Your little boyfriend is going?" he asked me with a snicker.

"IT'S A DANCE YOU PSYCHO. I'M NOT DATING HIM," I yelled at Trey'von for the last time. He sent me a careless shrug.

"I'm going with you then," he told me, but I shook my head "no."

"No, you aren't. Go home!" I snapped, but he sent me a look that told me he wasn't going to back down from this fight.

Chapter 25

Back and forth

TREY'VON

"I can't believe you won that fight," Elly complained as she sat in the passenger seat. I smirked, looking over the see her knees facing to door and sitting as far from me as she could. I won the fight about coming with her. She won the acid fight, and I got the dress shopping one. I wanted to make sure her dress wasn't revealing, since I wouldn't be there, and I wanted to make sure Travis knew she was mine.

"I can't believe you shoved 600 dollars' worth of drugs down your kitchen sink," I said, glancing over at her, but she just shrugged and looked at her phone.

"You don't need to be doing drugs or drinking. Where are we going? This is not how you get to Gabby's," she barked. I rolled my eyes as I pulled over to park in front of Lil Smiley's house and laid on the horn. After a couple seconds, Elly leaned over and brushed my hand off the horn, giving me a dirty look.

"Give them a minute, damn," she snapped. Fuck, I'm gonna need this weed to get through this day because her attitude, this fucking Travis guy that's going to be checking her out all day and flirting with her, and then the fact that I'm pissed at her over the acid thing.

"Come on kid," I said, laying on the horn again and looking at the house. Soon enough, the front door opened to reveal Smiley in pajama pants, and slippers. He looked out at my car rubbing his eye and then jogged down.

"DUDE WHERE THE FUCK DID YOU GO LAST NIGHT?" Smiley yelled, strolling up to the car. He bent down and saw Elly in the passenger seat, looking out of the window. He looked at me with a confused smile. He wiggled his eyebrows at me which made me laugh.

"Yo, I was fucked up last night. I ended up at my girl's house," I smirked as I reached over and tried to touch Elly's hair, but she smacked my hand and sent me a glare which made me laugh.

"Yeah, looks like you gonna have a fun day," he commented. Suddenly Elly leaned over me, her hand landing on my thigh as she shoved a finger in Smiley's face.

"I should fuck you up Smiley. You were with him and let him drink and do coke, and then you didn't even bother to take his fucking keys," Elly snapped at him. I laughed as I rubbed her back, trying to relax her.

"I can't control that man Elly, no one can. What the hell was you talking about when you pushed the stripper off? What were you seeing?" Smiley asked me. I looked at Elly with wide eyes as she moved back to her seat, shaking her head.

"Damn Smiley, you already see she's fucking pissed. Why the hell would you bring up the strippers? I need some weed," I demanded as I rolled eyes and looked over at Elly who just glared at me while shaking her head.

"Go get some from yo crib," Smiley shrugged. I sent him a glare, making him gulp.

"My house is a half hour away and I'm not going that way. I'll get you back, just give me some, damn," I snapped. He sighed, nodded his head and went back inside the house.

"Strippers Trey'von?" she asked me. I sighed, closing my eyes. This kid just doesn't understand girls.

"Baby, I was drunk and high before I even let that hoe touch me. I kept telling her to fuck off and then I got a little wild and I wasn't thinking clearly. I swear all that happened is she started to give me a lap dance and then I saw you behind her. I pushed her off and she hit her head and that's all I remember," I explained as I looked over at Elly. She turned, facing me, and looked like she was trying to read me.

"Be real, how nasty did the dance get?" she asked me with crossed arms. I cringed, grabbing the wheel and looking back over at her.

"It got nasty. She didn't use her leg like most strippers. She actually used her vagina and then I did get a little touchy feely but, I swear, I wasn't gonna do anything with her. I haven't even thought about sleeping with another girl since you. There was the one at the bar, but I was just trying to get over you. Even then, I wasn't gonna sleep with her." I told her nothing but the truth. She looked at me with a poker face as I watched her bite her plump unpainted lip. After a moment, she nodded her head, grabbing my hand and sending me a small smile.

"Thank you for being honest with me," she said. I looked at her, shocked, because that was not the reaction I expected.

"Aren't you mad?" I asked her curiously. But she just shook her head "no."

"Nope, you were honest and I believe the only reason you let her on you is because you were drunk and high," she told me with a shrug. I smiled, reached over and grabbing her hand. I leaned down to kiss her knuckles. I looked up to see her smiling at me.

"You know last night I slept better than what I have in weeks," she whispered. I smiled, leaning over and pushing her hair behind her ear.

"It's because we were meant to be with each other. Driving each other crazy, screaming at one another. We can't function without each other," I spoke lowly. She smiled, looking down and bringing my hand to her face.

"Yo, here," Smiley said, making me jump and take my hand from Elly's.

"Thanks, I'll give it back. I didn't want to drive to the crib," I said taking the weed, and he nodded. We shook up, and I pulled off heading towards Gabby's house.

ELEANOR

I sighed as I looked at Gabby's house and then down at my phone. I texted her to come out because we had a ride. She told me to hold on like 5 minutes ago. Tony or Nicole hadn't even walked out. I looked over at Trip as he broke apart the weed Smiley had given him.

"You're going to get arrested," I warned him. I watched him open the middle compartment and dig around. Seconds later he slung a card at me. I grabbed it, seeing that he had a medical Marijuana card for anger issues.

"That makes sense," I commented, putting it back where he got it from. I looked over to see all three of them finally coming out of the house. I rolled down my window and waved at them. Gabby groaned dramatically as they walked up.

"Who's car? That's hella nice," Tony said looking at it as they walked over. Trey'von scoffed in the driver's seat. Gabby opened the back door sliding in and Nicole and Tony followed. When they saw Trey'von, their eyes grew wide. He smirked and waved at them, as he held the blunt to my lips.

"Lick it," Trey'von told me, looking back at Tony. I knew what he was trying to do. He was trying to prove I was his no matter what so, I played along just to amuse him. I leaned forward, licking a bold strip up his thumb while sending him a seductive look. He licked his lips, watching me. I smiled, leaving a sloppy kiss on the tip of his thumb.

"Damn, Baby Girl," he groaned, watching me. I laughed, licking the blunt the way I've seen him do before.

"Y'all smoke?" he asked looking back at them through the mirror. They all quickly shook their head "no," making him laugh.

"So, you guys are like together now?" Nicole asked, leaning up and looking at me as Trey'von handed me the blunt and a lighter.

"No, not even close to it. He forced himself upon our shopping trip," I said, rolling my eyes and lighting the blunt as I inhaled the smoke. It burned my throat slightly as it filled my lungs. The familiar bitter taste had never tasted better. I couldn't lie, I did miss smoking with him. I blew the smoke at Trey'von making him grin.

"What are you doing?" Gabby asked me. I coughed a little on the smoke and hit it again, passing it to Trey'von.

"Smoking, it's actually pretty nice," I commented, grabbing Trey'von's water. He reached around and offered it to Gabby, but she just turned her nose up to it. I shook my head at my friends, taking the blunt hitting it again.

"So, I found this cute little boutique in Hollywood, look," Nicole said, handing me her phone. I hit the blunt again, looking at it. I quickly hit it again, making Trey'von laugh.

"Ok Smokey, run it," he teased me. I smiled, passing him the blunt as I looked at the shop. I nodded, telling Trey'von the address so he could take us there.

"Can we listen to music?" Gabby asked with attitude lacing her voice. I looked over at Trey'von as he nodded his head. I hooked up to the bluetooth.

"Play Pussy Fairy" Nicole commanded. I looked through my playlist found the song and played it as I turned up the radio. As Nicole and Gabby sang along, me and Trey'von passed the blunt back and forth, listening to the song. The higher I got, the better the music sounded. Trey'von snuck his hand to my thigh. I looked down at it gave him a dirty look but left it there. I didn't want to argue in front of my friends.

"Can I try?" Nicole asked. I nodded, handing her the blunt. I watched her take one hit and shake her head "no." My favorite part of the song came up. Gabby and I shared a look that made us giggle. I hummed along to the dirty lyrics.

"I aint never had dick that good," Nicole said referring to the song. I smiled amazed at how bold she is talking about this stuff.

"Girl me either, every time it's trash," Gabby said, I glanced over at Trey'von. Part of me just wanted to mess him off and agree, but I couldn't do that.

"Shit, I can't relate. The last person that gave me dick damn near got me crazy," I admitted. Trey'von sent me a glare, looked back at Tony and then at me.

313

"WHO?" He yelled at me. I rolled my eyes at him, laughing, as he put out the blunt.

"You pendejo" I said. He nodded his head visibly relaxing and making us all laugh. He's so annoying. He wants to believe I messed with someone else after him so bad, but I didn't. I grabbed my phone just as the song ended. I scrolled through my playlist turning on 'None of your Concern" by Jhene Aiko. The car fell silent once they realized which song I was playing. I saw Gabby and Nicole giving me worried looks, but I just shrugged as I looked at my phone. I knocked Trey'von's hand away from my thigh, making wave me off. As the song played, and I hummed along, I watched his jaw clench as his knuckles began to turn white from how tightly he was holding the steering wheel.

"Fuck you and that subliminal ass music," Trey'von snapped. Fuck me? So that's his energy? I could have said fuck him last night and let him go out and get into a car wreck, but instead I let him sleep in my bed and gave my dad 50 g's to keep him from calling the police.

"No, fuck you Trip. Tell me another person that would have taken care of you how I did? You can't, but you still fucking left me and had a whole other bitch," I snapped at him. The tension in the air was growing thick our tempers spiked.

"I ALREADY TOLD YOU I WASN'T GOING TO DO ANYTHING WITH HER. IT DOESN'T MATTER IF I DID OR NOT! YOU AND WHATS-HIS-FACE BACK THERE GOT A THING. YOU MOVED ON LIKE I WASN'T SHIT WHILE I LAID UP IN THE HOUSE EVERY NIGHT THINKING ABOUT YOU!" he yelled. Something about his accusation shot right through me. It wasn't true and I hated that he thought it was. I felt my eyes burning with tears of anger and hurt as my hearing faded in and out.

"I DIDN'T FUCKING MOVE ON FROM YOU. YOU DIDN'T STRUGGLE WITH SHIT MOTHERFUCKER. YOU JUST GOT HIGH AND PASSED OUT EVERY FUCKING NIGHT. I WAS THE ONE LAYING IN BED SOBBING OVER YOU!" I yelled as hot tears ran down my face. He sucked his teeth and shook his head.

"IT'S A DANCE. I'M NOT GONNA FUCK HIM!" I yelled at Trip. He looked over at me and made a face that told me he was calling me a bitch and a liar.

"Yeah, I fucking bet. That all you females are good for," he spat. I wiped away my tears which were only being replaced by more. His words rattled around in my head, pissing me off even more. Before my brain caught up with my movement, I was hitting him not in his face just in his arm and ribs.

"STOP, I'M DRIVING DO YOU WANT TO DIE AND KILL EVERYONE ELSE?" he yelled, grabbing my wrists with one hand and trying to stop my attack that I know didn't hurt him.

"I DON'T CARE TRIP. UNDERSTAND I HAVEN'T CARED ABOUT MY LIFE IN WEEKS AND I'M NOT SUDDENLY GOING TO CARE BECAUSE YOU SNUCK INTO MY BEDROOM, HIGH, LAST NIGHT---." He cut me off, sending me a glare as I fought to get my hands free from him.

"WHAT ABOUT EVERYBODY ELSE?" he yelled as I got my hands free and hit him again.

"I DON'T GIVE A FUCK TRIP. FUCK ALL OF THEM AND FUCK YOU!" I yelled as he swerved on the street.

"Hold up, let me pull over cause you trippin," he said, making me shake my head. I gave him a dirty look as he pulled over, parking next to the curb. I watched as he ripped his seat belt off, turned and glared at me.

"SAY IT! SAY WHATEVER THE FUCK IS BOTHERING YOU SO YOU'LL STOP FUCKING TRIPPIN!" he yelled. His voice seemed almost louder due to the small space in my car.

"MY PROBLEM IS YOU AND HOW YOU DON'T GIVE A FUCK ABOUT ME. YOU JUST RAN OFF DOING DRUGS AND GETTING FUCKING DRUNK WHILE MY WHOLE LIFE STOPPED. DID YOU EVEN THINK ABOUT THAT GIRL LAST NIGHT? THE GIRL YOU STOPPED DRINKING FOR. DID YOU THINK ABOUT ME ONCE BEFORE YOU SNORTED FUCKING COKE AND MESSED WITH STRIPPERS?" I screamed. I didn't even realize it was bothering me so much until the words escaped my lips, but it honestly hurt worse than him leaving me.

"Wait, there was another girl?" Gabby asked, leaning up and looking at us with wide eye eyes.

"STAY OUT OF IT!" Trey'von and I yelled together at her which made her slink back.

"Look, right there is a cute little dress shop. Let's go," Nicole said, and Tony practically bailed from the car along with Gabby. Once they were out me and Trey'von glared at each other.

"NO, I DIDN'T THINK ABOUT HER AND I WON'T THINK ABOUT HER AGAIN UNTIL I'M WRITING THE CHECK FOR HER COLLEGE TUITION. AS FOR YOU BABY GIRL, YOU'RE ALL I EVER FUCKING THINK ABOUT. THAT'S THE WHOLE REASON I DRANK BECAUSE I COULDN'T GET YOU OUT OF MY HEAD, BUT I KNEW I FUCKED YOU UP ALREADY. YOU DON'T TRUST ME SO HOW AM I SUPPOSED TO BE WITH YOU? AND I KNEW YOU WASN'T COOL ABOUT THE STRIPPER!" He yelled, punching the steering wheel, making his knuckles bust open. I wanted to keep the adrenaline flowing so I could tell him how much I hated him, but I didn't hate him. It was the exact opposite of hate. I wasn't really angry anymore over anything he did. I was hurt by it. I was so hurt it was like I couldn't breathe. I closed my eyes, burying my face in my hands, just sobbing.

"Why Trey'von? Why am I not good enough for you? If you were thinking about me why didn't you just come home to me? I waited every damn day for you to come back," I sobbed. My chest ached so bad I didn't know how I'd live through it. I tried to bring my knees up to stop the aching, but he pushed them down.

"Baby, come here," he whispered, touching my side. I uncovered my face, unbuckling, I moved over the middle part as he adjusted his seat back. I crawled onto his lap straddling him, hiding my face in his neck sobbing as I wrapped my arms around him.

"Shhh Baby Girl, don't cry. I'm not going to leave you ever again, even when you get tired of me," he whispered, grabbing a handful of my hair and kissing my shoulder. I held him tighter, shaking my head.

"That's the problem. I'm never going to get tired of you. I can't even hate you like I did before, and I want to so damn bad" I cried as he rubbed my back.

TREY'VON

I hated this. I hated how upset she was and how much she wanted to hate me. I didn't want that. I wanted to be her everything, like she was to me. I squeezed her tighter, taking in that heavenly fruity marijuana smell that lingered on her.

"I don't want you to hate me. You are my everything Baby. I can't even do my day-to-day without you. I'm so caught up on you I can't function, and I don't know how to deal with that," I admitted, playing with her curls as she snuggled further into me, which felt nice.

"That's all you ever had to say. We could have went as slow as you needed to go, but instead you pushed me away," she cried. I pushed her to sit up. She moved, looking away from me with black streaks running down her face. I wiped away the makeup stains, grabbed her face and made her look at me.

"Baby, I'm not going anywhere. I'm gonna sit back and let you have this boyfriend but at the end of the day I'm gonna be the one you come back to," I promised her. She shook her head "no," grabbed my face and squeezed my cheeks together.

"For the last time he is not my boyfriend. What do I need to do to prove that to you? I just told them how good your dick is. What, do I need to suck it in front of him too?" she asked sarcastically. I mean that would be hot. I couldn't help but laugh. Her chocolate brown eyes burned with raw truth and the need for me to believe her.

"Only if you want to. It's all yours. I believe you," I told her. She let out a breath and connected opening the car door and getting out. I followed her, shutting the door. I smiled as I fixed her makeup, making her blush.

"There, now you don't look like you was suckin dick," I teased. She laughed elbowing me playfully as we walked across the street.

"Oh, Baby Girl. Don't ever hit me again," I warned her, she looked at me with an embarrassed tint to her cheeks.

"I'm sorry. I shouldn't have done that," she said, but I waved it off. She didn't hit me hard, but it was enough to piss me off. I probably deserved to get the shit beat of out me for how I've been treating her, but that's about to change. We walked over to the dress shop and I opened the door for her. I stared at her ass as she walked in. I followed her in and saw Travis sitting on a couch, so I walked over and sat next to him. I got on my phone while the girls shopped for dresses.

ELEANOR

"We need to do something bold like an animal print, so we'll stand out," Tony told me as I tossed dresses onto my arm. I looked up giving him a 'hell no' look. I was not wearing no ugly ass animal print to a dance I didn't even want to go to.

"No, I want to be a simple red and black," I told him shaking my head "no." He groaned, opening his mouth to argue with me, when suddenly hands grabbed the dresses from me. I looked up, to see Trey'von sending Tony a scary glare.

"Red and black sounds perfect Baby," Trey'von said. I couldn't stop the smirk from finding my face as Tony nodded.

"Totally agree," Tony said, making me smile. Trey'von pushed me towards the dressing rooms. I followed him to a room as he walked in and put the clothes down. Without a word he walked out, shutting the door behind him. I sighed, looking at all the dresses, but there was one I grabbed to just strictly mess with Trey'von. It was sexy, like too sexy. It was a deep red one piece. The skirt was short like coochie out if I bent down short. The top was like half and half. One side looked kinda formal in a sexy way and went into a choker while the other was a bra. Once I managed to get the dress on I turned, looking in the mirror at myself and liking what I saw. My ass looked amazing. I hid my grin, as I walked out, looking down.

"What do you think?" I asked, spinning around in front of Trey'von and Tony but I didn't care what Tony thought.

"Yes," Tony said without a question, shaking his head up and down in the goofiest way possible. Trey'von's jaw was wide open as he looked at me. His heavy nearly black eyes made goosebumps rise on my skin as they looked me up and down from head to toe.

"Fuck no, dude. I'm about to shoot you for even looking at her. Baby, no please put on clothes. You can't wear that without me around," Trey'von complained as I spun looking at my butt. I was about to make a sassy comment when I heard a female voice.

"Champagne?" I heard. I looked up to see a girl standing in front of Trey'von, but his eyes were steadily on me. She looked like she belonged at Hooters. Her top was so low it was practically screaming "look at my boobs." Her shorts were so short and tight she had a whole camel toe. She was thin, curve-less. Her skin was snowy white. Her blonde hair looked wiry and not soft at all.

"Excuse me handsome. Champagne?" she asked him, again touching his shoulder.

"He's 19. Underage" I retorted at her. She glanced back at me rolling her eyes sending me a dirty look, as she stared back at Trey'von, but his eyes were still scanning me up and down.

"So, our secret," she batted her eyelashes at him. I looked over at Nicole and Gabby who looked back at me, amused.

TREY'VON

Elly looked amazing in that dress. It was the sexiest thing, and we weren't leaving this store without it. She just wasn't wearing it to that stupid dance. I couldn't help but glance up at the desperate store girl who was trying so hard to get my attention. I didn't give a fuck about her and it was taking everything in me not to cause a scene. I didn't want to upset Elly anymore than she already was.

"So, our secret," she batted her eyelashes at me. I gave her a look of disgust as I looked back at my baby. Elly looked at her friends and then at me, smiling.

"Papi what do you think?" she asked, walking over to me. I opened my arms and let her sit on my lap. I saw the jealousy in her eye, but she had no reason to be jealous because she's the only one I care about.

"I like it, but not for what you got going on," I told her. She smiled, touching my cheek and leaning into kiss me. I was taken back by the action. I felt my eyes grow wide as she moved her lips on mine. I felt the connection spark between us without even kissing her back. I quickly shook away my shock, smiling. I grabbed her pulling her even closer and kissing her back. The feeling was even more intense than any kiss we've shared before. I felt my head spin as a natural high filled my body. It was better than any acid, coke, weed, molly anything like that. I saw fireworks behind my eyes. My heart skipped a beat as her fingers ran through my long curls. My knees grew weak and if I wasn't sitting, I knew they'd dare to give out. My stomach twisted in a way I had never felt. Sparks flew in every direction as I heard explosions off in the distance.

Elly reached up, grabbing my jaw. She pulled away with a lustful glint in her eye. She licked my lips in the sexiest way, pushing her tongue into my mouth. I couldn't stop the throaty groan from escaping into her mouth as her tongue traced mine, teasing it. I grabbed her butt making her giggle as she glided her tongue across mine. I felt my jeans tightening as I moaned into her mouth once more. She pulled away laughing, leaving a hot wet sloppy kiss on my neck.

"Papi, I need help with the back of my dress. There is a zipper and a hook," she pouted. I smirked, glancing up at the shop girl who looked at us in total shock and disgust. Fuck, that was the best kiss I've gotten. She can keep getting jealous if it means I get more of those. It was nasty and sexy. I wanted her more than anything right now.

"Of course, Baby," I smiled, kissing her lips again, making her giggle. She got up, grabbed my hand and rested it on her butt.

"Actually, there is only one person allowed in the dressing rooms," the shop girl snapped. Elly looked her up and down with a smirk.

"So, our secret," Elly shot as the venom dripped from her tone. She shoulder checked the shop girl which made her drop the tray. I laughed following Elly into the dressing room, shutting the door behind us. I went to grab her, but she moved, giving me a look.

"Nope, we still have a lot to talk about. I just didn't want her flirting with you," she told me, undoing her dress. I sighed, sitting on the bench and watching her undress.

"So, you mean to tell me that nasty kiss was just for her?" I asked. She shrugged, turning her back to me and grabbing another dress.

"No, I wanted to kiss you. She just gave me the reason to," she told me. I nodded, grabbing the skirt and fixing it.

"The jealousy is hot," I commented. She turned, fixing the top of a dress I already hated. It was ugly.

A FEW HOURS LATER

We're at like our third dress shop. The first one Elly got mad because the shop girl came back to flirt with me again, so no one was allowed to buy their dresses from there. The other two girls already found their dresses, but not Elly. I loved watching her play dress up, but I was tired. I was ready to go home and sleep off the rest of my hangover.

"BABY GIRL LET'S GO. I WANT TO GO TO BED, I'M STILL HUNGOVER!" I yelled after her. Her friends gave me dirty looks but I didn't care.

"Ok, ok. What do you guys think?" she asked. I looked up to find my jaw fall instantly. Her dress was sexy but covered everything. It was a red two piece. The top sparkled like it was made of diamonds. It was high necked but cropped and sleeveless. The skirt was silky and floor length. There was slit in it showing her her beautiful russet leg.

"That's the one!" Tony told her as I just stared. She smiled but looked over at me as goosebumps rose on her skin.

"Trip?" she asked. I got up and walked over to her spinning her around.

"I'm gonna have to go to that stupid dance just to fuck you in the bathroom," I teased her. She gasped, hiding her face in my chest making me chuckle.

"Get it Baby Girl. You look gorgeous," I whispered, kissing the top of her head. She pulled away going back into the dressing room.

"HURRY UP!" I yelled after her. I looked at the other three as I pulled out my wallet and tossed a 20 at them.

"Can you call a cab?" I asked them and they nodded quickly.

"Thank God. I did not want to get back in the car with you guys. I think I'm high," Gabby said as Elly walked out, handing me her dress as she asked her friends if they were riding with us. I snuck off as she talked and paid for the dress. Then I handed her the bag.

"I was gonna pay for it," she told me, but I just smiled at her, shaking my head "no."

"I got it. Come on let's go, I'm ready to go home myself," I admitted. She said "bye" to her friends, and we walked out to get in my car. The ride to her house was peaceful. No argument at all. Just two people talking. Once I pulled up to her house, I saw Zeke and her mom standing outside.

"Can he see us?" she whispered but I shook my head "no." The windows were too dark. She smiled, leaning over to kiss my cheek.

"Thank you. Text me," she said as I smiled

"For sure, I'll see you tomorrow, beautiful," I said, and she nodded getting out of the car with her bag. I waved at Zeke pulling out to go home.

Chapter 26

Fight for us

ELEANOR

I woke up to the loudest high-pitched noise coming from downstairs. I whined, rolling over and covering my ears with a pillow. Soon enough the noise stopped. I let out a breath and tried to fall back asleep, but the noise started ringing out again. What could they possibly be doing down there this early in the morning? I just wanted to sleep. I finally had gotten a full night's sleep and I wasn't ready to get up. The annoying loud pitch hiss continued until I sat up mumbling curses under my breath. I was literally going to murder whoever was making that noise. I got up, gathering my hair into a messy bun. I looked down at my outfit, I wore a thin spaghetti strapped crop top that said, 'No Bra Club' and a pair of tiny maroon, tight fitting, velvet shorts. I thought about changing, but honestly, I was just going to silence the noise and then go back to bed. I walked out of my room and dragged myself downstairs to find the living room empty, but music was coming from the kitchen. I rubbed my eye as I walked into the kitchen. I froze in the doorway when I saw the source of the noise.

Kneeling on my kitchen floor was Trey'von. In front of him was a huge white sheet of dry wall. He had a tape measure and a marker in hand. I couldn't lie, he looked fucking sexy as he focused on his project. His long black curls were pulled back into a bun and he wore clear work glasses. His eyebrows were pulled together in concentration. He wore a thin white wife beater and a pair of basketball shorts. The muscles in his arms were strained, making them look even bigger. His broad exposed shoulders were

323

tense. You could see each muscle move under his tattooed skin. His normal bronze skin glistened in the kitchen lights from the layer of sweat covering him. There was white paint on his arms, hands, and a stripe going across his forehead. I don't know what it was about seeing him like that but in the matter of seconds I felt the hungry pit for him form deep in my stomach as the needy tingles took over between my thighs. I felt the soft wetness pooling inside my panties. I crossed my legs trying to ease the burn for him as I bit my lip, watching him. Just as whatever song he had been playing ended, he looked up to catch me staring at him. I blushed, looking away, making him chuckle.

"Good morning Baby Girl." His eyes held amusement as they wondered over. I swallowed hard, walking further into the kitchen. For the first time, I noticed the whole wall missing. It wasn't just the part he had punched, but the whole thing. The other three were painted white, they were no longer yellow. What was he doing? Why is he doing it?

"Yeah, good morning. What are you doing?" I asked, raising an eyebrow. He stood up and looked back at the missing wall. His wife beater was hugging his lean muscular body and showing off his pecks and abs. I could see the black, blue and red ink through his tank top, which only made my hunger for him grow.

"Well, besides being eye raped by you, I'm fixing the wall," He teased. I blushed, looking up at his nearly black eyes. I knew my eyes were wide from his words. He chuckled at me, shaking his head.

"When I said you had to fix this, I meant write a check and let a professional do it," I told him. His eyes scanned my body, the weight of them felt so nice after being without them for so long. I felt a shiver run up my spine as goosebumps covered my skin. He licked his lips looking at my top and then finding my eyes.

"Yeah, I could have, but then I started thinking, why let some stranger come into my girl's house and do a half ass job when I could do it myself?" he shrugged, looking over my outfit again and then up to my face. I felt like the blush was permanent at this point. Just as I went to tell him he didn't have to do all this, my mom and Izzy came into the kitchen with shopping bags.

"Oh Elly, you're awake finally. You got a real keeper here. He showed up at 7:30 in the morning and asked to come in and fix the wall. Then when I told him I didn't really like the color in here, he offered to paint the whole kitchen and has been giving me the best home improvement ideas. Good trait to have in a husband," Mom said suggestively making our eyes grow wide. We looked away from each other with a blush. Marriage? To Trey'von? Yeah, right.

"Ok Trip, this is the last one," I heard Mateo call as she walked in carrying a gallon of paint. He motioned for her to put it with the others.

"I've been helping him, Elly. I don't know why Dad hates him, he's super cool," Mateo boasted. My Mom laughed as Izzy sent me a teasing.

"I second that. You're welcome here whenever, Trip. Now Elly don't be a distraction," Mom scolded, making me look at her with an opened mouth as Trey'von laughed, turning back to the dry wall. Mateo sat next to him trying to help with the tape measure as mom and Izzy walked out.

"Can I help?" I asked, looking at the pair. Trey'von looked up at me with a smile.

"Nah, Baby Girl, we got it. But thank you," he said. He was rejecting my help? I don't know why that bothered me. Maybe because I wanted to spend time with him.

"Ok," I said, walking over the freezer to pull out waffles.

"Don't eat. I'm taking you out to breakfast once I get this hung and mudded," Trey'von told me. I looked at him raising an eyebrow. How long was that gonna take?

"Can I go?" Mateo asked, looking up at him, making him laugh.

"Sorry kid, but no. I have to make your sister love me again," he playfully whispered to her. I scoffed, rolling my eyes in annoyance. I do not love Trey'von Walker and I never have.

"How long is that gonna take? I'm hungry," I complained. He got up, took the box from me and put it back.

"A couple hours. Come on Baby, please?" he asked pouting his lip. I crossed my arms with a look. He laughed, opened a cabinet and pulled out a pack of Oreo's tossing them to me.

"Pancakes after I'm done. I promise," he said. I sighed nodding my head as I tore open the pack and grabbed a juice from the fridge. I walked out of the kitchen and back upstairs to my bedroom.

TREY'VON

A COUPLE HOURS LATER

I looked at the wall, approving my and Mateo's work. I didn't let her help mud because it's just too hard of a process and she'd be in the way. Now to go make things right between me and my Baby Girl. I grabbed my phone walked through the living room and up the stairs. I went to Elly's bedroom door. I tried to listen in, but I just heard the TV. I opened the door to see Elly in bed laying on her stomach watching TV. My eyes wandered down to her butt. It was hard not to stare at it. Her ass was literally falling out of those shorts. It was the biggest fucking tease.

"You all done?" she asked, pulling my eyes away from her butt. She looked over at me, her chocolate brown eyes scanning my body as she bit her lip.

"For now. I have to let the mud dry and then paint," I explained with a shrug. She nodded, looking up at me again. I looked over to the TV away, from her sexy body.

"What are you watching?" I asked her curiously

"Gotti. Come watch it with me," she invited, opening her arms for me to come into them. She wanted to cuddle with me?

"Baby, I'm sweaty and covered in mud," I warned, looking down. She shrugged, pouting her lip at me.

"Trey'von," she complained, waving me over. Who was I to tell her "no?" I couldn't lie, I wanted her cuddles too. I walked over and got on the bed. She smiled, making me lay down. She rested her head on my chest, as her thigh settled on my waist. I smiled, pulling her hair out of its bun and playing with her curls as my other hand went to her thigh.

"You do stink," She giggled, looking up at me.

"I was going to take a shower, but you wanted to cuddle," I defended. She hummed closing her eyes. I know she was not trying to go to sleep right now, we are going to breakfast and talking.

"Don't go to sleep," I said, tapping her leg and making her laugh.

"You're comfy," she whispered wiggling around, getting more comfortable. I chuckled, closing my eyes and just enjoying this time she's letting me be close to her.

"It was sexy watching you work," she told me. My eyes opened in surprise. She was looking up at me with a sly smile.

"What about it was sexy?" I asked, pulling my bottom lip between my teeth. She sat up so she was full on straddling me. She slipped her hands under my tank top.

"Seeing you all sweaty and focused. Then your muscles were like, popping," she whispered leaning down to kiss me, but I looked away, not letting her. It was obvious she was wanting sex, but I couldn't until we talked about everything.

"Trey'von, don't reject me," she whined grabbing my face, trying to kiss me. I laughed swiping her off my lap and onto the bed.

"We need to talk first because you'll regret anything we do unless we talk about this. I want us to be good. Can I use that soap that I used last time? It smelled good," I asked, getting up. She groaned getting up going to the closet to grab a towel and the body soap.

"Do you need my hair stuff?" she asked, but I just waved it off.

"Nah, I'm gonna throw on a beanie. Just wear sweats. That's what I'm about to wear," I told her as she handed me the towel and soap.

"You know where the bathroom is," she sassed. I smiled shaking my head, walking out of the room and down the stairs, I walked out to my truck, unlocking it. I grabbed sweats, a t-shirt, a beanie, and boxers. I put extra clothes in my truck because I knew we were going to go out. I shut my truck door, and went back inside and upstairs, just as I walked into the bathroom, I saw Elly standing inside looking at the mirror.

"Oh sorry," I said, starting to walk out.

"No, you're fine. I was washing my hands," she said, walking past me and out the door. I looked at her ass, closing my eyes. I let out a breath, shut the bathroom door, and stripped out of my dirty clothes. I got in the shower doing what I needed to do and then got out. I grabbed the towel drying off and then tried to get my hair as dry as I could. I changed into my grey Nike sweats, my white t-shirt, and my black beanie that said, 'Bad hair day'. I tossed back on my shoes and grabbed my dirty clothes and walked back to Elly's room to find her sitting on the edge of her bed looking up at the TV. She looked amazing. She had on a pair of baggy grey sweats that said "Playboy" down the side with a black shadow of a curvy woman. She wore a maroon lace bralette, with a black velvet choker and a pair of fluffy maroon Ugg sandals. Her hair was pulled up in a messy styled bun with strands framing her face and she wore no makeup.

"Damn Baby Girl, even in sweats you make me look like a bum," I said. She looked over at me her eyes falling to my dick. I laughed, shaking my head throwing my dirty clothes in her basket.

"I mean, you're just wearing male lingerie to breakfast," She teased me as she got up grabbing her purse. I looked at her, shocked, as she looked down at her shoes, trying to hide her smile.

"As long as you're going titties out, I'm going dick out," I joked, making her laugh. I bit my lip looking over her outfit one more time.

ELEANOR

I took another hit from the joint and passed it to Trey'von. I blew out the smoke, grabbing his water and taking a drink. I looked over to see him hit it fast twice and then put it out in the ash tray. He coughed slightly, so I handed him the water.

"You ready?" He asked and I nodded. I opened the door jumping down out of the huge truck that Trey'von had to help me get into. It was white and so tall I literally had to climb to get in. When I asked him where he got it he told me it was his. I wasn't sure what brand it was, but it was nice.

"I want French Toast," I told him as we walked into 'The Griddle'. He held open the door for me and I walked over to the little hostess booth as a waiter came over. His eyes wandered my body as a smile spread across his lips. He was kinda cute, I can't lie. He was tall like 6'9, light skinned, and covered in tattoos. His hair was buzzed and bleached.

"How many? I'm sure a beautiful woman like yourself isn't dining alone?" He flirted. I began to tell him there would be just two but arms wrapped around my waist, stopping me.

"Two," Trey'von told the waiter as I looked up towards him. He kissed my cheek, making me giggle. I knew he was trying to claim me, which was annoying because we aren't together, but I wouldn't reject him in front of a guy that was clearly flirting with me.

"Follow me," the waiter said. I moved from Trey'von's arms with a glare. I followed to waiter a table, thanking him.

"What would you like drink?" he asked, smiling at me. Trey'von sucked his teeth as he started growing impatient.

"Just a coffee please and I'm sure he'd like water," I said. He nodded, handing me the menus, sending me a wink and walking away.

"Alright, I'm gonna shoot him," Trey'von said, standing up. I laughed, grabbing his hand and pulling in down into the booth with me.

"Not in public," I joked. He rolled his eyes at me, grabbing my leg and putting it over his own. I already knew what I wanted, so I didn't bother to look. Soon enough Trey'von figured out what he wanted, and the waiter came back with our drinks and looked at my leg on Trey'von.

"What can I get you, beautiful? It's on the house," he flirted. I couldn't help but laugh and shake my head.

"Maybe a new fucking waiter," Trey'von growled. I forced a smile, resting my hand on Trey'von's arm.

"I'll just take French toast and bacon. Trip?" I ordered, grabbing Trey'von's shaking hand as the waiter looked at my boobs.

"Yo, I'll fucking kill you. Stop eye fucking my girlfriend," Trey'von snapped as he tried to get up, but I didn't let him.

"He'll just have pancakes with a side of bacon," I ordered giving him an "are you kidding me" look. The waiter walked quickly away and once he was out of view, I ripped away from Trey'von.

"Really Trip? Why do you have to be so rude? And I'm not your girlfriend. If you don't remember, I'm still mad at you" I retorted, crossing my arms. He looked at me, shocked, but I mean, there is no reason for him to talk to other people like that.

"You're joking. He was flirting with you right in front me Baby Girl. It's clear you're here with me. It's disrespectful," He shot back at me. I rolled my eyes giving him an unamused look.

"But was I flirting back? No, I wasn't---." He cut me off, slamming his hands on the table. For the first time I noticed how busted his knuckles truly were from our fight.

"IT DOESN'T MATTER," he yelled. I sank lower in the booth, covering my face from the questioning eyes. I felt my cheeks burn with embarrassment. He put his head on the table.

"Baby Girl, I'm sorry for yelling. I don't want to fight, I just want to talk," he sounded tired and defeated when he spoke. His nearly black eyes burning into me. My skin shivered with goosebumps as I lowered my hands, rubbing my arms.

"I don't want to fight with you either Trey'von. I genuinely miss being around you, but I'm still so hurt by everything you did and now all we've been doing is fighting," I told him, using my hands to talk. I just wanted to go back to how we were when we sat in my living room playing Monopoly, or how I thought we were gonna be after "that night."

"Then Baby, let's not fight. I know you are hurt, and I know how much I fucked up. I regret that shit every single day," he said. I felt the sting of tears at his words. It hurt to hear him say all of this because I still didn't understand why he did it. The last time I tried to talk to him, we blew up on each other and this was not the place. I grabbed my coffee, taking a sip and trying to hide my tears.

TREY'VON

I watched Elly take a drink of her coffee as she tried her hardest to hold back tears. I hated how she cried when we talked about this, but I knew she was still hurt. She cleared her throat, looking back up at me.

"I just don't understand Trey'von. You told me after we had sex that you had feelings for me, that you got scared, but what is there to be scared of? Especially when I told you I felt the exact same way?" She asked me, her long nails hitting the table with each word she spoke. I saw that they needed to be done. One was broken and they were grown out. I pushed away the thoughts about her nails, sighing and hiding my face in my hands.

"I told you I had never been in this situation before," I defended myself. But she just shook her head, tears slipping from her eyes. I watched her close her eyes, her long lashes brushing her cheek.

"That's an excuse, that's not the reason," she said as a sob ripped from her, making me groan. Just as I started to wipe her tear away, I heard a throat clear. I looked up to see the waiter looking at me with a smirk. I will literally gut him in the parking lot. Elly cleared her throat, wiping her tears away.

"French toast and bacon. A napkin for your tears," he said, pulling one out and handing it to Elly. She smiled, thanking him quietly as he sat my food down. I rolled my eyes looking back at Elly, grabbing her hand, but she ripped away from me, glaring.

"Can you stop staring at me and just go. You brought our food. It looks good. Thanks." She had misplaced all the anger she felt for me onto the waiter. He looked at her, shocked, but nodded and walked away. Dumb ass.

"Tell me the truth, that's all I want. I'm not going to judge you. It's not going to change the way I see you or feel about you Trey'von," she promised but it would. She'd think I was a monster. Hell, my own mom told me I was Lucifer in the flesh and my siblings, that I fucking raised, ditched me the moment they could. I wasn't worthy of her, and she'd see that the moment I let her in and it scared me.

"You will though, everyone does. I try to forget about it, but I can't because without that, I wouldn't be where I'm at in life," I explained. She'd leave this time. It wouldn't be that I tell her my biggest skeleton and she would stay. I felt her move closer, her hands grabbing my face. But I just brushed them off.

"Trey'von, I don't know what you're talking about, but I just want to be there for you. Nothing but you right here, right in this moment could change the way I feel about you. I care what happened to you in the past, but I wouldn't leave you over it," she said. I grabbed her, and pulled her closer, hiding my face in her neck taking in the fruity/marijuana smell she carried. She wrapped her arms around me, holding me tightly. I had to feel it one more time. I pulled away, pushing back a strand of her hair.

"I'm scared history will repeat itself and I'll become him. I don't want that, and I don't want you to take the role of my mom. I never dated because of that, but I never gave a girl the time of day before you," I told her. She looked at me confused, not knowing what I was talking about. She grabbed my hands, kissing my busted knuckles.

"You don't want to become who?" she asked me quietly.

"Paul, my fucking step-dad," I said. She reached up, grabbing my face, her chocolate brown eyes staring directly into mine. She had a serious, but concerned, expression.

"You are not Paul, you are your own man," she assured. I nodded my head, cringing, knowing I had to tell her.

"My mom was strung out on crack. She'd prostitute and bring her nasty ass client's home. She'd fuck them anywhere in the house, regardless of me, my brother, or my sister being home. Then Paul, he was a drunk, and a fucking mean one. He used to beat the shit out of my mom and me. He'd try to go for my brother and sister, but I wouldn't let him. I'd provoke him. One time he set out a cane, a hammer, or a belt and told me to pick one. I picked the hammer because, fuck him, he wasn't going to break me," I told her, tears filling my eyes at the memory. Every part of me wanted to lash out at her, but it wasn't her fault. She looked at me with wide, shocked eyes. She moved to hug me, tucking my head in her shoulder. I let the tears slip as I hugged her back tightly.

"Then he did break me. Later, one really bad night. I was 9 years old. I had been doing little jobs for Los Prophets for money. He came home and went into my sister's bedroom, but I was sleeping with her. She had nightmares. He tried to pull down her pants. I fought him. The fat bastard ended up tying me up and putting me in the bathtub. He tased me off and on for two hours. That very next day, I went and got jumped into Los Prophets. After I healed, I had one of the guys take me to Paul's work and I shot him in the head 5 times. He was the first person I ever killed," I admitted. She pulled away, wiping my tears and kissing my cheeks and nose. Her eyes were filled with tears, but she was trying to be strong for me.

"Fuck him, he deserved it. You were just a kid," she told me. I knew she couldn't handle any more stories. That wasn't even the worst that had happened to me.

"I was never a kid. I couldn't be one, but that's ok. So that's why I'm scared to love you because what if I am him? What if one day I decided to pick up the bottle again, and you're at home waiting for me. Then what if my life becomes too stressful for you, being gone and risking my life. What if you decide to pick up a pipe and then we bring kids into this world?" I asked her, shaking my head, trying to push away from her, but she wouldn't let me.

ELEANOR

I was trying so hard to not cry, but to finding out what he had gone through all of that at just 9 years old was too hard for me even to think about. He tried to push me away, but I just held his hands and refused to let him go. I didn't care that he killed his stepdad. He deserved it. I just wanted Trey'von. I wanted to be there for him.

"Trey'von, I am not your mom, and you are not Paul. You don't drink anymore because you saw him in yourself. I can promise you I will never smoke crack. You are a better man than what he could ever have been. I promise you we will not be your parents. Don't push me away over them," I begged. Trey'von couldn't ever become that. He might have a hard outter shell, but inside he wasn't that.

"How do you know?" he asked, his voice cracking. I moved to straddle his lap and made him look at me.

"Because I won't let us. I won't let you drink, do drugs, or become Paul and I know I won't become anything like your mother. As for you not knowing how to be a boyfriend, that's ok. I'll help you learn. We can move at your pace. Trey'von, you are so much more than your past. You are violent and scary sometimes, but that's who you've been forced to be all your life. You're not that with me, you are gentle and a softy," I teased, poking his nose. He chuckled, hiding his face in my chest. I messed with his beanie, leaned down and kissed the top of his head.

"You don't think I'm a monster for killing the man that raised me?" he asked. I shook my head "no," kissing his head again.

"You aren't a monster, you never were. He was, Trey'von. Did someone tell you that you were?" I asked him, moving to make him look at me. He scoffed, shaking his head, licking his teeth.

"My brother and sisters are older, but I was always street smart, so I took care of them. When I was 12, my sister turned 18. She took my older brother with her and moved out. She left me with my mom because I was in a gang, and they all swore I was dangerous. My mom put me out on the streets of South-Central LA. She told me she hated me because I killed the love of her life and I was Satan in the flesh," he told me. I shook my head, feeling my temper spike. What type of mother is she? Her fucking boyfriend was beating on her kids, and she didn't care.

"You aren't. You were just protecting the people you loved and I'm sorry they didn't see that, but I do," I told him. He nodded, looking at my boobs, making me laugh and cover them with my arms. He smirked leaning up leaving a sloppy kiss on my neck.

"Fight for us Baby Girl because I'm using everything in me to fight, but I feel like I'm losing," he whispered as he left another kiss. I smiled, leaning into him with a hug.

"I'm going to. Thank you for opening up now let's eat. I'm starving," I said, making him laugh. I got off of him to take a bite of my now cold bacon. We dropped all the heavy and just talked and joked around with no arguments.

"Babe, look," Trey'von called. I turned around to see he had painted a huge heart on the wall and inside it said "Trip + Baby Girl." I pouted my lip, looking at him like he was the cutest thing ever. Don't get me wrong, I still am hurt by his actions. I knew he had a bad past, but I didn't know it was that level of abuse. It made sense that leaving was his reaction to actually having feelings for me, but I needed time.

"You are so cute," I said as Mateo playfully gagged, making me laugh. I heard the front door slam shut. I went back to painting my section of the wall in the kitchen.

"What's going on in here?" I heard my dad. I turned to look at him smiling and walking over to Trey'von, who just kept painting.

"Trip fixed the wall and he's painting the kitchen, but let me and Mateo help," I smiled, hugging him from behind. He laughed, reaching around touching my leg.

"Only because you wouldn't stop crying about being left out," he said, making me gasp and shush him.

"And you got 50 g's I need you to run back," Trey'von said, and I stepped away, seeing he was about to become the business him.

"That was payment to keep you out of jail," my dad spat. Trey'von pulled his gun out, sitting it on the table.

"You broke our deal already. Baby Girl is going to the dance, so technically you are a dead man walking. Now the cash," Trey'von demanded. I went back to painting the wall. I didn't know what they were talking about, but I'd find out.

"Elly," Dad tried to chime me in, but I shook my head no.

"Nope, I don't know anything about a deal," I dismissed him.

"THE CASH!" Trip yelled. Dad walked over to a cabinet and pulled out my duffel, tossing it in front of Trip who nodded.

"Damn Babe, that ass looking fat," Trey'von teased. I started to turn to look at him, but I felt something cold and wet roll over me.

"TRIP!" I seeing paint covering my sweats which made him laugh. I laughed, dipping my hand in the paint. He pointed at me, warning me not to. But I slung it at him anyway which led to a huge paint war between me, him, and Mateo.

Chapter 27

Trust Issues

TREY'VON

A WEEK LATER

I yawned running my hand over my face as I parked in front of the bar. Zeke was freaking the fuck out because he wanted to talk to me, and I wasn't up at the ass-crack of dawn for once in my life. Elly insisted I catch up on some sleep instead of taking her and Mateo to school this morning. Being back in my spot and trying to show Elly I'm never gonna leave again was a lot of work. I've never had to juggle a relationship and work before, and Zeke has been taking a lot of heat from the higher ups (Big Rico, Carlos, and Daniel aka Big Honcho). He won't tell me what's up, but it's nothing good. It never is when with those guys. I got out of my car to see Antonio at his mailbox sending me a death glare. I sent him a malicious grin, waving at him as I walked into the bar. I saw the usual guys already here. Some of them were already getting hammered. In the back corner, at his usual table, was Zeke surrounded by the regular guys. I walked over shaking up with everyone and taking my usual spot.

"I'm here, what's up?" I asked, kicking my feet up on the table. He glared at me for my action, but I just shrugged. No one had told Zeke about me and Elly, although everyone here had heard her yell out that we had sex, and still no one told. I couldn't figure out if it was because they were scared of what I'd do or if they were just loyal. Regardless, I was happy for it.

336

"What are you going to do about Antonio?" Zeke asked me. I raised an eyebrow at him in question. I didn't know what he was talking about. As far as I knew he's just a fuck up and hadn't done anything to attract my attention. Recently, at least.

"Elly is going to the Homecoming dance. Don't play stupid. I know you went dress shopping with her," he snapped. I looked at him, confused about what the big deal was. When I threatened Antonio about the dance, I was the bad guy. So, what changed?

"So? Wasn't you the one preaching about how she's a high school girl that should lavish in every experience?" I mocked. My phone vibrated in my pocket. I pulled it out to see that Elly had texted me.

Baby girl😇😊- Good Morning Handsome😳

I couldn't help but smile at my phone. I pressed the lock button and sat it down. I'd text her back after I finished with Zeke.

"Are you even listening?" Zeke barked, making me look up at him with wide eyes. I laughed at him, shaking my head "no."

"Nah, sorry start over. Why is it a big deal she's going? She's not even dating that dude," I told him, looking up at him as my phone vibrated again.

"BECAUSE SHE SHOULDN'T BE GOING!" he yelled, standing up. I glared at him as he paced around like an idiot.

"You got one more fucking time to yell at me Zeke and this petty ass dance gonna be the last of your fucking worries," I warned leaning forward. He stopped pacing, and came over, pressing his palms on the table leaning down so we were almost nose to nose. His black eyes piercing mine, which only making me angrier.

"Is that a threat? Boy" he growled. I jumped up, throwing the table and getting face to face, chest to chest with him.

"Keeping trying me and find out Zeke. The higher ups already on your shit. I bet there wouldn't even be any punishment for it," I challenged. He sent me one of the hardest glares he ever had as my phone vibrated from the ground where it had fallen and was probably broken.

"I don't want Elly at that dance. Take care of it," he barked his order at me. But I wasn't doing that. It would only piss her off and I'm not tryin to do that.

"Nah, she aint my responsibility like that anymore. She's just my friend, you don't want her to go, be a man and stop her!" I snapped. He looked at me for a minute and then licked his lips.

"Ok, then you can go with her," he said dismissively as he started to walk away. He had me fucked up. I was not going to that dance. I would lose my mind watching Travis drooling over MY FUCKING GIRL and while he danced with her. I wasn't dumb. Elly was sexy, and he was gonna try something. I didn't want to lose my cool at some school dance. I wasn't going to spend my night watching someone throw themselves at what's mine and not being able to do anything about it.

"Bullshit! I'm not wasting my night at a high school dance, and she already has a date. Maybe you should spend more time with the girl you see as a kid." I kew that was going to hit a soft spot. He came storming over to me as I pulled my gun and held it up to his face.

"Watch how you steppin," I warned. He grabbed my wrist, throwing my hand out of the way.

"You're going to go. I caught word Nightmare is going as one of the girl's dates. You know those filth El Diablos don't travel alone. She'll have a target on her back. Smiley will buy you both tickets and get you in. He can sell rock to the kids," he said as he walked away. Whoa, we're selling to minors now? The strongest thing we're allowed to sell to them is marijuana, on his order. Nightmare wouldn't get around Elly and that was a promise. He got his name for a reason.

"Since when we sell to kids? Stop walking the fuck away from me!" I spat. He turned, looking me up and down, closing his eyes.

"SINCE SELLS ARE LOW TRIP. WE'RE NOT EARNING. IT'S COSTING MORE TO GET THE DAMN DRUGS HERE," he yelled. Why the fuck didn't I know about this?

"YOU DIDN'T THINK I SHOULD HAVE KNOWN ABOUT THAT? THAT'S WHY THE HIGHER UPS ARE ON YOUR ASS, HUH? DON'T WORRY, I'LL GET YOUR BITCH ASS OUT OF IT"

I yelled at him, kicking the table and making it fly a couple of feet. This gang is to be mine one day and if he wouldn't push our runners, I would. I would keep this gang alive for him so I wouldn't be moving into a train wreck when it became mine. He glared at me as my phone buzzed two more fucking times on the floor.

"You only worry about the dance and keeping Elly safe. Don't forget Lucas could be a problem, and pick up your damn phone," he shot, walking out of the bar. I shook my head and picked up my phone to find Elly was freaking the fuck out on me.

Baby girl😊😇- You're really going to leave me on read? Everything ok?

Baby girl😊😇- Did I say or do something?

Baby girl😊😇- Trey'von, if you're getting scared again just talk to me don't do this to me again please!

Baby girl😊😇- You promised you'd never leave again and look at what you're doing. You're leaving me, I should have known you would. I just don't get it because we've had a good week.

Baby girl😊😇- DON'T COME BACK THIS TIME!

Damn, this girl is over dramatic. I knew she didn't trust me, but fuck. I was meeting with Zeke who is fucking everything up and forcing me to crash her dance.

Baby girl😊😇- I didn't mean that, I always want you to come back. I missed you this morning

I laughed, shaking my head at how fast her tone and attitude changed. That was for real my Baby. A little bipolar, but shit, I wouldn't have it any other way.

ELEANOR

I walked through the lunch line behind Nicole and just grabbed random foods. My stomach was twisting and turning as I replayed the last week in my head. Everything seemed to be just fine with me and Trey'von. Actually, we've never been better. He's still adjusting to letting me in, but we haven't argued. We've been moving super slow, like not even kissing, slow. I've been working at his pace, and he's been trying to prove to me that he can be solid. I didn't understand why he was suddenly dipping out. I didn't know what could have scared him off this time. Once we got through the line and sat down. Just as Nicole started talking, my phone vibrated in my pocket. I quickly pulled it out to see Trey'von had texted me back. I let out a sigh of relief closing my eyes.

Trey'von😼😵 - Yooo baby chill😖 I was in a meeting with Zeke. I'm not going anywhere, I already promised you I'm not going anywhere, and I meant that shit. I miss you too but fuck you just broke up with me and got back with me in a 10-minute span😂

I blushed at my phone while reading his message. Ok, maybe I did overreact just a little bit, but I was so scared he'd disappear again. I couldn't handle it. Broke up? We aren't even together, are we?

Me- Sorry, I just get scared you'll get scared and leave

"ELLY!" Gabby yelled, making me jump and look up from my phone to my three friends staring at me. They laughed, eyeing me up and down.

"Tomorrow is the dance. I need shoes and makeup to go with my dress. Do you want to go shopping with me after school?" Gabby asked. I needed that stuff too. My phone vibrated again, but I ignored it for just a moment.

"I actually need that stuff too and a new set of nails. Nicole, you want to go?" I asked her, but she just smiled at me.

"Sorry Elly, I got a shift tonight," Nicole said. She recently got a job at Starbucks, so she hadn't been hanging as much. Gabby has been picking up more and more shifts. I've been with Trey'von, so I didn't know who Tony has been hanging out with.

"Tony, you want to go?" I asked him, but he just sent me a friendly white smile.

"No, you guys have a girl's day because tomorrow you are all mine," he smiled. I laughed at him as I picked up my phone and texted Trey'von back.

"Is that gang friend?" Nicole asked. I looked up at them and gave them a 'leave me alone' smile, making them roll their eyes.

"Elly, give him time to breathe. You are with him 25/8. You're going to scare him off. You said it yourself, he isn't used to all the attention," Gabby pointed out. Was I smothering Trey'von? I've been trying to go slow but what if I am around too much? That could scare him because he'd feel like it was getting serious too fast. Maybe I should give him more space.

"So, I got my suit for the dance and I'm going to have the best one there," Tony said confidently. I shook away my fears for now, smiling at Tony.

"Does it match my dress? Tony, please tell me it's not animal print," I asked nervously. I was not about to let him embarrass me. Tony tried too hard to standout sometimes and it could be so embarrassing.

"It matches your dress perfectly but has some of my own flare. You'll like it Ellles, I promise," Tony assured me. The rest of us all hummed looking at him.

"So, Nicole, who are you going with?" I asked her curiously

"No one has asked, but I mean, I'm cool going alone," she shrugged. Me and Gabby had tried to hook her up with different guys at the school, but she wasn't feeling it.

TREY'VON

I leaned against the bar, watching the guys shoot dice. Back in the alley, we had a kid getting jumped in, so I'm watching for the feds. The on top of that, Zeke and the higher ups were in the bar, so no one was allowed in unless they said so. I didn't know what they were doing here. They never come to you. You go to them. I saw the school bus pull up. I knew my little Baby would be getting off. I smirked, watching the crowd flow out.

She was one of the last one out and, fuck, she looked way too fine to be anywhere without me. She had on ones of those boob holder crop tops, but it looked like a newspaper, with light blue high-waist shorts. She had on a gold shiny body chain which drew my attention to those curves. She matched it with white vans and had those bouncy curls styled perfectly. I watched her and that Gabby girl start to walk over to me.

"Baby Girl," I smiled, starting to open my arms for her, but she just sent me a small smile and wave as she went to walk past me. Is she mad at me? Was it over the text messages? Hell no. She wasn't going to walk past me. I reached out, grabbed her belt loop and spun her over to me. She stumbled, hitting my chest hard, which made her giggle and me smile.

"You not about to walk past me like I'm a side piece," I teased, wrapping my arms around her tightly and looking over at the door to make sure no one was coming out. She grabbed a handful of my shirt, hugging me back, and then pulled away, looking up at me with a smile

"Of course, you're not just some side dude, I just thought I'd give you a little space," she said. I felt my eyebrows scrunch together at her words. Space? I don't want or need space from her. We've had enough space.

"Space?" I asked, and she nodded looking down at our feet.

"Yeah, I'm with you all of the time. I didn't want you to feel smothered by me," she said. Where would she get that she was smothering me from? I wanted to be around her all the time. I didn't like these thoughts in her head.

"Elly, can we just go?" I heard Gabby's attitude-laced voice. Then it hit me where she was getting that from. That bitch was in her ear, and I'd take of that later. I glanced to the door, cupping Elly's cheeks making her look up at me.

"Baby, we've had way too much space in our relationship. If I could have it my way, you'd be glued to me all of the time. I want to spend every second with you that I can. Plus, I get space while you're at school and asleep. That's all I ever need. Don't let someone fill your head with shit," I told her. She smiled, hugging me tightly, making me laugh. I kissed the top of her head, looking at that booty.

"You wore this to school?" I asked her, and she nodded against my chest.

"Is it ugly?" she asked, backing away and looking down.

"It's too sexy. All them high school muhfuckas probably been making moves on my girl all day," I said spinning her around. She laced together our fingers, smiling up at me.

"Well, I don't want any of those *"high school muhfuckas,"* I just want my little gangster," she teased. I smiled, shaking my head at her while looking at her ratchet ass nails.

"Yo, I'm about to take you to get your nails done. They've been driving me crazy, and you don't like them that long," I complained. She smiled, leaning up kissing my jawline.

"Thank you, but I'm going with Gabby, Mateo, and Izzy. I've been putting it off because of the dance," she said but I just scoffed.

"And Trip. Plus, I need your help, I got to go shopping for a suit," I smirked, pretending to straighten a tie. I knew she'd be pissed about me crashing the dance, but I didn't have much of a choice.

"And who you tryin to look sexy for?" she asked. Just as I went to answer, Smiley came running up.

"Yo, I just asked Nicole to the dance like you said and she said yes," he told me, doing a dance.

"MY FUCKING BOY!" I yelled, shaking up with him.

"So, you ready to see us dressed up for the dance Elly?" Smiley asked, putting his arm around me which made me cringe. She looked at me shocked, and I saw the anger behind her eyes.

"You don't trust me? Is that why you're gonna baby sit me?" she snapped, crossing her arms, which made me close my eyes.

"No Baby, I trust you with my fucking life. I wasn't gonna go but Zeke---." she cut me off with a shrug.

"You took back your spot, tell him to fuck off," she told me with nothing but attitude. I laughed, shaking my head.

"Zeke got word that there is going to be a potential issue there. You can have fun and pretend me, and Smiley aren't there. I tried, but when he said you could be in danger, I couldn't say 'no'" I told her with a shrug. She looked at me, squinting her eyes and then sighed.

"Fine, you should wear a Scarface suit," she suggested, I sent her a look of disgust. She smiled, trying to grab my hands, but I pulled them away. I was getting nervous that Zeke and the higher ups would come out.

"Zeke is inside with the higher ups. I think they're about to finish up. Smiley, go tell them that girl has had enough," I ordered waving him off, and he took off towards the alley.

ELEANOR

I watched Smiley run off to the alley were someone was getting jumped into the gang. Higher ups? I thought Zeke was as high as you could get.

"Higher ups?" I asked Trey'von, raising an eyebrow, and he nodded his head.

"They are a selected three. They're above Zeke. They deal with territory wars, new suppliers, everything goes through them. They practically own us, they're like gods," He explained with disgust in his voice. I started to ask another question, but the door to the bar swung open. Guys I had never seen before came out looking at Trey'von. I watched his posture change. He looked down at me with an expression that he always had on his face before he said something that crushed me.

"Nah, I'm cool but I'll hit you the next time I want my dick sucked. Get the fuck outta here," he snapped at me. I looked at him with wide, shocked, eyes. I looked back at Gabby who looked just as shocked.

"Who's your friend, Trip?" One of the guys asked, walking over shaking up with him. Was he acting like that because of those guys? Who were they? Where they the higher ups?

"Just some neighborhood slut I go to for a good time every now and then," Trey'von said, making me scoff. I shook my head, as tears filled my eyes at his words. Just because his bosses were here didn't mean he got to be mean to me.

"Trip, I---." He cut me off with a glare that cut right through me. I couldn't help but slink back.

"Get the fuck out of here. I'm done wasting my breath and time on you. Now go while you still can." His threat was cold and filled with hatred. The men laughed as I took a step back out of shock. That was not the Trey'von I know. He was throwing away all our progress, for what?

"You gonna ride with us for a little bit" One of the men ordered. Trey'von nodded his head, pushing off the bar. He was going with them? What about happened to him going with me or trying to find a suit for tomorrow?

"Let's go then," he said, and they all sent a smirk to each other. I was in such a state of shock I couldn't do anything besides watch him walk over to a Cadillac and get in the backseat. Before I knew it the car was leaving with Trey'von in the back.

"Yeah, looks like things have been amazing," Gabby retorted. I closed my eyes, as tears fell down my cheeks. I turned, walking away before Zeke walked out and saw me crying...again.

"He's never done that before. We were good. I don't know who those guys are," I told her as we walked up on my porch. I wiped my tears, taking a deep breath.

"The higher ups. Maybe he's embarrassed for them to know about you," Gabby said as we walked in. But that wasn't it. Maybe it had something to do with me being close to Zeke? Or Gabby was just right.

"You girls ready?" Izzy asked, standing up with a smile.

"Actually. I need a minute, sorry," I told her, going upstairs with Gabby following me. We went up to my room and shut the door. I sat down on my bed as my brain spun with reasons for him to act that way.

"You're wasting your time Elles. You need to be with someone who actually cares about and wants to show you off as theirs," Gabby whispered, brushing my hair behind my shoulder.

"I really believe he wants me," I told Gabby, as her arms slid around my waist. Her fingers tracing my side gently. It was such a comforting touch. I laid in my head on her shoulder as tears sprung to my eyes.

"Then why did he get in the car? He only wants you for what's between your legs," she said, but he already had that. My phone vibrated with a text message. I pulled away, grabbing it to see it was Trey'von. I sucked my teeth, thinking about ignoring him, but decided against it.

Trey'von😈😺- Baby, I am so so so so sorry. I didn't mean any of that shit and I will explain it to you the moment I get back. It killed me to say that but just know I had to. It's complicated and I will uncomplicate it in person. I will have a suit by tomorrow too, I promise. Here is some cash to get your nails done. I'm so sorry.

Cash app: $1,000.00 from Its_Trip.W180

I bit my lip, rereading his message over and over again. Maybe he had a really good reason. I needed to give him a chance to explain everything before I freaked out on him.

Me- You better have a good excuse. I'm done letting you hurt me. I don't want your money

"He just texted me," I told Gabby, handing her my phone. She took it reading over the messages. Her face showed nothing but disgust and distrust.

"Wow, he really tried to buy your forgiveness," she shook her head. I knew she didn't like Trey'von, so she saw the worst in everything.

"I'm going to let him explain. I don't want to talk about this anymore, let's just go," I said, not wanting to listen to Gabby bash him. My phone vibrated with a message from Trey'von.

Trey'von😈😺- I didn't ask if you wanted it. Use it, I'll talk to you later

I sighed rolling my eyes and grabbing my bag. Me and Gabby walked downstairs, told Izzy and Mateo we were ready, and we set out to get ready for the dance tomorrow.

TREY'VON

2 IN THE MORNING

Big Rico pulled up to my car which was parked in front of the bar. I leaned up, shaking up with them. My mind had gone to Elly, knowing I had to get to her and explain what the fuck that was about earlier.

"Think about what we said Trip. This could all be yours and we could even set up your boy, Smiley," Carlos said and I nodded my head. They had offered me Zeke's spot. They think he's ripping off their drugs and cash. I knew what it meant since they had offered me his spot. They were going to take him out. Then they said I was a good fit to take one of their spots one day. I never thought I'd get that high but if I could, I wanted it.

"I'll keep it in mind. You fellas have a good night," I said, getting out of the car. I got in my car and acted like I was messing around as I watched them pull off. Once they were gone, I got out just as Elly's mom pulled up and got out of her own car.

"MOMMA SANCHEZ!" I yelled jogging up. She looked back at me, smiling as she walked toward the sidewalk.

"What's up, Trip? You're out late," she commented. She was wearing scrubs. She must be getting off work.

"I need to talk to Baby Girl right now. I said some stuff I didn't mean but I was trying to protect her," I explained. She nodded, motioning me to follow her. We walked up to the door, and she unlocked it, letting me in. I went straight upstairs to Elly's room to find her sound asleep in bed. I smiled seeing her hair in a bun, no makeup, and all I saw was a bra. I smiled as I walked over and got in bed next to her. She was wearing a bra and thong. I pulled her into me, kissing her all over her face. She moved around, opened her eyes and jumped when she saw me.

"How'd you get in?" She asked, sitting up and rubbing her eyes.

"Your mom let me in. I had to talk to you tonight. I am so sorry," I told her, grabbing her and pulling her onto my lap. She snuggled into me, getting comfortable and hiding her face in my neck.

"Why did you say all of that?" she asked, yawning and closing her eyes. I laid back down with her, watching as her lips twitched up slightly.

"Because those were the higher ups Baby. I didn't want them to know about you. I didn't want them to think you matter to me. Because if I fuck up which I will it takes one thing I do that they don't like and they'll come for me. They won't come to me personally. If they know about you, they'll start with you. I can't even think about the things they'd do to you. I was just trying to protect you, and they bought it. They just thought you were a neighborhood hoe. I'm sorry for hurting your feelings," I told her, as she buried her nose into my side and put her leg over my waist. It pressed against my gun as she hummed, inhaling deeply.

"Did they hurt you? Where did you go?" she asked me. I knew I should tell her about their offer, but right now wasn't the time.

"I went with them to take care of some things. They told me I could be one of them one day. You got to be selected from the whole gang. Hell, people can come from overseas, so to know they're looking at me is amazing," I told her, letting my hand, drop to her butt rubbing. She jumped at my hand but then relaxed again.

"Is that what you want?" she asked me, sleep still in her voice. I nodded my head, pressing my nose into her hair, closing my eyes.

"Then I hope they pick you. What did you take care of? You smell like gun powder," she whispered. I grabbed my shirt smelling the powder smell. I wasn't going to tell her what I did with them. She knew I killed people, but I didn't want to tell her about it.

"Nothing for you to worry about. If it's bothering you, I can take the shirt off," I told her, but she shook her head "no," snuggling closer to me.

"No, it used to bother me, but it's nice to smell after not being with you all day. You're ok though, right? They didn't hurt you?" she asked, opening her sleepy eyes and looking at me. I smiled, leaning over and kissed her forehead.

"No Baby Girl, they didn't hurt me. I'm ok. Is this how you normally sleep?" I asked, looking under the cover to her curvy body.

"Do you like it?" she asked with a playful hint in her voice, running her fingers over my covered abs.

"Yeah, I do. I could get used to sleeping with a handful of booty," I snickered at her. I've never slept in the same bed as someone else before. I always went to the girl's house, hit and left. I've never had any female at my house or actually slept with them. It was scary to think that it was something I wanted now, but I couldn't be scared to love her.

"So, you're staying the night?" she asked me with a smile. I wanted to say "yes," but I just wasn't ready yet, I couldn't. I shook my head "no," blushing from my fear, but she just smiled kissing my cheek.

"That's ok. We'll get there. I've never actually had a guy stay the night anyway. I don't think it would fly with my parents," she told me. I couldn't help but smile knowing I'd be a first for her too. I smiled rolling on top of her, hovering over her. She laughed at me, reaching up touching my cheek.

"Did you get a suit?" she asked, but I shook my head "no."

"I'll go in the morning. I'm about to match you," I told her, but she shook her head "no."

"I have a date. You can't, that would be weird, and you aren't picking me up. Tony is and we're going to dinner without you." She gave me a pointed look. I groaned, hiding my face in her chest. She laughed, hugging me tightly. Oh well, Smiley would be at dinner, so he'd have my back.

"Your tits are so perfect" I whispered, biting down on one. She laughed, pushing me off her.

"Alright, I'm leaving. Sweet dreams Baby Girl," I whispered, kissing her shoulder. She nodded, touching my face and then rolling over to go back to sleep. I smiled, shaking my head as I walked out of her room and the house, making sure it was locked and headed home for the night.

Chapter 28

Pre-Dance

ELEANOR

I swung open the front door to find Gabby and Nicole standing there in sweats with dress bags in their hands. I smiled, opening the door for them. We were all going to get ready together and Smiley was coming to pick up Nicole. I assumed Trey'von would be driving them. Tony was coming to pick me up and I think Gabby was going to drive. She was scared to drive, so she hardly ever did, but she was going to tonight.

"I'm so nervous," Nicole squealed, as they walked in.

"I bet! You're 18 and going to a dance with a 15-year-old," I commented, shooting her a look of disgust, shutting the front door. She looked at me, shocked, as Gabby giggled.

"Just as friends! And he's the only one that asked!" She defended making me hum and give her a look.

"You should have just gone alone" Gabby commented, as Nicole's face turned bright red.

"Stoooop guys!" she complained, making us laugh and shake our heads at her.

"You guys, leave the girl alone. Isn't your date 19 or 20 Elly?" Mom said, coming into the room. I looked back at her, confused. I knew she was talking about Trey'von, but I already told her that Tony was my date to the dance.

"Tony is only 16," I told my mom as Nicole and Gabby looked at her just as confused.

"I thought you'd be going with Trip. You guys have been spending a lot of time together," Mom said as Dad walked in. He scoffed, as he sat down in his lazy boy chair.

"Tony is a much better anyways. Savannah, you should be happy she's not out with that thug," Dad said. I shook my head and just went up the stairs. I wasn't about to argue with him over Trey'von, today of all days. I just wanted to get ready for the dance and enjoy myself. So that's what I was going to do. I walked into my room, shutting the door as the girls hung their dresses in my closet.

"I'm so nervous. I hope Smiley got the right color. He said he was going suit shopping today," Nicole said, sitting at my desk with a stressed out-look. Her color was navy blue. I was sure Smiley got the right color. He probably went with Trey'von so that he had supervision while picking it out.

"He probably went with Trip. Trip isn't gonna let him look stupid," I told them shrugging it off while plugging in my straightener and pulling out all of my makeup for them to use along with what they had brought.

"Wait, why is Trip suit shopping? You're going with Tony as friends," Gabby reminded me with more attitude than I appreciated, but I let it go. I didn't know what her beef is with him, but it was annoying, and she needed to watch it because Trip's temper can be unforgiving. I sat down next to Nicole at the desk as Gabby walked over and started to section my hair to straighten it for me.

"I am going with Tony as friends, but Zeke is making Trip go too. Zeke thinks something might go down and when Trip found that out, he was going no matter what I said," I told them with a shrug. Nicole awed, but Gabby just rolled her eyes in annoyance.

"Gabs, he isn't going to dinner with us or anything. I already told him I was there with Tony," I explained to her trying to ease her mood.

"That's who you should be going with. You guys are dating," Nicole commented. I blushed, looking down at the makeup.

"Nothing is official. Can we please talk about anything else?" I asked, wanting to stop talking about my personal life.

"Ok, can I stay the night after the dance? I want best friend time," Gabby asked. I smiled, looking at her through the mirror. It's been forever since we had a sleep over and I loved the idea.

"Of course. Movies and snacks all night long," I said, holding up my hand. She smiled, shaking up with me.

"You remember the hairstyle I want right?" I asked, grabbing my phone and scrolling through Instagram.

"Yes Elly, just straight," Gabby said in a "duh."

"How are you doing your hair?" I asked Nicole curiously. Both of them thought I wasn't putting enough thought into my hair, but I did put thought into the dress and makeup. That was enough for a dance I still don't want to go to. I would much rather be riding in Trey'von's car with him or just hanging out and watching movies.

"It's this cute curled up look," Nicole told me and I nodded my head getting complaints from Gabby for moving, which only made me laugh as I started my makeup along with Nicole.

I bent down, applied more lipstick and smacked my lips together. I couldn't lie, I looked good and that made me feel great. My dress looked even better than it did in the store. It really showed my body off nicely. I did a reddish smokey eye that I was kinda obsessed with and shocked at how well it came out. My lip was a darker nude, but so perfect, and my shoes were red strappy high heels. My hair was sleek and straight.

"Elly, you look so amazing," Nicole gasped. I turned to see her in her navy blue-off-the shoulder gown. I smiled at how gorgeous she looked. Then Gabby walked into the room wearing her black off the shoulder mermaid fitted gown. Gabby's hair was in a classic bun which looked so good.

"Girls, you look even more amazing," I said walking over to them to just admire them as they did the same.

"ELLY, NICOLE, GABBY. TONY AND LIL SMILEY ARE HERE!" Mom yelled, interrupting our moment. I still couldn't believe no one asked Gabby to the dance.

"After you, ladies" Gabby said, motioning for us to go. Me and Nicole smiled at each other, and I let her go out first. I followed Nicole out of my room and down the stairs with Gabby following me. I saw Smiley smiling his usual big smile as he looked up the stairs at Nicole and me. Then my eyes went to Tony, and I instantly regretted letting him pick out his suit alone. His suit was neon red. It didn't have pants, but instead it had shorts that hung like four inches above his knee. His button up shirt was bright orange. His blazer matched neon red shorts. He had on white, red, and orange stripped knee high socks, and a pair of neon red Crocks. His tie was cheeta print just to pull it all together.

"What are you wearing?" I asked, rushing down the steps, looking over his outfit in a panic. I could not walk into that dance, or a restaurant, with him looking like Bimbo the Clown.

"I told you that you'd love it," he smiled, spinning around, making me cringe. I looked back at my mom, dad, and sisters who were trying not to laugh.

"Jealous? You didn't go with my idea, huh?" he asked me with a smile, but I just closed my eyes taking a breath. I knew this night was going to suck, but man it was just turning into a joke.

"Picture time. You all get together," Mom said, waving us together. I started to stand next to Smiley, but Tony took the spot next to him. Tony grabbed my hand pulling me into his side, wrapping his arm around my shoulders. Gabby giggled next to me. We all smiled, and my mom took the picture.

"Now, Elly and Tony," Mom said. I sent her a glare for forcing this. Tony grabbed my hips trying to pull me closer to him, but as I started to smack his hands away, Smiley ripped him back with a "Trey'von Walker famous glare."

"Keep yo hands off my boy's girl," Smiley snapped. I sent him a thank you look. I stood next to Tony forcing a smile as mom took the picture. She took picture after picture, which was driving me crazy.

"Ok last one, Elly and Gabby," Dad said. I smiled at Gabby as she came over to me. I grabbed her hands, wrapping my leg around her waist. We tilted out heads back sticking our tongues out. Of course, that earned giggles and chuckles from everyone in the room.

"That was so you, two," Dad cheered. All of a sudden, a gasp escaped Mom's lips, catching our attention. She ripped open the front door, smiling the biggest smile I've ever seen.

"GET YOURSELF IN HERE!" Mom yelled out of the door. We all gave her a confused look, not sure who she was yelling at.

"BOY YOU BETTER STOP IT. YOU SHOULD BE HER DATE ANYWAY. GET IN HERE, AND I'M NOT GONNA TELL YOU AGAIN," Mom yelled with "that" tone, making us all look at each other. Moments later the screen door was opened wider and Trey'von stepped in. His eyes found me right away. I couldn't help the gasp that escaped my lips. My hands shot to my parted lips as I smiled, looking at my handsome man. He had on an all-black suit. It held no tie which made it look even better. His button up was clearly silk, which was a beautiful touch. His suit only held accents of red, like the pocket hankie, or the rose pinned to his fitted tailored fitted buttoned up blazer. His cufflinks were red roses. He looked breath-taking.

"GAHDAMN!" He yelled the moment he was completely through the door. I blushed as he turned away from me and then looked back at me with his fist covering his beautiful lips.

"Yo Baby," he said, bending down and resting his hands on his knees while he looked at me. I looked away, knowing my cheeks were redder than Tony's suit.

"Aw hell, I just nutted from looking at yo fine ass," he said, making my jaw drop as my friends fake gagged and my dad glared at him.

"Perverted like always" I rolled my eyes playfully as he walked over to me. He smiled, licking his lips while grabbing my hand and spinning me around. I laughed, catching my balance by grabbing his suit jacket.

"Always, when it comes to you, but trust me, you haven't heard anything perverted yet," he snickered, grabbing my hips and pulling me in close for a kiss on my cheek.

"You look so sexy. You really do clean up nice," I teased. He smiled, spinning us around.

"Don't get used to it because I'm never wearing one of these again," he told me with a smirk. I laughed rolling my eyes playfully at him.

"You didn't go with the Scarface option," I pouted, but he just shook his head, smiling down a huge white smile. Suddenly, a flash went off. We looked over to see my mom smiling at us with the camera.

"You were about to have me lookin as dumb as Bimbo the Clown over there," he snickered, nodding towards Tony. I brought my hand to my mouth, trying not to laugh, but he just laughed at me. It astonished me how we thought alike sometimes.

"Actually, Elly likes my outfit," Tony said in defense of his choice, but Trey'von just scoffed shaking his head. He smiled down at me touching my hair.

"Your sexy curls are gone," he gaped, letting my hair fall between his fingers. I couldn't help myself for just staring at him and take in his outfit.

"They'll be back in a couple hours, trust me. I can't get over how hot you look," I said, stepping back to look at him.

"You guys look so cute together. Your red matches. You guys just look like a power couple. Everyone move, I want a picture of Trip and Elly," Mom said as she pushed my friends to the side. Trip groaned, as I just sent him a look that made him smile.

"Bring that fine ass here," He grinned at me. I smiled, wrapping my arms around him and resting my head on his chest as he hugged me. I smiled widely, looking at my mom, but Trey'von just looked down at me smiling as she took the picture.

TREY'VON

I couldn't stop staring at Elly. She looked so fucking good. That dress and her curves. That slit letting me see that russet leg. I didn't even want to go to the damn dance. I just wanted rip that dress off of her right now and put it down. Those sassy, bouncy curls that I loved were gone and replaced with a silky blanket of black hair.

"Yo, you know where these flicks would look fire at?" I asked. She hummed looking me over again.

"Out in front of my car. Our outfits with the murdered-out Audi," I told her. She looked at me with a look that said she was thinking about.

"We have reservations. We don't have time for pictures with someone that isn't your date," Gabby snapped at Elly. I looked down at Elly as she rolled her eyes. I couldn't stop my temper as much as I tried.

"Fuck her date. He looks like a fucking clown. He can't even dress good enough to be around her, so what makes you think he's worth any of her time?" I spat at Gabby. Familiar hands shoved me back, attracting my attention. I looked down at Elly as she sent me a look.

"Be nice. Tony has his own style, just like you do. If he likes the way he's dressed, then so do I because I don't care about that stuff," she told me, trying to be nice like she always is. I went to snap at her, but she covered my mouth with her hands.

"No fighting. Let's go take the pictures so we can make dinner," she directed. I sighed, nodding my head as she uncovered my mouth.

"Momma Sánchez you up for more pictures?" I asked her mom, pulling Elly into me.

"Of you two? Always," she said, making me and Elly laugh. I motioned for Elly to go as I let go of her. We walked outside to my car. I pulled it out more into the middle of the street and got out.

"I have an idea," Elly said going over and getting into the driver's seat. I quickly reached in snatching up the keys. She was not wrecking my car.

"You're annoying. Go stand to the side up there and pose," she instructed. I complied, standing to the side a couple feet in front of the car. I put my hands in front of me looking off to the side clenching my jaw. Elly sat on the driver's seat of my car with one hand on the wheel looking forward. She had her leg out of the car for the world to see. Momma Sánchez snapped the picture.

"That was hot," Smiley said, impressed. I looked him up and down with a 'of course it was' look. He waved me off, making me chuckle.

"One more than we have to go Trip," Elly told me, getting out.

"Let's just do a basic one in front of the car," I said with a shrug. I had never been a 'picture person' before, but for Elly, in this moment, I was. As Momma Sánchez showed me the pictures, Elly ended up with Travis.

"You should be her date," Momma Sánchez whispered, looking up at me with a look I couldn't read.

"She made these plans when we weren't even looking at each other. Plus, I wouldn't have ever gone to something like this if she asked me," I admitted looking down at my uncomfortable dress shoes. I knew I wouldn't have gone no matter how many times she asked me. I was crashing her day for her safety, and that was it.

"You're going and she didn't ask," Momma Sánchez pointed out. I smirked throwing my arm around her shoulders.

"Only because a rival I got big beef with will be at the dance and it'll be over my dead body he touches her," I told her, watching Elly laugh with her friends. Travis's outfit was such an embarrassment, I felt bad for her.

"You would have gone without that. You can't tell me that's not driving you crazy," she called me out, looking at Elly and her date. Travis went to touch her hip, but Smiley smacked his hand away.

"You're probably right. I'm gonna get this night over with, thanks," I told her shaking up with her. She laughed stumbling through it making me chuckle. I walked over, hugging Elly from behind which made her blush.

"You riding with me Baby Girl?" I asked, hugging her tightly. She turned in my arms resting her hands on my chest.

"I already told you I'm riding with Tony because he's my date," she told me. I looked Travis up and down and then scoffed.

"I thought you were scared of clowns though?" I asked. She sent me a pointed look which only amused me.

"Ight babe, I'll catch at the dance. You look fine as hell" I reminded, her kissing her cheek. I missed her lips, but I didn't think she was ready for that step.

"Thank you. So do you," she told me, pulling away. I got in my car along with Smiley and Nicole.

"Why don't any of you know how to drive?" I complained, pulling off.

"I do know how to drive. I just wrecked my car," Nicole told me and I nodded my head. That didn't surprise me by any means. Smiley was too young, but he was getting his L's when he turned 16. I've been teaching him to drive. I liked that Elly couldn't drive. I liked that she needed me sometimes.

"Why aren't you fighting for Elly?" Nicole asked me. Nosy bitch, she doesn't know anything I'm doing for Elly. I glanced back as Smiley looked at her, shocked.

"Yo, Nicole chill" Lil Smiley said with more annoyance than I would have thought was possible from the kid.

"No, Elly is hooked on him and he's just letting her go to a dance with someone else," she said. When you put it like that, it sounds bad, but I was just trying to respect Elly. I was trying to show her I trusted her and this was my way of doing that.

"She made these plans after me and before I came back. I'm not gonna tell her what she can and can't do. I'll be there. She wants me, she knows she can come to me," I said with a shrug, gripping the wheel tighter. I hated the idea of Elly dancing or being with that joke of a date, but if I started acting like a jealous lunatic, I might just scare her off and I couldn't do that. Finally, Nicole and Smiley fell silent, ignoring each other.

ELEANOR

I laughed along with Tony as he pulled into Langer's. It was a deli type restaurant that we all liked, and it was pretty cheap, so it was kinda perfect.

"Thank you for going to the dance with me Elles," Tony said, squeezing my knee making me smile and grab his hand.

"It's no problem. We're best friends Tony, and I always have fun hanging out with you," I told him. He smiled at me as he took his hand from mine and parked. We both got out as Gabby got out of her car shaking her head. I looked back and saw Smiley and Nicole getting out of Trey'von's car. Trey'von unbuckled, pulling out his phone. I couldn't lie, I was feeling really bad for leaving him out.

"Let's go," Gabby commanded and we all started to head to the restaurant. I couldn't help but bite my lip and look back at Trey'von. I know I told him he couldn't come to dinner because I didn't want things to be awkward, but now I felt like a piece of shit. It wasn't like me to leave anyone out and he'd never do this to me.

"Guys," I said as I stopped walking. They all looked back at me with a questionable look. I knew it would make Gabby, and maybe Tony, mad but I didn't care.

"I can't do this. I can't leave Trip out here. He would never do that to me or you, Smiley" I said looking for back up on this.

"Elly, it will make things weird. Your boyfriend and homecoming date together," Gabby said. But I just shrugged. I'd rather feel awkward than feel like I'm picking someone else over him or betraying him.

"He gets it Elly, it's ok," Smiley tried to comfort me. But I shook my head "no," running my fingers through my hair.

"No, it's not. I'm not leaving him out here alone. If him coming in is a problem, then I'll go somewhere else with him. I've never been the type to leave someone out and I'm not going to do it now. He'd never do this to me and I'm not being a very good friend to him right now," I told them, shaking my head as I backed away. If Trey'von wasn't welcome, then neither was I. We're a package deal.

"Elly, he probably doesn't want to come in anyway" Tony said. But I just shrugged.

"He doesn't want to do a lot but does it for me. It's either Trip or nothing from me," I told them. Gabby stormed off inside the restaurant, clearly mad about my choice. I looked at each of them as they waited for my next move. I turned away, walking over to the familiar black Audi. I pulled open the passenger side door and got in. Trey'von looked at me, confused, and then towards my friends who were heading inside.

"Baby, your friends are going inside, what are you doing?" He asked, pushing his phone back into his pocket. I smiled, leaning over to kiss his cheek which left a lipstick mark that made me giggle.

"I'm so sorry. I shouldn't ever have told you that you can't come to dinner. I hate leaving people out and you'd never leave me out. Please come inside?" I asked pouting my lip. He chuckled, shaking his head. He reached over, running his fingers through my long-straightened hair.

"Baby Girl, you aren't leaving me out. I wasn't even invited. I was forced to come. Go have fun with your friends. Plus, I can't watch Travis drool all over you," he told me. I smiled at him, grabbing his hand lacing together our fingers.

"His name is Tony and he's not going to. We're friends that's it. But if you don't go in then I'm not either," I told him, shaking my head "no" and letting go of his hand to get comfortable in the passenger seat.

"You're going to miss dinner over me?" he asked, raising an eyebrow. I nodded my head "yes," pulling out my phone to get on Snapchat.

"Baby Girl, don't be stubborn, go have fun with your friends," he encouraged. But I didn't care how many times he told me to go, I wouldn't go without him.

"How long you think they're gonna be?" I asked him casually. He got out of the car making me grin. I watched as he walked around the car, opening my door.

"Come on cry baby, let's go inside," He sighed. I smiled, getting out and hugging him making him chuckle and kiss the top of my head.

"I sit next to you, deal?" he asked, and I nodded my head.

"Deal. Now let's go because I'm starving" I complained, touching my stomach as I pulled away from him. We laced our fingers together and went inside, joining everyone for a sorta awkward dinner. But I didn't care because we were together.

Chapter 29

Homecoming

TREY'VON

I got out of the car and looked around the school parking lot. I didn't see Nightmare or any of his guys yet. I licked my lips, looking over to the old beat-up car that Elly was getting out of, smiling. Right away her eyes scanned the parking lot to find me. I watched that small smile grow into a big one. I waved at her looking back at Smiley climbed out of the car, ignoring Nicole completely.

"Yo, Nicole catch up with everyone else. I need to holla at my boy," I told Nicole. She looked at me, confused, and then nodded. Me and Smiley watched her walk over to Elly who looked at me confused too, but I just focused on Smiley.

"You got the rock?" I asked him and he nodded his head, patting the inside his jacket.

"I got more in a duffel in the trunk too," he told me. I nodded my head, glancing back at Elly who was laughing with Travis.

"Get as much product moved as you can but for the love of god do not let Elly find out. That is not a beef I am tryin to have with her. Then the moment we get in here we find Nightmare and don't let him out of your sight," I ordered. There was a lot tonight and, honestly, I needed more guys than just Smiley. But all of Los Prophet rollin up in a high school dance would draw attention.

"Don't worry dawg, Elles isn't going find out and Nightmare or his boys isn't getting close to her. I came prepared," he smirked leaning down as he rolled up his pants leg to show me the gun, I gave him. Yeah, Smiley with a gun in a room full of kids makes me feel a whole lot better.

"Put that shit down. Don't pull that shit unless you see me do it," I snapped, and he nodded his head quickly.

"TRIP!" I heard Elly yell. I turned, looking to see her waving me over. I looked back at Smiley who grinned at me.

"Dude, instead of lecturing me, go get your girl," he laughed, and I sent him a glare.

"Don't lose focus. We aren't here to have fun," I snapped at him walking toward Elly. I smiled, wrapping my arms around her waist and kissed her cheek which made her blush.

"What was that about?" she asked, touching my cheek. I just shrugged.

"Business. Nothing for you to worry about," I brushed her question off, kissing her cheek one more time before pulling away. She looked up at me with squinted eyes, like she didn't believe me. I sent her a smile.

"Elly let's go," Gabby called as Travis walked over to her. I looked away to hide my annoyance, but Elly locked her arm with mine waving for Travis to go. I smirked at him as I looked down at Elly who was fixing her dress. We walked inside following Gabby to a table in the back. I pulled out Elly's chair for her and looked around the gym for Nightmare, but there was no sign of him yet. Suddenly, Gabby gasped as Nicole's eyes grew wide. They looked behind me and Elly towards the entrance. I turned to see Lucas with some blonde girl. They were looking at each other smiling. I started to look back towards Gabby and Nicole, but I saw Elly staring with tears in her eyes.

"Yo, Baby Girl what's wrong?" I asked, bending down to her eye level. She rested her hand on my shoulder as I touched her legs. She shook her head "no," got up and walked away, leaving us all there. I started to follow her, but Travis grabbed me.

"Get off me bruh, that's my fucking girl," I snapped at him ripping away as I followed Elly once again.

"Trip, give her a minute. Lucas just showed up with Novah," Gabby snapped at me. This girl got one more time to talk disrespectful to me and they'll find her body in the fucking river. I turned, looking at her, and then back to the skinny blonde girl.

"That's the girl that's been messing with her?" I asked them and they all nodded their heads. That girl was ugly. She was curve-less, and her head is fucking huge. Why would Elly let Bobble-Head-Barbie mess with her? The Novah girl saw me looking at her and sent me a wink.

"They've had beef since elementary days. It was kindergarten and there was a 'prettiest girl' list that the boys made. Elly was on top and Novah wasn't, and they've had beef ever since," Nicole told me as I shook my head. That's the most childish shit I've ever heard in my life, a list in kindergarten. I couldn't see Elly holding onto something like that, but maybe Bobble-Head-Barbie was.

"I mean, Elly has always been prettier than Novah," Gabby said with a shrug and she wasn't wrong. I looked at Smiley and he looked at me already knowing who I wanted him to sell to. I nodded my head, and he smirked looking over at Novah. She wants to fuck with my girl, I'll fuck up her life. Getting her hooked-on crack cocaine was just phase one.

"Novah is the whole reason Elly quit soccer," Travis stated as I sat down in Elly's chair. I looked in the direction Elly took off in, but I didn't see her coming back yet. I'd give her a couple more minutes.

"Part of that is my fault," I admitted. I knew Elly threw her season away the moment I left.

"Why we sittin here if that bitch is messing with Elles. Let's show her what happens when you mess with one of us," Smiley said, talking like he was hard. I looked at him raising an eyebrow. He held out his arms like 'what'. I scoffed, flinching at him. He jerked back so hard his chair fell, making us laugh. Nicole leaned over to high five me.

ELEANOR

I looked in the mirror at my reflection as my mind replayed every great and bad moment me and Luke ever had. I missed him as a friend. A boyfriend, not so much. But I miss him being my best friend. Let's admit it, Tony is far from Lucas, and I wouldn't even compare Trey'von and Lucas because they're two different breeds. Out of all the people he could have gone with, Novah was his choice. He knows the history there. He knows how much she torments me. He gave her that video. The one that almost ended me. Was this his final way of telling me he was done with me forever? Or was he just trying to get my attention back? Regardless, of what he was doing it hurt like a bitch. I took a couple deep breaths deciding I wasn't going to let Lucas and Novah ruin my night. I collected myself and walked out of the bathroom to see that Trey'von had taken my seat. I walked over, touching his shoulder and getting everyone's attention.

"You good Elles?" Tony asked me, standing up with a worried expression. I smiled, nodding my head as he came over and pulled me into a friendly hug, making me laugh.

"I'm good, really. It was just a shock, that's all," I said, pulling away before Trey'von would go all Trey'von on Tony about touching me. I looked back at Novah and Lucas to see Dior and Yara walking in behind them. Novah saw me. Her eyes traveled to Trey'von, and I saw the smirk. I moved, standing in front of him to block her view and sent her a glare. I watched as the four of them begin to walk up to me. Novah front and center, as always.

"Don't worry Elly, I'm not going to take both of them in one night," she snarked as she walked past me. I scoffed, looking her up and down, Lucas tried to avoid eye contact with all of us as her brain-dead minions giggled.

"You didn't steal anything, Novah. You got my sloppy seconds, like always." My tone was too sweet. It almost sounded vicious. She stopped, turned around walked over me. I couldn't lie, she and Lucas did look good in the plum color they wore together.

"Baby Girl--," I cut Trey'von off, as he put his hands on my hips. I pushed them off me, sending him a look. I didn't need help with Novah and her goons.

"I've never come second to you, and I never will. Don't you have a gang to be a toy to?" She spat at me. She's used the same thing since middle school. You'd think she'd come up with something new by now.

"Say that shit again, I fucking dare you," Trey'von warned, pushing in front of me. I smiled, pulling him back to the table.

"Aw look, she brought a body-guard guys," Novah mockingly pouted. I watched Trey'von's dark brown eyes go black as his body shook.

"He's cute. Maybe you should come hangout with someone who isn't ran through," Dior snickered at Trey'von. I spun around sending them a glare, but then I just started laughing.

"You really think you can handle Trip? Ask Lucas about Trip---," Lucas cut me off

"Stop it. Let's go Novah." Lucas pushed Novah along. She rolled her eyes and stormed off, making me smile. Gabby squealed, almost tackling me in a hug.

"YOU STOOD UP FOR YOURSELF!" She yelled, as I hugged her back.

"I am so done with Novah walking all over me, but I'm not going to spend this dance focused on drama. We're here, so let's have fun," I declared. My friends cheered making shake my head.

"So, you're just letting her get away with stepping to you like that?" Trey'von asked. His anger was evident. I shrugged my shoulders, looking up at him.

"Nothing she said was new. Don't let her get to you, Trip. Now let's go dance," I said looking at Gabby and Nicole pulling them out to the dance floor.

AN HOUR INTO THE DANCE

I laughed as I danced with Tony. They were playing "Crew Love" by Drake and the Weeknd. Tony knew Drake was my favorite, so he made it a point to dance with me. I laughed as he spun me around making my dress fly up. I pushed it down which made him chuckle.

"Marilyn Monroe vibes," Tony joked.

"Does that mean I get my very own Kennedy?" I asked playfully, making us both laugh.

"I mean, you kinda got one, just he's a high member in Los Prophets," Tony teased as we danced horribly together. I smiled, looking at Trey'von who had his glare set across the gym. I turned to see a guy. He was at a table looking down at one of the cheerleaders, smiling. He wasn't dark skinned nor light skinned, but the perfect in between. He had a fade with some of the best waves I've ever seen. His dark brown eyes were focused on the girl he was with that sat in the chair by his feet. His facial features were average. They weren't a perfect fit, but not a bad fit either. His full lips were pulled back into a smile. He had huge diamond studs in his ears. There was a gold chain around his neck. His suit was elegant and looked expensive.

"So, is that his wife?" I asked playfully motioning towards the guy Trey'von was staring down. The song changed to one of mine and Tony's favorites.

"I can't thank you enough for coming with me. I'm having so much fun. It's been a while since we just hung out," he told me and I nodded my head trying to spin him around, but he way too tall so it was just awkward.

"Me too. I'm actually glad I came," I laughed as we struggled. Nicole and Gabby walked over to us laughing and drinking punch.

"Someone spiked the punch bowl and it's strong" Gabby giggled. I smiled thinking this dance was only going to get better. But then I remembered Trip and his old drinking problem. I looked up with wide panicked eyes as he made his way to the punch bowl.

TREY'VON

I watched Lil Smiley sell to Novah. Elly might not care, but I do and ruining that little slut's future was on the top of my "to do" list. I looked at Nightmare, who sat on a table staring at some girl. His eyes glanced up to find mine, and his smile fell. I glared, staring him down. He shook his head, looking back at the girl. I looked over at Elly who was dancing with her date, laughing and having a nice time. I looked back at Smiley who held up some cash in the air. I nodded my head, as he put it in his pocket. Everything seemed to be under control. Nightmare was controlling his guys, Smiley was making money, Elly was having fun without Bimbo the Clown all over her. I wasn't going to let my guard down, but I think this might go smoothly. I got tired of just standing there like secret service and decided to get a drink. I started to walk over to the punch bowl when I saw Nightmare heading my way. We met at the table, he smirked as he looked me up and down.

"Schools are a neutral place," Nightmare reminded me. I nodded my head, sucking my teeth and trying to keep my cool.

"So why are you here? Just checking everything out Trip?" he spat at me. I shook my head, getting a cup of punch.

"Why are you here? You're right, it's neutral, but yet here you are, too" I pointed out as I looked him up and down.

"My sister's here. Your excuse?" He countered. I started to take a drink of my punch. He was stupid if he thought I'd actually tell him about Elly.

"TRIP!" I heard Elly scream. I looked over, just as she smacked the cup from my hand, making it land on the table. I gave her a 'what the fuck' look as Nightmare smirked, checking her out.

"There's alcohol in it," She choked out. I looked at the cup and then back at her my eyebrows scrunching together. How did she know it was spiked? I haven't even seen her have a drink. I cringed, realizing Nightmare knew about her.

"Gabby had some. Just don't drink it," she pleaded, nothing but worry in her eyes.

"Damn Trip, aint nobody in the hood told me you had such a fine ass girl. Aye baby---." I cut Nightmare off by taking a step forward with a death glare.

"Say one word to her and you'll end like your boy, Lil Psycho," I snapped. He smirked stepping forward so that we were nose to nose. Smiley ran over, grabbed Elly and pushed her away, sending her off to be with her friends.

"Is that a threat?" he asked like I should have been scared of him.

"It's promise," I told him, sizing him up. I wasn't the type to shoot at a school but this muhfucka wasn't gonna try me. He lifted his shirt showing me his gun.

"And I got more than a kid with me," he threatened, as I opened my jacket showing him my gun. Smiley did the same.

"All I need is that kid to take out your bitch ass and your friends, so what's good?" I asked him. He looked me up and down licking his lips. I knew his bitch ass wasn't gonna do anything at a high school dance.

"Watch yo back and yo girl," he warned, walking away. I watched him, already making a plan for how I was going to handle him after this stupid ass dance.

"You good bro?" Smiley asked me and I nodded my head, sucking my teeth and looking at Elly. She was staring at me while she stood with Nicole. She smiled, waving at me and I waved back, looking at Smiley.

"Yeah, I'm good. Nightmare isn't gonna do shit. Get back to selling. I'm gonna keep an eye on him," I said. He nodded, shaking up with me. I walked away from the drink table and sat down at our table, keeping an eye on Elly and Nightmare.

45 MINUTES LATER

I watched Elly dance with her date. She looked like she was having fun. She was keeping it clean, and he was keeping his hands off her, which helped my sanity. The song changed to a slow song. Elly looked up at Travis with an uncomfortable glance and started to dance with him. But I kinda wanted this dance. I got up smoothing out my jacket. I walked out to the dance floor over to Travis and Elly, tapping his shoulder.

"Can I cut in?" I asked, smiling at Elly. She smiled, as she looked up at me in the cutest way, with the sweetest sparkle in her eyes.

"She's all yours," he told me. I smiled, grabbing her hand and resting my other on her hip as her hand went to my shoulder and the other interlocked with my fingers. I gave her a sly smile taking the lead of the dance, which was just small circles.

"I can't believe you wanted to dance with me," she whispered making me snort.

"Of course, I did. I can dance Baby Girl," I smiled down at her. She laughed at me, but her smile never fell. We were quiet and I started listening to the song and decided it honestly described what Elly was to me.

The song talked about being lost in life and how everyone who ever did me wrong led me to her. To the person, I was always supposed to love. Then, it talked about regretting the time I wasted without her and wishing I could give it to her, and it was right. I wish I could give her all the time I spent just doing whatever I wanted.

All of it was perfect for us. I couldn't even explain it, but it was. The combination of the lyrics and the way the lights fell on her, made her look even more goddess-like. I smiled at her, spinning her around. I couldn't figure out how I got so lucky for her to even want me in that way. I let my eyes wander over her as she spun. She smiled, looking at me like I was the most important person in the world to her. She moved closer, wrapping her arms around my neck and shoulders.

I pushed back her hair, snuggling my nose against her neck as my hands went to her waist. I left a kiss just a couple inches below her ear. I felt her shiver against me as the goosebumps rose on her skin. I smirked as she rested her head on my shoulder and I left another kiss on her neck. She pulled away, looking up at me. I smiled, spinning her around again just so I could take in how gorgeous she looked. She giggled that beautiful giggle as she placed her hand back on my shoulder.

Her plump full lips caught my attention. I had to feel them against mine even if it meant ruining our moment. I ran my fingers through her long straightened, hair cupping her cheeks. I leaned in connecting our lips and to my pleasant surprise, her lips moved in sync with mine, sending those electrifying and additive feelings through me. Our kiss was slow and tender, and I could feel every emotion she was feeling. Her hands rested on my chest and after another blissful moment, we pulled away looking at each other.

"I missed that," she whispered, making me chuckle and rest my forehead against hers. She leaned up connecting our lips in a rougher kiss, I groaned against her lips as she pressed her body more into mine. She wasted no time slipping her tongue into my mouth. She traced my tongue in the most pleasurable way. I wrapped my arm around her waist and tangled my other hand in her hair, pulling it slightly, making her moan as our lips and tongue moved together. She lined kisses over my jaw to my ear.

"I want you now, Papi," she whispered in my ear, pulling away and looking at me. I looked at her with wide eyes as her hand dropped, rubbing me through my pants.

"Let's go to your place. Mine's too far," I whispered leaning in kissing her lips.

"That's too far too. Come with me," she whispered, grabbing my hand and leading me through the crowd up towards the stage doors.

"Aye, no one is allowed back there," the DJ said giving her a pointed look. She reached into my pocket, grabbed my wallet and handed the guy a hundred. I went to complain about my money, but the guy smirked at her.

"Hurry up," he waved us back and she led me back behind the stage.

"You owe me," I joked. She shrugged, leaning up and kissing me lustfully. I smiled reaching behind her grabbing her butt making her laugh. We stumbled back until my legs hit something. I looked down to see a huge amplifier. Just as I looked back at Elly, she pushed me down, making me sit. She climbed on top on my lap straddling me and not letting that long ass skirt get in the way. She leaned down running her tongue over my lips, before pushing it into my mouth giving me a nasty kiss. I couldn't help but moan, she smiled leaving a trail of kisses down my jawline to my neck. Her tongue left a bold stripe before her lips wrapped around the sensitive skin.

"Baby Girl, are you sure?" I asked running my hand through her hair, tugging at it. She only responded with a moan, and I felt her grinding against my leg. I could feel how wet she was through my pants leg, which made me even more excited. I knew there would be a wet spot which was an even bigger turn on. I unzipped her top and she let it fall down her arms.

"We don't have much time before someone catches us," she whispered, getting off my lap and dropping between my legs. I bit my lip watching as she undid my pants, but she stopped touching a wet spot.

"What is on your pants?" she asked as I licked my lips.

"You," I flirted. She looked up at me with wide eyes and red cheeks. I laughed shaking my head.

"Trey'von, I am so sorry. That's so embarrassing," she blushed, covering her face. I leaned down, uncovering her face. I hated how shy she got with me, but it was a work in progress.

"Baby, no that is so fucking sexy. Like you said, we don't have a lot of time," I reminded her quietly. She nodded and finished unbuckling my pants pulling them down. She grabbed my length making me moan. She gave it a couple pumps and then grabbed the condom from my pocket. I grunted out in pleasure as she put the condom on for me. She moved, straddling me again. I rubbed her through her panties, making her throw her head back in pleasure. I moved her panties to the side, and she grabbed me, lining up. She slowly slid down on me, and I can't even explain how good she felt. She was tight and practically drooling on my dick. It was nice and warm. I swear at that moment, my eyes rolled back in my head.

"Fuck. Baby Girl" I grunted out and grabbed her hips as she moaned. She slowly moved her hips slowly making me sigh.

"You're so big," she whined in pleasure, touching her upper stomach.

"Is that where you're feeling it?" I smirked, thrusting my hips into her hard. She gripped my shoulders as her eyes rolled back with a moan.

"Yes, oh my god" she stammered as I repeated the action. She grabbed my hands locking together our fingers as she slowly bounced her hips up and down on me.

"Look at me. Fuck you're so wet," I grunted, reaching up grabbing her throat squeezing just enough.

"Papi," she choked out as she bounced faster and harder on me. She was so tight it felt better than it had ever with anyone else.

"This pussy is so fucking good and it's all mine. Do you understand Baby Girl?" My voice came out more forceful as I bucked my hips into her hard. I let go of her throat watching her boobs that were securely in her bra bounce slightly. I leaned forward biting them as her hips moved against mine. We both picked up the pace slamming into each other harder, only making the pleasure feel more blissful. Her hands slipped down my arms, lacing together our fingers. I looked up to her chocolate brown eyes as she stared down at me. It was the most intense intimacy I had ever felt. Her eyes giving away emotions I couldn't even read.

"It's all yours. Fuck, your dick feels so good." She threw her head back in pleasure. I felt her body began to shake as her movements got sloppier. I knew she was close. I drove myself into her harder and faster than I have before. Her nails dug into my back as her moans grew louder.

"Tell me how good it feels," I demanded wanting to hear the dirty words I knew she was capable of.

"You feel so good inside me," she struggled as she fought to keep her eyes focused on me and not rolling back.

"Cum for me baby." Suddenly I felt her tighten around me. Her body shook, she gripped handfuls of my jacket. Her eyes rolled back in the sexiest way as her back arched pressing her body against mine.

"TREY'von, fuck, papi, you feel so good," she groaned and that was enough for me. I felt the tension in my lower abs and back and before I could even slur out that I was close, I felt myself pulse and empty into the condom.

"BABY GIRL!" I yelled out a little louder than I meant to as I pulled her closer to me, enjoying the bliss her body gave me.

ELEANOR

My breath came out unevenly as I rested my head against Trey'von's shoulder, trying to catch my breath. His arms were still wrapped around me as he nuzzled his nose into my hair, kissing my temple. I swear that was better than the first time. I know the first is supposed to be the best it gets, but WOW. It was like a PTSD attack, and I saw him leaving me all over again. My breathing picked up as tears filled my eyes. He's not going to leave, he's not going to leave, he's not going to leave. Even though I fought to hold back my tears they fell with a sniffle, catching his attention.

"Are you crying? Did I hurt you?" he asked, trying to pull away but I shook my head "no," still hiding in his shoulder.

"Seriously, look at me, now!" He demanded. I pulled away looking away, wiping my tears. He easily grabbed my cheeks, forcing me to make eye contact with him.

"Why are you crying? Hold up, let me get my dick out first," he asked/told me seriously. I moved, cringing as I felt his fullness leave me. I looked at him biting my lip sitting back down on his lap.

"You're going to leave me now," I cried, covering my face with my hands. I heard him huff out as he grabbed my wrists pulling my hands away.

"Baby, I am not going anywhere. I'm gonna be right here with you, I promise." He leaned into kiss my nose. I smiled as I wiped my tears and interlocking our fingers.

"Good, because I couldn't handle you leaving again," I told him honestly. He picked me up and set me on my feet.

"I'm not going anywhere. Come on, get dressed," he pushed me as he fixed himself. We walked out, joining everyone else at the dance like nothing happened.

I laughed as I threw it back on Trey'von. He was moving in sync with me, grabbing my butt making me laugh. Tony kinda just gave me and Trey'von space, which I was thankful for. I felt Trey'von poke me, making me giggle. I turned, wrapping my arms around his neck connecting our lips in a lustful heated kiss.

"Already wanting more?" he hummed against my lips. I smiled, rubbing him through his dress pants, making him grunt out in pleasure as I leaned in close to his ear.

"I want as much of you as I can get Papi," I purred into his ear, nipping at his earlobe. He groaned pulling me even closer.

"You want to go to my place?" he asked. I was shocked by his offer because Trey'von has never invited me to even see what his house looked like. I couldn't lie, I was curious, and my parents didn't except me back until late anyway.

"Yeah, let's go," I whispered, kissing his lips once more. Without letting my friends and date know we were leaving, we just grabbed my purse and dipped out to Trey'von's house which turned out to be way more than I had ever excepted.

Chapter 30

The rising Phoenix

ELEANOR

I woke inside an island sized messy bed that almost hugged my nude body. It was soft and fluffy. The thick comforter wrapped around most of my body made it even more relaxing. Getting out of this bed was something I was going to find impossibly hard. I rolled over onto my stomach, peeling open my eyes. I looked into the wall sized mirror on left wall that was aligned perfectly with the bed. Of course, the mirror proved to be fun and useful last night. I couldn't help but bite my lip trying to hide the smile that came with the memory of the mirrors last night. The way Trey'von made love to me. How his hands were so gentle, but rough against my skin. How he took his time and did the freakiest things. It was like I stepped into a full night of my very own fantasies, and I was not complaining. I hummed at the memory, sitting up taking in the bedroom for the first time since I got here.

It was giant. This room alone was probably the size of my entire house. The walls were a beautiful sandy color. The floors were polished cherry wood with white area rugs under the bed and sitting area. On Trey'von's side on the bed, resting on his table, was a picture of us. Just the idea of him wanting, at least, a picture of me next to him while he slept sent butterflies fluttering in all the right places. In front of the white sectional couch and glass coffee table was a glass balcony. It revealed a beautiful view of the Beverly Hills mountains and the backyard which was nice to wake up to.

Also, along the right wall, towards the farthest corner, was a hallway. That hall held an entrance to a bathroom, a walk-in closet, and a private retreat.

I pushed myself out of the comfort of the warm bed. I found one of Trey'von's white t-shirts on the floor. I grabbed it and slipped it on to find that it fell mid-thigh, like a dress. I smiled looking at myself in the mirror. My straightened hair was beginning to curl and looked a mess, but other than that I was presentable for just waking up. I looked around to find a rubber band on the bedside table. I grabbed it putting my hair up in a messy bun. I walked out of the room and down the hall to the double doors. I wandered down the long turny halls until I found the stairs. I walked over to the edge and looked down in amazement. The foyer was white with black wire metal framing. There was giant a crystal chandler hanging from the ceiling and to my right were the twisty stairs.

I walked through the downstairs of the house listening for Trey'von. Before I knew it, I heard the faint sound of music. I followed it through the huge house into a kitchen that took my breath away. The floors were polished hardwood. The walls were white and lined with grey cabinets. The island stood in the middle of the kitchen with white bar stools and a built-in sink. Hanging over it were two beautiful big cage-like lights. Closer to the entrance, directly across from the island, oddly enough, was my giant stainless-steel fridge. Against the right wall behind the island, was my stove and marble countertops. By the entrance was a door which, I assumed, was the pantry. Further from the island and fridge sat a small round glass breakfast table with a light hanging over it.

To top off the look was the most attractive part. Trey'von stood in front of the stove with spatula in hand, looking at his phone. He wore basketball shorts that sagged down, showing the band of his boxers. He wore no shirt, giving me a view of that beautiful, tattooed body. The only thing he had on his upper body was a gold chain. His hair was still messy. I watched as he bit his lower lip looking at his phone.

"I thought you didn't cook for hoes?" I asked, crossing my arms playfully. He turned looking at me with a huge smile, putting away his phone.

"You aren't a hoe so look at that, you get to taste my mad cooking skills," he joked. I laughed, walking over to him, hugging his torso and looking at the food. I didn't know what I was looking at, but it looked so good. He had egg whites cooking in a dome formation, some kinda red sauce, and he had what looked like waffle mix with powdered sugar and strawberries.

"Damn chef," I joked, and he scoffed, leaning down to kiss my forehead.

"Gordon Ramsey don't have shit on me," he said, and I laughed. I moved, letting go of him to get a look at the sauce he was cooking.

"Can I help?" The moment the words left my lips I was being lifted from the ground. I squealed, grabbing the t-shirt trying to keep it down. I was put down on the island. I looked up at Trey'von with a smile as he came between my legs and kissed my lips passionately.

"Nope, you just sit here and look gorgeous," He whispered against my lips, pulling away to open the waffle iron. I watched him pull out a Belgian waffle and put it on a plate. I was so excited. I looked at the tattoos on his back while he worked with the food. A few of them caught my attention. There was one that looked like a knife going through the middle of his spine. Then on his right shoulder blade, there was a dragon. In the middle of his back was a woman's lips with finger to them. like they were telling him to be quiet. I squinted to see words written around the lips in small print and it said, ‹If you›re quiet, he won›t hear›. He has so many, and I always wondered what they meant.

"Are you mad?" he asked turning to face me with his eyebrow raised. I blushed bringing my hands to my cheeks. He just caught me staring.

"No, I was looking at your tattoos," I confessed, he smirked looking down at his body coming over to me.

"You like them?" I reached out, tracing the tattoo of Pablo Escobar that was on the right side of his ribs. I assumed he had this tattoo because he wanted to be like him.

"Yeah, but there is one I'm curious about," I admitted, tracing the dead, thorny rose vine that started at his waist band on his right side and curled around to the collar bone. I couldn't help but wonder why it's dead and so thorny.

"Which one?" I ran my nails across to the tattoo of the little boy trapped inside his ripping away skin. He swallowed hard, nodding.

"The phoenix will arise from the ashes," I read aloud running my nail across each letter. I looked up to see the panic in Trey'von's eyes. I began to tell him he didn't have to answer when he started to speak.

"It's me as a child. One day my mom had taken a picture of me after Paul beat me to remind me of what happens if I'm bad or tell anyone what happens. I was 7. That boy is still a part of me. The broken and bloody one, so I had it tattooed to show he's still inside me. The phoenix is a powerful bird, one that can't die no matter what you did to it. I mean it would die for a moment but rise again, even stronger. I feel like I could have given up so many times in my life but every time I bounce back, I'm stronger. Like a phoenix," he told the story behind it. I couldn't help but feel bad for making him share that.

"I'm sorry," I whispered, looking up at him. He leaned down kissing me easily.

"Not your fault, Baby. Taste this sauce," he said, moving to grab a wooden spoon and putting sauce on it and then bringing it over to me. I tasted it like he had asked. I looked at him with wide eyes, humming. It was a tangy but sweet flavor and it kinda had a spicy kick to it.

"Oh my god, that's so good" I said making him smirk as he walked over to the stove. He glanced back at me his eyes growing wide.

"You're not wearing panties," he stated, turning to look at me. My cheeks heated in embarrassment as I crossed my legs looking away from him.

"I, uh, I didn't see them on the floor when I woke up and didn't want to look for them," My voice came out higher than what I meant for it to. I looked over as he smiled shaking his head, turning to get back to the eggs.

"You don't even have to wear clothes while you're here," he commented. I hopped off the counter watching as he plated the food. He had one plate for the waffles which he sprinkled powdered sugar and put fresh cut strawberries on top. The next plate was the dome shaped egg whites with the sauce poured over the top. Basil leaves topped of the dome.

377

"Papi, that looks amazing," I said, looking at the food. He grinned, leaning down and kissing my cheek while handing me my plates. I followed him into an average looking dining room. There was a long table and some painting of famous gangsters, real and fictional. I sat down with my legs tucked under me in the chair.

"So what's in the dome?" I asked him curiously, looking at it.

"Bacon, sausage, ham, peppers, and a shit load of cheese," he told. I broke it open taking a bite. I couldn't help but moan and close my eyes, which made Trey'von chuckle.

"Now I'm starting to think you was fakin all them moans last night," he teased. I opened my eyes sending him a 'shut up' look. I quickly chewed my food and swallowed, shaking my head "no.

"You know I wasn't faking anything. I didn't know you could cook this good. I'm gonna have to wife you up," I joked. He made a face at me, moving his chair away. I gasped, looking at his playful shocked expression making him chuckle.

"Hell no, don't ever say that shit again. I'm a husband," he scoffed. I rolled my eyes taking a bite of my waffle, which was as good as it looked. This man could really cook and I was not complaining. My man can cook, fix things around the house, is a provider by nature, and a beast in the bed. Ya'girl got the whole ass package.

"I know you made it clear you wanted to be a husband since you snuck into my bedroom," I teased. He fought a smile, flipping me off, making me giggle. I went back to enjoying this bomb ass food.

TREY'VON

I loaded the last dish in the dish washer. Elly threw a fit because I wouldn't let her help. She ended up storming off saying something about taking a shower. I put the dish washing pod in and closed it and started the load. It was weird having Elly here. I've never had a girl here before. I've never slept with someone or shared a bed with them but, yet, when I woke up next to Elly this morning it was something I found myself wanting for the rest of my life. I decided it would be a good time to just watch movies and talk. I pulled out my phone, going to my Elly's text messages.

Me- Hey I'm going inside the movie theatre if you need help finding it let me know

I walked down the hall, turning left and going all the way back by a set of double patio doors. Right next to them, on the other wall, was another door that led into my home theater. I opened the door jogged down the four or 5 steps to the ground level. I turned on the popcorn machine even though I doubted Elly would want any, but just in case. I grabbed the glass jar of sour patch kids and turned on the screen going to Disney+, because it was Elly's favorite. I sat down on the front sectional relaxing, waiting for my Baby Girl to join me, or get lost in my house.

I groaned as I pulled out my phone to text Elly to find out if she was about done in the shower when the door opened. I turned to see her walking into the theater. Her eyes were wide as she looked around. She wore a pair of my boxers and one of my Supreme t-shirts. Her bouncy curls had returned, and they were dried and styled, telling me she found my hair stuff. I was worried she wouldn't, but I should have known she was fine going through my things. I couldn't get over how good she looked in my clothes. How badly I wanted that to become her everyday wear was crazy.

"Dude, your house is insane," she told me, making chuckle.

"It's not that crazy. It's getting kinda small honestly," I told her with a shrug. She scoffed, coming over to me and taking a seat on my lap. Her arm snaked around my neck as she played with my hair.

"Small isn't the word I'd use," she told me shaking her head. I tugged at the boxers she wore. I saw her blush the cutest blush. I noticed the hot goosebumps on her skin already. I loved the reaction she had to me.

"My boxers?" I asked. Her blush grew even hotter, making me chuckle.

"Your shorts kept falling off and when I tried to tie them, they hurt my hips," she complained. I smiled, leaning up to kiss her cheek.

"I don't care if you wear my things baby. I thought we could watch "Cars." It's my favorite movie as a kid, but I got to keep it gangster. This way I can say you forced me to watch it," I snickered, leaning back and grabbing the remote as she giggled at me and pushed back my messy curls. I started the movie and turned down the lights. Elly snuggled into me more resting her head on my shoulder as we focused on the screen. After about 10/15 minutes I decided to break our silence.

"You know you're the first girl I've brought here or that I've ever actually slept with, like in the same bed," I told her. She looked at me, shocked, but it was quickly replaced with a smile.

"I would have thought you've had a ton of girls here. You're the first guy I've slept with too. I was honestly nervous. I felt like I was taking up too much room on the bed or too much of the blanket," she admitted with pink tinted cheeks. I smiled, leaning over to kiss her adorable cheek and hugging her closer to my body.

"No, you didn't. There was one point during the night you grabbed my hand and just snuggled it to your chest," I told her with the biggest smile. That gesture alone made me feel so loved because she wanted to touch me even in her sleep. Elly leaned in, kissing my lips easily and then hugged me securely around the torso. It was somehow in this moment I knew this sassy, attitude filled, know it all, beautiful women had stolen something from me I didn't know was possible. I was in deep. I couldn't picture not having her around again, that was fucking torture. I was completely and hopelessly in love with Eleanor Valeria Sánchez. I didn't know if I should tell her because what if she didn't feel the same way?

"What are you thinking about?" she asked, pushing back my mess of curls. I smiled, leaning down to kiss her neck.

"All the dirty things I want to do to you right now. You look so fucking hot in my clothes," I whispered, nipping at her ear. She squealed with laughter and pushed me away playfully.

"Ya'nasty," she said in her accent, making my eyes close. Imagine never hearing that again...I wouldn't be able to survive it. I needed her more than I've ever needed anyone and that scared me to core, but I don't think I could run even if I wanted too.

ELEANOR

A FEW HOURS LATER

I laughed as Trey'von splashed me, I tried to hide most of my body behind the big swan float's neck, but I must have put too much weight because it flipped sending me into the cool water. I swam to the top flipping over the float as Trey'von howled with laughter. Trey'von insisted we go swimming, but when I so kindly pointed out I didn't have a bathing suit next thing I know, some guy showed up with a Louis Vuitton bikini. So, we're in the pool.

"Shut up, it's not funny" I giggled, splashing him.

"Yes, it is. That's why you're laughing, and you got one more time to splash me and you'll regret it," he threatened. I pushed the float out from in front of me, taking a step closer with a smirk. I splashed him, fighting back my laugh.

"Oh, it's so on," he said turning his back to me. I watched him go to the edge of the pool. Was he getting out? I raised an eyebrow, standing on my tippy toes trying to look.

"SAY HELLO TO MY LITTLE FRIEND!" he yelled, swinging around with a super soaker. I went to turn to run but he shot me right in the eye. Right away I felt pain and started seeing spots of colors like I had rubbed it too hard.

"TREY'VON!" I screamed, turning around covering my eyes taking a couple breaths so I didn't cry.

"Fuck" I heard him say mumbling along with a splash.

"Baby I'm so sorry, I didn't mean to get you in the face. Are you ok?" he asked touching my shoulder. I turned hiding my face in his chest. He wrapped his arms around me tightly kissing the top of my head.

"I didn't mean to Baby Girl. Does it hurt?" He asked. I nodded pulling away looking up at him forcing my eye open. He touched it tenderly and the next thing I knew he was picking me up, forcing my thighs around his waist. I wrapped my arms around his neck and let him take me from the pool. He walked us inside even though we were soaking wet and sat me down on the island.

"Everything is getting wet," I complained. But he just shrugged as he went to the freezer. He pulled out a bag of peas and touched it to my eye, making me flinch.

"Am I going to have a black eye?" I whined, taking the peas from him. He looked at it, shaking his head "no."

"No, you should be good. I'm sorry," he pouted his lip in the cutest way.

"Stop saying sorry. I know you didn't mean to. Gimme a kiss," I demanded. He smiled coming between my legs kissing me easily. I hummed as his lips touched mine. Ugh I couldn't go without his kisses. I can't go without him. If our time apart and this recent time together has shown me anything, it's that Trey'von Walker is the man I have to marry. Everything in me screamed he's the one and I'd fight for that no matter what.

"One more," he smirked kissing me again making me giggle.

"I am in so much trouble when I finally leave your paradise," I sighed. He scoffed giving me a playful look.

"Who said yo fine ass was going anywhere," he joked, grabbing my legs wrapping them around his waist.

"Me, Bud," I shot back playfully, he smirked at me nodding his head. Next thing I know his hand is on my throat cutting off my air supply in just the right way to make the needy tingles erupt between my legs.

"Sorry, what's my name? *Baby*," he growled as he leaned into my ear. His warm breath washing over my neck making me want him even more.

"Papi," I moaned with my eyes closed. I tightened my legs around him as my lady parts pulsed from wanting him so badly. I opened my eyes to see him staring down at me with lustful eyes.

"Are you going to stare at me or give me that dick?" I asked him and without another word his lips were hungrily attacking mine.

I looked in the mirror trying to comb out my hair, but it was just so tangled it was impossible. I needed my detangler spray and my special brush at this point. I groaned throwing the comb just as Trey'von walked into the bathroom. He looked at me raising an eyebrow.

"That guy fucking with you? I can show him what's up," he joked, sitting on the counter holding clothes for me to change into. I smiled, shaking my head and looking at my hair once again, grimacing.

"My hair is too tangled to comb. I'm just gonna put it up," I complained grabbing the rubber band that I found earlier. I put my hair up into a messy bun that turned out way messier than I wanted it to be. I looked in the mirror, tears filling my eyes as I ripped the rubber band out of my hair.

"I swear if you don't go up, I'm gonna cut it all," I grumbled to myself trying to use the comb to make it better.

"I know you are not crying over your hair. Cry baby," Trey'von pushed. I flipped him off, getting it up semi-decent and then wiped my eyes. I took the clothes from him and slippes on my thong. I threw on the grey sweatpants he gave me and the black t-shirt.

"Leave me alone. Am I taking that bathing suit?" I asked him, moving between his legs kissing his cheek.

"No, leave it here for the next time. I'll get you real hair ties, Pajama's, and a toothbrush to leave here too," he told me. I looked at him, shocked unable to stop the smile.

"You really want my stuff taking up your space?" I asked, shocked.

"I want you with me all of the time. My space is yours. Now let's take a walk around the neighborhood before I take you home and beef with yo pops," he told me. I nodded my head, grabbing my heels from last night. I looked so stupid walking through Beverly Hills like this, but oh well.

HEADING HOME

I looked out of the window nervously as Trey'von drove. I knew I was in trouble when I got home, I just didn't know how much yet. I was out all night. I was with Trey'von. I spent the night with him. I have a bunch of hickeys on my neck, so I was gonna be murdered. Trey'von pulled up in front of my house. I took a deep breath, looking over as he put the car in park.

"You're not coming in. You and my dad hate each other," I reminded him, shaking my head "no" noticing that everyone was home and probably waiting for me.

"Yes I am. No one in that house is gonna make you feel bad, now let's go," he said opening his door. I grumbled, opening my door getting out as well. Trey'von took a my dress from my hands and let me lead the way. I walked through the gate up to my door and then inside to find my family inside waiting in the living room.

"WHERE DO YOU THINK YOU'VE BEEN?" My dad's voice boomed the moment the door opened. I bit my lip walking in all the way, smiling at him.

"I fell asleep---." He cut me off, throwing his hands up in the air.

"I KNEW IT. I KNEW YOU'D BE WITH THAT LOW LIFE---." Trey'von cut my dad off.

"YO, FUCK YOU. NAH, WE AINT DOIN THIS. BABY GIRL GO GRAB A BAG YOU COMIN WITH ME. SIT DOWN!" Trey'von yelled at my dad, going towards him. I watched my dad sit down as anger filled him even more. I quickly went over to Trey'von grabbing his arm.

"Trip, it's fine. Please, we had an amazing day. I don't want it ruined by fighting," I pouted my lip at him. He looked at me sighing, leaned down and kissed my lips.

"Fine, then I need to get out of here. I'll be at the bar if you need anything, Beautiful," he whispered, leaning down to kiss me one more time. We watched him walk out and I let out a breath of relief.

"Are those hickeys?" Mateo asked with wide eyes. My dad sent me a glare, but I just shrugged as he stood.

"I love Trip and I want to show him that. It's my body," I said defensively, but my dad just shook his head.

"Your phone. Give it," he snapped. I opened my mouth to argue, but my mom cut me off.

"NO. WE'VE BEEN WORRIED SICK. I DON'T CARE IF YOU'RE WITH TRIP AND YOU KNOW THAT. BUT I CARE WHEN MY DAUGHTER DISAPPEARS WITHOUT A PHONE CALL. SINCE YOU CAN'T USE THE PHONE, YOU DON'T NEED IT," Mom yelled. If they wanted this phone. They could have it. I didn't care if they took it or not, they couldn't take my laptop because of school, and I can text off that. I sent them a 'I don't care' look and held it up in the air dropping it to the floor.

"There, it's yours. Now if you don't mind, excuse me, I'm tired. I didn't get much sleep," I snapped at them turning to walk up the stairs to my bedroom while ignoring their yells for me to come back. I spent the night on my laptop texting Trey'von, telling him what happened and watching TV until I fell asleep.

Chapter 31

Grounded

ELEANOR

"ELEANOR, WAKE UP AND GET DOWNSTAIRS NOW!" I heard my dad yell, making me sigh. I opened my eyes, laying there for a moment. I knew I was going to be in trouble the moment I stepped foot down there. It was going to be over yesterday and the hickeys I was covered in. I sat up, running my hand through my messy curls, I grabbed a hair tie and threw my hair into a bun. I looked down at the the skin-tone bralette and night shorts I was wearing. I shrugged, not worrying about changing my clothes and headed downstairs. I walked into the living room to find my mom and dad waiting for me.

"Have a seat," Mom demanded. I rolled my eyes, knowing she was only acting like this because of my dad. She liked Trey'von so I didn't know why she was making it into a bigger deal than it was. I walked over to the couch, sitting down as my parents stood in front of me.

"To start, I am very disappointed in your behavior. You never stay out all night without calling or with a boy. Do you not see what type of influence Trip is having on you?" my dad asked in a very fatherly tone. I didn't mean to stay the night. Around 3 a.m., after one of our many rounds of euphoric sex, we ended up falling asleep.

"Neither of us meant for me to stay the night. We fell asleep," I offered, but they didn't seem to buy it.

"Why didn't you call when you woke up in the morning or when it was late enough for the dance to be over? We found out you left the dance

386

when Gabby showed up here saying you said she could stay the night, but you disappeared with Trip," Mom snapped. I cringed, remembering my girl's night with Gabby. I didn't mean to ditch her. I just forgot. But I knew she wasn't going to take that as an excuse.

"I didn't think about it. Honestly, I wasn't thinking about anything other than what I was doing," I admitted with a blush. I didn't want to just come out and tell them I was too worried about sucking Trey'von's dick to call.

"WHAT WAS THAT ELEANOR? HAVING SEX? HOW LONG HAVE YOU EVEN KNOWN THIS GUY?" my dad yelled, making me jump. Mom touched his shoulder, sending him a look and I watched him calm down. I shook my head as my cheeks filled with a blush.

"Long enough for me to consent and that should be all that matters to you guys. That should have been your first question when you saw the hickeys, especially if you don't trust him. It will be my first question to my daughter and making sure she's comfortable with the situation and that her birth control is working for her," I spat at them. They couldn't stop me from having sex, but they could be smart about it. I watched my parents freeze and look at each other, shocked, like that thought never crossed their minds before.

"Was it consensual?" Dad asked his voice up tight as he looked at me, unsure. I nodded my head "yes."

"It was my idea," the annoyance was thick in my voice as I crossed my arms, wishing they'd get to the point already.

"I have a question. What are you going to do when Zeke figures it out?" Mom asked me. I froze looking at her with a dangerous glare. I watched a small smile tug at her lips along with an adoring look which filled her eyes. Weird.

"Zeke won't find out and I'll make sure of it. Both of you are going to leave this out when you talk to him, if you do. Me and Trey--Trip having sex, dating, hanging out, isn't Zeke's business," my voice dripped of authority as I leaned forward. I almost used Trey'von's real name, but I caught myself, so I should be ok.

"What will happen if he finds out?" Dad asked, truly not knowing.

"He'll kill Trip. He sees Elly like a daughter, and you don't mess with the boss's daughter," Mom explained, eyeing me. I stood up, looking her up and down trying to figure out her end game here.

"And we're not letting that happen right?" I questioned my mom, squinting my eyes at her.

"Right," she agreed, and I nodded, sitting back down, looking up at my dad who shook his head.

"You're grounded two weeks. No phone, TV, friends, going out, you're on lock down in this house. School and home, that's it" Dad told me. I sighed putting my face in my hands. All this because I stayed out.

"You are overreacting. I was safe, I was with Trip," I complained, not understanding the big deal.

"Safe, that's what you call him? He's not safe" Dad snapped at me. Trey'von was safe when it came to me. To him, not so much.

"I don't care if Jesus or any of the other Gods makes you go with them, you are still to call us. We're done here," Mom dismissed us, walking away. I rolled my eyes getting up going upstairs to my bedroom to sit and think. Two weeks without Trey'von? We are just now becoming really good, I don't want a step back because of this. Two weeks without going out with my friends and being locked in this house? I'm going to die. I groaned, throwing myself back on my bed, closing my eyes and thinking about the weeks to come. After a couple minutes I got up and went to my closet. I grabbed a pair of short high-waisted light shorts, and a black Motley Cru concert t-shirt. I went over to my dresser grabbing underwear and a black Nike sports bra. I made my bed, laid out my outfit, and grabbing a towel and body wash. Then I headed down to take a shower to get on with my boring day.

TREY'VON

I pushed open the broken russet gate that stood as a guard to my girlfriend's home. I heard loud music coming from the house. I walked up the stairs to the door and knocked. Not even a second later, it swung open to reveal a very pissed off Mama Sánchez.

"She's grounded," she told me, crossing her arms and sending a dirty look over her shoulder.

"Well, she's supposed to be, but I'm the only one trying to enforce it. You can be my guest to try to shut down their little party," she snapped, storming away and left the door open. I chuckled, walked in and shut the door behind me. I heard old 80's hair rock coming from the kitchen along with laughter. I walked into the kitchen to see Elly standing on the table with a duster in hand and Antonio holding a mop. Elly had her back to me, and her hips were swinging side to side as she held a red solo cup up in the air. Antonio was using the mop as a guitar. My eyes followed that cup. I was not letting her drink and Antonio should be a better fucking father. What are they even doing or listening to?

"WHOOO!" Elly yelled, swung her hips and slowly turning around as she pulled off her t-shirt which made my eyes grow wide. I relaxed, seeing the sports bra covering her sweat-coated skin. She turned, saw me, and smiled, tossing her t-shirt at me, picking up her cup again.

"TRIP, COME DANCE!" she yelled, stepping off the table to come over to me. I sent her a glare, roughly snatching the cup from her which made her stop.

"You better not be fucking drinking," I snapped at her, smelling the cup. It was just Coke. She took the cup from me and stood on her tippy toes, wrapping her arms around my neck. I grabbed her hips and smiling down at her.

"I'm grounded," she told me lovingly, but I scoffed.

"I don't care. You want to go to Beverly Hills with me?" I asked her, slipping my hands into her back pockets. How are they really going to stop her from leaving with me?

"Go to your house you mean? No, dance with me," she said, pulling away as another song came on. She went back over to her dad, both of them dancing. Elly tossed her kinda straightened hair around. It looked like she straightened it, but the curls were making their way back.

"Baby, what are you guys listening to?" I complained, going further into the kitchen. She walked over, moving her hips and laughing.

"Motley Cru," she cheered as she and her dad continued to dance together. Elly whipped her hair and Antonio mocked her not having any hair to flip. I shook my head and went into the living room, sat on the couch, and grabbed the remote. I'd let her and Antonio have whatever moment that is. I turned on "Criminal Minds" and leaned back into the couch, watching the TV. Elly made me watch it when she stayed the night and now, I'm hooked. Of course, that was the little brat's plan. Just as the episode started getting good the older one came downstairs and plopped down next to me. I looked over at her and then back at the TV.

"She got you watchin this shit?" she asked, and I nodded.

"It's not bad. I'm kinda into it. I wonder what the FBI has me profiled as?" I commented. I knew they followed me and were trying to get me, so what did they have me profiled as? Was I considered a serial killer? I've killed more people than I have fingers and toes so...yes?

"Probably a narcissist. I mean your sleeping with Elly even though she's close to Zeke, and you're flaunting it," she told me. Eh, I could see it. She did have a point. What I was doing was dangerous and if Zeke did find out I'd have a problem. If he did anything to me, the higher ups would come for him. They already wanted me to take his place. Fuck, I haven't told Elly about that yet. She walked into the room, sat on my lap and kissed my cheek. She wrapped her arms around me, hugging me. I smiled, wrapping my arms around her waist and hugging her closer to me.

"Spencer is so fine in a nerdy way," she commented, and her sister agreed. I scoffed, looking up at Elly who just smiled at me.

"That fed aint got shit on me, Baby Girl," I said shaking my head. Elly "awed" leaning down and kissing my lips.

"Of course not, but just know he's coming to steal me away one day," she joked, I rolled my eyes, attacking her with kisses all over her face, making her scream out in laughter. She grabbed my face giving me one of those nasty kisses. I tried to fight my groan, because of her sister, but I couldn't.

"YOU GUYS ARE GROSS!" she yelled, and we both pulled away. Elly shushed her as Savannah and Antonio walked in to see what we were doing.

"And Izzy, you're a whore, but you don't see me saying anything," Elly retorted, getting up. Her outburst shocked me. It wasn't something I was excepting from Elly, but they're siblings.

"ELLY!" Antonio yelled. I looked at him with my eyebrows scrunched together. He was not gonna yell at my girl. I watched Elly cross her arms. I watched amused knowing Antonio was about to catch hell.

"You don't talk to your sister like that," Antonio scolded. I watched the familiar fire ignite in Elly's eyes as a glare crossed her face.

"What are you going to do ground me longer? I don't care" She dismissed Antonio. I couldn't help but smile as I watched the feisty attitude directed towards anyone but me.

"Trip, Elly's grounded. I think it's time for you to go," Izzy chimed in, but I just scoffed, looking her up and down. Who the fuck does she think she is? I started to say something, but Elly cut me off.

"Shut the fuck up Izzy. You aren't my mom, or my boss and you definitely are not Trip's. He only has to listen to Zeke," she snapped at Izzy, her voice holding a different growl than I've ever heard from her. But I've heard it somewhere else. Just were?

"YOU AREN'T GOING TO TALK TO ME LIKE THAT!" Izzy yelled, getting up and sending Elly a glare. I smirked, leaning back knowing there was about to be a show.

"I'LL TALK TO YOU HOWEVER I WANT. YOU'RE 21 AND LIVE WITH YOUR PARENTS. LOSER!" Elly yelled back at her. I covered my mouth, trying not to laugh. I mean, she wasn't wrong. 21, living at home, ehh. They both started yelling at each other, slowly moving to get in each other's faces.

"ENOUGH YOU TWO!" Savannah yelled, as Antonio grabbed Elly's arm easily. I watched her freeze in a ridged way I've only seen one other person do. I leaned forward studying my girlfriend as she slowly looked over with a harsh deadly glare that would get the hardest of men (like myself) to listen to her every word. I've seen the person that freezes exactly like she just did...Zeke Santiago. My eyes grew wide as it all started to fall into place. She had his skin tone, nose, chin, cheek bones. Even, come to think about it, she has his smile. Of course, hers was beautiful and had an effect on me, unlike Zeke's. That's why Zeke is so protective because Elly isn't *like* his daughter. She *is* his daughter. I looked at Savannah with wide eyes. She saw my look and her skin paled. She knew that I figured out the truth and I had to tell Elly. I couldn't keep that from her.

"Trip, Elly is grounded. It's time for you to go," Savannah said in a shaky voice. But I wasn't going anywhere, unless she wanted me to blurt it out right here and right now.

"Yeah Trip. I'm grounded. I have a Volleyball game on Friday. I hope to see you there," Elly's voice was low, calm and bone chilling. She was Zeke's and I knew the truth. Everything pointed to it. I don't know how I hadn't seen it before. I saw Savannah panicking, and rightfully so. I was a dangerous person to know that kinda information. I stood up as Elly turned, storming off upstairs. I smirked at Savannah looking her up and down, laughing.

"Don't check out my wife," Antonio barked as Savannah tried to hush him. I took a step towards him with a glare.

"Back off before I ruin your whole life. This grounded thing is to be over by tomorrow. Me and Elly have plans," I said staring at Antonio. he scoffed, shaking his head.

"Ok," Savannah said. I smirked looking over at her and letting my eyes travel over her one more time, nodding.

"Nice working with you," I snickered and turned to walk out of the house an back down to the bar where I spent most of my night.

Chapter 32

Conspiracy

ELEANOR

"GOOD JOB GIRLS! We're going to kill it on Friday," I cheered in the middle of the huddle and the girls screamed. We just finished recruiting the new girls and we had a superstar team. We were going to state this year, I knew it.

"Hit the locker rooms," Coach called, breaking up our huddle. We shook up and walked over to the bench and I grabbed my water bottle.

"Elly," I heard Coach call. I turned, taking a drink from my bottle and looked at her with an eyebrow raised.

"A UCLA scout is coming to watch you play on Friday. I know that's not your choice school, but I thought I'd forewarn you," she told me with a friendly smile. I wanted to go to Harvard for Law. Being around Zeke and all those guys since I was young made me want to be a defense attorney. Zeke and my parents loved the idea, so I worked hard for it academic-wise and sports-wise.

"I'll make sure to impress. Thank you, coach," I said. Harvard was hard to get into, so I had to keep my options open.

"Hit the showers," Coach smiled and I nodded, walking into the locker room. I pulled out my dress, and my heels out of my locker. I changed into my tight-fitting red flower printed dress that had frilly tank top straps and my white strappy heels. My makeup didn't look bad, and my curls were fine when I took them out of their ponytail. I made sure I smelled good and gathered my bags, walking out as I said bye to my team. Outside I saw Zeke's car waiting for me. I got into the passenger seat, smiling.

"Hey Zeke," I smiled, kissing his cheek. I turned, throwing my bags in the back and jumping when I saw Trey'von.

"Whoa, no hi for me? I just get hit with the bags?" He teased.

"What are you doing here?" I asked him, shocked. This was beyond dangerous, and he knew that.

"He insisted on coming to our dinner," Zeke grumbled. I gave Trey'von a look of disapproval, but he just smiled at me. I rolled my eyes and turned to face the front. He was going to get caught and it would be his life and my heart. Wait, we're having dinner? I mean I love having dinner with Zeke and spending time with him, but I'm grounded.

"I'm grounded," I told Zeke, looking over at him. He nodded his head, glancing over at me.

"I know and we're going to talk about it. Who is this boy you stayed out with all night?" he asked. I felt my breath leave my body as my mind scattered. Was that why he let Trip come? Was he going to kill him right in front of me to teach me a lesson?

"You stayed out all night? Naughty naughty. Sounds like you do need a babysitter. Again" Trey'von snickered from the backseat. I turned, sending him a glare which made him laugh.

"If anyone needs a babysitter, you do. All you have done since you came here is cause trouble" I snapped at him with a wink, so he knew I was just making it up. He licked his lips and leaned forward. His nearly black eyes staring at me. I felt the goosebumps rise on my skin, which just made his smirk grow. Ugh, he's so sexy, and those lips. Everything in me wanted him more than I could have ever expected.

"You two are so strange. One minute you like each other, the next you don't. I can't keep up," Zeke commented.

"Don't be silly, she loves me," Trey'von joked. I clicked my tongue, turned in my seat, and didn't say anything. He was right. I did love him, and I would never deny that. He's had enough denied love in his life.

"Whatever, you're like obsessed with me, which is why you're here now," I shot back at him playfully. He watched me with an amused expression.

"Girl, no one is obsessed with you," Trey'von said, both of us bursting into laughter shaking our heads.

"Let's get Chinese. I could go for an egg roll," Trey'von suggested. I groaned, shaking my head "no." Chinese was his favorite and we just had it two days ago.

"No, we just had Chinese like two days ago. I want a burger," I complained, looking back at my handsome boyfriend. He leaned back crossing his arms with an attitude.

"Wait you guys went to dinner together?" Zeke asked as he pulled up to Berri's Pizza, which I loved. They had the best lobster pizza there.

"Yeah, me and Trip are really good friends," I told Zeke, smiling. Trey'von nodded in the back, looking at his phone while smiling. Zeke parked and we got out. I walked over to Trey'von and glancing at his phone to see that he had a picture of me sleeping up.

"Delete it," I whispered, but he just smirked at me.

"Nope, you're cute and the moment he's not watching, I get a kiss," he whispered. I smiled and walked towards Zeke.

"I never thought I'd see the day when you and Trip went to dinner," Zeke commented, making me giggle, but I just shrugged.

"He's not that bad. He brings a different prospective to each situation and I'm sure I do the same for him. We even each other out in a nice way," I told Zeke with a shrug. He surprised me by nodding in agreement.

"That's why I put you guys together in the first place. Its good you guys are friends. You've never been safer," he told me as we were seated. Moments later Trey'von came over, as he hung up his phone and sat down, smiling at me.

"What I miss?" he asked, as he slid across from me. He locked his legs around my foot and I fought off my smile as I mumbled "nothing."

TREY'VON

The corners of my mouth tried to twitch into a smile seeing Elly fighting her smile. I knew she loved my attention just as much as I loved her. I couldn't help but tag along with Zeke. I missed Elly and he was taking up her time, so I had to come. Was it dangerous? Yes. But I had the upper hand. If he found out, I'd kill him first and deal with Elly hating me later. It wouldn't be the first time I bounced back from her hating me, but it would be me or him. I'd chose me every time. Then Elly's little dress looked so fucking sexy, I couldn't wait to rip it off of her later. A waiter came over and Zeke ordered something called a lobster pizza, gross.

"Baby Girl," I said, and she hummed looking at me.

"Later there's a party. Come with me," I asked looking her up and down. There really wasn't a party. I just wanted to hang out, but I couldn't ask her to come to my place when Zeke was right there.

"I'm grounded, Trip," she reminded me, making me groan.

"Who was the boy?" Zeke repeated his question. I held back a cringe. I knew Elly wouldn't tell, but still.

"He's just a boy I go to school with, it's no big deal. We were safe," she told him with a shrug, but Zeke scoffed, not having it.

"Is this kid going anywhere in life?" he asked. She glanced at me, smiling brightly but I just looked away with no reaction.

"Yeah, he's gonna run a business one day. CEO status, maybe higher," she said, making me smirk. Fuck, I needed to tell her about the higher ups offer. I had a lot to tell her and no fucking time right now. The waiter came back to our table with the pizza and cups. The drinks must be self-serve. The pizza smelled so good and, I couldn't lie, it looked good. It didn't sound good, but it looked good.

"Trip doesn't like seafood," Elly said as if she had just remembered that I didn't like it. Zeke looked at me, raising an eyebrow but I just shrugged.

"I'll try it and if I don't like it, I'll get something else. It's no biggie. Where do you get drinks at here?" I asked as I moved my feet to let go of Elly. She smiled, got up and grabbed my glass.

"I got it." I smiled, leaning back watching Elly walk away. She is so fucking sexy, and that dress stopped just below that fat ass. I bit my lip looking at my girl. How I got that lucky. I don't know.

"What's going on with you?" Zeke asked, forcing me look at him.

"The fuck you talkin about?" I spat with him a glare. I hated being questioned and he knew that. He was pressing my buttons.

"You, you're different with her and she's getting your drink? Is she going to throw it on you?" Zeke asked. I couldn't help but chuckle, thinking about all the drinks she's made me wear. I shook my head, smiling at the memories.

"Nah, she better not, we're not fighting. We're just friends," I remided him with a shrug. Elly came bouncing back over and handed me the glass. She moved like she was going to sit on my lap, but I stood up.

"I got to piss," I said sending her a look. I saw her catch her mistake. She blushed, nodding and sat down next to Zeke as I walked into the bathroom, washing my hands just messing around for a couple minutes before I rejoined my girlfriend and the man she had no idea was her real father.

"I ordered you chicken strips just in case," Elly told me with the cutest look. I nodded my head in a thank you, holding her foot with mine again. I grabbed a slice of the pizza as Zeke and Elly bickered about her being out all night. I took a bite of the pizza and tried not to gag at the taste of seafood. I spit it out, shaking my head "no" and tossing the slice of pizza onto Elly's plate.

"You didn't like it?" Zeke asked raising an eyebrow. I shook my head, "no" taking a drink of the sprite that Elly got me.

"No, that shits gross," I said, shaking my head. Not even a second later, the waiter brought me chicken strips and fries. I thanked him and grabbed the ketchup.

"Trip, what do you think about her staying out all night?" Zeke asked as he eyed Elly. I was actually pleased with it. I had a lot of fun. We had sex, played in the pool, cuddled, watched movies. It was nice but he couldn't know that or that I planned for her to stay this weekend too.

"I think you better hope I never find out who it was, cause he's dead," I said looking at Elly who just laughed at me. I fought back a smile and laugh of my own, I couldn't wait for us to finally ditch Zeke. I wanted proper attention from my girl. She wiggled her foot in my grasp, making me smirk and look away. She knew I wanted her, and she was just dangling right in front of me like a prize to be won.

"You couldn't have called?" Zeke asked her in a fatherly tone.

"I forgot, but I mean I'm practically sneaking out right now and I have no phone to call," she shrugged, taking a bite out of her pizza. She did have a point, and a valid one.

"No, your mother knows you're with me," he told her which only proved my theory even more. I knew I was looking at Elly's real dad. He was much more respectable than Antonio anyway.

ELEANOR

AFTER DINNER

I laughed as I sat next to Zeke on the hood of his truck. He was just shaking his head at me. I looked up at Trey'von who was doing some little dance out of boredom. I still couldn't believe he tagged along and risked us getting caught.

"He's a character," Zeke said watching Trey'von and I nodded, smiling at him. He was a character, but he was mine and I loved him.

"Yes, he is," I said looking from Trey'von to Zeke. He smiled at me and then groaned.

"I got to take a leak. Stay with Trip," Zeke demanded as he walked away. Trey'von turned, watching him disappear into the woods.

"Come on," Trey'von said grabbing my hand and pulling me into the woods too. He stopped, grabbing my face and kissing me which made me laugh and kiss him back.

"Baby, I need to tell you something. Well, a couple things, but if the first one's true, then it effects the second thing," he rambled, confusing me more. I've never seen Trip like this before. I was worried. I reached up, grabbing his face and kissing him easily.

"Trey'von calm down and just tell me," I said looking at him with my eyebrows drawn together. He closed his eyes, taking a deep breath and grabbed my hips, pulling me closer. I was nervous, I'd never seen him like this before.

"I think Zeke is your pops." I looked at him with wide eyes, holding back a laugh. Zeke is like my dad, but he isn't biologically. Antonio was my biological dad. My parents were way too much in love to have that kinda secret. I nodded my head, looking at Trey'von. It was clear he really believed this.

"Why do you believe that?" I asked him, curiously, holding onto his shirt.

"Because yesterday at your place you were making his facial expressions like the ones, he gives me when I fuck up. You look like him and when I figured it out, your mom knew and that's why she told me I had to go." He gave me his reasons that were too easily dismissed to be true.

"Trey'von, I'm around Zeke a lot. So, picking up his facial expressions are bound to happen. I don't think I look like Zeke and my mom made you leave because I had an attitude," I told him, disproving each point he had made. He closed his eyes, shaking his head "no."

"No, I'm telling you Baby Girl, he's your pops. You should have seen the way your mom looked at me when I put it together. After you went upstairs, I confronted her. I told her I knew her secret, and she didn't deny it," he told me I just gave him a look of disbelief.

"She could have thought you meant anything. Everyone has secrets. It's just a conspiracy that I don't believe. I'm sorry," I told him, shaking my head.

"Trey'von, it's just not enough for me to believe my whole life is a lie. I respect you and every thought you have, but I can't turn my whole life upside down over this. I hope you understand," I told him, grabbing his hand and kissing his scarred knuckles.

"I'll prove it. I don't know how, but I will," he promised. I nodded my head, smiling up at him.

"You do that. What's the second thing?" I asked him, curiously. He sighed nodding his head.

"I was offered Zeke's position by the higher ups. If I accept, I think they're gonna kill him but if I don't, I don't know what will happen," He admitted. I took a deep breath, nodding my head and biting my lip. This was a lot. The idea of him thinking Zeke is my real dad and having his life dangling in his hands at the same time.

"You can't let them kill him," I told him seriously, and he nodded. He pulled me into him, hugging me and kissing the top of my head.

"They think he's stealing Baby. I don't know what I can do." I cringed, closing my eyes, hugging him tighter.

"I know you'll do the right thing. I believe in you with all my heart," I told him. I moved, leaning up to give him a passionate, loving kiss. Maybe my love was clouding my judgement when it came to this power-hungry man, but I will put all my trust into him.

"Let's get back," he whispered, and I nodded giving him one more kiss before pulling away. We walked through the woods back to Zeke's car. I didn't see him there, so I took a seat at the picnic table in front of the car. Trey'von sat on top of the table looking at me smiling. I smiled resting my head against his leg closing my eyes.

"You tired?" He asked me and I nodded my head.

"Then we should get going, take you home," Zeke said. I sat up nodding in agreement. We headed back to my house. We didn't talk about anything important on the way back. The ride was long but ended well. Once we finally got to my house, I saw that no one was home. Part of me hoped Trey'von would sneak in.

"Well, thanks for today," I said, kissing Zeke's cheek

"Bye Trip," I said, getting out. I walked up to the door, unlocked it, and went going inside. I walked straight up to my room, stripped to my underclothes and got into my bed, letting sleep take me over faster than it had ever before.

Chapter 33

Game Day

TREY'VON

I walked into the school with Smiley, Loco, and Ugly. There was a lady in the lobby selling tickets. We walked over and I bought my ticket while waiting for those clowns to buy theirs. Once they got their tickets, we walked into the gym, and I saw the Sánchez's in the stands. I thought about going over but decided against it. Smiley excitedly picked our seats and we sat down.

"Volleyball. This is your life now, high school games," Ugly commented. I shrugged, running my hand over my hair.

"I didn't go to any of her soccer games because I was too busy being a dick, so I figured Volleyball was the move. Plus, there is some recruiter from UCLA here for her," I said with a shrug and looked down on the court where I think the team managers were moving around.

"When Elly comes out, I'm gonna cheer so loud. Hell, might even air the place out," Smiley said, making us laugh and shake our heads.

"Shut yo dumb ass up," Loco laughed at him. Smiley was so fucking stupid, but he was cool.

"So be real, why aint y'all tell Zeke I was fuckin her?" I asked, looking at Loco and Ugly. I already knew Smiley was on my side more than anyone, so it didn't shock me with him.

"Cause you my boy and you already know how I get down," Smiley said. nodding his head matter-of-factly. We laughed at him again and I looked at the higher ranked guys that should have Zeke's back.

"If we're being real, the power is changing. Everyone can feel it and everyone wants to be on the winning side, which is you," Ugly admitted. I nodded my head, thinking about their words. Was it that obvious that the higher ups wanted me? I got lost in that thought. I didn't even notice Momma Sánchez come sit in front of me. She tapped my knee, drawing me from my thoughts and I saw her sitting there.

"What?" I asked her. I didn't like liars and I didn't like that she had Elly thinking I'm lying about who her dad is.

"Thank you for not telling her." I scoffed, shaking my head and leaning forward so we were eye to eye.

"I did, she didn't believe me. I'm not doing this here. Get the fuck back over to your family," I growled, not wanting her over here. I was pissed. Elly didn't deserve to live her whole life as a lie. Of course, she didn't believe me. Who would want to believe that?

"Antonio better never tell me to stay away again. He aint shit but a step-daddy now. Ask around about me and find what I did to my own step-pops." I didn't care how mean I was being to her, she deserved it. Elly would be pissed, but so am I.

"Yo Trip, chill. That's yo girl's mom," Loco said, trying to push back my shoulder. I jumped up, glaring at him.

"Stay in yo own damn lane, Loco. You don't know shit that's going on so sit down and shut up," I ordered. My guys weren't stepping out of line in front of that fucking slut.

"Trip," I heard Elly. I turned to see her standing there looking fucking sexy. Her shorts were so short. Her jersey hugged her upper body snugly. Her hair was up in bun pulled out of that beautiful face and she wore knee pads.

"Damn, Babe, those knee pads could be fun," I smirked, walking over to her as she laughed at me, kissing me passionately.

"Why's my mom with you?" she asked, looking at her mom.

"She was just leaving. She was asking me if you wanted to stay the night tonight and I told her yo fine ass was welcome whenever," I said, spinning her around and looking at that ass.

"I'm grounded though," she said, looking at her mom, confused. I pulled her into me, grabbing her butt leaving a kiss on her neck.

"Go have fun," her mom said, walking away. She looked at me squinting her eyes. I smiled, kissing her again.

"Go, you have a good game," I said, pushing her away. She smiled, stealing one more kiss and walking down the bleachers.

"Tell me I don't have the baddest bitch and I'm getting laid tonight," I said, punching my hand. They laughed at me, shaking their heads. But I was serious. I knew if she stayed the night, she was gonna let me get some.

"Yo, the sex is so good. I aint never hit more than once before, but fuck! She's freaky and that shit is fire," I grabbed, sitting down. They all gave me a look and then looked down at the court.

"Zeke gonna kill yo ass if he catches her with a hickey," Ugly said, but I shrugged.

"Just know I died up in that shit," I said, making us all laugh. Suddenly the lights shut off and the screens above the court lit up.

"WELCOME TO THE JAMES A. GARFIELD HIGH SCHOOL KICK-OFF VOLLEYBALL GAME. PLEASE ENJOY THE PLAYER VIDEOS." A man that looked like a news anchor on the screens announced loudly. Suddenly the old time count down started from 5. Once the countdown was over music started playing and it showed a girl's back. She was holding a Volleyball on her shoulder. The number was 18 and from the figure, I knew it was Elly.

It showed her spinning around fast, grabbing at her face and then the screen went black. It came back on when the beat dropped to show her holding a weighted ball, throwing it around her body, and then flashed to her using big-ass chains as training ropes. It flashed again to show sweat dripping from her beautiful lips, and then it showed her eyes in the fiercest way.

"Eleanor Valeria Sánchez. 17 years old, 3-time state champ and team capton." Her voice echoed through the gym and then the screen went black, and the song ended. Another song started and a different girl popped up. I was still shook from Elly's video. It was sexy, fierce, and it made you scared to challenge her on the court.

"Elly is so dope," Smiley said and the others agreed while I sat there just staring. I saw Gabby's video, but I didn't pay much attention. None of them was as cool as Elly's video. Elly's was in a dark tone, almost black and white, and everyone else's was too bright and doing too much. Finally, the teams came out shaking hands. Elly was in line, doing a little dance, acting up and making her team laugh. Her coach scolded her, but she just kept dancing anyway, which made me laugh, and the game started. My baby wasn't giving them a break on the court either.

ELEANOR

AFTER THE GAME

I spiked the ball just as the whistle blew, ending the game, at was 46-27. We won and I had a bomb-ass game. I had to show out because Trey'von was here and so was the recruiter. UCLA wasn't my first choice but was a good back up. I walked over to the bench, grabbed my water bottle and shook up with my teammates as I squeezed the water into my mouth.

"Sánchez." I heard my last name. I turned to see a guy I've never seen before. He was too old for high school, but too young to be the recruiter. He was cute too. Like if me and Trey'von wasn't a thing, I'd be all over this guy. He was tall like 6'2 muscular and even than bigger than Lucas, and I was feeling it. He was light skinned. His hair was perfectly styled on top and faded on the sides. His eyebrows were perfectly groomed as his black eyes stared intently at me. His nose and cheek bones fit his face. His plump pink lips were pulled back into a movie star smile.

His body, even covered, was so attractive. His sweatshirt hugged his broad muscular shoulders and pecks. His abs weren't hidden either. He had a nice even build. Even though this guy was sexy and one of the hottest people I had ever seen, he still didn't manage to hold a candle to Trey'von. When I thought about how cute this guy was, Trey'von came to mind, and he looked even better to me.

"Do I know you?" I asked. His dark eyes scanned my body as he shook his head "no."

"No, I'm QB1 at UCLA. I heard the recruiters were coming to look at you and I had to see for myself what the hype was about. That was a hell of a game," he said, standing way too close. I nodded and took a step back.

"Thanks. What's your name?" I asked, curiously, taking a drink of my water.

"Jayden Bowery. Next NFL quarterback," I gasped, playfully.

"Oh my god! NFL. I so need a picture and autograph," I pretended to fan-girl, making him chuckle and shake his head.

"Ok, smart ass. You might just be the reason I start watching Volleyball," he flirted, looking me up and down. A blush filled my cheeks at his words, and I nodded. Suddenly arms looped around my waist, spinning me around.

"Baby, you had an awesome game," Trey'von gushed. I smiled, wrapping my arms around my handsome man, kissing his lips passionately.

"I had to show out, knowing you were here, and I was excited to spend the night," I rambled pressing my body against his, which made him chuckle and kiss my cheek.

"Who's your friend?" he asked, seeing Jayden behind me. I smiled, pulling away from Trey'von.

"This is Jayden Bowery. He is the UCLA QB1 and came to watch me play along with the recruiter. Jayden, my boyfriend, Trip," I put emphasis on "boyfriend." Like I said, he might be cute, but don't got shit on Trey'von and never would.

"My girl got skill huh? What you think the recruiter thought?" Trey'von asked pulling me into his side.

"I think she's in. There is a party tomorrow night at the frat house on Gayley Ave. Starts at midnight and doesn't end till everyone is passed out. I hope to see you both there," he said, nodding at me walking away. I looked up at Trey'von with a smile, but he just rolled his eyes.

"He was flirting with you," he snapped at me, and I nodded my head.

"He was, but I wasn't. I only have eyes for you Trey'von," I told him. He squinted his eyes at me and then huffed.

"Don't be grumpy, you're my favorite man ever," I told him, leaning up to kiss him. He smiled, kissing me back, laughing.

"You're my favorite women ever. You need a shower though girl, damn," he said, waving his hand across his face, making me gasp and swat at him as I laughed.

"I know I'm stinky. I just played a game. Wait for me to finish showering?" I asked him, hopeful. He smiled, leaning down and kissing me one more time while he grabbed my butt.

"Of course. Now go before I say, "fuck it" and just get your fine ass home," he smirked. I was actually excited for him to do whatever his dirty mind was thinking to me. I walked away making sure to sway my hips to grab his attention. I went back into the locker room where the team was celebrating, and I joined them. We started talking shit about our next game and how we were going to kill them too. I was excited for the next game and just to be back in my flow.

TREY'VON

I sat on the bleachers waiting for my girl. Smiley stood on the bleachers next to me talking loudly to Loco and Ugly. The Sánchez's were also waiting for Elly, but on the other side of the bleachers, away from me, thankfully. Antonio caught my eye and I saw him waving me over to him as the other girls walked off. I scoffed, looking away and back up to Smiley who was doing some dance off Spongebob. Elly forced me to watch it, don't judge.

"Sit yo dumb ass down," I barked at Smiley. He quickly sat down. Me, Loco, and Ugly all shook our heads and waited quietly for Elly. Soon enough she came out and grabbed my face, kissing me. I laughed, pulling her down on my lap, pushing my tongue into her mouth which made her moan.

"Your parents are watching," Smiley gagged. Elly pulled away. When she saw her parents, she stood up.

"Let me go see what they want," Elly said. I stood up, hugging her around the waist and kissing her neck.

"I'm coming," I told her quietly. We walked over to her parents' hand in hand. She smiled at them as Antonio glared at me. Fuckin step-dad.

"You had an amazing game," Izzy told her as Mateo hugged Elly, forcing her to pull away.

"Thank you for coming Trip, but we're heading home now, and Elly is still grounded," Antonio told me. But I just scoffed, looking him up and down.

"Sorry, but you don't get that say so want-a-be. Yo wife already said she was mine for tonight, we'll be there to get her overnight bag," I dismissed him, viciously. Elly grabbed my hand, giving me a 'quit it' look. I just looked away and locked my jaw.

"What did you just call me you little punk?" Antonio snarled. I grabbed Elly, pushing her behind me and stepping up so that we were nose to nose.

"Call me that again and I'll show you what I did to my own step-pops. Don't got a problem doin it to hers," I threatened. He stepped up to me with what he probably thought was a deadly glare. Suddenly, I was pushed back and hugged.

"Trey'von let's just go. Let's get out of here," Elly begged me. I leaned down, kissing her head.

"Let's go," I said, looking at Antonio. She grabbed my hand, trying to pull me out. I looked at Ugly, nodding my head telling him to take care of business.

"He is not my step-dad, Trey'von. Zeke is not my real dad," Elly insisted, but I just shook my head. I knew he was. Hell, her mom told me.

"Your mom practically told me today that he was," I defended myself. Elly sent me a 'please stop' look. I huffed, storming over to my car and got in, waiting for Elly to catch up. She got in the car and sent me a glare.

"You need to stop; I don't want this to be a fight," she snapped at me, but I just rolled my eyes.

"Then believe me. I wouldn't fucking lie to you Baby Girl" I spat at the love of my life, who just did not believe me. It wasn't fair. I've never lied to her, so she had no reason not to believe me.

"You know what Trey'von, just take me home. I don't want to stay with you when you're acting like this. That's my dad and if you can't accept that, then maybe we shouldn't be together." I looked at her, shocked. I took off my seatbelt and turned to face her. So, she didn't want to be with me? She was probably already fucking that guy that was talking to her in there. UCLA my ass, and he was just her type. The big alpha male I should have known she'd never love me the way I love her.

"SO, THIS IS WHAT THAT'S ABOUT? WHO WAS THAT GUY IN THERE?" I yelled, losing my temper with her like I so often do. I knew I should be more patient, but it was so hard, especially when I knew she didn't love me.

"YOU'RE JOKING RIGHT? I TOLD YOU I DIDN'T KNOW HIM. HE WAS FROM UCLA" She yelled back at me, but I just shook my head.

"Yeah, he might be from UCLA but how long have you been seeing him, huh? How long have you been fucking him behind my back?" I accused. She looked at me, shocked, and then laughed, shaking her head.

"IF ANYONE IS CHEATING IT WOULD BE YOU. I'VE NEVER CHEATED ON YOU OR ANYONE FOR THAT MATTER. I'm not even going to argue with you about this. If you want to act insecure that's fine. All of this because I said you can't talk to my dad like that. Ya'know what? Fuck you, Trip. Sleep alone tonight." She got out, slamming the door so hard it shook the whole car. I punched the steering wheel, resting my head against it as the door swung open.

"OR INVITE THAT HOE YOU'RE SLEEPING WITH. ONLY CHEATERS ACCUSE SOMEONE OF CHEATING BECAUSE THEY

FEEL GUILTY," she yelled and slammed my door. Me? Cheating on her? Oh hell no. I got out, storming over and grabbing her flinging her into my car.

"GET OFF OF ME!" she screamed, punching me in the chest. I pulled my gun and held it to her throat with a murderous glare. She froze, as a scream came from across the parking lot.

"What Trip? You gonna shoot me?" she mocked chocolate eyes hypnotizing me as they studied my face. I closed my eyes, pushing my gun into her neck further.

"I'M NOT CHEATING ON YOU---!" I started to yell, but she cut me off as another scream came across the parking lot.

"YOU'RE RIGHT YOU AREN'T CHEATING BECAUSE WE'RE NOT EVEN TOGETHER. YOU NEVER ASKED ME TO BE YOUR GIRLFRIEND. YOU JUST STARTED CALLING ME BABY!" she yelled. What the fuck ever. We are together and she knows damn well she's my girl. Just because I didn't ask doesn't mean shit.

ELEANOR

He lowered his gun looking at me, shocked. I can't believe he pulled his gun on me. I pushed him back, shaking my head with a glare.

"You know damn well you are my girl, Elly!" he snapped, using my first name for the first time since I've met him. I was always Baby Girl, never Elly. I looked at him fully hurt by that. I don't know why it hurt so much, but I felt the pain in my chest. Tears rushed to my eyes and fell before I could stop them.

"Why are you crying?" he sneered with a dangerous glare. I didn't care about the glare or the gun. I cared about the name he used.

"You called me Elly," I sobbed covering my face. I felt the energy change in the air it was no longer angry but confused. I slid down the car and sat on the pavement, hiding my face in my knees sobbing.

"You're crying because I called you by your government name, not that I held a gun to you?" he asked, confused. I felt his hand on my knee and then his fingers going through my hair.

"Baby Girl," he whispered. I looked up at him. He smiled, wiping away my tears.

"Don't cry, you call me Trey'von all the time. You've never called me Baby or Babe," he said, I thought back to it and realized that I haven't unless we're having sex then I call him papi mostly.

"You never asked me out. I didn't know if it would weird you out," I complained wiping away my own tears. He groaned, closing his eyes.

"Will you be girlfriend?" he asked with a sharper tone. I rolled my eyes at him and his lack of patience. I nodded my head "yes," moving to hug him.

"Are we done fighting now?" he asked, kissing the top of my head.

"Are you going to let the Zeke thing go?" I asked, him pulling away as I looked up at him. He groaned, hanging his head low, but nodded his head.

"I will for tonight because I want cuddles," he admitted. I smiled, standing up and pulling him up with me.

"Gimme me a kiss *Bebe*," I smirked. He smiled, leaning down to kiss me roughly, pushing me against the car.

"I'm gonna fuck you so good when we get home," he whispered against my lips. I felt the softness pool between my legs as the tingly/needy feeling took over.

"Can't wait," I grinned moving to get in the car. I heard him chuckle as he came around the car to get in.

"You are something special," he said. I smiled, grabbing his hand and kissing his knuckles.

"If you ever hold a gun to me again, I will have you killed" I threatened, more than serious. He leaned over, pushing my hair back and kissing my lips.

"That's my girl," he whispered against my lips, kissing me again. He pulled out as I messed with his phone, trying to find a good song to listen too.

"I do think we should go to that party tomorrow. It could be fun for us" I suggested. He scoffed rolling his eyes.

"No, he was flirting with you. Let's not slip back into our fight. We were on our way to amazing makeup sex," he pouted his lip, glancing over at me. I laughed, shaking my head playfully at the amazing man next to me.

"We aren't going to fight but I want to go and, if he was flirting, who cares because you will be there," I told him with a shrug. I pouted my lip back at him, but he shook his head "no."

"Plus, tomorrow night I have to work. Big moves are happening," he said. All I wanted to do was go and have fun. We were always at his house or mine, or at the bar. I wanted to go and dance, be shown off and have fun.

"Trey'von, I want to go and have some fun. We're always cooped up in one of our houses or at the bar. Show me off" I complained, letting go of his hand. He groaned, stopping at a stop light and putting his forehead against the wheel.

"I'll take you to a party, just not that one. Los Prophets have a party every weekend. I'll take you to one of those." I mean, he was trying, so I'd give him that.

"Ok," I smiled at him. He sighed, shaking his head at me, but I was just happy we found a middle ground.

I stepped out of the shower, kissing Trey'von's lips, laughing, he chuckled following me out. I smiled as I walked to the sinks and grabbed his blow drier.

"Don't do your hair, it's 1 in the morning," he complained. I smiled up at him, squinting my eyes playfully.

"I'm not, but I'm not letting my hair air dry and get huge," I turned on the blow drier. I blew my hair and put it up in a bun. Trey'von walked past me, smacking my butt making me jump and smile.

"Hey, can I wear your clothes?" I asked him hopefully.

"Only if you come to McDonald's with me. I want a Big Mac" I smiled as I walked out to his closet. I grabbed my clean underwear and slipped them on. I grabbed a pair of track pants and tied them to fit. I grabbed a white wife beater, tying it so it fit like a crop top. I walked out throwing on my Airmax's.

"How do my clothes look better on you?" Trey'von asked coming over to kiss me.

TREY'VON

She smiled against my lips pulling me down closer, kissing me again. I couldn't believe she forgave me so easily for pulling a gun on her. Either she had to really love me or was just stupid. Either way I was happy for it.

"Let's go Papi," she whispered. I closed my eyes pushing her back on the bed, hovering over her kissing her again.

"Maybe I just need you to eat," I whispered against her lips, making her laugh and push me off.

"Come on horn dog, let's go get you real food. You can get between my legs when we get back." She sent me a wink. I laid back, closing my eyes with a smile. She is so perfect and doesn't even realize it.

"COME ON!" she yelled, walking out of the bedroom. I got up, following her down to my car. I pulled out the keys, but she snatched them from me.

"Fine, just don't kill us," I said getting in the passenger seat. She happily got in the driver's seat and pulled out of the driveway skillfully. Mindless conversation took us over while she drove us to McDonald's. I couldn't lie, she was a good driver and ready to get her license. When we got to McDonald's, she stopped in the middle of the parking lot.

"I don't know how to park," she said with nervous eyes and shaky hands.

"You're fine, just pull into a spot. You got this Babe," I encouraged her. I reached over, grabbing her thigh. She slowly started to move into a spot but didn't cut the wheel enough. I grabbed the wheel, turning it more to help her park.

"You did it," I said, high-fiving her. Her eyes lit up as she turned off the car and leaned over to kiss me. I smiled as we got out of the car. I grabbed her hand, leading us inside.

Elly laughed, taking a bite out of her fry. We were just joking around and enjoying one another like we always do when we're together. That was one reason why I loved her more than anything in this world.

"Have you ever thought about kids?" she asked me out of random. I choked on my shake, looking at her, shocked. Kids? Where did that come from? I don't want kids and I refuse to have kids. I mean what do I know about being a dad? All I know how to be is an abusive piece of shit, like Paul.

"No, never. I'm not having kids," I told her quickly. I saw pain flash across her face. She looked down at her food, tossing down her fry, nodding.

"Why? Is that something you want?" I asked her. I thought it was obvious if she was with me, we wouldn't have kids. What type of life would I bring to a kid? Not coming home one night because I've been killed or arrested. What type of life could I honestly give Elly?

"Well yeah, I'd love to have a mini us running around," she said with a shrug, not looking at me.

"I don't know how to be a dad. I couldn't give them a good life." I was not budging on this topic. I was a changing man but not that much.

"Why not? You said the same thing about being a boyfriend but look at you now," she said looking up at me with sad eyes. Kids and being a boyfriend or husband are completely different.

"You have the choice to leave if I start acting like Paul, a child doesn't. They depend on us, kids aren't happening," I told her with a shrug. I was ready for this topic to be over with. I don't know what in her brain thought of it but that needed to be let go.

"You aren't him Trey'von. You know how it feels to have that happen. Break the cycle. Actually, I'd make you. I wouldn't stay with you if you treated our child even an ounce like that," she told me, shaking her head no. So, a kid would make me lose her.

"Even more of a reason not to have one. I'm not losing you over a little shit that can't wipe themselves," I said with a shrug. She sighed, looking at me crossing her arms.

"Are you trying to break my heart today?" I looked at her with wide eyes. How am I breaking her heart? I've never wanted kids. It didn't suddenly change because I can see myself being married for the first time in my life.

"How am I breaking your heart?" I asked her offended. She shook her head, pushed away her food and looked away from me. Tears filling her eyes. She was so dramatic sometimes. It wasn't like I had ever planned to have kids. I thought it was a given. I mean, if I've never cared to date why would I care about kids.

"Don't cry," I groaned, reaching out to touch her hand, but she jerked it away.

"You don't see a future with me," she cried, hiding her face in her hands.

"Baby I do. I see myself marrying you. I just don't want kids" She looked at me through her fingers still crying.

"So, it's just going to be us forever? Who is going take care of us when we're old? Who is going to carry your family name?" I just shrugged my shoulders. She sighed, wiping her eyes looking at me.

"One day Trey'von Matias Walker, *you will be begging me to have your children. Mark my words*" She smirked. I laughed, nodding my head. Yeah, totally will I be begging for kids. We dropped the kid topic and started to joke around and enjoy each other. Once we finished eating, we went back home and cuddled most of the night.

Chapter 34
UCLA Party

ELEANOR

I laid on my bed looking up at the ceiling. I was beyond bored. I didn't have a phone or anything. I had my laptop, but Trey'von was busy with Zeke so I knew I wouldn't get a text back anyway. Tonight, is the UCLA party, in like two hours, and I couldn't go. A. I was grounded B, Trey'von was busy. C, he didn't even want to go in the first place. I sighed, getting up and grabbed my laptop I logged into my iCloud, messaging Gabby.

Me- Gabs what's up???

Gabby Boo♥- Getting ready for the UCLA party like you should be doing

Me- I can't go I'm grounded, and Trip didn't want to go. He had to work

Gabby Boo♥- What's his work? Killing puppies? Since when has being grounded stopped you ever?

She had a point. I was only listening so well because I was worried one of my parents would tell Zeke about Trey'von. I really did want to go to this party and just enjoy myself for a little bit.

415

Me- What do you have against my Bebe 😫 I'm only listening because I'm worried, they'll tell Zeke about me and Trip

Gabby Boo🤍- You know damn well they wouldn't do that. Be ready I'm gonna come swoop you for the party

I guess what Trey'von doesn't know won't hurt him. I'll just go for a couple hours. I'll be back before he's done doing whatever he's doing. I bit my lip getting up and walking to my closet to look for something to wear. I grabbed my black leather skinny jeans and a salmon colored off the shoulder long sleeved crop top that showed plenty of under boob. I grabbed a thong and went to get into the shower. I did what I needed to do and got out. I dried off, wrapping the towel around my body and went back down to my room. I sat down at my desk, I blew my hair dry, and straightened it. I put it in a cute half up and half down bun. I did my usual makeup just a little bit more glammed up. Once I approved of my look I got up and changed. I grabbed a pair of black lace-up heeled open toe boots. Just as I finished with my college party look, my laptop dinged. It was Gabby.

Gabby Boo🤍- Out here boo😚

I grabbed my backpack, put it on and went to my window. I opened it, climbing out onto the tree. I shut the window before edging down fully. I ran through the yard and out to Gabby's car, getting in the backseat.

"Yo, I'm so excited," I said, taking off my backpack.

"You look good, Elly," I heard Lucas's voice. I looked up to see him sitting next to me. I sent Gabby a glare, but she just smiled.

"Thank you, Lucas, you always look good," I whispered grabbing my seat belt and buckling up. Awkward silence took over, so I just looked out of the window while he played on his phone.

"That's my favorite top that you own," Gabby said. I looked down at the amount of under boob and blushed.

"Thanks, I figured since we were going to a frat party, might as well dress like it," I told her with a shrug, and she nodded her head.

"You look like you're in college. How'd you meet this guy?" Tony asked, curiously.

"He came up to me after the game. His name is Jayden. He's super cute, Nicole," I suggested. She looked over Lucas and winked at me. I laughed, rolling my eyes playfully.

"Why don't you try to get with him?" Nicole asked.

"Because if my Bebe finds out I'm even here, he's gonna air that bitch out." All of us laughed except for Lucas.

"Have you guys dropped the L bomb yet?" Gabby asked with a hint of disgust in her voice, but I ignored it.

"I want too, but I don't know if he'll feel the same. I'm kinda just waiting for the right moment that won't freak him out," I explained with a shrug as they nodded their heads.

"I bet he already feels the same and he's scared too. I saw the way he looked at you at the dance, like he was in love" Tony said. I laughed, shaking my head smiling at the memory of us dancing together.

"Yeah, it hurt to watch," Lucas commented, ruining my moment. I scoffed, looking him up and down.

"But it didn't hurt to watch Theo almost rape me?" I countered. He started to touch me, but I slapped away his hand with a loud smacking noise. Gabby pulled up to the frat house and I got out of the car, storming past the drunks and into the house. I was shocked right away. It was dark with strobe lights. There were people drinking and dancing everywhere. The smell was so sweat-and-alcohol-laced, I thought I'd puke.

"Elly," I heard my name. I turned to see Jayden smiling down at me with that superstar smile. I smiled back and went over hugging him.

"Hey Jayden, this party is sick," I said looking around the house. He chuckled, putting his arm around my shoulder.

"Let's get you a drink. What do you drink?" But I wasn't much of a drinker, so I didn't know.

"Anything brown." I faked my confidence. He looked down at me, impressed.

"Alright, Jack and Coke?" He led me into a giant kitchen. The counter was covered in different kinds of alcohol. I watched him mix a drink and then hand it to me. I smiled while taking a sip and looked up at him.

"I didn't think you were coming. I want you to meet some of the guys," he said, putting his arm around me again and pulling me through the frat house to a couch filled with guys.

"Are you sure you want to introduce me to your friends?" I asked, pushing his arm off me and taking a drink of my alcohol.

"Of course. I did invite you, remember?" he asked, sending me a wink. I blushed and followed him closer to the couch. Right away my eyes caught onto a super cute dark-skinned guy. He had the Will Smith box cut from Fresh Prince, thin eyebrows, piercing black eyes, and perfect facial features. He was buff, not like Jayden, but like he worked out.

"That's Darius Moore, CW, Jamie, and Zo" He introduced me to all of them. They all had the jock, which didn't surprise me.

"This is the girl I was tellin you about, Elly." I smiled and shook their hands.

"Aren't you pretty?" CW asked. I nodded my head, looking around the party and back to the men.

"Where's Noah?" Jayden asked, sitting down and patting his lap. I scoffed and moved to sit on the arm by Darius.

"I don't know, we were just talking about him. He told me I looked like a wet dog last night. What type of Australian slang is that?" one of the guys asked and they all laughed. I zoned out of their conversation. I looked across the room as I took a drink of my Jack and Coke.

My eyes caught onto a guy across the room. He was gorgeous. His smile was bright as he laughed with another guy. His dazzling blue eyes found mine across the room. My stomach turned into butterflies as I bit my lip with a blush. His dirty blonde, almost brown hair, was styled. His straight hair falling to his forehead, the sides shaved like every other guy's hair in the world. His eyebrows were thick. The fact that his blue eyes did not leave me only made the butterflies more intense. His features fit his face perfectly. His thin pink lips weren't really eye catching, but I had a feeling that they held some amazing kisses.

He was muscular, not like Jayden's or Lucas's. He was the perfect size down from them. His arms were thick. I knew he had an amazing body under that shirt, but it was hidden. He had a nice even build. He was tall, like he had to be 6'4. I thought I looked short next to Trey'von. Him, I'd look like a kid next to. I saw him walking over to me. I blushed, looking away and back to the couch at the boys who were laughing.

"Hello mates," I heard an Australian accent. I looked up to see the beautiful guy shaking up with the football players. His blue eyes finding me and making the butterflies stir.

"And who might you be? I'd remember such a beautiful face," he flirted, extending his hand. My cheeks burned as I shook his hand, but he brought my hand up to his lips, kissing my knuckles. My blush grew even brighter.

"That's Elly. She's Jayden's date," CW announced and he looked at Jayden and then me.

"Actually, I'm not Jayden's date. I have a boyfriend. I came with my volleyball team," I corrected CW. The whole couch "ohhhed," looking at Jayden as he blushed. I stood up, dropping my drink and closing my eyes in embarrassment. I needed to get out of here. I shouldn't be looking at anyone other than Trey'von with this kinda lust. He'd never do that to me, and I won't do that to him. Plus, if I did, Mr. Fine here might die.

"You dropped your drink. I can get you another one," he offered, but I shook my head "no."

"Actually, I shouldn't have come. Jayden, thank you for inviting me," I said. turning on my heels and walking away fast, trying to find Gabby. If I had to call Trey'von all hell would break lose in my life and I can't have that right now.

"ELLY!" I heard an accented voice yell. I tried to keep walking, but a warm hand grabbed my wrist, spinning me and I saw that guy in front of me.

"Hey, are you ok?" he asked. I shook my head "no."

"I need to go," I told him, but he laughed and pulled me closer. Lord, please move your hand and protect this stupid, stupid, fine man from my Bebe's temper.

"Before you Cinderella me, just one drink?" He pleaded I looked at him, confused, taking a step back.

"Why? You don't know me." Gabby was looking at me with a smirk. I sent her a "help me" look, but she just laughed and turned back to the girl she was talking too.

"I want to change that. You're very attractive." His beautiful blue eyes looking me over.

"You are too, and that's the problem," I mumbled, but he just laughed at me.

"Don't worry about your boyfriend. I'm a gentleman. Friends are a thing." I blushed bringing my hands to my cheeks. He laughed, putting his arm around me and pulling me into another direction.

"One drink and then I have to go," I negotiated. He smiled and nodded.

"One drink. My name is Noah Lane, by the way." "Noah," I like that name. He pulled me into the kitchen, which was empty, and the loud music was muffled.

"What's your boyfriend's name?" He asked me, curiously, as I pulled myself up onto the island.

"Trip. He's busy tonight," I told him, and he nodded trying to hold back a laugh.

"That's his street name. He's a gang member," I teased. Noah gave me a faked scared look.

"Oh my god, I'm shaking in my socks" He joked making me giggle and shake my head. He handed me a drink, which choked me. It was straight tequila. I looked up at him with watery eyes.

"Wow! Straight tequila. Is this one drink supposed to get me drunk?" I asked, playfully. He licked his lips, looking over my body.

"If it means you stay longer," he flirted. I rolled my eyes playfully, taking another drink.

NOAH

She was beyond gorgeous and wasting her time with some loser in a gang. She needed to find someone who wouldn't ruin her life. I was a gentleman and gladly would respect her relationship. But when she came to her senses and realized she was too good for that life, I'd here waiting.

"You're flirty," she commented, swinging her legs.

"Only when I see a beauty like yourself," I flirted, watching a blush come across her face. She sat her cup down with a guilty look.

"Listen, my boyfriend isn't someone to play this game with. He will literally kill you, so maybe I should go," she said, getting down to walk away. In a panic, I grabbed her and pushed her against the island.

"I'm not scared of your boyfriend. Just hangout for a bit." She looked up at me with a challenging look.

"Then stop flirting with me and get off of me!" she snapped, pushing me back harder than I thought she could. I laughed, biting my lip and nodding my head. Me flirting was her issue? I could chill out.

"Tell me about you Elly," I said leaning against the counter.

"What do you want to know?" she asked, suspiciously. I shook my head, smiling. She didn't trust me, but let me make her drink? Interesting.

"Everything, favorites, dislikes, goals, anything," I asked with a shrug. She took a sip of her drink and then looked at me.

"My favorite food is Tacos, color is peach, person is my sisters. I don't like anything blue or purple flavored, it's just gross---," I cut her off.

"Not even blue juice?" I asked, shocked, but she shook her head no.

"Blue anything. Candy, juice, toothpaste," she told me with disgust.

"I thought everyone liked blue stuff," I said. Who doesn't like blue Jolly Ranchers? Or juice?

"I'm a weirdo," she said with a shrug. I scoffed, looking over at her and shaking my head "no."

"No you aren't, you just don't fuck with it," I said with a shrug. She looked at me with something in her eye, but then just shook her head, smiling and taking another drink.

"You're drinking the tequila like a champ," I chuckled. She smirked, putting the cup up to her lips and tilting back her head. I watched with wide eyes as she gulped down the alcohol and then crushed the cup in her hand.

"I can drink like my dad," She grabbed the bottle of tequila and took a drink straight from the bottle. Wow, that was impressive, but it made me wonder how much she drank.

"How old are you?" I asked her curiously

"17. You?" she asked. my eyes grew wide, and I took a step back, putting more space between us.

"23. I take back every flirt," I said. She laughed, shaking her head.

"But when you turn 18..." my voice wondered off which made us both burst into laughter.

"Join the line, Bud" she joked. But I was cutting to front of that line.

"Shit put me right behind the boyfriend," I teased. She laughed, nodding her head.

"Yeah, totally," she said sarcastically. A guy walked into the kitchen that I didn't know. Elly rolled her eyes at him.

"Can we talk Elles?" He asked so they know each other.

"Go talk to your El Diablos," She spat at him and moved to the other side of me, away from him. El Diablos. That's a gang in the hood. She must be from around that area. I looked at the attractive girl, shocked. I know she said her boyfriend was in a gang, but I thought she meant one of those fake ones were you just claim to be in a gang not a real one.

"I'd rather talk to my Los Prophet," he openly flirted. She's part of Los Prophets. I've heard about how deadly they are.

"Well, I'm not in a gang and Trip isn't here, which is lucky for you," she snapped at him and moved behind me. I rested my hand on her leg and looked at the guy.

"I think it's time for you to go, she doesn't want to talk to you," I said, stepping forward. He looked me up and down, shaking his head.

"And who are you?" He asked with a strict tone, like he had authority over me.

"Don't worry about who I am. Go, party before you're kicked out," I spat. He looked back at Elly and then at me, shaking his head.

"Theo was an El Diablos, not me" he told her, walking out. I turned, looking at the girl a little more on edge.

"When you said "gang," I didn't think you meant a real gang, I thought it was just someone claiming to be a gangster." She shook her head "no."

"Real life," she said, I nodded my head, taking a few steps back. She giggled at me.

"So how dangerous is your boyfriend?" I asked, unsure if I really wanted this problem in my life or not.

TREY'VON

A COUPLE HOURS LATER

I held the gun up to the smuggler who stole from me and pulled the trigger. Blood splattered back into my face and neck. Zeke nodded his head as we took everything of value from his boat before we sank it with the smuggler on it. We had smuggled virgin prostitutes from Europe, and he had raped his way through them. That's stolen product and money. He just took the value of these girls down.

"STOP FUCKING CRYING," I screamed at the girls. This shit was annoying, and I didn't want to hear it from some whore. I barely can stand it when my own girlfriend is crying around me. I love her. These hoes I could shoot in the mouth and not think twice about it.

"What should we do with them? They're worthless," I said, looking at the beaten, raped women in front of me.

"Dispose of them with the boat," said Zeke and I nodded at Ugly to take care of them. Gun shots and screams rang through the air as he killed each worthless product.

"I can't believe that fucker just messed with my money," I growled in anger, kicking his body.

"Move on Trip. There is nothing we can do about it now but cut our losses. We still have ten girls." Yeah 10 out of 60. The profit would have been stupid, but now it's cut in half because he couldn't keep his dick put up.

"We have two more boats of girls to unload. Chill out" Zeke commanded. But I couldn't just chill out. They were messing with my money. None of these other girls better be touched or I swear to God. My phone vibrated in my pocket. I pulled it out to see an unknown number. I opened it, biting my lip.

Unknown- Hello Trip, it's Gabby. Would you like to see what your girlfriend is up to right now?

Up next was a picture of Elly standing on a table with a bottle of Patron. The bottle was lifted above her head. Her eyes were glassy, and her smile was wide as she laughed at the guys surrounding the table. The anger I felt pulsing through me was like nothing I have felt towards her before. I told her not to go to that damn party but, of course, she didn't listen. She never does.

Me- Where are you?

Gabby wasted no time texting me the address of the party.

"I have to go and take care of something" I told Zeke, putting my phone away. He looked at me raising an eyebrow.

"What could be more important?" He snapped. Well, your daughter getting wasted at a frat party. I couldn't tell him that. He'd figure out we were together.

"A girl," I told him. He looked at me, shocked, and started to say something, but I just turned and walked away, calling Smiley for back up.

AT THE PARTY

I pulled up looking at the house. There were people littered on the lawn, stumbling around drunk. The lights were bright, the music was loud. It was your stereotypical frat party.

"This looks lit," Smiley said excitedly. I turned, sending him a glare. He sunk back into the leather seat.

"We're here to get my Baby Girl, and that's it," I reminded him, my tone coming out a lot shittier than I meant for it too. But I was pissed that Elly was here after I told her not to go. I got out, slamming the car door shut. Smiley followed me as I stormed into the house. I pushed past the drunk partying students into a dining room to see Elly near a couch filled with a bunch of guys.

"Elly, let's do body shots" some white boy said, holding up a shot glass. She laughed, shaking her head "no."

"My boyfriend will shoot you," she giggled and, damn right, I'm going to shoot him and his little prick friends.

"I'LL AIR THIS BITCH OUT, IF YOU TOUCH HER!" Smiley yelled, catching their attention. Elly turned and gave me a drunken smile.

"Bebe you're here!" she cheered, coming over to me. I finally saw her outfit. She had on my favorite pants and a shirt that her tits were hanging out of. Any other time I'd want to fuck her right here, but I'm pissed.

"Why the fuck are you here and dressed like that?" I growled. She laughed, grabbing my face and pushed her tongue into my mouth. The alcohol so strong on her breath that I couldn't taste anything else. I pushed her away, sending her a glare.

"Oh! sorry Bebe, I forgot about your problem," she said, covering her lips, which only angered me more. I didn't tell her that for her to get drunk and announce it.

"We're leaving now." I grabbed her wrist.

"No Trey'von, I don't want to" She whined, trying to pull away from me as I sent her a glare.

"Aye man, she said 'no,'" the white boy pointed out. I turned, glaring at him as Smiley pulled his gun on the guy.

"Who are you?" I snapped. He looked at Smiley then back at me and stood up with four more guys. I smirked, about to pull my gun, when Elly jerked away from me.

"I SAID I DON'T WANT TO LEAVE!" she yelled at me, her words slurring together. I looked at her stunned, shaking my head.

"I'll carry you out of here," I threatened, but she just sent me a smile and went back over to the dude she was with.

"LET'S DO SHOTS!" Elly yelled, and they all cheered. The white boy handed her a shot glass.

"ELEANOR!" I yelled slapping the glass out of her hand, letting it fall to the floor where it shattered. Elly looked at it, stunned, and then up at me with a glare.

"JUST LEAVE TREY'VON, I'M HAVING FUN WITH MY FRIENDS. YOU'RE JUST THREATENED BY NOAH BECAUSE HE ACTUALLY ASKED ME THINGS ABOUT MYSELF AND DOESN'T JUST WANT SEX ALL OF THE TIME!" she screamed at me. What the fuck is she talking about? I knew everything there was to know about her. I didn't sit and ask questions, but I learned them from spending time with her and watching her. I saw what she liked and what she didn't. I knew her like the back of my hand and it's not just about sex. It hadn't been about that in a long time.

ELEANOR

I was so drunk I could barely make out Trey'von's face. I knew I wouldn't remember this in the morning. I didn't care though. I was having fun and Noah made me feel a type of way. He actually wanted to get to know me. Trey'von never asked questions like that. It was nice to have him want to actually get to know me.

"IT WAS NEVER JUST ABOUT SEX BABY GIRL, FUCK, WE'LL TALK ABOUT THIS WHEN YOUR FUCKING SOBER, NOW LET'S GO!" As his attractive voice screamed at me, I felt the needy tingles between my legs. I watched as the anger took over his face. He grabbed his curls like he does when he gets frustrated. It was the sexiest thing and it made me want him more than anyone else in the room, but I didn't want to leave.

"OF COURSE, IT IS TREY'VON, THAT'S WHY YOU DON'T WANT TO HAVE KIDS WITH ME. JUST LEAVE! I'M HAVING

FUN WITH MY NEW FRIENDS. THEY'RE NOT ASHAMED TO BE SEEN WITH ME LIKE YOU!" I yelled at him, as Noah filled my shot glass and I threw my head back I took another shot, laughing.

"You want me to make him leave?" Noah asked me, his eyes wandering over my body. I looked at him laughing shaking my head.

"Aw cute, you think you can make Trip leave? I appreciate the thought but that's blood on his clothes. He'll kill you. SMILEY PUT UP THE DAMN GUN!" I yelled at him, throwing the shot glass at him.

"AYE, BACK OFF MY GIRL!" Trey'von yelled pushing Noah back as he pulled his gun. I rolled my eyes pushing Trey'von away as I grabbed the bottle and took a drink.

"I'm not ashamed of---." I cut him off because I didn't want to hear whatever bullshit was going to seep out of his mouth.

"LIES. YOU ARE ASHAMED OF ME OR ELSE YOU WOULD HAVE COME WITH ME TONIGHT. INSTEAD, I HAD TO SNEAK AND COME BECAUSE MY BOYFRIEND WANTS TO HIDE ME!" I yelled, stumbling and almost spilling the liquor in my hand. I giggled, taking another drink of it.

"I'M TRYING TO PROTECT YOU FROM WHAT WILL HAPPEN IF WE GET CAUGHT----." I cut him off, shaking my head.

"THEN STOP PROTECTING ME----." He cut me off, it was like neither of us could get anything out.

"I CAN'T, BECAUSE I'M IN LOVE WITH YOU ELEANOR. YOU CHANGED EVERYTHING ABOUT ME. YOU SNUCK IN AND MADE ME SOFT. NOW LOOK AT ME STANDING IN A PARTY SCREAMING AT YOU WHILE ZEKE UNLOADS FUCKING HOOKERS," he screamed. I choked on the liquor going down my throat. He loves me? Trey'von Matias Walker was in love with me.

"You love me?" I asked, astounded. Even drunk it shocked me. I brought the bottle to my lips as the guys around me stared.

"FUCK YES I LOVE YOU. NO, I DON'T ASK STUPID QUESTIONS----." I cut him off because it wasn't stupid to me. It meant a lot more than he thought it did.

"IT'S NOT STUPID, YOU PROBABLY DON'T EVEN KNOW MY FAVORITE CANDY OR BOOK BECAUSE YOU NEVER FUCKING ASKED ME! YOU'RE SUCH A LIAR! YOU CAN'T LOVE SOMEONE YOU DON'T KNOW!" I yelled. I felt my temper spike. He didn't love me. He lies all the time. He didn't know me to love me. I grabbed my hair walking in a circle. He opened his mouth to speak, but I threw the bottle at him.

"SHUT THE FUCK UP, YOU'RE A LIAR. YOU CAN'T LOVE ME!" I screamed, Noah went to touch me, but I pushed him off me.

"It's time for you to go," Noah slurred but I shoved him onto couch.

"STAY OUT OF IT" I yelled at him. Suddenly I was grabbed around my waist and thrown over a muscular broad shoulder. I recognized the letterman jacket. It was Lucas. I screamed, punching his back.

"GET OFF OF ME. I HATE YOU MORE THAN I HATE TRIP AT THE MOMENT! LET GO OF ME LUKE!" I screeched, trying to kick him, but he grabbed my legs.

"Elly drunk and upset isn't fun. Where is your car?" Lucas asked Trip as I squealed punching him in the back.

"LET ME GO, FUCK YOU!" I yelled as he carried me out. Once we were outside and by some cars, he sat me down. I pushed him away with a glare, but Trey'von grabbed me and pushed me against the car.

"What's your mom's number?" he demanded. I rolled my eyes telling him the number. He typed it into his phone, opening the passenger door.

"GET IN NOW!" he yelled at me. I pushed him away and almost fell, but he caught me.

"I GOT IT TREY'VON. I'M DRUNK NOT DISABLED!" I yelled stumbling into the car. He shut the door and pressed the phone to his ear. Why was he calling my mom? Soon enough he got into the car and putt up his phone.

"Why the fuck did you call my mom?" I questioned him sending him, the nastiest glare I could muster

" I told her you were staying with me, I'm trying to save you from getting into trouble," he chastised me as he pulled out, but I didn't want his help. I looked out of the window with nothing but attitude. Suddenly everything started blurring. My vision was going in and out along with my hearing.

"I feel funny" I slurred. I burped and the next thing I know everything went black.

Chapter 35
Warfare

ELEANOR

I woke up to my stomach churning in the most undesirable way and my head pounding against my skull. Even with my eyes closed, I could feel the whole room spinning. I felt the bile in the back of my throat creeping closer with each churn. I cupped my mouth, jumped up, and ran to the bathroom, puking up nothing but alcohol from last night. Moments later, I felt cool fingertips against the clammy skin on my neck and pulling back my hair. Once I felt like I was done puking, I groaned and rested my head on the toilet seat.

"You deserve that." I heard Trey'von's deep sleep-laced voice. Trey'von? How did I get here? How did he find out I was at the party? I was already grounded for not coming home and yet here I am at my boyfriend's house, and he was probably pissed. I lifted my head to find I was only in my underwear and one of his shirts. I flushed the toilet as he handed me a glass of water and stormed out of the bathroom, slamming the door as hard as he could which made my head hurt worse. Well, he's pissed, and I had so many questions. I wandered if everyone at that party was safe when I left. I stood up, rinsed out my mouth and threw away the little Dixie cup. I went back into the bedroom to see Trey'von laying in bed on his phone. I rolled my eyes and walked back over to the bed where I laid down and closed my eyes.

"I barely fucking slept last night because you smell so damn bad," he spat at me. I covered my head with his comforter in annoyance.

"I don't even remember coming here, so not my problem," I snapped back, trying to fall back asleep. I was still drunk. Once I slept it off a little more, I'd talk to him but not until then.

"It IS your problem. You went to that party after I told you not to," he countered. I held my tongue, choosing not to have this argument at the moment. Before he was able to continue, sleep overtook my body. I was already in trouble for sneaking out, being out all night, and being with Trey'von. So, I might as well sleep off the hangover and then call my parents.

A FEW HOURS LATER

I woke up to the sun shining brightly into the bedroom. I sat up still feeling bad but not as bad. I saw I was alone. Trey'von must have gotten up after I fell back asleep. I pushed the comforter off my alcohol smelling body and stumbled into Trey'von's closet. I grabbed a pair of track pants and a t-shirt, and then going into his bathroom to take a shower. Once I was clean and out of the steamy shower, I felt better. Almost normal, but for a faint headache. I changed into the outfit and just ran a comb through my curls, leaving them to dry naturally. I walked downstairs to look for Trey'von and found a door cracked open. I pushed it open. He was sitting behind a CEO desk with a pair of black rimmed hipster glasses on. I couldn't lie to you the look was beyond attractive.

"Hey Bebe," I whispered. His head snapped up and he sent me a glare and then looked back down at his papers.

"I don't have time to fight right now. I'm busy," he dismissed me. I wasn't going to push him because I knew I was the one in the wrong.

"Can I use your phone and call my mom? Mine is dead," I murmured quietly. He threw the papers in his hand and slammed his fists on the desk which made me jump.

"I already called her, Baby Girl. She knows you're with me. Now, get out of my study," He demanded. I nodded quickly, walking out of the study and shutting the door. I went into the living room, sat on the couch, turned on the TV trying not to overthink the upcoming argument I was going to have with Trey'von. After about 30 minutes, he walked into the living room and sat next to me while looking at the TV.

"I was working," he told me quietly, and I nodded my head as I picked at the pants I was wearing.

"I didn't want you to hear and since you can't be trusted alone----". I cut him off with a glare.

"I didn't do anything to break your trust. I made everyone stop flirting with me and everyone's hands stayed to themselves," I corrected him. The only thing I did was go to a party he had told me not to. But he's not my dad and I had real fun from what I can remember.

"Bullshit, I told you not to go in the first-place Baby Girl," Trey'von growled. I looked over at him, crossing my arms. He sent me a warning glare, but I was not scared of him, and he was not going to push me around.

"You're my boyfriend not my dad. It's not like you would have gone even if you didn't have to work." I knew he was going to be mad, but I had to defend myself.

"Yeah, just like I don't know you either?" He snapped, standing up. What was he talking about? Of course, he knew me. Sometimes it was scary how well he knew me. Even when he pulled away from me, he still knew me better than anyone else ever did.

"What are you talking about? Stop acting crazy." He jumped up and looked at me with wide eyes, his arms out to his sides.

"I'M NOT ACTING CRAZY ELEANOR, THAT'S WHAT YOU SAID. I DON'T FUCKING KNOW YOU AND ONLY WANT YOU FOR SEX. ALL BECAUSE I DON'T ASK YOU DUMB ASS QUESTIONS!" he screamed. I was taken back when he used my name. It hurt so bad to hear Elly or Eleanor come from him. I had been 'Baby Girl' since the day we met. It was his giveaway as to how angry he was at me. It took everything in me not to burst into tears over the single name.

TREY'VON

Elly stopped just looking at me. I saw tears fill her eyes as I watched her fight them back like a pro. I knew using her name would hurt her just as much as I was hurt right now. It bothered me that she thought I didn't know her, and I only wanted her for sex. I told her I loved her. That was big for me, and she threw something in my face that hasn't mattered for so long and claimed that I did not know her. Then that guy was all over her. She didn't give a fuck and just let it happen. Don't even get me started on that fucking top she was wearing.

"I was so drunk. I don't even remember Bebe. Calm down and let's just talk and not scream at each other," She begged. She leaned up to touch me, but I ripped back with a glare.

"NO, YOU DON'T GET TO MAKE A MISTAKE AND HAVE IT GET SWEPT UNDER THE RUG. IF I DID THAT BULLSHIT, YOU'D BE PISSED!" I yelled. I didn't want to remind her of the time that I came to her house high and drunk. Her reaction then wasn't much different.

"ACTUALLY, YOU DID DO THIS REMEMBER? RIGHT AFTER YOU DITCHED ME THE FIRST TIME, WE HAD SEX!" she screamed. I rolled my eyes at her comment. I have made up for that, so why she held onto that, I won't ever understand.

"Yeah, remember your reaction? You were just as pissed. It took me all morning and part of the afternoon for you to lose your fucking attitude," I retorted. She rose to her feet from her anger or surprise or whatever the fuck she was feeling in her hungover state.

"I REACTED PRETTY FUCKING GOOD IF YOU ASK ME. I LET YOU SLEEP IN MY BED, I MADE SURE YOU WOKE UP TO CLEAN CLOTHES, MEDICINE FOR YOUR HEADACHE. I FUCKING BABIED YOU WHILE I FELT LIKE MY HEART WAS BEING RIPPED OUT. THEN I BOUGHT MY DAD SO HE WOULDN'T HAVE YOU LOCKED UP---." I cut her off, shaking my head. Yeah, she might have done all that but there was hell for me to pay over that too.

"WHY THE FUCK ARE YOU SHAKING YOUR HEAD 'NO?'" she yelled. I started to walk away, but then I couldn't help but turn and glare at her.

"YEAH, BUT I DIDN'T TAKE YOUR MOST VULNERABLE MOMENT AND CHEW IT UP AND SPIT IT BACK AT YOU IN FRONT OF EVERYONE. JUST GO FIND THE FUCKER THAT ASKS YOU QUESTIONS. SEE IF HE KNOWS YOU AS WELL AS I FUCKING DO. YOUR LUCKY YOUR LITTLE BOYFRIEND IS STILL FUCKING ALIVE," I screamed. That British guy, or whatever the fuck he was, all over her and she was just letting it happen.

"I DON'T KNOW WHAT YOU'RE TALKING ABOUT TREY'VON. WHAT DID I DO THAT HAS YOU SO PISSED? AND WHO ARE YOU TALKING ABOUT? NOAH?" She yelled. But I didn't know the Fucker's name, and I didn't care to know him. Actually, I might put a hit on him just to prove a fucking point that Elly was mine and only mine.

"I DON'T KNOW THE ASSHOLE'S NAME ELLY, BUT YOU SURE WERE ALL OVER HIM, AND YOU KNOW WHAT I'M TALKING ABOUT!" But she just rolled her eyes and threw her arms in the air.

"I know for a fact I wasn't all over anyone. I made it clear I had a boyfriend that was extremely dangerous, and I didn't want them flirting with me. You get so jealous, you make things worse than they have to be," Elly bit back. Oh, so now it was my jealousy that was the issue? Could you blame me for being jealous? Elly deserved better than me. She deserved someone who was going to be a doctor or a lawyer not some fucked up gang member with a past that fucked him up even more. She'd realize that one day and leave me. I knew it and it drove me crazy because I loved her.

"Yeah, that British guy was practically eye fucking you all night. You are mine Baby Girl and I'll make the statement known," I growled, taking a dominating step closer to her. She sent me a glare. The look almost dared me to do something.

"That's Noah, and he's Australian. He's 23 and I made it clear I had you and didn't want anyone else. He was just being nice." Elly's arms crossed with attitude. Nice my ass! He was probably hitting on her all night, not to mention the way he tried to kick me out.

"HE ASKED YOU QUESTIONS THOUGH REMEMBER? HE KNOWS MORE ABOUT YOU THEN I EVER WOULD!" I yelled. she rolled her eyes shaking her head as she tried to walk past me. But I stepped in front of her, which stopped her. I wasn't done with this argument, and she wasn't going to walk away from me before I was done saying what I had to say.

"MOVE TREY'VON. I'M DONE FIGHTING OVER SOMETHING I DON'T REMEMBER AND YOU WON'T TELL ME. WHEN YOU WANT TO ACTUALLY TALK TO ME LIKE A GROWN UP, I'LL LISTEN BUT I DON'T FEEL GOOD AND I'M NOT DOING THIS ANYMORE!" Elly scolded. Her words made my temper flare. I should grow up? She's the one who snuck out to party last night and who acted like a child who didn't want to leave the park when I went to get her.

"FINE ELEANOR, YOU WANT ME TO BE AN ADULT ABOUT IT. I TOLD YOU I LOVED YOU. I STOOD THERE IN THAT PARTY AND ADMITTED THAT I AM IN FUCKING LOVE WITH YOU. THEN YOU PRETTY MUCH CALLED ME A LIAR. YOU SAID I DIDN'T KNOW YOU TO LOVE YOU, SO, YEAH, I'M PISSED THAT SUDDENLY I DON'T KNOW YOU AND SOME RANDOM CUNT DOES IN YOUR MIND!" My whole body was shaking from the anger coursing through my veins. She looked up at me with wide eyes. Her jaw gaped open. I laughed, shaking my head and waving her off, knowing she didn't care. She never did care about me.

ELEANOR

I watched Trey'von laugh at me. He waved me off and stormed into the house and away from me. He just dropped the L bomb. Trey'von Matias Walker admitted to loving me. I never expected that from him. I loved him. I knew for a long time he was the love of my life, but to hear the words come from his lips? What happened last night when he told me? Did I really react badly? I was dying to hear those words from him and when I finally did, I was drunk. I sat on the couch processing his words.

"He loves me," I whispered to myself, smiling. It was the best feeling in the world to know he truly loved me, but I was filled with regret, too.

The moment he told someone he loved them for the first time in his life, I had to be drunk and mean about it. I had to make this up to him and talk through this with him. I got up off the couch and walked in the same direction he went. The door to his study was open. I walked into the doorway. He was at his desk rolling a blunt.

"I don't want your pity," He remarked. I bit my lip as I walked into the study, shutting and locking the door. We had to talk about this. I had to let him know how much I loved him too.

"I'm sorry Trey'von. I don't even remember you telling me you loved me. Please talk to me. Tell me what happened," I begged as I went over to the desk. He focused on the blunt he was rolling.

"Bebe, I don't want to argue. I want to talk about this," I told him seriously. He leaned back into his chair looking at me with nothing but attitude on his face.

"We were fighting. I came to the party to get you and bring you home. You started talking about how that guy asked you questions about yourself and that I never did that, so I didn't know you and that I am ashamed of you. When I tried to tell you, I was far from ashamed of you, you told me that I was and that's why I hid you. I tried to explain to your drunk ass that I was protecting you because I loved you." He looked at the weed on the desk and went back to rolling it. I quietly moved over to the desk and sat on it.

"You yelled and told me I didn't know you to love you. I just wanted sex from you. You claimed I didn't know your favorite candy, book, anything really. I was nothing but a liar in your eyes. But the truth of that is that I know all of that. Your favorite candy is Sour Patch Kids not the blue ones. You don't like anything blue, or purple favored. You leave them in the pack for me. Your book is the "Wuthering Heights" or anything by Emily Dickinson. I know your favorite cheeseburger is from McDonald's of all places. You'd rather have sushi than anything else, but you're scared you'll get sick if you eat too much," he rattled off little facts that I hadn't even realize he'd picked up. I smiled, biting my lip and looking at him as he put the blunt to his lips, lighting it. He took a couple hits from the blunt, passing it to me. I smiled taking it, hitting it a couple times, blowing out the smoke and handing it back to him.

"Bebe, I don't know what to say." My heart was full, and I was so happy he knew all of that. I knew Trey'von as much as he would let me know him. I always thought I was open with him so of course he'd know everything. Maybe he really didn't need the questions. He'd rather just pay attention to me and learn that way.

"Well, for starters an "I love you" would work," he snarked. I cringed, face palming myself. I moved to straddle his lap, steadying us in the roller chair. I grabbed his face, making him look at me.

"Trey'von I've loved you for so long now. I was just afraid I'd scare you away with the words. I am sorry I was drunk and had a bad reaction to it. I'm sorry I let Gabby convince me to go to that party." He stopped hitting the blunt looked at me with a raised eyebrow. I bit my lip, messing with his messy curls.

"Wait, Gabby convinced you to go?" he asked me suspiciously. I nodded my head, leaning in kissing his lips passionately. As expected, he lazily kissed me back. He was still mad and rightfully. I would be pissed if I told him, I loved him in front of people, and he called me a liar. He pushed me back. I sighed and looked up at him.

"Yo, uh--," he stopped shaking his head, adjusted himself under me, and passed me the blunt. I took a hit while looking at him.

"I think Gabby might like me," He suggested. I couldn't help but burst into laughter. Yes, Trey'von is sexy, and most females would be all over him, but Gabby would never. She doesn't even like being around him.

"No Baby Girl, I'm serious. She just caused this whole fight between us." I stopped laughing and looked at him, confused.

"What are you talking about? How did Gabby cause this fight? I'm the one who went to a party you told me not to go to," I asked him as I hit the blunt again and handed it to him. He nodded his head, pushing back my messy curls.

"Yeah, but Gabby convinced you to go, right? Like you weren't gonna go but she talked you into it. Then she texted me this:" He pulled out his phone, tapped around and handed it to me. I saw that Gabby had sent him a picture of me with a bottle dancing on a table surrounded by a bunch of guys. And then she texted him.

Unknown- Hello Trip, it's Gabby. Would you like to see what your girlfriend is up to right now?

I looked at the number to see if it truly was Gabby's. Why would she get me to go to the party just to text Trey'von? How did she get his number anyway?

TREY'VON

Elly stared at my phone in shock. Her chocolate brown eyes looked up at me. Her lips parted slightly. She shook her head as she looked back down at my phone.

"I don't understand," she whispered. The hurt in her voice telling me that she really did understand. I pushed back her hair, kissed her cheek and tried to comfort her. Her best friend just betrayed her. I couldn't picture how that felt. I would never know because Smiley was down for me no matter what, and, honestly, that kid was my best friend.

"She just tried to break us up Baby Girl. Us fighting plays right into her plan," I explained. She got off me and paced around in front of my desk. I leaned forward and saw tears spring to her eyes.

"THAT BITCH!" Elly yelled. I couldn't help but smile as I watched her pace around. She's so fucking attractive. She tied her hair up in a bun.

"She's supposed to be my best friend, Trey'von. But, instead of being that she's a backstabbing slut who's trying to break us up so she can fuck you. She's going to regret that Monday morning and that's a promise," Elly foamed with anger which made me chuckle. My little Baby Girl thought she was so bad. I couldn't help but find it funny and cute at the same time.

"So, I'm going to school Monday. Who we fighting?" Smiley asked, busting into my study. I rolled my eyes as he walked over to Elly, shaking up with her.

"Gabby. She's trying to break me and Trip up," she explained to Smiley as he came over to me.

"Damn, for real? Y'all good?" He asked, looking between us. I looked up at Elly as she stared at me waiting for my answer. I smiled at her and waved her over to me.

"You know we good. No hoe gonna break us up," I said as Elly smiled, came over to sit on my lap, and kissed my smiling lips.

"The only thing I'm not good with is that shirt you were wearing. That is going in the trash," I scolded. She nodded her head quickly, making me chuckle. She looked at Smiley and then at me. This girl. I knew what she wanted. Makeup sex. It was always what we did after a fight, but Smiley was here.

"What you need Smiley?" I asked him curiously, but he just shrugged.

"Nothing, I got bored at the bar. Zeke is with the higher ups who are pissed you had those hookers killed," he said. I cringed, looking at Elly who looked back in shock.

"Go, I don't talk business in front of you," I told her tapping her thigh. She nodded, kissing my cheek and walking out of the study as the door closed behind her.

"Why are they pissed? They weren't any good," I asked Smiley, but he just shrugged his shoulders.

"I guess they could have brought in more money still. So, I know y'all had a fight... spill," Smiley pushed, but I just shrugged my shoulders.

"We did. It wasn't that bad really. We've had worse fights. Right before you got here, we put together the Gabby thing. You goin to school on Monday?" He nodded affirmatively, his head running hand over hair.

"Keep her out of trouble. Let her and Gabby go at it, but don't let it get stupid." I gave him the call on what I wanted. I knew they'd just argue. There is no way they would get physical. This was Elly we were talking about and if that little slut touched her, I'd have her head.

"Got you bro. Let me hit," he said pointing to the blunt resting on the desk. I handed it to him just as the study door opened to reveal Elly.

"I actually just came for that," she said, pointing towards the blunt. I nodded my head, and Smiley handed it to her.

"Why don't we all go and get breakfast. I'll take you home Baby Girl and deal with the higher ups," I suggested to everyone, and they nodded their heads. I smiled getting up and kissing Elly's cheek which made her blush.

"You are beautiful. I'm gonna go shower and then we'll go," I promised, and she nodded, kissing my lips.

"I love you," she told me. I closed my eyes at the sound of the words. I wanted to hear them again, but I didn't want to seem soft in front of Smiley.

"I love you," I told her as I kissed her cheek once more and walked out of the room to get ready for my day. Hopefully, it's better than this morning has been, but I had a feeling I was about to have a shitty day and there was nothing I could do to change it.

Chapter 36

Human Emotion

ELEANOR

I woke up to my alarm screaming in my ear. It was Monday morning, which meant that it was time for school. I groaned, rolled over and turned off my alarm, tiredly. I didn't get in until late last night. I was doing a run with Zeke. We went all the way to Canada and back. Of course, Trey'von was pissed because he doesn't want me in gang business. His words were "I swear this will be the last run you do Baby Girl," and then stormed off and got on his phone.

I sighed as I got up, turned on my light and shuffled to my closet to look for something worth wearing. I knew there would be major drama today because I was going to confront Gabby. I ignored her all weekend. No one is going to try to break me and my Bebe up. I picked out a pair of black high-waist skinny jeans, a plum color tank top, and underclothes. Lastly, I grabbed a towel and my body soap.

I went down to the bathroom to shower. I dried off with my white fluffy towel and wrapped it around my body. I went back to my bedroom, sat at my desk, and blew my hair dry. I decided to straighten it today and just change it up a little bit. I did my usual makeup. Once I approved of my look, I stood up and changed into my outfit, throwing on my all-white Nike Air Forces. I gathered my homework and laptop and went downstairs where I shoved everything into my backpack. I went into the kitchen and found my mom, dad, and Mateo.

"Good morning," I chirped, sitting down my backpack. They surprisingly weren't mad about the party or staying the night with Trey'von. They didn't say anything to me when I got home. They just went on like it never happened, so I did too.

"Morning. After school we're going shopping," Mom informed. I smiled, nodding my head and grabbing my water bottle from the fridge.

"When do I finally get my phone back?" I asked my dad. I feel like it's been forever since I have had it.

"Next week. You guys better get going," Dad said. I groaned loudly, as I picked up my things and walking out to see Trip waiting for me. I smiled and skipped down the steps towards him. His dark brown, nearly black eyes ran over my body and sent tingles of goosebumps over my skin.

"Beautiful as always," he complimented me, smiling. I went over and hugged him, kissing his lips easily.

"I love you," I declared. He smiled widely, grabbing my butt and kissing my lips passionately.

"I love you more," he whispered. I think it was impossible for someone to love anyone more than I loved Trey'von. I snuggled into him. He chuckled, hugging me close him.

"I miss the curls," he pouted. I smiled, standing on my tippy toes kissing his lips.

"Hey Romeo, can I have a ride too?" Mateo asked. Trey'von pulled away and smiled down at Mateo. He opened the back door for her, and she got in. He looked back at me snuggling his nose in my neck.

"Say it again," he asked. I giggled, running my hands up his shirt and tracing his abs.

"I love you Trey'von Matias Walker," I whispered into his ear. He groaned, grabbing the back of my thighs and picked me up, putting me on top of the car. He pushed back my hair and kissed me roughly. He shoved his tongue into my mouth, making me moan and grip his shoulders.

"I'm gonna fuck you so good later." I felt the thrill of excitement from his dirty words. I smiled, wrapping my legs around him and pulling him closer.

"Maybe I should ditch school," I suggested. He chuckled, shaking his head "no."

"I have to meet with the higher ups. I'll be done by the time you get out. Come on let's get you there," He said. I nodded, getting off the car. He opened the door for me, and I slipped into the leather seat. I watched Trey'von walk around and get into the driver's seat. He smiled leaning over to kiss me.

"The sexual energy is so high in this car right now," Mateo faked a gag. We laughed as Trey'von rested his hand on my thigh.

"Leave us alone, we're in love," I said playfully to my younger sibling. She stuck her tongue out at me which made me laugh.

"What are you meeting the higher ups about?" I asked. He looked over at me and shook his head "no."

"I don't want you in the middle of it." I laced our fingers together, kissing his scarred knuckles.

"I just want to be there for you," I told him. He nodded his head, glancing over at me.

"I know, but I'd rather you not know gang business." I respected his decision. It was one Zeke would make too. Soon enough we got to school and to the drop off point. Mateo yelled a "thanks" as she got out and I looked over at my love.

"See you when you get out of school," he said, leaning over kissing me.

"Sure will, be safe today," I told him. He smiled kissing me longer than before.

"I will. I love you," he told me. I felt tingles of butterflies in my stomach from the words.

"I love you too," I murmured kissing him one more time before getting out and grabbing my backpack. I started to walk into the school when I heard the car horn. I turned as Trey'von rolled down the window.

"THAT ASS LOOKIN FAT!" He yelled. My cheeks ignited in embarrassment as my eyes grew wide. I laughed as I turned to walk into the school, purposely swaying my hips. Once I got to my locker, I saw Smiley standing there looking at his phone.

"You're early," I commented, opening my locker. He shrugged, looking at me with a goofy smile.

"Instead of timing me, fix yo lipstick. Look like you sucked dick the whole way here." I looked at him stunned as I fixed my lipstick. I grabbed my homework from my bag and put it away.

"That's happening later," I teased, sending him a wink. He looked at me with a smile never leaving his face.

"MY FUCKING BOY!" he yelled, making me laugh. I shut my locker and my mind went straight to Gabby. She wasn't getting away with trying to break up me and Trey'von.

"Stop screaming, Lil Smiley." I blushed as we started to walk down the hallway. He chuckled at me, shaking his head.

"So, there is a party in South Central, Trip's old neighborhood. You guys got to come through." I shrugged my shoulders, not sure. Trey'von was picky about his past, so I didn't know if he wanted me that close to it. Then there was that whole party thing that just happened.

"If Trip is up for it, then we will. But I'm not gonna push it after the frat party and it being so close to his past," I told Smiley. He nodded his head, shoving his hands in his pockets. We turned the corner and I saw Gabby, Nicole, Tony, and Lucas all standing by Tony's locker and just talking. I pushed my things towards Smiley, and he was quick to take them with a confused look. I ran over and pushed Gabby against the lockers hard, making a thud fill the hallway.

"HOW LONG HAVE YOU HAD A THING FOR TRIP? YOU'RE A HOME WRECKING BITCH!" I yelled as Lucas tried to grab me and pull me back. I swung on him, but he ducked down, and I missed. I turned my attention back to Gabby who looked at me with wide eyes.

"What are you talking about?" she asked. I just shook my head, trying to stop my temper from spiking, but it was climbing fast.

"YOU KNOW WHAT I'M TALKING ABOUT. YOU TRIED TO BREAK ME AND TRIP UP WITH THAT PARTY. Trip is mine, so keep your hoe ass away from him!" I growled, shoving her back against the locker again. She started to push me back, but I hit her with a quick two piece and then hit her with a hard right hook and she fall to the floor.

"WHY'D YOU DO IT GABBY? HOW LONG HAVE YOU WANTED MY BOYFRIEND?" I screamed at her as tattooed arms wrapped around me, pulling back.

"YO, ELLY, CHILL," Lil Smiley yelled as I fought against him to get back to Gabby. He chuckled, which only made me angrier. Gabby slowly sat up, probably dazed. Her nose and lip bleeding from my violent punches. She looked at me blinking a couple times, anger showing on her face.

"ELLY, STOP! I DON'T WANT TRIP. I NEVER DID NOR WILL I EVER!" Grabby screamed at me. She was liar. Why else would she have sent him that photo after convincing me to go to the party?

"HEY, BREAK IT UP NOW!" I heard Mr. Dean, the Principle, yelled from down the hallway. I stopped fighting against Smiley, staring at my former best friend in disgust. I couldn't believe that she'd do something like this after all this time that we've been friends.

"You're such a fucking liar, Gabby. The fucked-up part is that I'd never do anything like this to you. Get off me, Smiley," I barked trying to jerk out of his arms, but it was impossible to get out of the hold he had on me.

"WHAT DID I JUST SAY? I said that's enough. Miss. Sánchez, you're coming with me," Mr. Dean's voice boomed as the crowd surrounding us started to disperse. Smiley slowly let go of me as Mr. Dean grabbed my arm and started pulling me towards the office. Another teacher was quick to come to Gabby's side to help her up and probably take her to the office.

I sat in the plastic chair waiting for my dad to show up. I knew I was in trouble. I just didn't know how much trouble I was in just yet. I heard footsteps down the hall. I expected to see my dad rounding the corner but, instead, I saw Gabby being led by a teacher. I shook my head, crossing my arms and looking away.

"Sit. I don't want to hear any talking between you two," the teacher told us and walked away. He didn't have to worry about us talking. Why would I want to talk to her? She was supposed to be my best friend, but all she has done is stab me in the back.

"Elly, please it's not what you think," Gabby broke the silence after a few minutes had passed. I didn't say anything, I just shook my head because I knew she was lying.

"Elly, please you have to believe me," Gabby begged. Finally, I snapped my body around as I shot daggers at her.

"Why I should I believe you Gabby? The only reason you had to do what you did was to break us up so you could get with Trip yourself. You were supposed to be my best friend." My hands moved wildly, and my tone was as mean as it's ever been towards her. I was betrayed and hurt by what she had done. She was supposed to be the person I could count on through everything and then she pulled something like this? She groaned, putting her head between her knees. She sat like that for a moment and then looked up at me. Her dark eyes were bloodshot. They revealed nothing but vulnerability and honesty.

"No Elly, I didn't send Trip the picture to break you guys up so I could get with him. I sent him the picture so you guys would break up, yes. But it's because I'm in love with you!" I froze in shock as the realization hit me like a ton of bricks. Gabby was in love with me? Gabby liked girls? I mean that did explain a lot, but me-out of all people me?

"He doesn't deserve you, Elly. You deserve more than some gang banger that's just using you and is bound to hurt you. You deserve someone who's going to love you and cherish you. So yeah, I tried to break you guys up. I thought once he dumped you, you'd come to me for comfort and maybe, just maybe, you'd realize you loved me too." Her tone was desperate for acceptance, which was crazy. Gabby should have known I would have accepted her for who she is.

I don't care that Gabby is gay. Everyone loves someone. Hell, I don't even really mind that she's in love with me. I'm a little weirded out right now by that but who wouldn't be shook if their best friend dropped a bomb on them like that. Even though she thinks she loves me, she doesn't. If she did, she wouldn't have pulled what she did.

"Gabby, I'm going to only say this once. I don't care that you're gay. I would have loved you as a best friend, regardless. Hell, I wouldn't even have minded if you had told me, you were in love with me, but I know you're not really in love with me---." She cut me off, wide eyed and shaking her head "no." She was stumbling over her words trying to defend herself, but she couldn't seem to form a sentence. After a few seconds I held up my hand and made her rambling stop with a snap of her jaw.

"No, if you loved me like you say you do, you wouldn't have done what you did. You would have wanted me to be happy. For trying to break Trip and I up I don't know if I can forgive you," I told her, shaking my head. Before she could say anything else, I heard the heavy steps of work boots around the corner and, moments later, my dad appeared. I opened my mouth to explain myself, but he held up his hand, shaking his head "no."

"I don't want to hear it," he snapped as he went into Mr. Dean's office. I sank lower into my seat waiting on my dad to come out and freak out on me over my fight. My dad was in Mr. Dean's office for about 30 minutes. When the office door opened, my dad walked out with steam rolling off of his head.

"You are in so much trouble. ALL OF THIS OVER THAT GANGSTER!" He yelled. I stayed quiet, trying to sink even lower into my seat.

"GABBY HAS BEEN YOUR BEST FRIEND--just wait till we get home," he shoved a finger my way, which scared me even more.

"You're suspended for a week, Miss. Sánchez," Mr. Dean told me. I nodded, looking back at my dad.

"Go get your things," He growled. I quickly made my way out of the office and to my locker.

"LOOK AT YOU THROWING AWAY YOUR FUTURE FOR SOME NOBODY. YOU HAD A PERFECT RECORD UNTIL NOW

ELEANOR. YOU THREW IT AWAY, FOR WHAT? HIM! ALL BECAUSE YOU THOUGHT GABBY HAD A CRUSH ON TRIP!" my dad roared as we drove home. I kept my eyes trained out of the window, praying we got home fast. I was ready to be out of this tight intense space.

"WHERE DID YOU EVEN LEARN TO FIGHT? WE HAVE A VIOLENCE FREE HOME! I ASKED YOU A QUESTION!" He shouted, not even giving me time to answer his stupid question.

"Zeke taught me because Novah was messing with me," I whispered, glancing over to only see the anger in his eyes grow hotter.

"ZEKE TAUGHT YOU HOW TO BRUTALLY BEAT UP YOUR CLASSMATES?" He yelled even louder as we pulled up in front of the house.

"THAT'S IT! YOU'RE DONE WITH THAT BAR, THOSE GANGSTER, ZEKE, ALL OF IT. DO YOU UNDERSTAND ME ELEANOR?" His voice boomed. But I wasn't done with them. Not even close to it, and I wasn't going to let him bully me out of my life. I sent him a glare, shaking my head "no."

"NO, I'M NOT. I'M ALMOST 18. SOON ENOUGH YOU WON'T BE ABLE TO TELL ME WHAT TO DO!" I yelled, getting out of the car. In seconds, he was out of the car too, the whipping noise of his belt coming out of his pants was the only thing I heard.

"I DON'T CARE HOW OLD YOU ARE ELEANOR. YOU ARE OUT OF CONTROL!" He stormed around the car with his belt in hand. I started to bolt down to the bar where I saw four men standing. I easily made out one as Trey'von, but I didn't know the others. Before I could take off, my dad grabbed my arm so tight it ached, and I knew there would be a bruise.

"YOU'RE SNEAKING OUT, PARTYING, STAYING OUT ALL NIGHT, GETTING DRUNK, HAVING SEX. I'M DONE WITH YOUR BEHAVIOR!" He brought back the belt and I closed my eyes tightly ready for the sting of the leather strap.

TREY'VON

I saw Antonio's car speed past the bar. I was standing outside talking to the higher ups, Big Rico, Carlos, and Daniel, aka "Big Honcho." We were talking business and they were telling me how much of a great fit I would be to take over. I couldn't help but zone them out as I watched Antonio's car pull into the spot. Moments later, I heard my girl's voice.

"NO, I'M NOT. I'M ALMOST 18, SOON ENOUGH YOU WON'T BE ABLE TO TELL ME WHAT TO DO!" Elly yelled, getting out of the car. Second later Antonio got out and ripped his belt out of his pants. Oh, he's lost his damn mind if he thinks he's going to hit her.

"I'll be fucking damned," I growled as I began to walk away, but Carlos grabbed me with a confused look.

"I DON'T CARE HOW OLD YOU ARE ELEANOR. YOU ARE OUT OF CONTROL!" Antonio yelled storming around the car with his belt. I ripped away from Carlos, pulled my gun and headed towards my girl. I knew it was dangerous for them to know about Elly but Antonio, being the fuck up he is, wasn't going to hurt her. I took off running over to them to stop Antonio.

"YOU'RE SNEAKING OUT, PARTYING, STAYING OUT ALL NIGHT, GETTING DRUNK, HAVING SEX. I'M DONE WITH YOUR BEHAVIOR!" Antonio screamed just as I got behind him. He brought up the belt. My Baby Girl closed her eyes ready to take the blow. I held my gun up to his head and pulled back the hammer.

"Hit her with it and I'll make your wife clean your brains off the sidewalk," I growled lowly, and he froze as Big Rico, Carlos, and Daniel calmly walked over to us. Elly opened those beautiful chocolate brown eyes to find me behind her dad.

"DROP THE FUCKING BELT ANTONIO AND LET THE FUCK GO OF HER!" I yelled. He dropped the belt and Elly at the same time and then brought up his hands. Elly ripped back, tripping, but Big Rico caught her. I laughed, shaking my head as I brought my gun back to hit Antonio, but I stopped when I saw Elly watching me.

"Baby Girl, go to the bar. I'll be there soon," I told her seriously. She shook her head "no" as she started to come closer to me, but Carlos and Daniel grabbed her and stopped her.

"Are you going to hurt him?" she asked. I nodded my head at the two men to take her away. I was done giving Antonio chances and he was about to learn my temper.

"Take her to bar, send out Loco, Ugly and Jose. Watch her, she's got a temper and can throw a punch," I warned them. Elly looked at me shocked, and then sent me a glare.

"Trip, don't send me away. TRIP!" she screamed as they drug her away. I watched as they pushed her into the bar. Once Elly was out of view, I hit Antonio hard with my gun and he fell to the ground where I kicked him.

"WHAT THE FUCK ANTONIO? YOU WERE GOING TO HIT THE LOVE OF MY LIFE WITH A BELT? WHAT IF I DID IT TO YOU? Actually, that doesn't sound like a bad idea," I growled as Lil Loco, Lil Ugly, and Jose came walking down the street towards us. Antonio groaned, holding his ribs. I smirked, kicking him where he held himself

"Pick his dumb ass up," I growled reaching down to grab the belt. Paul used to have the same one. Memories of the abusive piece of shit I grew up with flooded my head.

"You know my old man was a piece of shit too. One day he came home drunk and laid out a cane, a belt, and a hammer. He told me to pick one so he could beat me with it. You know the one I picked?" I asked Antonio. He looked up at me with a glare. I could tell he wanted nothing more than to swing on me. He tried to get away from my guys, but they forced him to his knees.

"The stick," he guessed. I shook my head "no."

"Nope, the hammer. Because fuck him. All I saw right then was that piece of shit AND I'LL BE DAMNED IF ELLY GOES THROUGH THAT WHILE I'M BREATHING!" I yelled; swinging the buckle which hit him in the face. I beat him over and over with the belt. He yelled out in pain and begged me to stop, but I wasn't even close to stopping. I threw the belt away. Lil Loco was punching him in the stomach, Jose was punching him in the face, and Lil Ugly was throwing him down.

"STOP, PLEASE"! He begged. But that only made me laugh and punch him harder in the jaw. Lil Loco kicked him one good time in the jaw and I pushed us all back. He was laying there in his own blood, groaning in pain.

"Pick him up" I ordered, and they did as I told them. Antonio lazily picked up his head and looked at me with blood dripping from his mouth. I pulled my gun, pressed it under his chin while keeping eye contact.

"Take this as a warning. I'm done fucking around with you. If I even hear you raise your voice at my girl again, this beating will be the last of your worries," I warned as I stood up straight. I nodded to Jose, and he pulled out his switch blade, stabbing him above the hip and then they threw him down. I kicked him hard one more time.

"You know the rules, Antonio. You talk to the police, and I'll kill everyone but Elly," I threatened, and he nodded, holding the spot where he had been stabbed. Pain was written across his face as he grunted. I smirked at him nodding for my guys to walk back down to the bar. Inside, I found Elly standing at a table with an attitude.

"Baby Girl, are you ok? Did that fuck up hurt you?" I asked, dropping my gun and rushing to her. I grabbed her perfect face, looking over her body. I didn't see any marks. I connected our lips in a rushed kiss, looking over her once again for any marks.

"My arm hurts a little but I'm fine. Is my dad alive?" she asked, worried. I pulled her into me, hugging her tightly and grabbed a handful of her hair. I hate the thought of her getting hit with that belt. If it had connected to her, I promise, he wouldn't be alive.

"Barely, but yes. If he would have hit you, I swear---." She pulled away, smiling at me, kissing me lightly.

"He didn't. You were there, saving me, like always," she whispered and then I remembered the higher ups. I turned, pushing her behind me, glaring at them as they smirked at me.

"You have a girlfriend, Trip. Interesting," Daniel snickered at me as they looked her up and down. I wasn't sure of my next move here. I didn't want them knowing about her. I needed her to be safe.

451

"I never took you as a one women type," Big Rico snickered as Elly held onto my shirt nervously.

"Trip, we're not going to mess with your girl. Introduce us," Carlos waved me off. I brought her forward still keeping her close to my side.

"Baby Girl these are the higher ups. Big Rico, Carlos, and Big Honcho. Guys this is my girl, Elly," I said nodding down towards her. They smirked at her, and she waved at them, snuggling into me more. I leaned down, kissing the top of her head as Smiley busted through the doors.

"YO, YOUR GIRL IS FUCKING CRAZY! LOOK AT THIS FIGHT!" Smiley yelled and she cringed into my side.

"Fight? You got into fight?" I asked her as I let go and moved over to Smiley. He showed me a video of her and Gabby. I couldn't lie, I was impressed. I looked up at Elly in approval as she looked down.

"If you're going to lecture me too, save it. I need to talk to you," she pleaded with urgent eyes. I nodded my head, handing Smiley back his phone.

"Excuse me guys. We'll get back to work in just a second," I assured, and they nodded. I pushed Elly towards the back of the bar and into the back room.

"What's up beautiful?" I asked her, shutting the door. She came over, kissing me roughly making me smile.

"Gabby told me she was in love with me," she whispered. I looked at her, stunned, pulling away.

ELEANOR

Trey'von pulled away from me with a shocked look. He pushed back my straightened hair and looked into my eyes sending the tingles of goosebumps through my body.

"What did you just say?" I bit my lip, messing with his shirt.

"Gabby told me after the fight that she loved me. Like was "in love" with me and that's why she was trying to break us up." He grabbed my hips and pulled me closer to him. He looked at me like he was thinking about my words or letting them soak in.

"I thought you guys were just best friends?" I nodded my head, biting my lip as I looked up at him.

"Yeah, well we were before all the whole frat party thing. I would send her my nudes before I sent them to you just to make sure they were poppin and now I feel weird about it" I admitted. He burst into laughter. He shook his head, kissing the top of my head.

"For one, you can't take a bad nude with this body, and for two she should have told you she was into girls before she let you send those kinda private photos, just so you could fully consent. How do you feel about that?" he asked, leaning against the wall. I sighed, running my fingers through my hair, shrugging.

"I have no idea how to feel. My best friend is in love with me. How do you react?" He just shrugged his shoulders.

"Well, you're my best friend and I love when you tell me that you love me." Those dark brown eyes were burning with truth. I couldn't help but "awe" at how adorable he is. I leaned up, connecting our lips.

"You are so sweet but think if Lil Smiley told you, he loved you." He made a face at me, making me laugh.

"Yeah, let's not even pretend that's a thing. I'm nervous," he murmured. I hummed, looking at him with questioning eyes.

"Why Bebe?" I asked, looping my arms around his neck. He traced shapes on my hips as he looked away from me.

"The higher ups are putting pressure on me to take Zeke's spot and now that they know about you, I'm scared they'll try to use you to force my hand." His tone shook with fear. I licked my lips. I knew I was in danger, but I wouldn't let him know how scared of the men I really was.

"And I feel bad for them if they do. Bebe you are the strongest person I know. I love you and I know you will protect me." My tone was more serious than I intended for it to be. He nodded, kissing my lips easily.

"Come on, they'll be getting restless," he whispered, letting go of me. I watched him open the door and followed him out to the main lobby.

"Elly is your name, right?" the man known as Big Rico asked. He must be the leader of the three of them. I nodded my head, sending them my best smile as I grabbed Trey'von's hand.

"Yes, and you're Big Rico," I said, looking at him. He kicked a chair out, nodding for me to sit down. I sent him a look, telling him I expected more manners and class.

"Please sit," he motioned to the chair. I looked up to Trey'von before I moved for the chair. I wanted to show them that Trey'von had the power in this situation. He walked over to the chair sitting down, pulling me into his lap.

"Bebe," I blushed. He chuckled, kissing my jawline.

"It's weird to see Trip so soft," Carlos said. I smiled, running my fingers through Trey'von's hair.

"Don't let him fool you. He's still very capable, especially when it comes to me," I assured. He smirked as he leaned back and looked away from the group.

"How'd you manage to catch the heart of our most feared?" Big Honcho asked me curiously. I bit my lip not really sure what I did to get him, but I had him.

"I don't know. We actually used to hate each other," I admitted. Trey'von laughed, nodding his head.

"I wanted to kill you so bad. You were so annoying," he chuckled, squeezing my thigh. I rolled my eyes looking at the big guys. I went to open my mouth when the door to the bar swung open. There was Zeke. Just as I went to jump up, Trey'von pushed me off him, making me fall to the floor.

"Trip!" I hissed at his feet.

"Sorry, Baby Girl" he whispered. I rolled my eyes, getting up as Zeke walked over to us.

"Princesa, what are you doing here? Why are you at Trip's feet?" Zeke asked, hugging me. I bit my lip, thinking of a cover story quickly.

"Trip saved me from my dad and then pushed me down, Zeke" I told him pouting. He sent Trey'von a glare. I stood behind Zeke, sticking out my tongue.

"What happened with your dad? Trip, touch my daughter again---." Big Honcho cut Zeke off

"And nothing will happen to him. We didn't know you had a daughter," Big Honcho said glancing at the other three. I moved to hug Zeke like I was scared of the guys.

"She's not really mine, but close enough" Zeke told them and they nodded sharing smirks with one another because they knew our secret. I was praying they wouldn't say anything to Zeke and ruin our lives.

"Her fuck up as a father tried to hit her with a belt but I took care of it," Trip smirked, leaning back as he pulled out a knife and played with the blade. What did he do to my dad? Was he laying out there in a pool of blood? No, Trey'von would never hurt me that way, would he? There was a lot of bad blood there, but he wouldn't.

"What did you do to him Trip?" I spat. He looked at me with a glare.

"Don't fucking worry about it Baby Girl, maybe you should be thanking me instead of being a bitch." I reached out for a drink, but he stood, grabbed my wrist and pushed me back sending.

"You two are so bipolar. Princesa, now is not the time, go home," Zeke ordered kissing the top of my head and I nodded.

"Love you Zeke," I said. He smiled, pulling me into a hug.

"I love you too. Dinner tomorrow night, just me and you," he said. I smiled nodding in agreement. I said goodbye to the higher ups and flipped off Trey'von. I walked out to see my mom getting out of her car.

"GET IN! YOUR DAD WAS JUST STABBED!" she yelled. Stabbed? I was just with him and he was fine. Trey'von...

Chapter 37
Backslide

ELEANOR

I rushed into the emergency room to find my dad laying on the bed with his shirt cut off and stitches in his side. His face was busted and stained with blood. I could see the imprint of a belt buckle on his face. He looked at me, shaking his head "no," and then looked away.

"Antonio, what happened?" Mom rushed to her husband's side. I quickly followed, but Izzy got up and pushed me back with a glare.

"YOUR BOYFRIEND DID THIS!" I looked at her with wide eyes and then back to my dad.

"Elly got suspended for fighting Gabby, of all people. When we got out of the car, I lost my temper and started to hit her with my belt. Trip and some other guys showed up. They drug Elly away, beat me up, and one stabbed me." I felt my blood boil at Trey'von. We've been doing so well. He knew this would be ruin us. How could I be with someone who would so easily hurt my dad?

"I didn't know Trip was going to stab him," I defended myself to Izzy, but she just scoffed at me.

"How many times are you going to let him beat our dad up before you get it through your head, he's dangerous!" Trey'von was not dangerous unless he was forced to be. There had to be another reason that he stabbed my dad. Maybe my dad tried to stab Trey'von?

"Dad, please tell me there is more," I begged, pushing passed my sisters. He grabbed his side, cringing and shaking his head "no."

"He said if I told the police, he wouldn't hold back next time." I was going to kill Trey'von myself. I grabbed my hair in anger, pacing around in a circle trying to think.

"I need my phone." I needed to get to Trey'von. He wasn't just going to hurt my dad and get away with it. He stabbed my dad and came back to me? kissing me? pretending that nothing ever happened?

"Are you crazy? Your dad is laying here in the HOSPITAL AND YOU WANT YOUR PHONE?" Mom yelled. I sighed, crossing my arms, and looking away. My dad cringed and all my sisters rushed to his side. I saw Izzy's keys on the chair. I walked over, grabbed them, and shoved them down my shirt as I went to my dad's side.

"Are you ok dad?" I worriedly asked, but he waved me away.

"Go, you've done enough" Mom scolded. I nodded my head, turned, and walked out of the room and out of the emergency room doors. I pulled Izzy's keys out of my top and pressed the panic button. I followed the noise to her car and got in. I drove the quickest route I knew back home. After several stop lights, I made it, and parked the car. I got out and stormed down to the bar, swung open the door and saw Zeke, Trip, and the higher ups laughing.

"YOU ASSHOLE, YOU STABBED MY DAD?" I yelled as I stormed over to Trip. He looked up at me with wide eyes and then back to Zeke, who glared at him.

"WHY WOULD YOU DO THAT? YOU COULD HAVE KILLED HIM!" He stood up to answer, but I pushed him back.

"AFTER EVERYTHING WE'VE BEEN THROUGH YOU ARE GOING TO TAKE THIS STEP BACK IN OUR RELATIONSHIP? WHAT IS WRONG WITH YOU? DON'T YOU THINK WE'RE IN A LITTLE TOO DEEP TO BE PUSHING ME AWAY. WHY WOULD YOU DO THAT TRIP? YOU COULD HAVE KILLED MY DAD!" I saw the anger growing in his face, but I didn't even care right now.

"IF YOU'D SHUT THE FUCK UP AND LET ME TALK, YOU'D KNOW I'M NOT THE ONE WHO STABBED HIM---." I cut him off by shoving him again.

"BUT YOU GAVE THE ORDER. YOU ALWAYS GIVE THE ORDERS. I'M NOT STUPID I KNOW HOW WELL EVERYONE LISTENS TO YOU," I screamed at him as tears rolled down my cheeks. I was so hurt and betrayed, I couldn't help but cry and the anger I was feeling didn't help. I knew we shouldn't be fighting in front of the higher ups, but here we are in another screaming match.

"Guys let's not do---" we both cut Zeke off sending him a glare.

"STAY OUT OF IT!" we yelled and glared at each other once again.

"DON'T TALK TO HIM LIKE THAT!" we both yelled. It only enraged me more when we said the same thing at the same time.

"STOP THAT!" we both yelled. The higher ups were laughing at our fight. I felt my anger begin to fizzle out and all that was left was hurt and betrayal.

"JOSE IS THE ONE THAT STABBED ANTONIO'S FUCKED UP ASS, NOT ME. I WISH IT WAS ME, HE DESERVED IT FOR TRYING TO HURT YOU!" Trey'von yelled as he took a step closer. He was shaking from anger. His dark brown nearly black eyes were wide and fully black. Most people would be scared of him like this, but not me.

"You let Jose stab him so it might as well have been you that did it. If you want to push me away just say so. Just tell me you're done and leave my family out of it!" My voice shook with each word. I turned to walk away, but he grabbed my arm and spun me around.

"WE AREN'T DONE UNTIL I SAY WE ARE!" his voice boomed so loud I felt it in my chest. Zeke came over and got between us with worried eyes.

"Is Antonio, ok?" Zeke asked with concern.

"Jose stabbed him as a warning, he's fine. Just a couple stitches," Trey'von rolled his eyes as if it was no big deal that he had my dad stabbed. That's a huge deal, it's my dad.

TREY'VON

She was freaking out over nothing. I knew that the stabbing was done in as safe a spot as possible. There was no vital organ right there, and it was a slow bleeding spot. There was no way he would have died from that unless he had made the choice to lay down and bleed out. I knew Elly would lose her shit over it the moment she found out. I thought she'd have enough sense to not do this in front of the higher ups. Who would have guessed that Elly would prove me wrong?

"Just a couple stitches, IT COULD HAVE BEEN HIS LIFE!" she yelled at me, but I rolled my eyes.

"NO, THE FUCK IT WASN'T. THE ONLY WAY HE WOULD HAVE DIED IS IF HE LAID THERE FOR HOURS. THERE WAS NO ORGAN THERE AND IT WAS A SLOW BLEEDING SPOT. IT WAS A WARNING TO NOT TOUCH YOU AGAIN. HE'S AN ABUSER BABY GIRL, HE WOULD HAVE DONE IT AGAIN!" I yelled at her. I knew for a fact he would have. I grew up with a man like that. It would have gotten worse, so bad that I might not have been able to save her. So, I stopped it before it started.

"Whoa, that's a big title to put on someone. Tell me what happened," Zeke said, trying to calm the waters between us. He's seen how bad things can get between us and I knew he didn't want that to show in front of the higher ups.

"Antonio tried to hit her with his belt Zeke. We already fucking told you this. I saw it and stopped it. Me, Lil Loco, Lil Ugly, and Jose jumped him and Jose stabbed him as a warning not to touch her again," I explained to Zeke with a shrug. He opened his mouth to say something, but Big Honcho cut him off.

"Zeke, let's go for a ride. Let's let them figure this out. It has nothing to do with you," Big Honcho said. I knew I'd owe them for not telling Zeke about me and Elly and giving us this alone time.

"You hurt her, and I'll kill you," he warned as he walked out with the higher ups. Once the door slammed shut, I looked back down at my girlfriend.

"I should dump you," she hissed. I felt my heart drop. I couldn't lose her. Not over this. I loved Elly too much to lose her.

"Wait no, Baby listen----," she cut me off shoving me back.

"WHY'D YOU DO IT?" she screamed. I was trying not to lose my temper as she shoved me. She started to shove me again, but I grabbed her wrists and spun her around and held her into me. She fought against me with tears falling from her eyes.

"Can you stop and let me explain my side to you. I know once you hear it you'll understand why I didn't stop Jose," I said seriously. If she just gave me a chance to explain my side, we wouldn't be fighting.

"Fine, but if I don't, we're over. I won't be with someone who hurts my family like you do," she said as she ripped away from me. I felt the pressure from her words. I didn't want to lose her over this or anything. If I did, Antonio would regret telling her I was involved with this stabbing. I would have already lost her. Losing her would be like losing my life, so I wouldn't have a second thought about killing him and spending life in prison over it. I pulled out a chair for Elly and she sat down. I sat next to her, grabbing her hands as I looked into those beautiful chocolate brown eyes.

"When I seen Antonio pull that belt on you, I thought about Paul. I thought about being locked in a closet with no food, taking beatings for my siblings, watching my mom get her ass beat by him. Hell, I smelled that nasty ass Everclear he used to drink again. Then I saw you and I couldn't stand the idea of anything like that happening to you---," she cut me off, making me groan. She could ever just listen, she always had to talk.

"My dad is not Paul, Trey'von. I love that you want to protect me, but almost killing him?" she asked me as tears rolled down her face. I leaned over wiping her tears away. I kissed her cheek looking into her watery eyes.

"Baby, I promise you where he was stabbed wasn't going to kill him. There was no vital organ there and it was slow bleeding. It would take him two days to bleed out. We use it for torture and to scare people into thinking they are dying. I just lost it when I saw him about to hit you and the way it so easily connected to Paul for me. I'm not going to apologize for protecting you. I stopped the abuse before it could have gotten bad. If you want to break up with me over that, fine but I'd do it again," I told her. I watched her eyes soften at my words. She sighed, moving onto my lap and kissing my lips while hiding her face into my neck sobbing.

"I love you Trey'von, please don't use this to push me away," she sobbed into me. I sighed, wrapping my arms around her, and shaking my head "no," kissing her shoulder.

"No Baby, that's not what I'm doing. I love you so so so much. I just lost my judgement when I saw him about to hit you. If he would have hit you, I would have killed him," I swore to her. Her arms got tighter around me. I shushed her crying, running my fingers through her straightened hair that was beginning to curl once again.

"Don't talk like that. I love him, he's my dad. I don't want to see him hurt," she cried. I knew she did, but I wouldn't let him hurt anyone I cared about.

IZZY

I turned to grab my keys, but they weren't where I left them. I made a face as I got in my bag looking for them just as my phone lit up with a text message from Anthony, my boyfriend.

Ol' boy Walker♡- Hey baby how's your pops? You need me to come out?

He was so sweet making sure I didn't need him right now. This isn't how I wanted my family to meet my love so even though I did need him, I wouldn't let him come. I dropped my phone back into my bag and looked around for my keys.

"Mom, my keys are gone." She looked at me, confused, and then looked around the room to see that Elly wasn't here.

"Let me go ask your sister if she's seen them, keep looking," Mom said. I dumped out my whole bag and looked on my dad's tray for them. I grabbed my phone to text Anthony back.

Me- You're too sweet but I don't think right now is the best time for you to meet my family.

Ol' boy Walker♡- I'm starting to think you like hiding me, we are having a baby. We have to tell them at some point.

I touched my stomach, biting my lip. I didn't like hiding Anthony, but Elly causes so many problems because of her boyfriend that I didn't think my parents would react well to me having a boyfriend too. I mean, in no way are Trip and Anthony the same. Anthony wasn't in a gang. He was in college. He had a job and would support me and our baby. Nothing about the two were the same. *They weren't connected in any way.* I touched my flat stomach thinking about the baby in there. Yes, I was pregnant, and no one knew but Anthony and his mom Celina.

"Izzy, what's wrong honey?" Dad asked. I turned to open my mouth and tell him "nothing," just as mom stormed into the room.

"She's gone. Elly is gone with Izzy's keys. This girl is out of control!" Mom fumed throwing her arms up in the air. It didn't surprise me. The apple didn't fall far from the tree there. She acts just like her real dad, a criminal. Add grand thief auto to the list of crimes she's committed.

"Next, she's going to join that gang," Mateo commented and, honestly, it wouldn't surprise me. She surrounds herself with them and she is blood-righted in. I thought it was wrong that they lied to her. I get it, they tried to stop her from following in Zeke's footsteps. But she's following them anyways, so they might as well tell her.

"Mateo, go get something to eat," said Mom, handing her money. We watched Mateo walk out and I stood up.

"I'm about to send her to live with her father for a while," Mom foamed out of anger. Dad cringed as he sat up in his bed and I moved quickly to his side.

"I am her father, not Zeke. I will handle this," He cringed again. I grabbed his hand and kissed his knuckles.

"You're her daddy and always will be, but Zeke is her real father. She's following him without knowing it. Maybe he can help her. I mean, she's too protected for you to do anything. Look at you." I tried to reason with him, but he just shook his head "no." My dad hated that my mom stepped out on him with Zeke. He tried to forget about it by forgetting the truth

462

about Elly, but she wasn't his and her genes were showing it. I looked up at mom who looked away cringing. I knew she wanted to tell Elly, especially now that Trip, himself, knew the truth.

TREY'VON

I pulled Elly closer as we made out right there on the bar. I wanted nothing more than her right now, but I knew Zeke was right outside. I would owe the higher ups for keeping my secret and giving me this time alone with her. I wasn't sure what they'd want in payment, but I knew it would be big.

"Oh, by the way" Elly said pulling away. I looked at her raising an eyebrow. She reached into her top pulling out a set of keys with a blush.

"Who's keys?" I asked her, confused.

"Izzy's. I kinda stole her car to come breakup with you." I looked at her with wide eyes and burst into laughter as I shook my head. Only Elly would steal a car to come breakup with me and then end up making out with me on the bar. I smiled, kissing her lips again which made her giggle.

"I'm not going anywhere Baby Girl. You're stuck with me for life." I was being honest. I wanted her for the rest of my life. I wanted to love her and hold her. Hell, I wanted to wake up next to her and call her Mrs. Trey'von "Trip" Walker.

"Only if you don't hurt my dad again and make an effort to get along with him," she smiled, kissing me again. I smiled back, moving closer to her, if that was possible. I held her legs that were wound around my waist.

"I will if you take my last name," I negotiated, pulling away and biting her lip. She moaned, looking up at me with a raised an eyebrow.

"Like marry you?" she asked with humor in her eye. But nothing about me was kidding. I wanted a future with her, and I wanted it now.

"Yeah, why not? We can go down to the courthouse, get married and then go to the hospital," I told her, biting my lip. She looked at me, speechless, and then burst into laughter shaking her head "no."

"No, I want more than a courthouse wedding and Zeke doesn't even know we're together." As if I cared about Zeke. I smiled, licking my lips, and kissing her again.

"Fuck Zeke. I'll go out there and take his spot right now. Then he can't tell me if I can be with you or not. You'll get a big wedding for sure, but I just want you to be Eleanor Valeria Walker right now," I told her. I watched a blush cover her cheeks at the idea of it. She smiled, kissing my cheek.

"You have to ask me the right way. I want a ring." I nodded my head. I could come up with a romantic way to ask her to be mine.

"Let's get Izzy her car back" I sighed, moving. She got off the bar and followed me as we walked out. I looked behind me to make sure she was there.

"Make up?" Big Rico asked us, looking between us.

"I just put her in her place," I scoffed. She hit me, making me laugh and bite my lip.

"But we got a problem," I told Zeke, taking the keys from Elly. He looked at Elly with wide eyes and she sank behind me.

"YOU STOLE A CAR?" he yelled at her. I moved to let her face what her actions had caused. She glared at me, but I just winked at her.

"Just Izzy's. I'm taking it back," she defended herself. He shook his head with a sigh.

"Your mother is letting you go crazy. I'll be talking to her. Trip, fix this," he ordered, and I nodded my head, giving her back the keys.

"See you guys later. I'll follow you, Baby Girl." walked over and got into my car, watching her get into Izzy's. She pulled out and followed her to the hospital. Once we got there, I parked right next to her and got out.

"You don't have to go in if you don't want to," she told me, but I scoffed shaking my head "no."

"Nah, I'm not scared of your family. Let's go," I said, waving her off. I grabbed her hand and we walked inside. She led me through the emergency room to a cubicle and opened the door. Everyone looked back at her, and I saw the glares.

"GIVE ME MY KEYS!" Izzy yelled. I walked inside, hugging Elly from behind and looking over to Antonio.

"Get him out of here," Antonio demanded but I just made a face, leaned down and kissed Elly's cheek as she tossed Izzy her keys.

"I took them to breakup with Trip," she said making me smirk. I let go of her and started to walk over to Antonio, but he spoke.

"If you guys broke up, then why is he here?" I went over to his bed and sat next to it.

"Because she loves me and didn't breakup with me. We talked out our problems and one thing we talked about was us getting along better. I shouldn't have let Jose stab you, but you shouldn't have tried to hit her. We're even." I shrugged. Elly huffed, looking at me. I gave her a 'what' look.

"Bebe, you were supposed to say sorry," she said as she came over to mess with my hair. I rolled my eyes looking at Antonio. I shook my head and stood up.

"Shit, we just gonna have to break up," I said. She laughed, pushing me down and giving me a look.

"I'm sorry for letting Jose stab you, he'll be punished," I said as I looked at him. He just looked away. I reached for his oxygen, but Elly grabbed my hand sending me look.

"Good news is, you weren't gonna die. It would have taken days to bleed out from that spot," I told him, but he scoffed, shaking his head, and looking away.

"Daddy, Trip is trying and so should you. I want you guys to get along because Trip is going to be around for a long time." I was going to be around for the rest of my life, I was marrying that girl.

"We're gonna get married," I announced, pulling her down into my lap and kissing her cheek so that she giggled.

"That will be a wedding I won't attend," Antonio scoffed. I wasn't to hurt by that. Elly just looked at her mom who smiled widely.

"I've always supported you two, but we can't keep doing this," Savannah said, motioning to Antonio. I looked at him with a smirk, tapping Elly to stand up.

"You know Savannah, he almost took a belt to your daughter. His words were...what again Antonio? Something along the lines of "you're sneaking out, partying, staying out all night, getting drunk, having sex, and I'm done with that behavior." Announced it to the whole neighborhood and then tried to hit her with a belt. But luckily, I was there to protect her, like always," I said looking back at Antonio. I saw the anger fill Savannah's eyes as she looked at Antonio.

"You tried to hit her with a belt? Kids, go to the waiting room." Savannah crossed her arms. I grinned as Elly shook her head at me, but I didn't care.

"Come on, troublemaker," Elly said, pushing me out of the room. I smiled, wrapping my arms around her and kissing the top of her head. Me, Elly, and her siblings walked out. Izzy's phone rang and she quickly walked away from us.

"She has a boyfriend," Elly gossiped and I nodded my head. The second we hit the waiting room. My phone started to ring. I pulled it out to see that Zeke was calling.

"Excuse me, Baby Girl," I said, walking away. I went to a corner of the room and answered the phone.

"What's up?" I asked Zeke.

"Problem with 67th street, meet me at my place."

"On my way now," I told him, hanging up. I walked over to Elly, kissing her lips easily and fast.

"I have to go, Zeke needs me. I love you," I rushed. She pouted her lip but nodded, kissing me again.

"I love you too. Be safe." I nodded and walked out of the hospital and headed straight over to Zeke's place.

Chapter 38

Pressure

ELEANOR

"Elly wake up! We're going to go visit dad," Izzy called as she opened my bedroom door. I sat up and groaned when I saw her already dressed. Her hand was laying on her stomach like she wasn't feeling well.

"You feel ok?" She smiled, nodding, and moved her hand away from her stomach.

"Cramps. Period," she told me. I rolled over and pulled a bottle of Pamperin out of my nightstand drawer and tossing it to her. She caught it and looked at it.

"Thanks, Elles," she said as she walked out of my room. I got up and went to my closet. We were just going to the hospital, so I grabbed my black sweats and a black bralette and headed down to the bathroom. I took a fast shower and then made my way back to my bedroom where I sat down at my desk. I did a "no makeup" look and then pulled my hair into a French braid, leaving strands out to frame my face. Once I approved of my lazy look, I changed into my clothes. I grabbed black socks and my Gucci slides that were a gift from Zeke. Downstairs, I found my family sitting in the living room.

Despite all that happened, my mom and dad are in an argument. She has never believed in hitting her kids. She had made it clear that none of us would ever be hit and now my dad had tried to beat me with his belt. I was 17 years old. I've outgrown spankings. It's inappropriate for my dad to spank me.

467

"Ready kiddos?" Mom asked us smiling as she stood up. We all nodded and followed her out the door. I locked the door, making sure it wasn't going to open, and then skipped down the steps as a long glossy black Hummer limo pulled up. My mom pushed back myself, Izzy, and Mateo back, eyeing the car. The driver got out, walked up to my mom, and looked directly at me.

"Elly, you've been summoned," I felt my heartbeat speeding in my chest. My palms began to sweat as my fingers shook from nerves. Who summoned me? Why was this so sketchy? Was I going to die? Did Zeke find out about Trey'von?

"I'm good," I dismissed him. The window began to closely creep down. My mom pushed further us back, but I caught a glimpse of Big Rico.

"You can't say "no," Elly. You owe me for keeping your secrets," Big Rico called from the window. My mouth went dry at his words as my heart raced. I knew these were not the type of people to owe a debt to. My mind rushed with the possible things they would want me to do. My mind jumped from murdering someone to running drugs. Whatever it is, it isn't good and Trey'von is going to be pissed.

"My daughter isn't going anywhere with you," Mom snapped, making my eyes grow wide. He laughed nodded his head "yes."

"Savannah Lopez, why am I not shocked you are this girl's mother? She's coming or else I'll tell Zeke about her, and Trip and I won't protect him. Then that husband of yours is under Prophet protection right now. After I heard about what was going on I thought I'd help Elly out, seeing she was with my best guy. But maybe they're both replaceable," Big Rico threatened. My eyes grew wide, and I shook my head "no," pushing my mom out of the way. I stumbled into the driver's arms by accident. I pushed him away and stood on my own.

"No, I'll go with you, just leave Trip alone," I begged Big Rico. He smiled, nodding his head as he rolled up his window. I took a breath as I stepped towards the limo when I felt someone grave my arm.

"Elly don't do this," Mom begged me. I had a million questions about how she knew Big Rico and how he knew her maiden name, but they'd all have to wait.

"I'll be fine, Mom. I'll meet you at the hospital," I promised. I was gently pulled over to the limo where the driver opened the door. I slid in to find Carlos and Big Honcho inside as well.

"How do you guys know my mom?" I asked curiously as the door shut.

"That's another secret we're holding onto," Carlos told me. I nodded my head, trying not to think too far into it right now.

"Drink?" Big Honcho asked, offering me a glass of alcohol. I smiled, shaking my head.

"No thank you," I declined. I didn't intend to be with them long enough to drink a whole drink. He nodded, downing the alcohol in one gulp. I looked at the other two and waited for them to say something, anything.

"Where were you guys headed to?" Big Rico asked, scratching his whiskers.

"The hospital, to see my dad." They smirked at each other and then looked back at me. I wished they would just get to the point of why I'm riding around with them.

"You're very protected, huh?" Carlos asked. He'd find out how protected I was if he made a move against me.

"Enough small talk. Why am I with you?" I asked, crossing my arms. They chuckled at me, but I didn't see what was so funny.

"You're much like Zeke I see," Big Honcho commented. I was more like him then they knew and Trey'von was rubbing off on me too.

"You have our two biggest players wrapped around your pinkie. Zeke and Trip," Carlos informed me. So...I was their weak spot. Were they going to take me out to send a message to them? Trey'von drops everything for them, so what could he possibly have done to make them angry?

"We have a certain vision for New York. We need big players there," Big Honcho filled me in. They wanted Trip to go to New York? No way. I would never tell him to leave me.

"Trip would never leave me behind," I told them, shaking my head "no." They all shared a look of amusement as Big Rico took a swig from his drink.

"Exactly, you ensure he stays here. Zeke, on the other hand, is perfect for New York. He leaves, Trip moves up and takes Zeke's spot. You guys can be together because he's a boss and Zeke can't say or do anything without a war." He explained their master plan, but I didn't want Zeke to leave either.

"This has what to do with me? I don't want Zeke to leave either," My voice was filled with attitude. I wouldn't let them push me around.

"Because you can whisper in their ears, and they'll do it. You start to convince Zeke that New York would be a good idea. Then, we'll protect you and Trip. You guys can be together, and Zeke won't be able to do shit about it without enraging us. If you don't do what we ask, we might not protect Trip, which would leave him vulnerable to certain attacks," Big Rico hinted. I bit my lip, trying to keep my breathing even. I didn't want Trey'von hurt, but I didn't want to manipulate the people I care about.

"Do we have a deal Miss. Elly?" Carlos asked as we pulled up in front of the hospital.

"Right now, we have our personal capo's working to protect your dad from rival gang members who just might hear that Trip's girlfriend's dad is here, laid up and vulnerable. If you decline, our protection will go away," Big Honcho threatened. My eyes grew wide as I looked towards the hospital. If I said no, they'd kill my dad and hurt Trip. They weren't leaving me with much of a choice.

"Fine, I'll get in their ears. I'll tell Trip to take Zeke's spot and Zeke to take New York." They smiled, nodding their heads and my door opened. I looked at them, regretting that I'd agreed to their plan.

"Good doing business with you," Big Rico said and I got out. I walked around the limo and into the hospital where I took off down the hall to get to my family.

TREY'VON

I woke up to my phone ringing. I groaned as I rolled over and saw that Elly was calling. I thought she got her phone taken away. I quickly answered it, putting the phone to my ear.

"Baby, are you ok?" I asked, my voice laced with sleep.

"The higher ups paid me a visit. Get to the hospital." Her voice shaking. The hospital? Why was she at the hospital? Did they hurt her?

"Did those assholes hurt you? Baby Girl" I asked as I got up and rushing to my closet. I grabbed a pink t-shirt, black skinny jeans, and new boxers.

"No, they didn't hurt me. They threatened yours and my dad's safety. Just get here and I'll tell you about. I love you." She hung up. I put down the phone and changed quickly. I grabbed my "Trippin" beanie, and a pair of pair of vans. I brushed my teeth, grabbed my keys, and rushed out of the house and into my car. I sped through the long drive to the hospital. I parked next to Momma Sánchez and got out. I rushed into the hospital and up to Antonio's room to find Knives and Ace standing in front of the door.

"What are you guys doing here?" I asked, shaking up with them.

"Big Rico put us here. He didn't want someone to come and finish the job," Knives told me. I scoffed, waving them off.

"My boy did it under my command. Go home. No one is coming for him" I said. They started to open their mouths to reply, but I grabbed Knives and slammed him into the wall.

"I said go home. Your services aren't needed," I growled. I pushed Knives away and they took off down the hall. I went into the room to see everyone sitting there, calmly, except for Elly who was pacing around.

"Baby Girl…" She turned, ran over to me, and hugged me tightly.

"They threatened you," she whispered with a shaky breath. I reached down and picked her up, letting her wrap her legs around my waist. I went over to a chair and sat down so that she straddled me. I knew the moment they found out about her, they'd use Elly to force my hand.

"What did they say?" I asked, pushing back a loose strand of hair. She looked at me and swallowed hard.

"They told me if I didn't get in your ear and Zeke's about a power move, then they'd stop protecting you and tell Zeke about us." I fought my temper, trying to not let it get the best of me. This wasn't her fault, and I didn't want her thinking I thought it was.

"What power move?" I had an idea, but I wasn't sure what they told her.

"Zeke takes New York and you take our streets. They know I'm a weakness for both of you. As they put it, I have you wrapped around my pinkie. I'm supposed to get into your ear and tell you take leadership here and then tell Zeke to go to New York. I'd love for you to become a boss, but I don't want Zeke to leave. If I don't do this, they'll hurt you, my dad, Zeke---." Her breathing began to pick up, which told me she was about to hyperventilate, so I cut her off. This wasn't a big deal. I could work around this without the higher ups even knowing she told me.

"Bebe, look at me" I said, grabbing her face. I had a plan, one that I knew would work.

"I'll pretend you're telling me to take over. They won't know you even told me. As for Zeke, you mention it. Let him flip out and tell the higher ups you are too scared to mention it again, but you'll keep working on me. That will buy us some time." I knew we'd be playing a dangerous game, but it's the only game I knew to play right now. I had to keep her safe. Clearly, she's going to do whatever she has to do to keep me safe too.

ELEANOR

He wanted us to play the higher ups, it was dangerous. Too dangerous, and I couldn't do that. They'd kill him. I shook my head in fear, he closed his eyes as he exhaled.

"Baby Girl, how else are we going to do this?" he asked. I bit my lip, not sure of what to do.

"We have to tell Zeke. He'll know," I told him, touching his perfect jawline. He looked at me with wide eyes, and shook his head "no."

"He'll kill me Baby Girl," reminding me of what would surely be his doom if this plan fell through. Then I remembered something. My mom knew Big Rico, but how? I turned to her as I got off Trey'von's lap.

"You know Big Rico," I stated. She nodded her head, biting her lip and glancing at my dad.

"Why didn't you tell me you knew someone so high up in Los Prophets?" I asked. Trey'von looked between us in pure shock.

"You know Big Rico? Damn, Momma Sánchez," Trey'von mused. I grinned at how cute he was but pushed away that thought off for the time being.

"I never bragged. He had a thing for me some years ago when I with the wrong set of people," Mom filled us in as she looked down. I looked over at Trey'von who smirked at me. I saw an idea swirling in his eyes.

"I got it," he told me with a smile. He stood up, kissing my lips, and happily clapping down on my dad's leg.

"You aren't gonna like this Antonio, which makes it a little more fun for me," Trey'von commented. I was not surprised he'd find a way to get under my dad's skin.

"Momma Sánchez, you're going undercover. Big Rico is the leader. I need to know why they want me to take over so badly. I hope you have nice lingerie. If not, you can borrow some of Baby Girl's." My cheeks ignited in fire. I had one set which I haven't worn. Maybe I should wear it for him though, that could be one hell of a night.

"No, I am not, he might not even like me like that anymore," Mom refused.

"Trip, I don't think that's a good idea either. I don't want my family involved." He turned to look at me and rolled his eyes.

"Then how the fuck am I supposed to take care of this?" He spat at me. I'm not real sure what to do either. They never told me not to tell Trip that they had picked me up. Maybe it was part of their plan for me to tell him.

"They never told me not to tell you. Maybe you should mention it to them like you would anything else," I suggested. He looked at me with squinted eyes, then nodded his head. He looked over at Izzy and Mateo and then back to me.

"Fine, I'll deal with it like I would anything else." He started to walk out of the room, but I grabbed his arm, stopping him.

"Wait, don't just rush out of here like you're invincible, let's talk about this" I said, panicked. I didn't see a way out of this. I needed Trey'von to talk to me and tell me what his plan was so I could see the light at the end of the tunnel.

"Why do we care about this? Why shouldn't I have the hospital throw you out now?" My dad snapped at Trey'von. He turned with a hard glare and began to storm towards my dad, but I put my hand on his chest to stop him from leaving my side.

"They threatened you too, dumb ass. I don't do what they want they'll kill all of you. FUCK!" Trey'von yelled as he paced around the room, his anger growing worse by the second. I stayed quiet, not wanting to catch the blunt end of his wrath.

"This is exactly why I didn't want them knowing about you, Baby Girl. Now everyone is in danger, and I don't know how to fucking fix it," He snapped as he paced, and then stormed over to my dad wagging his finger in the air.

"THIS IS ALL YOUR FAULT. IF YOU JUST WASN'T A FUCK UP FOR ONCE IN YOUR LIFE THEY WOULDN'T EVEN KNOW ABOUT ELLY AND ME!" Trey'von yelled as I grabbed his shirt and tried to pull him back, but he was stuck in place and refused to move.

"NO, IT'S YOUR FAULT LIKE ALWAYS. I WAS BEING A FATHER AND YOU CAME STORMING OVER GETTING INVOLVED---." Trey'von cut my dad off just as nurses came running in to see what the screaming was about.

"YOU AREN'T EVEN HER REAL FUCKING DAD. MOMMA SÁNCHEZ ALREADY FUCKING TOLD ME THE FUCKING TRUTH!" Trey'von screamed, reaching for his gun but I laced together our fingers.

"TRIP!" my mom and I yelled at him. Finally, I was able to push him back. He stumbled a couple steps and then turned his attention to me.

"I ALREADY TOLD YOU TO DROP THAT, IT'S NOT TRUE," I yelled, but he shook his head "no." His mouth opened, but he was cut off by the nurses.

"Sir, we need you to leave please," a nurse told him. Trey'von shook his head and started to walk out of the room, but I grabbed his shirt, stopping him.

"You need to leave or else we're calling security," the other nurse snapped at Trey'von, as he turned to look at me.

"Whatever you're going to do, be safe. Please?" I begged. He leaned down kissing my lips and then walked out of the room to do God only knows what.

TREY'VON

I pulled up in front of the mansion I knew Big Rico, Carlos, and Big Honcho would be at. I was pissed for so many reasons and I was ready for a fight. I got out of the car, slammed the door, and walked towards the house. I banged my fist so hard on the front door it's a wonder my scarred knuckles didn't break open. The door slung open to show Stab Happy. I pushed right passed him

"Yo, Trip you can't---." I pulled out my gun, glaring at him. I wasn't in the mood to "wait my turn," not when they're threatening the love of my life.

"Finish that sentence and I'll put a bullet in your skull. I'll do whatever the fuck I want," I snapped. He nodded quickly and I stormed down the hall as I put away my gun. Once I got to the huge table room, I kicked open the door with a force that got the three men's attention.

"I see Elly called you," Big Rico said. I stormed over, pulled my knife and slammed it into their table as I looked between the three men.

"You guys might practically own me but you're going to leave Elly out of this," I growled. Big Rico smirked, leaning back, and looking at me. The look on his face pissed me off even more.

"So, I see she talked to you about taking over?" he asked. I exhaled glaring at him.

"I already told you, I'm not taking over until Zeke steps down on his own or moves by his own will. Elly doesn't have anything to do with us," I snapped. I was not backing down until they left Elly alone.

"Actually, she owes us. We didn't tell Zeke and that comes with a price" Carlos snickered at me which only pushed my anger.

"Then you come to me. I don't appreciate you threatening her family either." They weren't going to back down with this idea, not until Zeke went or one of us ended up dead.

"It's just business, Trip. I hope we have your attention now. We want you to take over our biggest money-making block in California. You should be proud of how fast you've been moving up," Big Honcho congratulated me. I had moved through the gang fast. I'm only 19 and able to take over if I wanted. It was a big deal.

"I'm not stepping on Zeke to get there. He might be a dick, but he's my friend and I'm loyal to those who are loyal to me," They rolled their eyes at me, but I was loyal and I always would be. Being loyal to the right people was how I moved up so fast.

"How loyal would he be if he knew you were fucking his *blood* daughter?" Big Rico asked. My eyes grew wide. I couldn't help but wonder how they knew the truth. They looked at me, laughing, and Big Rico shook his head.

"The moment I saw Savannah was her mother, I knew she was actually Zeke's. Everyone remembers how hooked Zeke was on Savannah and still is," Big Rico told me. So, Savannah and Zeke did get together. I didn't know she was the reason Zeke didn't date. I knew there was one girl he never got over, but Momma Sánchez?

"Trip, everyone looks to you as the leader already. We watched the way they look at you right after Zeke gives an order. You're leading them without even trying and New York needs someone like Zeke. It's a win for both of you," Big Honcho said. I bit my lip thinking about his words. I knew the guys looked at me as their leader. Hell, Lil Ugly told me that when we were at Elly's game. Still, Zeke was our leader.

"I can't double cross Zeke, even if I wanted too. Like you said, that's Elly's dad, even if she doesn't believe it. She'd be heartbroken over him leaving. I've hurt her enough. I'm stuck between my girlfriend and a hard place here, guys" I groaned while squeezing the bridge of my nose. I knew they didn't give a fuck what happened to Elly and I as long as they got their way.

"Then get Zeke to decide for himself. Tell Elly her debt is paid to us, but yours is not," Big Rico told me. I looked at them, confused.

"I thought she was supposed to get into my head?" I asked, confused. They chuckled, looking around and then back at me like I should know what they were thinking.

"She did. You're here actually discussing this offer with us. Get Zeke to go to New York and you're clear. See your way out," Big Rico directed. I shook my head and turned to leave without pushing them any farther than I already had. I walked past Stab Happy out to my car and called Zeke.

Ring

Ring

Ring

"Yo, Trip," Zeke answered fairly quickly.

"I need you to meet me at my place now." I had to talk to him about the higher ups. He needed to know they had pulled up on Elly and weren't letting this New York thing go.

"Everything ok?" he asked as I pulled out of the driveway.

"Not even close, I'll see you at my place," I said hanging up, then dialed Elly next to deliver the message for the higher ups.

ZEKE

I looked at Trip as he paced back and forth behind his desk. He grabbed his long curls which in my opinion, needed a trim. He looked at me, shaking his head.

"The higher ups picked up Elly today," he informed me. My jaw tightened at his words, they picked her up? I didn't want her anywhere near them and she was in a car with them.

"Why? What could they want?" I asked, suspiciously. He looked over at me as he sat in his chair.

"They know she's a weak spot for both of us. They're trying to force my hand to take your spot," he explained. I wasn't shocked by the news. They wanted me to take New York. They needed more structure there. They thought I could bring that, but I couldn't leave Elly or Savannah behind because they needed me. Savannah and I still co-parented, differently than most people of course, and I wouldn't leave either of them behind.

"That doesn't surprise me. What are we going to do to get Elly away from them?" I asked. I didn't understand Trip and Elly's friendship. I knew Trip would do anything for her. I've seen him do things he never would have done before simply because she smiled at him. I worried there was more between them than friendship, but I knew Trip would never betray my trust like that.

"They're done with her. Her job was to get into my head and get me to think about taking your spot. When I confronted the higher ups, they said the thought was in my head. What are we going to do? I'm not taking shit from you. You have to step down or willingly move before I take anything from you," he said forcefully. As his phone started to ring, he looked down and rolled his eyes.

"Excuse me," he said as he got up and walked out of the office to answer his phone. Trip was loyal. He'd never take my spot without my blessing. I knew he'd watch after Elly and Savannah for me, but I couldn't bring myself to leave them. Not while Elly was acting like a wild child, which I still needed to talk to Savannah about. Moments later, Trip came back in smiling at his phone and shaking his head. He tossed his phone down. The smile never leaving his lips.

"What's got you so happy?" He just shrugged.

"I got a bad bitch pulling up on me later, so we got to wrap this up. What are we going to do?" But I had no idea what we were going to do. I bit my lip thinking about it.

"Pretend we're considering it. It will buy us some time to figure it out from there," I told him. He nodded his head.

"That's what I was thinking, too. Buy some time and figure it out from there," he agreed. I stood up and shook up with him. I wanted to take Elly out to lunch and talk to her about the higher ups to make sure she ok.

"I'm gonna go get Elly for a little bit and just check up on her. Have a good night," I said heading towards the doors of the office.

"Yeah, you too. Hopefully they buy it," he sighed. Hopefully they didn't figure out we were playing them. We said our goodbyes and I walked out to call Elly and tell her to be ready because I was coming to get her.

Chapter 39

My Brother's Keeper

ELEANOR

A WEEK LATER

I stood in the school bathroom looking at myself in the mirror. I had my usual makeup done, my curls perfect and I wore a simple grey Calvin Klein sports bra, a pair of baggy black sweats with pink and purple butterflies on them and the top said 'Baby Girl" across the front. When I woke up this morning, I had a killer headache and just wasn't feeling it. As the day went on, I began to feel better, but I still don't feel 100% the best. All day my stomach has felt wheezy, like I was going to puke, and certain smells have been making it worse. Finally, the last bell rang dismissing everyone else from class. I grabbed my laptop and books and walked out of the bathroom. I went to my locker and opened it.

"You feeling better?" I heard Nicole. I touched my stomach, shrugging.

"My headache is gone but my stomach still feels funny." I pulled out my backpack and put my laptop and books into it. I grabbed my binder filled with homework and put inside my bag as well.

"You're probably pregnant," Nicole hummed, wiggling her eyebrows at me. I burst into laughter, shaking my head "no."

"Nicole, me and Trip use protection and I'm on birth control. There is no way I'm pregnant." We always use condoms. Lately, he hasn't wanted to but I won't let us have sex without one. Even though I'm on birth control, the idea of having a baby right now still freaks me out.

"I call dibs on being it's godmother," she teased, touching my stomach. I laughed, slapping her hand away and shutting my locker.

"Girl, I'm not pregnant. I'll text you later though," I said, and she nodded. We said our goodbyes and I headed out to the bus. Trip has been busy with Zeke, and I was skipping practice today. I felt like shit. It felt like forever before the bus was full and started on the way home. I joked around with the people that sat around me but mainly just looked out of the window. After what felt like forever, we made it to my neighborhood, I seen Trip standing outside the bar with Smiley smoking a blunt. I got up with my backpack, filed off the bus, and walked over to my man. He saw me, and gave me a confused smile, opening his arms for me.

"I thought you had practice. You're wearing the sweats I bought you," he commented as I went into his arms. I hugged him, resting my head against his chest, and closing my eyes.

"I skipped. I don't feel good" He brought the blunt to my lips which made me giggle. I smiled and took a hit. I inhaled the odd tasting smoke and blew it out.

"What's wrong with you?" he asked curiously, his hand tangling into my curls in the most loving way.

"I woke up with a headache, but it's gone now. My belly feels funny. I feel like I could throw up and certain smells are bothering me today," I complained as he kissed my forehead.

"Aw Baby, I'm sorry. You must be getting that bug that's going around. You want to come over and I'll take care of you?" He asked. That sounded so good. Just to be babied.

"Yes, can I just stay the night with you?" I asked and he hummed hugging me tighter. I heard the roar of a loud motor and I looked over to see a motorcycle fly past the bar and stop in front of my house. On the back of it was Izzy and in the front was her boyfriend...what was his name again? I stayed snuggled into Trey'von and watched them get off the bike. The guy looked back at Izzy, smiling, but then he did a double take when his eyes landed on Trey'von. I watched his dark brown nearly black eyes grow wide. His white smile spread across his face in the goofiest way. He side-stepped Izzy, keeping his eyes locked on my Bebe.

"TREY'VON" He yelled, which only confused me more. How did he know Trey'von's real name? Why was he using it so freely? I pulled away from Trey'von as he looked at the guy who was jogging over to us.

"You have to be fucking kidding me," Trey'von groaned rolling his eyes just as the guy stopped near us. He smiled, holding out his hand to shake up with Trey'von. I could see how annoyed he was, but he still shook up with the guy. How did Trey'von know my sister's boyfriend?

"Anthony," Trey'von said, eyeing him. I couldn't help but notice the matching curls, bronze skin, cheekbones, and nose structure. Trey'von's lips were plumper and more eye catching, but Anthony's weren't too far off either.

"Bro, it's been years. I miss you. How have you been? Still running with Los Prophets, I see," he said motioning to Trey'von tattoo. Izzy walked over and was just as confused as me. Trey'von nodded, sucking on his teeth.

"Yeah, they've been a real family to me. How is our whore ass mother doing? Found dead in a ditch yet?" Trey'von asked. My eyes grew wide, along with Izzy's, as I looked up to the look alike. He was Trey'von's brother? Well, that explained the looks. I knew they weren't close because of the past. Anthony rolled his eyes at his brother, waving him off.

"Mom is doing good. She went to rehab. I bet she'd like to see you," Anthony said. Trey'von sent him a glare, his mouth opening to spit out the most viscous words, I'm sure.

"Trip, are you going to introduce me?" I asked, interrupting whatever mean thing Trey'von was about to say.

"Of course. Baby Girl, this is my older brother, Anthony. Anthony this is my girl, Elly." I smiled, extending my hand happily to the man in front of me.

"It's nice to meet Trip's family, finally," I said excitedly. He looked at me surprised, and then at Trey'von.

"It's nice to see Trey'von has someone to tame him," Anthony smiled. Trey'von grabbed me, pulling me away from his older brother.

"Ok, now you can disappear like you did when I was 12," Trey'von spat harshly at him. I took a step back next to Trey'von and looked down.

TREY'VON

I didn't want to be around any of those people. Not my brother, my sister, and especially not my crackhead-ass mom. I was still mad at how my brother and sister just ditched me the moment they had a chance. I supported them from 6 years old until they left me behind. Even when our bitch-ass mom threw me on the streets at 12, they didn't help. I've always had to fight, and I didn't need them now. The only person I've ever needed was Elly.

"I was a minor Trey, come on. There was nothing I could do, and we were scared of you. You murdered Paul and then had all these sketchy guys around----." I cut him off, taking a step closer. His eyes grew wide, but I watched as a serious look took over his face and he actually stepped up to me.

"I killed Paul to protect you, mom, Yasmine, and most importantly myself," I snapped at him. Instead of holding that against me, I should get a fucking thank you. But they didn't see it that way. Maybe if I had let Paul beat their asses a couple times then they would understand. I'd see him going for one of them and I'd push every button until he beat me instead.

"Anyways, you should know. You're about to be an uncle and I wouldn't mind you being around," Anthony announced. My jaw fell open as I looked over at Izzy. Her hands went protectively to her stomach.

"YOU'RE PREGNANT?" Elly and I asked at the same time. She nodded her head, biting her lip nervously and eyed me and Anthony. Elly burst into laughter. I looked over at her with an eyebrow raised.

"My dad is going to kill you both. Oh my god, Bebe my dad hates you and now my sister is knocked up by your big brother. I can't breathe." Elly was doubled over laughing at the irony of the situation. I mean it was kinda funny just because Antonio was about to eat shit. Then it hit me, the news. Anthony was having a baby. He was bringing a life into this world, and he didn't know how to be a dad. Hell, none of us knew how to be a parent. He'd be a fuck up like Paul.

"What do you know about being a dad?" I asked, crossing my arms with a smirk. He looked shocked by my words. I leaned back into the bar looking my older brother up and down.

"Exactly, you don't know shit about being a dad. Hell, I don't either that's why I'm not stupid enough to bring a life into this world. Izzy get the fuck out before he has you out here on the streets like a whore and that baby locked in a closet." Just as I finished the jab at my brother, he pushed me back with a glare.

"Say that shit again and see what happens," Anthony growled. I grabbed him, slamming him into the brick wall, hard. I saw the pain cross his face.

"WE AINT KIDS ANYMORE ANTHONY. YOU COULDN'T BEAT MY ASS THEN AND I KNOW YOU SURE CAN'T NOW. WHAT? YOU DON'T LIKE THAT TRUTH? TELL ME WHAT THE FUCK DO YOU KNOW ABOUT BEING A PARENT? YOU SHOULDN'T HAVE BEEN STUPID----." He tried to throw me off, but I refused to move.

"SHUT THE FUCK UP TREY'VON! I'M NOT PAUL, YOU'RE NOT PAUL, YASMINE ISN'T MOM. YOU CAN'T BE SCARED OF THAT MAN FOR THE REST OF YOUR LIFE!" Without a second thought, my fist connected to my brother's jaw.

"TRIP!" the girls yelled as Anthony stumbled back, holding his bleeding nose.

"SCARED OF HIM? IF ANYTHING, PAUL SHOULD BE FEARING ME FROM THE GRAVE. I WAS NEVER SCARED OF THAT MUHFUCKER!" I yelled as Izzy moved to his side, looking at his nose.

"Seriously though, all you know about being a dad is to lock them in a closet the moment they misbehave. They're gonna need more then bread shoved through a crack," I spat as Elly grabbed my arm, pulling me back.

"Trip, calm down," Elly said, moving in front of me in an effort to keep me away from Anthony.

"What is he talking about Ant? Why didn't you tell me Trip was your younger brother? What else aren't you telling me?" Izzy asked him. It's nice to know I was hidden, even now, with my family. After everything I'd done for them fuckers and they're still ashamed of me. But now they can't lock me away and pretend I'm not there.

"You know, forget it. FORGET I EVEN CAME OVER HERE TO TALK TO YOU. I THOUGHT AFTER ALL THESE YEARS MAYBE WE COULD BROTHERS AGAIN!" I forced back a laugh at the idea of us being "brothers again."

"Yeah, sounds like. You're hiding me from your girlfriend. I told Elly about you and Yasmine. Not names but she knew you guys existed," I snapped, but he waved me off as he looked at Izzy.

"Come on, let's go so I can meet yo pops." Anthony waved for Izzy to follow him.

"Wait, I want to be there when you tell him. Shit I need popcorn," Elly said. I chuckled, pulling her into me and smiling. She smiled up at me, kissing my cheek.

"You're going with them?" I asked. I didn't want her to leave my side. I needed her right now. I wanted to rave and rant about my brother just randomly showing up.

"My dad can't stand you, Trip, and now your brother has my sister pregnant. He's going to lose his shit. I need to be there to make sure he gets out in one piece, and I want to see Izzy get in trouble," she smiled up at me excitedly. My little troublemaker. I chuckled, shaking my head at her. Anthony and Izzy walked towards the house leaving me and Elly alone.

"Who cares what happens to him. He's never cared about me," I told her with a shrug. She squinted her eyes at me shaking her head.

"You don't mean that. You know he's walking into a death match. I'm gonna go. After I make sure your brother survives this meeting and see Izzy get in trouble, I'll be back," she promised as she pulled away. I felt my temper spike even higher at the idea she rather be with Anthony right now then me. That she thought Anthony needed *my* girlfriend more than I do right now.

"Fine, go. But don't come back here. I don't want to see you if go," I seethed. She looked at me surprised and then shook her head.

"You don't mean that. I'm disappointed in you. You know my dad is about to rip him to pieces in there and you never let someone you love go through that. You might have not seen him in years and there might be bad blood, but I know deep down you still love him. When you come to your senses, the front door will be open." With that, Elly turned and jogged down the street.

"FUCK!" I yelled, punching the brick wall that busted open my knuckles while the blood dripped down my wrist.

ELEANOR

I walked into the living room as Izzy held a rag to Anthony's nose. My dad stood in front of them with his arms crossed as my mom sat next to Anthony with a worried look. Mateo came out of the kitchen with a baggie of ice.

"I'm guessing this has Trip's name written all over it," Dad commented. I sent him a glare as I sat in the chair looking at the couple. Soon enough the bleeding stopped.

"I'm fine guys, thank you," Anthony said, pushing them away. He stood up smiling at my dad and extended his hand.

"It's nice to finally meet you, Mr. Sánchez. I've wanted to meet you for a while now. Along with you, Mrs. Sánchez. You're as beautiful as your daughter." I couldn't help but envy the way he introduced himself so politely to my parents. My boyfriend storms in with a gun and threatens everyone. They were brothers but they acted so differently, Anthony was open to the idea of a family while Trey'von refused to have one. Even with me, the love of his life, he still didn't want it.

"Daddy, this is my boyfriend, Anthony Walker. Ant, this is my dad, Antonio," Izzy introduced. My dad eyed, him nodding his head. I watched him roll his eyes.

"Great, another boyfriend. Hopefully this one is better than someone's" Dad said glancing over at me.

"My boyfriend just has a rough outer edge," I said defiantly. Dad and Mateo hummed as they all took their seats.

"How did you guys meet? If you say a bar, I might stab my own self," Dad said. I laughed, shaking my head along with Mateo and mom.

"School, Daddy. Not all of us are wild children," Izzy commented smugly, but I didn't care.

"School? What are you going to school to be?" Mom asked, curiously. I saw that Dad was happy that Anthony was in school. Part of me wanted to knock down his acceptance and tell him about Trey'von, but I decided to wait until my jealousy peaked.

"Literature. I want to be a high school English teacher," he told my dad, who seemed very impressed. Yay! That Walker brother really likes kids, and I got the one who hates them.

"Teaching. I'm so glad to hear that. How many years do you have left?" Dad asked with satisfaction in his voice.

"I do my student teaching next year and then I graduate," Anthony explained proudly, that was something to be really proud about. I didn't know him and I was proud that he found something he loved.

"Daddy we actually have----." Izzy's words were cut off by the door slamming shut. We all turned to see a pissed off Trey'von storming into the living room. My dad looked at Trey'von with a harsh glare and stood up.

"You are not welcome here and Elly isn't supposed to be around you," Dad bit out at Trip. I looked up at Trip, ready to grab him if need be.

"Shut the fuck up, Antonio. I'm not in the fucking mood. I'm only here to make sure you don't step out of your place with my big brother," Trey'von growled. Everyone except for me and Izzy looked surprised as our eyes darted between the two Walker siblings.

"I thought I was just a fuck up to you?" Anthony asked with an attitude. Trey'von sighed as he looked over at his brother.

"Anthony, you might be living your life differently than me, but you are my brother and I love you. I've always protected you and Yasmine. That isn't going to change now. This muhfucka forgets his place sometimes," Trey'von said. I couldn't stop the smile as I squealed, jumping up to kiss him.

"I knew you'd do the right thing," I told him happily. He smiled at me, sat down in a chair, and pulled me down onto his lap, kissing my cheek. I smiled, running my hands up his tattooed arms.

"Brothers? You can't be serious Izzy? This isn't happening. Sorry young man, but I have enough issues and you are not causing anymore. Get out of my house," Dad spoke sternly. He looked at my dad stunned as Trey'von squeezed me tighter.

TREY'VON

I glared at Antonio from where I sat. He wasn't going to talk to my brother like that. Just as I opened my mouth to say something, Izzy spoke up.

"They're nothing alike, Daddy," Izzy pushed the topic.

"My brother might make a lot of mistakes like joining a gang, dropping out of school, and being a dick. But he has a good heart, and that shows because he is here. I've turned my back on him once and I won't do it again. But I'm not going anywhere until you hear me out, sir," Anthony said. I snickered at him calling Antonio "sir."

"Square," I teased my brother who just sent me a glare, making me laugh.

"Izzy, you see how this has been working out," Antonio said, motioning to me and Elly. I shrugged, leaning back. It's been working out great for me and Elly.

"Daddy, I'm pregnant," Izzy said. Elly looked back at me with wide eyes, but I focused on Antonio. His look mirrored Elly's wide eyes and parted lips except with bewilderment instead of amusement. He looked at Anthony and then back at Izzy. I tapped Elly's thigh and she got up to sit on the arm of the chair as I leaned forward, watching Antonio.

"By him?" Antonio asked, pointing towards Anthony.

"Yes, we're starting a family. We've applied for a house and are waiting hear back. Anthony got a job and is letting me focus on school. Dad, Anthony is not Trip---." I cut Izzy off. She wasn't going to explain this for me and Anthony.

"She's right, he's not me. I protected him from becoming me. You don't know me how you think you do Antonio," I told him. I knew the judgement he passed on me, but he wouldn't to my brother.

"You do seem more put together than Trip. One chance," Antonio said sternly. What was he going to do? He couldn't even get rid of me.

"Thank you, sir. I'm going to be the best dad. I didn't have a positive father figure but I'm going to figure it out. Hopefully with my brother there helping me?" Anthony asked, looking at me but I just scoffed.

"Nah, just because I got your back doesn't mean I'm about to hang around you," I said, seriously. I haven't needed them in years, and I'm not about to need them now.

"How's Yasmine?" I asked him curiously.

"She's great. She's got three kids. The dad is a piece of shit. In and out of their lives, but she's a nurse now." I knew Yasmine would be a nurse or something like that. She was always playing doctor on us. Now, the kids was another thing I didn't understand. She didn't know how to be a mom either. Ours was a prostitute crack whore that would have sex with her clients in front of me.

"Y'all having these kids and don't know how to be anything but abusive." I shook my head at them, standing up. Antonio was acting right, so I didn't need to be here.

"Actually, Yasmine doesn't even spank her kids, she's a good mother. You know, Mom's clean and off the streets," He explained. I made a face, looking away from him to my baby girl with a smile.

"Go get your things Baby Girl, I've had enough of this family reunion," I told Elly. She nodded her head and stood up to hug me. I smiled, wrapping my arms around her tightly.

"Can I stay over at Trip's house today?" Elly asked her mom. Momma Sánchez nodded her head. Elly kissed my cheek, walked out of the room leaving me with everyone.

"Where you staying at now?" Anthony asked me curiously.

"Beverly Hills. I own a house over there," I told him, sitting down. He looked at me impressed, nodding.

"How you go from our two-bedroom house to Beverly Hills?" he asked just trying to keep conversation going, which was going to drive me insane.

"Los Prophets, I moved up fast. I'm almost running it," I explained as a knock came from the door. Momma Sánchez walked out of the room to answer it.

"They pay that much?" I sent him a look, warning him to stop asking questions.

"I catch you even thinking about joining, I'll beat your ass myself. This isn't a life for you and now you got a baby to worry about. My life expectancy is 25, if that," I shot at him, glancing away to make sure Elly couldn't hear the statistic.

"I wouldn't, that's your life. Trey'von, I'm sorry about how we just left you. We were scared and---." Suddenly a voice came from behind me.

"Trip, Zeke wants to see you at the bar," I heard Smiley. I turned to see him lighting a blunt. I got up, nodding my head and shaking up with my brother.

"It was nice seeing you, bro. Tell Elly to wait here for me." I nodded at older brother. He returned the nod and I walked out with Smiley, hoping to never see Anthony again.

ELEANOR

I pulled up to Trey'von's house and parked in front of the garage. I smiled as I looked over at him. I earned a high five from him because he let me drive all the way home.

"You killed that Baby Girl," he encouraged. We got out of the car and Trey'von grabbed my bag. We walked inside the house and straight upstairs to the bedroom. I laid on the bed while while Trip put my bag in the closet. I wanted to talk to him about how he was feeling after seeing his brother. Soon enough, he walked into the bedroom, pulled off his shirt and exposed those attractive lean tattooed muscles.

"Bebe, you are so sexy" I complimented him. He smiled, getting in bed, and kissing me. He grabbed my thighs and forced me to lay back. I giggled which made him smile.

"You are the sexy one. How are you feeling? Any better?" he asked, pushing his fingers through my curls. His dark brown nearly black eyes gazed into mine. The tingly goosebumps ran over my skin and made me shiver. I didn't feel much better. My stomach felt worse if anything.

"No, my stomach feels even more gross," I complained. He pouted his plump pink lip at me.

"Maybe you need food. Let me go cook you something," he said as he started to get up. I grabbed his arm, rolling over onto my side and pulled him back down. I traced the thorny dead rose bush that started at his waist band and curled up to his collar bone. This tattoo always caught my attention. I always wondered why he chose a dead ugly bush instead of a beautiful live one?

"How are you feeling after seeing your brother?" I asked, worried. He sighed, looking down to my legs and then back up to my eyes.

"I don't know. Confused. He wants to be around me but yet he ditched me when I was 12 and actually needed him and Yasmine." I lacing together our fingers, kissing his busted open knuckles that would surely scar.

"You never told me the full story" I whispered, not wanting to push him. I knew Trey'von's past was ify for him. He didn't like revisiting it. But I'm sure he was revisiting it now even without me pushing him.

"When I was 12 my sister, Yasmine, turned 18. She took Anthony and moved out but left me with my crackhead-ass mom. Once Yasmine and Anthony were gone, my mom threw me on the streets with a trash bag full of my stuff. She told me she wouldn't have the person who murdered the love of her life living with her anymore. I went to them and asked for help, but Yasmine told me she wouldn't have a murderer living with her, either, and I was left homeless." I felt my blood boil at the idea. He killed his abuser. Trey'von was in the right in every single way possible. Paul locked him in closets, withheld food from him, and beat him. He took the beating for his siblings, and they still had the nerve to turn him away and leave him behind?

"But he abused you, why would your mother choose him over you?" I asked. He shook head and then shrugged his shoulders.

"Not everyone has a mom like yours. Honestly, I think Anthony's going to be a piss poor dad. Hell, I'm sure my sister is a horrible mother too." It bothered me he thought that. I knew Trey'von would make a great dad. He's learned what not to do on a level other people don't.

"You really think that?" My tone slipped indicating how hurt I was. He nodded his head, looking down to my stomach. I watched him shake his head and look up at the ceiling.

"Well, I think you'd make a wonderful dad. Years from now, of course, after I have a law degree and you take Los Prophets. Imagine a little us running around." I tried to convince him it was a good idea. He looked over at me and kissed my lips.

"Baby, you'd make a wonderful mother, but I'm not having kids. I don't even want to take the chance of turning into Paul. Let's talk about this another time. You just rest while I make you something to eat," he whispered. He kissed the top of my head and got up. I sighed, not done with the conversation. But I didn't want to fight with him after everything that he'd been through today.

"Ok. Wake me up when it's ready." He nodded, walking out of the bedroom. I moved under the covers. I laid there imagining a life where Trey'von was willing to have kids. One day I wanted to me a mom. Not anytime soon, but one day. A mini me and him would be the cutest thing ever. Soon enough a dream plagued sleep took over.

Chapter 40

The Black Widow

ELEANOR

I added my last layer of lipstick as Trey'von got out of the shower, I looked at him through the mirror in awe. The water droplets dripping down his tattooed body made it glisten in the light and sent the dirtiest thoughts through my head. I couldn't help but let my eyes wonder down to his long friend. I bit my lip checking him out. I heard him chuckle as the towel went around his waist, blocking my view.

"Like what you see Baby Girl?" he asked, his voice husky and seductive. I fought to keep my eyes open and to stay standing on my wobbly knees.

"I always do," I whispered. He smiled as he came behind me and kissed my cheek.

"We're going on a date tonight, like a real one," he told me. I looked up at him impressed, grabbing my setting spray. I sprayed it on my face, opening my eyes as he made a face waving away the spray.

"We are? What are we doing Bebe?" I asked excitedly. He grabbed the setting spray from my hands and tossed it on the counter, shaking his head and making me giggle.

"We're going out for a steak dinner at a nice restaurant here in Beverly Hills and then I have a surprise for you." I looked at him interested. I hummed as I picked up my clothes. I dropped my towel and slipped on my thong and bra.

"What's the surprise?" I asked curiously. I looked up to see his eyes roaming my body. I smirked as he licked his lips.

"Don't worry about it, just know we gonna have a nice-ass date and I'm getting head at the end." I burst into laughter as he chuckled at me. I grabbed my black tight fitting crop top, and my dark short high-waist shorts and put them on.

"Yeah, what makes you so confident about that?" I asked him with a raised eyebrow as he grabbed my curl crème along with his blow drier.

"Because I'm about to be so romantic that it's all you're gonna want to do," he bragged.

"Whatever finish getting ready," I laughed at him. I walked to the bedroom and slipped on my black vans. I sat back on the bed looking at my phone and scrolled through Instagram as I waited for Trey'von.

"Baby Girl, I almost forgot that your birthday is two months away. We're about to get so lit for your 18th," Trey'von said coming out of the closet as he looked at his phone. He looked amazing in his simple outfit consisting of a dark grey Gucci t-shirt, faded skinny jeans, and a pair of the newest Jordan's. He, of course, wore his usual silver rings on almost every finger, his thick diamond gold chain, and diamond studs in his ears. The tattooed sleeves were on full display, which was very much to my liking. I brought up my Snapchat, recording him.

"Damn baby, you look so sexy" I said. He saw me recording him. He smiled, shaking his head and looked back down at his phone.

"Let me have that---." Trey'von stopped the dirty words from flowing from my lips.

"AYE, STOP THAT!" he yelled, grabbing my phone and making me laugh. I stopped recording as he snatched the phone from my hands. He smiled, leaned down and connected our lips in a passionate kiss.

"I love you," he whispered. I blushed, taking my phone back and looking up at him.

"I love you Bebe," I told him with a smile. I looked down at my phone, captioning the video "My Bebe is soooo fine" and posted it to my story.

" I'm serious, your birthday. Let's take trip. A baecation," he said plopping down on the bed next to me. I smiled, straddling him, and running my fingers over his tattooed arms. I couldn't help but giggle hearing him say "baecation."

"Where would we even go? Zeke would kill you before we got on the plane," I reminded him. He groaned, covering his eyes with his arms.

"I'm so tired of hiding. I'm about to just take up the higher ups on their offer so he can't tell us we can't be together," Trey'von complained. I leaned down, kissing his neck, and moving his arms away from his beautiful face.

"The law still applies. No messing with the boss's daughter or sorta daughter," I reminded him. He ran his hands up my thighs, shaking his head no.

"Nope, I'd be a boss then. He can't tell me shit or make a move without sparking a war and for you Baby Girl..." he flipped us so that I was laying on the bed. He hovered between my legs, his nearly black eyes staring down looking at me so lovingly. I watched as his hands traced my curves, every part of me screaming for him.

"I'd go to war any day," he whispered kissing my lips. I smiled, wrapping my arms around his neck. He pulled away, standing up to fix his pants. I groaned, sitting up with a questioning look.

"I need to meet with Lil Loco for a run," he told me. I groaned, getting up to grab my phone. I decided to just leave my clothes here.

"Can I leave my stuff here?" I asked Trey'von. He nodded his head waving me to follow him. I followed him through the bedroom and out of the house to his glossy black Audi. We got in and right away his hand went to my thigh. I was a little sad about him doing this run with Lil Loco. I wanted the whole day with him. I get it he has to work, but I wanted attention.

"Can't you send someone else?" I asked as he pulled out of the driveway.

"No Baby, it's my job. Why what's up?" he asked, tracing shapes on my thigh as he shut the gate behind us.

"I want attention," I whined. I didn't care how needy I just sounded, not when it came to Trey'von. I wanted his attention all of the time, but today I was craving it like a crack fiend needing a fix.

"Aw Baby Girl, you'll have all my attention later tonight. I promise." He smiled, squeezing my thigh assuredly. I grabbed his hand, kissing his scarred knuckles and looked out of the window with a smile. Too soon, we pulled up to my house, I saw Zeke outside of the bar, but I knew the car windows were too dark for him to see me inside.

"Well, since you just have to leave me. I love you," I pouted, leaning over to place my lips on his easily. He chuckled and kissed me back passionately.

"Stop being such a baby, I'll see you in a few hours. I have a surprise upstairs in your room." My eyes grew wide as the smile took over my face. He had a surprise for me inside? What could it be? Did it have something to do with our date? I was getting more and more excited about our date. He chuckled, shaking his head.

"Stop looking at me like that and go see what I got you," he urged. I nodded excitedly, kissing his lips once again. I grabbed his face, sending him a serious look.

"Be careful," I demanded. He didn't say anything, and I wasn't getting out of this car until he promised to come back to me.

"I always am," he said, kissing my lips once more. I smiled as I got out of the car and called "goodbye" over my shoulder. I saw Zeke looking at me, but I walked straight into the house to avoid questioning. Once inside, I saw my dad coming down the steps in his jogging shorts.

"You have a couple packages upstairs, they were left at the door," he said. I nodded my head as I started to go upstairs but I stopped to grab my dad's arm.

"Are we ok?" I asked, worried. Me and my dad hadn't been the same for a long time. We didn't go out and have father-daughter days. He barely would be in a room alone with me. I knew it was because Trey'von and I were together, but I loved him and Zeke just like I loved my dad.

"We're fine Elles. Things around here are going to change, starting with our relationship. We're pulling away from one another and I want to fix that," he told me. I smiled and came down the steps to hug him, kissing his cheek.

"I'd like that dad." He smiled, kissing the top of my head. As I released him and went upstairs to my room to find three boxes on my bed, stacked from biggest to smallest. I walked over and naturally grabbed the biggest first, opening it. There was blue tissue paper and a note that read

I hope you like the gifts enough to wear them for me tonight. Be ready by 8 o'clock. I love you Baby Girl

~Trip

I smiled and pulled back the tissue paper to find a beautiful dress. It was deep blue with a red holographic tint to it when the light hit it just right. It was spaghetti strapped and would show off a nice amount of cleavage. The dress looked as if it would be tight fitting. It flowed to my ankles and had a slit going up the thigh on the left side. It was beautiful. It was something I would have picked out for myself. I could tell I'd feel sexy and pretty in it, I couldn't wait to wear it tonight. The next box held a pair of Louis Vuitton which were deep blue strappy heels with red bottoms. I was taken by the expensive brand. In the last box was a golden necklace that said "Trip." I smiled, touching the necklace. I laid out my new outfit and just admired it.

"ELLY, YOU HAVE A VISITOR!" Mom yelled. Who would be here for me? I wasn't expecting anyone. I wasn't even excepting to be home yet. I turned on my heels and went downstairs to see a woman standing in the doorway. She was gorgeous. She had light brown hair with blonde highlights. Her light bronzed skin glowed in the light. She had eyes that looked so familiar...they were such a dark brown that they were almost black, but something else about them was eerily familiar. Her pink plump lips were pulled back into a smile as she looked at me. She had a bold hourglass figure. Her abs were on display beneath a crop top. She was average height, about 5'5. She was probably around my moms, age if not a little older.

"Elly Sánchez?" she asked, pointing at me as I stepped down the last step. I looked at the strange women, confused about how she knew me.

"Yes, do I know you?" I asked. She smiled at me, shaking her head "no."

"I'm looking for my son, Trey'von Walker. They said you were his girlfriend and you'd be my way to find him. My name is Celina Pedro-Velazquez." My eyes grew wide as I took in the woman's looks again. This was Trey'von's mom? The woman I had a vendetta against even without having met her. Judgement passed through me as I looked at her. She was a horrible person. She chose to let some man abuse her son and didn't do anything about it. She blamed him for protecting her.

"You got to go," I said crossing my arms, looking at her. She looked back shocked and confused, but she should have known that would be my reaction.

"I just want to see my son. Anthony told me about you and how you've...tamed him," she said, as if he was a wild animal, and that only fueled my anger towards her.

CELINA

The girl in front of me was so beautiful. From her long bouncy curls, her glowing russet skin, to the rosy painted lips and chocolate brown eyes. Her figure was amazing as well. She had that ideal body that most girls only dreamed of having. I couldn't help but wonder how my heartless, cold son got someone so beautiful wrapped around his finger. She looked at me with distrust, which only made me wonder what horror stories Trey'von had filled her head with.

"He's not an animal that needed to be tamed. He needed love. He's not going to want to see you. So, you need to leave and not come back," she demanded, her tone full of authority. But I couldn't leave without at least seeing that he's alive, that he's happy with his life and this girl who seemed like she was trying too hard to protect him.

"Elly, I know you want to protect him from whatever he's told you about me, but I didn't come to hurt him. I just want to see my son and see how he is if he's happy. Please don't take that from me," I begged the teenage girl in front of me. She was my only way of getting to him and, from what those guys at that bar said, she was the safest way too.

"Celina?" I heard my name. I looked at Izzy as she walked into the foyer of the house with a surprised look. I was shocked to see her, as well. I smiled, opening my arms to my future daughter-in-law come into them.

"What are you doing here?" I asked her. She pulled away with a laugh.

"I could ask you the same. I live here, this is my little sister, Elly," she told me, and I nodded my head as I looked at Elly, who's jaw was locked.

"I'm looking for Trey'von" I told Izzy hoping maybe she could help me instead but she just seemed confused.

"He goes by Trip now," Elly spat. He's changed his name? Well, most gangsters do, I shouldn't be surprised. Izzy looked back at Elly who looked away and crossed her arms. I reached out and grabbed her hand.

"Elly, I'm begging you to let me see my youngest son. You're going to be the only way I get to that, please," I begged. She looked at me like she was thinking and then sighed. She nodded her head which made me smile. She motioned for me to follow her. So, I did with no questions asked.

"Your son stirs up quite the issues around here," the older man, who I learned is named Antonio, told me. He was Elly, Izzy, and Mateo's father, and Savannah was their mother. Right now, everyone was in the living room. Elly handed me a mug of warm tea.

"Thank you, Elly. He's always been like that. He's always caused chaos wherever he goes," I told Antonio, taking a sip from my tea and sitting it on the table.

"Well, I think he's a joy to have around. He's really brought out a more confident stride in Elly. Have you gotten a hold of him yet?" Savannah asked Elly, but she shook her head no.

"He's on a job with Lil Loco. He's not answering. We're going to have to wait," she said as she eyed me. I nodded my head, smiling at her.

"Thank for trying. I bet he's a handsome man." I hadn't seen Trey'von since he was 12.

"I was actually shocked to hear he had a girlfriend," I told Elly as I played with the tea bag in my cup.

"Trey'von was always such a loveless boy growing up. When they said he had a girlfriend, I couldn't believe anyone would put up with him or that he'd open himself up like that." I looked up to see her chocolate brown eyes boring into me with a deadly, almost scary glare.

"He became what he was forced to be. Don't sit there and call him loveless when I can prove all he's ever wanted is to be loved," She snapped and shook her head, the anger growing in her eyes. I knew whatever Trey'von told her wasn't good. Her phone began to ring. She looked away from me as she answered and got up.

"Bebe, I need you to get to my house now---." She walked out of the room, leaving me with her parents and sisters.

"Loveless, what do you mean? Like serial killer?" Antonio asked, a little too excited to get dirt on my baby boy.

"He was so cold, even as a child, causing fights, joining a gang at 9. He was hard to raise, always in trouble. Never caring about myself, his dad, or his siblings. It was like we were pawns in a game he was playing," I explained to them as I grabbed my tea and took another drink. Elly returned, hanging up the phone.

"He's about 20 minutes away but I will warn you, he's not happy," Elly said cautiously, sitting back down in the chair she had been sitting in before.

"How did you guys meet? I'm really happy he has someone as protective as you Elly," I praised her. I wanted to know the girl that could get through Trey'von's outer shell. It was something I could never do and I was his mother.

"We met at the bar. I have friends down there. I hated him at first. I thought your son was the most narcissistic, annoying, self-righteous, dickhead I've ever met," She laughed and shook her head. I watched a bright loving smile spread across her face, which made me smile. I loved seeing how much she loved him, even though I wondered if he was capable of that type of love.

"He does rub wrong," I agreed, and she nodded her head.

"Somehow, he made his way into my heart, and I can't live without him now. We need each other." Seeing how happy she was made me sure of his happiness for a moment and it warmed my soul. After everything he's been through, he found someone he could be open with.

"I'm glad you have that, Elly. I did too, but he was taken from me too early. Cherish it while you have it," I told her, thinking back to my Paul and how much I loved him. Suddenly a bang came from the foyer which made us all jump.

"BABY GIRL!" A rough voice boomed and moments later I saw an older tattooed version of my baby boy storming in. He looked at me with wide eyes, blackened with rage. His body was shaking, his upper lip snarled in the deadliest of ways. His muscles were tense, his hands balled in fists. I could smell the rage oozing from his pours. I saw the bulge of a gun in his pants, which sent even more fear through me.

"Did that *bitch* hurt you?" He spit the word "bitch" out with so much venom and anger, it physically hurt. I watched Elly stand as he approached her. He easily took her small face in his large shaking hands. His blackened eyes delicately wandering over her seeking an injury. He was so tender and caring with her. It was amazing to watch.

"I'm fine, she hasn't touched me. Are you ok?" Elly asked, worry lacing her eyes. I couldn't help but stare at my cold boy who was now grown and being so gentle with someone.

TREY'VON

I looked into Elly's chocolate brown eyes trying to calm myself down before I dealt with the whore who was trying to force her way back into my life. I leaned down and pressed my lips to Elly's. I felt the cool sting of my gun leave my waist band. She knew me well enough to know I wouldn't make a good decision right now. I let go of my Baby and looked over at my whore of a mother, feeling rage fill me.

"Son, you are so handsome. Elly----." I cut her off. I didn't want her calling me "son," or even speaking Elly's name.

"SHUT THE FUCK UP. I'M NOT YOUR SON! REMEMBER, I'M A FUCKING MURDERER, AND DON'T SPEAK HER NAME," I screamed at my mom. Her eyes grew wide as she sank further into the couch. She shook from fear, as she should.

"WHAT MOM? YOU DON'T GOT SHIT TO SAY NOW? I'M NOT A LITTLE FUCKING KID YOU CAN BEAT UP ANYMORE AND NOW YOU'RE SCARED, HUH? THAT'S HOW I FELT EVERY FUCKING DAY!" I screamed, getting closer to her and backing her more into the couch. Elly grabbed me, pulling me back and putting herself between me and my mom. I could easily move her, but I'd let her think she was doing something.

"Trip that is---." I cut Izzy off. Just because my stupid-ass brother got her knocked up didn't mean she was a part of this or my fucked-up family.

"Izzy, why don't you shut up and go suck off my brother," I spat at her, looking back at my mom and glaring.

"Trey'von, I just wanted to see you. It's been years. Can't we put that behind us and start over? I'm not on the streets anymore. I'm clean with a real job at a club," she explained. I scoffed, shaking my head "no." I never wanted anything with her. The day she kicked me out was the best thing that could have happened. How was I supposed to put years of physical, mental, and emotional abuse behind me like it didn't happen? She didn't steal my wallet. She stole my childhood.

"You want me to put it behind me. YOU WANT ME TO JUST FORGET HOW YOU AND YOUR ASSHOLE BOYFRIEND LOCKED ME IN A CLOSET, DIDN'T FEED ME UNLESS IT WAS LITERAL SHIT. LET'S NOT FORGET ABOUT THE SICK FUCKERS YOU'D BRING HOME AND MAKE ME WATCH YOU HAVE SEX WITH. YOU RUINED MY LIFE BEFORE I COULD EVEN EXPERIENCE IT," I screamed at her. I saw the familiar rage fill her eyes. She jumped up in the way that used to terrify me as a child, but not anymore. I grabbed Elly, picking her up, and put her in the chair, and took another step forward with a smirk.

"I WAS STRUNG OUT TREY'VON AND PAUL WAS THE ONLY WAY WERE GETTING BY. YOU WERE A BAD KID. I WAS

AT MY WITS END WITH YOU. WHEN PAUL SAID HE KNEW
HOW TO FIX THE PROBLEM, I DIDN'T THINK TWICE ABOUT
IT," She yelled back. I started to reach for her, but Elly wiggled between
us and grabbed my hands, lacing together our fingers.

"TELL ME THIS TREY'VON, DOES YOUR LITTLE
GIRLFRIEND KNOW EVERYTHING YOU'VE DONE? DOES SHE
KNOW YOUR A THIEF AND ALWAYS HAVE BEEN? HE WAS
PICKED UP AT 6 YEARS OLD FOR STEALING AND LET'S NOT
FORGET HOW YOU MURDERED THE LOVE OF MY LIFE AT 9,"
she screamed which only pushed my anger more. I wanted nothing more
than to put a bullet in her. It wouldn't bother me by any means.

"GET OUT OF MY HOUSE. YOU'VE OVERSTAYED YOUR
WELCOME!" Elly yelled at my mom, trying to push me away from her. I
burst into laughter at the idea of Paul being the love of her life. I spun Elly
around, shoved her into a chair, and sent her a look that told her to back off.

"WHAT ABOUT ALL OF THE WHORES TREY'VON? DOES
SHE KNOW ABOUT THEM? DOES SHE KNOW HOW YOU
WERE JUST LIKE PAUL AND A FUCKING DRUNK----." That was
her deadly mistake, comparing me to him. I spun, grabbed my mom and
threw her against the wall. I picked her up and slammed her into the dry
wall, which made pictures fall. I pulled out my knife and held it to her
throat. She froze, feeling the chilled blade against her jugular. I didn't
know how she knew that stuff. Elly would have never told her anything.
It didn't matter though, because these were her last few moments on earth.

"The only reason, Mom, there isn't a bullet between your eyes right
now is because Elly has my gun. She knows everything about me. You
can't come here and destroy my relationship. You're just bitter I shot that
disgusting fucker WHO YOU LOVED MORE THAN YOUR KIDS!"
I screamed, digging the knife into her flesh sending blood down her neck.

ELEANOR

I stood behind my dad, scared of Trey'von at the moment. I'd never
seen him like this. I knew this was a bad idea, having these two together.
I didn't want to call him, but she wasn't going to leave.

"Do something," Izzy demanded, but I shook my head "no," flinching as Trey'von screamed at his mom. I took a step back as my breathing picked up, my heart banged against my ribs.

"You're the only one he won't hurt Elly. He's going to kill her," Mom urged. She was right, Trey'von would never hurt me. I slowly walked over to him and grabbed his arm gently. His head snapped down at me. His skin was burning hot, he was shaking, and his eyes were completely black. I saw the veins in his arms and neck poking out.

"Bebe, stop doing this. You are making it seem like she's right about you. That you're a monster and I know you aren't. Please, come back to me," I whispered the last part as I touched his face. He looked over at his mom and then back at me.

"Show her that you are more of a man than Paul could have ever been. Don't let her bring you down to this level," I told him. He dropped the knife, taking a step back. I quickly pulled him into my arms. He hugged me tightly, burying his face in my neck.

"I'm sorry for losing control," he whispered, but I shook my head "no."

"You were pushed Bebe, that's not your fault. Are you ok?" I asked. He just shrugged, leaning down to pick me up by my thighs. I looked over to see my mom showing Celina out. Trey'von sat on the couch with me on his lap. I ran my fingers through his hair, kissing his shoulder.

"You are so amazing Trey'von. Nothing she said mattered, she's wrong. You are nothing like Paul. You know that don't you?" I asked. trying to move away to look at him, but he wouldn't let me. I hugged him tighter as he stayed quiet. My whole family was quiet too, thankfully. They were seeing him in a time of weakness.

"Fuck her, I'll show her I'm nothing like him," he whispered. He pulled away, moving back my hair and looking me in the eyes.

"I'm gonna do that by marrying you and giving you whatever you want, even if it's a house full of kids. I'll show her I'm twice the parent she'll ever be," he swore. I felt my stomach flip at the idea of him wanting to have kids with me. I smiled, grabbing his face excitedly.

"You mean it? You really want kids with me now?" I didn't even care that he only wanted them to prove a point to his mom. I wanted kids and if he was willing to have them, I'd take as many as he'd give me. Hopefully just two, but if he wanted more, then I'd pop out more than two.

"Not right now Baby Girl. Let's get you through school first. But one day. We're gonna show her I'm nothing like that asshole and you'll never be her. I'm sorry for scaring you," he said, kissing my lips. I nodded my head, pushing back his curls.

"I've never seen you like that before," I whispered.

"Are you ok Trip?" Mom asked, coming back into the room. Trey'von smiled, kissing my cheek.

"Yeah, Momma Sánchez, I am. I just lost my temper. Thank you for taking my gun," I told Elly. She smiled, running her fingers over my lips. I smiled, biting them tenderly and making her giggle.

"But I want it back shorty," I teased tickling her side. She burst into laughter, wiggling away from me. She got up and gave my gun back. I looked at it, knowing I would have shot my mom. I would have shot her in front of Elly without a second thought. I never wanted to be violent like that in front of her again. Ever since the day she saw me shoot that racist skinhead and the day with Lil psycho in the alley, I swore not to be violent in front of her. The way her chocolate brown eyes looked at me with such fear, I just couldn't do that in front of her again.

"If you don't want to go out tonight, that's fine" Elly told me. I scoffed, kissing her cheek.

"We're going out, Baby Girl. That crack whore isn't going to ruin our first date. Are you ok with the things she brought up?" I asked Elly nervously. We never really talked about the girls that came before her, mainly because I never met one that meant anything until Elly.

"What did she say that you think is going to bother me? That you used to have a drinking problem? I already knew that you've never hid from me," she told as she kissed my lips. That's not the part I was talking about.

"The other females," I whispered. She looked at me, shocked, but shook her head "no," kissing the tip of my nose.

"No, Trip you're attractive. Of course, other females wanted some of you, but they were all before me and they'll stay right where they belong in your past. They have your past, but I have your future and that's all the matters to me," she assured me. I smiled, pulling her into me to kiss her roughly and make her laugh.

"I have to finish what I started with Lil Loco, Baby, but tonight you're all mine in every way," I whispered, kissing her neck. She got off me, with an easy kiss.

"I love you," I reminded her. I felt like I couldn't tell her enough.

"I love you too," She whispered. With that being said, I walked out of the house and got back inside my car to meet back up with Lil Loco.

Chapter 41

First Date

TREY'VON

I sat on the floor in sweats and a tank top as Babycakes braided back my hair. She was a 16-year-old girl in the gang. She smuggled our drugs through airports. She was putting my hair in 5 tight-ass French braids. I thought about having curls, but I wanted to switch up my look a little for our date. This was my very first date ever, and I was nervous. I had no idea if I planned this out right or not.

"You're awful quiet down there," Babycakes commented, pulling on my hair harder than she needed to.

"Damn, Babycakes, I'd like my hair to stay in my head," I spat. I could feel her amusement as she kept braiding my hair.

"You nervous or something?" she asked me. I ran my sweaty palms down my sweats, biting my lip.

"Yeah I am. This is my first date ever. I'm sure Elly has been on dates before. I just have no idea what I'm doing," I admitted. I didn't feel soft when it came to Elly, because everyone knew one wrong look at her, and they'd be dead by my hand.

"You have a nice little dinner planned and you said she always looks at the hot air balloons in the sky. She'll love it, just be yourself," Babycakes told me and then sucked air in through her teeth.

"Well not yourself, you're a dick. Be nice and charming if you can," She joked. I faked a loud laugh, flipping off the teenage girl. Fuck, I wish

507

she'd hurry the hell up with these braids. I looked at the time to see it was only 7 o'clock. I still had an hour to get ready. I grabbed my phone and found to Elly's number.

Me- Send nudes

"Trip, you guys are about to have a romantic date and that's what you gonna text her?" Babycakes asked, laughing, but I just shrugged.

"Just trying to get in the mood for tonight," I said carelessly. My phone vibrated and I saw that Elly had sent me a phone. It was of her boobs. She was in the shower. Water running over her russet skin as her arm was placed under them pushing them up in the sexiest way. Another picture came in of her butt and, fuck. It was fat. The water droplets made it glow. I couldn't wait to get home, already.

Me- Just wait till I get yo fine ass home tonight

Baby girl😇😽- Can't wait 😈

I smirked, tossing my phone to the side. I groaned loudly, running my hand over my face.

"Oh, shut up, I have one section left," Babycakes snapped. This one section is going to take another fucking hour to do.

"It's taking forever," I complained. Babycakes didn't say anything, she just kept braiding. Soon enough, she slapped my head.

"Done," she chanted. I stood up, running my hand over the braids. She opened the camera on her phone to show me. I couldn't lie they looked good.

"These look good. Thanks, Babycakes. Here." I pulled out my wallet and handed her a hundred dollars.

"Thanks Trip, now go get ready," she shooed me away. I smiled, knowing she could see herself out. I went upstairs to my bedroom and grabbed my suit from the closet. I went into the bathroom to look at my braids once again. I honestly liked them. I might keep them for a few days instead of bringing back the curls tomorrow like I planned. I unzipped my suit bag and looked at the new clothing. It was an all-white suit with a white silk button up shirt. I changed into the suit and brought out my chain to rest on the white fabric. I walked out to my bedroom and put on my new black glossy dress shoes. I looked at myself in the mirror, fixing my jacket. I was nervous. My palms were sweating as my hands shook. I licked my lips, making sure I had my wallet. I grabbed my keys and headed out to my car.

After what felt like a forever drive, I found myself in front of Elly's house. I parked, got out and walked up to the door. I knocked, hoping Antonio didn't answer. I was nervous enough without him starting shit with me. The door opened to show Momma Sánchez. She smiled as she looked me up and down.

"Don't you look nice? All of this for your date?" she asked, moving to the side to let me in. I ran my hand over my braids nervously.

"Yeah, I'm tryin to make it special," I told her as Izzy walked into the foyer looking at her phone.

"Mom, Anthony is coming over," Izzy announced. I bit my lip holding back my comments.

"Ok, that's fine. Go tell your sister Trip is here and ready for her," Momma Sánchez told Izzy. She smiled at me as she walked up the stairs. I kept up small talk with Momma Sánchez until a blue heel on the steps caught my attention. I looked up as smooth russet legs came into view and then she was in full view. Elly looked breathtaking. Her dress hugged her curves, her skin glowing a heavenly way. Her hair was straight, and she had a side part. Her makeup was glamorous. She truly looked like a model coming down the steps. She looked better in the dress than I thought she would. My name hanging around her neck sent a sense of pride through me. It made me feel like she was completely mine. Of course, she couldn't wear it any other time because of Zeke, but, damn, it looked good.

"Bebe, you look so handsome," she smiled a bright white smile as she walked the rest of the way down the stairs. I smiled, grabbing her hand and spinning her around.

"You look even better than what I pictured. I thought you'd keep your curls for me though," I pouted my lip. I loved her sassy bouncy curls.

I loved watching them move while she was yelling at me or laughing at something I said. Don't get me wrong I liked her straight hair too, but her curls had a flare to them that I adored.

"Yours are gone too," she commented with a smile. I nodded, touching my head once again.

"My head is kinda cold," I admitted. She giggled at me leaning up to kiss my cheek. I smiled, wrapping my arms around her waist and hugging her tightly as I spun us around.

"We better get going. We have reservations." She nodded her head, grabbing a bag by the door. I took it from her and looked at Momma Sánchez.

"You good with this?" I asked, holding up the bag. She smiled, nodding her head.

"You kids go have fun," she pushed us out of the door. I smiled, grabbing Elly's hand and leading her to the car.

ELEANOR

I was so nervous about this date. It was our first date, and the butterflies were showing me no mercy. Trey'von looked so great in his suit and his braids. Every part of me just wanted to rip it off of him. I glanced over at him as he drove, touching my necklace. He's so handsome.

"What are you thinking about?" he asked, resting his hand on my thigh. I rested my hand on top of his.

"You and how much I love you," I flirted. I watched the blush spread across his cheeks which only made me giggle. I leaned over kissing his cheek. He squeezed my thigh, keeping his eyes on the road.

"I love you too," he whispered shyly. I laughed looking back out of the window just as we entered Beverly Hills. Every time I came here, I was amazed by the luxurious lifestyle that was being lived here. Soon enough, we pulled up to a fancy looking restaurant. A valet came over, opened my door and extended a hand. I took it thanking him as he helped me out of the car, Trey'von came around and tossed his keys at the man. He grabbed my hand and led me into the restaurant and to a podium.

"Reservation for Walker," Trey'von told the girl. She typed on her Ipad and then smiled at us.

"Yes, right this way," she said. We followed her to the far back of the restaurant. Set away from everyone else in a dim corner was a table for two. The white tablecloth had rose pedals spread on it. There were lit candles in the middle of the table. There were also champagne glasses filled with what looked to be champagne. Trey'von must be crazy if he thinks I'm letting him relapse and drink. I walked straight over to the table and grabbed both glasses.

"What are you doing?" Trey'von asked with an amused look as I handed the glasses to the waitress.

"You are insane if you think I'm letting you drink," I told him, crossing my arms. He looked at me with an amused look and grabbed the bottle from the ice bin.

"It's Apple cider." He showed me the bottle. I blushed as an "oh" escaped my lips. He chuckled, taking the glasses back from the girl. Trey'von pulled out my chair for me. I sat down, moving my chair in as he pushed. Trey'von took a seat across from me as we were given menus.

"I'll be back to take your order," the girl said, walking away. I looked at Trey'von with a smile and then around to the beautiful scenery.

"This is gorgeous Trey'von. Did you do this all by yourself?" I asked, happily.

"Of course, I did all by myself. I can be romantic," he snickered. I smiled, reaching across the table and grabbed his hands. I played with the silver rings I've grown so used to being on his fingers. I was so content in the moment with him.

"What are you going to get to eat?" he asked, I looked down at my menu shrugging. I forgot to look, honestly.

"I don't know what are you getting, Bebe?" I asked him, biting my red painted lip.

"The T-bone steak with a baked potato and salad." I couldn't help but notice how expensive this restaurant was. The soup was 20 dollars by itself. I looked up at him and back at the menu.

"Are you sure you want to spend this kind of money? I'm good with pizza," I told him, looking at him nervously. He rolled his eyes, waving me off.

"Get whatever you want. I got the bill," he told me with a shrug. I decided on the sirloin steak, fries, and a salad. I lifted my glass of apple cider, taking a sip and sitting it back down. Our waitress walked over to us with a smile.

"You guys ready to order?" She asked as she looked between us.

"Yeah, I'll have the T-bone with a baked potato and the house salad. Baby Girl?" Trey'von asked, his eyes never leaving me. I blushed as the goosebumps formed on my skin.

"I'll have the sirloin with fries and a salad," I said shyly. She nodded, taking back the menu's and walked away. I couldn't help but wonder how he was feeling after the last couple days with his mom showing up and his brother popping up. I knew it had to be hard for him. He hated revisiting his past and it was just being forced on him.

"How are you feeling after everything that's happened these last couple of days?" I asked curiously, and worried for him. I watched Trey'von look away from me, licking his lips like he was thinking. He grabbed his glass and took a drink of his apple cider and then looked back at me.

"Honestly, I'm angry. My mom just showing up the way she did, with the nerve to try to cause problems between us just because she was mad at me. Then Anthony having a kid. I'm worried about him more than angry." I knew Trey'von loved his brother, even if he didn't act like it.

TREY'VON

I did not want to be talking about this right now, but Elly was worried about me. I could see it all over her face. Once she knew I'd be ok, she'd drop the topic and move on like it never happened.

"Why are you worried?" she asked, being her nosy little self. I leaned forward, I loved Elly, but she was so damn nosy.

"Aren't you being nosy," I smirked at her. She smiled, leaning forward with a challenging look.

"I'm allowed to be nosy with you. You're my boyfriend," she reminded me. I couldn't wait for the title to change. I was no longer content with being just her boyfriend. I wish she'd agree to just go to the courthouse with me. Once we were married, Zeke couldn't do anything. Killing me and leaving Elly widowed would cause my boys to retaliate against him in my name.

"I want to be your husband," I said, suggestively. She rolled her eyes smiling at me.

"Not this again," she whispered. I nodded my head grabbing her hands.

"Just us, at the courthouse. We wouldn't have to hide anymore. Once we're married, Zeke couldn't kill me or you for this," I reminded her once again of this detail she already knew. We could still have a real wedding, just formalize it first.

"I want a real wedding, Bebe, and to be asked properly with a ring," she said. I groaned, leaning back. I tried to fight the attitude that was beginning to form because she was telling me "no."

"Don't get grumpy," she whined, but I just shrugged my shoulders.

"I'll buy you a ring, that's a given, and if you want a real wedding, we can have one, but I want to be with you without hiding from Zeke. Us getting married or me taking his spot is the only way to do that. He's going to figure it out sooner than later, Baby Girl," I told her with attitude lacing my voice. Her smile turned into a glare. Just as she started to open her mouth, our waitress came over with the salads.

"Thank you," Elly said as I just glanced at the girl. She smiled at me, walking away. Then Elly turned her attention on me.

"Do not ruin our night Trey'von. If you really think that, then take over. I am not going to settle for anything less than the wedding and proposal I deserve. I think we should drop this topic for the night," she snapped back at me. Of course, that would be her response. She was right though. I didn't want to ruin our first date by throwing a fit because she wouldn't marry me.

"Fine, but we're not done with this conversation," I said jabbing a finger towards her. She nodded her head, messing with her salad.

"Ok Trey'von, please, let's go back to having a good night," she begged. I nodded my head, pouring ranch over my salad. Right now, wasn't the time to fight her over marriage and how to save myself from Zeke.

"Who did your hair?" she asked me quietly, taking a bite of her salad. I laughed at how she took her bite while trying to avoid messing up her lipstick. I mocked her bite, making both of us burst into laughter.

"A girl in the gang. Her name is Babycakes, she killed it huh?" I asked, touching the braids. Elly leaned across the table, feeling them.

"She did. How long did it take?" We got lost in conversation about my braids until the waitress showed up with our food.

"Go ahead and cut into them and make sure they are cooked well enough for you," The waitress asked. As we cut into them, we assured the waitress that they were perfectly cooked, and thanked the waitress as she walked away.

"This is perfect," Elly sighed, taking a bite of her steak.

"Not as perfect as you," I flirted. Her cheeks blushed to that perfect rosy color. We spent the rest of dinner flirting with each other and just joking around.

"Bebe, do not let me fall," Elly squealed holding onto my hands that hid her eyes. Her back was pressed against my chest as I walked us forward. I chuckled, kissing her cheek.

"Never," I promised as we neared the top of the hill. There stood a hot air balloon ready to take off with us inside. I smiled, knowing how much Elly was going to love this. Every time she had seen one fly past my house, she'd just stare at it with a longing look.

"You ready?" I whispered in her ear as we stopped walking.

"Yes!" she said excitedly. I grinned, leaning in close to her neck and leaving a hot kiss on it. She shivered under my touch which made me chuckle.

"You sure?" I asked in a low, seductive voice. She pushed me away with a gasp. She looked back at me with wide excited eyes and then back to the balloon.

"How'd you know?" Her smile was the brightest I'd ever seen in my life.

"I just know you better than anyone else ever could. Come on, let's go get in," I urged, grabbing her hand. We walked over and I helped her into the basket and then climbed in myself. I saw her looking at the apple cider bottle. She smiled looking back at me happily. She was really making sure everything was non-alcoholic. I liked that she supported my recovery and kept me on track.

"Surprise!" I said happily. I grabbed a chocolate covered strawberry and held it to her plump lips. She beamed up at me as she bit into it making me chuckle.

"You are beautiful" I gushed, pushing back her straightened hair. The balloon made us stumble slightly as it took off. Elly went to the edge and looked over. I quickly grabbed her waist, making sure she wouldn't fall.

"Awe, are you worried about me?" she teased. I smiled, kissing her shoulder.

"Always." She smiled, touching my cheek as she looked out to the fading ground.

ELEANOR

I looked at the stars as we floated through the sky. This night has been so perfect. From dinner to the surprise hot air balloon ride. Music started to play from behind me. I recognized the song. It was the song we danced to at homecoming. I turned, glanced at Trey'von with a confused look as he came over and grabbed my hands. He slipped my hands around his neck and grabbed my waist.

"You recognize this song?" he asked as we danced slowly together. I nodded my head telling him I knew it.

"It's our song, Baby Girl. This was the song playing at homecoming when we got together. It's how I feel about you," he whispered wrapping his arms around my waist pulling me closer. I couldn't believe had he remembered such a small detail. I couldn't stop the tears from filling my eyes out of happiness. He had made this night so special. I didn't think it could ever be topped. Trey'von spun me around and then pulled me right back into him.

"I know we've only known each other for about a good 7 months, but these have been the best 7 months of my life, Baby Girl. I love you so much." I couldn't believe it had only been 7 months either, but it had. It felt longer than that. I felt like I've been with Trey'von my whole life.

"I love you," I whispered leaning up on my tippy toes, connecting our lips in a soft, sweet, and tender kiss.

My back hit the wall roughly as our lips moved too lustfully and hungrily against one another's. All that was going through my mind was Trey'von and how much I needed him. My arms were around his neck feeling his braids as my legs were wrapped tightly around his waist. I felt my core pulse for him as the tingles reminded me how badly I craved the feel of him. His lips moved from my mine to my neck. Right away he found my sweet spot, earning a low moan. I pushed the jacket off of his shoulders and started on the buttons of his shirt.

"Papi," I moaned as his teeth sank into my neck. I ran my hands over his shoulders, pushing down his shirt and leaving nothing but skin and tattoos. He pushed up my dress running his hands over my butt. He stumbled back sitting down on his couch. I groaned pulling away from him.

"Baby---." He stopped as I slowly let the straps to my dress fall. I stood up, stripping out of the dress, letting it pool at my ankles. It left me in nothing but my bra and thong.

"So sexy," he groaned, reaching out to grab me. He pulled me back down on his lap. I grabbed his face, shoving my tongue into his mouth and taking control of the kiss. He groaned running his hands up my back to my bra strap. He popped it with no problem as he always does. I let the straps fall as he grabbed it slinging it to the side, his hands going to my breasts, palming them right away. I peppered kisses down his neck getting to his sweet spot. I smirked, licking a bold stripe up his neck and then biting down seductively.

"Fuck," he groaned in my ear as his dick jumped, poking me. I moaned at the movement. I got off of him and got on my knees between his legs. I ran my hands over his growing bulge. He groaned as he watched me. I undid his pants and pulled them down to his ankles.

"I told you I'd get head," he snarked. I rolled my eyes playfully, kissing his tip through his boxers.

"Joke's on you, I wanted to suck your dick this morning. You could have gotten head twice in one day," I teased, sticking my tongue out at him. He grabbed my throat choking me in the sexiest of ways, making me moan.

"And you didn't tell me?" he growled seductively as the dominance poured off of him. I moaned wanting nothing more than him at the moment. He let go of me, pulling off his boxers and letting his friend spring to life and hit his belly button. I grabbed him rubbing my hand down his long length. I left a hot wet sloppy kiss on his tip and ran my lips down him. I touched my tongue to his base and slowly licked up his length, making eye contact with him.

"Baby Girl," he moaned watching me. I swirled my tongue around his tip, taking him into my mouth. I slowly moved my head up and down on his length, running my tongue across it. I watched his eyes close as pleasure took over his face. It was my favorite time to see Trey'von, in his most vulnerable and primal state. He ran his hand through my straightened hair, forcing my head to move up and down faster.

"Oh shit, just like that," He groaned. I sucked in, making my cheeks hollow out. I moved my head up and down faster building the confidence to go all the way down. I pushed my head all the way down until my lips touched his base. He groaned out in pleasure as I gagged coming up. I licked my lips, pumping my hands. I took his tip back into my mouth bobbing my head up and down fast as my hands worked the lower half.

"Fuck, keep sucking," he groaned. I sped up, finding courage in his words. I moved my hands faster as drool went from my mouth to my hands.

"Oh fuck, I'm gonna cum," he groaned. I moved back, leaning up to kiss him, smiling.

"Not yet, Baby," I said, kissing him again. He groaned into my mouth which only intensified my need for him.

TREY'VON

I groaned as Elly shoved her tongue into my mouth. I grabbed her legs, pulling her down onto my lap. I ran my hands over her ass, grabbing it, and smacking her hard, making her moan.

"I want you," she moaned into my mouth. I bit her lip, pulling away and groaning at her words.

"Let me hit without a condom," I groaned, I didn't want to use the condom. I wanted to be as close to her as humanly possible and the condom stopped that. I've never went in raw on anyone. I've never trusted the person enough or even wanted to be that close to someone.

"No, it's too risky," she whispered, kissing me again. I pulled away letting my eyes wander her body as I shook my head "no."

"I'm clean, you're clean, so what's the risk?" I asked, licking my lips and kissing her breasts. She ran her hand over my head, sighing.

"I don't want to get pregnant. I have to finish high school, go to college---." I cut her off, she wasn't going to get pregnant. She was on birth control.

"You're on birth control and have been for a while. You won't get pregnant. Come on, please I want to be close to you," I begged against her breast. She pulled back making me look up at her. She looked at me, biting her lip, unsure.

"What if I do though? Birth control doesn't always work," she worried. I sighed grabbing her and laying her back on the couch as I hovered between her legs.

"You won't. I promise, Baby Girl. Don't you want to feel closer me too? I want to feel you, all of you without something in the way," I told her quietly kissing her jawline. She sighed, running her hands down my arms.

"Ok, fine, we won't use the condom." I smiled excitedly, grabbing her thong and pulling it down. I looked at her and groaned in pleasure at what I saw. She was so tight and looked so soft. I watched her wetness drool down, promising it was going to feel good.

"Are you sure?" I asked, licking my lips. I leaned down running a bold stripe with me tongue over her, moaning at the taste.

"Yes," she gasped as my tongue worked its magic on her. After getting her close, I sat up kissing her lips, lining up with her entrance. I looked down and slowly slid in. About halfway, my arms shook, threatening to give out as a pleasurable moan escaped my lips. I couldn't describe this feeling. It was so warm, wet, and tight, but that's not what got me. It was how close I felt to her. I felt like we had entered another level of our relationship and trust. The closeness and intimacy of it was what got me and made it so much better.

"Baby," I sighed against her shoulder. She rubbed my back, wrapping her leg around my waist and pulled me even deeper inside of her. I thrust in roughly, both of us moaning.

"Fuck, this feels better," I moaned, repeating that action. Her hands traveled up my arms to my chest and down to my abs.

"I can make it feel even better," she whispered, pushing at my abs. I pulled out, groaning at the action, and sat back down on the couch. She moved on top of me. I watched her line up with me. She slowly slid down on my length sending the shock waves of pleasure back through me. She moved her hips slowly against me at first. I moaned grabbing her breasts. She grabbed my hands lacing together our fingers and moved up and down on me faster and harder. Our moans filling the room. Her chocolate brown eyes found mine as she rode me.

"You feel so fucking good, Baby. I know you feel that," I moaned. I couldn't even think of anything dirty say. My mind was so focused on the pleasure. I took my hands from her, grabbing her hips and lifting mine as I slammed in hard.

"Trey'von, yes Baby," she moaned loudly gripping her boobs as I pounded into her. She bounced on me as I slammed my body into her.

"Oh my god, don't stop Bebe," she moaned, her nails sinking into my shoulders. I went faster and harder than before. She might not be able to walk in the morning but that was a good price to pay for how good this was feeling. I began to feel the pressure in my lower abs. I couldn't lie, I was embarrassed at how quickly I was starting to feel my ending come, but she felt so good.

"Trey'von, I'm so close," she moaned out and not even seconds later I felt her tighten around me. It was even better without the condom blocking it. Her body tightened and shook. Her eyes rolled back as she gripped my shoulders. Her back arched as she took my whole length inside her.

"Trey'von, I love you," she moaned in her state of bliss. Her words pushed me over the edge. I felt the pressure release in my abs, my eyes squeezed shut as I pulled her closer, releasing inside of her.

"BABY GIRL!" I groaned loudly. She moaned, collapsing down on the couch. I threw my head back with my eyes closed, catching my breath. Once my heart rate slowed and I was breathing normal again I looked over at Elly to see my cum running down her russet leg. Her eyes closed, her breathing still labored, her hair messy. It was one of the sexiest sights I had ever seen.

"You are so gorgeous," I murmured, kissing her lips. She smiled, kissing me back as she got up and looked down in disgust.

"I'll be back." She grabbed my shirt and wiped her leg off. I watched her walk back to the bathroom. I laid back on the couch closing my eyes. I was tired. Not long after I closed my eyes and sleep took over.

Chapter 42

Daddy Issues

ELEANOR

I woke to the sound of snores from under me and the bright sun light. I groaned, opening my eyes to find Trey'von and I were still on the couch. The sun was streaming through the windows. I looked up at Trey'von. He was still soundly asleep with his arms wrapped around me. My head laid on his chest as my legs were tangled with his. I hummed in content, looking at the tattoos on his arm. They all seemed so random, but when I really looked at them, I could see a deeper meaning behind them. His arms were covered completely just like his chest and abs. He had tattoos on his back but nothing like those on his front. I looked at his left arm and all of the tattoos which told a story of their own. I shook my head as I looked at the thorny dead rose bush on his stomach. I placed my nail on his boxer waist band and slowly drug it up, tracing the vine.

"You're awake?" Trey'von complained. I jumped at the sudden boom of his voice. I didn't even notice that he had stopped snoring. I looked up to see his nearly black eyes were still closed, and I couldn't help but just stare. He was truly so attractive.

"I didn't mean to wake you," I whispered. He shrugged, pulling me closer to him as he brought his free arm up to rest behind his head.

"You're fine." His voice was husky. I looked back down to the tattoo, my curiosity getting the best of me.

"This tattoo of the rose bush. Why is it dead?" I asked curiously as his eyes opened. He sighed as he closed them again and covered them with his arms.

"Because life is shit, like that bush," he said, both carelessly and annoyed. Trey'von wasn't a morning person, so my questions were probably bugging him, but he'd get over it. Did he still think life was that bad? He always tells me I've changed him so much. Did I change that outlook on life for him as well?

"Do you still think that?" I asked, snuggling closer.

"Baby Girl, go back to sleep," he grumbled, but I wasn't tired and wanted to talk to him about his tattoos. I was always so curious about them but had never had the courage to ask.

"No, I'm not sleepy anymore. Answer my question," I whined like a child. He made an annoying grunting noise and looked down at me.

"Sometimes. It's more when I get upset about something. You gave me a reason to live," he said, I blushed knowing it would be his answer, but I loved hearing it over and over again. He has changed me as well. I wasn't that weak little girl anymore. I could stand on my own feet now.

"Now, let me sleep" He commanded. I laughed, getting up to straddle him. He covered his eyes with both of his arms. I ran my hands over his tattoos, tracing certain ones that caught my attention.

"Baby," He fussed, I smiled leaning down kissing his chest.

"I want attention," I whined, kissing his chest again. He opened his eyes looking at me with an irritated look. He shook his head as he reached out for the remote to the TV.

"You've been needy these last couple of days," he commented but I just shrugged my shoulders and ran my hands down his abs.

"Would you rather me just sit here with an attitude?" He sighed, resting his hand on my thigh as he looked away from the TV and back to me.

"Of course not, but I'd like to sleep." I giggled, grabbing his face kissing his lips. He pushed my hand away kissing me back. I laughed and looked at the TV. He was watching the GodFather.

"You live that whole life, why watch it?" I asked him curiously. I didn't mind watching it personally. I liked the GodFather. He shrugged his shoulders as he looked at the TV, and traced shapes on my thigh. I went back to tracing the tattoos on his chest. I slowly ran my hand up to his neck where his Los Prophet tattoo was when my phone rang. I leaned over to the table to see my dad calling.

"Hey, Dad," I answered. Trey'von moved under me to sit up slightly and looked at me. I smiled at him, making a kissy face.

"Elly, I'd like you to come home now. I thought we could go get ice cream and just talk," Dad said. I smiled at the idea of spending time with my dad, we haven't spent much time together since things had gotten intense because of Trey'von.

"Yeah, for sure. Let me take a shower and get ready. I'll have Trip drop me off at the house," I said excitedly. Trey'von looked at me, confused. I started to get off him, but he grabbed me and kept me on his lap.

"I can just come pick you up. Where does he live?" Dad asked me, curiously.

"Beverly Hills. I'll text you the address. Just ring at the gate and he'll let you in. I'm going to go get ready. Love you," I said. My dad told me he loved me too and we hung up.

"What's going on?" Trey'von asked as I texted my dad his address.

"My dad is going to come pick me up. We're going to go have ice cream and just spend time together," I told Trey'von, lacing our fingers together and kissing his knuckles. He sighed, closing his eyes in annoyance.

"Babe, I love you but not your dad. I don't want him in my house," he complained. I smiled, leaning down to kiss his lips.

"He'll only be here for a second. Come shower with me?" I asked, pouting my lip at him. He chuckled at me, shaking his head. He tapped my thigh, telling me to get up. I excitedly lead the way upstairs. I felt clingy in this moment, but I just wanted to be close to him. When we went into the bathroom, I turned on the water to let it warm up. I stripped out of my underclothes and stepped into the shower. Moments later, Trey'von joined me, leaving a kiss on my shoulder.

"So fucking gorgeous," he sighed out, running his hands over my curves. I turned in his arms, smiling, and placed my arms around his neck, kissing his lips. He pushed me through the water until my back hit the wall. I smiled, jumped up and wrapped my legs around his waist, making him chuckle.

ANTONIO

I pulled in through the gates to a gigantic house. I was shocked at what I saw. The house was beautiful-all white with plenty of windows. In the middle of the drive was a fountain with water pooling beneath it. There were bushes and trees around the house. A man was trimming them. I knew Trip was high up in Los Prophets, but I didn't realize he made this much money. Why was Zeke living in our neighborhood? Zeke was the boss, so he had to make more than Trip, right? I parked my car, got out and walked over to the glass double doors. I pushed the doorbell and waited patiently. After a few moments, the door swung open and there stood a shirtless Trip. He wore low saggy sweats and his whole body covered in tattoos. On his neck and throughout the tattoos were hickeys. I tried to convince myself that Elly wasn't having sex. She was too young, but now he was just flaunting it.

"Elly is still getting ready, come on in," Trip said moving to the side. I stepped inside the foyer and looked around. I found myself just as amazed with the inside as I had been with the outside. I followed Trip into a living room. Right away, my eyes caught a picture that was by the TV. It was of him and Elly. Elly sat on his lap laughing as he kissed her cheek.

"You can sit down, Antonio," Trip said, sitting on the couch. I sat down next to him and saw that he was watching the Godfather.

"That's a good movie," I commented. He nodded agreement as he adjusted himself to get more comfortable.

"Yeah, it's not bad. I missed half of it because of Elly," he said, annoyed. I chuckled, nodding my head.

"She can talk when she wants to," I said, shaking my head. I hated when Elly got into those talkative moods. It was hard to keep up with what she was even going on about.

"She woke me up like that this morning. The moment y'all leave I'm getting back into bed. I'm fucking tired," he complained, crossing his arms and closing his eyes.

"Oh, shut up Trip. It's your job to give me attention," Elly's voice came from behind us. I turned to see her holding her shoes as she looked at her phone.

"Man, you about to have all these guys looking at you. You look way too fine to be out of this house," Trip said, waving her over. I bit my tongue as Elly blushed and walked towards him. I looked back at the TV. It was no secret I didn't approve of this relationship, even more so now that he knew the truth about Elly's DNA. Zeke came to the house late last night and told Savannah that Elly was out of control and he wanted to tell her the truth. He wanted Elly to come stay with him for a while. I couldn't lose my daughter. Zeke didn't raise her. All he's done is drive her into the arms of this criminal and teach her the ways of the streets.

"You ready to go, Dad?" Elly asked. I nodded, standing up and watching Trip who had his eyes glued to my daughter.

"Gimme a kiss and then you can go," he said. I watched Elly lean down and kiss this disgrace of a man.

"I love you. I'll call you later. Let's go, Pops" Elly bounced over to me. I smiled, putting my arm around my daughter as she and Trip exchanged goodbyes.

"I used to love this place as a kid," Elly reminded me as she added gummy bears to her ice cream.

"I remember. We used to come here after every game you played. We should start doing this more," I said as we walked over to the scale. We each weighed our ice cream and I paid. Elly ran over to the monkey-shaped booth like she did even as a child. I smiled and sat across from her.

"So, what made you decide to get ice cream?" She asked curiously, licking her spoon.

"Just to spend time with you. We've been distant since everything with Trip, and it shouldn't be that way." She nodded her head in agreement, looking down at her ice cream. She was silent but I could see the thoughts crossing her face. I'm sure I didn't want to know what she is thinking at the moment.

"Speaking of Trip, that is something I want---." Elly cut me off, shaking her head "no."

"I don't want to talk about Trip or Zeke. I just want us to enjoy our time together without talking about them." But that was the whole reason I wanted to come and get ice cream. I was going to put an end to Zeke trying to 'co-parent,' as he calls it, and this obsession with this gangster she had.

"Well, Elles, they are one of the reasons I wanted to come out and get ice cream," I admitted. I watched her smile fall as her eyes grew wide. The shock on her face only lasted for a second before I saw irritation take over. She was so much like Zeke. Her temper matched his. Zeke was more deadly, but we had gotten that temper tamed in her until Trip came along encouraging it.

ELEANOR

I should have known there was another reason why my dad wanted to get ice cream with me. I should have known he didn't want to just spend one-on-one time with me. I didn't want to hear anything he had to say about Zeke and Trip. Zeke has done nothing but be a second father to me. He was a good man. Trip did his damage, and I could understand my dad's resentment towards him, but it didn't change the way I felt about him.

"It's more about Zeke then Trip--." I interrupted my dad.

"Why can't I just be enough for you? Why can't us sitting here talking about Volleyball be enough?" I asked him, my tone breaking from anger to show how hurt I was. My dad reached over the table and grabbed my hands. His brown eyes bore into me, but I saw the seriousness behind them. He wasn't going to let this go. He had pulled me away from my blissful morning just to start an argument with me.

"You are enough Elly. I love you, but I can't have you around Zeke anymore. He's a criminal and a bad influence," I looked at my dad with wide eyes. A bad influence on me? A criminal? I couldn't help but laugh at these things. Yes, Zeke was gang leader with a record but it's not like he was shooting people in front of me or encouraging me to live the same life he is. Hell, he wants the complete opposite for me. Influencing me? How has he been a bad influence? He talks to me about college, law school, and being a strong independent woman.

"Zeke has been nothing but a second father to me. He preaches college to me. He's taught me how to fend for myself, so I don't have to depend on anyone else. You're talking about someone you don't even know. Zeke never says a bad word about you but you, on the other hand, always have something disgusting to say about him," I spat at my dad, pushing away the ice cream. I no longer wanted it. I crossed my arms, glaring at my dad as I waited for his rebuttal.

"I'm the only father you have Elly, and I will not put up with you even giving him the privilege of that title. This is the last time I'm telling you nicely. You stay away from Zeke, or else," my dad growled. I sent him a challenging look. I mean what was he really going to do if I didn't listen? I was 17, 18 in two months.

"Yeah, and what are you going to do about it, Dad?" I asked, crossing my arms. He glared at me, leaning forward.

"Try me Elly and see for yourself," he dared. I laughed, shaking my head and leaning back into the booth.

"Maybe you should try me, Dad. You know what. Take me home" I demanded, getting up from the booth. This was a mistake to even come here with him. I should be with Trey'von snuggling on the couch and getting attention, not arguing why I wouldn't stay away from a man that is like my father.

"Sit down now. We aren't done talking!" My temper flared at his tone. He might not be done talking, but I was.

"WELL, I AM DONE TALKING. FORGET IT I'LL JUST WALK HOME!" I yelled, turning on my heels and storming out of the ice cream parlor.

"ELEANOR!" My dad yelled, following me. But I just shook my head and kept walking.

"IF YOU DON'T STOP, YOU'LL BE GROUNDED UNTIL YOU TURN 18 AND I'LL TELL ZEKE ABOUT YOU AND TRIP!" he yelled. I stopped dead in my tracks. How dare he use that against me? Sometimes I wonder if he forgets that I'm the only protection he has from the gang. I turned on my heels with a glare. I stormed over, shoving my dad back.

"If you do that, we aren't father and daughter anymore. ALL YOU'LL BE TO ME IS A SPERM DONOR!" I screamed. He glared at me, grabbing my arm so tightly it ached. He drug me over to the car, throwing me in. He slammed the car door. I screamed out in anger, kicking the door.

"I'M DONE ELEANOR. EVER SINCE YOU'VE BEEN AROUND TRIP YOU'VE BEEN A NEW PERSON. FIGHTING IN SCHOOL, STAYING OUT ALL NIGHT, DRINKING, FIGHTING ME AND YOUR MOTHER ON EVERYTHING. I'M DONE WITH YOU, TRIP, AND ZEKE. YOU ARE *MY* DAUGHTER AND YOU'RE GOING TO START ACTING LIKE IT AGAIN!" Dad yelled the moment his door opened. I bit my lip so hard I could taste blood. I was trying to keep myself from lashing out even more because I knew that once I calmed down, the guilt would consume me. I looked out of the window as my mind ran with all of the vicious things I wanted to say to my dad. I wanted to hurt him. I wanted him to feel the betrayal and pain I felt. I wanted him to feel like he wasn't good enough, just the way he made me feel.

"YOU'RE BREAKING UP WITH TRIP AND GOING TO FOCUS ON SCHOOL, SPORTS, AND COLLEGE. YOU'RE DONE GOING TO THE BAR AND I MEAN IT THIS TIME. IF I CATCH YOU DOWN THERE AGAIN, I SWEAR TO GOD YOU'LL THINK I'M THE BIGGEST BASTARD THERE IS!" he screamed as he ran a red light in anger. I couldn't stop my rage from bubbling over. I knew the end result of this fight, but I didn't care.

"WHAT ARE YOU GOING TO DO DAD? HIT ME WITH YOUR BELT? REMEMBER HOW THAT ENDED LAST TIME? IF YOU DON'T REMEMBER, WHY DON'T YOU TAKE A LOOK AT THE SCAR. DO YOU NOT REALIZE I PROTECT YOU!" My hands moved as I yelled at my dad. I ran my hand through my curls trying to calm myself down. He stayed quiet, just driving. I looked out of my window trying not to spiral. As we got close to the house I saw Zeke and Trip outside the bar talking. I glanced at my dad as he pulled into his spot in front of the house. Just as I went to make a break from the car to Zeke, my dad grabbed my arm.

"Go over to him and I'll tell Zeke how you gave Trip all of those hickey's and you stayed the night with him. You'll watch a bullet end his life," my dad growled. I sent him a glare, jerking away and got out of the car.

"I HATE YOU ANTONIO. COUNT YOURSELF WITH ONE LESS DAUGHTER, I FUCKING HATE YOU!" I screamed, backing away as he came near me.

"STOP MAKING A SCENE AND GET IN THE HOUSE," Antonio ordered but I just laughed at him, shaking my head. He walked around the car. His eyes filled with rage. His hands balled into fists as his side. I heard the front door open and heard my mom, Izzy, and Mateo calling out to us.

"WHEN I TURN 18, I PROMISE YOU WILL NEVER SEE ME AGAIN. I LITERALLY HATE YOU SO MUCH!" I screamed. Suddenly my arm was grabbed. I looked to see a russet tattooed hand pulling me back.

"Princesa that's no way to talk to Antonio," Zeke scolded, sending me a fatherly look. I saw Trip slowly making his way towards us, sending Antonio a warning look.

"You have no idea what he's done, Zeke. You know he demanded I stay away from you because you're a criminal and a bad influence, along with Trip. BUT YOU KNOW WHO WAS THERE PROTECTING ME WHEN LUCAS'S BIG BROTHER ALMOST RAPED ME? THAT'S RIGHT, ANTONIO, IT WASN'T YOU! IT WAS ZEKE AND TRIP. YOU DON'T KNOW ANYTHING ABOUT MY RELATIONSHIP WITH THEM!" I yelled. I watched the anger fade from his face as he looked at me, shocked.

"THAT'S ENOUGH PRINCESA. Go inside while me and Antonio talk," Zeke ordered, kissing my cheek. I shook my head, shooting Trip a look. I could see he was confused and angry.

"No, you don't get to tell my daughter what to do. I want you stay the hell away from her," Antonio snapped at Zeke. Zeke shot me a 'follow my order' look. I swallowed hard, turning on my heels and walking inside past my mom and sisters. I went straight upstairs to my room where I screamed out in anger, throwing anything I could get my hands on.

I laid in bed looking at Trey'von's text message. I didn't even have the energy to talk to him right now. My room was destroyed. There was broken glass and ripped up family pictures everywhere. I laid on my torn-up bed lost in thought about how me and Antonio got to this point. I hated this. I just wanted to have a good relationship like we did before, but I wanted to live my life for me too. My stomach growled loudly telling me I was hungry. It was 7:30 and all I'd eaten was a couple bites of ice cream. I got up, tip toeing past the broken things in my room and out the door. I walked downstairs to the kitchen where I heard Izzy and Antonio talking about me. I dipped behind a corner, hiding.

"Daddy, you can't keep doing this. Her genes want her to be close to Zeke. She's following his footsteps without even realizing that's what she's doing. You need to tell her the truth," Izzy told my dad. The truth? About what? My genes? What did my genes have to do with Zeke and how was I following in his footsteps?

"No Izzy, that is my daughter," Antonio snapped which confusing me more. I heard Izzy slam a hand on the table and then shoes clicking on the kitchen floor like she was pacing.

"But she's not your daughter, Daddy. You helped raise her, but Zeke has been in her life since she was 7. It's time you tell her that Zeke is her real dad. Zeke and mom have always wanted the truth to be out, but you keep standing in the way. I know it's a hard pill to swallow, Daddy, but her daddy raised her just as much as you did," Izzy explained. I felt the world under me shake. My hearing blocked out whatever else was said while I just stared ahead in shock. Zeke was my real dad? Trey'von was telling me the truth all along and I called him a liar. Everyone I loved and trusted has lied to me my whole life.

Everything made sense now. The reason Zeke took such an interest in me. It wasn't because I didn't snitch, it's because I was his. Why he waited for me to turn 7 to come into my life I will never know, but it didn't matter. It wasn't Antonio's right, or my mom's, to hide that from me. I don't understand why Zeke didn't just tell me the truth himself when I got older if he wanted me to know so bad. I also understood now why Antonio didn't want me around Zeke, for fear their dirty little secret would come out. I walked into the kitchen looking at the two stunned. They both fell silent and looked at me with wide eyes.

"Elles---." I stopped Antonio from speaking to me.

"Zeke is my dad?" I asked trying to make sense of this all.

"Daddy, don't you dare lie to her," Izzy warned Antonio, sending him a glare. I looked to Izzy and back to my dad. Mom and Mateo walked into the kitchen, looking at the scene unfolding. Antonio's shoulders slumped and he looked down, nodding.

"Yes, Elles. Zeke your real father but I raised you..." Everything he said after that mixed together and I didn't care. My confusion and betrayal hurt so much it took nothing for it to turn into the fire of rage. I looked up at Antonio with a deadly glare.

"YOU LIED TO ME. ALL OF YOU HAVE LIED TO ME MY WHOLE LIFE! THAT WAS NOT YOUR DECISION TO MAKE. I can't even look at you right now," I said, shaking my head and turning out of the kitchen. Everyone called my name, begging me to come back, but I couldn't. I needed to confront Zeke. Hot heavy tears fell down my cheeks as I walked out of the front door. I stormed over to the bar. My hands shaking. My vision blurred from anger. My jaw was locked so tight it hurt. Once I hit the bar, I slung open the door with force making it bang.

"YOU LIAR!" I screamed, looking directly at Zeke. He looked at me surprised. I saw Trip next to him groaning, but I ignored him. I started to storm over to Zeke, but Lil Ugly got in my way.

"Move," I demanded, but he sent me a look. Before he could speak, Trey'von spoke up.

"Baby Girl, I don't know what you think I did---." I cut my simple-minded boyfriend off as I pushed Lil Ugly out of my way.

"NOT YOU. FOR ONCE IT'S NOT YOU FUCKING UP. IT'S YOU!" I screamed pointing at Zeke. He looked at me stunned. He started to speak, but I grabbed his drink and threw it on him.

"ALL THIS TIME, YOU'VE BEEN MY REAL DAD. YOU KNEW I WAS YOUR DAUGHTER THAT'S WHY YOU TOOK ME IN THE WAY YOU DID. IT WASN'T BECAUSE I DIDN'T SNITCH, WHY DIDN'T YOU TELL ME?" I screamed, picking up Trey'von's bottle of water, which was instantly snatched from me. Trey'von grabbed me, pulling me back away from my real dad. I hit his chest. I tried to pull away. I tried kicking my way free, but he had a good grip on me.

"GET OFF OF ME TREY'VON. IT HAS NOTHING TO DO WITH YOU. YOU LIED TO ME MY WHOLE LIFE, ZEKE. I THOUGHT I COULD TRUST YOU MORE THAN ANYONE ELSE!" I screamed, still fighting off Trey'von, who just stayed silent. I watched Zeke pick up a napkin and try to wipe himself clean.

"Princesa, I didn't tell you because I thought that was the only way of keeping you safe from my enemies." He gave me a poor excuse as he stood up walking around the table towards me. I fought Trey'von harder, wanting nothing more than to slap the mug look off of Zeke.

"Baby Girl, calm down. Breathe," Trey'von whispered, but not even he could calm me down in this moment. I had so many thoughts running through my head, I couldn't even think about what I was saying until it left my mouth.

"THEN WHY EVEN COME AROUND? IF IT WAS JUST TO PROTECT ME?" I yelled, looking at Trey'von and trying to push him off of me.

"Trip let her go, she's fine," Zeke ordered. Trip released me and I moved away, sending him a dirty look. I crossed my arms. looking at my new-found father.

"That was the plan all along. Your mother decided Antonio was the safe choice and left me for him. She was scared of you being in this life, just like I am, Princesa. The deal was I stay away from you and keep you safe. I'd make sure you were taken care of. Antonio sadly, got to be the father I thought I'd never get to be. Then one day you saw me shoot somebody. It broke my heart that you saw me like that. Then, when you didn't choose anyone from the lineup, I knew you were more like me than I thought you'd be. I knew I had made a mistake agreeing to those terms, so I started coming around----." I stopped his talking by shaking my head. He couldn't just decide for me that he was too dangerous to be in my life.

"So what? You just decided to be a father. WHY DIDN'T YOU TELL ME THE TRUTH?" I screamed, closing in on the space between us so that we were standing about a foot apart. I wanted him to see the pain in my eyes.

"I COULDN'T ELLY. Antonio has damning evidence of me being a gang boss, evidence that could get me locked up for a long time. WHAT GOOD AM I TO YOU IN PRISON? He told me if I ever told, he'd turn it in to the FBI," Zeke argued. Just when Antonio couldn't be any worse. I shook my head, backing away and grabbing my hair. This can't be true or happening right now. It was all too much. I hadn't even realized I was crying until the hot tear slid down my neck.

"Trey'von, get me out of here," I said, looking at Zeke with wide eyes. I didn't want to be around Zeke, or anyone inside my house, right now. I saw Trey'von look to Zeke who nodded his head.

"Come on, Baby Girl. You're going to be fine," Trey'von whispered, wrapping his arms around me. He pulled me out of the bar where I completely broke down. My knees gave out, making me drop as blood curling sobs left my lips. I saw Trey'von's eyes close in pain. He bent down, picking me up, bridal style.

"I got you, Baby. I'm right here," he murmured, putting me inside his car and kissing my makeup-stained cheek. I hid my face in my hands, sobbing as my brain ran so fast, I couldn't keep up with it. The rest of my night I spent sitting in Trey'von's bed, staring off, or crying, having a total downwards spiral.

Chapter 43

Caught in the Act

TREY'VON

I woke to the sun shining brightly into my bedroom. Before I could even get my morning groan out, everything that happened to Elly came flooding back. I quickly opened my eyes to see that she was still soundly asleep next to me. I let out a breath, laying back down and closing my eyes. She was such a mess yesterday. I couldn't even pull a word out of her. Not even when I made a perverted joke. Those always get comments out of her. I looked over at the love of my life. Her makeup had run down her face, her curls were tangled and hanging in her face. She had deep dark circles under her eyes from crying. Even with all of that, she still managed to look breathtaking.

I rolled over onto my side and pushed back her hair, just admiring her. I hate everything she had to go through. All this time I was trying to convince her that Zeke was her real dad, I had no idea she'd react the way she did. I wanted to take the pain from her and burden myself. I knew I was strong enough to handle it. When I saw Elly, I saw my fragile future wife, the one I never wanted to know pain.

"Good morning to you too," she whispered with closed eyes, making me jump. I smiled, running my fingers over her cheek.

"You scared me," I whispered. She giggled, snuggling into me and hiding her stained face in my chest.

"Sorry, Bebe," she murmured. I smiled, pulling her closer into me, playing with her hair.

"How are you feeling today?" I asked, I just wanted to be there for her. Today, Antonio wasn't coming and taking her away from me. She was so upset and heartbroken by him, it made me want to kill him. But she still protected him. If I was loyal to anyone and their protections, it was Elly. I'd never betray her like that.

"I don't know. I'm still so confused and hurt. I don't understand why they lied. I don't understand how my mom and Zeke even happened," She admitted, keeping her face in my chest. I rubbed her back. I left a kiss on her shoulder, squeezing her tighter.

"Talk to Zeke today. He seemed like he was going to be honest with the information you wanted. I'll even go with you," I offered. I could just go and be a supportive friend. I didn't even think it will make Zeke question our relationship.

"Yeah, I will today, but right now I just want you." Her leg wrapped around my waist making me laugh and kiss the top of her head. I smirked flipping us over. She giggled, pulling her face away from my chest. I snickered, shaking my head and leaning back on the bed.

"You have makeup all over your face," I laughed. She gasped, pushed me away and ran to the bathroom. I grinned, laying back on the bed. Moments later, Elly returned with her face freshly washed. Her messy hair in a bun. She had ditched her clothes and was now wearing my red pajama pants along with her chocolate brown lacy bra. I licked my lips, looking over her sexy curves.

"I looked a hot mess. Do you even still love me?" she asked me jokingly. I scoffed, grabbing her and pulling her down on the bed. I moved, hovering over her and looking into those chocolate brown eyes.

"Don't ask me dumb shit like that. You know I'm gonna love you until time ends." I leaned down and placing a hot wet kiss on her stomach. She inhaled sharply, running her hands over my braids. I smirked, kissing just below her bra. I playfully flicked my tongue on her skin.

"Ew, Trey'von," she giggled, pushing me away. I chuckled, leaning up and kissing her lips. I ran my hands up her curves to her neck. I gripped her throat gently.

"You came out here dressed like this trying to start something," I growled into her ear, kissing her lips. She moaned into my mouth, making the corners of lips twitch up. I swear Elly is so sexy. I had no idea how I got this lucky. Hell, I didn't even think I was capable of love. When I find out I am, it's with the baddest chick around. Her hands ran up my body to my shoulders and she tried to push me down. I knew what she wanted, but she wasn't getting it without those sexy dirty words coming from her lips.

"Aht aht Baby Girl, what do you want," I promoted, moving my hand and kissing her neck.

"You're talking too much," she complained. I laughed, lifting myself to hover over her. I got the dirtiest, most annoyed look I've ever seen cross her face. I shook my head, smiling down at her.

"Wow, aren't you just being pushy?" I asked. She rolled her eyes, wrapping her legs around my waist as her hands ran down my arms. Her eyes softened and she pouted her lip at me in the most adorable way.

"Bebe, just be my distraction like I am for you," she whined. She had a point. Anytime I got upset and needed a distraction, she was there letting me do whatever I needed to do. I wanted to be that for her, but I wanted her to know I was more than willing to listen too. She always pushes me to talk so maybe I should try that with her.

"Baby, I'm happy to be that for you trust me. But are you sure you don't want to talk about it?" I asked. I moved away from her to my side of the bed. I watched Elly groan, pulling a pillow over her face. So dramatic.

"I don't want to talk, Bebe. I just want you," she grumbled. I smiled, grabbing her and pulling her on top of me. Both of us laughed. I wrapped my arms around her thin waist.

"You know I'm here for you though, right?" I asked. She nodded her head, grabbing my face and kissing me. I smiled, rolling us over so I was on top of her again. She giggled against my lips, making me smile. I peppered kisses down her neck, nipping at her earlobe.

"Tell me what you want, Baby Girl." I watched a shiver run through her body as goosebumps formed on her skin. I smirked at how responsive she was to me.

"I want you to taste me," Elly moaned. She didn't have to ask me twice.

ELEANOR

I moaned into Trey'von's mouth as he popped the strap to my bra. I let the straps fall down my arms. He wasted no time snatching it away and kissing my collar bone, palming my breasts. I slipped out of the pants I was wearing, leaving just my thong.

"Someone's excited," Trey'von snickered. I rolled my eyes playfully, smiling. I was excited. I needed the bliss of him before I had a nervous breakdown. Sloppy wet kisses traveled down my stomach. His warm, wet tongue ran across my pantie line. I closed my eyes and reached for his curls, only to find those damn braids. I was ready for the curls to come back. I missed them so much.

"Trey'von," I whimpered as he left kisses on my inner thighs. He blew my clit nerves through my panties, making me jump. He chuckled, rubbing me. I gripped the sheets in pleasure.

"I'm about to make you feel so good, Baby." His warm breath washing against me in the most desirable way.

"Please, Papi," I begged. He grabbed my thong and pulled it off, tossing to the side. He grabbed my knees, spreading my legs wide. My cheeks flushed at how wide he spread them. My embarrassment didn't last long, due to the wet kiss he left. I sighed in pleasure as his tongue flicked across my ball of nerves.

"You taste so good," he groaned, pushing his tongue deeper into me earning a string of moans and groans. I grabbed the sheets, pulling at them as his tongue worked wonders. I looked down at him just as he slipped in a finger.

"Trey'von," I squealed, running my hands over his shoulders. His fingers sped up along with his tongue. My moans grew louder, my back arched off the bed as my eyes closed.

"WHAT THE HELL IS GOING ON IN HERE?" we heard Zeke yell. Trey'von jumped off me and I quickly sat up to see Zeke standing in the doorway with three guys I didn't know. My eyes grew wide as I looked at Trey'von and back to Zeke.

"I TRUSTED YOU TRIP. THAT'S MY FUCKING DAUGHTER. SHE'S NOT A TOY FOR YOU TO PLAY WITH!" Zeke screamed, storming over to us. I quickly went behind Trey'von hiding my body with his. His hand rested on my thigh as he watched Zeke and the guys.

"Zeke, let's just calm down and talk ab---." Zeke cut Trey'von off with a look that sent fear cutting through me. Zeke leaned down, grabbed Trey'von's sweats and my tank top and slung them at me.

"DON'T TELL ME TO CALM DOWN WHEN YOU BETRAYED ME. YOU WERE SUPPOSED TO BE THE PERSON I COULD TRUST, BUT INSTEAD YOU MANIPULATE MY DAUGHTER INTO BED WHILE SHE'S UPSET. ELEANOR GET DRESSED NOW!" Zeke screamed as I grabbed the clothes that hit me. Zeke looked at the men with him and they pulled their guns.

"Baby Girl, get dressed and go downstairs. I'll be right down," Trey'von assured me. But he wouldn't be right down, not if I left him.

"No, I'm not leaving you. Zeke, he didn't manipulate me---." Zeke waived me off

"Princesa, you don't have to lie for him. I knew what type of man Trip was, but I didn't think he had a death wish" Zeke growled at Trey'von. Trey'von stood, his body shaking from anger. I'm sure his eyes were completely black. I quickly pulled on the clothes, hiding my body from Zeke and the strange men.

"YOU DON'T KNOW SHIT ZEKE. IF YOU DID THEN YOU'D KNOW HOW MUCH I LOVE HER. WHAT ARE YOU GOING TO DO, KILL ME? Go ahead because Big Rico will kill you and your buddies here," Trey'von threatened, standing toe to toe with Zeke. I got up and slid behind Trey'von, grabbing his hand and lacing our fingers together.

"Zeke, he didn't manipulate me. I asked him for that. We've been dating for 5 months," I pleaded for the love of my life. I watched the rage grow in Zeke's eyes. Trey'von must have noticed too because he took a step back, pushing me back.

"Get him," Zeke growled and, before I could even register what was happening, Trey'von's fist was connecting with the jaw of the biggest guy in the room. He wasted no time swinging on the next guy.

"TREY'VON!" I screamed, looking around. My eyes landed on the gun on the nightstand. I looked at Zeke who sent me a look, telling me "no." I ran for it, but Zeke grabbed me, slinging me back.

"STOP ELEANOR!" he yelled. I went to lunge past him, but he grabbed me and spun me around just as the two men got Trey'von down on his knees. They drew their guns and he stopped fighting them right away.

"Zeke, please don't do this I love him. Be my friend or my dad, just please don't," I begged him, grabbing his shirt. Zeke looked from Trey'von to me. He pushed me back towards the exit doorway. I was in a panic. I didn't know how to help Trey'von, and I'd do literally anything to help him right now.

"He's not dragging you into this life. He doesn't love you like he tells you, Elly. He just wants in your pants," Zeke spat. But that wasn't who Trey'von was anymore. Before-maybe. Hell, I know at one point that's all he wanted from me, but not anymore.

"Baby Girl, don't argue with him, just go downstairs. Please, I don't want you see what's going to happen," Trey'von begged. Zeke pushed me out of the room into the hall. I grabbed my hair as he turned around. I heard him talking to Trey'von about his upcoming death when an idea hit me. It might be like throwing a live grenade into my relationship, but at least Trey'von would be alive.

"STOP ZEKE!" I screamed, running in to the room. I grabbed Zeke, pulling him back and forced him to turn and look at me.

"If you kill him, you're going to kill me and YOUR GRANDKID!" I yelled at him, my tone giving away how desperate I was. Zeke's eyes grew wide, his lips parted, and he looked back to Trey'von. Trey'von was pale, his jaw dropped open, his nearly black eyes staring at me with fear and shock. I swallowed hard as Zeke looked down at my stomach.

"You're pregnant? By Trip?" Zeke asked, taking a step back stunned. I brought my hands to my stomach nodding my head "yes."

539

"Yes. I was going to tell Trip about the baby today. I'm only a couple weeks along, but if you end his life, I promise you, Zeke, I will swallow a whole bottle of pills or slit my wrists or hang myself. I can't live without him. It was obvious before when we broke up. So, unless you want my blood and this baby's blood on your hands, you'll let him go." I was completely lying. I wasn't pregnant, but maybe it would be enough to save his life. My life and a baby's being linked to his, maybe, hopefully, Zeke wasn't the monster Antonio swore he was. Zeke sighed, looking over at Trey'von.

"You're lucky," Zeke sneered. I exhaled in relief, running over and pushed the huge guys away from the love of my life.

"GET AWAY FROM HIM. Bebe," I gasped, dropping to my knees and hugging him. His tattooed arms wrapped around me tightly as his nose nuzzled into my neck.

"Baby Girl," He breathed out, pulling me into him as he dropped down to his butt. I hid my face in shoulder, squeezing him even tighter.

"Princesa, get changed. We're leaving," Zeke ordered. I pulled away from Trey'von but didn't move too far away. I didn't want to go anywhere with Zeke. He lied to me my whole life and just now tried to kill Trey'von.

"I'm not going anywhere with you. You can't lie to me my whole life and then threaten to take away the only person who's ever been honest with me," I snapped. Trey'von stood up, grabbing my hand. His glare fixed on Zeke. I saw the anger in his eyes. I knew he was going to lash out at Zeke. Trey'von wasn't the type to take treatment like this quietly...not in his adult life at least.

"Baby, go downstairs and get something to eat. Me and Zeke need to have a conversation," Trey'von demanded. I nodded my head, kissing his cheek and walking out of the bedroom. I didn't want to leave him in there alone, but I had a feeling I bought his safety until my lie came out. I nervously went downstairs to the living room. I sat on the couch with the TV off trying to listen for yelling. I felt horrible for lying. I knew Trey'von was freaking out about the baby news. I knew it was a lie and I was freaking out over it.

"GET THE FUCK OUT OF MY HOUSE ZEKE!" I heard Trey'von yell. I stood up from the couch just as Zeke walked into the living room with Trey'von following him.

"Can you just please go get dressed, we're going to breakfast. We have a lot to talk about, Princesa. More than you just betraying me," Zeke snarled at me with his hands in his jacket pockets. I betrayed him? How did I betray him when he's the one who kept the biggest secret of my life from me? I scoffed, shaking my head as I locked my jaw.

"Yeah, I betrayed you by sleeping with your boy, but you totally didn't betray me by hiding you were my dad? Next." I waved him off, turning on my heels to go into the kitchen.

"Zeke, I'm not fucking with you, leave her alone. I could kill you and the higher ups won't look at it twice, but you kill me, and she loses the both of us. I have the advantage, now get out," Trey'von demanded. He reached out to grab Zeke but stopped, looking at me.

"Princesa, don't push me away without knowing my side first," Zeke begged. Maybe there was more to the story. He did admit to not being able to tell me about the truth before. I sighed, nodding my head as I looked back at Trey'von.

"Fuck no. We got shit to talk about first. If our house isn't in line, then fuck Zeke's." Trey'von stormed around Zeke to me. He lightly pressed his palm against my stomach looking at it and then up to my eyes.

"You aren't going anywhere," he growled that sexy growl. I knew it was out of anger, but it was so sexy.

"I need to hear him out. Please don't make this any harder," I whispered, grabbing his hands and lacing together our fingers. He groaned, putting his head down and then glared at Zeke.

"I don't give a fuck if you go with him, but we need to talk," Trey'von snapped at me. I smiled, touching his face and kissing him easily.

"Come upstairs with me while I get ready?" I asked with a shrug. He looked back at Zeke with a glare.

"Tell your boys to fuck off and stay down here," Trey'von barked at Zeke. Zeke glared, and started to say something but stopped when he looked at me. He glanced back at Trey'von with a calm, cool look.

"Hurry up," he demanded. I grabbed Trey'von's hand, pulling him out of the room before they got too heated. We went upstairs and to the bedroom where I knew Trey'von would lose his mind. Part of me wanted to let him believe I was pregnant just for a little while, then maybe he'd actually want kids with me.

TREY'VON

"So, when were you going to tell me your pregnant?" I questioned, slamming the bedroom door shut. I was terrified. I didn't know how to be a dad. I didn't even want to be one, but now she's pregnant and I found out in the worst way. Elly turned, looking at me nervously. I raised an eyebrow, expecting her to answer.

"Bebe, I'm not really pregnant. I lied," Elly confessed. I looked at her completely lost. I couldn't even tell you what was going through my head. Was she pregnant or not? I shook my head, walking around her and sitting on the bed trying to sort through all of my thoughts. She came over, pushing me back on the bed. She climbed on top of me in a straddle.

"I lied to Zeke. It was the only way I knew to save your life. We're not having a baby." I let out a breath in relief. I closed my eyes, covering my face with my arms.

"Baby," I said, relaxing. She giggled, leaning down and kissing my neck. The only problem we had now was Zeke finding out she had lied. He would be expecting a doctor's appointment, a big belly and an actual baby. I couldn't think of a way out of this. We were actually going to have to have a kid. I did not want a kid, but there was no way out of the mess she had just created trying to fix my mistake. I rolled us over, so I was hovering over her. She laughed, running her hands down my chest.

"Problem. Zeke is going to expect a baby and we don't have one," I pointed out. She looked at me squinting her eyes like she was thinking about it. I watched the smile spread across her face. I raised an eyebrow as she burst into laughter.

542

"Well, I guess you better fix that problem," she snickered. I rolled my eyes, smiling as I got off of her. She was always playing some kinda game with me. She was never serious unless she was pissed. Don't get me wrong, I loved that the most about Elly. I loved that I could be a playful boyfriend with her, but I was freaking out.

"You make everything so hard. Seriously, Baby, what are we going to do?" I asked. She sighed, sitting up, looking at me like she was thinking.

"Ok, we'll let him believe I'm pregnant until he calms down about us being together and then tell him I lost it." That could work. It was manipulative as fuck, but it just might work. If that didn't work or if he didn't get over it in time, I'm just going to have to become the boss with or without his blessing. I'm going to have to burn that bridge.

"What are you thinking about?" Elly asked. I walked over and sat on the bed, pulling her onto my lap and kissing her cheek.

"How I'm going to keep you and myself safe. We'll do your idea and if something happens and it falls through, I'm taking over." It was the only plan I had. She smiled at me touching my jawline.

"I love a man in power," she teased. I smiled, pulling her down on the bed and kissed her all over her face.

"I love you, Baby Girl. Thank you for saving my life." She smiled, rolling over to her side grabbing handfuls of my shirt.

"Always, Bebe. I love you too," she murmured, kissing my lips. I smiled, making the kiss harsher, biting her lower lip and earning a moan.

"Fuck it, he's about to wait," I groaned grabbing Elly's hips and rolling her over so her back was flat against the mattress and I was hovering over her. I trailed kisses down her neck to her collarbone a moan slipping from her lips. Elly's nails, traveled over my braids, lightly scraping my scalp.

"Bebe, we don't have time," she hummed. I shrugged grabbing her throat and kissing her roughly. I wanted her right now. I wanted her earlier, but we got interrupted. She giggled, pushing back my shoulder slightly. I groaned, pulling away and looked down at her.

"I need to figure out my family. I need to understand why I've been lied to my whole life and then when I get back you can give me that baby we need." She sent me a playful wink. I groaned loudly rolling off of her onto the bed.

"Fine, I'm going to go down here with Zeke while you shower," I said. She nodded her head and walked into the bathroom without another word. I went downstairs to find Zeke on my couch.

"I trusted you Trip and for you to betray me like this---." I cut him off. He wasn't going to finish that sentence. I never meant to betray him. I really didn't even like Elly at first, but she unlocked a part of me I didn't know I needed.

"You have no idea how me and Baby Girl even started. It wasn't like when I first seen her, I was like 'oh yeah I'm about to fuck with Zeke.' I actually didn't even like her but the more *you* put us together, and I got to know her, she wiggled her way into my life. I love her Zeke. I've put my life on the line for her. I'll die for her. If you think falling in love to the point you can't live without someone is betraying you then, whatever," I snapped, taking a seat on the couch. I was surprised at my own words. I've always admitted I couldn't live without Elly and that I love her but to tell Zeke?

"You're going to get her hurt. How much of the life have you drug her into?" he snarled. I looked at him, shaking my head.

"None, because I don't let her into that business. Hell, I went and flipped out on the higher ups for picking her up. Which they know about me and Elly and trust me. They want me a hell of a lot more than they want you at the moment," I fired back. I knew this was the craziest thing we've fought over, but I was aware of the law. I wouldn't back down from this, and I wasn't breaking up with Elly, either. He'd have to kill me first.

"See how long that lasts. I didn't care that you guys were friends, but then you had to go and make yourself more and then have sex with her!" he shot. I nodded my head, grabbing the remote to the TV.

"If it makes you feel any better, we're still best friends. Zeke, that's the girl I'm going to marry. She's it for me. I'm not gonna hurt her how you think I am. Elly trusts me, so why can't you?" I asked. He scoffed, shaking his head "no," I watched him grab the hood to his hoodie and put it over his head. He was beginning to get upset, but I was telling the truth. Elly was my endgame. It was her or nothing for me. I knew that and I'm almost sure Elly knew it too.

"Yeah, I thought that too and was left behind. I don't trust your temper," he admitted. I rolled my eyes at his dramatics. I'd never hurt Elly. If she ever wanted to leave me, she was free to go.

"I love that girl way too much to hurt her. I can't hurt anyone in front of her. I know I say fucked up things to her sometimes, but physically hurting her would never happen. If she came down these stairs and broke up with me right now, I'd let her go. I would spiral, but I'd never force her to be with me," I explained with a shrug. I didn't care if he approved of me and Elly or not. I didn't care what Antonio thought and I didn't care what Zeke thought. Zeke just scoffed, shaking his head as if he didn't believe me. With that, no one said anything else. We just let an intense silence fall between us because that was better than the deadly rage that would have burst out if the conversation continued. All I knew is that Elly couldn't get ready fast enough.

Chapter 44

Clarity

ELEANOR

The restaurant felt oddly quiet as I sat across from Zeke. My eyes continued to glance at my phone. My fingers moved nervously. I felt awkward. I mean, this man, who I had always looked at like a father, turns out to be my real father and then tries to murder my boyfriend. I guess it would be strange if it wasn't awkward. I glanced at Zeke who was staring at his phone, his thumb easily gliding against the glass.

"One sweet tea and one water with lemon and mint leaves," our waitress announced as she set the drinks down in front of us. I looked at her with a small, uncomfortable smile. Her eyes glanced at Zeke and then back to me. She must be noticing the tension between us. She cleared her throat, pulling out a notepad.

"Are we ready to order?" she asked. I didn't even look the menu. I was too lost in my thoughts about how uncomfortable I was. Zeke looked up from his phone to the waitress with a nonchalant look.

"We'll both take an order of French toast with sausage and hash browns. We'll need hot sauce and she'll want her syrup hot," Zeke ordered for the both of us. I couldn't help but smile. It was my favorite breakfast since when I was like, 8. I would beg him to cook it for us and then cry when he wouldn't give me enough hot sauce. The waitress looked at me to make sure I was ok with that order. I nodded my head, looking back down to my feet. I needed to get my toes done again. I wiggled and them my strappy heel dug into the marble flooring.

"Princesa, are we going to sit here in silence the whole time just sneaking glances at each other?" Zeke asked. That was the first time he'd spoken to me since we walked out of Trey'von's house. I just shrugged my shoulders, biting my lower lip. I was nervous and I wasn't sure why. Part of me wished Trey'von would just have invited himself and forced his way onto our breakfast. I would be much more comfortable.

"Princesa, I will answer every single question you have. I will explain everything. Just please, I'm begging you, do not shut me out. I made the choices I made because I love you," Zeke pleaded. But if he loved me so much, why not just tell me the truth? I swallowed hard, leaned forward taking a drink of my tea, and then looked at Zeke.

"Why didn't you ever just tell me the truth? You know I already saw you as a father figure. Why lie to me my whole entire life?" I asked. I crossed my arms, leaning back in my chair and waited for him to speak about why he had made this choice. I watched Zeke's body language change. It showed guilt and remorse. He sighed, closing his eyes. Moments later his black eyes opened, staring directly at me.

"I wanted to tell you the truth, but I couldn't---." I cut him off, feeling my temper flare. Zeke was a notorious gangster. He did what he wanted when he wanted, so I wasn't buying it.

"That's a bullshit excuse," I snapped. His eyes narrowed into that fatherly look that sent shivers through my body. I cleared my throat, sinking into my seat.

"Watch your tone, Princesa. I couldn't tell you because, like I said yesterday, Antonio has damning evidence against me and swore to turn it into the FBI if I told the truth. I wouldn't have been any good to you in prison. I couldn't protect you from my enemies in prison," Zeke explained, but I was still lost.

"What kinda evidence does he have against you? Do you still think it could be played against you?" I asked, my tone was nervous and worried. If what Zeke says was true, I wouldn't put it past Antonio to use it against Zeke, now that I know the truth. Antonio hated my relationship with Zeke. He'd do anything to destroy what's left of it. Zeke sighed, running his hand over his face and nodding his head "yes."

"Yes, it could be used against me. Back in the day, my temper was much shorter. I was very much like Trip. Little things would set me off into a violent unforgivable rage. There was only one woman who was ever able to tame my temper." I watched the biggest smile spread across Zeke's face as he looked up towards the ceiling. A glow had come over his cheeks. I could see how happy he was even with the thought of this women. I couldn't help but smile, seeing how happy he was.

"That woman was your mother. She left Antonio for me. She calmed me down and I gave her the excitement she craved. Well, when she got pregnant, she knew you'd become a target for every enemy I ever made, so she left me for Antonio. He was the safe choice. I wasn't very happy about it, but it made sense. You would have been safe, so I didn't fight. But I made it known I'd be in your life. Antonio hated that idea. One day he came into the bar and told me I'd never be a part of your life or your mother's, so I needed to stay away," Zeke explained. I watched him bite his lip and move around uncomfortably in the chair. I stayed silent because I had a feeling the next part of this story wasn't going to be like the Zeke I knew.

"I didn't like that. I had a temper very much like Trip's. So, I had some of my men grab him and drag him to the back of the bar where I strung him up like a piece of meat. That's where I had him beat and tortured and reminded him that it was my family. I reminded him how I run Los Prophets and could have his face on a missing person poster so long that everyone forgot about his existence. We beat him until he was almost dead, then dropped him off at the hospital. He only lived because I love your mother and she loves him." let out a breathe, unable to even picture Zeke like that: angry and covered in blood. Every part of me could picture Trip like that easily, but not Zeke.

"That doesn't explain the evidence. He didn't tell people at the hospital what really happened, clearly," I said. He smiled, reaching across the table and moving a curl from my eyes, his fingertips lingering on my cheek.

"Orders up," the waitress sang, making both of us jump. I didn't even see her coming over. She set down each plate and we thanked her. I wasn't very hungry, the imagines of Zeke covered in blood torturing Antonio made my stomach churn. Once the waitress was out of earshot, I looked at Zeke, imploring him to explain this evidence.

"He was wearing a body cam, Princesa and we didn't see it. He has video evidence of me torturing him and admitting to running the streets. A week later, I got a copy of it in the mail and note that said if I ever tell anyone the truth, he'd give the video to the FBI." My head was spinning at how far Antonio would go. He knowingly and willingly got tortured just to keep me and my mom away from a man that just wanted his family. Would he still be willing to go that far to keep me away from my biological father? He did all that because his ego was hurt because my mom left him and got knocked up. What if it hurts his ego that I know that truth now? He could turn the video into the police and have Zeke taken from me. Even though I was angry, I didn't want that.

"Zeke, if he still has the video, he could turn it in. Antonio always hated me being around you and now that I know the truth, he could turn it in just prove that he has power over you," I expressed, staring directly into his eyes so he could see how serious I was. He licked his lips, taking another bite out of his French toast.

"Eat. You and the baby need it," Zeke said, motioning to my stomach. I nodded, taking a bite out of my food that was getting cold.

ZEKE

Elly was right. Antonio could turn in that video at any moment. Now that the truth was out, I definitely wasn't staying away from Elly. She needed me more than ever now that she was pregnant, and I didn't trust Trip with her at all. I didn't know how well Trip would treat her or the baby and, honestly, Savannah and Antonio didn't have enough money to support their house full of kids and a baby. It was time for me to step up more than ever, as a father and now a grandfather. Elly looked up at me her head tilting in confusion. I could see the confusion and curiosity in her chocolate brown eyes. I raised an eyebrow, but she shook her head "no," looking back down to her French toast.

"Princesa, ask your question. An unanswered question just turns into paranoia and that's the fall of every great leader," I reminded her. I watched the small smile spread across her lips as she looked down. I mocked her smile, seeing that she remembered the saying I used to tell her all time when she was younger.

"You and my mom are like polar opposites. How did that happen?" She asked. She looked up at me with an amused look. I chuckled, shaking my head. I could say the same thing about her and Trip. Elly was a sweet, innocent, pure soul who couldn't hurt a mouse. On the other hand, Trip is an angry, violent, narcissistic, unfeeling person. I've seen him snatch the life a 16-year-old girl just because he felt her street value had run out.

"I could ask you the same. You and Trip are ice and fire," I pointed out with a shrug. She squinted her eyes at me and then smirked. She leaned forward, her pink painted lips parting slightly into a devilish smirk.

"Do you know what fire and ice have in common?" she asked. I shook my head "no," seeing a new light behind her eyes.

"They can both burn you." I chuckled, nodding my head. Elly did have my temper and manipulation skills. She was my daughter at the end of the day. I sighed, thinking back to the day I met the love of my life... Savannah Sánchez.

"Your mom and Antonio had just moved into the house you guys live in now. I pulled up to the bar in my most bad-ass Cadillac, at the time. When I got out of the car, I heard a women yelling in Spanish. When I looked over, I saw your mom and she was, and still is, the most gorgeous women I had ever laid eyes on. I'll never forget those little jean shorts and that thin sports bra she wore. I was smitten right away." I couldn't help but smile thinking back to that day and that moment I knew I found my soulmate.

"Awww, it was love at first sight!" Elly squealed, making me chuckle and nod my head.

"It was more than that," I said, smiling like the softy I am when it comes to Savannah. I couldn't help but close my eyes and picture the day we met scene for scene.

FLASHBACK

I pulled into my usual parking spot at the bar. The moment I put my car in park, I saw her. The neighbor, she was so gorgeous. She was bent over in her yard planting flowers, she wore short denim shorts, a black sports bra and her hair was pulled back into a braid. Her daughter was sitting on the sidewalk drawing with chalk. I tore my eyes away from the woman and got out of the car, ready to go handle business with Mad Max. Just as I circled around the car and stepped onto the sidewalk, I felt a tug on my basketball shorts. I looked down to see the daughter of the gorgeous girl.

"The ice cream truck is coming. Can I have a dollar, please!!!!!! My mommy won't give me one," She begged. Before I could respond to the little girl, I heard a musical voice.

"Isabella, you do not run off like that. I am so sorry sir," the voice chimed. I looked up just as the gorgeous woman from the house down the street snatched up the little girl. I chuckled, shaking my head and sending her a charming smile. Her deep black eyes caught mine and I swear, for a moment, it was like everything around us stopped spinning.

"Don't be, she's adorable but I'm guessing she gets that from her mother," I flirted as I reached into my pocket, pulling out my wallet. I watched the woman blush and look towards the bar away from me. I smirked, dropping to one knee in front of the little girl I now know is named Isabella.

"I'm one of the good guys. If you need anything, feel welcome to yell for me, but not every guy here is as nice as I am, ok? Stay with your mommy from now on. Here's three dollars," I smiled, handing her the money. I watched her eyes light up in excitement as she snatched away the money and ran to the curb for the ice cream truck.

"You didn't have to do that," the woman told me. I smirked, standing up and leaning against my car, licking my lips.

"Honestly, I was just trying to buy myself a few more minutes with her fine ass mom. You care if I get yo name?" I asked, confidently. She blushed once again, looking at the kid and back at me.

"Savannah. I'm married though," she said, embarrassed as she held up her hand to show me a pathetic diamond. I chuckled and shrugged my shoulders.

"If that diamond isn't weighing down your finger, in my book, you single. I'm Zeke Santiago," I introduced myself. She looked at me impressed. Her eyes going to my car and then back to me.

"That beauty yours?" she asked curiously. I looked back at the car and then back to her, nodding my head.

"Wow, such a nice car for someone who can't be much older than me. What are you, 23?" She asked. I smirked, opening the passenger side door to let her look at my custom interior.

"24. I don't have your 'usual job'." She looked up at me, raising an eyebrow.

"Yeah? What are you? An assassin?" She joked as she easily shut the door to my car.

"Better than that. I'm a gangster. The boss actually." She looked at me, bursting into laughter, but I gave her a serious look. Her laughing stopped and she looked at me with surprise.

"Oh," she muttered, her eyes scanning my body. I watched her thighs press together as she bit her lip. She wanted me as much as I wanted her. In one slick movement I pushed her against my car. I pressed my body against hers, her butt pressing against me in just the right way. I let my breath brush against her neck which earned me a shiver of delight.

"When you're ready for a real man to show you how someone as gorgeous as you should be treated, you know where to find me," I whispered huskily against her exposed skin. I didn't miss the moan that escaped her lips.

"Mommy, look Spongebob," Isabella called, and I let Savannah off the car. She looked at me flustered and panting. I sent her a wink and simply walked into the bar, leaving them both outside.

FLASHBACK OVER

"Wow, your guy's meeting was so chaotic and sexy. I understand why she wanted you, now." Elly grinned, which made me chuckle and shrug.

"I was very wild back then but your mom seemed to like that about me," I shrugged. She giggled shaking her and then smiled at me.

"I guess that's where I get it from. Who would have thought me, and my mom would both have a thing for the bad boys," Elly teased. I wanted to know how her, and Trip happened, but I couldn't handle the deals right now. The waitress came back, dropping the bill and collecting our empty dishes.

"So did my mom come to you or did you go to her?" Elly asked curiously.

"She came to me, and the rest of that story isn't meant for your ears," I told her, standing up. She rolled her eyes, following me over to the counter to pay the bill.

ELEANOR

I watched the streets pass by while my mind ran wild with how I was going to get that video away from Antonio. I had a pretty good idea where it was. He had a lock box hidden under the floor in his bedroom. We weren't allowed near it, and I almost promise, if I get it open, it will be in there. Within seconds, a plan hit me but I'd need Zeke's help.

"I know how to get that video away from Antonio," I said looking over at Zeke. He looked at me and then shook his head "no."

"No way. You are to stay out of this. I'll handle it, I'm the adult," Zeke said in his fatherly tone. But it wasn't up to him. I needed Zeke. I always have, so I was going to fix this.

"Ok, let me reword this. I'm getting the video. So, either you help me, or I have Trip meet me at my house and help me," I explained to Zeke just how it would be. He looked over at me sighing, nodding his head. I smiled and leaned back in my seat.

"Ok, I'm going to stay the night with you because I don't even want to be around Antonio right now. You're going to distract my mom and Antonio because I have a really good idea where he's keeping it. Keep them downstairs, no matter what, and I'll take care of the rest," I instructed as he pulled onto my street. He nodded his head, looking at me as he pulled up in front of my house. I saw my mom, Antonio and all my sisters on the front porch.

"You really are mine," he said. I smiled as we fist bumped. I got of the car. Right away Antonio's eyes landed on me with a glare. My mom looked relieved to see me and, clearly, my sisters were just waiting on the tea.

"What are you doing with him?" Antonio boomed before we even touched the front gate. My mom sent him a warning look but stayed quiet like she always does.

"Getting answers about why my life has been a lie. I've lost all respect for you," I snapped at Antonio, pushing open the gate. I heard Zeke suck on his teeth, but he didn't say anything to me about my attitude, which surprised me. Antonio stood up, sending me a devilish smirk.

"Zeke do you know what *your daughter* has been up to with your right-hand man?" Antonio smirked, keeping eye contact with me. I rolled my eyes as I walked up the stairs to the porch, stopping right in front of Antonio with Zeke behind me. Antonio really thought he was going to drop a bomb, but that bomb already went off and is unarmed for the moment.

"She's been sleeping with him and they're dating. How you feel about that?" Antonio asked, looking up at Zeke. I looked over my shoulder to see him shrugging.

"I already know, and it's handled as best it can be since she's pregnant," Zeke announced. I cringed, looking down to my heels. I felt eyes on me. I glanced up to see my whole family staring at me with the same stunned faces.

"YOU'RE WHAT? BY THAT COMMON THUG?" Antonio yelled. Zeke's hand landed on my shoulder as he stepped up in front of me, eyeing Antonio.

"Princesa, go pack a bag while I talk to Antonio," Zeke commanded. I nodded, stepping around the man I thought was my biological father for so long. I walked into the house and up the stairs. I went straight into my mom's room. I quietly shut the door, locking it. I looked around the room nervously. I couldn't believe I was in my parent's bedroom. We have never been allowed in here. I bit my lip nervously and quickly went to the closet. I opened the door, ripping up the area rug that was in the closet which exposed a hidden door. I lifted the heavy wooden carpet-covered door and found Antonio's lock box. I dropped to my knees, reaching into grab the heavy box. I pulled it up and rested it on the floor. I tried pulling on the locks, but they wouldn't budge.

"Fuck, what would he make the combo?" I whispered to myself. I tried my mom's birthday, my dad's birthday, mine, Izzy's, and Mateo's, but none of them worked. I groaned, hitting it as I looked around the room trying to think on the fly. My eyes caught my dad's toolbox across the room. I got up, running over to the toolbox and slung it open.

"Yes, Elly you are a genius," I praised as I grabbed a flat head screwdriver and a hammer. I went over to the lock box. I shoved the screwdriver under the first lock and hit it with the hammer, popping the lock. I smiled, repeated the action and broke the second lock. I dropped the tools and opened the box as I looked through all the papers and found a flash drive at the bottom. I smiled, as I grabbed it and stuffed it in my bra. I quickly got up, leaving my mess behind and sneaking out of my parent's room to mine so I could pack a bag.

I walked down the stairs and heard yelling coming from the front porch. Right away, I knew it was Antonio and Zeke. I opened the front door and saw my mom with her hands pressed against Zeke's chest, trying to push him back.

"YOU THINK I WON'T DROP YOU MYSELF ANTONIO? THAT'S MY FUCKING DAUGHTER. GET OFF OF ME, SAVANNAH" Zeke yelled, grabbing my mom's wrist and lightly pushing her against the house. I dropped my backpack and ran over to Zeke.

"ZEKE, ZEKE LET'S GO!" I yelled, pushing him back. His usual black eyes seemed demonic. His russet skin was so hot, it almost burned my hands. It was scary to see Zeke like this. I had never seen his temper spike like this.

"Come on, I got what I came here for, let's just go. He's trying to get a reaction out of you, lets go," I urged Zeke, pushing him towards the steps. He looked at me, shaking his head clear of whatever thoughts were going through his mind. Without another word Zeke turned and walked towards the gate. I let out a breath, picked up my bag and started to follow him.

"So, you're just going to turn your back on us? I raised you, Eleanor. He didn't!" Antonio spat. Yeah, he raised me, but he turned his back on me the moment he threatened Trey'von and then truly tried to have him hurt. He turned his back on me before I was even born by denying me my father.

"I'M TURNING MY BACK ON YOU? YOU TURNED YOUR BACK ON ME THE MOMENT I TOOK MY FIRST BREATH ANTONIO. YOU DECIDED TO LIE TO ME AND FORCED EVERYONE ELSE AROUND YOU TO LIE AS WELL. THEN DON'T EVEN GET ME STARTED ON HOW YOU WERE GOING TO HAVE THE LOVE OF MY LIFE KILLED. YOU KNEW WHAT WOULD HAVE HAPPENED IF YOU TOLD ABOUT TRIP. You were just a little too late," I growled the last part out in pure anger. Antonio sent me a glare, one that had scared me into behaving as a child, but oddly, enough it sent only anger coursing through my body now. I dropped my bag to take the last few steps closer to him so we would be face to face, but Zeke grabbed my arm, stopping me.

"I give up on you Eleanor. If this is what you want, the gangsters, the life where you're always looking over your shoulder, have it. But just know you are no longer my daughter. Don't even bother calling me dad anymore and don't ever come back here." If I wasn't already so angry with him, that would have hurt worse than anything he's ever said to me before.

"ANTONIO!" my mom yelled. But I don't know why she was trying to correct him now. I shook my head, picked up my backpack and nodding my head as I looked him up and down.

"You really know how to pick them, mom. That's fine Antonio, but when I leave, so does my protection, and I won't stop Trip from anything anymore. I'll be here to get my things another day." I turned on my heels, blowing past Zeke and out to his car. I got in and threw my things into the backseat. I saw him say something to Antonio and then he got into the car. He sped out, driving toward his house.

I hung up my last piece of clothing in my closet. This was now going to be my home. I didn't plan to go back to my mom's. I mean, I wasn't even welcome there anymore. Oddly enough, I hadn't cried, or anything, over it. Maybe I was just numb from everything that had happened today, and it hadn't really set in yet. There was a knock at my door. Zeke walked in holding a grocery bag.

"Here's your flash drive. I didn't watch it," I assured, picking the small silver drive up from my dresser and handed it to him. He nodded it, took it and shoved it into his pocket.

"Thank you, Princesa. How are you feeling?" he asked, but I just shrugged as I shut my closet door.

"Numb, but that's good for now," I told him, moving over to sit on the bed. He nodded, looking at me and crossing his arms. I watched his black eyes travel over my body, stopping my stomach.

"I want you to take a pregnancy test," he said holding the white plastic bag out to me. That broke through the numbness. My stomach churned with nerves. I forced my breathing to stay as normal as I possibly could make it. My palms were already starting to sweat as I tried to hide how shaky my hands were. I didn't want Zeke to see how nervous I was. Maybe I could convince him that I didn't need to take it.

"Why? I'm pregnant, Zeke. I already took a test," I lied, looking into his black eyes. But all I saw was distrust. He tossed the bag onto the bed, nodding towards it.

"Then prove it." I bit my lip, looking at the bag. I couldn't take it. It would come back negative, and he'd kill Trey'von. The idea of that sent me into a total panic attack which I couldn't hide. My breathing began to get heavy and shallow. My chest started to hurt, and my body shook as tears fell from my eyes. Zeke watched me have a total melt down without saying anything. My thoughts raced to find a way to get out of this, but I couldn't think of one.

"I'm not pregnant. I lied so you wouldn't kill Trip," I whispered through my panic. Zeke looked at me with a hard look. He started to walk out of my room. I ran to him, grabbing his arm, stopping him.

"No, please Zeke, please, please don't hurt him. I love him and I don't know if I can live without him, please. I will do anything for you to spare his life, please," I begged my biological father as sobs ripped through my chest. My knees wobbled and I fell to them as I looked up at him.

"Please, I need to know he's out there and he has a chance for a perfect life. Please," I begged Zeke. He looked at me, letting out a sigh. I watched him pinch the brim of his nose. He opened his eyes, looking down at me nodding affirmatively.

"On one condition I will let that trader live." I looked at him with wide eyes, nodding my head "yes" quickly as I got up. I'd do anything to keep Trey'von alive because he'd do anything to keep me alive.

"You have to break up with him and stay away. No "friends" or anything. This isn't the life for you Elly. You are to marry a doctor, a lawyer, a judge, someone successful that has a life for themselves. Not some gangster that probably won't live past 25. You deserve more than the gang life and you will have more than that." I felt the last remaining piece of the Earth I had left under my feet crumble away. I didn't want a doctor or a lawyer or a judge. I wanted Trey'von. But I couldn't keep him if it meant he'd die. My sobs grew worse as my tears blinded me with the reality of what had to be done. The last sliver of Earth and sanity I had collapsed under my feet, plunging me into the darkness. I did the only thing I could do and nodded my head.

"Ok, I'll break up with him tomorrow, just please let him live," I begged. Zeke nodded, pushed my hands off of him and walked out of my room, slamming the door. I melted onto the floor screaming out sobs as complete, unescapable darkness surrounded me.

Chapter 45

The ending us...of me

ELEANOR

I sat on my bed looking at my phone with Trey'von's name pulled up. I had to do the thing I never wanted to do. I had to end my happiness to save the person I love the most in this world. My whole body ached with the weight of this decision. I knew my eyes were puffy and red from all the tears. I had on a pair of baggy grey sweats and a stained white t-shirt. I didn't care about looking cute. I didn't care about anything anymore. A knock came at my bedroom door. I looked over as it opened to show Zeke, bright eyed and ready for his day.

"Have you gotten ahold of Trip to end this whole thing yet?" Zeke asked. Pain shot across my chest. I closed my eyes as tears slipped from them. I shook my head "no," trying to hold back a sob.

"Well get on it. I have to meet with Knives about the underboss position," Zeke informed me. My head snapped over and I looked at him with wide, shocked eyes.

"What? That's Trip's position," My voice was raw as shaking my head "no." Zeke couldn't take Trip's position. I was breaking up with him. This would all be over soon enough.

"Not anymore. I can't have him as my underboss. I can't trust him. He's lucky he's still alive. I'm only letting him live because I can't afford to lose you anymore than I already have", Zeke said, shaking his head. He was wrong. He was losing me the more I learned about his plans.

"The higher ups won't let you do that. They want him bad," I told Zeke. But he shrugged his shoulders, looking me up and down.

"It will already be done by the time they find out. Get it done Eleanor, the sooner the better for all of us," He demanded. walking away and closing the door. I bit my lip and scrolled to Trey'von's text messages. I was going to tell him Zeke's plan. He could go to the higher ups and stop this.

Me- Meet me at Starbucks now. We need to talk.

With the message sent, I ordered an Uber. I reached over grabbed my Adidas and threw them on. I didn't know how I was going to survive this. From breaking up with Trey'von to living without him. He gave me something I've never had before. He gave me a passionate, fiery, dangerous, adventurous love that I'd never find again. I didn't want to find it again. I didn't want anyone but him and now I'd never have him again. I sank to the floor just sobbing. My phone was ringing like crazy, and I knew it was Trey'von calling me to find out what was wrong. But hearing his voice would break me even more. Soon enough a horn, sounded outside. I left my phone where it lay on the floor. I wouldn't be talking to Trey'von after this and my family hated me, so I didn't see the point in even owning a phone anymore. I walked outside, wiping my tears. I made sure the door was locked and walked over to get in the Uber. The man talked to me the whole way to Starbucks, but I was completely silent. Once we finally got there, I got out of the car without a word and walked inside. I sat at a far-back table, just waiting to hurt the man I love the most.

After about ten minutes, I saw Trey'von walk in. His nearly black eyes scanned the café for me. He looked so good as he always did, and it hurt me even more to do what I was about to do. His heavy eyes found me. They immediately filled with concern. My skin erupted in the familiar goosebumps for the last time. It was almost enough to make me burst out into tears all over again.

"Baby Girl, what's going on? What's wrong?" he asked, rushing over to me. I stood up as he pulled me into his warm, strong, tattooed arms that screamed "home." I hugged him back, snuggling my nose into his chest and taking in the smell of his cologne one last time. I didn't pull away for what felt like for years, but I needed to remember this: how his arms felt, how he smelled. His lips connected with the top of my head just as I pulled away.

"What's wrong, Baby?" he asked, his velvet voice laced with worry which only broke me more. I grabbed his smooth hands. I was going to miss everything about him.

"Zeke is trying to replace you as underboss with Knives," I blurted out. He looked down at me, surprised, and then nodded his head. He sat down at the table, and I reclaimed my seat.

"That doesn't surprise me. I'll call Big Rico. He'll put a stop to it. Listen, I'm just going to take over. This lie isn't going to work---." I cut him off, shaking my head "no" as I closed my eyes. Tears fell as a sob ripped through me. I hid my face in my hands.

"Baby Girl, why are you crying?" I had to tell him. I just needed to rip the band-aid off and get away from him.

"Zeke knows I lied. He tried to make me take a pregnancy test. I had no choice but to tell him the truth." I wiped my eyes. He leaned back in his chair looking at me with wide, frantic eyes. He looked around and then back at me. I watched him swallow hard and nod his head.

"Baby, it's ok. He won't touch me or you. I'm going to Big Rico's now. Come on you can stay at their place until I'm done," he said, standing. I shook my head "no," grabbing his hand and pulling him back into his seat.

TREY'VON

Elly shook her head "no,' pulling me back into the seat. She was so upset. It didn't make sense for her to be this upset because Zeke found out our lie. I was going to take care of it, like I always do. I'd just dethrone Zeke and then he couldn't do shit. I don't know who he thinks he is giving my position to Knives. Knives couldn't be me. He was too much of a pussy. Plus, all of that has to be approved by the higher ups. Zeke is on a power trip, and I was going to bring him down real fast.

"It's not ok, Trey'von. He was going to come after you last night after I told him, but he didn't on one condition." I felt my nerves grow. My whole body stiffened as I looked at my girlfriend with questioning eyes. What did she agree to for me to be sitting here with her right now? I felt my temper spiking towards Zeke. I swear, I will leave him in a pool of his own blood.

"Baby Girl, what did you agree to?" I was trying to keep my tone as calm as possible, but you could hear the anger. Elly cringed at the sound of my voice and then looked down to her hands. I reached across the table to touch her, hoping to calm her down, but she just jerked away from me. My temper grew more intense as the hurt washed over my body. I looked at her, biting my lip.

"To break up with you and never to see you again." Her voice was emotionless, like she was numb. I scoffed, shaking my head "no." I couldn't stop the anger.

"No, fuck him. He isn't keeping us apart. I'll fucking gut him like the rat he fucking is. Who the fuck does he think he is trying to take my girl and my position? I swear to God, Baby Girl, when I'm done with him, he's going to wish he never walked into my house uninvited." I laughed a dangerous laugh. Elly looked at me taken back. I don't know if she's ever seen me so ready to kill someone, other than the time I actually killed someone in front of her.

"I can't take that risk Trey'von. I love you too much to risk your life. So, if being away from you will keep you breathing, then I'll stay away. But you have to stay away from me too." I looked at her with a glare. Her words sent such a shock through me that I stood up, making the chair I was sitting in clatter to the floor. I knew people were looking, but I couldn't even bring myself to care.

"So, what? You're just gonna dump me like I'm not shit to you?" I asked. She closed her eyes, letting more tears fall. I could see this was killing her, but I couldn't live without Elly-and I wouldn't.

"No, you know I love you, Trey'von. This is why I have to do this," she whispered. I closed my eyes, running my hands over my braids. I didn't want to explode on her when she was just doing what she thought was right. She was wrong, of course. She was so wrong.

"Don't do this, Baby Girl. Let me just fix this," I begged. She looked at me, shaking her head "no."

"You can't fix this Trey'von. You're going to die if I don't do something and this is the only thing I can fucking do," she sobbed as her own anger slipped into her tone. I grabbed my chair and sat back down as tears filled my eyes. She wasn't leaving me. I wasn't going to let her.

"Baby Girl, I need you. I can't live without you. I've already tried, remember? I'm a mess without you. I can fix this, just give me some time, please," I begged, my voice cracking as tears slipped from my eyes. She looked at me with the most painful look I'd ever seen her on her face. She shook her head "no," standing up.

"I don't know how I'm going to live without you either. Hopefully, over time, the pain will just fade into a faint memory of what was and what could have been. I love you Trey'von and I always will, but I can't be with you if that means you could die over it. I love you but this is it, I'm so sorry," she said, standing up as her tears came even faster. I closed my eyes, putting my head down and letting the sobs escape my lips. I didn't care how weak I looked right now. If anyone said anything I was likely to shoot them where they stood.

"This is goodbye," she whispered, touching my shoulder. I felt her hand move and then heard her walk away. Seconds later, the doorbell sounded, and I knew it was Elly leaving me forever. I was going to kill Zeke in the most painful way I could. I stood up, grabbing my chair and throwing it as I stormed out of the coffee shop I'd now forever hate. I got into my car, ripping out and racing to the only people who could help me get my girl back. I was finally going to give into them. Why should I show Zeke any loyalty when he wasn't showing me any-or even a sliver of respect?

Halfway to my destination my anger had consumed me, and I was ready to make an example. Zeke wants to take away my reason for living every day, maybe I should take his away. Knives wants my position? He has to be alive to have it. Without a second thought I swerved into the other lane of traffic and changed my direction. I sped to the bar and saw Zeke's car. I whipped into my parking spot. I saw my brother standing at the gate of the Sánchez home. I didn't even bother to shut off my car I just got out.

"TRIP!" I heard Izzy yelling for me.

"FUCK OFF IZZY!" I was not in the mood for my family. I stormed to the bar and threw open the door. Zeke was at his table laughing with Knives. His eyes slipped across the bar to me, and he sent me a devilish smirk.

"YOU DON'T KNOW WHO YOU'RE FUCKING WITH ZEKE. GIVE ME ONE REASON NOT TO FUCKING DROP YOU RIGHT NOW!" I yelled! Lil Ugly went to get in my way, but I punched him in the jaw, tossing him to the side.

"ANYONE ELSE WANT TO STOP ME?" I screamed as I heard my name from the door. I didn't even need to glance back to know it was my bitch-ass brother, but I wasn't in the mood. Everyone moved away from me, leaving me a path to Zeke. I stormed over, glaring at him.

"I see Elly spoke with you," he said calmly. I laughed, shaking my head at him.

"You really think she's going to stay away from me Zeke? We've tried that. It doesn't work. Everything in me is telling me to end you," I barked at him. He looked at me, raising an eyebrow and nodding towards me.

"Do it then? What? Scared Elly will hate you?" he teased. I picked up the table and threw it, stepping towards him, but Knives got in my way.

"Back off Trip," he growled. I looked at him shocked. I burst into laughter shaking my head at Knives. I saw him pull a knife which only made my laughter grow.

"You're a fucking joke. You want my position? YOU THINK YOU CAN BE ME? NONE OF YOU MOTHERFUCKAS IN HERE CAN BE ME!" I yelled. My anger was boiling over. Knives looked me up and down, shaking his head "no."

"No, I don't want to be you. You're a disgrace to Los Prophet's. You were so respected and threw it away, that's embarrassing," he growled. He started to shove me back, but I punched him which made him fall. I grabbed the knife he dropped and stabbed it through his hand and the floorboards, making him scream out in pain as I laughed evilly. I pulled out my gun, aiming it between his eyes.

"To be me, you have to be alive," I said, and without hesitation, I pulled the trigger, planting a bullet between his eyes. I looked up at everyone in the bar, including my big brother, who was looking at me with the most fearful look I've ever seen from him.

"WHO ELSE WANTS TO BE ME? YOU, UGLY? WHAT ABOUT YOU, LOCO?" I yelled. Everyone shook their head "no," backing away with frightened eyes. I looked at Zeke who looked shocked. I smirked storming, over to him as he stood.

"Count your fucking days, Zeke. I'm taking this gang from you. I'm getting my girl back and you won't be able to do shit without me ending you, like Knives. THE ONLY REASON YOU'RE ALIVE IS BECAUSE SHE'S ALREADY SO CRUSHED I DON'T THINK SHE CAN HANDLE ANYTHING ELSE," I yelled at him, but he just laughed at me, shaking his head.

"You think you can do this? What are you going to do when you fuck up and they come for Elly?" he asked, but I just shrugged my shoulders, looking him up and down.

"I won't," I snapped, storming past my scared shitless brother and out of the bar. I got into my car and pulled off, going straight to the men that could help.

I stormed through the halls of the giant house. No one dared to stop me. It must have been the look on my face, but I wouldn't hesitate to put any one of these assholes down for even stepping in front of me. I got to the double doors and threw them open. Big Rico, Carlos, and Daniel all looked over at me.

"You seem upset, Trip," Carlos commented, taking in my appearance. I nodded my head, laughing. I couldn't stop the crazed thoughts of how I wanted to torture Zeke for taking the only good thing in my life away from me.

"I'm in," I told them all. They looked at me, confused. Big Rico leaned forward eyeing me.

"In what? Sit, talk to us to, Trip," Big Rico said, motioning to a seat at their table. I sat down looking Big Rico in the eye.

"I want Los Prophets. Fuck Zeke. Fuck his blessing. I don't even give a fuck if you guys kill him in order for me to take over. But I want it." They looked at each other shocked by my new-found attitude, but I couldn't lose what was mine.

"What has brought this on? Talk to us. After all, we are all friends here," Daniel said, calmly. I knew these fuckers weren't my friends, but I didn't care about anything other than my girl right now.

"Zeke found out about me and Elly. He was going to kill me, but Elly lied and told him she was pregnant. Well, he tried to force her to take a test, so she came clean. The only way he agreed not to come after me is if she broke up with me and stayed away," I explained. They looked at each other with a look I couldn't read. M=My protectiveness for Elly was no secret to them. My love for her was no secret either and if they are the only people who can help me, then fine.

"Oh, and then his dumbass was going to give Knives my underboss position. I killed Knives for even entertaining the idea, of course. Who is that low profile dick to go against me? I'm Trip. I've worked my ass off for this gang. I'm done being under him. I'm done watching him fuck up our gang and covering for him. Taking Elly from me was the last fucking straw," I ranted. They were surprised, but I saw how impressed they were by my commitment and that meant everything when dealing with them.

"Ok Trip. We will get the motion started for you to take over. You taking over makes you even more important to us. We will protect Elly. Don't worry about her right now. Just worry about taking over the neighborhood and getting these men to bow to you. We will be back," Big Rico said, standing as the other two followed his lead. I watched them walk out of the room, leaving me. Who knows what the fuck they were going to do, but I didn't care. I needed these streets to be mine.

I spun in the chair, looking at my phone. I kept sending Elly text messages, but they failed to send. It was like she had blocked me. I yelled out in anger, throwing my phone across the room, surely busting it to pieces. I looked around the room and saw bottles of whiskey lining the bar. I bit my lip, got up and walked over to grab one. I ripped open the top and took a swig. The smoky flavor was addicting. The burning feeling that slid down my throat reminded me of how alive I was, just like Elly does. I looked at the bottle, bringing it back to my lips and making the decision that I didn't want to be sober anymore.

ELEANOR

I sat my desk just staring at the wall with my knees to my chest. Everything hurt. My body, my throat, my lungs, my heart. I couldn't even cry anymore. Everything just hurt too much. My chest felt like there was a weight crushing down on it. It was one I'd never be able to escape. There was a knock at my door. I knew it would be Zeke and he was literally the last person on this earth I wanted to see right now.

"Hey, Princesa, what are you doing?" Zeke asked, but I didn't answer. I didn't even look away from the wall I was staring at. I heard the bedroom door close and seconds later a hand landed on my shoulder. It wasn't warm, inviting, smooth, or addicting. It wasn't the hand I wanted to feel touching me.

"You talked to Trip. I'm proud of you for keeping our deal," he said. But I didn't have a choice. If I didn't keep his deal, then he would have killed the only person I love, that I'm ever going to love. Zeke sighed, taking his hand off me. I heard the bed creak, telling me he had sat down.

"Really Elly, the silent treatment?" Once again, I did not waiver. Both fathers in my life have hurt me more than I've ever been hurt. From hiding something so important from me, disowning me, to threatening the man I loved and making me leave him behind. I didn't know how I'd ever recover enough to forgive either one of them for this. Everything in me screamed to get away from East LA, maybe California all together. Everywhere I go was going to remind me of Trip and how we couldn't be together. Then my family, if that's what you even all this mess of people. I didn't want to be around any of them.

"Trip killed Knives. Right in front of everyone at the bar, in front of Izzy's boyfriend," Zeke informed me. I couldn't stop the scoff from leaving my lips. Anthony would be alright. He's saw Trey'von violence before, and, as for Knives, he deserved it.

"Good, he deserved it," I spoke quietly, not looking away from the wall.

"What? The Elly I know would have never been ok with something like that," Zeke said. But I was starting to gather that he never really knew me. I shrugged my shoulders, resting my chin on my knees.

"Well, she's dead. You all have killed her over and over again. Knives deserved what happened to him for trying to take Trip's spot. He should have known Trip wouldn't have taken the challenge quietly," I told Zeke as if it was obvious. I did feel different. I felt like that Elly from the end of summer was truly gone. She had grown and blossomed into something beautiful until she was poisoned by the people around her. I had was strong, confident, and independent. I had learned to love so recklessly. Then Antonio and Zeke poisoned everything I had grown into until I was shattered and left with nothing but weeds.

"He's threatening to take my place. You know I could die if the higher ups truly want him." I turned to look at Zeke. His face gave away his shock and hurt. But I didn't care. I didn't care about anything anymore.

"Yeah, well they want him, so I guess you better step down willingly. I've talked to them personally and I know how bad they want him to run these streets," I said with a shrug. He nodded his head, eyeing me.

"Are you even worried about me?" he asked, hurt. I shook my head "no." I got up to look out of the window to the street below where kids were riding their bikes. What I would do to go back to that age, before Zeke, before Trip, before my dangerous, fiery love developed, before I knew the truth.

"No, I'm not. Whatever happens, happens. I don't care about anything anymore," I admitted. He scoffed from behind me and soon enough I felt him looking out at the kids over my shoulder.

"You sound ridiculous. All of this over some guy that's not even good for you. He would have chewed you up and spit you out the moment he got bored. I saved you from that. You'll get over it. I wouldn't be surprised if he was already in bed with some whore." That sent me over the edge. I pushed him back with a screaming glaring.

"YOU DON'T KNOW HIM LIKE I DO. HE'S NOT LIKE THAT ANYMORE, I'VE CHANGED HIM JUST AS MUCH AS HE'S CHANGED ME. JUST LEAVE ME ALONE ZEKE! I HATE YOU AS MUCH AS I HATE ANTONIO, IF NOT MORE!" I screamed as hot, angry, and hurt tears fell from my eyes. He looked at me stunned but stormed out of my room. The door slammed so hard it made me jump. I sank down to the floor, curling into a ball and sobbing, crying out for Trey'von until I fell asleep right there on the floor under the window.

TREY'VON

I took the last swig out of the bottle. I sat back in my chair and threw it across the room, letting it shatter against the wall. I lifted my head as the room spun and I felt lighter than I have in a long time. I looked around the room. There were about 5 or 6 bottles laying around that I had drunk until the last drop was gone. I honestly had no idea how I was still conscious, but I was. I looked over at the bar. I wanted more. I got up, staggering over to grab another bottle, ripped the top off, and took a drink. I looked at the bottle as I saw Elly's beautiful laughing face flash before my eyes. I missed her already. I knew I was disappointing her by drinking my pain away, but I didn't know how else to deal with her absence in my life. The higher ups had yet to return, and I was losing my mind.

I took another swig of the liquor as my mind swam with thoughts of Elly. My arms burned to feel Elly's curvy figure in them. I craved hearing her musical laugh, her sassy curls bouncing, and her beautiful smile. I wanted to lay down with her and just sleep off the all the liquor. I looked around the spinning room. I saw my keys on the table by an empty liquor bottle. I stumbled over and almost fell, but I caught myself on the table. I grabbed my keys and staggered through the mansion and out of the front door into the night air. I went to my car and got in. I groaned as I grabbed my stomach. I felt the need to puke. I burped, tasting it. I shook my head, pressed the start button and pulled out.

"Oh fuck," I slurred as I almost hit the pole by the gate. I jerked the wheel over, avoiding the wreck, and got on the main road. Everything was spinning. The lines on the road were blending together and moving. My focus was on Elly and how much I wanted her. I knew she was at Zeke's. If he tried to stop me, I'd just kill him. I needed her just like she needed me. I squinted at a pair of lights speeding towards me. I couldn't figure out what it was. Suddenly a horn blew, and I saw a truck. I jerked my wheel, trying to move, but the truck jerked as well. I watched it run off the road into the grass. I looked over to see I was headed right for a house. I quickly jerked my wheel again which put me back onto the road. Suddenly, I heard sirens and saw lights flashing behind me. I looked in my mirror to see a cop behind me.

"Fuck, shit. I'm just trying to get to my Baby Girl," I groaned. In my drunken state, I tried to pull over, but my car jerked which told me I was way up on the curb. I slammed my car into park, opening my door to get out.

"GET BACK IN YOUR VEHICAL!" a man's voice yelled at me as lights shone in my eyes.

"FUCK YOU MUHFUCKA, NOBODY TELLS ME WHAT TO DO!" I yelled back at him, slamming my car door shut, stumbling. I lost my and fell falling over onto the street. I groaned laying there for a moment.

"You ok kid?" the cop asked as he shined a light in my face. I sent him a glare, getting up and stumbling but stabilizing myself the best I could as my whole world spun.

"Am I ok? Fuck no. The love of my life just fucking left me. Both of her dads are fucking fuck ups, and I just need to get to her. Get that light out of my fucking face," I spat at the cop as I tried to stumble back to my car. I tripped over my own feet but caught myself on my car.

"Sir, are you intoxicated?" he asked me shinning that stupid fucking flash light on me. I shook my head "no," looking at the cop.

"No. I'm fine," I slurred but he looked at me, unimpressed. He shook his head "no," looking me up and down.

"Why don't you step back here to my car sir. We'll get you a breathalyzer. What's your name?" he asked, but I just scoffed at him. I wasn't answering any of this pig's questions.

"Fuck off, dude," I spat as I started to get back into my car. He reached out and grabbed my arm, trying to stop me. I turned and swung, letting my fist connect to his face and then I hit him with my other fist. Just as he fell and I stumbled back losing my balance, I was grabbed from behind and slammed against my car.

"GET THE FUCK OF ME YOUR FUCKING PIG!" I yelled, fighting against the other one that had me.

"TASER, TASER!" I heard and then I felt the barbs of a taser, and the electricity flowed through my body. I collapsed to the ground as my body jerked violently from the voltage. The second it ended, before I could recover, I was grabbed and rolled over. Knees on my back and neck kept me pinned down.

"You are under arrest. You have the right to remain silent. Anything you say can and will be used against you in a court of law. You have the right to an attorney. If you cannot afford an attorney, one will be provided for you. Do you understand the rights I have just read to you?" the cop snapped. I groaned, closing my eyes as I felt the darkness daring to take me over. I felt the cool sting of my gun being pulled out of my pants.

"He's a Los Prophet. Look at the tattoo," that was last thing I heard before everything around me went completely black.

Chapter 46

The burnout

ELEANOR

TWO MONTHS LATER

I groaned, laying in bed. I felt horrible today. Well, I have felt horrible every day since the breakup, but this one takes the cake. My stomach was churning and daring me to puke. I had the worst heartburn I've ever felt. My breasts hurt, and my head hurt. I haven't felt good in weeks but today was the worst day to feel bad. It was the day of Trip's trial. He was arrested two months ago for a DUI, resisting arrest, assaulting an officer, having an illegal firearm, possession of a firearm by a felon, and public intoxication. I didn't even know Trey'von was a felon. I mean, I guess I should have just assumed so. I was disappointed that his first instinct was to drink the minute he was hurt, but he was pushed to it, so I didn't hold any ill feelings towards him for it. I wanted to be there for the trial. I wanted him to know he had my support, even though it was dangerous for him to have it.

I groaned, as I felt the bile in the back of my throat. I got up, putting my hand to my lips. I ran down to the bathroom and dropped to my knees, emptying my breakfast into the toilet. I didn't understand what was wrong with me. I'd been throwing up for a week now and little things set it off. Smells, the look of some things, and, sometimes, nothing at all. I've been tired and moody. I know Zeke is beyond worried about me and keeps pushing me to go to the doctor, but honestly, part of me was hoping I was dying. Once my stomach was empty and had nothing else to discharge, I wiped my mouth and flushed the toilet. I rested my head on the seat for a minute, letting the stars and dizziness pass. Once I felt good enough to look up, I saw a pack of unopened tampons and pads sitting on the back on the toilet. I felt my heart drop as I touched my stomach.

"When was my last period?" I questioned. I picked myself up off of the floor, rinsed my mouth, and went back to my bedroom. I grabbed my laptop and opened it up to the calendar where I tracked my period. I went backwards to discover that I haven't had my period in two months. I've been so busy worrying about Trip, and dying inside without him, that I forgot about my period. I touched my stomach as my mind went a million miles per-hour. It was hard to keep up with. I couldn't be pregnant, not right now. Not while Trip was about to go to prison. Not while I'm in school. Not when I can barely function because I miss him so much. I got up, went over to the desk and grabbed my phone. I went to the one person's number I was praying would help. If I hadn't ruined that relationship too.

ring

ring

ring

"Elly?" I heard her calm but surprised voice. I took a shaky deep breath, not sure how to even say it without just saying it.

"Gabby, I need your help. I think I'm pregnant. I haven't had my period in two months and Trip is going to go to prison today," I said, unable to stop the sob or the tears of panic. What am I going to do if I am pregnant? How am I supposed to take care of another human when I can barely keep my own head above water? I'm not ready to be a parent. I don't want to be a parent yet.

"Hey, calm down Elles. I'm on my way now. You're still at Zeke's, right?" she asked me, and I nodded, completely forgetting she couldn't see me. I sank down onto the desk chair, crying out of fear and pure terrified panic.

"Yes," I choked out as if it was the most painful word, I've ever spoken.

"Ok, I'm on my way now," she promised and hung up. I put my head down, sobbing begging God to give me a break for once.

I sat in Gabby's car looking up at the Walmart. I wore a pair of black spandex shorts and one of Trip's hoodies that I had I kept. It still smelled like him and brought me the comfort I needed right now. I was terrified to buy this test and to take it. I didn't know if I really wanted to know the results. Gabby reached over and grabbed my hand. I looked over at her as she sent me a small smile.

"Look, whatever it says, you'll be ok. I'm here for you and our little bun in the oven if it's there," she promised I appreciated Gabby right now more than she'd ever know. I took another deep breath and put my hood up.

"Let's go." We got out of the car and walked silently into the Walmart. We went over to the pregnancy the test looking at all the different options.

"Which one is the best?" I asked, looking over at Gabby, but she just shrugged her shoulders.

"I'm gay, remember? I've never had to buy one," she told me. I looked at her, confused. I thought she had hooked up with guys before. Maybe she lied so no one would find out she was gay. I shrugged it off, looking back at them.

"I've heard of Clear Blue," I said, grabbing it. Gabby shrugged, and picked up another box, reading the back as I did the same.

"Sounds good to me." She put hers back and we walked over to the self-checkout. I bought the tests and we walked out getting back into her car.

"You know, I've missed you as my friend," Gabby said as she pulled out of the parking spot. I nodded looking back over at her.

"I've missed you too Gabs, and right now I really need a friend." She nodded, sending me a smile and grabbed my hand, squeezing it. I looked back out of the window, letting the tears fall as my thoughts raced. If I was pregnant, would I go visit Trip in prison and tell him? Would I wait until he got out? How would he react? How would Zeke react when he found out I wasn't lying about it anymore? Was I going to a raise a child by taking it to a prison to see their dad?

I sat on the edge of the bathtub while Gabby sat inside the bathtub wearing Zeke's sunglasses. We were waiting on the test to finish doing whatever it does to get the results. My anxiety was out of this world. Part of me couldn't help but be excited because having a baby would mean having a piece of Trey'von and, just maybe, I could live my life with that. Maybe it would be enough, but the majority of me was terrified of this fate.

"Hey, you're going to be ok." I nodded my head and just continued to stare ahead in total fear and panic. The alarm on my phone went off. I pressed the button, silencing it. I took a deep breath and stood up wiping my sweaty palms on my hoodie. I walked over to the test. I picked it up and saw the word *'pregnant'* written across the little screen in clear letters. I gasped, dropping the test in the sink. I backed away, I didn't know what to do or how to react. My breathing picked up until I was full-on hyperventilating. My thoughts were so loud I could barely hear anything in the room, my chest started to hurt, and my knees gave out, making me drop to the floor. Gabby was by my side in seconds, hugging me as I sobbed into her.

"I can't do this Gabby," I cried. She hushed me by rubbing my matted hair which was hidden under my hat.

"We'll do this together. You're going to give this baby the best life," she promised, but I didn't know how I'd do that without Trey'von by my side. I didn't know how I could do anything without him and now I was going to have another human fully dependent on me.

TREY'VON

I walked out with my hands in cuffs and shackles around my ankles. I looked out to the seats and saw Zeke, the higher ups, Lil Smiley, and Momma Sánchez. I didn't see Elly, though. I couldn't lie, that hurt. Even with everything going on, I was hoping to see her chocolate brown eyes and sassy curls sitting out there for me, but she wasn't. She really meant it when she said I was never going to see her again. I looked over at my lawyer with an emotionless expression, I knew I was going away. I walked over and stayed standing as the asshat in a gown walked out and sat behind the bench.

"You may be seated," the judge called. I sat down rolling my eyes. I've had more court cases than I can count, so this didn't scare me at all. My worst fear had already come true and that was losing my baby.

"Who were you looking for when you walked out? Big Rico has arranged for you to get an hour of private visitation after this," my lawyer whispered lowly. Big Rico was pissed at me, so I'm surprised he did that. I was finally about to take over Los Prophets, but then I decided to get wasted, drive, and fight a cop. I'm facing charges for something I don't even remember doing. I watched the dash cam, so I know I did it. I just don't remember it. I couldn't help but wonder what Elly thought of me right now. She was probably disgusted with me for drinking and getting arrested. Maybe that's why she wasn't here.

"Nobody. Don't worry about it, I don't want it," I whispered not taking my eyes off the female judge. She looked at me, squirming uncomfortably under my gaze, making me smirk. She's scared of me. Good.

"Trip don't--." I cut the lawyer off, sending him a deadly glare. He sank into his seat, and I looked back at the judge.

"We are here for the hearing of Trey'von Matias Walker," she announced to the court. I already pled guilty for less time. I knew this was about to be total bullshit. The state would pull the fact that I'm a gang member to try and put me behind bars longer. I half listened to the case against me. I glanced back to Momma Sánchez. She sat between Zeke and Lil Smiley. I saw Zeke moving around nervously, looking at her. Then I looked at Smiley who nodded his head. I knew he was telling me he'd watch after Elly for me. I mouthed a "thank you" to him.

"Mr. Walker are you even paying attention?" the judge snapped. I looked back at her with a sly smile, I couldn't stop the chuckle from leaving my lips.

"Aw you aren't the first judge I've been in front of, and this isn't the first case I've heard against me. I'm a gang member, oh no. The prosecutor will run with that, then use my very long track record to show that I'm a common nuisance to the public. Then my attorney will take his turn and explain how I went to AA and just had a little back slide and he'll talk about how I've changed and how I'm working on myself, and my childhood trauma. He'll try to convince you all I need is anger management and therapy. So no, Your Honor, I'm not listening," I said coldly. My attorney was looking at me like I was crazy while the courtroom broke out into murmurs, but I didn't care. I lost my only reason to care about anything.

"Mr. Walker, are you trying to find yourself in contempt?" The Judge roared, slamming her gavel down, making everyone quiet down. I just shrugged my shoulders. My attorney was quick to jump to use the excuse that I was anxious, and I would behave.

I was growing impatient as the trial continued to drag on. I was ready to get my verdict and get back to the cell where I could be a dick to everyone and mope around. I was ready to go lay in my bunk and pretend I was at home in my huge bed with Elly. Fuck, I missed her so much it wasn't funny.

"Please stand for the sentencing of Trey'von Walker," the judge ordered slamming her gavel down. About damn time we get this over with. I stood looking at her carelessly. She looked at me, shaking her head and then looked at her paper.

"I find Trey'von Walker guilty on the charges of Driving under the influence, assaulting an officer, resisting arrest, possession of an illegal firearm, possession of a firearm by a felon, and public intoxication," the judge rattled off my charges. I knew that was going to happen, so I didn't even care.

"I sentence you to four years in a maximum-security prison. You're remanded to custody of the state," she told the court slamming her gavel down again. I felt a tap on my shoulder, and I saw Momma Sánchez. I smiled at her.

"I'm shocked you came. How's my Baby Girl?" I asked. She smiled, pulling me into a hug. I laughed, hugging her the best I could.

"Of course, I did. You are my family and always will be. She could be better," she whispered, and I felt her slip something into my jumpsuit pocket.

"Tell her I love her," I whispered, and she nodded, pulling away just as a guard grabbed my arm. I let him lead me away to the truck that would carry me to the prison that would be my home for the next four years. Once I was securely put in the back of the padded truck and left alone, I reached into my pocket and pulled out a picture of me and Elly. I smiled at it. We were standing outside of the bar. She was looking at me with the biggest attitude and I was laughing at her. I shook my head, folded it up as small as I could get it and hid it in my mess of curls so it wouldn't get taken from me.

End of book one

ACKNOWLEDGMENTS

As I sit here in my bed, watching my cat play with a bobby pin he has randomly found on my floor, I don't even know where to start with my thanks. I have learned much during this publication process. Each person I encountered was friendly and willing to help at a moment's notice. There is a lot to be thankful for.

I will start by thanking my readers first of all. Without you guys, picking up the book and actually reading it (if anyone does. Hopefully they do.) then it would have partially been a failed effort of a dream. I am thankful for each and every single person who saw my book sitting on a shelf at a store or saw it as they scrolled on their kindle and stopped to give it just a chance. Thank you.

Next, I would like to thank Writers Republic for all their help. From the design team for making my cover to designing my pages. To Grey, who was so hopeful and kind in each and every single email we shared. Thank you for making sure I loved the final product of everything we worked on together. Then, there was Scarlet who was so kind over the phone. She helped start the publication process and talked me through each step of the way. Thank you to everyone at Writers Republic for giving me the opportunity to make my dreams of being a published author come true.

Kath Khamis. An amazing friend who took the time out of her days to edit my book. I can't thank you enough for that either. Without your support and help editing, I don't know if I would have ever truly been able to get "Cold Blooded" off the ground. Thank you so much for everything.

Then my Mom and Dad. I've always hidden my writing from you guys. Well, everyone really. Only strangers on the internet had ever been able to read anything I had written before, until now. I hope you just skipped over the sex scenes, and I prefer to not talk about them with you guys LOL! They were very detailed, I am aware, next topic in the book please! The bickering on the back porch over who was "prouder" jokes or not made me feel really good. So, thank you guys for not knocking down the idea of publishing when I presented it to you.

I hope you all stick around for the next part of Trey'von, and Elly's lives. Cold Blooded is just the beginning of their story but nowhere near the end. This isn't a goodbye but a simple, see you next time.

CPSIA information can be obtained
at www.ICGtesting.com
Printed in the USA
BVHW031554050821
613614BV00051B/101